What Readers Sa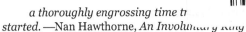

Absolutely brilliant! —Bridget, 1

a thoroughly engrossing time tr .... *; it*
started. —Nan Hawthorne, *An Involuntary King*

a delightfully intricate tale of time travel, life lessons, challenges of faith, and redemption...moving, witty, and captivating...a page-turner...I highly recommend this novel. —Jennifer, Rundpinne.com

Vosika spins a captivating tale.... The pacing flows from a measured cadence...and builds to a climatic crescendo reminiscent of Ravel's Bolero. I become invested in the characters. Both Shawn and Niall are fully fleshed and I could imagine having a conversation with each. Write faster, Laura. I want to read more. —Joan Szechtman, *This Time*

fast-paced, well-written, witty...Captivating! —Stephanie Derhak, *White Pines*

Ms. Vosika wove these aspects...together in a very masterful way that...kept me spellbound. I could hardly put it down. —Thea Nillson, *A Shunned Man*

Original& intelligently written. I couldn't turn the pages fast enough.
—Dorsi Miller, reader

Ms. Vosika spins the web so well you are a part of all the action. If you love history, romance, music and the believable unbelievable...this book is for you. I couldn't put it down until I closed the cover on an ending I never expected.
—Kat Yares, *Journeys Into the Velvet Darkness*

...best time travel book I have ever read. Fantastic descriptive detail and a sweet love story are combined beautifully. —Amazon reviewer

some of the best writing it has been my pleasure to read....
—JR Jackson, *Reilley's Sting, Reilley's War,* and *The Ancient Mariner Tells All.*

a very exciting tale.... —Ross Tarry, *Eye of the Serpent,* and other mysteries

Vosika is a master at creating engaging characters...a riveting plot, well-drawn cast, and the beautiful imagery of Scotland.
—Genny Zak Kieley, *Hot Pants and Green Stamps*

I love books on time travel, but this is so much more. The characters come to life in your heart and mind. —Jeryl Struble, singer/songwriter, *Journey to Joy*

One of the most intriguing stories of Scottish history I have ever read...riveting.
—Pam Borum, Minneapolis, MN

I found myself still thinking about the characters after finishing the book.
—Goodreads reviewer

For J. Al

Thank you for your encouragement and belief in me

The

Water is Wide

Blue Bells Chronicles Three

by Laura Vosika

Contact editors@gabrielshornpress.com

Published in Minneapolis, Minnesota by Gabriel's Horn Press

Publisher's Note: This novel is a work of fiction. Names, characters, places, and incidents are either products of the author's imagination or used fictitiously. All characters are fictional, and any similarity to people living or dead is purely coincidental.

First printing: January 1, 2014
Printed in the United States.

For sales, please visit www.bluebellstrilogy.com

ISBN-10: 1938990005
ISBN-13: 978-1-938990-00-7

Acknowledgements

I am deeply indebted to the Night Writers: Judy, Genny, Judd, Janet, Stephanie, Sue, Ross, Lyn, and particularly, Jack, who did a great deal of extra work outside of our weekly meetings in seeing this book come to life.

Thank you to Deb, my editor, who has put countless hours into reading, re-reading, editing, suggesting, and reading again.

.

~The Water is Wide~

The water is wide, I can-not cross o'er.

And neither have I wings to fly.

give me a boat that can carry two,

And both shall row, my love and I.

♫

A ship there is and she sails the seas.

She's loaded deep, as deep can be;

But not as deep as the love I'm in

And I know not if I sink or swim.

♫

I leaned my back up against an oak

I thought it was a trusty tree

but first it bent and then it broke

Thus did my love prove false to me.

~Traditional Song

PRELUDE

Glenmirril Castle, on the shore of Loch Ness, 1314

The sun rose over Glenmirril Castle, its rosy fingers touching Shawn's eyes, where he slept in the tower. He woke slowly, growing gradually aware of the deep chill in his bones. The cold from the flagstones cut through his cloak. Winter air brushed his cheek, like his mother had years ago, whispering to wake up. He stayed in the dark behind his eyelids, locked in hope. The past days and weeks drifted through his mind, of midnight raids, MacDougall's gallows, pretending to be Niall at Niall's marriage, just days ago. He'd asked God, he'd defended God to Niall, setting him straight that God was Love, not Hell. He'd learned his lesson about Amy and treating people better. So God would surely work the magic in the tower again, slide the centuries up, one against the other, and tip him back into his right time.

His head thrummed with alcohol. He opened his eyes cautiously. The wineskin lay flaccid by his side. The tower walls rose around him, etched against dawn. Mist floated over the flagstones. It looked as it had last night, in 1314. It looked as it had the night he and Amy fought, months ago, in the twenty-first century.

Voices sounded on the stair. He strained to hear if they were medieval Gaelic or modern English. He sat up, slowly, putting off the moment of finding out whether the switch had happened, hoping. Footsteps fell on the stairs, light feminine steps. He scrambled to his feet, his heart beating. It was Amy! By some miracle, it was Amy, come back for him!

Bannockburn, Present

I stare in shock at my violin student and her family: Sinead, her parents, her brothers—and a sister she's never mentioned. They look up at me, smiling, from their table at the pub. The other girl has blue eyes, freckles, and black curls bouncing around her shoulders—just like Sinead. The baby kicks inside me, as if sharing my agitation. I press a hand to my stomach, just starting to swell.

"They dinna tell ye, did they?" Mr. Gordon shakes his head. "This is Siobhan. Sinead's twin."

"You're not angry, are you, Miss Amy?" Sinead pipes. She fails terribly in her attempt to look contrite.

I gather myself. "No, they didn't, but...." I stop.

The shock is not Sinead's twin. It's the implications. Angus waits at our table. We're leaving for England, to follow Niall's trail as he raided Northumbria with James Douglas. But now I wonder....

Sinead and Siobhan giggle. Their brothers roll their eyes. Mrs. Gordon huffs. "Really, you two, playing tricks on Miss Amy."

"We played no tricks, Mam, honest," Siobhan protests.

"She never asked," Sinead adds, her eyes wide.

"Imagine that!" I smile, and hurry past, sliding into the booth across from Angus. Thoughts swarm my mind like Scotland's midges, too swift to touch. Sinead has a twin!

I've spent months grieving Shawn's death, while reading of Niall's amazing exploits, twenty-hour work days, speedy recoveries from horrific injuries, being everywhere at once—all the while being amazed at Sinead's many talents and quick movements. I know now: Sinead didn't do it all.

Neither did Niall.

Glenmirril Castle, 1314

She appeared at the top of the stairs, framed in the stone arch. Sorrow lay across her face like a shroud over her pale skin. The sun blazed, a red halo through her flyaway hair.

His hopes crashed.

"Shawn," she whispered. "'Tis sorry I am. We hoped. For your sake, we hoped...." Her words hung in the cold air.

Niall appeared in the doorway behind her.

Shawn crumpled to the floor. His face dropped into his cupped hands. Scenes of battle and flames and women screaming and men dying filled his head; and images of crowds cheering him, far away, centuries from now, and Amy, waiting, waiting...always waiting for him to come back from his foolishness, waiting with comforting words and accepting arms. His shoulders shook with the effort to hold it in. Not even at his father's funeral had he cried. Not even at the trial for his father's murderer. A warm arm slid around him.

Allene pressed his head against her shoulder, her hands in his hair, sitting on the cold floor beside him, and he cried.

Bannockburn, Present

My heart pounds; my arms tremble as I slide into the booth. Angus is smiling, the smile of secrets, of kissing behind a castle, lying on the floor last night with a board game pushed to the side. I barely register his ruddy cheeks or close-cut dark curls. My thoughts spin. I've come to love his deep, gravelly voice, the light in his eyes when he looks at me, his gentle humor. But I loved Shawn, too—and not so long ago. I loved his laugh, his warmth, his generosity. I watched him throw himself before a charging warhorse to protect a child. I've grieved his death.

And now—he's alive! If I'm right, he's alive!

Angus holds my hand across the table. He speaks, a buzz of sound over my head. I answer, smile back. But inside, I'm a volcano roiling with implications.

Angus cocks his head. "You're pale. Are you aw' right?"

I nod quickly; too quickly. "Sinead. She has a twin."

Shawn survived!

Anger flashes through me, as quick and white-hot as lightning. Shawn has caused upheaval in my life from the moment he walked into that rehearsal on his hands, twisting his head up to grin at me, see if I was watching; and even now, when he's supposed to be dead and seven hundred years distant, he's still turning my life upside down!

But he's alive!

"Well, now, that explains a lot," Angus says. But his eyebrows furrow.

"Yes." I speak brightly. He survived. Maybe he'll be here for his child! "Obviously one person couldn't do so much." Another thought whips through my head like a boomerang. Records prove Niall survived MacDougall's gallows. What if Shawn died on that noose instead? I blanch.

Angus jumps up, bumping the table, setting the tea things clattering. "You sure you're all right?" He reaches for my arm.

"Fine. Great!" I take a hasty bite of toast. "Just surprised, that's all." Leave it to Shawn not only to survive such a thing, but to become part of a legend! My amusement fades. Did he survive the knight only to die months later at the end of a rope? I lift my cup with a shaking hand.

"Tea is to be sipped," Angus teases. But his forehead wrinkles.

I set the cup down with a rattle. "What did the book at Glenmirril say about Niall?" I ask. "We thought he must have survived, right? I mean," I add hastily, "if he even was at Creagsmalan."

"Which I don't believe he was." Angus scratches his jaw. "It said he walked the shore with his son. What's this to do with Sinead's twin?"

"Nothing," I lie. "It's just—it doesn't seem like the kind of thing a medieval man would do."

"'Twould have been unusual." Angus butters a thick slice of bread. "A nursemaid would have cared for the children, not Allene. Certainly not Niall."

I swallow.

"Why should that upset you?" Angus sets his bread down.

Questions tumble inside me. It must have been Shawn walking the shore. So was Niall hanged? "Not upset," *I hedge.* "Baffled. Remember the serving the servants incident? What year was that?"

"It didn't say."

"So it could *have been...."* I stop. Angus doesn't believe Niall was ever in Creagsmalan's dungeon. Shawn would never quote the Bible or serve anyone. If it happened after Creagsmalan, then they both survived, regardless of who was in the dungeon. I want to sort through it with Angus, but I can't tell him this insane story.

"What?" Angus waits, fork poised.

I stare at my plate. "Nothing."

"You're still afraid Niall somehow died on MacDougall's gallows." He reaches for my hand. *"I don't understand* why, *Amy! He was knighted by Bruce. We already* know *he went to Ireland after 1314."*

I bite my lip, a nervous gesture I developed with Shawn, one I hate. I stop. Angus is right. Except—he doesn't have all the facts. If Shawn took over Niall's life, then it was him in Ireland. The touch of Angus's fingers startles me.

"How did we get from Sinead's twin back to Niall?" He squeezes my hand. *"And why are you so upset?"*

"I'm not upset." My heart pounds. My emotions shift again, tossed in a tornado. Shawn, who loved to barbecue who brought parties to life, who made people laugh till their sides ached, who pushed love letters under my door and left roses—Shawn survived!

CHAPTER ONE

Bannockburn, Present

Angus warmed the car while Amy used the restroom. He tapped gloved fingers on the steering wheel, a tight frown creasing his forehead. After a minute, he pulled out his phone and dialed his partner on Inverness's police force. "Clive," he said, moments later. "Here's a riddle. What's the link between Shawn Kleiner, twenty-first century missing person, and Niall Campbell, fourteenth century laird?" His mind flitted around Rose, Amy's mentor, teacher, and friend. *Think outside the box,* she had told him.

But Kleiner was not living in two centuries, regardless of his cracks at his last concert.

"Two of a kind," Clive said promptly. "If Kleiner'd lived in Niall's time, he'd'a' mooned MacDougall, too." He laughed. "Seriously, MacLean, Kleiner called himself Niall Campbell—the day she found him, and again at his last concert. You know that."

"Seriously," Angus said. "When she told me she was pregnant, I thought that's what she'd been hiding. But she just found out her student has an identical twin, and it's got her agitated over Niall Campbell."

There was a brief silence before Clive's voice dropped. "What's he to do with her student's twin?"

"Aye," replied Angus. "It's like when we talked to her at the hotel. She's not saying something. She knows a great deal about Campbell but evades when I ask for her sources." He cleared his throat. "Being pregnant doesn't explain her saying Kleiner's never coming back. Why do these twins get her upset about a medieval knight?"

"I'll think on it," Clive said. "Though how I'd even begin to research such a thing, I'd not know. Ancestor? Family curse? Buried treasure?"

"I'd say don't be ridiculous," Angus said, "but I can think of no rational connection." Watching the door, he lowered his voice. "There's something else. I didn't want to say it before. I feel disloyal."

"If she's lying, you've no reason to," Clive said

"You've met her," Angus shot back. "Do you believe for a minute she's a bad sort?"

"No," Clive said. "But clearly she's hiding something."

"Why does a good person hide things?" Angus asked. "Because the timing of her break up with him has been bothering me for a time now."

"I've been thinking on it, too," Clive said. "And it can't be as she told you."

"You see the problem, too." Angus drummed his fingers on the steering wheel, watching the door. "She said they broke up the night before he disappeared."

"Witnesses say he spent that evening playing harp at the re-enactment in Bannockburn. His phone was with her, over two hundred kilometers away at the hotel in Inverness."

"Could he have called her from someone else's phone?"

"Possible," Clive said. "But unlikely. Hold on."

"I'll have to hang up if she comes out." Angus listened to the soft shuffle of paper over the line, and muffled tones of Clive speaking to someone. The door of the pub swung open. He took a quick breath, but Sinead's family emerged. He relaxed against the seat, listening to the girls chatter as they passed. He watched them, identical in their black, bouncing curls, dark eyes, and sprinkle of freckles, and smiled.

"Here," Clive said. "That Rob fella said she broke up with him in the tower."

Angus frowned. "I don't remember that."

"Pat down the hall overheard him and mentioned it to me but last week."

"But that can't be," Angus objected. "That was two weeks *before* the re-enactment."

"He was quite put out that they were back on such good terms. *Very* good. Kissing-backstage-after-the-concert good."

Angus frowned, less than pleased with the image himself. For a fleeting moment, he sympathized with Rob. "So 'tis odd she'd break up with him again. Apart from the lack of a phone or any witness to him using one." He watched the twins argue beside their car, wondering which was Sinead. One girl grinned at him, waved, and hopped into the vehicle.

"Angus?"

"What?" Angus snapped his attention back to Clive.

"I asked, are you sure you want to be involved in this?"

"Don't think badly of her," Angus said. "I've always had a good sense for character, and I don't believe she's done anything wrong." He watched the second girl stomp around her family's car.

"She seems a good sort," Clive agreed. "But you're on shaky ground already, seeing someone you were assigned to on a case."

"Aye," Angus admitted.

"Have you found out why she believes he's not coming back?"

"I've not asked," Angus said. "I'm not here as an inspector."

"Come now, Angus, you ought to know what you're dealing with."

"She'll tell me when she's ready."

"She's suggesting he's *dead!* You're losing your professional sense for personal reasons!"

"I am," Angus sighed. "But I like being with her."

"You mightn't have a choice, in the end," Clive warned.

The pub door swung open again. "Text me if you think of anything." Feeling guilty, Angus stowed the phone as Amy appeared, her white hat snug over thick, black hair spilling the length of her back. She smiled. He jumped from the car, rounding it to open her door. He desperately wanted her in his life, the Glenmirril Lady who'd brought his feelings gloriously alive after eight dormant years.

Stirling, Present

"Alec, what are these?"

Alec looked up to see his intern holding a medieval helmet, sword, and heavy puddle of iron. "Chain mail?" Alec's forehead wrinkled. "Where'd you find that, now?"

"The old lockers down at the end," the boy answered.

"Those haven't been used in months," Alec replied. "Did you find paperwork on them?"

The boy shook his head. Alec swiveled his chair to a cabinet and dug through. He pulled a file, read it, frowning, and reached for the helmet atop the pile in the lad's arms. It tumbled from his hands, its weight surprising him. Dirt fell from it, dusting his desk. He brushed at it, smearing his report, before lifting the helmet and irritably shaking filth to the floor. The boy waited, silent but for the clink of chain as he shifted under the weight of mail and sword.

Alec ran his finger along the swirls of artwork adorning the helmet's edges. He scratched at a dark fleck, before realization hit him. "It's blood!" He yanked his hand back. The helmet rattle to his desk. "Whose are these?" He snatched the papers from under the crusty helmet. "The re-enactment," he murmured. He looked up to the boy. "I'm no expert, but they look real."

"My Uncle Brian works in the Creagsmalan archives," the boy volunteered. "Will I call him?"

Alec pondered only a moment, before nodding. "And find out what happened to whoever owns these."

CHAPTER TWO

The Road to Stirling, 1314

"Enjoying married life?" Shawn asked with a wink and a leer. Cold wind whistled down the wooded, mountain path, flinging his words away. Clouds and forest canopy left the trail gloomy.

"'Tis none of your affair." Niall smiled, as his pony trotted up chilly wooded hills toward Stirling. A coif covered his head, shorn of the long, golden-brown hair like Shawn's own, during his escape from Creagsmalan, barely a week hence. The hood of his cloak covered the coif. His eyes, golden-brown like Shawn's, twinkled with humor.

"Yeahhh, you're loving it." Shawn tugged his cloak close, hunching over the bobbing neck of his pony, a shield against cutting wind. "Imagine, an altar boy finding it's not so bad after all."

"What's this altar boy business?" Niall asked.

"Altar boys serve Mass. You don't have altar boys in this holy, holy time?"

"Acolytes serve with the priest," Niall said.

"Yeah, well, in my time, it's boys." The path narrowed, fir trees closing in on either side. "Stop grinning like an idiot. Don't you get that it's an *insult?*"

Niall regarded him quizzically. "An insult from you, now, 'tis hardly surprising. But why accusing me of serving our Lord should *be* an insult, I've no idea."

Shawn rolled his eyes, not seeing the low-hanging limb.

"Watch the branch," Niall murmured, as it swatted him in the head.

"Oh so pure and holy, can't even touch a woman."

Niall smiled again, a self-satisfied grin.

"Before marriage, I meant," Shawn snapped.

"Purity as an insult," Niall mused. "To each his own."

"Come on, spill the details," Shawn goaded. "We've got a long ride. We need to talk about something."

Niall shook his head, still grinning. "Then I'd have to kill you."

Shawn ducked the second low-hanging limb. Riling Niall had not been the fun he'd expected. The man just kept grinning like an idiot staring at a pot of gold no one else could see. "Toto...." Shawn intoned.

Niall snatched a pine cone off a tree and whipped it at him, laughing. "We're not in Kansas because it'll not exist until the 1800's. You thought I couldn't learn as quickly as you, did you not?"

"Oh, yeah? What year did Toto become a state?" Shawn challenged.

"'Tis not a state, but a dog, or a quartet."

"A band, not a quartet. Big difference. Toto is a dog. Nice to know at least you're learning something, too."

"Though nothing as useful as what you're learning." Niall ducked as two pine cones sailed back at him.

"I'll get the details out of you sooner or later." Shawn returned to his favorite subject. "You may as well tell me now. Is she...."

Niall flipped a pine cone at him with a sharp flick of the wrist. They reached the crest of the hill and started downward. "I'm surprised to find you in such high spirits," Niall said.

"Shouldn't I be?"

Niall shrugged. "The tower failed you. You're trapped here."

"Yeah. Well." Shawn dug a hunk of bread from his sporran, while his pony jolted rhythmically beneath the trees. "When I hung around the tower after you and Allene left, I stood there looking out over the hills, trying to throw a pity party, but instead, I kept thinking about you waking up in my time." He swallowed the hard bread. "In the last six months, you've been shot in the rear, nearly died of infection, sucked into the twenty-first century, had your best friend sell you out, killed him, and barely escaped MacDougall's noose. But *you're* still cheerful."

"Arrows, battles, hanging." Niall shrugged. "These things happen. But you—you've lost everything."

"Your best friend selling you out *happens*?"

Niall stared straight ahead as their ponies trotted, side by side, down the slope. "He's not the first man to betray a friend. Nor will he be the last."

"You just take it for granted you can't trust anyone?"

Niall turned. "Like Amy trusted you?" They stared one another down for a full minute, Shawn's eyes hard, before Niall shrugged. "I'm sorry. 'Twas unnecessary." He cleared his throat. "I imagine they offered him land."

Shawn's shoulders relaxed. "I didn't sell her out, much less kill her. And for *land*? Why not just buy it?"

"One can't just *buy* land," Niall exclaimed in disbelief. "One must be given it. He was offered what most men only dream of."

As their ponies plodded up the next slope, the trees thinned. The way opened to a pass, looking down into a valley. A river ran through it, steel-blue against the browns and Kelly greens of the glen.

"So it's okay, then?" Shawn let the sarcasm flow. "Thou shalt not murder, unless thou wantest land?"

"I *understand*," Niall corrected. "I killed my best friend. Naught will make that right."

"He didn't leave you much choice."

"No. Which is why it does no good to think on it. We can't change the past, aye?"

Shawn chuckled. "Well, actually, we did."

Niall smiled, but the sadness didn't leave his eyes. He tapped his heels against his pony, and they started down the steep slope to the glen.

A memory came to Shawn, of his first morning in medieval Glenmirril, when all had thought him to be Niall. "He tried to save you."

Niall turned, hope flickering in his eyes. "Why d' you think so?"

"That first morning, he came to my room—your room—and said he wanted to go with me, with you, whatever. He said I was injured and asked me to let him go instead."

The flicker of light grew. "He'd have stopped Hugh's men joining Bruce, without killing me."

Shawn nodded eagerly. "Is it possible MacDougall had something on him to pressure him?"

Niall shrugged. "Kin who could be turned over to the English, a youthful indiscretion, many things. Though I'd think I'd know of those. We were close." He snapped the reins, and the small garron trotted more quickly. "'Tis over and done. I've understood, these past months, that he envied me. I didn't see it, for I never envied anyone. I was content with my lot, even before the Laird took notice of me. But Iohn always felt his lack. He always wanted to have and do and be more."

"No, no, *no!*" Shawn shook his head hard. "Quit *excusing* him!"

Niall's voice, when he spoke, was low, tinged with shame. "I am but saying—I had my faults, too. I riled him when I didn't need to. I was always a wee bit faster, stronger, smarter. And I needled him about it. When he could get a sound from the sackbut and I couldn't, I dismissed it as a foolish instrument."

"Well." Shawn guided his pony to the stream, and reined it in. "Those *are* fighting words."

Niall laughed. "We all have our faults, aye? I've seen mine more clearly in the last six months than ever before. I pray for his soul, and mine. He lived in envy and died of it, while I'm alive, married to the woman I've loved for years. What have I to complain of?"

As they reached the bottom of the slope, the grim sky lightened, spilling weak sunlight across the valley floor. They guided their animals to the snaking stream. It bubbled happily against thin ice at the edges. Shawn held his tongue. If Niall could move on, he supposed it was best to let him. The ponies nuzzled at silver water with velvety lips. Shawn slid from the animal's back to his knees, and cupped his hands to drink beside it.

"But you." Niall, too, slid to the frosty ground. "You're caught far from home and Amy."

Shawn shrugged, letting Iohn go to his grave. "Next time, right? If you did it twice, I can, too. What's the secret?"

Niall pushed the hood of his cloak back, gulped from the cold stream, and shook his head, sending glittering droplets of water flying. "I've thought on it a hundred times."

Shawn nodded, squatting back on his heels. "And?" The horse pushed its nose against his ear. He scratched its bristly chin.

"There've always been stories of men disappearing and coming back years later, when they thought but days or hours had passed. They come from somewhere, aye?"

"Aye," Shawn said. "What places?"

"Fairy hills." Niall climbed to his feet, and swung back onto the horse. "They're all over. Erceldoune. The Eildon Hills where Thomas the Rhymer disappeared, a wee bit south of Melrose."

"Yeah, I know where it is." Shawn planted his foot in the stirrup and swung up onto the garron. His travels with Douglas had taught him a great deal. "So your next brilliant idea is a fairy hill?"

Niall grinned. "'Tis one way of getting rid of you before you conjugate a verb poorly and make me look like a fool before the Bruce."

Shawn laughed. "Too bad for you I'll be talking to Bruce before you can push me down a fairy hole."

Road to Northern England, Present

I'm quiet as we drive into the world of James Douglas's raids, trying to unknot this mess Shawn has left me. He survived a charging knight. Afterward, he and Niall lived, both, as Niall. One of them raided with Douglas, one was in Creagsmalan's dungeon. Shawn's mark is at Creagsmalan, where MacDougall built gallows—for 'Niall.' My hand goes to my stomach, to Shawn's child. Modern men don't hang from gallows. It's too awful to think of.

Mist wreathes the brown hills. It thins as the sun climbs. Angus points to a road, telling me about the castle there. I barely hear, my mind stuck on this puzzle: Shawn's mark is also on papers signed by 'Niall' as Douglas left for these raids. So was it Shawn *on the raids? But then how did his mark come to be at Creagsmalan? Would MacDougall take a prisoner to the chapel? If Shawn was with Douglas, he didn't hang. But that means Niall did. Niall who played harp. Niall who wrapped his arm around me on the train and rested his cheek on my head and spoke so warmly of those he loved. "That supply list," I ask abruptly. "He'd have signed it before they left, right?"*

"What?" Angus turns in surprise.

I shrug. "Just thinking about these raids, that's all."

"They moved fast," he says. "They traveled light. They'd not carry unnecessary papers. Yes, I'm sure he signed at Stirling."

My heart rises for Niall; it sinks for Shawn. My mind trails, like a child's finger on a frosted window, through my life with him, the good and the bad, gazing out the window into memories as Angus guides the car up twisting, hilly roads.

"Sure you're aw' right?" Angus reaches between our seats to lay his big, warm hand over mine. I relax under his touch. I was so tense, by the end, with Shawn. I was different before I met him. Can I tell Angus about it? We've talked, we've kissed, we've shared secrets and fears. But telling him my weaknesses, mistakes, the parts I'm ashamed of—that's a deeper intimacy than the world approves—the intimacy of letting that mask slip, the one we keep on even with our closest friends, not trusting even them to really accept us as we are.

The car rounds a bend, bursting onto a straight shot through high Northumbrian hills, as my mind shoots onto another question. Niall crossed twice. So can Shawn. Will he? Now, when I thought he was dead? When I've built a life without him?

It's not as if I have to choose between them, I told Rose. It would be horrible to be put in that position.

Angus glances at me, concern on his face. "Something's eating you."

"Just tired." I stare out at desolate hills, brown with November decay. Mist floats over the moors. Shawn signed Douglas's forms. His mark proves it. If it was him in Northumbria, I'll find his mark there. Right? And if I do—what does it mean, and what then?

Glenmirril, 1314

MacDougall's demeanor grew stormier as the walls of Glenmirril rose into view over the next hill. Christina kept her face passive, daring show no relief or joy. They wouldn't hang her at Glenmirril. She remembered the people there as kind.

MacDougall unfurled his raven banner a mile from the castle. It snapped, blue and gold, in the cold November wind. They trotted down the hill, and the envoy halted, tack jingling, hooves stamping the powdery snow at the edge of the moat. Water flowed, inky and black, below. Helmeted guards peered down from the parapets.

"'Tis MacDougall!" one of Christina's guards bellowed. "Open up!"

Christina's heart pounded, fearing her reprieve would evaporate like morning mist. She shivered in the cold.

MacDonald himself appeared on the parapets, distinctive with his bushy red-streaked beard. "Have you brought the lass?" he called down. Archers appeared, stretching out on either side of him. They lifted their bows, a fluid and deadly ballet; arrows whispered back alongside a dozen ears.

"She's here beside me," MacDougall shouted up. "You can see her! Take her and let us be on our way."

"Move your men back two furlongs."

MacDougall grumbled, but signaled his men with a jerk of his head. He and Christina waited, their horses snorting cold breath into the winter air, while his men backed up with a rustle of horseflesh and squeak of leather. The winches creaked. The great drawbridge trembled high above their heads, dropping inch by inch. The archers stood, immobile, watching, while MacDonald disappeared.

Christina felt MacDougall's eyes on her. She held her head high, her face passive, eyes straight ahead, hiding the shaking inside. She wanted to bolt, to throw herself across the drawbridge, to safety, before it touched ground. But MacDougall must not see how badly she wanted to flee.

The bridge hit the ground with a heavy thud in the snow-dampened earth. MacDougall's horse clopped halfway across and stopped. Astride his own horse, with men guarding the gatehouse behind him, MacDonald met them in the center. Christina searched faces, keeping her own impassive, for any sign of Niall or Shawn. Wind roared in her ears. MacDonald's horse bumped its nose up against MacDougall's. "Has Duncan harmed her in any way?"

"Duncan harmed her in many ways, of which I knew naught till two nights ago. She has had a physician's care. Duncan will answer to me in kind."

"Christina." MacDonald turned to her. "Does he speak the truth?"

"'Tis true he did not know." Her voice echoed hollowly in her own head. "He stayed Duncan's hand and sent for a physician." She trembled, fearing MacDougall would somehow snatch her back.

"Are you satisfied he will deal with his son?"

"I am." She kept her face still as a rock, looking at neither man, refusing to say anything that might delay the moment of crossing those last precious feet to safety.

"Send her in and be on your way," MacDonald said.

"Give us a moment," MacDougall replied.

MacDonald spoke a silent question to Christina with his eyes. She nodded, though her insides trembled. "Two minutes." MacDonald backed his horse, clopping on hard wood, into the shadow of the gatehouse, watching them.

Christina turned to MacDougall, staring at a spot above his nose and freezing her face into the expressionless mask that had protected her from the worst of Duncan's rages.

"You're safe," he said. "Whatever your answer. Did you mean what you said in the stable or was it a ruse to get me out of the castle?"

"I spoke the truth." Her mare sidestepped beneath her, and shook its head. She had indeed longed for a kind touch. She thanked God she'd not had to endure his.

"I cared for you, Christina." The words came out a whisper, as dry as the winter air around them.

"Thank you, My Lord."

"Alexander."

She bowed her head. "Thank you for protecting me from Duncan."

"Christina…"

The trembling inside her grew. "Thank you, My Lord." She touched her heels to the mare, guiding it across the bridge and into the gatehouse. Cold air shimmered around her. Darkness closed in, narrowing her view to a steadily darkening tunnel. She kept her eyes straight ahead, vaguely aware of MacDonald's hand falling on her reins, and the creaking of winches as they pulled the bridge up behind her. Steel held her spine straight and her chin up, a gracious smile frozen on her face for those thronging the courtyard. Allene appeared. It must be Allene with red hair, easing her from her horse, an arm around her back. Stone walls rose around her. Stairs moved, slid drunkenly under her feet. The door of a bed chamber clicked behind her. Dark blue hangings wavered before her eyes, her knees sagged.

"Nobody is to know," she heard MacDonald say, over and over. The sound echoed in a dream-like tunnel. "Nobody must know. There is only Niall. D' you understand?"

She nodded, and sank into darkness.

CHAPTER THREE

Stirling Castle, 1314

He could fool anyone about anything, Shawn reminded himself for the tenth time, as he rose to his feet. But Bruce, mighty king of Scotland, taciturn in his gold-threaded lion tabard, and his battle-hardened commanders with scarred faces and daggers in their boots, seated around a great oak slab, were not Conrad and the orchestra directors with whitened teeth and baby blue Polos, sipping coffee around polished mahogany.

Sunlight poured through the window, flashing off the discreet gold circle that marked Bruce as king. "Tell us, Sir Niall, what you learned," he said.

Shawn swallowed. He and Niall had gone over the story a dozen times, combing it for inaccuracies. The less said, the better. "John of Lorn and Duncan MacDougall are gathering ships to re-take the Isle of Man."

Edward Bruce stroked his chin. "How do you know?"

It was the question Shawn had hoped not to hear. They all believed Niall had spent autumn with James Douglas in England. "I learned it both from MacDougall's kin, and from one at Creagsmalan who is overseeing preparations." His stomach clenched, hoping the answer would satisfy.

"Who?" Edward persisted.

The other lords leaned forward, waiting.

"To say would endanger the person," Shawn hedged.

"To send our men into battle on poor information," said Lennox, "would endanger *them*."

Shawn cleared his throat, buying time to think up an answer.

"It's rumored," Edward inserted into the silence, "that you were in MacDougall's dungeon. What say you of that, My Lord?"

"I was not in MacDougall's dungeon." A smile stretched across Shawn's face. Lying became significantly easier when he could grasp on a point of truth. "I've heard it myself, and 'tis laughable that MacDougall makes such claim when all know I was with Sir Douglas. I've barely had time to cross the country, get the information, and be back here."

"Not to mention he was married in his short time home," Douglas added. "MacDougall seeks to cause trouble."

Shawn's stomach loosened its death grip on his bowels.

Douglas leaned forward, his black beard brushing the scarred, wooden table. "Though I, too, am curious how you did it."

"I sent a messenger ahead to summon my informant," Shawn said. It wasn't a lie. His 'messenger' just so happened to be the real Niall. He turned to Bruce. "I am confident 'tis as accurate as possible, short of coming from Duncan, MacDougall, or John of Lorn, themselves." He bowed low, hoping, praying almost, that this would be the end of it.

"Step forward, Sir Niall," Bruce said.

Shawn's stomach resumed its fidgeting. Blood trickled like ice in his veins. He was on this man's good side, he reminded himself, but still he felt the shadow of steel blades all around him. He forced reluctant steps around the table, around the commanders. With each step, the table grew longer; the blades in their boots sharper. He reached Bruce on shaky legs, though he held his back straight, and told himself it was only Conrad. He bowed. "Your Grace?"

"Name your informant," Bruce ordered, *dolce piano*.

"Christina." Shawn met Bruce's *piano* and lowered him a *pianissimo*. His nerves settled. He trusted Bruce. "Duncan's wife. She's no cause to love him. He ill-treats her, Your Grace."

"So I've heard." Bruce reached for his belt. Shawn's heart thumped a double beat, fearing a knife.

"For your service." Bruce held out a leather bag, swollen with what could only be gold.

"Your Grace." Shawn bowed low, accepting the bag. He would live!

St. Bee's, Cumbria, England, Present

"It's huge!" Removing her gloves, Amy stared up at the massive arch framing the altar of St. Bee's. But her mind was on her research of the previous months, trying to think of a piece she'd forgotten, something to tell her, definitively, that neither Shawn nor Niall had been hanged.

"You're pale." Angus touched her cheek. "I'm worried, you being pregnant and all. Was this long trip a good idea? Do you want to sit down? Or get water?"

"I'm fine." Her mind skittered back to someone who looked like Niall walking the shore with his son—like a twenty-first century father.

Angus watched her.

"I was expecting ruins." She ran her hand over the smooth edge of a baptismal font, hoping to distract him. "You said James Douglas burned and looted the churches." Her hand tightened around Bruce's ring. Which of them had stood here, maybe looked up at the altar, or to the roof soaring high, supported by gray stone columns, maybe touched this very font? Niall would have hated ransacking a church. Shawn, not so much.

"Sometimes," Angus said. "But there was a great deal of restoration in the 1800's." Angus checked his watch. "The reverend said he'd meet us here."

Amy scanned the pews marching in stately splendor toward lacework grills framing the altar. At that moment, a slight, middle-aged man in a black suit and white collar emerged from a side door. He bustled across the front of the altar, smiling. "You must be Angus," he said. "Let me say how much nicer cross-border visits are today than in the time you're asking after!" He skipped down the stair to join them, proving to be barely Amy's height, and shook hands. "Come along to the chapel." He led them to one side of the church, a rising wall of silver-gray stone, shimmering with stained glass set high above, as he launched into the church's history.

Amy's mind danced between Niall, Shawn, and the vicar's story of St. Bee, an Irish princess fleeing a forced marriage. A chieftain promised her all the land covered by snow the next day—a safe, if cruel, promise on Midsummer's day. At dawn, however, three miles lay under a frosty, white blanket. The land became hers to offer in God's service.

"The baptismal font and piscina," he said, as they passed, "were here during Douglas's raids. "The windows are much newer." He pointed to the stained glass, pouring down jewel-colored patches of light on the stone floor, as he led them back toward the church's main door.

"What was there in Douglas's day?" Amy could imagine a cloudy night with a sliver of pearl-white moon peering in. Her mind stuck on the one question. Which of them had been here to see it?

"'Twould have been open or maybe glazed glass—white or green. Here's the flood." Green and brown light shimmered through the bearded man in the window, his arms upraised. "Abraham and Isaac." Blues and reds shone, as the man raised his knife over his son. "I know you are a God-fearing man," quoted the vicar, "for you have not withheld your only son. Take the ram instead."

"It seems cruel." Amy thought of the child within her, and the other one, the first time she'd been pregnant with Shawn's child. Irritation at Shawn blossomed and burst into the familiar anger.

"It shows how far God Himself went for us," the vicar replied. "He watched *His* only son die." His smile never left. "Here, Joseph meeting his brothers in Egypt. Forgiving everything."

She had plenty, she thought, to forgive Shawn for—the child she'd never know, and pressuring her into so many things. They passed below each window, the length of the peaceful church: The Sermon on the Mount, the Annunciation, the Transfiguration. Long-forgotten stories came back to Amy. She felt audacious, being in a house of God after ignoring Him for so long. And she hadn't come for God at all. She touched the crucifix, under her thick sweater, wondering if Niall would have given it to her, if he'd known how far she was from his world and his beliefs. She should have insisted he keep it. It had meant a great deal to him and Allene.

Angus touched her arm. She looked up. His dark eyes met hers, questioning. "Are you all right?"

She nodded, her eyes sliding away from his. The abortion was more she hadn't told him. The vicar had moved ahead. They hurried to catch up, through jewel-colored sunbeams dancing with dust motes.

"Relics from the fourteenth century, now," the vicar was saying. "The door has been here since long before that. The pride of our local historians." He tugged at the heavy doors, and stepped out into biting November air. Amy pulled on her hat. With a strong breeze grappling with her hair and whipping her coat around her legs, the vicar's fascination caught her in its grip. She backed up to get a full view of the five red stone arches zeroing in on the door.

"Up there, do you see?" The vicar pointed up to a small carving. "We believe 'tis the face of Christ."

Amy ran her hand along the arch, wondering if Niall had put his hand here, if he'd leaned against the wall, cleaning his fingernails with a dirk, or shouted at his men to follow him.

"The raids went on for years," the vicar was saying. "St. Bee's was close enough to Scotland, we got our share. They'd storm down from that ridge." He pointed to the northern hills. "They came in the night, burned the town and fields, drove off the cattle."

And what, Amy wondered, had happened between Shawn and Niall, caught together. How had they explained Shawn's presence? Her eyes fell on the mark. Seven hundred years had softened the lines, but there, in the red stone, were three slashes: a long middle line, short ones above on the left, and below on the right. No curves connected them this time. She traced the lines. Her thoughts tumbled one over the other.

"I see you've found our mystery graffiti. There's another, of an archer, inside." The vicar touched Shawn's mark, his hand by hers on the door frame. "Nobody can explain it."

"I can," Amy whispered.

Glenmirril, November 1314

"Did they send nothing with you?" Allene asked. Christina had slept the better part of three days, before Allene insisted she rise, eat, and stroll in the gardens.

"He did not even tell me where I was going." Christina pushed at the bread before her. The fear of the last weeks had not fully receded. "I feared he was taking me to hang me in the forest."

MacDonald paced the room, filling the space with his heavy cloak, thick beard, and agitation. "'Tis no matter. You'll be provided for. You are Morrison's kin, after all. Now is it clear there must be no word, ever, of Shawn? There is only Niall."

Christina nodded.

"They are *both* Niall, you understand?"

"She *understands*, Father!" Allene said. "Now do leave us in peace!"

He let out a grunt, and left them.

When the heavy door had swung to, Christine asked, "How does it happen my father-in-law brought me here instead of bringing Niall back to Creagsmalan?"

"Shawn did it."

Christina leaned forward. "Who is this Shawn?"

Stirling Castle, November 1314

"He gave me go-old! He gave me go-old!" Shawn danced around the middle of the small cell he shared at Stirling Castle with Niall, swinging the bag of gold over his head. "Oh, yeah, I'm the man! I'm the *man!*" He gyrated his hips, and lifted the bag high over the table, letting the gold coins spill out, winking in the noon light pouring through the arched window. He let out a boisterous laugh. "As rich as I was, I never actually had a handful of gold! This is great!"

Niall cleared his throat. "Aye, well, if you're done acting the fool...." He stood against the wall, cleaning his fingernails with his dirk.

Shawn laughed. "It's called having fun." He lifted a handful of gold high in the air, letting it spill through his fingers, clinking, clattering, and rolling into the pile on the table, and kissed the last remaining pieces in his palm. "Oh, yeah!"

Niall jabbed the knife back in his boot and came to the table. "It seems you've once more gotten credit for my work."

"You think so?" In the small room they shared, Shawn grinned as he spun a chair around and dropped on it, arms crossed on its back. "Niall Campbell gets the credit, regardless of who stood in front of Bruce today." Shawn reached into his tartan for the bread and meat he'd hidden in its folds, and tossed them on the table before Niall. "I did everything with Douglas, but it's Niall Campbell who's a knight. My name means nothing. I don't even exist."

"Aye," Niall acknowledged. "Still, 'tis no great craic, knowing my name is a lie and I didn't actually do those things." He lowered his eyes to the food. "The Bruce was pleased, then?"

Shawn lifted a handful of coins, grinning. "Ya think? They found out who told MacDougall you'd be heading his way, and I understand he'll be swinging from a rope himself if he ever sets foot in Scotland again." The gold lay warm in Shawn's palm. In six months here, he'd had nothing of his own. He ate what lord or land provided. He wore what was given to him. He missed having his own things. He missed being able to walk into a store and buy what he wanted.

He missed—he saw in a flash of insight—not the things themselves, but the power to have all he desired with almost less effort than snapping his fingers.

His grin slipped. "The chain, you know," he said, "I did those things. I earned that. But the gold is yours."

Niall stared at it, not touching it. "He gave it to you."

"You got the information. Why wouldn't you take it?"

Niall said nothing. A guess formed in Shawn's mind, culled from months in the environment. "You're a future laird. It would be like taking money from a commoner, wouldn't it?"

"'Twas given to you," Niall said, tersely.

"Only because I'm the one who went down. Because I have hair, and we don't want your clansmen and Bruce comparing notes and asking why you shaved your head on the way to Parliament." Shawn pushed the gold across the table. "You'll have a castle to run, people to care for."

Niall stared at the wall beyond Shawn's head.

"He intended it for the man who got the information," Shawn said. "Take it. Use it to help Adam's widow and her new baby. It's your duty as laird-to-be." *Duty,* Shawn had found, was a useful word in this time. Especially with Niall. "Otherwise, I'm using it to buy ale and prettier company than yours."

Scowling, Niall scooped the coins into his sporran. "For Adam's widow, then." He gulped his wine.

"Great." Shawn paced the room. "So parliament then on to the Eildon Hills. I have even less faith in fairy hills than in God. So what's our plan when that fails?"

"I'm traveling a full day's ride out of my way to help you," Niall snapped. "Without my laird's permission or knowledge. Must you be so negative?"

"I'm being *realistic*," Shawn shot back. "And having a plan B never killed anyone."

Niall sat silently for half a minute, before saying, "I'll ask the Bishop."

"B for Bishop." Shawn rolled his eyes. "I had to ask. Do they actually *teach* history in your schools? Because, you know, asking a medieval bishop about time travel might get us labeled witches, which would get us hanged, which, in case MacDougall wasn't clear, would *kill* us."

"Did you not ask for a plan B?" Niall glared.

"Yeah, but what does a *medieval bishop* know about time travel?"

"A bishop is wise in God's ways." Niall stood, shoving his chair back. "I've no way of knowing what he can tell us, but the other choice is to do naught." He glanced around the room, grabbed the coif, and pulled it over the tight cap of hair that no longer looked like the flowing chestnut mane the world expected of Niall Campbell.

"You're going now?" Shawn asked. "What if he hangs you for asking about time travel? I don't think...."

Niall stopped, a hand on the door, and pierced him with a hard stare. "Stay here. Don't show your face."

"Don't be...."

Niall slammed the door in his face.

"...stupid!" He glared at the door, hands on hips. He considered going right out after Niall, pulling him back. He decided, finally, against it, throwing his agitation instead into carving his mark. Asking a medieval bishop about time travel seemed like the only thing that could possibly be worse than doing nothing.

CHAPTER FOUR

St. Bee's, Cumbria, England, Present

Angus leaned close, studying the scratches. He lifted his eyes to Amy's. "'Tis very like the one at Creagsmalan, is it not?"

Amy nodded, mutely.

"You're pale," said Angus. "Shall we get in from the cold?" He tugged the doors, ushering her inside. The vicar followed, talking about a bowman scratched on another wall.

Amy finished the tour in a daze. When the vicar left them, she collapsed in the back pew.

Angus chafed her cold hands. Their knees touched. "What's wrong, Amy?" he asked softly.

"Nothing." She shook her head, unable to look at him. The realization of Shawn's survival, and the questions it spawned, overwhelmed her. And she wondered how Shawn had lied so easily, because she felt she'd be sick if she lied to Angus one more time.

"Clearly summat's wrong." His hands wrapped around hers. "You've been agitated since you saw Sinead's twin."

She stared into the dusty sunbeams slanting down from the windows. He would think she was crazy. But she couldn't stand the lies.

"Amy," he pressed. "Trust me, finally. What's going on?"

Tears pricked the corners of her eyes. "You promised me once you would never think I'm crazy."

"I won't."

"I warned you you might be put to the test," she said. "In a house of God, of all places, can you believe I'm telling the truth, no matter how crazy it sounds?"

"I trust you. Sinead's twin brings us back to Niall. The three lines have startled you twice now. You said they're Niall's mark. Why does that upset you?"

Pulling her hands from his, Amy dug in her purse for a softened sheet of pink paper—Shawn's last letter to her, with the words *mo gradh* and his mark at the bottom. She stared at Bruce's ring on her finger as Angus took the letter.

"Shawn signed his letters with Niall's mark?" He looked up, brow wrinkling. "He called himself Niall Campbell at the last concert, and when you found him at Glenmirril. What's his thing with Niall Campbell?"

Amy reached inside her sweater for the crucifix out, lifting it over her head and down the length of her hair.

"How does this answer my question?" he asked as he accepted it.

"Look at it closely."

He took his time, turning it over, holding it up to the light, before saying, "'Tis medieval or an excellent reproduction. Will you tell me now who gave it to you?"

"Could you prove it was a reproduction, or if it's real?"

"It looks authentic." Angus touched the carved Christ. "And yet too new to be so."

She slid the ring from her finger, and handed it to him, watching as he studied it, too. Sunlight shot down from the windows, glinting off Bruce's garnet in the cavernous church. "Look inside," she said.

He squinted at the inscription. *"Roibert de Briuis 1298?"* He raised his head. "Where did you get it? I'd swear 'tis real gold, and a real jewel. And this is how he'd have spelled his name."

"Let that sink in." Amy pushed the ring back on her finger. "Tell me what the police reports said about Shawn's injuries. You wrote them yourself."

"An arrow wound in the posterior." He shook his head, like something had lodged in his ear. She felt she could read his thoughts. Living and breathing Niall as they did, how could he not be thinking of Niall's identical injury?

"What else?" she asked. "I need to hear you say it. *You* need to hear *yourself* say it."

"He had an infection that could have come from such a wound," he said. "But the doctor said—he was very insistent—the wound was older than the few hours you'd left him, the infection more advanced. He was very clear, either you weren't telling all you knew, or you didn't know he was wounded when you left him."

"Could he have hidden an arrow wound?" Amy asked.

"No," Angus said decisively.

"Did he climb over walls and up to the tower with an arrow wound?"

"No."

"Did the doctor see the scars on his back?" she asked.

He nodded, frowning. "What were they from? You didn't mention them at the time."

"Because I didn't see his back until later. So I had no reason to tell the police Shawn's back was perfect. Do you understand? *Perfect.* Not a mark."

Angus's frowned deepened. "It wasn't Shawn."

Her respect for him jumped. He looked at the facts, saw the answer, and accepted his conclusion, far more quickly than she had, with her eternal self-doubt. "It wasn't," she agreed. "Do I sound crazy yet?"

His eyebrows creased more fiercely over his nose. In the still church, the air hummed, dust motes hummed, sunbeams shooting through the windows hummed in expectation.

"Who had an arrow wound?" she whispered. "You never found a maniac with a bow."

"Aye, and it's continued to be a concern in Inverness," he said.

"Who had flogging scars on his back?" she asked. "Who played harp?"

Shock registered on his face, an unnatural stillness. "No, now, listen to yourself." Angus laughed. Then he frowned. "You're overstressed. Niall died in the forest of...." He stopped, staring at her.

"You remember telling me that, that day in the hospital?"

"Aye, but why would I've said such a thing?"

"Because at the time it was true." She leaned forward. "As history happened *at the time*, he never reached Bannockburn."

"But that's impossible."

"Then why did you just say it?"

Angus pressed his fingers to his forehead, blinking in bewilderment. "But that can't happen."

"Do you remember that first day behind the Heritage Centre?" Her words rushed now, heedless of the reverence she should display in a church. Dust motes jumped, disturbed, an accented staccato, on the sunbeam. "Do you remember saying you kept feeling at the re-enactment that it ended all wrong, that the English were supposed to have won? I spent a week with Niall—*Niall Campbell*—researching why the Scots lost, and I rode a train to Stirling with Niall—*Niall Campbell of Glenmirril*—telling me he knew what went wrong, and he was going back to fix it. Do you remember the reports of two Bruces, and someone killed on the field?"

"A hot day, dehydration, mass hallucinations," Angus sputtered.

Amy slid the ring from her finger. She held it before his eyes. "Conrad saw two of Shawn that day. I saw them. It was Shawn and Niall. Shawn ran toward me. He yelled and threw this, just before he threw himself between a horse and a child. Then it was just the re-enactors, and a statue of Robert Bruce where it had been Edward II of England." She pushed the ring a half inch closer to him. "Is it possible I stole it from a museum or found it on the sidewalk?"

He said nothing.

"We've done a lot of research together," she pressed. "Where did I find out Niall was devout or that he was the spitting image of Shawn? Or whose cattle those were?" Her voice rose. "You notice I never get back to checking my notes." She knew she was becoming agitated, needing him to believe her. "I *couldn't* tell you where I got it without you thinking I'm crazy."

He shook his head, stood up, stared at her, frowning.

"Historical records say Niall Campbell played harp." She held out the ring and crucifix. "Watch the last concert. The man onstage played harp like he'd been doing it all his life. Shawn learned fast, but not that fast. Watch the video.

He *tells* us who he is."

She waited for an answer she knew he couldn't give. "Ask anyone in the orchestra. 'Shawn' came back from Glenmirril obsessed with Bannockburn. He got internet and a computer, he went to museums, he printed up a hundred maps." Her words tumbled out, racing to be heard before he dismissed her as crazy or walked away. "He was trying to reach the Laird's brother, Hugh, to call him and his men to fight at Bannockburn."

Angus shook his head, still looking dazed. "'Tis impossible." He took the ring, gingerly, turning it over, squinting again at the inscription.

"The letter," she said. "Shawn wrote lots of them. That's not Niall's mark. It was a double entendre, a flattened S, or a trombone. Can you see how it would come out as three lines, carving it in the middle of a raid?"

Angus thrust the ring at her. He shook his head sharply. The letter fluttered to the pew.

"Do you think I'm crazy?" Amy whispered. "Overstressed? I'm holding the ring. You've read the medical records. Lots of people saw strange things that day."

"Just give me a minute." Angus stood, looking from side to side, then backed out of the pew. "Just give me a few minutes." He spun, striding heavily from the church.

She dropped her gaze. The crucifix lay in her lap. She lifted it, staring at Christ. Everything drained out of her, all the proof, all the energy.

All the desperation.

Her hand, clutching the crucifix and ring, sagged to her knee. *He thinks I'm crazy.* The thought wobbled in her head. But underneath flowed words like a strong current: *The evidence is all there.* She felt the humming, as if God whispered, *Give Me a chance.* She lifted her head to the crucifix far away down the aisle. She didn't deserve God's help. She'd ignored Him so long, betrayed her beliefs and faith for Shawn, had an abortion. Even now, coming to church for the first time in years, it was for Niall and Shawn, not for God.

Her fingers grew stiff. Her legs and back ached. Angus didn't come back. She crossed her arms on the back of the pew before her, staring unblinking down the long aisle, to the altar, and finally dropped her head on her arms.

Stirling, November, 1314

In an airy solar, with a fire roaring in the grate near the bishop's chair, and November's dead landscape showing through the window arch, Niall greeted the old cleric with uncharacteristic nervousness. He didn't entirely trust Shawn to stay in their room. And he was sure MacDonald would not approve. He was equally sure he couldn't do nothing, after all Shawn had done for him, rescuing him MacDougall's gallows.

The bishop's lush white beard brushed his chest as he extended his hand for the traditional kiss of the ring. His withered body relaxed back in his throne-like chair.

"You know me." Niall took the seat offered. "You know I've ever been faithful to the Church and our Lord Savior Jesus Christ."

The bishop nodded. "Have you done aught that needs confessing, lad?" His voice rasped like stones washing against stones on a pebbly shore.

"I've questions that may raise concerns," Niall hedged. "I'm looking for miracles, for unexplained happenings around Glenmirril."

"Is it the one or is it the other?" the bishop asked. "If 'tis a miracle, then 'tis explained. God intervened."

Niall smiled, imagining Shawn's response to the man's logic. He himself saw sense in it. "What of that which may or may not be a miracle?"

"What sort of thing?" the bishop queried.

"D' you mind the stories of Thomas of Erceldoune?"

"Ah, I knew Thomas well, in the days of Alexander." The bishop stared into space. "A remarkable man. True Thomas, we called him, for he was unable to tell a lie. Yet he claims the most remarkable story of spending only three days in Elfland, while those of us who knew him knew he was gone for seven years."

"What d' you make of it?"

The bishop heaved a sigh, and let his watery gaze drift to the window, and the bleak trees beyond. Niall felt sweat coat his palms. Shawn waited in their room—hopefully. Niall wondered if he should call him in and tell the whole story. MacDonald would definitely not approve. Finally, though, the man answered. "There are things we don't know of this world. We don't understand God's ways. Thomas's prophecies have come true, no?"

"Some of them," Niall said.

"On the morrow, afore noon," quoted the bishop, "shall blow the greatest wind that ever was heard before in Scotland." His eyes met Niall's, full of grief. "This he did say to the Earl of Dunbar, and indeed before noon, we knew our good king Alexander was dead. And his death has indeed brought a great and bitter wind."

"It has, My Lord." Niall's head bowed in sorrow. The bishop had lived a hard life, these years of fighting. But, unlike Niall, he had known a free and prosperous Scotland. Niall could not remember such a thing. He wished Shawn knew from history if he would ever know it—but then, he and Shawn had changed history.

"The rest," spoke the bishop, "time will tell. None have proven false."

"So you believe 'tis possible for time to behave strangely?"

"It seems to have done so for Thomas."

"Was it fairies or a miracle?" Niall asked.

The bishop shrugged. "If fairies exist, they are created by God, and their powers, if unlike our own, are given them by God."

"So you're saying 'tis one and the same, fairy hills or miracles?"

"No." The bishop rose and strode to the fire. He held his hands out to the crackling flames. "If fairies exist, their ways are their natural order, as are ours to us. A miracle goes outside the natural order."

Niall's jaw tensed. He wanted to be back in his room with Allene, not here discussing the difference between miracles and fairy magic. It was all word games, so far. He tried to think of a way to get information without telling the story. "Do you think Thomas had any control over the changes in time?"

The bishop sighed, and Niall wondered if it was his questions or the man's age that were such a trial. He consoled himself it was the latter. The man had lived a harsh life, and suffered greatly in the wars with England. "He'd no control of seven years passing. But he had control over going in with the Queen. And they say he went back in future years and never returned. If so, he had control over that."

"Do you believe he could have moved back and forth across time?" Niall leaned forward, sure he'd get no helpful answer, yet eagerly hoping.

"No," the bishop said. "He lost seven years. He never got those back."

"What if a man did such a thing?" Niall asked. "Jumped ahead by centuries like King Herla—but came back? And what if another man moved backward several centuries from his proper time and wanted to return to his own year? How would he find the natural order that would accomplish that, or how would he re-create the miracle that made it happen the first time?"

The bishop, wilting in his chair, stared blankly for so long that Niall feared he'd drifted off to sleep despite the wide-open watery blue eyes. Then he frowned. "You speak true, Sir Niall. Your questions trouble me. Though, I'd rather your questions be my biggest concern, than our troubles with England." He leaned his head back on a wrinkled neck, stroking his lush white beard, and stared at the ceiling. "You'd first need to know if the act resulted from the natural order, or if it was a suspension of the natural order, that is, a miracle."

"If it happened twice, does that not suggest something in the natural order which can be controlled?"

"Mayhap."

Niall restrained himself from rising from his seat and pacing the room. He tried again. "Are there sacred places around Glenmirril or Bannockburn that might affect such things?"

The Bishop nodded, eyebrows raised. "There are standing stones and such. We couldn't say what they really were. Some believe they were sacred. I'm afraid I can't help you. But there's the wise woman, Sorcha, who lives in the hills east of Inverness. Talk to her."

St. Bee's, Cumbria, England, Present

I wait in the quiet church. Maybe I hope to hear a Heavenly Voice, I chide myself, raining down wisdom. I hear nothing. Maybe I hope Angus will come back. He doesn't.

Irritation washes over me. He keeps walking away. But then, I've dropped a few bombshells, haven't I? Maybe he wouldn't walk away if I had normal things to tell him, like, oh, I forgot the plumber is coming today instead of, by the way, I'm pregnant, or, my ex-boyfriend got sucked into a time void and I spent two weeks with a medieval warrior.

With the softening of my heart toward Angus, another emotion washes over the sands of anger, one I last felt the minute before Shawn walked into my life: Peace. The weight of lies has evaporated.

*November's chill reaches in, trailing icy fingers down my arm. A shiver racks my body. I rise, leaving the peaceful interior. Outside, bare limbs scrape gun-flint clouds. I tug my scarf tight as I pass red stone walls, and under the ancient Beowulf lintel. Did Shawn or Niall glance up at the carved warrior, centuries ago, in the midst of their raid? Beyond the lintel lie the autumn remains of a garden. I follow a path past dead vines and wilted blooms, to a stone sculpture of a woman surrounded by children. A bare shrub arcs behind them. My hand goes to my stomach; my thoughts to the other baby. But the statue wraps comfort around me—*your baby is at peace, *the woman in the statue seems to say.*

Tears sting my eyes. That baby is still more Angus doesn't know.

Angus hunches, elbows on knees, on a wrought iron bench in the curve of the sculpture's embrace. He clasps his wool hat. Compassion is the next wave washing up over the rocky shore of my wild emotional landscape. I take the hat from his unprotesting hands and tug it over his wind-stung ears. "I'm sorry," *I say.*

He looks up with dry, red eyes. Furrows carve his forehead.

"I want to be mad at you," *I say.* "You keep walking away."

Angus squints up as if I speak a foreign language.

"Say something," *I whisper.* "Please. Do you think I'm crazy?"

He clears his throat. He turns to the statue. "I don't think you're a liar. You seem quite sane."

I hold my tongue. I thought much the same of Niall.

"I've been trying to think, did someone pull a horrible prank?" *He squints at the woman and her children, as if they withhold the answer and he can't figure out why they would do that to him.*

I wait, clutching my arms in the chilly breeze.

"But I've gone through all the possibilities, what it would take to get old scars on Shawn's back or find a man exactly like him with Niall Campbell's injuries." *He falls silent. After a minute, he pats the stone bench. I sit down. Cold bites through my long coat and jeans. He wraps his arm around me.*

Relief rushes from my body. He's not running away.

"It explains the Glenmirril Hoax, aye?"

I nod. Yes, Shawn or Niall drew the pictures of airplanes and skyscrapers found at Glenmirril by archaeologists.

He pats my hand, and rises. "Let's find a pub. It's cold and I need a pint."

Maybe two." He leads me down the path, under the bare branches.

I clutch his arm more tightly than I ever have, my stomach in knots. I still haven't told him everything.

CHAPTER FIVE

Stirling Castle, November, 1314

It was Niall, posing as Brother Andrew, who learned that Brother David had returned to Stirling from his journey to Rome to petition the Pope.

It was Shawn, posing as Niall, who met Brother David in their chamber. He was as tall and slender as Shawn remembered him. He gripped Shawn's hand in a strong clasp, clapped his shoulder, and said, "Welcome back to the land of the living. When I left Stirling, I thought I'd only see you on the other side. I'm eternally grateful to you for saving my life, at least twice."

"Don't mention it," Shawn said. "But maybe you can help me this time. I need information, any wisdom you might have. I need to know what the Church thinks of Thomas of Erceldoune."

"Thomas the Rhymer?" Brother David moved to the window, staring out over bleak barren hills frosted with a powdered sugar dusting of snow. "A man who could not tell a lie, but claims to have gone to Elfland with its Queen. What is there for the Church to think?"

"Do you believe it?"

"Do I, or does the Church?"

"Either," Shawn said.

Brother David turned from the window. The sun burst in a halo around his brown woolen robes and tonsured head. "I've never heard the Church discuss it. I could not say. I've not given the story much thought. I would fear the fairies may be demonic, but that they appear to have given him gifts of prophecy and honesty."

"And time travel, of sorts."

Brother David's narrow face showed concern. "Time travel. You spoke of such a thing on our journey. If a truthful man's strange story is true, then time was indeed different in Elfland."

"Do you know of any other place where such things have happened?"

"One hears tales." Brother David tilted his head, studying Shawn. "What is it you seek?"

"A way—an explanation. You know my reputation?"

"I've heard, here in Stirling, that you are a man of God."

"So what if I told you I had an experience as strange as Thomas's?"

"Then I should believe you."

Shawn's shoulders relaxed. Being believed was good. He dared more. "I'm looking for an explanation."

"It involved moving through time?"

Shawn picked his way through the conversation as through a field of daisies studded with landmines. "I saw the world centuries from now." To Brother David, there was only him, and he was Niall. "I spent time there."

Brother David stared, just short of open-mouthed, and Shawn heard his words of months ago: *'twould be witchcraft.* "Surely 'twas a dream from the head injury?" Brother David said.

"It surely 'twas not." Shawn hoped he wasn't condemning Niall, or himself, to yet another attempt at hanging. "I was there. And I got back." He must tread carefully, unable to explain how Niall had arrived back during the battle when Brother David had been with 'Niall' prior to it. "It was no dream, and no witchcraft. I fell asleep in the tower of Glenmirril and woke up in a different time, with different people."

"How did you get back?" Brother David's interest crept out over his wariness.

Shawn told Niall's story as his own. "I looked for places that are there both now and then, and I ended up here again." The problem was, it left out the connection between himself and Niall that might be responsible, and without good information, Brother David couldn't give good advice.

"You do not jest?"

"Oh, no! I'm serious indeed. Because I've a wee problem. Suppose...." He tried to think of a way to explain the rest, the need to return to the twenty-first century. He pressed a hand to his forehead. Niall would have to show himself. They'd have to try the truth. "Suppose a man from that time crossed into this time with me. We would need to get him back where he belongs." Niall would not be happy. This was not in the plan. MacDonald would be furious—if he found out. So they'd just have to be sure he didn't.

Brother David said nothing. His eyebrows furrowed. His jaw worked. He fingered the beaded cord hanging from his belt.

"Brother David, please," Shawn said softly. "I need your help. Are there sacred places where strange things happen? Are there fairies? Was it a random miracle both times? Is there a way to make it happen again?"

"Where is this man?" Unease laced the edges of the monk's voice.

Shawn closed his eyes. Niall would not like this. But there was no other way. He opened the door between the adjoining rooms. Niall stood on the other side, shielded from Brother David's view, shaking his head sharply. "It's too late," Shawn said. They stared each other down, Shawn with the golden hair they'd once shared, and Niall with his stubble.

Brother David appeared behind Shawn, staring from one to the other. The look on his face told Shawn the resemblance was strong. "This is Niall

Campbell," Shawn said. "You might say he's the real Niall."

Brother David went pale. He made the sign of the cross. "Then who are you?" He stared at Shawn, his eyes wide. "And who traveled with me in the forest?"

"It was me in the cellar and forest," Shawn said. "My name is Shawn." A weight lifted from his shoulders. It felt good to speak his name, if only for one other man. At the same time, the weight of the situation settled on him. He crossed the room, dropping heavily into one of the chairs at the table. "Niall, you want to tell the story this time." It wasn't a question.

Niall came through the door. He held his hand out to Brother David, who took it as if shaking the hand of a wraith. Niall quirked a smile, and indicated Shawn with a jerk of his head. "It's him you ought to fear."

"But I know him," Brother David said. "I've seen his character."

Niall smiled at the irony. "Sit down. I've a story to tell."

Cumbria, England, Present

As we walk the wind-whipped streets of Cumbria, Angus recounts, as if reporting to his unit, the evidence supporting this impossible story: scars on back, arrow wound, infection, ring, crucifix.

"The change in personality." I tug my white knit hat against the wind chafing my ears. Relief fills me when we stop before a leaded glass window framing a Currier and Ives interior, complete with a fire blazing in a small hearth. A wooden sign with a steaming kettle hangs over it. "When you have eliminated the impossible," Angus says, "what remains is the truth, however improbable." He pushes the door open. "We learn that both as detectives and historians." The breeze whistles in around our ankles; the fire hisses back, and shoots angry sparks up the chimney.

The waitress appears, wiping her hands on an apron. "Well, now, what'll we be having?" Her smile is as welcoming as the crackling fire, as comfortable as the dog that wanders from the kitchen, dropping its old, withered shanks before the hearth.

Angus glances at the unopened menu. "I hear the steak pie is good."

"'Tis indeed!"

"One for you?" he asks me, and at my nod, adds. "Tea, and two Guinness."

"I shouldn't drink," I murmur.

"I did say I'd need two," Angus replies, and the waitress leaves.

I laugh weakly. "If ever a man was entitled to two, it's you, today."

"Niall Campbell." He says it as if posing a question. "You spoke with the actual man."

I nod.

"Niall Campbell from the fourteenth century?"

I nod again.

Angus leans forward, his eyes shining. "What was he like? Did he tell you about Glenmirril?"

"He spent the train ride from Inverness to Stirling talking about it."

Excitement lights Angus's face. It's what I feel when I start a new solo. I smile, falling more in love with him.

"D'you know what I'd give to be able to talk to someone from Glenmirril's past?" he asks. "And by some miracle, it seems you've done just that!" He touches the ring on my finger, almost reverently. "Did he tell you how they built their siege engines? Was it oil or water they boiled? I've heard both."

I shake my head. I knew a man who was gentle and funny, not one who sent boiling anything down on anyone. "He talked about his mother and brothers. Two of them were executed by the English. His father died at Falkirk."

"The people?" Angus says people the way I'd say out of tune? Or...cheating?

I cock my head. "They were his family, his friends. History said they all died."

"Hm." Angus tries to see Niall's side, but Niall is not real to him. "What did he say about the Laird?"

We fall silent as the waitress returns, bearing a tray with a tea pot, china cup, and two beers, amber on the bottom and frothing on top. When she leaves, I tell him all I remember, of the Laird, the MacDougalls, Allene. They feel like people who climbed halfway from a fairy tale into real life, but remained tangled in the pages of their book. Except for Niall. Niall putting a necklace around my neck. Niall smiling in the dim light of the pawn shop, Niall's eyes alight as he looked at me.

"There's so much we don't know about the time. I'd give anything for the chance you had." Angus takes a long sip of his Guinness, and asks, "What was he like?"

My eyes soften, remembering him backstage after the concert. "He was kind."

There's a heartbeat of silence. Angus's fingers touch mine across the table. "You were in love with him."

My eyes re-focus on the present, on Angus leaning across the table. Warmth creeps up my cheeks. "I thought he was Shawn."

"But now you know he's isn't, you miss him."

I stare at my hands, warmth in my cheeks.

The waitress backs through the kitchen door, a tray high over her head. At the hearth, the dog thumps his tail. She slides steaming plates in front of us. Thanking her, Angus takes a mouthful of steak pie, his expression confirming that regardless of never having heard anything about it, it is, in fact, delicious. He sits back. "Tell me everything. From the start."

I tell him, from leaving Shawn in the tower to the apology carved on

Hugh's rock. The stress of the last months melts with each word. No more lying, no more evading. And he hasn't left! He's here, talking to me as if I'm not crazy! "I thought he was dead," *I finish.* "I saw him cut nearly in half. I thought Niall left the mark in Creagsmalan's chapel before he got thrown in the dungeon."

"But now you know he's alive."

"He *was* alive." *Tension creeps back in, hugging close to its good friends, Worry and Fear.* "Someone who looked like Niall was in MacDougall's dungeon. Gallows were built for whoever it was."

He leans forward, as if it's an exciting movie we're talking about. "Niall in England with James Douglas! Niall in MacDougall's dungeon." *He lifts an eyebrow.* "Niall marrying Allene and walking the shore with a child."

We reach our conclusions at the same time. He's a cop, after all, but I see it, too. It's a small world, medieval Scotland. "What happens," *I ask,* "if MacDougall hangs Niall and then hears Niall has just married Allene and Niall has a son? What kind of uproar would that cause?"

"No." *Abruptly, Angus backpedals, shaking his head.* "We can't assume that because we haven't read about any such uproar, there wasn't one."

"A thing like that?" *I argue.* "Wouldn't it be in that book? If it remarked on him walking the shore with his son, wouldn't resurrection from the dead rate a sentence or two?"

"But anything could have happened!" *He leans forward again, eyes alight with the hunt.* "Maybe MacDougall didn't live much longer himself, so he wasn't alive to notice the man he killed is married and fathering children."

I blanch, thinking that could be Shawn, the father of my child, we're so blithely discussing swinging from a rope. My stomach knots realizing that if Niall died, then Shawn married Allene and fathered her child. I stick with the issue. "Everyone at Creagsmalan knew Niall Campbell was hanged. He was their mortal enemy. So unless the whole castle suddenly dropped dead, somebody *would have noticed.*"

I hope...I pray...that this proves they both lived.

"As likely as that is," *counters the cop sitting across the table,* "likelihood is not proof."

I stare at Bruce's ring, heavy on my finger, seeing Shawn's face in the moment he threw it. I don't want either him or Niall to have died. We fall silent. Our steak pies sit, half-eaten, their wisps of steam gone. The dog by the hearth lifts his head, watching us. He thumps his tail once, twice, then drops his head on his paws with a heavy sigh.

Angus reaches for my hand. "Let's assume," *he says,* "that Shawn survived. He's living in medieval Scotland. What would we do?"

"Get him back." *I don't even have to think.* "But I have no idea how."

"You?" *He raises his eyebrows.* "What about we? That's a big problem to leave you alone with."

The enormity of his words hits me. My shoulders sag in relief. But worries jump back, determined to be heard. *"You'd do that for me? He's my boyfriend."*

"Ex," he says. *"Remember, I'm assigned to his case. 'Tis my* job *to find him."* He squeezes my hands. *"But apart from that—the chance to meet someone who* lived *history! How could I not?"* His eyes light with excitement. *"Maybe he knows something about the Glenmirril Lady!"*

"He couldn't draw," I say.

"Maybe he knows who did." His face becomes serious. *"Apart from my own self-interest, though, I know too much of medieval times. They were brutal. A modern man isn't equipped to live there."*

"Okay, then." I don't want to think of the deaths that may await Shawn. *"Where do we start?"*

"Right where we are. Following Douglas; see if we find more of his marks."

"They could have been left by either Shawn or Niall," I point out, *"since we've now found them here and at Creagsmalan."* My heart tingles, feeling close to him, as I once felt close working side by side with Shawn.

"Let's see what turns up," Angus says, *"and go from there."*

"But what do we start with?" I sip my tea, now lukewarm. *"Do we look for a way to get someone back across time when we don't even know if he's alive? Or find out if he survived the gallows when we have no idea how to get him back anyway?"*

"Both," he says. *"When someone's missing in the mountains, we launch the rescue on the assumption they're alive."*

I'm doubtful. *"Getting lost in the wrong century is a little different than getting lost in the mountains."*

He squeezes my hands again. *"We'll go with the only precedent we have. How did Niall get back?"*

"They switched the first time when they were in the same place at the same time—I mean, same date. So he put himself where he thought Shawn would be. And it worked."

Angus frowns. *"You see the problem?"* he asks.

I nod. *"They're both on the same side now. So what's left to make the times overlap?"*

"Ah, that's our job, now, isn't it?" He raises his Guinness to my china teacup. *"Here's to an incredible adventure together."*

Stirling Castle, 1314

"So was it fairies?" Shawn asked Brother David, when Niall finished. "Magic? A curse? A miracle? How do I get back?" He resisted the urge to knock his heels together and say, "There's no place like home."

"We must pray," Brother David said. The crease in his brow had deepened with the telling of the story. "And fast."

"I'm on it." Shawn jabbed at his forehead, chest, and each shoulder.

Brother David and Niall stared at him with wide-open eyes. Then Niall laughed out loud.

"What!" Shawn looked up from carefully folded hands. "You said pray fast."

"Pray *and* fast," Niall said.

"I heard you the first time. How much faster could I have done it? It's you two holy rollers sitting there doing nothing. Excuse me, *naught.*"

Niall's mouth twitched upwards. "He means don't eat for a day." He turned to Brother David. "Just in case you'd any doubt who's who."

Shawn glared at them both. "Very funny. I save his life, I earn you knighthood and save *your* neck, and you criticize my vocabulary."

"Peace, Shawn." Brother David's mouth twisted up at the corners, too, though he fought it down. "You've the right of it. We ought pray fast." He made the sign of the cross, and repeated ten *Aves* in Latin, while Shawn sat with bowed head, disinclined to believe answers would shoot through the window or knock at the door.

And they didn't.

They looked at each other in the silence that followed the last *Ave*, no wiser than before. "Blessed Mother Mary," Brother David added, "Grant us guidance." To Niall and Shawn, he added, "I will ask my superior leave to pray before the Blessed Sacrament tonight. May one or both of you do the same. We will fast on bread and water and meet again on the morrow."

It was more than Shawn had hoped for, and far, far less.

CHAPTER SIX

Northern England, Present

"Appleby, Brough, Richmond—James Douglas hit them all in 1314." Angus guided his car around the curving road.

"With Shawn or Niall in tow." With soft medieval music from the radio washing over her, Amy gazed out the windows at rough, rolling hills, trying to imagine Shawn riding up and down them. The towns weren't far by car. They were able to visit two a day, searching churches and castles. She tried to imagine the same distance on ponies, perhaps driving cattle ahead. As she listened to Angus's stories of border raids, burning, raping, looting, she wondered how much of it Shawn had done. He wouldn't have raped, she was sure of that, at least.

"Most likely Shawn," Angus said. "MacDougall's dungeon records...."

"...prove nothing," Amy reminded him. "MacDougall would believe he had Niall either way."

"True. But we've found three marks. It has to be Shawn." Twice, they'd been at the door. In one church, with only walls standing, its window sockets staring out emptily at the land, and trees pushing up through the floor, he'd gouged the mark deep in the steps leading up to the altar.

"Unless it was some sort of communication between them," Amy said. "Then it could be either of them. He seems to have always been in the churches," she added. "Do you think that means anything?"

"'Twouldn't have been his decision," Angus said.

"Unless he sneaked off each time?" She laughed, without humor. "Maybe he's desperate to pray?"

"I would be in such a world," said Angus.

His words reached inside Amy with a cold touch.

"They'd have looted the churches," he added, "along with the rest of the town. Or, depending how co-operative the clerics were, taken the treasures as protection money."

"Stealing from churches!" Amy shook her head.

"Come now," remonstrated Angus, his eyes on the curving road. "They had to fund the war until Edward agreed to a treaty." Reaching Kirkoswald, he slowed, navigating narrow streets crowded with old houses, with lace in their windows. "Suppose Shawn gets back, and you find he's been sacking churches. Surely, you'd not be so hard on him."

Amy turned to him in surprise. "You of all people advising me to go easy on Shawn!"

Angus smiled. "Perhaps only in this matter. I'm a fair man, after all, and you can't judge by our times. You must judge by the standards of 1314. The English didn't stop at sacking churches. They liked to nail the local priest to the door and set the whole thing on fire. And Berwick—'twas awful slaughter. Longshanks called it off only when he saw one of his knights killing a woman even as she gave birth!"

Amy's hand flew to her mouth. Nausea boiled in her stomach.

Angus jammed on the brake as he slid into a parking place in alarm. "Now, then, I'm that sorry! Open the door! Get some fresh air!"

She leaned out into the cold, trying to erase the images of crucifixion, burning, and pregnant women being hacked to death. "I'm sorry," she said. "That normally wouldn't nauseate me—I mean, not literally—but...."

"'Twas tactless," Angus said. "I've thought of them as naught but stories for so long. You've not had lunch, and that can't help."

Michael Chapel, Stirling Castle, 1314

In Stirling's small St. Michael's Chapel, Niall knelt on the hard floor before the Blessed Sacrament. The monstrance glowed, softly golden in the gleam of candles lit through the night. The host shone large and white in the center. Stone walls and heavy columns rose all around, supporting the timber-beamed ceiling. Statues shone pearl-white in their stone niches, Mary on the right and Joseph on the left. He poured out *Aves* and *Paters*, thumbing through his beads, head bowed. His stomach rumbled.

Beside him, Brother David's lips moved silently, lost in his own prayers. On his other side, Shawn dug a finger in his ear, coughed, and stared at the ceiling. He spun the crucifix, dangling from a Rosary, in small circles. "Give me patience," Niall prayed. He put out a hand to stop the spinning Rosary. "Some reverence is due," he whispered. He followed it immediately with another silent request to God. "Give me humility. 'Tis not mine to judge."

The smell of wax hung heavily in the air. Although he remained motionless on his knees, hands clasped, his mind jumped like a red squirrel. His life had changed. Having Shawn here had done great things for him. Even apart from earning him knighthood and a reputation unmatched among men, it was like having a brother, a replacement for the six who had died of illness, drowned, and been executed; someone with whom to laugh, work, compete, and fight. He'd learned to play another instrument. At night, Shawn told stories of the continent that would be found across the ocean beyond Ireland, of wars against the

English, and a battle against crates of tea. He soaked up every detail of a man named William Allen who would write music called *The Resurrection*, Verdi who would write about Elijah, and Bach who would write *The Hallelujah Chorus*. Shawn taught Niall every part. He told him about big bands and rock bands and a boy younger than Taran who would write a piece for brass instruments, heard and loved around the world.

An incredible universe of knowledge had dropped into Niall's eager mind—stars falling to earth, into his outstretched fingers. When Shawn left, the knowledge would go with him, slipping back out into the night sky, beyond his reach forever.

He tried to envision life after Shawn's leaving, and what had once seemed normal and good, now seemed empty, ordinary. He bowed his head lower over clasped hands. Having always thought himself good, his own selfishness hung heavily on him. He vowed he'd listen for God's voice and do whatever he could to help Shawn, and hoped he wasn't only trying to convince himself.

From down the hall came the far off chanting of men's voices. The monks moved through the early morning halls, coming to the chapel for matins. Frustration crouched on his shoulders like the gargoyles high on the church walls. Despite all his efforts at prayer, his mind had strayed repeatedly back to his crucifix, the crucifix he had intended for Allene—the one he'd left back in the twenty-first century for Amy to sell. God, forgive my selfishness, he prayed. How can I be worrying about that all night, when I'm supposed to be praying for Shawn?

Kirkoswald, England, Present

"Remarkable men for any time," Angus said over fish and chips, "but especially their own."

Amy ate hungrily of steak pie while he praised his national heroes.

"Bruce was known for mercy, a thing in short supply in medieval times. Normally, you'd want to crush your enemy, so they'd never harm you again. But Bruce had seen years of clan feuds resulting from that. So he forgave, and welcomed his enemies back into his peace. Even Ross, who betrayed his wife and daughter to the English."

"But James Douglas," Amy said. "How can a man be both the Good Sir James *and* the Black Douglas?"

"*Hush ye, hush ye, do not fret ye, the Black Douglas will not get ye,*" Angus quoted. "They sang it to their children for centuries afterward. Can you imagine being sound asleep of a night, and waking to the skirling of raiders, and flames rising around your town?"

"Yet he's called the Good Sir James."

"He *was* good." Angus stabbed at his golden battered cod. "They burned, they took hostages, gold, food—all in an attempt to put a permanent end to the war. But they didn't slaughter and murder as the English did."

After lunch, they walked hand in hand through the village, across fields to a stand of trees surrounding a single broken-down tower piercing the November sky. Dead vegetation climbed the walls. Come spring, it would be a picturesque, ironic burst of life clinging to decaying ruins. Now, it heightened the desolation of the place. A window remained, high up. Amy wondered if a woman had stood on a long-gone floor, watching Scottish raiders approach. Had she rocked her child in a cradle, waiting anxiously, or hugged it in fear, perhaps locking her doors and hoping they wouldn't climb so high? Had she watched Shawn himself storm down from those hills? Amy's gaze drifted down to the lone doorway. She crossed the frosty grass and touched the doorway, running her hands and eyes from top to bottom, on the front, back, and inner edges of the arch. Angus followed, doubling her search, scanning every surface, and examining the doorway. There was nothing.

"Douglas burned the castle in 1314." Angus stepped back. "'Twould have made no sense to leave his mark on a building that was to be burned."

"It's still a disappointment," Amy said. "Of course, what finding these marks is accomplishing, I don't know." She pulled her hat tight.

He put an arm around her shoulder, blocking the worst of the wind. "You didn't know why you stayed, you just followed your gut, and look what's come of it."

She nodded, her head on his shoulder, exhausted from days on the road, constant cold wind, months of searching and grieving, and the drain of pregnancy.

"Most of the marks have been in the kirks," Angus reassured her. "This one has parts from 1314. Let's go see."

They cut across the stubble of autumn fields, to the church. It was a small, ancient structure, nestled in a hollow, surrounded by trees. Sheep huddled in the pastures beyond. A bell tower rose on a hill behind them. Wind blew across the fields, cutting through Amy's long blue coat as they crossed the small churchyard, through tumbled-down gravestones straight off a movie set. She shivered, sheltered in Angus's arm, while they examined the edges of the door. They found nothing. He pushed the door open, the stiff breeze trying to tear the heavy beams from his fingers.

Amy sighed with relief in the warmth wrapping around her as he closed the door. She looked around in wonder. "It's beautiful," she breathed. "Who would have thought so from outside?" It was small, nothing like St. Bee's. But the inside was whitewashed, apart from the natural stone of the arches. Stained glass windows shone light down on the nave.

"Some arches are Norman, some are thirteenth century." Angus walked down the aisle between dark wooden pews. "The baptismal font is Norman. The base of the chancel arch is Saxon. They'd have been here in his time."

"What's a chancel arch?" She followed him, lowering her voice.

He pointed to the altar. "The chancel's there, where only the clergy went.

So that's the arch, in front of it. You look there, while I search the columns."

At the front of the church, she knelt to examine the dark, shining wood of the stairs. They were far too new, she decided. If he'd left a mark there, it was long gone. Still, she examined the grain. There was nothing. She rose, studying the cool taupe stones. She glanced back to Angus. He was running his hands over every inch of the first stone column, searching with fingertips and eyes.

He moved to the second arch. She turned back to her work, trying to imagine Shawn here, dressed as a medieval raider. Instead, images filled her head of Shawn on stage, Shawn the first night he'd taken her out, somehow leaving a rose in her apartment for her to find afterward. And opening Shawn's phone to see another woman's name. The familiar pain dug, a tiny knife point pricking her heart, drawing blood.

Angus was running his hands over the third column. She finished searching the left side of the arch, as high as she could reach. Shawn's memory walked beside her, with that same grin he'd used on the promotional posters, self-assured, cocky, telling her of course he'd been home sick; it must have been someone else her friend saw downtown. He could show her the bottles of medicine, or the rumpled bed. He was crushed she doubted him. *Crushed.*

The sick feeling that always accompanied the stories rose in her throat. She crossed to the right side of the arch. She'd never had any proof, nothing but the kicked in the gut feeling that the story was off; the uneasy feeling that conversations stopped when she entered a room, *Shawn* being the last word spoken before her friends in the orchestra saw her—and fell silent.

The shame, humiliation, self-doubt, and recriminations pressed down, heavier than her growing stomach. Anger ate at her insides, the blind rage she'd felt at catching him in lies, when he'd stare at her with wide-open eyes, insisting on stories that couldn't possibly be true. But no one in his right mind would try to get away with such insane stories if they *weren't* true.

She looked to Angus, examining the fourth column. He'd shown himself in every way to be good and decent, a giver to Shawn's taker. She stopped, her hands flat on the arch, her head against the stone. She felt Shawn.

She swore she felt him beside her, silent. *I like him*, she thought to the presence at her shoulder. *He deserves my love more than you ever did, so why am I here looking for a sign from you?*

Because I loved you as well as I was able, and I'll love you better when I get back. She pulled in a deep breath. It was her imagination, she told herself. But it was true he'd loved her as well as he'd been able. She raised her head, her eyes dry and itchy, searching the empty air. She saw nothing, but she felt him. *I like him a lot,* she told the unseen presence. His face was the last thing she thought of at night, even after pondering Shawn's and Niall's fate.

Give me a chance.

She didn't know if she heard the words or only imagined it's what he would say. It irritated her. *If it weren't for you, my life would be very different,* she thought back. She studied the wall, her eyes traveling with her fingers. Yes, her life would be different. He'd also given her this child she already loved. He'd filled her life with color and music and warm embraces and love letters and the knowledge that he *did* love her—as well as such a broken man could love anyone. Her fingers trailed farther up, over cool stone.

And there it was—fainter, and smaller than the others. Excitement leaped in her throat! She studied the mark, the long center line, and the shorter ones above and below. "Angus," she breathed. A smile grew, saying his name. "He was here."

Angus turned from his exploration of the farthest column; she realized how familiar he'd become, the shorn black curls, ruddy cheeks, and dark eyes. They filled her with warmth.

The baby kicked just then, hard, taking Amy's breath away. She stopped, clutching her stomach.

Angus jumped forward. "Are you aw' right?"

Joy lit her face. "It's kicking!"

He smiled. He looked nervous. They stood as still as marble statues, staring at each other across the empty church. Shawn's ghost stood between them, looking from one to the other, waiting.

Stirling, 1314

Once again, Shawn bore the brunt of their efforts. Being recognized as Niall, he mounted his pony almost as soon as he climbed up off his knees in the cold chapel, and rode through the cold, misty dawn to Cambuskenneth Abbey for Bruce's full parliament of nobles, prelates, and bishops. He wondered if it was his imagination that the elderly bishop watched him through narrowed eyes.

Niall, trying to do his part, remained on his knees before the Blessed Sacrament, robed and hooded as their alter ego, Brother Andrew.

When they met again in Shawn's room that evening, Brother David brought a loaf of bread, meat, cheese, and ale. He blessed the food at some length, while Shawn's stomach growled, and finally passed it around, asking, "Have either of you had any insight?"

"Yeah. Fasting is no fun," said Shawn.

Niall shook his head. "I imagine he meant something beyond hunger."

"I'm way beyond hunger. I could eat a horse."

"I'd not advise it unless there's famine." Nothing in Brother David's demeanor suggested he was joking. "They're not so tasty."

"Not at all," Niall agreed, before adding, "I could think of naught but the crucifix I gave Amy."

"Perhaps we are to meditate on the death of Christ?" Brother David suggested. "Shall we pray again tonight?"

"I'm going to bed." Finishing his small meal, Shawn leaned down to unlace his boots. "Not that I don't appreciate it and all, but I don't really see where it did any good. My personal belief is we'll think better on a good night's rest and full stomachs. I gave it a fair shot, but this just didn't work for me." He tore off his second boot and tossed them both into the corner.

Brother David and Niall stared at each other and shook their heads. "I'll be down to the chapel soon," Niall said, and Brother David collected the remains of the meal, and bid them goodnight.

"What are the Bruce's plans?" Niall asked.

"Get his ships hence to the Isle of Man." Shawn stretched. "Edward Bruce is gung-ho. Angus Og likes any excuse to use those galleys of his. The men of Glenmirril are cordially invited."

"That means me." Niall groaned, pushing a hand through the stubble crowning his head. "I've had two days of marriage."

"Lucky for you, they only expect someone who looks like you."

"If you're still here," Niall pointed out. "What else?"

"Only those loyal to the King of Scots can have land here. Henry Beaumont's lands were taken. The Earl of Atholl's lands were given to Gilbert Hay."

"A fine man, Gilbert Hay," Niall said. "Though 'tis a shame about the Earl. He sided with England because Edward Bruce jilted his sister. A fine price all have paid for Edward's behavior."

"Yeah, well. I hate to think how many women's brothers I've driven to side with the English. America won't exist by the time I get back." Shawn stripped off his vest, down to the *leine* that served as nightshirt, and was about to drop the garment on the floor when Niall's stern look stopped him. He hung it in the wardrobe. "So have fun praying. I need some sleep."

Niall pulled his monkish hood over his face and stepped into the hall as Brother Andrew. Several minutes later, as Shawn began to pull his vest off, a knock whispered at the door. Surprised Niall would knock, he went to answer it. A tall, hooded figure stood in the hall. It wasn't Niall. Shawn's hand slid to the knife at his hip.

Kirkoswald, England, Present

Angus breaks into action, striding down the aisle. Shawn's presence, if it was ever more than my imagination, fades, leaving me and Angus and this baby. Shawn's baby.

He touches my stomach tentatively, smiles. I hug him tightly and finally, pull back, reaching for the mark, softened with age. Seven hundred years! "How can his marks be here," I ask, "and at Creagsmalan, too?"

"We know when someone called Niall was in the dungeon," Angus says, "but we don't know when the mark was actually made. And the raids went on for years."

"So Shawn could have left marks in both places—at different times." I

frown. Does that mean Niall was hanged?

"We'll believe they both lived." Angus reads my dark thought. "Until we find proof otherwise." He genuflects before the altar, and turns to leave. He pulls out his phone as he walks.

Following him outside, I hear him say, "Could you dig through your archives? See if there's more on our man Niall Campbell?" Chirps buzz from his phone. In the cold November wind, I tug my coat close. We've hit dozens of ruins, for four marks. And we have no idea what they mean.

"You'll ask around?" Angus smiles. "Thanks, Brian."

"Brian your obnoxious friend from Creagsmalan?" I ask as he hangs up.

Angus laughs. "Brian's a fine man, even if he is on the wrong side of the great cattle debate."

"He defended MacDougall cheating!" *I object.*

"'Tis but colorful characters in thrilling stories to him. He'd never defend Shawn." Angus wraps his arms around me, shielding me from the wind. "He'll do his best to help you."

"Thank you." I rest my head on his chest. "We've searched a dozen ruins and haven't found much."

He smiles. "But we're searching together."

Stirling, Present

"Sorry, Alec!" Brian gave a high-pitched laugh as he slid his phone into his pocket. "Everyone's on about the early 1300s. Me mate's just after asking about Niall Campbell, you know, of Glenmirril. He fought at Bannockburn in 1314."

"Of course," Alec murmured. "The sword and mail...?" He indicated the items on his desk.

"Ah, yes!" Brian touched them almost reverently, his eyes shining. He'd been giddy with excitement when he heard about them from his nephew, and raced to Stirling as soon as he'd had a free day. "They do indeed look authentic. The hilt, now. Early 1300s." He pointed to an engraving. "This rearing lion— see the forked tail? Castle Claverock, Northern England, late 1200s."

Alec rubbed his chin. "It hardly looks so old."

"No, indeed," Brian agreed, smiling. "Did you track down the owner?"

Alec rose from his desk. "Aye. Would you like to see him?"

Brian's eyebrows shot up. "Very much!" He let out a high-pitched giggle. "Hopefully he's nothing like the original owner. Legend says it was the lord of Claverock who hacked to death the pregnant woman at Berwick."

Alec nodded, the corners of his mouth tight. "I'll take you there now, although it'll take some doing to actually get you in."

"Get me in where?"

"The psych ward."

Stirling, 1314

A chuckle came from under the hood. "Your king comes in peace, Bard."

With a gasp, both of relief and of shock at threatening his king, Shawn pulled back, ushering him in. He cleared his throat. "My, uh, Your Grace. Come in."

Bruce waved him aside, sinking into a chair at the table as he pushed back his hood. His auburn hair fell to his shoulders, unencumbered by the crown. "Let us talk, Sir Niall."

Shawn's heart thumped, wondering why Bruce would seek out Niall, wondering if he'd given himself and Niall away. He bowed, and waited until Bruce waved at the other chair before seating himself. He'd done Scotland no harm, he assured his itchy neck. He'd helped the cause. There was no reason Bruce should hang him, even if he did learn of the deception.

He saw the empty flagon before Bruce, and rose again to pour him wine. "Your Grace, my apologies." As always, Shawn found it hard to tear his eyes from this living, breathing man, standing in glorious life and vivid color before him, a man who should have been no more than words in a history book, dust in a grave.

Bruce took a long swallow, set the cup down, and regarded Shawn thoughtfully, giving him plenty of time to fear what was coming. Regardless of what he *should* be, he *was* a man with power to execute. The torch flames cast dancing shadows over the table and golden flagons.

"A remarkable man," Bruce finally said. "I was amazed, as were my lords, at how quickly you were up, after your injury at the joust."

Shawn swallowed, wondering if he dared poured himself wine. He could use something to steady his nerves. He decided not knowing if he'd just committed a medieval faux pas would negate any calming benefit the wine might have. He gave a small incline of his head. "Thank you, Your Grace. By God's blessings."

"Indeed," Bruce said. "It so amazed me, that I asked about, and it seems you experienced an even more remarkable recovery after Bannockburn."

"The injury was not as severe as some say," Shawn told him. "But 'tis to our benefit to have the English think so, aye?"

The wall torches made a small sizzling in the momentary silence. Bruce smiled. "I read the physician's reports. In truth, 'twas *more* severe than is said. Yet you were on your way to England within days, strong as a war horse."

Conrad, Shawn told himself. He plastered a smile on his face. "'Twas indeed a miracle, then." He waited, smiling.

"MacDougall may be my enemy," Bruce said, "but he is no fool. I understand he apprehended a man in the hill country, shortly before battle, thinking him to be you. Yet this man played sackbut."

"You are well-acquainted with my harp," Shawn replied.

"He found a man in his castle whom he believed to be you."

Shawn felt the sweat prickle his back under his *leine*. "Mayhap his eyes are poor?"

Bruce sipped his wine. "I think not. It seems he saw the scar across your midsection well enough at Glenmirril."

"I was not in his dungeon," Shawn asserted. "You knighted me yourself in England at the time he claims I was there."

"*Someone* was in his dungeon." Bruce leaned back, regarding Shawn as he twisted the cup slowly between his fingers. The flames cast small golden glints off its curved surface as it turned. The nerves tautened in Shawn's legs, in his back. He refused to let it show, but waited for Bruce to speak.

"Be that as it may," the king said at last, "I know a great deal of you, from your youth onward. I've made it my business to know, since the remarkable events at Bannockburn. I am a good judge of character, and of this I have no doubt: Niall Campbell is loyal to Scotland. He is hardy, quick, and clever. I'm glad he fights for me, and not against."

"Thank you, Your Grace. You do me great honor." Shawn noted Bruce's use of third person, but hid his hammering heart behind a smile, thinking instead how much his father would have loved speaking those words to a real king, rather than a re-enactor.

"I've another mission for you."

The November wind whistled against the window. The smile slipped from Shawn's face. He was supposed to go to the Eildon Hills, figure out how to work a fairy hill, and go home to hot tubs and Amy. Saying *you do me great honor* hardly made up for Jacuzzis. His mind raced. Niall could drop him off. Or he could go alone. He realized Bruce was watching him waiting. "Your Grace?" he asked. "What mission?"

"You must take word to my people. Next summer we lay siege to Carlisle. From there, go to Carlisle. You excel, Sir Niall, at charming women and they delight in helping you. Learn all you can that may help us." He rose.

Shawn scrambled to his feet, bowing. "Aye, Your Grace." A string of curses spun through his head, but none of them changed what he—Niall—had just been ordered to do. Now what?

Stirling, Present

Alec's longer legs worked to keep up with Brian's enthusiastic near-skipping. He filled Brian in as they hurried between antiseptic white walls. "He was injured at the re-enactment. In a coma for weeks."

"No family, no friends, no missing person report?" Brian asked.

"Only the American musician." Alec lowered his voice and added, "Strange things afoot that day. My sister swears she saw a man run through with a sword."

Brian snorted, as good-natured and cheerful a sound as a snort had ever been. "'Twas a hot day. People riled one another up, imaginations went wild. There were no dead bodies on the field afterward."

"No," Alec agreed. "But yer man in the psych ward has a nasty wound."

"Did he fall off his horse?" Brian asked. "Or get kicked by one?"

Alec shook his head. "Reports suggest a blow with a long, heavy, blunt instrument." He cast a sideways look at Brian. "A sword fits the description."

A frown flickered across Brian's plump face. "Did one of the re-enactors get carried away? Did our man run in front of someone?"

Alec shrugged.

"How did he get from the hospital to the psych ward?"

"When he woke from the coma, he was agitated, speaking gibberish," Alec explained. "When they made out words, he seemed to think he'd been at the actual battle."

Brian's mind flickered to Angus and the girl with the long black hair, asking after Niall Campbell.

"He was aggressive; attacked the staff." Alec stopped before a steel door. Its multi-layered glass window was criss-crossed with wires inside. "They brought him here."

Brian stretched on tiptoe, peering in. One man sat in a wheelchair, staring out the window. Another pounded his fist on the table before him, yelling at an orderly dressed in white. Two men played cards.

On a couch sat a man of average height. His broad shoulders and muscled arms strained the fabric of his robe. He sat almost eerily still, but for his toe tapping a steady tattoo. He watched the screaming man steadily, his eyebrows furrowed in thought. His head had recently been shaved, revealing a long scar, slanting from the tip of his widow's peak, across his forehead, and down toward his ear.

He turned, slowly, like a cobra lazily watching its prey. His eyes met Brian's. Brian blinked, and steeled his spine against the urge to step back.

"Simon Beaumont," Alec said.

Southern Scotland, 1314

"A medieval bishop didn't call you a witch. Neither of us has been hanged." Shawn recounted their progress as their hobins climbed yet another hill. "Chalk those up in the good column. But this praying all night thing didn't work so well."

"'Tis not a magic charm," Niall said irritably.

Ignoring him, Shawn continued. "And now, instead of going north to a wise woman who may get me home, I'm going south to an English governor who may hang me."

"We're going toward the Eildon Hills. Perchance they'll take you home."

Shawn snorted. "Fairy hills! Somehow, I think I'll end up in Carlisle with you." He rubbed his neck, already feeling the shadow of a rope around it.

"Do you ever quit complaining?" Niall glanced at the gray bank of clouds piled thick in the sky, and spilling down to enclose the tops of the hills.

"Yeah," Shawn said. "There was this day when I was six...."

"By nightfall, you may have a different perspective."

Their ponies trotted into the thick wall of cloud. They fell silent as they rode through gray mist, two ghostly figures abreast. Shawn shivered. It had been cold enough without the damp blanket pressed around him. The animals angled downhill.

"Are you sure we're going down the right side?" Shawn asked in hushed tones. The cloud thickened.

Niall faded to a wraith. "Trust me," he muttered, in a *sotto voce* attempt at indignation.

Shawn coughed. "Yeah. *Trust* you. Thanks to you and your tower, I'm stuck in medieval Scotland on a smelly horse."

"'Tis not a horse. And thanks to me, your two worthless halves got dragged off the battlefield and sewn back together. I'm regretting that, at the moment."

"I don't know why, because I saved your worthless...." He broke off as the cloud opened abruptly, displaying a valley spread far below. Mist curled along its floor, and twisted in wisps up the mountain side. A handful of cottages clung to one another, with a dirt track running between them.

"Let us speak no more of worthlessness," Niall said softly. "We've a sad job before us."

Shawn pulled the hood of Brother Andrew up over his face, while Niall adjusted the coif that hid his shorn head. They rode down into the valley to summon Bruce's men to war.

CHAPTER SEVEN

Scottish Borders, 1314

A gaunt woman set food on a table in the center of a nearly bare room. The small yard had held a single goat and two chickens. Shawn doubted the woman would eat that evening. She bowed, and said, in an accent thick even by medieval and Gaelic standards, "'Tis an honor, My Lord; my good brother."

She set smaller portions of bread before her two sons, and husband. Shawn wondered, uneasily, if it would be an insult to give them some of his. He suspected it would be. Her husband poured ale all around. "We'll be at our king's side," he assured Niall.

Careful to keep his face hidden, Shawn peered from under his hood. The older son might be starting college, in his own time. The younger son—Shawn swallowed—was a boy. Lank hair fell over his eyes. He wore tattered clothes. If he went to a modern emergency room, they'd be debating if he was young enough to be given a teddy bear. Shawn thought of the boy he'd pulled from in front of the charging warhorse, just months before. Had he saved the child only for the day a Scottish knight would enter his family's home and order him back to the field to die before another charging horse?

As he lifted his ale to his mouth, he heard a sniff. The woman stood before the hearth, stirring the pot, her back bent, her head bowed. She pressed a hand to her mouth. As if she felt his eyes, her back straightened; she turned, saying brusquely, "Now, then, Wat, Aymer, your king needs you. We've a great deal to do before you go." The younger boy looked up to her, hesitation in his eyes. She knelt before him, gripping his chin. "You'll serve your king well, aye, Wat? And when ye come home with your da and brother, we shall have such a feast as ye've never seen!"

She smiled, then rose and hurried abruptly from the room, the hand to her mouth once more.

Shawn wanted to take Niall's arm, say, *Let's go. Leave these people alone.* He hated himself for bringing this upon this woman.

Bannockburn, Present

Searching together. I smile, in the warmth of my office, at images of crossing pastures, and searching ruins. Together. The memory of his hand warm over mine and his laugh and his humor, and the way he looks at me and hugs me all keep me smiling as I pull up my e-mail.

Where are you? Rob asks in his first message. Are you okay, in another. What are you up to, in a third. I dash off a summary of Niall's adventures. I don't mention that it might have been Shawn. Rob was there when I broke down and told this insane story to the cops. I don't need to upset him again by saying I believe it.

I send off e-mails to my mother—yes, I'm seeing a doctor, yes, I know what I'm doing staying here when I'm pregnant—and to Celine and Dana, and finally, I open my notes from the previous months' research. I compare them against the places we found Shawn's mark. Ten to one ratio, I read somewhere. Archaeologically speaking, whatever is found, it is likely there were ten times as many. Did he leave forty marks across Northumbria? I plot the locations on a map. I compare it to Douglas's raids, but there's no pattern, no clue jumping out. Should I put together the first letters of the locations? Search for a code entwined in all of it? No. I press my fingertips to my forehead. He was carving in the middle of raids. There was no time to plot some elaborate DaVinci code. They're simply marks crying out, I am here!

Or maybe it was Niall, using a mark he knew meant something to me to tell me...what?

Either way, what do I do with that information? What good does it do me to know there were likely many more marks, now destroyed by time?

He appears to have lived as Niall, I remind myself.

I open a browser and search for Niall Campbell, Niel Campbell, Glenmirril, or any other term even remotely related to him. The hours pass, twisting into the familiar labyrinth of the web, one site leading to another. I find facebook pages and lawyers and doctors and government officials named Niall Campbell. I find sources about Bruce's friend. But there is almost nothing about Niall himself. I take a deep breath, quelling the frustration. Think, I command myself. There are forums for medieval enthusiasts. I find three and leave queries regarding Niall. I stare at the monitor as my third request flashes up on the screen. I know myself. I'll flip from site to site, waiting for an answer, if I don't walk away.

I go downstairs to my violin, losing myself in the beauty of a Mozart Concerto, for a time; then I make tea and curl up in the leather wing chair to review what the professor's books say about Glenmirril. A ghostly woman who keens on the loch. Longshanks passing by in 1296. There's fighting there in June, 1316—the same day I went back to the castle last summer, thinking I'd found Shawn. Something about a monk called Brother Andrew. I scan the meager stash of entries on Niall's home. There's not much.

Upstairs, I check the forums. Two of them have no answer. The third has a response! I click in excitement, scroll, and read.

Never heard of the guy. Sounds interesting. Can't wait to see the responses.

Frustration replaces the flare of hope. I try to remember more of Niall's time. Maybe, with the right terms, I'll find something. I try Bruce Niall Campbell; Douglas Jedburgh Campbell; Arbroath Campbell. I follow a dozen links, wade through more sites, return to the results, and try again. Failure follows failure. The baby kicks. My head hurts.

I head downstairs to try to relax in front of the fire. As I do, my phone rings. It's Angus. His voice tumbles out in excitement. "Me mate in Ayrshire did some digging in the archives there, talked with a historian, met an old member of the MacKinnon family...he found something."

"About Shawn?" I hardly dare believe it as I stoop, careful with my growing size, and put kindling in the hearth.

"About Niall. But if Shawn lived as Niall, 'twould be about Shawn. Our friend Niall was at the Parliament of Ayr in April, 1315. He went from there to Jura."

"Which was...?" I touch a match to the twigs. Niall would have used flint to do the same job.

"Didn't you say something about Niall and water?" Angus asks from my phone.

"He avoided it if he could." I watch small flames curl around a twig.

"Maybe he forgot, in the midst of battle."

"What do you mean?" With the newborn blaze chirping pianissimo crackles, I head to the kitchen for a vase, phone to my ear.

"Jura was a sea battle. Niall fought valiantly and well." His voice lifts in excitement. "Let's make another trip!"

Eildon Hills, 1314

Niall kicked his pony into a gallop. It suited Shawn fine. In his past life— make that his future life, he thought irritably—he would run from trauma with alcohol and women. But leaning into the racing hobin, knees around its body, its mane flying in his face, the cold whistling around him—he could almost believe he could out-ride the women crying, and hugging their sons; their gaunt husbands, with weathered faces, and missing teeth, wanting to protect their wives from this grief, wanting to protect their sons.

They stopped, at last, to eat. He hadn't outrun a thing.

"You've had no complaints since the last village." Sitting on the frosty ground, leaning against a bare-limbed tree, Niall rubbed his pony's muzzle as he ate hard bread sent with them by the last family whose sons they'd gone to claim.

"What's to complain about?" Shawn stared up at cloud banks rolling like aircraft carriers across the sky.

"Surely there's good complaining value in being drenched for three solid days."

"Nope." Shawn shook his head. "I'm good. My work here is done. Another family destroyed."

Gray mist wreathed the hills sloping up on either hand. Niall dropped his goading. "You've a peculiar notion of destroy. Is English more changed in your time than I knew?"

"Destroy," Shawn intoned bitterly. "Verb. To ruin. Wreak destruction. Tear a boy from his mother's arms and tell her you're throwing her kid in front of English lances." Wind whistled down the hills. He pulled his cloak close, desperately wanting a second one, even as he thought uncomfortably of the threadbare cloak, much thinner than his own, worn by the father of the family they'd just left. It wouldn't give the man much warmth as he tended his livestock through the winter.

"Destroy," Niall returned. "Verb. To send armies against a small country to kill her defenseless people. To hack to death a woman at Berwick in the very act of giving birth, when her husband, a tailor, has but a needle against your sword!" His face grew dark. "Hope. Noun! To bring good news of the king who will lead us against oppression!"

"Hope is what you see when women burst into tears?" Shawn asked incredulously.

"My own brothers were executed by the English," Niall reminded him. "I kept watch through the night with my mother, over my father's body. Do you not think I *know* what we're asking? And do you not understand *yet* what will become of these families if we *don't* ask it? Now about those complaints you had?" His anger at the English flew out at Shawn.

"You need to hear me say it out loud?" Shawn snapped. "I have no cause for complaint, okay? Are you happy? My life is pretty damn good compared to what I've just inflicted on these people. Making women send their little boys out in front of charging knights! They're just *boys!*"

Niall bowed his head. After a moment, he raised it, and placed a hand on Shawn's shoulder. "No, my friend, we did not inflict this on them. Longshanks did so."

"If the English came storming in by night," Shawn said, "at least they'd see England take their sons. But they saw us."

"'Struth, they saw me." Brushing crumbs from his hands, Niall rose.

"For all practical purposes, I am you," Shawn snorted. "Only better looking." He, too, climbed to his feet.

Niall sighed heavily. "Apparently the blow to the midsection has affected your vision as well as your wits." He stowed the bag with the last of the bread under his saddle, and mounted his pony. "We'll be at the Eildon Hills by nightfall."

"Yeah, great." Shawn placed a foot in one stirrup and threw his leg over his own pony. "Families destroyed. Boys sent to be killed. Women pretending they're not running to cry behind the chicken coop. Now let's get me home to hot tubs and champagne." With a nudge of his heels, the animals began a steady trot to the south.

"You can do naught for them by staying here," Niall reasoned. "Your place is there. I'm rather surprised at your concern."

"I'm surprised myself," Shawn said. "Life is about having fun. That's my philosophy, and it's served me well."

Niall said nothing.

"You're not going to point out that it didn't serve Amy so well?"

Niall shrugged. "I needn't say it."

They rode under heavy leaden skies, across broad valleys, with hills rising around them. Their saddles and jerkins squeaked. Harnesses jingled.

After a time, Shawn asked, "How are you going to explain Brother Andrew's disappearance if Bruce asks?"

"Tell him a wild boar got the poor sod. I'll tell him Scotland's better off without a monk who can't keep a vow of silence." As the sun lowered, they trotted past a frozen loch with mist dancing on its glassy surface. A mountain rose to three sharp points. "There it is," Niall said softly. "The Eildon Hills." He turned to Shawn, grinning. "Perhaps now we can be done with one another."

"Thank God," Shawn returned. "If I'm lucky, I won't drag too many of your stick-in-the-mud fun-killing morals with me. You probably killed my reputation in your two weeks pretending to be me."

Niall snorted. "It couldn't have gotten much worse. Thanks to me, they'll be happy to have you back."

"Have your fantasy," Shawn said. "It's all you got. Now how do we work this thing? Is there a fairy door? A magic chant? What did Thomas the Rhymer do?"

"The fairy queen rode past while he sat under a tree." He pointed. "They say 'twas halfway up to the Trimontium."

"What's *that?*" Shawn demanded.

"An old Roman fort."

"That's your plan?" Shawn asked in disbelief. "Sit under a tree and hope an elf queen rides by? And you realize, he went to *Fairyland,* not the twenty-first century. Are you seeing the same flaws with this plan that I am?"

"What's *your* plan?" Niall challenged. "Complain until God takes pity and delivers me from your eternal grousing?"

"That's got a better shot than sitting around waiting for a fairy to ride by," Shawn shot back.

Their hobins came to a stop where the land began to rise. They stared up at it. "They say she came on a gray horse," Niall said, "wearing a gown of green silk, and a velvet mantle, and her horse wore fifty-nine silver bells."

"Well, then." Shawn slid off his hobin. "We may as well make some of those delicious oatcakes while we wait for her and her fifty-nine bell horse. Should we shout her name or something? Maybe there's a fairy ticket counter. One way ticket to the twenty-first century, please."

Niall scanned the countryside. He nodded to a stand of trees. "We'll build a shelter there."

"And do what?" Shawn asked.

"We'll spend two days here. We'll hunt and gather food for our journey. We'll pray."

Shawn snorted.

Niall glared. "I can do no more. If you're still here grousing, God forbid, we go on to Carlisle as Bruce bids, and from there, to Sorcha."

"Assuming this spying expedition goes better than the last one, and we don't end up in a dungeon," Shawn muttered.

CHAPTER EIGHT

Bannockburn, Present

Angus arrives Monday evening as my last student leaves. I throw my arms around his neck. "You weren't supposed to be here until tomorrow!"

"Surprise!" He laughs. His delight reminds me of Shawn's love of surprises. He gestures to his car, filled with boxes. I turn to him questioningly. "Help bring it in," he says with a smile.

We carry in baby clothes, blankets, diapers. My amazement grows with each box. We talk as we carry them in. "I still have this idea of being in the same place, same time—that seemed to bridge times for Shawn and Niall," I confess. "Which means we should go to Ayr on April 26. But it's not true, anyway. The connection seems to be Niall and Shawn. Why can't I seem to keep that in mind?"

Angus lifts tiny white undershirts from a box, folding them carefully into a drawer. "Never mind why. Your instincts have served you well. The first thing is, all the information we can possibly gather. Who knows what we'll find out about him by searching records there, where he was." He sets a picture frame on top of the dresser, smiling and saying, "You'll have a lovely picture to put in it soon."

We're putting bottles away in the kitchen when an engine sounds outside.

Angus puts formula into my cupboard. "Better see what that's about."

"Just the neighbors," I say.

He shakes his head decisively. "That's not their car."

"How would you kn...."

"I'm trained to be observant." He's holding back a smile.

With a questioning look, I go to the door. Mike is pulling his truck to the curb, loaded with a crib. Tears sting my eyes. Angus hugs me, whispering, "I told you you'd be fine." In my room, Angus and Mike sit amidst tools and bars and nuts and bolts, laughing and talking and drinking Guinness. I brush at hot tears after Mike leaves, as Angus and I pull the crib sheet tight together, spreading out a quilt made by Angus's sister, and tucking a white velveteen rabbit into the corner. I rub my thumb and finger against the baby blue silk lining its ears; tears flow.

"What's wrong?" Angus pulls me close. "Aren't you happy?"

I nod and hiccup and laugh and cry all at the same time. The last pianissimo whisper of loyalty to Shawn refuses to let me tell him I'm crying because Shawn rejected this baby, his own, that last night up in the tower, while Angus welcomes this child that isn't even his.

Eildon Hills, 1314

Dawn rose on the third day, pink rays streaming over the eastern mountains, lighting the night's mist into a magical morning landscape. Shawn sat against a tree halfway up the slope, staring down the mountainside. He hadn't expected anything, he told himself. Through days of climbing the hill, traipsing through the valley, exploring the old Roman fort at the top, and searching for anything unusual, for anything to explain Thomas the Rhymer's disappearance, he hadn't expected anything. The story was too ridiculous.

And yet—he'd hoped.

Images of Amy had burned before his eyes and in his heart, as he climbed each slope, and searched rocks, and followed streams, as he hunted with Niall and gathered berries and fixed more oatcakes. Thoughts of her home in the States with Rob had plagued him. That he'd never see his child, never even know if he had a son or daughter, haunted him. That they were heading into enemy territory to spy terrified him. If they both ended up in a dungeon, there was no one to rescue them this time.

He threw a stone, hard. It hit a boulder with a sharp crack, and bounced off. Shawn stared after it, his lips tight, as it bounced down the mountainside. A hart stood, far away, stock still, looking up at him. Suddenly, it bolted.

Shawn turned. Niall climbed the hill, bannocks in hand. He offered one to Shawn. "I cannot wait longer. I'm sorry."

"Yeah, well." Shawn climbed to his feet, accepting the offering that would be his only meal until noon. He fought against the disappointment welling painfully in his chest, trying to make light of it. "These fairy queens, you can't count on them, you know?"

Niall smiled sadly. "Aye, a temperamental lot. What say we figure out what to do in Carlisle without her help?"

They descended the hill, leather boots slipping in the damp, cloaks fluttering in the wind. He was stuck with it, Shawn told himself. He may as well come up with an idea, if he wanted to get out alive. "Music has worked well," he suggested, as they approached their garrons, standing in gloam up to their fetlocks by the stand of trees that had sheltered them for two days.

"We haven't an instrument." Niall untied the animals, and they mounted, setting off into the west, with the rising sun at their backs.

"We do, however, have a bag of gold, which can be spun into an instrument." The meal and the crisp morning air began to work their magic, and

Shawn felt his spirits lifting. There was still the wise woman. He just had to get there. He couldn't resist adding, "And Bruce specifically ordered me to charm women." He polished his nails on his cloak, smirking at Niall. "I don't mean to brag...."

"You do indeed."

"...but I must humbly acknowledge my charm is world class when a king orders me to use it to save his country."

"He thought he was talking to me," Niall retorted. "We need to find out what weapons, siege engines, how many mounted and foot soldiers. We'll spread rumors to create fear and demoralize them. Your idea is good. We'll find an instrument and pose as a minstrel again."

They refined their plans as they rode, coming at last to a small village. Shawn pulled his cowl up and lowered his head, as they passed people in the streets. It didn't take long to find food. Finding an instrument was not so easy. The innkeeper, they were told, had a harp.

"He has a triangle of wood with wires hanging off it," Shawn mumbled from under his hood, when they found the rumored instrument.

"Can you fix it?" Niall asked.

Shawn snorted. "I'm a musician, not a miracle worker."

The innkeeper sniffed. "'Twas not me asked you a-come lookin' at it, now." He slammed it back on its peg on the wall.

"Do you know of other instruments?" Niall asked.

"The smith's son plays the pipes. I doubt he'll part with them, but that doesna stop the English."

"I'm not English." The irony occurred to Niall that protecting these people against the English would be easier were he more like the English.

When they approached the smithy at the far end of the street, the smith lifted his great bull head from his bellows. Despite the cold day, his bare arms glistened with sweat in the heat from his forges. He eyed them suspiciously, as the wind, blowing down off the mountains, lifted a heavy lock of hair from his forehead.

"He's no doubt had bad experiences with knights," Niall murmured to Shawn, "being so close to the border." He stepped forward, raising his voice. "My good smith, we come on the Bruce's business."

"I've barely food for my family," the man grumbled. "There are no women here."

Inside his cowl, Shawn grimaced, taking the man's meaning.

"We come in peace," Niall assured him. "We hope only that you'll sell us your son's pipes."

"His pipes?" Disbelief replaced the man's wariness.

"To play music," Niall clarified.

"A knight on the king's business wants pipes?" His heavy forehead wrinkled.

Shawn noted movement at the window, a quick flash of a pale face and long hair.

Niall sidestepped the question, saying instead, "We've gold. I wish to buy them."

A boy raced from the house, throwing his arms around the man's waist. "Don't let them, Da!"

The smith's arm tightened around the boy's shoulders. He shook his head and spoke bitterly. "It's all he has since the last soldiers came on king's business."

Shawn's throat tightened.

"I'm sorry," Niall said softly. "Do you know where we might find another instrument?"

"The miller over the hill." The smith regarded them warily.

They took directions, and headed over the hill, passing a fresh white stone in the kirk yard as they went.

"There lies our choice." Niall stared straight ahead, speaking tersely as they trotted past the stone and the new mound of dirt. "Leave the sons safe with their mothers, and the mothers may not live long to care for their sons."

Shawn's lip tightened. He had no answer.

They crossed the hill in silence, coming at last to a small mill on the river. Sheep dotted the hillside beyond it. A goat bleated. As they approached, two girls in woolen capes ran, laughing, from the mill, carrying sacks. Their breath hung, frosty, in the November air. They skidded to a stop, staring at Niall and Shawn. Their laughter froze. A burly man followed them. He, too, stopped, and gave a sharp word to the girls. They dropped their bags, sending up white puffs of flour, and hastened back inside the mill.

"Milord." The man's words were courteous. His tone and posture were not.

"We come in peace," Niall said. "We were told you've an instrument we might buy."

"Buy?" He raised one bushy eyebrow. "I'm familiar with the way knights purchase goods. I've naught to sell, since the last group *bought* everything."

"We're not English," Niall said.

"The last group didn't bother to mention if they were," retorted the man.

"I have gold." Niall reached inside his cloak for a coin.

The man studied him an interminable minute, before grunting, "Bide a moment."

He returned with a lute.

Niall accepted it, turning it over, studying it. "Can you play this?" he murmured to Shawn.

"I play a little guitar. I'm sure I can figure it out." Shawn took it, keeping the hood over his face as he studied the bowled back for any sign of cracks, and the strings for sign of wear. He plucked a few notes, tuned them as he would a guitar, and played. Inside the cowl, he smiled at the rich sound. "It'll do well," he said.

Niall passed over the gold, and they left with the lute on Niall's back.

Ayr, Scotland, Present

A web site named Niall at Bruce's parliament in Ayr on April 26, 1315. But two days hunting through delicate scraps of parchment at the Ayrshire archives turns up nothing. We slide down an emotional roller coaster. A visit to an old titled family, introduced by Angus's friend, turns up records verifying that Niall Campbell of Glenmirril did indeed attend Parliament in Ayr. The roller coaster swoops up. We continue hunting with renewed hope, at his lamp-lit mahogany table, in his massive old-money home library, but the trail goes cold again.

The next day, we run through December's drizzle to another archives. Angus greets the director, a friend from his days at Stirling. Hope wars with my stern reminder to self that information from that time is sparse. As we settle to reading, I'm drawn in by lives lived long ago. They stretch from their graves, brought to life by ghostly whispers of faded ink and the deep, rich smell of old vellum. They blink back at us in surprise. I move each parchment aside, and Robert, ordered to pay recompense for killing his neighbor's cow, and Alexander, sent to London with a message, settle back to rest. But just for a moment, they stood beside me, Robert old and stooped with a drooping white mustache; Alexander tall and gangly, only 15.

Late in the afternoon, our shoulders ache with hunching over faded, spidery writing. I sit back, easing the discomfort in my growing stomach. "How long can we keep this up?"

"Three more," Angus says, "and we'll have dinner."

I glance out the windows. The moon is a pale crescent on the blue-gray sky. "Four more," I counter.

"Four apiece." He returns to his pile.

I adjust a lamp and study a note apparently to the lady of the castle from a soldier in Bruce's service. What a story! But it's a story for another day. I'm tired and hungry. I want to know about Niall and Shawn. The second is a letter from father to son. Neither is Niall, and there's no reason Niall's letters would be here in Ayrshire. The third concerns siege equipment. The fourth is a will. I sigh.

Angus glances at me. "No luck?" I shake my head. "I've one left," he says.

As long as he's still working, I scan one more document.

My insides lurch at the name on the top: James Douglas! I give a little laugh. Am I really touching ink laid down by that great man himself?

Angus looks up. "You've found something?"

I shake my head. "No. I mean, yes, but not about Niall. It's James Douglas."

"A note from him?"

I look more carefully.

To My Lord Douglas, from Glenmirril.

My stomach drops! "It's from Glenmirril!" I lean in, deciphering ancient script.

My Lord Niall has received your request and makes all due haste to meet you at Carlisle.

"Angus!" My words come out in a breath. "I found him!"

Angus scans it, a slow smile growing on his own face. "You did indeed!"

The roller coaster shifts into motion again. My heart tingles! I break into a grin. I'm once again grazing Niall's fingertips through this veil of time, once again seeing him in the narrow, cobbled street in Inverness, running his hand down my hair, smiling at me. Angus and I read together.

He will arrive shortly with his monk and thirty men.

We glance at one another. "He was quite devout," I say.

"Maybe he traveled with a confessor?" Angus guesses. We lean in to read further.

He offers the services of his monk to....

We search for whom, or what, Niall offered the services of his monk. Or who this monk is. Or why he is 'Niall's' monk. But the words dangle, swallowed by time-faded ink, and a torn, charred edge.

I sit back, disappointed. "What's Carlisle?"

"The siege in July of 1315," Angus explains. "'Tis only a wee hike." His eyes shine with excitement.

"Siege?" I clarify. "Battle. People die in sieges."

"He walked the shore with his son," Angus reminds me. "Do the math. That had to have happened after *the siege.*

"But we don't know if it was Shawn or Niall with the son," I remind him.

"One answer at a time," he says. "Maybe we'll find he did something heroic at Carlisle."

I bite my lip. "Maybe we'll find he died there."

"So far, he's alive. We're still on his trail, aye?"

I smile, my excitement growing just a little. "Yes, we are."

Near the Border, 1314

With the lute bumping on Shawn's back, they galloped through woods, and beside the racing River Esk, shooting sprays of blue and white, as the sun sank into the west, till finally, south of Langholm. Niall slowed his mount. "'Tis but hours before we reach Carlisle."

"Or, as I like to call it, Outer Hades," Shawn said. "At least MacDougall isn't there."

"We'll stay the night in the next town, just on the border, maybe three hours." Suddenly, Niall's pony gave its head a hard shake, and stumbled. Niall slid off quickly. The animal lifted one foreleg, and snorted. Niall touched its nose, calming it, and dropped to one knee, feeling the leg.

Shawn dismounted. "What's wrong?"

"He needs rest."

Shawn glanced around the woods on their right, the river on their left, and the sun waning in the west. "For how long?"

"I can't say." Niall rose, his hand on the reins, stroking the pony's nose, and looked around, too. "Let's walk a bit," he said. "We'll have to take it slow."

They continued south, on foot. As the shadows lengthened, Shawn cleared his throat. "Any thoughts on where to spend the night? Is there a Holiday Inn around here?"

"There's no inn of any sort."

"Yeah, and that's a problem," Shawn said, "because last time I slept in the great outdoors, a wolf climbed into bed with me, and it didn't really end well for either of us." He rubbed his thigh, where a long scar would forever remind him of the night.

"You did well." Niall cocked a grin at him. "It almost makes me glad to have you at my side, despite your infernal complaining." The sky over the leafy canopy grew grayer as they climbed another hill.

"I haven't complained for half an hour, and considering I'm stuck with you, that's pretty impressive." An owl hooted, low and mournful. "I'm pretty sure that knocks a couple months off any Purgatory time I'd racked up." The river crackled along, cold water splashing against thin ice on the edges, beside them.

"*Any* time?" Niall chortled, a candle against the darkening wood. "You'll be fortunate to get as high as Purgatory, and if you do, you've racked up so much time there, they'll have to kick the rest of them straight into Heaven to make room for all the Purgatory you need!"

"I don't think it works like...." Shawn stopped at the top of the hill, staring at the sight before them. "Holy ruins, Batman. What is that?"

Niall and his pony halted by his side. The animal tossed its head, and nuzzled Niall's arm. Before them stretched a wide expanse of broken stone walls, stone buildings with mouths and eyes gaping wide in the twilight, on either side of a long road. One vast length of wall held numerous niches. Thirty yards away, crumbling walls enclosed rows of short, stout, stone posts. Beyond it, a stairway led down into a dark maw. Bushes sprang from cracks. Trees grew in and among the abandoned structures. Shadows stretched everywhere, as the sun sank, sending fiery orange and pink rays down the center road, lighting the mist that swirled along it.

"That," said Niall with a smile, "is our inn. God provides." He touched his heels to his pony, starting down the gentle slope.

Shawn coughed loudly. "Uh, yeah, He sure does. The question is *what* has He provided? What *is* this place?"

"A Roman fort." Niall led his pony down the center path, the remains rising on either side. A bird called somewhere in the trees.

"The *Roamin' in*." Shawn used English for the last two words. "God has a sense of humor."

Niall smiled, pointing to the stairs leading down. "There. 'Tis indoors."

"It's a pun," Shawn clarified. "It's a whole lot funnier if you see it spelled out."

"No doubt," Niall agreed. "Shall we gather firewood? Keep any more wolves from climbing in bed with you?"

"Yes, let's. And what keeps away the ghosts of the Roman legionnaires? Or their victims?"

"One sight of your face ought to scare any spirits back to the underworld."

"If that doesn't work," said Shawn, "your pathetic attempts at music will."

"Perhaps you could brag of your exploits with women." Niall grinned. "Even Hades is better than having to listen to that."

Shawn laughed. "You're jealous."

They picked their way over the darkening path strewn with stones. In the trees above, an owl hooted.

"What happens tomorrow?" Shawn stooped to gather twigs.

Niall's mouth was taut. "We hope he's better. If not, we let him rest, and spend the time learning to play the lute. We've shelter, walls and a roof, which is more than we expected."

They stopped before their intended room. Shawn sighed. It would do no good to stay in the open, but the stone structure, with its empty eyes and stone stairs descending into darkness, was hardly welcoming.

"We'll need wood," Niall said. They tethered the ponies to a tree springing up near the ruin, left the lute beside them, and set out to gather branches.

The sky was now deep blue, the ruins cloaked in shadow. A wolf howled in the distance. The air grew chillier as they worked, till a night among ghosts looked inviting, even homey, as long as it was warm. They piled the kindling on the lowest step outside their chosen abode, where it would warm the room, but send its smoke up into the sky. Niall scraped flint, and soon, they had flickering light by which to eat their hard bread and berries. Shawn settled back, content with his stomach less than empty, and pulled out the lute. He adjusted a couple tuning pegs, tried a few chords, and began one of the songs he'd played on guitar. Niall relaxed against another wall, watching his fingers, humming along. "Let me try," he said at last. Shawn handed it over, giving instruction as Niall leaned over the strings, working his fingers into unfamiliar positions for chords, and picking out melodies.

Outside, a pony whickered. Niall and Shawn froze, looking to the doorway, where they could see only black night beyond the glowing fire. Niall laid the lute down gently. "We've been careless," he said softly. They reached for their knives.

"I'm kind of hoping it's only a ghost," Shawn whispered back. The familiar tingle of adrenaline began, a tremoring of the nerves in his arms. His muscles tightened. "Do we wait for whoever it is to come in?"

Niall shook his head. "And wait for a whole army to come in on us? If I'm to die tonight, 'twill be fighting for my life." He rose, back against the wall, and inched around till he stood pressed by the doorway, where the fire crackled. On the other side, Shawn did the same, his heart pounding hard. Niall pointed to his chest, then to Shawn, and held up fingers in a silent count: *One. Two. Three.*

He sprang over the small flames, into the night. Shawn leapt behind him, knife ready, heart beating triple time, nerves screaming! The fire threw shadows across the pony, who balked against his tether. Shawn saw nothing. But he heard the crack of a twig just beyond the light. He and Niall lunged. The single crack grew into a panicked flurry of rustling leaves, cracking twigs, branches snapping back in their faces as they gave chase. Shawn ducked and swerved, saw Niall ahead, veered, and suddenly, there was a pile of arms, legs. He dropped his knife.

"Get down!" Niall roared. Shawn threw himself to the ground, hands over his head.

All became silent for a heartbeat...two.

Then the forest erupted with sound!

"I didn't mean *you!*" Niall said indignantly.

"I've done naught, Milord! Don't kill me!"

Then Niall was laughing, great gusty roars of merriment. "Shawn, get up! You're hiding from a *boy!*"

"Don't kill me! I can help you! I can help your hobin, Milord!"

Shawn inched his hand from over his eyes to see the dark shape of Niall sitting astride a boy who managed to flounder, fight, and cower, all at once, while protesting. He climbed irritably to his feet. "You *said* get down!"

"I meant him."

"You staged this because your lute-playing sucks!" Shawn threw back into the night. "You needed a distraction."

"Thank goodness at least you can play a lute, because the way you fight, a mouse would have gotten the better of us!"

The boy looked back and forth between them. He stopped struggling. "Milord?"

Shawn realized both their faces were showing. He recoiled into shadow. Niall climbed to his feet, his knife at the ready. "Get up."

"He's just a boy," Shawn sighed. "Put your knife away."

"Aren't we sending boys to war?" Niall asked. "What makes you think a boy can't kill?"

Shawn had no answer. He could think only of the boys to whom he'd taught trombone, so many years ago in the future—boys in sports jerseys, with trimmed hair, worrying about who to ask to prom. This boy stood before them in tatters. He wrapped his arms around his skinny body. His hair hung past his shoulders. *Clarence.* His father's killer, as he'd last seen him, flashed through Shawn's mind. Yes, boys could kill. He didn't want to believe this one would. He just didn't want any more ugliness in his world.

"What's your name?" Niall demanded.

"I have none," the boy said.

"No name? How can you have no name?"

The boy shrugged. "My parents died long ago, my mother in childbirth, and my father in battle. A farrier found me and took me in. He didn't know my name."

"Surely he called you something?"

"Red." The boy's shivering increased.

"Niall," Shawn said.

Niall pressed the boy, ignoring Shawn. "And why are you not with him now?"

"He was...." Red's teeth clacked together. He clenched them tight, rubbing his hands up and down his arms, and tried again. "He was killed when the soldiers came through. I ran into the forest and hid. They were afraid to follow me into the ruins."

"Niall, he's *cold*."

Niall's knife remained pointed at the boy. "Which soldiers?"

"They were English, Milord. Meaning no offense, Milord." His teeth clattered again. "If you're English."

"Niall!" Shawn stepped forward, his anger growing. "He's just a *kid!* He's about to...."

Before he finished, the boy collapsed. Shawn was under him, catching his sagging body before it hit the ground.

"Do you understand naught?" Niall demanded. He jabbed his knife into its sheath angrily, but helped Shawn take up the slack. "We cannot blindly trust! It'll get us killed! And *that* will get Allene killed!"

They slipped their arms under the boy's, and half lifted, half carried him back through the dark wood. "There are times," Shawn said, tersely, "I think I'd rather be killed than descend into an animal that coldly—no pun intended—watches a boy drop of *hypothermia!*"

"We're alive, aren't we?" Niall snapped back.

"Which is possibly more than can be said for him." They inched down the steps, and lifted him carefully over the flames.

"Go build that up so we can get some warmth into him," Niall barked.

"Yes, my *liege!*" Shawn threw the last of his adrenaline, and fear-fueled anger into the word. He and Niall glared at one another before Niall eased the boy to the ground, putting his own cloak over him, and Shawn stomped into the dark to gather larger branches. He knew Niall was right. And he resented it. He resented being caught in a day when he had to hold a knife on a shivering kid. He resented being caught in a time when he couldn't even play a few songs without suddenly being back in a fight for his life, and the fear of dying. He slammed a handful of twigs into the bowl of his cloak, angry at his failure at the Eildon Hills. *Damn fairy hills!* He stooped for a tangle of dry branches, furious at God for leaving him in the wrong century in the tower back at Glenmirril.

The boy now lying in the Roman ruins, and the knives, and Clarence who had killed his father, all swirled in his mind, creating a maelstrom of confused emotions he couldn't even name. He wanted a drink. He wanted to be at one of his parties, flirting with a beautiful woman, covering his own pain with the promise in her eyes, with thinking about anything other than Clarence and his dead father.

He leaned against a tree, wanting everything to be different. *He needs your help.* As if he'd heard the words audibly, he looked up, looked around the dark trees. Something rustled in the forest. He turned, making his way back. He stepped over the flames and laid his offerings on the fire. It crackled, rose, and grew warmer, consuming his pain and anger, and melting it away. It was not Clarence lying there, but a boy without a name. His face was pale and waxy. Shawn touched his forehead, cold as ice, and removed his own cloak, adding it to Niall's, and wrapping the hood around the boy's corkscrew curls.

"Play the lute for him," Niall said softly. "Music may help."

Shawn lifted it, his eyes prickling with tears. He wasn't sure why. He played, and sang an old love song. At least, old by his standards. For Niall, it was probably too new to exist for another couple centuries. He played and sang, and the boy's breathing evened out.

"I'm sorry," Niall said. "I should have brought him in anon."

Shawn nodded sadly. "You were right. Boys can kill."

"But not this one."

"Do you think he'll be okay?"

"Morning will tell," Niall said. "I'll take the first watch."

CHAPTER NINE

Carlisle, Present

We head south early the next morning. I teeter on a cliff of expectation, as we drive up into rough border hills, holding hands across the gear stick, trading stories and philosophical questions about life and faith—things Shawn never cared about.

As we leave the hills behind, Angus brings the siege of Carlisle to life, describing the wet, soggy summer in which Bruce's men fought as much against rain and mud as against stones and arrows zinging over the castle walls. The great fortress was two hundred years old when Niall—or was it Shawn?—stood there at Bruce's side, not knowing how the battle would play out, who would live or die. I swallow hard. I don't know, either. Maybe Shawn survived MacDougall's gallows, only to die at Carlisle.

We visit the castle first, focusing on the dungeon. "Some of the Scots were captured," Angus says, apologetically. "If he's left a mark inside the castle, 'twould be here."

My stomach quivers as we search. A mark would mean he didn't die at Creagsmalan. But neither do I want to think of him or Niall chained in this dank pit, licking moisture off the walls to survive.

We find nothing. I decide I'm thankful.

Searching outside turns up a pair of deep scratches on an outer wall. It could be two-thirds of Shawn's mark—a long one and a shorter one on top.

Or it could be two scratches.

"They tried to mine under the walls," Angus says. "But he'd not be scratching while they did so."

I close my eyes, trying to dislodge the brutal image of medieval men huddled together under a mining cat—Shawn among them—digging, in mud and rain, filth and stench, digging as arrows hail down, piercing the unlucky ones on the edges of the cat. This is the father of my child, a man I loved. For all his faults, I loved him. It's all too easy, and far too distressing, as I stare at this mark that could be his, to see him there, desperately scratching as arrows hail down, as men dig and shout and cry in pain all around him. The baby kicks in agitation.

"It's just scratches, Amy," Angus says. "He wasn't here. Come away."

English Border, 1314

Shawn lay restless through the night. Adrenaline, fear, and cold kept him awake, even during Niall's watch. Every time he closed his eyes, he saw Clarence, with the corkscrew curl falling over one eye, sneering at him in the courtroom. And his mother's voice came back to him insistently, softly. *His mother's boyfriend. Shawn, I know it hurts, but you have no idea what he came from. You have no idea what was happening in his life. If you must fight, fight against the evil that drives a boy to such desperation!*

He's not desperate, Mom! The young Shawn had roared back—perhaps the only time he'd ever yelled at his mother, one of the few times he'd been angry with her. He lowered his voice, tried to remember she was hurting, too, trying to cope, tried to make her see. *He wasn't desperate, Mom. He just wanted drugs.*

In the medieval firelight, he listened to the boy, Red. His breath came softly, evenly. He was just a kid, who had lost both parents, who had lost the man who took him in. Shawn sat up, watching him, and wondering—what had happened to Clarence's father? What had it been like, living with the mother's string of boyfriends? What had his own mother been trying to tell him? The doorway of their ancient Roman chamber grew gray. He touched the boy's forehead, felt the pulse in his wrist.

Niall stirred. "He's well?"

"He's alive, anyway."

"I'll go find food. He'll need it."

Shawn played the lute, singing softly, while he waited, wondering, what next? They couldn't just leave the kid. But he couldn't come with them. And if the pony was lame, what then? They couldn't walk into a town from which they might need to escape fast. The light grew, as melody filled the small chamber, and he saw why the farrier had called the boy Red. His hair was nearly clown-red. Shawn smiled. He hit a wrong note, and tried again, playing the phrase over and over until he was sure it would come out right in Carlisle.

"What a bollox." Grinning, Niall appeared at the doorway, a skinned squirrel skewered on a stick. He held it over the flames, even as he added more twigs.

"Yeah, well." Shawn grinned back. "At least I never tried to serve roadkill for breakfast at a five-star Roamin' Inn." He switched from their medieval Gaelic to modern English, trusting Niall had retained plenty. It was one language they could be absolutely sure Red wouldn't understand. "We better decide quick before he wakes up who's Brother Andrew and who's Milord Niall as long as he's with us."

"You've the hair," Niall said.

"And it never looked better," Shawn cracked. He peeled off the robe he wore, and tossed it to Niall. "What do we do with him?" he asked, as Niall pulled it on. "We can't leave him, and we can't take him with us." Shawn studied the boy. He guessed him to be about fourteen. They'd tackled and pulled knives on a fourteen-year-old. Was that about how old Clarence had been when he first met him? About. He'd been a kid himself. He'd never thought about where Clarence was when he didn't live with them.

"As long as the pony is lame, we're not going anywhere," Niall replied.

"He said he could help it. Do you think he was just talking to try to save himself?"

Rotating the squirrel over the flames, Niall shrugged. "Time will tell."

Shawn turned back to the lute, working on another piece, sounding out chords, while the smell of roasting meat gradually filled the small cell, and pink sunlight glowed through the door. The boy stirred. Niall pulled his hood up, and lowered his head over the squirrel. Red opened his eyes first in a daze, looking confused, then suddenly scrambled up, scooting across the floor, till he bumped up against the stone wall, staring at Shawn with wide eyes. "Don't kill me, Milord!"

"I'm not going to kill you." Switching back to medieval Gaelic, Shawn put the lute down. "Listen...Red. You want me to call you Red?"

The boy shrugged. "As you please, Milord."

"No, really, as you please," Shawn said. "It's your name, after all."

"Milord, I've been called nothing else."

"Frank, Benjamin, Joe, Gene Krupa, Glenn, Benny, Amadeus. You could pick anything."

From under the hood came a grunt, and Niall spoke in their modern English. "'Tis naught but a name. We've bigger things to worry about."

"A name is important," Shawn argued, using the same tongue.

"Not as important as getting information. Which means healing this hobin."

The boy looked back and forth between them. "Milord," he asked softly. "What manner of monk is this? What language does he speak?"

"Brother Andrew," Shawn said. "He's a manner of monk who is completely unable to keep his vow of silence. I hope you'll pray for him."

"Find out what he can do," Niall said irritably.

"Red it is, then," Shawn addressed the boy. "Unless you change your mind. The world's your oyster, Kid."

"Milord?"

"Ask him," Niall hissed from under the hood.

Red glanced at him fearfully; his eyes traveled to the squirrel, now roasted dark.

"You said last night you can help our pony," Shawn said.

Red's eyes lingered on the meat.

"Give him something to eat," Shawn said.

Red shook his head quickly. "Oh, no, Milord. Only if there are scraps."

Shawn rolled his eyes. "'Tis my royal command. Eat."

The boy paused only long enough to attempt to look courteous, before his hand flashed out to the skewer Niall offered, nearly burning himself as he dug in. Shawn watched, wondering how long ago the soldiers had killed the farrier, and how long it had been since the child had eaten. He ripped with his teeth, gulped, wiped at his chin, digging around the bones with his fingers for the smallest pieces of flesh still clinging there. When he finished, he looked up, suddenly abashed. Sunlight cast rosy shades over the stone walls behind his head. "My apologies, Milord. 'Tis sorry I am. I was hungry. I forgot myself."

"It's all right, kid. Red. You said you know horses."

The boy nodded enthusiastically, eager to redeem himself. Niall rose from his place by the fire, and the boy stepped over the low flames. He hurried up the short flight of stairs to where the ponies were tethered, and dropped to his knees before the lame one. It stepped back skittishly, but he touched its leg gently. He whispered to it, ran his hand down its leg, and lifted his head. He was no longer a fourteen year old boy, Shawn noted, but a man, confident in his work. "Milord," he said, "might I go into the wood to seek herbs?"

Shawn glanced at Niall, who nodded subtly.

"You won't find much in November, will you?" Shawn asked doubtfully.

"Milord, I believe I can find what I need. I'll not run away."

It hadn't even crossed Shawn's mind. But he felt he ought to be a little stern. He cleared his throat and spoke forcefully. "Be quick about it, then! I want you back in...." He lifted his wrist in the habitual motion, before remembering he had no watch. "Before the sun gets even close to noon!"

"Oh, well done," Niall muttered in modern English.

The boy bowed low. "Yes, Milord. Your monk can come with me, if it please you, Milord. To assure you I'll come back."

"Go with him, Monk," Shawn ordered, thoroughly enjoying himself now, "and learn what it is that will help my hobin."

"You'd best not sleep too soundly tonight," Niall muttered, and followed the boy into the forest.

CHAPTER TEN

Carlisle, 1314

"Persistent, isn't he?" Niall murmured from under the hood. They watched the boy kneeling on the bank of the racing river, scooping water into his mouth. "I'm not sure you've done him any favors by letting him come along." They spoke, again, in modern English for privacy.

"Throwing rocks at him like a stray dog and making him stay behind in an abandoned ruin was better?"

"Getting hanged beside us if we're caught is surely worse."

Shawn shrugged. "So we don't get caught."

"A good plan," Niall remarked dryly. "I'd not thought of that."

"Good thing I'm here to think of it. Lucky for you I couldn't find the remote control to work Thomas's fairy hill."

Red lifted his head from the water, grinning.

Shawn smiled. It was nice to see him acting like a kid. He'd worked with the pony, putting some poultice or other on its leg, and giving it massages, and after two days, it had seemed rested and healed. Now, they stood on the banks of the River Eden. "Still determined to come with us?" Shawn asked.

The boy's smile grew. "Milord, it seems you need me."

They left the ponies in the care of an innkeeper, forded the river at a shallow point, jumping from stone to stone over icy waters, and before noon, were passing into Carlisle. Niall went first, saying he came to stay with the Gray Friars. Shawn watched from a distance, ten minutes later, as Red followed, seeking work in the garrison's stables. After another half hour, Shawn walked in with the lute strapped to his back. After much questioning from the men at arms, he was directed to the castle at the far end of town. "You'll need permission to play, and they may be wanting you to play there," he was informed.

Trying to ignore his quaking knees, he headed north, walking the long city streets, memorizing layouts, noting what soldiers he saw, seeking sign of war preparations or equipment—all while trying to pretend he wasn't the enemy taking note of everything. There was a large gate on his left. He scanned it for signs of weakness, for anything that might help the Bruce break through, until a burly knight stepped forward, growling, "What are you looking at, Minstrel?"

Shawn bowed his head humbly. "'Tis only that my small town has nothing so grand, Sir!"

His last experience posing as a minstrel, when he'd been apprehended by MacDougall's men while playing sackbut, made his knees quake. He inched away, his heart pounding, trying not to look guilty; trying not to set off the man's Invader Warning Instinct—and noting the six guards at the gate as he did so, along with the barred gate, and the murder trap, into which they might pour boiling oil. A part of him hoped Bruce's men would never get through that gate, so they wouldn't meet that fate.

"Where are you going!" the man demanded. His tabard flapped around his knees in the chilly day.

"To the castle, Milord. They told me at the south gate I must ask permission. Please your lord, sir, send a man to ask them. They'll tell you 'tis true. I seek but to play earn my bread."

A young woman approached, a girl in green silk with a dark woven cloak thrown over her shoulders. She glanced at Shawn, letting a small smile slip.

"Emeline!" The knight barked her name.

Her eyes danced coyly away from Shawn's. She lowered them demurely, and gave the knight a swift curtsy. "My mam sends you bread, Bertrand. She bids me wish you good morn."

Shawn summed things up quickly. Their body language spoke words neither of them ever would. Bertrand was besotted. Emeline's mother envisioned a lord's knight for a son-in-law. Emeline was laughing at both of them, and if he hadn't lost his sixth sense about women, she was, rather, enjoying the attention her looks garnered from any number of men in the town.

And Bertrand suspected it.

"Bring it here." His face softened into a smile. Then he scowled at Shawn. "Be off with you! Make haste to the castle! My men will be watching you!"

Satisfied he'd shown Emeline who was more manly, he leaned close, whispering in her ear. She giggled.

Smiling at Bertrand's need to prove his prowess by belittling a minstrel, Shawn headed to the castle. Emeline was the first place he would try for information.

He spent the next two hours waiting in a chilly stone hall, and another hour in a chilly ante room, while the sun climbed high outside the Gothic windows, while officials in thick beards and heavy fur-lined cloaks hurried on their business, bidding him wait. He listened. He watched. He learned Andrew Harclay commanded the place. Two men strode by, one issuing commands. They glanced at him and switched to French. But he recognized, 'gather stones....'

Stones? For warfare? What were they, cavemen?

Finally, a harried man with a great beard and greater belly, and gold chains hanging around his neck, entered the ante room. "You. Minstrel. You may play each day in the market place." He named the fee. "You'll play for our dinner each night. You'll be fed, given a room here, and...." He looked Shawn up and down. "Clothed appropriately. See the tailor in town and tell him he shall be paid."

"My Lord." Shawn rose and bowed. "Thank you."

"Go!" The man flapped his hands as if at a flock of geese. "Be back before the evening meal."

He found the tailor—noting more of the layout of the town and soldiers as he went—made arrangements, and took up a spot in the market, where he could see the citadel. He began playing the pieces he'd worked out during their enforced stay in the ancient ruin. *All things work to good,* Allene would say. *Dumb luck,* he'd respond. He smiled, thinking of Allene, of the Laird, of Hugh; thinking of Christina, and hoping she was safe at Glenmirril.

He turned his wandering thoughts back to the matter at hand. If all went according to plan, Brother Andrew would not be seen again until they left. But Brom, minstrel from Durham, would be meeting a couple of girls every evening. He'd watch, and choose likely candidates, as he played.

It didn't take him long to spot a comely young girl sashaying through the town with a basket of wool. His eyes followed her as he switched to a farcical love song. She pretended not to notice, but he saw her throw looks over her shoulder as she spoke with a woman in the market.

A monk in a gray robe stopped before Shawn. "You think she knows about military preparations?" came Niall's voice in modern English.

Shawn strummed a chord, and murmured back, "Bruce told me to use my gift."

"For *information.*"

The girl glanced at him again, and this time, gave him a fleeting smile.

"Judging by the come-hither looks over the shoulder, she knows plenty about the men around here, and half of them are military." He let his fingers drift over a simple melody he'd once known quite well on guitar. It sounded all right on a lute, he decided—at least on a lute tuned like a guitar. More or less.

"Do your job."

"I could do it better if you'd get out of here. Having a monk hanging around is like having my grandmother in the back seat on a date." He strummed another chord and added in a soft undertone, "Plan on meeting her tonight as Brom. I'll be meeting someone else."

Niall glided away. Shawn began singing another song. Something about mushrooms. Gathering mushrooms. He sang it in English, played an interlude, and sang it again in modern Gaelic, all the time watching the girl. A man at arms approached her, leaning close, touching her arm. She laughed, leaning into him, and turned quickly, moving away to another stall. She glanced back over her shoulder at Shawn, and her eyes darted away again.

He turned his attention to the gate of the citadel, seeking any girls who came and went, who might also know things. There were several, he decided. A girl with flaxen hair talked with a guard at the bottom of the steps. Another, down the street, laughed with a mounted soldier. He made eye contact with each of them, letting his eyes slide over the soldiers, too, as he did so. He calculated their comings and goings, studied their horses, and when two stood not far from him, he reverted to the familiar guitar melody, closed his eyes, and listened to their talk. When he opened his eyes, another beautiful girl stood before him, watching him play. He smiled at her, sang to her, and saw Red behind her, holding the reins of a horse, that nuzzled his cheek as he rubbed its nose. He resisted the urge to sigh. How was he supposed to charm women with monks and kids hanging around!

After a time, he slung the lute on his back, and wandered down the street. It took twenty minutes, but he found a shop, dim in the afternoon light, where a gnarled woman spun at a wheel. She looked up, peering at him with rheumy eyes. He gave his most charming smile. It could be his grandmother. Well, maybe his great-great grandmother, he amended. "I've heard you make the most beautiful wool here," he said.

She narrowed her eyes at him, and didn't answer.

"I'd like to buy some," he said.

Again, she didn't answer. He looked around. A counter barred him from the back of the place. Shelves behind it held skeins of wool in various hues. He wasn't sure what more to say to a woman who wouldn't answer him. He wondered if she were deaf, or mute. He pointed to a skein of wool, and took a small coin from the bag at his belt.

"Now what would a minstrel be wanting with such a thing?" asked a light voice behind him.

He spun. She stood there, laughing at him. "'Tis used for lasses' under garments."

He grinned. "You're having me on."

She gave a saucy laugh. "Perchance I am, but then again, maybe not. Have you a lady for whom you'd like such a thing?"

"I don't. But 'tis best to be prepared, for I've hope there will be soon."

She smiled. "I rather envy her. I think, though, that perhaps you and I should discuss wool more thoroughly, so that you might make the best possible choice."

Shawn bowed. "My Lady, I must go now to play for the commander's dinner. Will you meet me in the east orchard when the moon rises?"

Her smile promised more than meeting.

Bannockburn, Present

"Sorry it took so long." Alec handed a bag, heavy with chain mail, to Brian.

Standing just inside the door of the psych ward, tingling with excitement to finally meet the owner of the Claverock sword, Brian waved him off with a cheerful, "No matter! We're here now!" He hefted the heavy bag in his chubby arms.

"Mr. Beaumont." The orderly softly, as if to a slow child.

The man in the hospital robe turned his bull-shaped head toward the orderly. He said nothing. His head swung again on a thick neck. His eyes met Brian's briefly before falling on the bag in Brian's hand. He lifted his gaze back to Brian's.

Nerves rippled down Brian's arms. The man seemed the personification of unbridled energy, ready to uncoil and spring. A fierce and dangerous aura hung about him. He barked a few short, guttural sounds. Recognition shot like electricity through Brian. He frowned. It couldn't be. "What...what did you say?" he managed.

The man spoke again, slowly, as if to a fool. The disdain in his eyes made it clear Brian had not misunderstood. *What do you hold?* he asked.

Brian recognized the words with a thrill that trembled, then bloomed into excitement. He turned to Alec. "You say he was speaking gibberish?"

"You didn't just hear him?" Alec replied, his eyes wide.

Brian laughed, as delighted as if he'd just discovered the Bruce's personal journal. "'Tis not gibberish at all! 'Tis perfect Middle English! Alec!" He turned to his friend. "I'll be wanting to speak with this man at length! What can you arrange?"

Carlisle, 1314

After playing for the commander's dinner, Shawn found Niall, his head bowed, face shielded, and working prayer beads through his finger, outside the Gray Friars monastery, and continued walking. Niall fell into step beside him. "Brom—that's me—is meeting Emeline in the west orchards outside the castle. Brom—that's you—has a date with Duraina in the east orchards. So ditch the monk's robe."

"You're wasting your time," Niall murmured, his head still bowed.

"Didn't we get information from Ellen and Christina?"

Niall grunted. "Let us hope Christina has not paid too heavily."

His words discomforted Shawn. Emeline and Duraina were anonymous faces to him, barely more than names. But Christina, at one time, had been, too. Now he worried about her fate. "What's your solution?" he asked. "Just walk up and ask the guys with bows and arrows?"

In lieu of answer, Niall ducked down a side street, and began pulling off his robe. "Tell me what Duraina expects of Brom."

Carlisle, Present

We move on to Carlisle's archives. Three hours' digging turns up a mention of Taran from Glenmirril, but nothing of Niall or his monk. It's as if they never existed, here at the siege of Carlisle.

At least we find no record of their deaths.

We eat dinner in a pub and turn for home under a new moon. "I can add Ayr and Carlisle to the time line," *I say.* "But really, what have we accomplished?" *Snow dances in the night sky.*

He grins. "A fun few days?"

I rest my head against the car seat, smiling as I watch moonlight play over his shadowed jaw, wishing he didn't have to head home again. "Anything that would answer our questions?"

"We know Niall was at Ayr and Carlisle."

"We already know he goes to Ireland after that time. And we don't know if it was Niall."

"We now know he traveled with a confessor."

My brow furrows. "Which tells us what?"

"Nothing new," *Angus admits.* "You knew from meeting him that he was devout."

"No." *I sit up straight.*

"He wasn't?" *Angus asks in confusion.* "You said...."

"No, we're missing the obvious! Niall *was devout."*

"Shawn wasn't." *Angus takes my meaning.* "Shawn *wouldn't travel with a confessor."*

The familiar ache starts in my stomach, fearing Shawn's death. Angus places his hand on mine. "Niall hated water," *he says.* "Shawn *fought at Jura and* Niall *traveled with a confessor."*

I shake my head. "But they can't both have shown up at Ayr, looking exactly alike, one of them with a confessor, one of them getting on a boat. How would they explain that?"

Angus stares straight ahead. "They both lived. You'll see." *He turns the radio to something soft and medieval.*

I stare out the window. My reflection stares back, the Glenmirril Lady with her hair falling down. I turn away. "It's bugging me," *I say.* "I know I've heard something about a monk with some connection to Glenmirril."

"It'll come back to you." *Angus glances at me as the car climbs the narrow, winding road.*

"And until it does?" *I ask.* "We can't even say we're looking for a needle in a haystack, because we don't even know if it's a needle we're looking for. We're just throwing hay around. Following Niall's historical trail is getting us nowhere."

"We'll have a nice dinner when we get home," *he says,* "take a wee break from time-traveling twins, and think about it fresh in the morning." *We drive for a time through dark hills, the soft medieval strains keep my mind on Niall and Shawn. I stare out the window at hills, ever undulating and rolling, wave upon wave of dark hills rising, one beyond the next, forever, wondering if the two of them rode these hills together, or if one of them rode alone.*

Carlisle, 1314

Flushed with moonlight, crisp night air, and a long, sweet kiss from Emeline, Shawn headed up to the room he'd been given. "Brom the Minstrel!" a man greeted him in the hall. "Did you not go up but a moment ago?"

Shawn smiled, frozen. "Uh, yes! Yes I did! Then—I came back down." He indicated the lute on his back. "I forgot it. And now I'm going back up!" He hurried upstairs before Niall could come down.

Niall lay on the bed, his hands behind his head. "As long as you've been gone, I hope you've learned all there is to know." By unspoken agreement, they had adopted the habit of using modern English whenever it was important not to be overheard.

Shawn cleared his throat. "I'm being cautious. Not giving Brom away."

Niall sat up and swung his legs to the floor. "Translation: you learned nothing."

"I learned medieval England has some pretty hot chicks."

Niall rolled his eyes. "The Bruce will no doubt find that helpful in planning the siege."

"What did *you* find out?" Shawn challenged.

"Naught." Niall sat up, kicking his feet to the floor. "It seems Duraina's folk have little business with the castle or soldiers."

"Where do the monks think Brother Andrew is?" Shawn asked curiously.

"He's taken ill. They saw Brom leave after visiting poor Brother Andrew."

"Brom's a great guy," Shawn said. "Next question. What do you expect to learn from *monks* about military readiness? Are they putting in nuclear prayers against Bruce or something?"

"Nuclear?" Niall moved to the table to pour ale.

"Mega. Big. Powerful."

"The Gray Friars live near the east gate," Niall replied. "They'll be in danger should Carlisle be attacked, and they talk. Particularly around a monk under a vow of silence. 'Tis human nature to forget that mute does not mean deaf."

"And?" Shawn poured his own ale and joined Niall at the table.

"Stones will be stored on the Gray Friars' grounds for the siege they believe is coming."

"*Okay*, stones! I'm scared!" Shawn smirked. "You're wasting your time. I'll get more out of girls chasing army men."

Niall smiled. "We'll see. There's a house of Black Friars on the west. I believe another wandering monk will stay with them."

"Where are you getting a black robe from?"

"I'll have to steal it."

Shawn clucked his tongue. "A monk who can't keep a vow of silence, and steals. Doesn't your conscience bother you?"

Niall rocked back in his chair, cleaning his fingernails with his dirk. "In light of the alternative, of my people being killed, no."

Bannockburn, Present

The week in Carlisle brings my dreams alive with battles and belfries, castles and kirks. I tape timelines, charts, and maps to my office wall, marking Douglas's raids, Ayr, Carlisle, and all we know of Niall's movements. I step back, the roll of tape in my hand, staring at the newly hung rubbing of Shawn's mark at Creagsmalan, and ponder the burning question: what now?

Devoid of answers, I play my violin. The familiar flow of fingers and bow frees my mind to roam wild thickets of thorny questions, laced with rose-sweet memories of long drives through the English hills with Angus, holding hands, climbing over ruined castle walls and exploring medieval churches; listening to his stories of Robert the Bruce, Angus Og, and James Douglas, until they feel as real as the people of my own life—flesh and blood, living, breathing men, as real as my parents, Rob, Celine, and Dana. As real as Shawn and Niall.

My mind drifts back to the strings biting into my fingers, the pull of horsehair against wire, the sweet thread of sound twisting up to the high notes, as my fingers creep toward the bridge. It's my favorite song from Cillcurran, *the musical about a mythical Scottish island. I try to remember the last time the orchestra played it. I can't. The thought floats away as I close my eyes, listening, swaying as the music describes a magical mist rising when danger threatens. Somebody left Shawn's mark. It could only be Shawn or Niall. Think, think, think, I tell myself.*

My bow jumps to a series of staccatos. Which of them left the marks? How do we find out if they both survived MacDougall's gallows, when both of them lived as Niall? Brian is looking for more information. I swallow my lingering irritation at Angus's munchkin friend. He is doing that for me, when I've been nothing but critical of him.

My bow slows; I turn to the other question: How do we get him back, if he's alive in medieval Scotland? They're on the same side now, yes; but no other story of time travel depends on two people being in the same place. So think, I admonish myself.

I open my eyes. My bow floats off the strings. Ideas swirl in my mind like the half-formed mists of Cillcurran. Mysterious events. Magic. How are they different? We live in an age that acknowledges one without believing in the other. Does it matters which I call it? It's a direction to search. I swish my polishing cloth over the honey amber face of my instrument, settle it into the case, and, hand pressed to my stomach, climb the stairs to my laptop.

The sun sinks, as I delve into the labyrinth of the web, searching Scotland's mystical past. One link leads to another till I'm lost in a hall of mirrors, forgetting where I started, and no idea where I'm going; only knowing Angus is right—it's better to start somewhere, anywhere, even if it's wrong, than nowhere. I wander through a virtual maze of cairns and stone circles, and end up staring at a site marked ley lines. As I reach for my notebook, I notice how gloomy the office has grown. I switch on the light, and jot notes.

> Ley lines connect points of mystery. Strange events
> happen along them. Melrose, where Bruce's heart is
> buried, is on one such line. The monks of ancient days
> are said to have traveled along another line to....

My pen stills. The breath hovers in my throat, going neither up nor down. Is it an amazing coincidence or no coincidence at all? There are dozens of these lines, after all. I hit Angus's name on my phone, draw a breath as he answers, and say, "Angus. You'll never guess what I found."

CHAPTER ELEVEN

Carlisle, 1314

The next days found Shawn playing lute with steadily increasing proficiency, and ever-chillier fingers, near each of the three city gates, smiling as more and more coins clinked onto a cloth spread before him. As he played, he counted soldiers, listened to conversations of passers-by, and watched which girls spoke with the men at arms. When he took breaks from playing, he prowled wood shops and the smithy, showing interest with good-natured foolishness. Pieces of a trebuchet leaned against the woodworker's shop walls. He was no expert, but his description, Niall said, sounded like at least five were being built. On the third day, in the smithy, he was lucky enough to catch a man wheeling out a bin full of arrow heads. Thousands of them.

He chatted up girls while he strolled the town, seeking out those who favored the guards. Red seemed always to be coming by with a horse when he did so. And when he wasn't working in the stables, Red sat listening to him play, or followed him through the streets. He swore Red was laughing at him, though he couldn't say why. The boy was too canny.

"Go away, kid," Shawn muttered. "I'm working." The carpenter's shop was nearby. His daughter was comely and had watched him play for two days now. She might know more of her father's work.

"What work?" Red asked. "You're not playing your lute."

"*You* have work to do."

"If you want a lass," Red offered, "I can help you get one."

Shawn stopped, turned, and snorted. "Listen, kid, *I* can get any lass I want. I've never had any problem in that field."

Red gazed up at him. The sun shone down into the narrow street, turning his curls into a vivid red halo. "Then why do you talk to a different one every day?"

"Go take care of the horses, kid." Shawn started moving again.

Red hurried after him, past the church. "You've a fancy for the same ones who come to the citadel."

Shawn stopped again, eyeing the boy. He was *way* too observant. He pulled him close, and leaned down. "You know Brother Andrew and I won't stay long, right?"

The boy nodded.

"Are you staying when we leave?"

Red looked aghast. "Milord!"

"Sh!" Shawn yanked him into a narrow lane between the houses, a finger pressed to his lips. "Don't say that!"

"Of course I go with you," Red whispered back.

"Okay, then."

He cocked his head. "*Okay*?"

"All right," Shawn clarified. "Have you seen Brother Andrew? You seem good at seeing everything."

The boy grinned. "Thank you, Mi...."

"I told you not to call me that."

His grin did not diminish. "He's wearing a black robe and staying with the Dominicans by the west gate."

"How did you know that before I did?"

Red's smile grew. "I pay attention."

Shawn laughed. "Yes, you do. I'm glad you're sticking with us. Be prepared to leave any time we come for you. Make it easy for us to find you, understand?"

He nodded. "I'll be at the citadel."

Shawn hurried to the carpenter's shop. His legendary luck held. She was just coming from the back of the shop with a basket full of long sticks. They might be shafts for arrows, Shawn thought. She twitched a cloth over the basket, and beamed at him. "What brings a minstrel to the carpenter's shop?"

Shawn indicated the lute on his back. "I hoped to talk to your father about making another one. But it looks like you're heading out. Maychance you need an escort to protect you?"

She laughed. "I think not. Though...." She paused, smiling at him. "I know lutes fair well, and perhaps could help my father by finding out what you need, as he's got a fair bit of work to do."

"But you can't talk to me now?"

She shook her head, smiling.

"Soooo...." Shawn drew out the word, "I would have to meet with you later."

"After you play for dinner? I could meet you in the orchards."

He beamed. Red thought he needed help getting a girl, did he! He lifted her hand to his lips, smiling into her eyes. "I shall not disappoint you, My Lady." He glanced at the sun. He should have time enough to find Niall before he had to be back at the castle. He found the west gate, and from there, the house of the Black Friars. He knocked, having no idea what he would say.

A porter swung the door open, and waited.

Shawn bowed, scrambling for an idea. "My good brother," he stalled. A story came, as it always did. "You've a visiting monk. I believe he's one I met on the road, who did me a great kindness. I wish to thank him with a gift."

The porter glanced at the sun. "'Tis close to prayer time. Make haste."

"Haste is my second-favorite thing to make." Shawn grinned, and followed the man down a short hall to a visitor's room. He waited, none too patiently, for the ten minutes it took Niall to arrive, shuffling and head bowed.

"The Black Friars broke through the wall at one time," he murmured softly, in modern English, "to build a conduit to the outside."

"A conduit?" Shawn was puzzled. Suddenly his face cleared. "A sewer? A *toilet?*"

Niall's lips pursed.

"You people are so weird about talking about bodily functions," Shawn said. "Are you seriously suggesting we tell the Bruce to send his men in through the toilet?"

"Not quite how I envisioned it," Niall snapped. "'Tis a weakness in the overall structure. He needs to know."

They exchanged news quickly, and Shawn made his exit, back into the town's narrow streets. He slid into his seat as the servants laid great planks across the trestles, making tables for dinner. Others followed with white cloths which they shook out in great billows that floated down and settled, turning the planks into banquet tables. He used the time to work out a couple of new pieces. Footsteps fell behind him, and stopped.

"We need two more tables." He recognized the steward's voice. "We've just received word of another two score arriving. They'll be here before the meal begins."

"Who is it?" asked his underling.

"My Lord of Creagsmalan, Alexander MacDougall and his son Duncan."

Shawn's blood went cold—colder than warranted by the chilly November castle. He'd rise, as soon as they left, pretend he had to...get something for the lute...change his clothes...anything...and get Niall and Red and flee Carlisle. They hadn't gotten nearly enough information, but Bruce would prefer them back alive with some information, than dead.

A hand fell on his shoulder. "Minstrel. The commander requests your presence immediately."

Bannockburn, Present

"Iona." With a large, square finger, Angus tapped the small western island, on the map stretched across the coffee table in Amy's living room. The fire in the hearth cast dancing shadows over their faces. "Ley lines. One of which the monks—supposedly—followed to Iona." He lifted his eyes to Amy.

"Which Shawn carved on the rock," Amy murmured. Before Niall had disappeared back into his own time, he'd called her from a hiker's phone to tell her Shawn had left a message carved on Hugh's giant rock, deep in the forest where Hugh had lived in hiding, centuries ago. *A so sorry. Iona J.* Sitting beside Angus on the couch, knee against knee, she knew no more about Shawn's meaning now than she had the day Niall called.

Angus's dark eyebrows met over his nose as he studied the map. "Explain these ley lines again. It's been a mad week."

"Crazy time directing traffic?"

He glanced up, too distracted at first to catch her meaning. Then he grinned, the corners of his eyes crinkling. "Aye."

"Clive told me you were in the mountains."

"He shouldn't have worried you."

She slipped her hand into his. "Don't you like knowing someone is worrying about you?"

He chuckled. "Aye. Now these ley lines...?"

"You don't want to tell me about it?"

Angus shrugged. "We got them out. Ley lines?"

She looked at him quizzically. He smiled back, waiting, showing Shawn's habit of refusing to discuss what he didn't wish to discuss. She sighed. "Okay, ley lines." She explained them again.

"Let me think." Angus leaned back against the couch, his arm around her.

Resting against his shoulder, Amy stared into the flames, seeing instead, tongues of fire licking up the sides of St. Bee's, and Shawn somewhere in the chaos. She saw him as he'd been on the battlefield, his face set and determined, striding forward, scanning the fighting around him. On the raids, there would have been horses, maces, swords slashing, knives stealthy and deadly, and flames everywhere, creeping up walls, curling up the spire; thatched roofs blazing, fire crawling through fields, screaming and shrieking....

She jolted, pulling her eyes from the small flames in her own hearth. "How long could he survive in a world like that?" There were so many ugly ways to die. She didn't want Shawn—didn't want the father of her child—dying in any of them.

"His odds of surviving increase greatly if he was with Niall."

"But if one of them died at Creagsmalan, he *wasn't* with Niall." The thought of him twisting on a noose sickened her.

He squeezed her hand. "Serving the servants had to be Niall; walking the shore with an infant is a twenty-first century man. They both lived. You *must* believe that."

She stared at the maps on the coffee table, her lips tight.

He cleared his throat. "Let's pick one and see what happens."

"Okay." Amy cleared her throat, and shuffled her papers. "This one runs from Killin, to Fortingall, to the Praying Hands of Mary."

"I know it well," Angus said. "It's in Glen Lyon—the Valley of the Sun God. The area was considered sacred. And...." He stopped.

"What?"

"It was a prime target of missionaries. From guess where?" He grinned.

"Iona?" She sat up straighter, intrigued.

"Yes. St. Adoman lived there for a wee bit. He wrote the first biography of St. Columba—who founded the monastery on Iona." Angus rose and rounded the coffee table to stir up the fire. "The Fortingall Yew Tree is there. Yews were sacred trees. Pontius Pilate played under this one."

"Pontius Pilate from the Bible?" Her eyebrows shot up. "What was he doing in Scotland?"

"His father was a Roman diplomat who came to visit a Pictish chief."

"Which has what to do with people disappearing in time?"

Angus added several small branches to the fire. It blazed up, snapping its new food with crackling teeth. He grinned. "Nothing a'tall. Just that strange things happen there, and it has a connection to Iona." He poked at a branch threatening to tumble onto the hearth. "There are standing stones nearby. And, come to think of it, Mount Schiehallion overlooks the whole thing." He looked over his shoulder at her, raising his eyebrows significantly.

"Meaning?"

"Meaning," Angus said, returning to his seat, "Mount Schiehallion is called 'the fairy hill of the Caledonians' and fairies like to play with time. Do you know of Thomas of Erceldoune? He lived shortly before our Niall." He gave a brief account of the man.

"He was real?" she asked in disbelief.

"Oh, aye."

Amy pressed her hand to her forehead. "And this might have some connection to Shawn and Niall? He disappeared near Mount Schiehallion?"

"In the Eildon Hills," Angus said. "What else have you found?"

"Here." Amy shuffled the papers again. "This one is convoluted, but it mentions Bannockburn." She pointed to a diagram of constellations overlaying a map of Scotland. "Orion, which pivots around the Island of Craigleith, rose in the east at dawn the day of the battle. These lines stretch from Menteith to various structures and it somehow relates to the Knights Templar and the Scots descending from the Egyptian Pharaoh's daughter."

The corner of Angus's mouth twitched. "Did we now? Her and who else?"

Amy lifted a hand in resignation. "He didn't say. This is crazy!"

Angus laughed out loud. "We're seeking a man who disappeared into time. Who are we to call anyone mad?" He rubbed her arm. "Pick one, and we'll start."

"What do we do when we get there?" she asked.

"No idea. They didn't cover this at the academy." He grinned. "But we weren't looking for anything at Creagsmalan, and look what happened. So where will we start?"

The baby kicked inside Amy, sending a ripple across her stomach. "Here." She thumbed through the printouts. "A ley line runs from Stirling to Iona. Why not start with the place he named?"

"Perfect," Angus said. "How early can you be up?"

Carlisle, 1314

"My Lord of Creagsmalan is partial to the lute." Harclay didn't look up from the pile of documents before him. A man at arms stood by his side, watching the towering pile as if it might topple and make a run for it.

"Yes, My Lord," Shawn acknowledged. Sweat prickled his forehead. He had to get out! He forced himself to speak calmly. "There's a piece he'd fain hear?"

"Aye, a few pieces from our neighbor to the north."

Shawn's heart gave a quick double-time thump, wondering if that was a veiled warning that they'd been recognized. "I'm not sure I know any."

Harclay scanned the paper before him, scratched his signature at the bottom, and moved it to the right. A boy there sprinkled sand on it to dry the ink, and carefully sifted it off. He looked up. "Aren't you a traveling minstrel? Why wouldn't you?"

"I've not been to Scotland." Shawn wondered if he should spit, just to make it clear he was no part of the enemy. That would be overkill, he decided. And he decided *overkill* was not the best choice of words in this situation.

"Regardless. He wants *The Orkney Wedding Song.*"

"You're...." Shawn stopped himself saying, *You're kidding!* It seemed very much the wrong thing to say to the guy in charge of the castle, even if he wasn't exactly a king. His mind churned. He *knew* that piece! He actually knew it! He'd done an arrangement of it for a senior project. He'd dug into his father's family history, and determined to do the oldest piece he could find from Scotland. But if he admitted he knew the piece, would that make Harclay think he'd been to Scotland?

Harclay signed another piece of paper and handed it to the boy before looking up. "I'm...what?"

He was a traveling musician, Shawn reminded himself. He was supposed to know these pieces. "You're right, Sir. I will play it." His mind scrambled. He *couldn't* play it. He couldn't be in the same room with MacDougall. He'd be dead before dinner was over. He smiled, "I'm not as well-versed in Scottish music as I should like." He cleared his throat. "Never having been there. I've a colleague who can show me more. I'll speak with him."

Harclay glanced at the sun barely clinging to the edge of the western window. "You expect to learn new pieces so quickly? Dinner begins anon."

"I'll bring him, an it please Your Lordship." Shawn said. "I'm a quick study, and he can play, too. Perhaps, however, you could have Rulf play the first pieces while I fetch my colleague? 'Twould be a treat for My Lord of Creagsmalan, to present him with a selection of his favorite music."

Harclay pondered only briefly. The boy waited, the freshly sanded documents laid carefully on the far end of the table. Shawn's heart pounded. Time was ticking away, and he'd not even be able to leave on the pretense of finding the fictional man, if Harclay didn't give an answer soon.

"Yes," Harclay said. "Yes, he's more pleasant to deal with when he's happy. Find your friend, but make haste. Rulf only plays the pipes, and I particularly want lute tonight."

Shawn bowed. "I'll be back ere it starts, Sir."

"You had best," Harclay said dryly. "MacDougall will be coming through the gate any moment. 'Twill take a bit of time to settle his men at table, but you haven't long."

Shawn retreated as quickly as possible, trying not to appear to be running, his mind racing ahead to finding a monk's robe to disguise himself, getting Niall from the Black Friars at the west gate, Red from the south gate, and getting out —all before dinner started.

Bannockburn, Present

Angus pushed aside the maps. "Now, let's pretend, while dinner cooks, that we're rational people in a rational world where men stay put in the era in which they're born. Tell me about your students. Tell me about Rob. Did he enjoy Colonial America?"

Amy laughed. "Yes. And he can't wait to visit Victorian England." She sobered. "That might explain why I haven't heard from him."

"Have you not?"

"Nothing," Amy said. "No angry outburst, no lectures, no pleading." Dana had written telling of her latest exploits. Celine had sent ideas from Aaron about the search for Shawn. But Rob had fallen silent.

Angus rubbed her back. The fire tossed flickering shadows over the lace curtains and leather couch. "Perhaps he's angry," he said. "Or hurt. Or finally decided to let go?"

Amy shrugged. "Or he thinks I'm crazy."

Angus smiled. "You can understand, surely."

She remembered, then, and climbed to her feet. "A package came with the orchestras' return address. But I had things on my mind, the doctor's appointment, my A string snapped." She called down the hall, rushing for the package and a knife. She returned to the living room, and lowered herself carefully, with her growing stomach, to the couch. "Yes, it's from him." She sliced through the tape with a satisfying snap and release of the tension, and shook the box. A pack of over-sized cards slid out.

Angus leaned forward. *"Playing cards?"*

"Strange," Amy said. Then her confusion cleared, and she laughed. "He got me the whole set!" She fanned them out, revealing face after face—the members of her orchestra. "It's kind of silly," she apologized. "Someone started selling them on the internet, when Shawn got to be so big."

Angus pulled a card out. It showed an older man in a tuxedo, posing with his violin. His face bore a look of wry patience.

Amy smiled. "That's Peter, our concertmaster. I sit behind him."

"Name: Peter Abbot." Angus read. "Instrument: Violin. Favorite saying...."

Amy finished it for him. "That's Abbot, not Rabbit."

"I don't get it." Angus looked up, his eyebrows furrowed.

"Peter Abbot. It sounds like Peter Rabbit."

Angus laughed. "He's a sense of humor."

Amy smiled. "Shawn never saw it, but he's very funny. Very dry. Sometimes I get his jokes a day later, and start laughing on my way to work."

"Where's yours?" Angus shuffled through till he found Amy's card. She posed in a black blouse, her violin propped on a black-skirted knee, her shoulder to the camera, her thick hair falling to her waist.

"Come on, don't!" She reached for it. "It's embarrassing."

He laughed, holding it at arm's length. "Does it say anything I don't know?"

"Come on!" She laughed, reaching for it, but her size made her awkward.

He grinned at her, before turning to read, holding it out of her reach. "Graduated from Juilliard. Played with the Catskill Quartet. Great kisser."

"It does not say that!" She lunged across him, grabbing the card. He caught her wrist, and pulled her in.

"Dinner's going to burn," she whispered.

"Who cares?" He dropped the cards on the floor, kissing her, and Amy forgot about Shawn.

Carlisle, 1314

He'd given Harclay his excuse, both for heading into town, and for hurrying. He jogged to the single gate leaving the castle compound. He had to get out before MacDougall came through. He had only to get past the orchards beyond, and through the next gate, and he'd be in the town's narrow, twisting streets, with plenty of places to hide. A flurry of light, feminine voices stopped him. He picked up the collective note of agitation. Past experience told him he might well be the target. He glanced behind—back inside the castle walls—and before—across the bridge where he'd be exposed. He couldn't see them. He ran for it, the lute thumping on his back, and just as they emerged from the twilight, at the far end of the orchard, he threw himself to the right, into the shadows of the west orchard.

Their voices came to him. "It seems he's met every one of us here!" That was Emeline.

Shawn pressed a hand to his eyes, stifling a groan. *Not now, Emeline!*

"He'll be playing at the castle for the commander's dinner." That was Duraina. The voices came closer.

"There's only one way in and out," said the carpenter's daughter. "He's met all of you here. He'll be back to meet me. Let's wait."

The voices came steadily closer, an agitated cacophony of agreement. He backed farther into the orchard, wondering if they would come looking for him; wondering if he could climb a tree silently enough to avoid detection. They were going to get him killed! MacDougall would be coming through any minute! But the orchards were wide and deep. There were only seven of them.

"You, Duraina," spoke Emeline. "Stand here in the path in case he comes. Lorelle, Maud, search the east orchard."

"He'll be playing for Harclay's dinner," Maud protested. "Do you not see the lights in the great hall?"

"It has not started yet, for the Scottish lord has only just come through the town gates," Emeline announced. "Gundred, Sabina, come with me to search the west orchard."

Shawn swore beneath his breath, and glanced over his shoulder, seeking a better hiding place than behind a tree. He was increasingly sure he didn't want to meet Emeline any more than he wanted to meet MacDougall. Their footsteps, their voices, the swish of their skirts against grass, came toward him. There were only three, he assured himself. He could evade them. But MacDougall would be coming, with a score, or two or three, of men. What if he joined the search? His heart pounded. MacDougall would have no reason to interest himself in these girls' search for a philandering lutar. He backed up another few steps. If he went too far, he'd bump up against the city walls and be trapped. He glanced again at a tree, considering climbing.

"I heard something!" Gundred shouted triumphantly. She emerged from the darkening evening, heading away from him. He pressed himself against the tree, thanking God.

Emeline hurried by, clutching her skirts up around leather boots. Shawn glanced up the tree. The limb was within reach. He could swing himself up. He could....

"'Tis but a squirrel!" Emeline announced disdainfully.

Shawn peered through the shadows. She was coming back. He ducked again behind the tree, holding his breath. The lute had to go. Maybe he could convince them he was someone else, without it on his back. He gritted his teeth. No, nobody would believe that! He heard her, on the other side of the tree. "Brom!" she called sweetly. "'Tis Emeline."

Okay, he muttered to himself, does she really think if Brom is here that he didn't just hear the calls for his blood?

"Brom?" It became quiet.

In the chilly evening, sweat prickled under Shawn's arms. Then her skirt swished, just on the other side of the tree, at the same moment he heard the first clatter of hooves in the streets beyond the orchard. He closed his eyes, begging, *God, just for a minute, could we forget all the things I've said and thought about You? Maybe we could come to some agreements, if You would just let me live another day?*

As if in answer, another voice sounded among the dark trees, over the growing sound of hooves ringing on cobblestone, coming from the town. "Emeline!" It was Red!

Shawn's heart pounded faster. Red was here. Good column. He wouldn't have to use more time going to look for him. Red was here. Bad column. Now *he* was in the middle of this! Would he flush him out unknowingly?

"Red?" From the other side of the tree, Emeline sounded more surprised than Shawn felt.

"You seek Brom?" Red's voice approached. "He's at the south gate."

"Why would he be?" Suspicion lined her voice. "He's to play for the commander's dinner."

"He's running late," came Red's barely-pubescent voice.

"Well, that means he's on his way back, and we mean to talk with him!" She sounded indignant.

The clatter of hooves grew louder. Soon, MacDougall and his men would fill the path between the two orchards.

From the other side of the tree came Red's sigh. "He'll be out after the evening meal. He's meeting Gusselin."

"Her!" Emeline was indignant.

Shawn wanted to lean around the tree and ask, "What's wrong with her!" He thought better of it. She was jealous, that was the problem. Gusselin was easily the hottest babe in Carlisle, *and* her father was wealthy. Otherwise, it wouldn't have taken him three days to convince her to meet him. Damn, he realized! He was going to have to stand her up! And she was *hot!* He leaned his head against the tree, breathing slowly, silently. He had bigger things to worry about, he reminded himself. MacDougall. Hanging. *Come on, Shawn!*

"He'll be here after dinner," Red repeated. "Bertrand is looking for you. He's suspicious, My Lady. Certainly you'll want to go to him and reassure him."

The clopping outside the orchard gate grew to a small thunder.

"Him!"

Shawn imagined she'd tossed her head. *Go on,* he urged her silently. *Come on, Red, think of something else.* Something brushed his nose. He sucked in his breath, looking cross-eyed in the growing dark, and saw a spider lowering itself from the limb above. *Great, just great.* He resisted the urge to brush it away as it settled. He could feel its little feet moving across his face. He tightened his lips; hoped it wouldn't decide to explore up his nose, or crawl down the neck of his shirt. He resisted the urge to fling the thing away. A spider was *not* going to be his death.

"We'll wait," Emeline declared.

The spider crawled up onto his nose, tickling, and making his nose itch with the need to sneeze. He held his breath.

"Then you ought wait by the path, where you'll see him," Red suggested.

Yes! Shawn wanted to shoot his fist into the air. *Good one, Red!* He waited, his eyes now closed in fear the spider would move upward, hoping she'd see the sense in that. Of course, that left him no way out.

Men's voices sounded now in the street, laughing and calling.

"Hm. Yes," she announced. "We shall."

Her footsteps and the rustle of leather boots and skirt swooshed away through the trees. Shawn lifted a hand carefully, flicking the spider away, waiting...waiting. He still didn't know how he was going to get out. From the gate came a loud whinny, and rustle of horseflesh. The clank of stirrups and bits, and creak of bridles filled the chilly night air, as suddenly MacDougall's mounted men swarmed up the narrow path.

"Milord?" came Red's frantic hiss. "Please be here, Milord!"

"I'm here," Shawn rounded the tree, grabbing Red's shoulder.

The boy jumped, yelped, and clapped a hand over his own mouth. The noise of MacDougall's men covered the small sound, as much as it filled them both with fear of being heard. "Praise be to God!" Red whispered, and pushed a bundle at Shawn. "Brother Andrew says you must put this on and get out. MacDougall is coming."

"So I noticed," Shawn said dryly, even as he shook out the cloth. It was a robe of the Black Friars. A coif fell from it. *Thank You,* he thought to God, as he yanked it over his tell-tale hair. *I'm hoping You can wait until tomorrow for that discussion?* He shoved his hair inside the tight-fitting hood, and struggled into the monk's robe, the lute dropped carelessly at his side. "Where's Ni...Brother Andrew?" he whispered as his head emerged from the neck of the robe.

He felt Red's hands, yanking the hem down, straightening it out. "He's in the east orchard."

Shawn pulled up the hood, shielding his face. "Great. There's an army between us. How many are there?"

"Three score?" Red guessed. "Four?"

"Sixty, eighty." Shawn leaned back against the tree, listening to the steady hoof beats rolling up the path not a furlong away, trying to reassure himself they'd march straight through to the castle. They had no reason to come into the orchard. But he still had to get out before Harclay sent someone looking for his lutar. "Does he have a plan?"

"Brother Andrew?" Red asked. "He said as soon as MacDougall's men go through, just walk out with me. The lasses saw me walk in with a monk, they'll see me walk out with a monk."

"That leaves Niall stuck."

"I'll come back for him and walk out again."

"These girls aren't going to wonder where you keep getting monks from?"

"He won't go as a monk. You've his robe, Milord. But they seek a lone minstrel, with a lute and long hair, not a lord with short hair. They'll pay him no mind."

"Not smart," Shawn muttered. "MacDougall might recognize him." The steady *thud, thud, thud* of hooves jarred Shawn's heart like the rattle of a drum announcing battle. His adrenaline raced, his nerves stood on end. "Here's the deal," he said. "I get out, give you the robe, and you go back for Ni...Brother Andrew."

"They've closed down all the gates for the night," Red said. "How will you get out?"

Shawn closed his eyes, listening to the cavalry passing between himself and Niall. "We hide out with the monks for the night and leave in the morning."

"Commander Harclay will not take kindly to his lutar disappearing," Red pointed out.

"Look, Kid, I *know* that." The cavalcade came to a halt. Shawn looked up in alarm, seeing their dark shapes through the trees, and backed further into the orchard, wondering if he could climb the walls. A deep voice called out. Another answered, and they began moving again. He turned back to Red, lowering his voice to almost nothing. "But why would he storm a monastery looking for a minstrel?"

"We'd best find a way out tonight," was all Red said. "Come along." He began moving, slipping from tree to tree. Clouds slid across the sky, freeing the moon. It shone down into the path, revealing the multitude of horsemen. Red crept stealthily, Shawn behind him, praying no one would look into the copse, to see Niall on the other side. They came, suddenly, up against the southern wall that stood between them and the town. It was too high to climb. That, Shawn supposed irritably, was the whole point. They waited silently, while more men streamed through the gate, till finally, the last one passed. They held their breaths, waiting, two minutes, three, five, as they filed north toward the castle. No more appeared. But the girls waited, as threatening as any army.

Shawn folded his hands into his sleeves, bowed his head, and followed Red, his heart thumping. There was no reason they should question a monk.

"Good even, Red," Emeline said cheerfully as they passed.

Reluctantly, Shawn followed the boy into the relative safety of the town. They slipped into a narrow lane between houses. "You have to take the robe back for him," Shawn insisted. He wiggled out of it, pressing it at the kid. "I'm waiting here. And if I have to get away, we meet at the Black Friars." The boy nodded, stuffing the robe into his bag, and returned to the orchards. Shawn waited in the lane, feeling exposed, as Brom the minstrel. A gaggle of angry women, Harclay's men, and possibly MacDougall, would soon be looking for him. And all he could do was stand here and wait.

Bannockburn, Present

In the front hall after dinner, I grip Angus's lapels. "You're really okay with this?"

"I've said I am." Angus's hand runs down the length of my hair, settling on

my waist. "Why do you find it so hard to believe?"

I stare at my toes. I know why.

"Because Shawn told you no one would accept your beliefs?" Angus suggests.

I nod, unable to meet his eyes. I can only barely make myself admit, "Dana, too. She said my expectations were silly, romantic, and unrealistic."

"They were wrong," Angus says, "and I don't think Dana is a true friend."

"No, we have a lot of fun together!" I look up, surprised. "She just has different views. That's all."

"And it seems you accepted hers."

I bite my lip. "She didn't mean anything by it."

"Even so," he says, "if you're silly, romantic, and unrealistic, so am I. In fact, there's a secret underground of us with silly, romantic, unrealistic notions." He winks. "Our headquarters is on a ley line."

I laugh; he pulls me close, giving a kiss that promises just the sort of temptation I'm trying to avoid. He pulls back, smiling. "I'll see you in the morning." He opens the door. December chill swirls in around my ankles. He pulls his coat tight and bends into the wind, turning as he passes under the halo of a street lamp to wave.

I wave back, missing him already, even as I shut the door against the howling wind. The house is cold. I stoke the fire and scoop up the trading cards from where they fell on the floor, hours before. I stop at Shawn's, studying his laughing face. Laughter was his normal state. He exuded life and joy. I miss that. It haunts me, not knowing what's become of him. But tomorrow—on Iona —we'll find answers. I push the cards into their box.

Upstairs, I check my e-mail. Still nothing from Rob. My mother has e-mailed again, questioning my wisdom in staying, and shouldn't I just come home. Six months ago, her words would have made me doubt myself. I smile as I assure her I'm very happy here, and hit send. Tea, I decide, a hot cup of tea in bed, then a good night's sleep under my warm duvet. Downstairs, the doorbell rings. I smile. Angus sometimes forgets things. I hurry down and throw open the door. My smile falls. My hand flies to the crucifix.

Carlisle, 1314

Harclay waited in the castle courtyard to meet MacDougall personally. There were rumors he was in a black mood these days—something about a prisoner escaping his gallows, and a false accusation against the young Niall Campbell, resulting in public humiliation. The Scots would be at Carlisle sooner or later, and he'd as soon not have to deal with MacDougall's moods, as they discussed the anticipated attack.

He greeted the lord as he rode in from the orchards. Reaching a hand on his reins, he said, "Welcome, My Lord! There's a fine meal being laid even now for you and your men, and I've a wonderful lutar for you, only recently arrived!"

As he dismounted, MacDougall smiled.

A good start, Harclay thought irritably. He disliked having to soothe grown men's tempers.

"A lutar *and* an orchard full of comely young lasses," MacDougall said. "It seems my stay will be pleasant indeed."

"My Lord?" Harclay questioned. "Lasses in my orchard?" MacDougall's men flowed past him, entering from the orchard path, their laughter filling the courtyard.

"Waiting along the walk. Were they not were there to greet me?"

Harclay frowned. He turned to the head groom. "Look into this and report back immediately." He turned to MacDougall, ushering him into the great hall, and the head table. He glanced at the silent gallery. It was empty.

"Your lutar is not here," MacDougall observed.

"Indeed," Harclay agreed. He turned, searching for the steward, but before he could find him, the groom entered, bowing.

"Commander, it seems the women seek Brom, the minstrel."

"Why would they be looking for him in the orchards?" Harclay asked.

MacDougall listened with interest, as the story spilled out, and glanced again at the empty gallery. "Pray tell, Commander," he said, "what does this Brom look like? Is he tall and broad, perhaps? Of fair looks? Long, golden hair?"

Harclay nodded. The story of the minstrel at Creagsmalan sat uneasily with him. He wanted no such trouble here.

"And he's quite a way with women, it seems." MacDougall gave a meaningful glance to the empty gallery. "Commander Harclay, did you by chance mention to your minstrel that I would be here?"

Harclay nodded again.

"I believe," said MacDougall, "that your lutar does not intend to play for me." His face grew dark; he turned and strode to the door, calling for his first in command. "Tell the men to mount up. I want this minstrel found, immediately."

Harclay's face, too, grew stormy. As much as he disliked MacDougall's attitude, he also objected to a minstrel breaking his terms of employment and making a fool of him. If it were indeed the same minstrel who had been in Creagsmalan's dungeon, he guessed there was also an issue of spying.

Bannockburn, Present

"Rob." Amy stared in shock. "*Rob?*"

He stood on her doorstep, tall and thin, his hair shining white blond in the night, his cheeks red with the wind, gripping a suitcase in each hand. "Can I come in?"

"Oh—yes!" She jumped back, swinging the door wide. Wind tore down the hall, before she could push it shut, forcing it against the elements.

"Come on, give me a hug." He dropped the cases, and wrapped her in a warm embrace. She twisted away. He stood back, looking at her growing stomach, and gulped. "Well, uh...that's.... Well! You've gotten big."

She was grateful he didn't pat her belly. "Uh, yes. That happens." She hesitated. "Did I miss an e-mail telling me you were coming?"

His laugh sounded forced. "I thought I'd surprise you."

"Oh." She clasped her arms over her stomach. "Yeah. I'm surprised. I was, um, about to put on tea. And go to bed." She led the way down the hall, snapping on the light.

He followed her to the kitchen, looking around. "Sit down. I'll make it. Put your feet up." He guided her, hand on shoulder, to a chair. "You don't want swelling. I've been reading up on pregnancy."

"Tea and sugar are in the cupboard," she said faintly. She didn't point out that he knew nothing about *her* pregnancy. "Milk's in the fridge under the counter."

In minutes, the kettle steamed, and he had tea on the table, in the cheap white mugs from the pound store. She clenched her fist, feeling Bruce's ring with her thumb. She always used Shawn's black mug or Rose's china cups.

"*Slàinte!*" He lifted his mug, grinning. "Are you surprised?"

"Very." She raised her cup weakly, and sipped her tea, scouring her mind for kind words. She could do no better than, "Why, Rob?" The kitchen light glared off hospital-white walls. She'd planned on taking her tea upstairs to the soft yellow glow of the lamp in her bedroom.

"I'm going to find him, and then we'll go home." When she didn't react, he cleared his throat. "We talked it over back home. We all agreed it was a good idea."

"Did you show them my e-mail?"

"Um, no." He blushed, looking with interest at a speck on the wall. "No, I did not."

"Rob." The word came out a sigh. "Please tell me you didn't quit your job."

He cleared his throat and stared again at the wall. "Sabbatical. I'm officially here to research and arrange Scottish music."

"Okay, good, because you're not going to find him."

"You've been under a lot of stress." He gulped his tea, his Adam's apple bobbing, and set it down. "I never should have left you, Amy. I'm sorry."

She set the white mug down. "Look, you need to know something. I'm sort of seeing Angus."

"Who?"

"The cop. From the hospital. And scratch the sort of. I *am* seeing him."

He gulped and looked away. His face flared fire engine red. "No, uh, no, that's fine. I didn't come for—I just, you know, you need a friend. I, uh, we didn't want you to be alone."

"I'm not alone."

"We all wanted you to have a friend from home. It's just I sort of got elected." He forced a laugh. "So here I am! We're going to set up a fund and a toll free number and find out what happened to Shawn. Someone must have seen something. There were hundreds of people there, and we all feel a little guilty we left you alone to deal with it."

"What else could you have done?" Amy rose from the table, pacing the small kitchen. "I didn't expect everyone to quit their job for me."

"Still, uh...." He swallowed, glancing from the wall to her to the stove. "It seemed like you could use someone."

"Okay." Amy dropped heavily back into the chair. "I just don't want you feeling obligated. Do you have a place to stay?"

"I thought, maybe, since you have three bedrooms...?"

Amy groaned. "Rob, this is my *home*. You can't just show up on my doorstep and move in!"

"I'll pay rent," he said quickly. "If that doesn't work, I understand. Could I just spend the night?"

She hesitated. "I'm going to Iona tomorrow."

"Great!" He beamed. "Now you won't have to go alone!"

She bit her lip.

His smile slipped. "No?"

"I wasn't going alone."

"Oh." His Adam's apple bobbed. "With...uh...that cop?"

"Angus. Yes."

"Is this about chasing down places you think this Niall was?"

She said nothing.

"This isn't healthy." He spoke gently, as to a child, reaching for her.

She backed up. The baby kicked; she put a hand to her stomach, wondering if her agitation was upsetting the child. She decided it was just awake and active. No need to blame Rob. She sighed. "Rob, you know I'm not going to kick you out in the middle of the night. But you have to find a place fast. I actually do have a life here."

Rob fell silent. His eyes narrowed. "He's not living with you, is he?"

"What? Who?" Realization dawned; she laughed. "Of course not. I spent two and a half *years* with Shawn and I wasn't living with him. You think I moved a guy in in five months?"

"Well," he said defensively, "you're *seeing* a guy in five months. But it's not serious, is it? You were just lonely, right?"

"Rob!" She wanted to wring his neck and cry for him all at once. "I like him. A *lot*. Don't do this to yourself." She stood up, leaving half a mug of tea. "You can sleep here for a night or two. But you have to find your own place."

"No, that's fine, no problem." He stood, swallowing, to follow her down the hall and lugged his suitcases, bumping, up the stairs.

Carlisle, 1314

In the dark, Niall edged toward the single lane, keeping to the far sides of the trees. Without his coif, without Shawn's longer hair which they recognized as Brom, he hoped the lasses would ignore him. They were closer to the northern end of the lane and might not even see him. Peering around a tree, he saw the last of MacDougall's horsemen ride through, and Red pass out, followed silently by a monk with bowed head, nearly brushing the horse's rump. But Emeline stood there. He drew a breath, letting it out slowly. She was too close. She would raise an alarm, and MacDougall's men filled the orchard. She paced. She stopped abruptly, looking to the castle, and headed up the lane toward the castle. Breathing a prayer of thanks, he made for the gate, but abruptly, a shout rang out from the castle gate. "Niall Campbell is here! Spread out! Search the orchard! Search the town!"

Niall made his decision before the next beat of his heart, before the last horseman could turn. He ran, swift, and low, along the dark wall. A dark shape sped past a tree, straight at him. His nerves shot a mile high, before he realized it was Red. He grabbed his arm, spinning him, and pulled him through the gate, back into the town. A horse snorted and stamped.

"You!" Behind him, MacDougall's man shouted.

"Where's Shawn?" Niall rasped. He pulled Red to the right, and ran. Behind him, shouts erupted, along with the whinnying of horses, and the sick, slick sound of metal rasping on metal as dozens of swords slid from their sheaths.

CHAPTER TWELVE

Carlisle, 1314

"Here, I'm here, run!"

"Black Friars," Niall gasped. He yanked them around a corner, out of sight of the orchard gate, and sprinted down the street. They could hear hooves thundering out the orchard gate. Red slipped, dropping to one knee, and Shawn yanked him up, half-dragging him as they sped. Niall skidded before a house, threw open the door, and they tumbled in, trying to be quiet. Red sprawled to the stone floor. Niall eased the door shut, doing a frantic head count. "The robe?" he demanded, already seeing it and yanking it from Red's hands. "Put it on, Shawn."

From outside came the sound of horses at the far end of the street.

With Shawn pulling it over his head, Niall glanced around. The monks would be at evening prayers. Niall led the way down a dark narrow hall, to the back of the monks' home. "They'll search every house," he said. "We need to get out."

"They're not going to let us walk through the gates," Shawn objected.

Outside, a man shouted up and down the streets: "A Scottish spy is in Carlisle! Open up! Anyone who harbors a spy will be hanged! Open your doors!"

"Now what?" Shawn hissed. "Do we find more robes and blend in with the monks?"

Niall shook his head. He opened a door, revealing a small room with a wide bench against one wall. A hole was cut in the top. From below came the smell of raw sewage.

Shawn looked at him in horror. "You're kidding, right?"

Down the hall, a fist pounded on the monks' front door.

"Would it be the proper time," Niall hissed, "to say *dead* serious?" He reached into a closet for a coiled rope, which he tossed at Shawn. "You first." He lifted the bench off altogether, giving them room to climb through.

The pounding at the front door grew louder.

"Milords." Red looked nervously from the latrine to the front. "I'll mislead them, and bring your ponies to the fort."

Shawn's head shot up from his work securing the rope. "You can't...."

"He's right," Niall's forearms flexed. "They're not looking for him." He glanced in frustration at the bench in his hand, and added, "You need to drop this back in place, first."

"Open up!" roared the voice at the front.

Grimacing, Shawn swung a leg over the edge, griped the rope, and shimmied down, down, down, fourteen feet down into the dark. The smell grew stronger. The shouting above grew louder. They must be in the house. His leather boots sank into soft mush at the bottom. Niall was above him, on him. He jumped out of the way, his foot landing in another soft, slippery mess. Niall hit the ground, yanked on the rope. It slithered down and landed at their feet, even as the bench overhead dropped with a solid *thunk*. Dark closed in around them, black as tar.

They stood, listening to the soft click of the door to the chamber. Then everything became quiet, too.

"Pardon my French," Shawn muttered, "but, *holy shit!*"

"The holiest there is," Niall agreed grimly. "Lucky for us, it was cleaned only yesterday."

"How are we going to find our way out in the dark?" His voice bounced off the stone walls.

"While you were dallying with the ladies, I was working." In the dark, Shawn heard Niall moving carefully, slowly. There came a soft whisper of skin against stone. Muffled, angry voices shouted far above.

"They won't search the bathroom, will they?" Shawn whispered.

"Hopefully we'll have light and be gone by then," Niall murmured back. A faint scratching whispered in the dark.

"What will they do if they see light glowing from the toilet?"

Niall chuckled. "I imagine they'll repeat your very eloquent words." Something sputtered, and a weak light flared. Niall's face shone ghastly in it, with great shadows beneath his eyes. "Let's find the exit fast before they consider the privy."

"Holy shit indeed," Shawn whispered. "They keep torches in their toilets?"

"I told you I'd been at work." Niall followed the stone wall. It took only a moment to find the maw of a tunnel leaving it. They hurried in, grateful their light would no longer show above. Still, Niall kept his voice low. "As soon as I discovered they had a conduit leading out of the city, I offered in all holy humility to clean it, saying I had great sins of which to repent. The monk whose job it is was more than happy to accommodate my penance. I thought to have it ready, in case we needed an escape."

The smell pervaded the tunnel. "We should have made Red come with us," Shawn said into the darkness.

Niall shook his head. "They'd have found the bench open and been waiting for us on the outside. He's saved our lives, and they're looking for me, not a stable boy."

"He's just a kid," Shawn objected. "We left a *kid* behind to save our skins."

Niall shook his head irritably. "Welcome to the fourteenth century, Shawn. In *your* day, he's a kid. Here, he's a man. He works like a man, he'll fight like a man."

They continued in silence for a time, following the flame held over Niall's head; their leather boots padded against slick stone. Shawn tried not to think about what made it slick, and hoped he wouldn't slip in it. "Think he'll make it?" he finally asked.

"He's smarter than we've realized. Notice he called us milords? He knows I'm not a monk."

"You don't think he'll turn us in to get a reward or something?"

Niall shook his head. "He's loyal."

Cool air whispered down the tunnel, edging aside the worst of the stench. "We'll be dousing the torch soon," Niall said softly. "Just in case they've thought of this."

They walked in silence for another five minutes. The chill grew, a shock after the stuffiness. A shiver racked Shawn. Never had he been so grateful for cold. At the same time, his insides began to coil in a tight knot, fearing what awaited them at the other end. Niall extinguished the torch. Once again, darkness pressed like a black cloth on Shawn's eyes. He put his hand on Niall's shoulder, following him in the dark. Another ten feet, and he thought he saw Niall's outline, black on black. Then he saw the glimmer of gray. The smell faded to a faint whiff of unpleasantness.

His heart pounded harder than before. If Red had betrayed them, they'd know in the next few minutes.

"We can wait a few weeks, or we can get it over with," Niall whispered. They inched together, to the edge of the tunnel, and peered out cautiously into the moonlit night. The air was cold and quiet. "You sure they aren't waiting behind a rock?" Shawn whispered.

"There are no rocks," Niall muttered. "The Caldew is half a furlong away. If we go through the night, we can be at the ruins before dawn. We step out, we run. Stop for nothing. As silently as possible. There are guards on the walls."

The Caldew was low enough to wade across. "On three," Shawn whispered. He closed his eyes, imagining a horde of archers and horsemen just outside the tunnel; imagined running a deadly gauntlet in a hopeless bid for freedom. But they'd still be searching the town. It wouldn't occur to them for a long time that Niall had so easily left a locked city. He drew a breath, hoping he was right. "One." They crouched low. "Two." They drew breath. "Three."

They sprinted from safety, into the night, barely noticing the cloud-shrouded moon overhead; ran low, in fear of being seen, till the wide expanse of river jumped out from the dark with a faint, silvery glint. They slowed, entered carefully, trying not to splash, trying not to alert the guards. In the town, a dog barked loudly. Icy water bit through their leather boots. Shawn sucked back a gasp of shock at the cold. It crawled up around his ankles. He sought footing on slippery rocks; he and Niall gripped hands and arms, steadying one another, picking their way across, their feet plunging now and again into water up to their calves, trying to stay low, trying to be silent.

A call sounded from the city walls. "Go, go!" Niall hissed. His foot slipped from a rock. He plunged in, past his knees. Shawn lunged ahead, holding on hand to hand, and hauled him along, scrambling the last two meters. They dared look back. A man patrolled the walls, small at this distance. Whether guards were gathering to burst from the city gates, they didn't know. Niall hauled Shawn up off the soggy bank, and they ran.

Bannockburn, Present

An early call brought Angus to Amy's door before dawn. "He just showed up!" At the bottom of the stairs, in her peach robe and bare feet, her hair escaping the long braid, Amy stretched up to give Angus a swift kiss.

Angus's face darkened. "Such presumption deserves to be kicked out in the middle of the night!"

"I told him only a night or two," Amy said. "But I've known him for three years, Angus. I'm not going to kick a friend out in the middle of the night!"

Before Angus could reply, a strangled sound erupted from above. With a curious glance at Angus, Amy hurried up the stairs.

At the end of the hall, Rob stood in the doorway of Amy's office. Amy marched the short length of the hall, Angus on her heels. Seeing it through Rob's eyes—charts, maps, and timelines in the lamp light—she realized it looked like a war room. Angus's hand tightened at her waist.

Rob turned to her, horror on his face.

"He's alive, Rob," she said. Angus started forward. She shook her head, stopping him.

Rob crossed the room to a timeline marked *Shawn*. "Appleby." He stabbed the chart. "Brough, Kirkoswald, Swaledale." He touched the stone rubbing and photograph taped above it, depicting Shawn's carving. He turned to her. "September." His eyebrows shot up. "*Thirteen-fourteen?*" He looked to Angus, and burst out, "She's been under stress, but *you*! Why didn't you stop her?" Anger flushed his face, red against his white-blond hair and eyebrows. "Why didn't you talk her out of it! This is *insane!*"

"Show him the ring and crucifix," Angus said.

She pulled them off her neck and finger, laying them on the table in the room. Rob looked from Amy to Angus, to the crucifix and ring, and slowly, as if they'd burn him, picked each one up.

"Look at the inscription in the ring." Amy tried to keep her voice even. "Shawn threw it to me, at the re-enactment. You heard Conrad say he saw two of them."

"It doesn't mean there *were* two of them." Rob squinted inside the ring. "It means it was hot, it was chaotic with you and the cops running into the middle of the battle."

"I have the history Niall wrote of the crucifix," Amy said. "The ring says *Roibert de Briuis, 1296* inside."

"I can see that." Rob cast the ring down. It spun on the table, and settled with a soft clatter. "It doesn't *mean* anything. I can get *Roibert de Briuis* engraved on my trumpet. That doesn't mean he played it."

Amy's heart beat triplets; nerves jangled up and down her arms.

"I can get it sewn on my underwear!" Rob's voice rose. "That doesn't mean he wore them!"

The baby kicked in agitation. She touched her stomach.

"That's enough." Angus's hand tightened on Amy's waist.

Rob rounded on him. "Who the hell are you, anyway? I leave her alone for five months and you're practically moved in, and convinced her of this insane story."

Thunder rumbled in Angus's chest like a bear pawing to charge. But he spoke softly. "No, she convinced me. Look at the marks. Look at...."

"I *know* what he signed his letters with. *I* was there. *I've* been there for her all these years! It doesn't mean anything, because this can't happen." His eyes snapped back to Amy. His voice softened. "Amy, listen, honey, we're going to set up a hotline, we're going to interview people, we'll find out what really happened. Then we'll go home."

"Don't call me honey." Tears stung her eyes, and she hated herself for it. She'd never been prone to tears. "Don't *patronize* me." Having to sniff back a suddenly runny nose gave the words a cruel irony.

"This is a sick joke." Ignoring her, Rob gave a sweep of his arm encompassing everything.

"Why don't you at least look, really *look*," Amy demanded, "before you dismiss it?" She pushed past Angus, into her bedroom, and dug in her drawer. "I have the necklace he gave me." She held it out, the garnet twisting on the end of the chain. "Shawn never would have chosen this."

Rob glared. "Okay, yeah, and why don't I look, really look, at all the evidence for the Loch Ness monster."

"You need to stop." Angus's voice dropped a minor third.

"It's stories, that's all!" Rob reached for Amy.

Amy shook her head, swiped the back of her sleeve under her nose, and rushed for the stairs. In the dark hall, she headed to the kitchen for tea, turned on her heel and stomped back to the front room, still dim in the pre-dawn, for her violin; turned again for tea. Angus stood halfway down the stairs, saying, "Amy, Amy, now, it's aw' right."

She threw herself into the front room, yanked the violin from its case, and launched into the chattering witches on *Bald Mountain*, leaning in, pressing the strings with all her strength, the bow cutting viciously, hacking, sawing, cackling, the garnet necklace jolting on its delicate chain, in her bow hand, as she poured her anger into the witches, spinning furiously around the cauldron in the dark on Bald Mountain. She played the scene over and over, until she felt Angus's hand resting, like the flute solo ushering in the peaceful dawn, on her shoulder.

She dropped the violin to her knee, the bow and her head hanging, the garnet dangling, the energy drained. "He's right," she said. "I'm crazy. I imagine things! Shawn said I did. How did this happen, because I don't feel crazy, but he's right. This is insane."

Angus knelt beside her, opening his palm. The crucifix lay there, its leather thong curled around Bruce's ring. She touched them, and lifted her other hand, letting the red stone of the necklace flash in the lamp light. "He was here," she said, quietly. "Shawn never would have picked this."

"You're not mad," he said, "Nor am I. Are we going to Iona?"

"Yes." She drew a deep breath. "Yes. We'll go to Iona."

Angus raised his eyes, looking over her shoulder. She turned. Rob stood in the doorway, glaring. "There's nothing *on* Iona!" he said.

"You need to go." Angus rose to his feet, stepping close to Rob. "Now. Me mate's looking for a roommate. Get your bags. I'll take you."

Bannockburn, Iona, Present

With Angus and Rob gone, my home falls silent. With shaking hands, I don a long-sleeved black shirt, and forest-green, tunic-length knit vest. Shawn carved Iona on Hugh's rock. I braid my hair the length of my back. Iona is on a ley line. I pull on my high leather boots like Niall's. We'll find answers there!

Angus returns. He wraps his arms around me in the dim hall. My stomach flutters at his touch. I feel safe. He helps me with my long blue coat; in his car, he twines his fingers between mine as we drive. "Don't let him make you doubt."

"I'm trying," I say. I relax against the seat, under the soothing strains of lute and harp from his radio. I think of Niall and Shawn and harps and trombones, as we pull onto the highway. Angus tells me a story about bagging a Munro that makes me smile. Light blooms softly in his rear view mirror, the sun climbing from rest and chasing us west as I tell him about a violin store Miss Rose always took me to, that I was sure was Geppetto's workshop. He tells me about a beloved instructor at the police academy as we climb into brown hills wreathed with mist on this gray morning.

The mist thins by the time his car rolls onto the ferry that will carry us over the ice-water fingers of the Atlantic curling around Scotland's islands. Gunflint skies lighten to pearl gray. We're going to Iona, a place of ancient mystery, monasteries, and miracle-working monks. Anything could happen! On deck, we watch the ferry separate from the dock. The doubt Rob stirred up shrinks with Oban's shore. I relax into Angus's shoulder, remembering who I was, in those few healing years after I left home, before I let Shawn spin his sticky web of lies around me. I feel free; able to breathe again. It feels good. Wind stings my ears. Shawn loved boating with his father. I wonder if he sailed to Jura over these cold, windy waters.

The ferry reaches Mull. As we drive across, Angus tells me of Columba, his miracles, and St. Oran's chapel where it's said the great saint buried a man alive. We talk of ley lines and time traveling twins. We talk as if it's a given we'll find answers. We don't know what we're looking for, but we're sure we'll find it.

A smaller ferry carries us on foot to Iona. The mist lifts, but December is still cold and windy. As we set foot on Iona, still feeling the roll of the sea, my excitement surges! We're here, on Iona, the place Shawn named! We walk The Road of the Dead to the ruined abbey and restored church. We search them, but find nothing. We traipse through the long, swaying grasses that cover the island, under skies grown blue, finding ancient stones and crosses, searching them for Shawn's mark. We find nothing.

At a pub in the tiny village, I sigh heavily. "Nothing."

"St. Oran's has been here since before Niall's time," Angus reassures me. "It's exactly where Shawn would leave his mark." Filled with hot food and new hope, we go to the Graveyard of the Kings.

"Cill Oran," Angus says. The chapel stands like Mother Ginger in a graveyard; tombstones tumble around her—leaning, cracked, gray children, playing in their morbid field above the sparkling sea.

Inside, I scan the small kirk. It might hold twenty people. Small arched windows at the front pour winter sunlight over a single pew, three kneelers, and a small altar. In a corner stands a large wooden cross. Bright scraps of paper cling to rough-hewn arms.

"Prayers," Angus says. Prayers, prayers, prayers. His voice echoes. He points to vertical stones hanging on the wall. "Those are grave slabs." Slabs, slabs. He pulls off my gloves, rubbing my hands between his. "Better?" Better, better?

A thrill surges through me. "Amazing!"

"I've never doubted my finger-warming abilities." He blows on my hands, grinning. "But you're the first to acknowledge it."

I laugh, swept back to my first days with the orchestra, when I felt free and confident. Joy lifts my soul. Laughing, I break it to Angus gently. "I meant the acoustics."

He feigns disappointment, but says, "Oh, aye, a recording was made here."

"Hello, hello, hello!" I sing a shimmering major chord. Rob and Shawn fade away. I turn to Angus, beaming. "What songs do you know?"

"Och, no." He holds up a hand. "Some things I'll not do until after the wedding." He winks. "When it's too late for you to run."

I laugh. "Seriously. You play bagpipes. You must know Amazing Grace."

"From memory." Angus wiggles his fingers as if on a chanter.

I lift my chin, and sing. "Twas there on the banks of yon bonnie braes." Arms wide, head back, I turn as I sing, drinking in rich harmonies, and lightness I haven't felt since that first year with Shawn.

Shawn.

The song falters. My arms drop. "This was the last place to look. What if there's nothing here?"

"We go outside and wait for the mother ship." He tugs at my long braid.

I smile, despite my frustration. "Thanks for taking my time-traveling ex-boyfriend problem seriously. Not everyone does, you know."

"Maybe we will *find something. If not, back to the drawing board, aye? And we've still had a lovely day."*

I smile, remembering the misty morning, his hand warm on mine, the stiff breeze on the open waters. I feel warm inside. "Yes, we have."

He begins the familiar routine of searching the chapel wall, with eyes and fingers double-checking one another. I turn to the first grave slab, looking for Shawn's mark. I miss the good in him.

My thoughts drift back to a spring day. He took me through the woods on his property, insisting I shut my eyes. His voice held the excitement of a child at Christmas. I knew one of his surprises was coming. I let him lead me, laughing at the stomach-dropping sensation of moving, unseeing, over rough ground, trusting him. I felt leaves, soft and half-decayed under my feet; heard the stream burble along beside us.

"Here," he said, and pulled me to my knees.

Anticipation tingled in my stomach. The breeze whispered across my bare arm. He pressed my hand into something soft, warm, moving. I gasped. A gentle mewl caressed my ear; delicate sandpaper scraped my fingers. Something soft rubbed my cheek. My eyes flew open.

Shawn held up a white kitten, fluffy as cotton candy. A black one, equally round and furry, peered up from a nest of pink blankets inside a basket. I turned to Shawn in amazement.

"You missed your cats." His face shone with love. Flecks of gold in his deep brown irises made them sparkle. "Next time, it'll be horses."

"You don't like horses."

"Look in the basket."

I recognized his dismissal, and knew no pressure would make him explain. I touched the black cat. Pink paper crinkled under its paws as it strained to lick my hand. I lifted the card out.

I need kisses and hugs every day.

The flattened S sparkled in gold ink below the words.

I smiled. "Which one needs kisses and hugs?"

"Hey!" Shawn lowered the white fur ball into the basket. "I admit these two are almost as good-looking as me, but—don't take this as arrogance— they're not quite as smart. I had to write the note for them. I get a percentage of those kisses and hugs."

I miss that day. I miss Shawn.

"Amy?"

Angus's voice, gravelly and half an octave lower than Shawn's, jolts me back to St. Oran's chapel. *I draw a sharp breath.*

"Did you find anything?" He stands close, warm and smelling of aftershave.

I lower my hand off the ancient carvings; I'm disoriented, pulled from the world of Shawn and all that was, to Iona and Angus and all that is, and all that might be. "I got distracted." *I study the grave slabs on the walls. He searches beside me. There's nothing.*

He takes my hand. "We've the gravestones outside, still."

I nod, without hope.

We squeeze through the narrow door, into a day grown sunny. Clouds glide overhead, like great white sails unfurled on the sea breeze. Water sparkles a rich blue; islands rise in the distance. The perpetual Scottish breeze takes a rest, leaving me almost warm. We round the small chapel, into the ancient graveyard, walking among tilting stones. Slabs peer up through long grass flattened by wind. Overhead, a raven shrieks and flaps away. A deep voice calls out down on the shore. None of it diminishes the wild isolation of the place.

We search, me lost in thoughts of Shawn, in each of his love letters signed with the flattened S which I now seek on medieval gravestones half a world away from our life together.

Mo ghaol. My love.

I lift my eyes to Angus, running his hands over a granite obelisk. Peace washes around the ancient resting place of kings. The same peace pervades the whole island. It has disturbed me all day. Suddenly I know why. "It doesn't feel like anything would happen here," *I say.* "The tower felt different that night. Unsettled."

Angus turns to me. "Next week, we'll try places on the same ley line as Iona."

"But he said Iona. So why isn't there a mark? Why doesn't it feel right?"

"I've no idea, Amy."

I return to one of our earlier guesses. "Maybe Iona J is a woman, not an island at all?"

"I think he got interrupted while he carved," Angus says.

I stare out at sparkling waters. Wind lifts my hair. I realize I wanted something to show Rob, to prove I'm not crazy. A gull squawks and rises against azure skies. Paper crackles behind me. Angus pulls out our map, and a red pen. He marks a red X over Iona, and looks up. "What now?"

"Follow these ley lines," *I decide,* "and see what happens." *I touch the crucifix. The ring is heavy on my finger. They dance an inexplicable waltz with Rob, in my mind. Ley lines are as elusive as the Scottish gloam. These are real, solid. Maybe there's a way to use that? If there is, it eludes me.*

Scottish Borders, 1314

A cold, nerve-wracking night and day in the ruins was rewarded with the sight of Red riding hard on an English horse, bursting from the evening mist, his vivid red curls flying, his face a mask of concentration. He led Shawn's and Niall's ponies.

"You stole a horse?" Niall asked sharply.

Red's face fell as his horse came to a sharp halt.

"He's *alive!*" Shawn reprimanded. "He saved our skins."

"I did not steal it," Red said. "They gave it to me to find the two of you."

Shawn and Niall glanced at one another, their prior fear leaping back.

"I'd not lead them to you," Red said indignantly. "If I wanted to, I'd have done so last night."

"He's right," Shawn said, and to Red, "I'm sorry. You can imagine we're a little jumpy."

"We'd best go," Red said. "They're organizing to search the roads to Scotland."

"It takes time to move a force out," Niall reassured Shawn, as they mounted.

Nevertheless, they did not tarry, but rode through the night, picking their way slowly in the dark, over muddy paths. As they climbed higher into the hills, snow hampered their progress. "It'll slow MacDougall's army, too," Niall reminded his companions. As night fell again, Red wrapped his hands in his horse's mane. His shoulders drooped over his saddle, and soon snores rose in the cold night.

"We didn't get much information," Shawn said softly after a bit. "We don't have a clue how many men they have."

"We know they're building siege engines."

"But not how many."

"Why did you not just ask me?"

Shawn jumped at the sound of Red's voice at his side. "You've been listening?"

"'Tis impossible not to hear," Red retorted. "While you two dallied with lasses and monks, I was with the soldiers. Would that not have been the sensible place to go for military information?"

In the sliver of moonlight, Shawn and Niall glanced at one another, abashed.

"They pay no heed to a stable boy."

Shawn could hear the pleased grin in his voice. "Well done, Red," he said.

"'Tis why it worked for you," Niall said in defense. "They'd have asked why I was hanging around."

"Sour grapes," Shawn prodded him. "The great Sir Niall has been bested by a kid!"

"As has Sir Ego, *The Best of Scotland,*" Niall shot back.

Shawn laughed. It was good to be alive.

They drank water cold and clear from a mountain stream as the sun rose, splashing pearly pinks over the mist that wreathed miles upon miles of rolling hills stretched out before them. The sight stunned Shawn with its beauty. He smiled, looking out over the miles they must cross, seeing the grandeur.

"Beautiful, isn't it?" Niall asked at his side. "If I must die today, I thank God I saw this first." He clapped Shawn on the shoulder, and they once again mounted their steeds.

CHAPTER THIRTEEN

Bannockburn, Present

"You're a whirlwind." Amy looked in dismay around Rob's office. She'd relented and come to see his new home, from which he would lead the search for Shawn. A phone waited silently, on a table against one wall; a laptop, pad of paper, and jar of pens its only companions. They shouted of money poured into finding a man who couldn't be found with telephones or laptops. Not that her own methods had accomplished much, she thought ruefully. She scanned Rob's efforts, bound to be even more futile than her own, and tried for conciliatory words. "I can't believe you did all this so fast."

Rob colored, grinning. "I'm forgiven, then?"

"Forgiven?" She crossed her arms over her rounded stomach. "*I can have it sewn on my underwear?*"

Rob swallowed. "Yeah, okay. I was upset."

"Try *I'm sorry.*"

"I'm sorry." He blinked hard, then abruptly crossed to the desk, touching the phone like a new Ferrari. "There's a, um, a hotline, and I've talked to a reporter about a follow-up story on Shawn's, uh, disappearance. I've got flyers all over Bannockburn and posts on the internet." He gripped her arm. His eyes bored into hers. "I'm going to find him for you. Then we'll go home. I'm looking at houses, old ones, like you like. You can help me...."

"Help you buy a house?" She pulled away. "Rob, you and I are *not* buying a house together!"

Rob's eyes softened. "You know how I feel about you, Amy. It's been crazy, you're upset, but when things settle down, I see a real future for us. As soon as we find him...."

"No." Amy shook her head. "I know you don't believe me, but it's hard to sit by and watch you put so much energy and money into this when I know you won't get any results."

Rob's jaw tightened. "He's not lost in a time void, Amy!"

Amy slid the ring from her finger, holding it up. "Explain this!"

Rob shrugged. "He won it gambling. It's fake."

Amy met his eyes steadily. The trio of Rob, ring, and crucifix stopped their dance, waiting, watching. Calm came over her. "Take it." She offered it to him on outstretched palm. "Have it verified by an expert!"

He plucked it up with two fingers. "The crucifix, too." He held out his other hand. "I'll have them both looked at." He bounced the precious artifact in his palm like a bauble from a gumball machine. "You'll see, Amy. If this is what you built the story on, you'll see they're not real. This Angus guy, he's sold you a bill of goods."

"No." Amy lifted the crucifix over her head, sliding the leather thong down the length of her hair. "Angus is a cop, a historical expert, and rational man, and he's convinced. Rose, too."

Rob snorted. "These road trips and archives—he's trying to buy you."

Amy gestured at the room, encompassing the money Rob had spent, and the thousands more he planned to. "And you're not?" She laid the crucifix in his palm with a clash of eyes and wills. "I'll bring you Niall's history of the crucifix, too. What are you going to say when they tell you they're real?"

Rob dropped the things on the table. "I'm not too worried about it."

"Put them somewhere safe." She met his eyes sternly. "They're seven hundred years old."

Sighing, he put them in a drawer. "What are you going to do now?"

She smiled. "I still have a few places to look."

Stirling, 1314

"Another bag of gold." Shawn grinned at Niall, as he spilled it across the table in their room in Stirling. "A third for you, a third for me, a third for Red?"

Niall glanced at the boy, sitting in the stone window ledge, wrapped in a new, warm cloak, gazing out over the snowy landscape. "I daresay more than a third for him, as neither we nor the information would be here without him."

Red turned, grinning.

"What do we do with him?" Shawn asked.

"Red," Niall asked, "would you like to come with us? The Laird will be glad to have one of your talents with his horses."

Red smiled. "I'll go with you, Milords."

Shawn lowered his head, staring at the flagon of ale he twirled between his fingers, and when Red had once again turned his attention to the snow outside, asked softly, in modern English, "What about that stop we have to make?"

"Hugh has returned from his own mission for Bruce," Niall said. "Brother David is returning to Glenmirril with us. He'll go ahead with them while we make our stop." He rose, stretching, and announced, "We'll be home before Christ Mass. We leave at dawn."

Scotland, Present

Scotland is a treasure trove of ley lines with connections to Bruce and Bannockburn. It's like the Narnian pool between worlds, wondering each time what wonder I might witness, wondering if today will be the day.

We start at Lindisfarne in the east, crossing the great causeway as the tide washes in. I shut my eyes, nervous of the water lapping closer to the wheels of Angus's mini with each surge of the tide. His hand covers mine. "We're fine." There's a warm smile in his voice. We reach Lindisfarne as the waters meet behind his bumper and swish out again. St. Aidan came here from Iona in 635. There's that Iona connection again.

We search the ruined priory and the gravestones surrounding it. We have no idea what we're looking for, apart, maybe, from Shawn's marks. We're seeking nothing in particular, and nothing is what we find. Angus marks a red X over Lindisfarne on our map. "We've only just begun," he says. "We've many more places to try."

While Angus works, I visit Rosslyn Chapel. I stand at Bruce's tomb in Melrose, intersected by the far end of a line that pierces Iona, and travel to Dunvegan. There's a fairy flag, but no time travelers. I put red Xs on our map.

On Angus's days off, we climb the wind-swept slope above the Bridge of Balgie, to the Praying Hands of Mary. We peer through the wrought iron fence protecting the Fortingall Yew Tree, walk among three sets of three standing stones each, across the road, and visit a stone circle in Killin. Red Xs spread across our map, marking each failure.

"Is he just supposed to pop out of thin air?" I ask in frustration. Angus lifts his hands in resignation.

I call Carol, Shawn's mother, every few days. Between my treks to ley lines with Angus, teaching, practicing, doctor's appointments, calls to Dana and Celine, and walking to the store for groceries, I read voraciously about time travel, ley lines, and standing stones.

I still have no idea what we're looking for.

"We weren't looking for his mark at Creagsmalan," Angus reminds me. It doesn't help. My frustration mounts with each red X.

Still, I love every idyllic day of holding Angus's hand as he helps me, in my awkward size, up hills, and through medieval towns. We search one ancient church and monastery and castle and graveyard after another, and sip hot tea in warm pubs, as we talk about our childhoods and growing up, our hopes and dreams, and what we believe and how we feel.

Rob visits routinely, eager for my approval and affection. He's found a professor of medieval history to look at my ring—Bruce's ring—and crucifix. Nerves shoot through my stomach. My finger and neck feel bare. I fear never getting them back. They're my only tangible proof.

We drive to Jedburgh, where James Douglas once roamed. Niall or Shawn roamed with him. One of them was here, too, we tell each other. We lift one another's sagging hopes. Still—we find nothing. It's another beautiful, but fruitless day. We drive silently for a time through rolling border hills as the sun sets. Suddenly Angus hits the steering wheel with the palm of his hand. "Cambuskenneth!" he exclaims, as if that explains everything.

"I'm lost," I admit.

"Niall—or someone passing as Niall—was at Cambuskenneth by November 6 of 1314, and at Ayr the following April." Angus glances at me. "Where was he in between?"

"We don't know. Or do we?"

"Traveling in winter was hard in medieval times," Angus says. "He'd either stay in Stirling or race home before winter."

I sit up straight. "He was newly married!" It hits me as fast and hard as Flight of the Bumblebee.

"Aye." Angus takes his eyes off the road, grinning at me. "And where was he just before Cambuskenneth...?"

I smile, knowing he's enjoying his detective work. "Creagsmalan's dungeon."

"Aye, south of Fort William. He marries Allene at the end of October, and...."

"...leaves immediately," I finish, "to reach Stirling by early November. So after Parliament, he races home to Allene. But there are lochs between Stirling and Glenmirril." I see what he sees.

"Going south is a hundred and twenty-five miles," Angus says. "North, a hundred and fifty. Twenty-five miles was a great distance in those days. Maybe a full day's travel."

"But he's just narrowly escaped death. He's not going anywhere near MacDougall's land."

Angus looks pleased. "And on that northern route, he'd pass very near some standing stones."

My mind jumps ahead. "How long would they have stayed in Cambuskenneth?" I note my use of they, though we know nothing of the sort. I don't correct myself. An idea has occurred to me.

Angus shrugs. "Parliaments didn't last long. They'd have left by mid-November."

I peer out the window at dark, frosty hills speeding by as we climb higher. I'm vaguely aware that we've just made several assumptions—that Niall and Shawn both survived, that Niall married Allene, that they both went to Stirling. There's no justification for any of these except our desire to believe. But my mind is too stuck on something else to back up and deal with that. "There's no chance they'd be there this late?" I ask.

Angus shakes his head. "Unlikely. Why?"

I sigh, seeing the flaw with my thought. "I'm still thinking of people on either side of this time shift. But that's Shawn and Niall. Us being there at the same time won't make any difference."

"No, I don't suppose so." Angus eases the car around a dark curve. The music on the radio jumps to a more lively tempo.

"But why would he go to them at all?" I ask. "He believed in God, not...whatever standing stones were about."

"Same reason we followed ley lines. If something mysterious happened, why not go to another mysterious place? We may not believe in ley lines, and he likely didn't himself, but if they travel together, if they stop at these stones...."

"That's a lot of ifs." Outside, mist curls across the road, and prowls up into the hills beside us.

"But if they did," he insists, "Shawn leaves his mark everywhere he goes. Maybe they go there and fail—but he'll still leave his mark, right?"

"Even if we find his mark," I say, "what good does that do us?"

"It tells us Shawn survived the gallows."

"It does?" I gape at him. "If the mark is there, Niall might have left it."

Angus shakes his head, excited by his deductions. "Niall, alone, has no reason to go to standing stones. It's Shawn who's looking for a way home."

I sag back into the seat, seeing his logic. And more. "So if we find it, maybe Niall died instead." A wisp of winter-gray cloud slides over the moon, cutting it in half.

"True." Angus is un-phased. Niall is only a name in history books to him. "But it would give us one answer. It would suggest Shawn is alive. I mean, was. After the gallows."

I think about a man who travels with a confessor, fighting valiantly on water. The confessor part is Niall. Water is Shawn. Valiant fighting is Niall. It's as if the two became one. Questions scream through my brain, spinning around and around and around, all the notes of a symphony, refusing to settle into sensible harmonies.

Angus squeezes my fingers. "Maybe the next answer will prove Niall lived, too." When I don't answer, he adds, "If Niall died at Creagsmalan, that means Shawn married Allene and had a son with her. So he wouldn't be looking for a way home. So a mark at the stones means they're both alive."

I shrug. "It's all guesses." Would he leave her? Leave his son? I barely knew who he was the years he was here, with me. I certainly don't know who he became.

"You don't want to go?" he asks, and suddenly says, "What am I on about? You're pregnant. Have I gotten too excited about this chase? Are you tired?" His brows knit in concern.

I lift a finger to the five o'clock shadow shading his jaw. "I'd love another day with you."

His face relaxes into the smile that has become familiar and beloved. "There are a few places in that area we can go, actually. My next day off happens to be the Solstice. A perfect time to go."

East of Inverness, 1314

Niall, Shawn, and their group traveled toward the northern tip of Loch Ness. It added to their travel time, wending up steep hilly passes and through thick forests, which Shawn didn't appreciate in the chilly Highlands. "'Tis better by far than meeting the MacDougalls," Niall reminded him when his grumbling grew.

"Did your mother never teach you to offer it up?" Hugh asked.

"Tried," Shawn said. "It didn't stick."

"Because your lives are far too easy," Niall muttered. "And you expect them to be easier still. 'Tis no good."

After fording the River Nairn, with the sun sliding into the west, they parted company with the others. Red looked dejected at being sent away.

"D' you think Christina will be there?" Niall asked, when they were alone.

"I've seen the Good Sir James when he's riled. MacDougall would be a fool to get on his bad side. And it's not as if Duncan loves her."

"Love does not always enter a man's determination to keep a woman," Niall said darkly. The wooded path narrowed ahead of them. Niall took the lead, pointing out a hill formation to their east, and another to the north. "Clan Ross's land," he explained. "We'll be safer here."

"A welcome change," Shawn said. "What do you know about Christina? She seems quite remarkable."

"Indeed." Niall's horse slowed, picking its way over the rough trail inching upwards. Pine boughs drooped over them, brushing close on either side till they all but shut out the sun. "I've been trying to think how she knew I didn't wish to meet MacDougall. I asked around Stirling. She is kin to Lord Morrison, and stayed briefly at Glenmirril after her parents died, before going to Creagsmalan. Though she must have quite the memory for faces, to recognize me years later."

"Who wouldn't remember a face as good-looking as mine?" Shawn asked.

"So she'd certainly remember one even better-looking," Niall retorted.

"Too bad she never saw such a thing," Shawn shot back. "What else do you know about her?"

"They say she goes to Iona each year to pray."

Shawn snorted. "Lot of good it's done her."

"Has it not?" Niall asked. "If all went as planned, she's away from him now, is she not?" He looked back over his shoulder at Shawn. "Why *did* you carve *Iona J* on the Heart?"

"Huh? What? Iona?"

"With the apology you left Amy."

"Why would I carve anything about Iona?" Shawn asked. "I barely know where it is."

Niall shrugged. "I suppose in seven hundred years perhaps someone else may have done it."

"Must have," Shawn repeated, "because I didn't."

"'Tis odd, though, that it's right there with what you carved. Look sharp here. Where the road branches, we go right."

"How much farther to this wise woman?"

"Not much."

"Her house isn't made of candy, is it?"

Niall peered back over his shoulder.

"Or sitting on chicken's legs?" Shawn gazed up at dark firs pressing around them, and tugged his cloak closer in the dim light. It was easy to see, he thought, how such stories had sprung into being.

"I'd not expect so," Niall said. "You do have interesting ideas."

"Not really," he said. "Modest Mussorgsky, *The Hut of Baba Yaga.* It's an orchestral piece about a witch." He flung words forth as candles against the dark forest, a relief from the silence, everything muffled by a coat of snow. He sang a few bars and stopped when he reached the trumpet's part. Thoughts of Rob and Amy sobered him more than the dark woods. She'd be very pregnant now, showing. He wondered if she'd visited his mother.

"Is there more?" Niall looked back.

Shawn's pony brushed a tree spattered with snow. It shook down like fairy dust, sprinkling his cloak and hair. "It doesn't matter," he said. "What do you think this wise woman can tell us? I thought in your day they were accused of being witches. Know how you tell if witches are made of wood? They float, like ducks."

"Don't be a bampot," Niall said.

"It's not like I believe that," Shawn clarified, with a strong undercurrent of irritation. "It's from a movie. A jest. It's kind of creepy here." When Niall didn't answer, he said, "You really think she might have some ideas?"

"We've none of our own," Niall replied. "She lives as a hermit and is known for holiness and wisdom." The road forked, and he led them to the right, onto an even narrower track, barely wide enough for a man, with wintery ferns spilling over it. "There's a stream nearby," Niall said. "Listen for it, and a mile upstream, we should find her."

Shawn followed, his pony's nose pushing into the rump of Niall's, shuffling along. He hummed a bit of the *Great Gate of Kiev,* thinking of witches and huts on chicken legs and Amy, pregnant with his child, maybe planning her wedding to Rob.

He stared up at the pine boughs arcing above, and heaved a sigh. Niall had told him she had no interest in Rob. Still, the idea persisted. She'd want someone. She'd need someone. She liked old-fashioned things. She'd wanted a 'real' wedding night, as she called it. She'd want to marry Rob before the baby was born, give it a name. His fingers curled around the reins. His pony balked, paused, and skittered backward a step.

Niall looked over his shoulder again. "What are you doing to him? Loosen up on the reins."

Shawn loosened his fingers and patted the pony's neck. She wouldn't really give it Rob's name, he decided. She couldn't just forget him like that. But then, maybe she could. He'd forgotten her easily enough when others had been available.

"There's the stream," Niall said. "D' you hear it?"

"No."

"You must learn to listen or you'll never be able to find your way." They paused, and suddenly Shawn heard it, clear as a piccolo sailing over a full orchestra, breaking through the darkening wood. Niall twitched his reins. His pony turned languidly, pushing into a patch of silvery birches and waist high ferns. Shawn's mount followed. Soon, they reached a silver creek rippling through the chocolate browns and hunter greens of the forest. Niall turned north, following it. Shawn tugged his cloak close, wishing for a little Thinsulate. Moments later, they broke out of the forest, into a narrow glen. Rocky hills climbed up against the evening sky on either side. On one slope, a light flickered. Shawn squinted, seeing that it came from a cave set in the hill's face.

Niall guided his pony to the foot of the slope and dismounted. Shawn followed, clambering to the ground in relief. Niall cupped his hands, calling up the hill. "Hallo! We seek Sorcha."

They waited while the wind sloughed down the valley, rippling their cloaks. The ponies shook their manes in irritation, and bent to tasting the frosted grass.

"Is this going to be some bent, old snaggle-tooth with scraggly gray hair?" Shawn asked. "Should we collect some eye of newt for her?"

The light flickered in the cave entrance.

"Berries would be more appreciated." Niall scanned the foliage. Spotting a bush spangled in dark blue, he picked handfuls, dropping them into the folds of his plaid. Shawn helped.

"'Tis Sorcha you've found." They turned to the thin voice drifting down the hillside. A figure stood at the cave entrance. "Come up."

Shawn took a last handful of berries, and followed Niall up a narrow dirt track wending up the hillside. The woman took shape as they approached. She wore bundles of nondescript clothing. Her face, beneath the folds of the *arisaid* covering her head, lacked the wizened features he'd expected. She had round, rosy cheeks and bright blue eyes shining with humor.

"I've little use for eye of newt," she said.

Shawn stared, uncomprehending.

Niall chuckled. "Surely you've learned by now how sound carries up the hills?"

"It was a jest," Shawn muttered. Niall nudged him, and he added, "My apologies."

"Accepted," Sorcha said. "Come in from the cold." She led them in, edging past the fire burning at the entrance. A large cast iron pot hung over it. "It holds only turnips," she assured him, and pointed to furs on the floor and bowls on a ledge carved in the rock. "You're welcome to food and shelter. I'd think you'd not be wanting to travel further with night coming on."

"Thank you." Niall seated himself on a fur, as did Shawn. Sorcha pulled the *arisaid* off her head, revealing dark hair wrapped in a heavy braid. Firelight played over her ivory skin. "You seem young to be a wise woman," he said.

She laughed, dishing stew from the pot into bowls. "Age and wisdom are not always related. Though I never claimed to be wise. 'Tis others say so. If I've helped anyone, 'tis God working through me."

Shawn was about to snort—his usual response to mention of God. Niall's hard stare stopped him.

Sorcha paused, the ladle over a bowl. She peered at their identical faces. "Brothers?" she asked. "Twins?"

"Not quite," Shawn said dryly.

She peered more closely at him. "You don't believe?"

"Believe what? Are we talking God? I believe I make my own destiny." But he dropped his gaze, unnerved by her scrutiny. Her eyes seemed to prod through his skin.

"Aye, we're both doing well at that." Niall's voice crackled with sarcasm.

Shawn glared at him. "My talents are my own doing and hard work."

Sorcha tipped broth into the bowl, handed it to him, and reached for a second bowl. "You've worked hard, no doubt. Yet you came to me."

"He thought you might know something." Shawn stared at the stew, and swirled it a little. It looked better than much of what he'd eaten in this time. He lifted his wooden spoon.

"Did your mother teach you no manners?" Niall asked as he accepted the second bowl. "Prayers." Sorcha finished spooning up her own meal and sat down on a fur, bowing her head, and saying grace.

"My mother tried," Shawn said, when she finished. "I found I got more out of life without them."

Niall snorted. "Like Amy's undying love and devotion, aye?"

Shawn set the bowl down hard, glaring.

"Peace." Sorcha's gaze rested on Niall, a gentle reprimand in her blue eyes. Faint color, barely discernible in the dim firelight, crept up his cheeks.

"Let us eat," she said. "Turnips taste fair good with tongue of owl. Would you'd brought some."

Shawn's head shot up, wondering if she was mocking him. She bent over her bowl, smiling a small, secret smile.

They finished the meal in silence, wooden spoons scraping the bottoms of their bowls. Shawn helped himself to seconds, despite Niall's disapproving stare. "What?" he demanded. "There's plenty of tongue of owl around here to make more."

Sorcha met his eyes. She laughed, her teeth flashing white in the firelight.

He grinned back, and remembered the berries tucked in the folds of his tartan. He took a bowl from the ledge and tipped them in, holding it out to Niall, who added his. "It's not much," Shawn said. "I don't suppose you have whipped cream to go with them?"

"Whipped lung of lizard mayhap." Sorcha finished her stew, swished the bowl in a pail of water, and reached for Niall's and Shawn's bowls. Returning to her seat, she said, "Now, your story."

Niall and Shawn glanced at each other. Shawn cleared his throat. "Well, it's now you, me, MacDonald, Hugh, Allene, Christina, Brother David, Red, and maybe Bessie. What can one more hurt? Wise women don't blab everything they know on twitter, do they?"

Sorcha waited silently, firelight playing over her features. For a moment, she looked older, wiser. Shawn blinked, and she was young again, her eyes twinkling with humor and patience as they flickered over his face.

Niall said nothing.

"Look," said Shawn, "it was your idea to come here. How's she supposed to help us if we don't tell the truth?"

"You arguing for the truth, me hesitating," Niall mused. "'Tis a change."

"Want to hear a funny story?" Shawn turned to Sorcha. "Last June, I went to sleep in the twenty-first century—like seven hundred years from now. I woke up here in 1314 with everyone thinking I was him."

"The likeness is uncanny," Sorcha replied.

"Leaving out all the other fascinating details," Shawn continued, "he woke up in my time and somehow crossed back. I'd like to go home, too. We figure if he managed it, so can I. But we don't know how." He smacked his forehead. "I don't suppose you have a *hot air balloon* and want to get back, too?"

"I've nothing of the sort," Sorcha said.

"What, you know what a hot air balloon is?"

Sorcha shook her head. "I don't, which suggests to me I've not got one." She glanced around the cave. "I've very little here."

Shawn grunted, and rose, pacing the cave. A candle flickered in a recess, illuminating a crucifix on a ledge. "What good is this?" he asked Niall. "We're on a wild goose chase. What could she possibly know?"

Niall shrugged. "Would you rather we did naught?"

"This is a crazy story. How can we expect her to even believe it?"

"There are many strange things in this world and out of it," Sorcha said. "He's the look of truth to him."

Shawn turned from the crucifix to see Sorcha staring at Niall. "Yeah, but I'm the one who told the story. And he looks just like me. Do I have the look of truth?"

Sorcha shrugged. "If you'd been lying, he'd have said so."

"Oh, I like this," Shawn huffed. "Mr. Perfect just sits there and gets all the accolades. What's he done to have the look of truth to him? You notice we look exactly alike?"

Sorcha turned to meet his eyes. His insides became still. Her steady gaze bored into his soul. His eyes dropped to the floor, as if it would prevent her seeing all his lies to Amy, to Celine, to so many others, the secret e-mail accounts, the drunken, tawdry escapades. A deep flush crawled up his neck.

Celine hadn't deserved it, either. The collar of his cloak felt tight around his neck. He remembered the nights he told Amy he was going for a six pack. Heat enveloped his face. He wondered how much Amy knew. She was better off with Rob.

He slid down against the wall, sitting under the tiny flickering flame of the candle, and dropped his face in his hands, his hands pressed to his bent knees, hiding, like a child, from her eyes, from his own misdeeds.

"And yet," Sorcha said softly, "I believe you about this. What will you do when you go back?"

"Tell her the truth," Shawn whispered. "Ask her to forgive me. I'll change."

"*Will* change? Will you wait till you get back to change?"

Shawn lifted his face from his palms, peering out cautiously. "Who *are* you?" His voice quivered. He saw nothing but her eyes, as old as the hills and streams, full of the wisdom of all time.

"I am who I am," she said. "I am Sorcha, I live in this cave, I pray, I give hospitality."

He stared at her. "Can you help me?" He tried to fight off the child, to sound tough again. "What could you possibly know of time travel?"

"I know 'tis under God's control. Have you prayed?"

"Yeah, we prayed and fasted. I'm still here."

She cocked her head at him. "You do expect strange things of God. He is not a jin."

Anger and despair pushed up against the shame. "Doesn't the Bible say ask and ye shall receive? I asked. I didn't receive."

Sorcha sighed. "Perhaps you are receiving even now and do not see. Was there nothing you needed besides getting home?"

Her eyes filled his vision, dark blue eyes, eyes like Amy's. The scenes of his life with Amy filled the cave: Amy in her peach satin robe, in her lace-filled apartment, at the top of the Ferris wheel; leaning into her violin making the witches chatter atop Bald Mountain. He'd loved the concentration on her face when she played, though he'd teased her about it. Amy, in his home, asking why it took so long to get beer. The first store was closed, he told her. The second store didn't have the brand he liked. He saw doubt and pain in her eyes. He'd convinced himself at the time he wasn't hurting her, that none of those women changed anything he felt about her or all he would give her and do for her; but now he saw the pain, flowing through Sorcha's eyes, as Amy struggled to reconcile his story with his lengthy absence. Her eyes filled his vision, the pain leaking out. How had he failed to see it?

"There was so much more you needed," Sorcha said softly. "Until you get that, there's naught for you at home."

CHAPTER FOURTEEN

Clava Cairns, Scotland, Present

"And I was worried about oversleeping!" Laughing, Amy leaned back against the headrest in the dark, warm cocoon of Angus's green mini. Deep blue velvet filled the sky outside

Angus chuckled. "I did warn you Gavin and Hamish rise early!"

"Early! They got up late! Late last night!"

"I'll talk to Mairi," Angus said.

"No, don't!" Amy touched his arm. "She's putting me up over Christmas." She gazed through the windshield at silver stars spangling the graying sky. A smile flitted across her face. "Gavin brought me a book as soon as I got there." She'd lost herself in a world of selkies between the pages of his book. "I forgot for awhile that life hurts."

Angus wrapped his hand around hers. "Gavin was a wee thing when Julia and I broke up. I spent a lot of time with him. Babies are very healing."

Amy studied his clean-shaven cheek in the pre-dawn. She could imagine him holding a baby. He said no more, his eyes on the road. He rarely spoke of Julia; she guessed he didn't want to now. "They're sweet," she said. "They made me breakfast."

"Is that why there's butter on your nose?"

"What?" She reached for the mirror, scrubbing at her nose.

Angus's laugh stopped her.

"That was a dirty trick," she said.

"I get it from Mairi. Best be on your guard with her." He winked. "How badly did they burn the toast?"

"The toast was fine, but I suspect they put too much coffee in the coffee press."

"They use instant," Angus said. "It comes out rather strong. Very courteous of you to drink it all. I never can. I've something more palatable in the thermos."

"Thank goodness." She grinned. "But please—don't tell them I said so. They were so proud."

Angus smiled as he eased off the highway onto a smaller road. Amy closed her eyes. It seemed only seconds later he touched her cheek, saying, "Wake up now. Gavin and Hamish have brought you burned toast and another cuppa."

She twisted against the seat, and opened her eyes to his, dark and piercing. He kissed her, ran a finger down her cheek, and said, "We're here." They got out of the car; glancing at the snowflakes trembling in the gray dark, Angus pulled a tarp and blanket from the trunk.

"What now?" Amy tugged her coat, but it no longer closed.

"I don't know." Angus wrapped the blanket around her shoulders. "'Tis a mysterious place, on a mysterious day." He leaned close, sheltering her from the wind, as it tumbled them toward a low stone wall. He helped her over, and soon they found themselves among the standing stones and cairns.

"Wouldn't it depend on Shawn actually being here?" she pressed. "For anything to happen?" The possibility burst inside her. What if Shawn *did* appear before her? The thought stirred irritation and excitement, both. She wondered if he'd look as he had at the battle—strong, determined, as he turned for the child. But she hadn't forgotten his betrayals and lies.

"Maybe." Angus shrugged. "I thought we'd look around and see what happens." He glanced at the sky, light gray now, and brushed snow off one of the stones. "Maybe he left a message to explain Iona. Something that'll mean something to you. Like his signature S."

Amy clutched the blanket. The whole place had an eerie stillness to it; magic and mystery quivered in the air. Wind sloughed through the pines, setting needles to rustling and whispering. Mist twisted around their ankles. Standing stones rose, wraith-like, from the gloam. Amy shivered. Someone could easily slide through time in such a place.

Angus nodded toward one of the cairns. "Let's have that coffee until it's light enough to see."

They entered the cairn, down a long, narrow passage. Stone walls rose on either side, but its roof had long since disappeared, leaving it open to the sky, and snowflakes dancing above. Angus laid the tarp on the chilly ground and helped Amy lower herself. With their backs against the stone wall, he took out the thermos and biscuits.

"It feels sacrilegious." She wrapped her hands around the thermos. "Wasn't it a grave of some sort?"

"A thousand years ago, maybe," he said. "They've never found any bodies. Some doubt they were graves after all. They're aligned with the sun, see. I'm surprised no one else is here on the solstice."

"Maybe they're all down at Stonehenge."

They fell quiet. She laid her head on his shoulder, and dozed. Shawn prowled her dreams, Shawn in the midst of stones, circling, looking to the sky, reaching for home. She had no idea if it was the stone circle by the cairn.

Highlands, 1314

"Sleeping in the tower, bishops, monks, wise women! What next?" Shawn tried to snap. But his heart wasn't in it. As dawn stained the sky pink, their ponies trudged northward into deeper snow. The wind whipped through the robes of 'Brother Andrew,' through his *leine*, even covered as it was by leather armor, and stuffed with Sorcha's old rags. He hadn't expected to be so cold. Niall glanced back. He couldn't fail to notice the missing cloak. Shawn was grateful he didn't mention it. Sacrificing his warmth for a strange woman with piercing eyes was not his style. He didn't want to talk about it. He'd been just fine the way he was, and didn't want Niall's approval for 'changing.'

"Standing stones," Niall said. "I talked with Sorcha after you left."

"A holy hermit suggesting standing stones." Shawn spit into the ferns huddled along the snowy path. He'd scrambled blindly to his feet, when her eyes became too much, and disappeared into the glen, not coming back till the cold became unbearable. "Just when I thought it couldn't get any stranger."

A bird of prey screeched overhead and wheeled away above the trees. He wondered uneasily if they'd see wolves in this forest. Niall's assurance that they only attacked when sick or hungry didn't comfort him. They'd *be* hungry in winter, and quite likely sick.

"No one knows what the stones were for," Niall said. "But she believes they were sacred places, where unexplained things happen. She is praying even now. She has promised you a novena."

"A novena, what's that?"

"Nine days of prayer."

Shawn spit again.

"You'd best not scoff at God," Niall said mildly.

"What's He going to do?" Shawn's irritation erupted. "Abandon me in a brutal era where people kill each other?" He laughed, a short, dry report with no humor.

They rode in silence for some time. Shawn draped his reins over the pommel, and rubbed his hands up and down his arms, trying to stop the shivering. *Please, just spare me hypothermia.* He hadn't planned to pray. It wasn't a real prayer. *Would it kill You to try?* His words echoed in his head. A flurry of wings sounded above, sending a draft of warm air down over him. From the corner of his eye, he saw, he felt, a phalanx of angels, not soft white-washed cupids, but solid ranks of warriors with wings eight feet tall, more powerful than eagles, solemn faces, shielding him.

He spun. Bare silver birches stretched behind him, a snowy track, fir trees with snow shimmering on green branches. A rabbit sat frozen, blinking with dark eyes. He swallowed. He didn't believe in angels. If they existed, they would have protected his father. They would have kicked him into shape before he'd done so many stupid things to Amy. He nudged his pony with his heels, urging it into a trot, till he caught up with Niall. The shivering stopped.

"There are standing stones not far from here," Niall said.

"Okay, that's great and all. But isn't MacDonald expecting us back?"

"'Tis on the way." Niall brushed snow from his pony's mane.

"What are we supposed to do, sleep in the middle of them? Say a prayer or something?"

"Or something," Niall said. They lapsed once more into silence.

Clava Cairns, Present

Amy jolted awake. A touch of Angus's soap and shampoo came to her.

He handed her a cup. "Why did you love him so?"

She drank deeply, letting the hot coffee warm her. "You mean, why was I so stupid?"

"You're not stupid. So what attracted you?"

Amy studied the plastic cup in her hands for a time before saying, slowly, "People outside it, they saw the wild parties, the drinking, just barely staying inside the law. You saw the cheating from the start. But that's not what it was like *for me*, that first year and a half."

"What *was* it like?"

"Nice. Good." She stopped. It had been romantic, comfortable, even domestic sometimes. She pulled away from him, studying his face. "I shouldn't tell you this, not you of all people."

Angus's dark eyes pierced hers. He touched her hair, her cheek. "Isn't that what friendship is? Sharing, honesty?"

"You really want to hear this?"

He nodded.

"Okay." She sipped her coffee. "He gave a hundred and ten percent." She stared up at the pink-gray sky overhead. "He made everything an occasion. He made people feel like he really cared."

Angus slid his hand under her hair, rubbing her back.

"He played flute."

"Flute?" He sounded surprised. "That's a wee bit different from trombone."

She nodded. "He played everything, really, at least a little. I went to his house, once. It was his dad's birthday, and I thought he'd like company—even though I wouldn't dare mention it to Shawn, because he liked to ignore it."

"Ignore his dad's birthday?"

"He was murdered. Shawn never talked about it. Like it never happened."

"Oh."

"But I made an excuse and went, and he was leaving with his flute. He wouldn't tell me where he was going, and he got mad when I wouldn't leave. Then he laughed. He was like that. He'd be furious, and then the sun just came out again. And he made me swear." She laughed. "First he was really serious, then he made me pinky swear. That's how he was—this hard-nosed businessman, this guy who partied, but then he'd show this child-like side, not afraid to be ridiculous, to laugh at himself."

"Where was he going?" Angus asked.

"A nursing home. In the parking lot, he told me to stay in the car."

"I take it you didn't?"

Amy laughed. "Of course not. I went in ten minutes later. I found him playing for Mass."

"Shawn Kleiner playing for Mass?"

"I think it was because it was his father's birthday, and faith was so important to his dad. I stayed back where he wouldn't see me, and after Mass, he sat with these old men, knee to knee, leaning forward, listening. I saw this grief in his face, even though he was smiling, and talking. It was one of those moments where you feel like a veil lifted and you're seeing something beyond what you're really looking at."

"I know that feeling," Angus said.

Amy stirred, her arms clutched around herself, caught in the memory. "I went back to the car. He came out and said, *These old people are too wily. I thought I could get a few bucks for this damn flute. I can't even give it away.* If he saw me, he never let on."

Angus sat quietly for a time, before handing her a biscuit. "How did it go from all these good things to what you know now?"

"Like the frog in the pot." She took a bite of the biscuit. "One little thing, then two. I guess I adjusted to each one, till I realized I was half-crazy with the stories. He disappeared, and I felt what normal was again." When he said nothing, she asked softly, "Why wasn't I good enough for him?"

Angus pulled her close. "You're good enough for anyone."

"Then why did he turn to them? How could he do this to me? I gave him everything he wanted."

"Because he was broken. It took me a long time to know that with Julia. But one day, all of a sudden, you'll know in your heart it was never about you."

"I wish that day would come soon," she said. "Because it hurts. I go back and forth between the cheating, and his apology on Hugh's rock."

Angus's arm tightened around her shoulders. His cheek rested on her hair. Suddenly, a ray of light stabbed her in the eyes. They both jumped up. Coffee sloshed from the thermos. He laughed at the sunlight streaming in, lighting up the stone walls. It poured over the roof, turning the world outside pink and white with sunlight pouring over the snowy field and trees and stones.

He hugged her tightly. "Let's see if we find Shawn here or at the standing stones."

East of Inverness, 1314

Shawn and Niall stopped at the edge of the field. Seven standing stones, in a rough circle, reached like jagged fingers into the sky. The ponies stamped in the snow, snorting out frosty puffs of breath. Shawn patted his animal's neck, wishing he could give some of his own warmth to it. His shivering had stopped hours ago and not returned. He'd wondered if he was in the beginning stages of hypothermia, that he no longer felt the cold. But he remained strong and alert. He'd adjusted to the weather, he decided.

"What now?" he asked Niall. The standing stones stood alone in the field, silhouetted against the western sky's streaks of pink and orange clouds.

"We pray," Niall said. "I've heard stories of these places. But I don't what they really are."

Shawn looked at him curiously. "It's unlike you to mess with things that might not be Godly."

"Anything to get you off my back," Niall returned.

"At least *you're* not constantly having to save *my* skin."

"D' you no mind me dragging your two halves off Bannockburn's field?"

"Well, my two halves did a better job earning knighthood than your one whole. Some of us were working while you lounged in Chez MacDougall."

"Aye, 'twas a pretty place." Niall twitched his reins, and they started forward. At the stones, they dismounted in choreographed silence.

Shawn glanced to the west, where sunset blazed behind the hills. "What do you think will happen?" he asked.

"I've no idea. I suppose if there's any chance they'll whisk a man into the future, I'd best not go in."

Shawn harrumphed. But it made sense. He took three steps. Two feet from the stones, he felt a force on his chest, pushing him. Cold swelled around him again, shooting shivers down his arms.

"I'll stay here and pray," Niall said.

Shawn turned, seeing his own face looking back. Niall's heavy cloak hung to his knees, wrapped tight against the chill.

"What if I disappear?" Shawn said.

"I must believe you disappeared to your proper time."

They stared at each other. Suddenly, Niall strode forward, grasping Shawn's forearm, placing a hand on his. "Thank you."

Shawn swallowed over a lump in his throat, not knowing what to say.

"For everything," Niall emphasized. "For taking care of Allene. For knighthood. For getting me out of Creagsmalan. You're a true friend."

Shawn swallowed again. He was feeling, in the last two days, like Rob, with his constant gulping. "I guess I owe you thanks, too," he said. "For taking care of Amy. For Bannockburn." He laughed. "Showing me the lesser-seen..." he coughed, "...and *smelled* sights of Carlisle!" He cleared his throat. "You'll look out for Red? I didn't even say good-bye."

"He'll be well cared for." Niall gripped him in a warrior's hug. "God go with you." He stepped back, smiling. "I hope not to see you again in the morning."

East of Inverness, Present

Amy shivered in the snow-whitened field, gazing up. Seven granite giants leaning against a gunflint evening sky streaked with oyster gray clouds. The smallest rose an inch over Angus's head. "Well then!" Angus clapped his large hands together, and glanced doubtfully at the waning light. "We'd best start!" Their failure at the cairn and the other stones they'd visited left him undaunted. "'Twas the more likely place, anyway."

Iona had been the most likely place, too, Amy thought. She rubbed her own hands together, trying to summon enthusiasm, but couldn't help asking, "What if we don't find anything?"

"We look elsewhere." Dropping his backpack to the ground, he entered the circle. He pulled off his gloves and shoved them into his pocket, baring his fingers to feel each pitted, weather-scarred, surface.

Amy began searching the outer face, lost in thoughts of Shawn, her child, the wild world of medieval Scotland, and the many failures surrounding the few scraps of information they'd found. Wind chafed her hands. She leaned around the stone. "Does it even seem real to you anymore?"

Angus's hands stilled. "No," he said. "And it makes me a wee bit sad. Imagine talking to someone who *lived* it!"

They continued in the silence of the barren field, the stones swaying above them like dancers frozen in the cold. A blackbird cawed overhead as they mirrored one another's actions on either side of the stone, brushing at snow, feeling with cold fingers, studying with wind-stung eyes, for any sign of Shawn's scratches.

Angus leaned suddenly around the fourth stone. "Want to see time travel?"

Amy looked up. "What?"

"Throw an alarm clock!"

She groaned, as she moved to the sixth stone. "Lame. Very lame."

He followed, on the opposite side of the monolith. "I found an advertisement this morning. There's to be a conference on time travel." He squatted down, studying the lower half of the stone.

"Really?" She paused, the granite rough under her fingers. "You're kidding. When?"

He looked up. "Two weeks ago. Shall we go?"

She laughed, flicking a dusting of white flakes into his dark hair. He shook it off, laughing, and scooped up a handful of snow. She stepped aside. The snowball landed in a puff and broke apart silently in the quiet landscape. A raven shrieked and lifted from a fir tree, leaving a green limb trembling. Amy watched it spin away, a shock of black against clear, blue sky.

"The ravens wheeling overhead...."

She turned at the sound of rich baritone singing. Angus cast song into the snow-muffled world as he ran his hands over the stone. She had loved listening to Shawn sing. And Shawn had loved singing.

"...above the ancient ruins...." He looked up, and stopped. "'Tis not what you're used to, no doubt."

"Don't stop," she said softly. "Your voice is incredible!" It was, if anything, better than Shawn's. "Why wouldn't you sing at St. Oran's?"

He smiled, shrugged, cleared his throat, and started a new song. *"Let me call my love to me."*

The wild call of the melody, ringing with sorrow and joy, pierced her heart. He took a great breath; his voice filled the snowy clearing. *"Ride with me forever more, you're my dearie, dearie-oh!"*

She moved to the last stone, thrilling to his rich tones in the twilight.

"Let me call my love to me, let me give her everything."

In the crisp solstice air, she searched every inch, with chapped, cold fingers. She closed her eyes, her forehead against the cold rock.

"Let me shower her with love, and give her cause to sing, she's my dearie, dearie-oh."

Amy looked up. Angus smiled at her. His love seemed to banish Shawn and his misdeeds to another realm, to shine light on who he'd been, not who he told Amy she was. The weight lifted. She smiled. "You were born to sing."

"Aye, well, don't tell the other officers, aye?" He grinned. Then he cocked his head quizzically. His grin melted. He touched her cheek. "Come and have a cuppa." He hefted the backpack from the ground, and, taking her hand, led her inside the circle. He pulled out a plastic tarp, and shook it out over the frosty grass. They sat, backs against one of the great boulders, and he poured coffee from his thermos into plastic mugs. Her thoughts spun around Shawn as she sipped.

His arm tightened around her shoulders. "You're disappointed."

"Your logic about Shawn and Niall coming here seemed so, well, logical." A heavy sigh escaped her lips. "But there's nothing here."

"He mayn't have left a mark this time," Angus reasoned. "Or it's worn away. Or 'twas on a stone that's gone." He sipped his own drink. "Or maybe I'm simply wrong and they didn't come here a 'tall."

"All this running around, for what?" Amy asked.

"We know they both survived."

"That's all a guess," Amy objected.

"But a good one." He grinned at her, the same way Shawn always had before strutting on stage, absolutely sure of himself. "I've done well in the department with gut instinct. They're both alive, we've a growing list of their movements, and we know Niall traveled with a monk. A professor of medieval history is looking at the ring and crucifix."

"None of which tells us how to get him back."

"Bits and pieces," he admitted. "But all of a sudden, they'll add up. You'll see." He screwed the lid back on the thermos. "Christmas is on us. Let's get you to Mairi's, and have a few days of normal."

East of Inverness, 1314

Niall sank to his knees, making the sign of the cross. He recited an *Ave* and *Pater*, before words fell from his brain, and he remained silent and motionless, the damp earth biting through his trews, watching. Shawn moved into the circle of stones, a dark figure melting into the dark interior. Unease settled on Niall's shoulders. He bowed his head. *Have I done the right thing? Am I dallying with things not of You, My Lord?* But a holy woman had told him of the place. *Though no one knows what they were for,* she'd said, *men do say the ancients worshiped there, and God is God by any name, is He not?* She'd promised the novena. She'd promised to pray that her advice was sound, that no harm should befall them if it wasn't. "But this is what my heart tells me," she'd said. "The urge is strong within me to send you there."

Niall stared into the stone circle. The seven stones were tall, wide, and close together. He squinted. Black shapes flitted inside the circle. No sound came out.

He rose, restless, and paced the outer edge of the circle. Each stone stood an inch or two above his own six feet.

He named them as he passed. James, hanged, drawn and quartered by the English. Thomas, hanged, drawn and quartered, his head staring out lifelessly from a pike above Berwick's gate. Adam, William, both taken by the summer illness that swept Glenmirril. Robert, dead as an infant in his cradle. Alexander, the one Niall remembered most clearly. The familiar sick feeling filled his stomach. The clamminess crawled over his arms.

He hastened away to the last stone. Himself. The youngest, and only surviving, of James Campbell's seven sons. Some called him blessed for having seven sons. Some called him cursed for losing six. Niall reached for his crucifix and touched bare throat.

He closed his eyes. It hit him even harder than it had in St. Michael's chapel. He didn't want Shawn to go. Long ago, he'd been surrounded by brothers. One by one, they'd disappeared and never come back. Pipes skirled, women keened while he and Alexander stopped fighting long enough to clutch one another's hands, too young to understand why their mother wept. Then Alexander had strayed too far into the loch and gone under, kicking and shouting. Men had rushed from the castle, while Niall stood on the shore, helpless. Pipes skirled, women keened, and Niall learned why his mother wept, as he watched them pull Alexander's lifeless, bloated body from the water; as he followed the wooden coffin the next day to the graveyard behind Glenmirril's kirk. Life had become strangely quiet without Alexander. He'd turned to Iohn, and Iohn had betrayed him.

Now there was Shawn. God had given him back a brother. And Niall had sent him away. But it was the right thing to do. He bowed his head, feeling the loss, and tried to pray.

♫

Shawn wandered inside the stones. They towered stark and black against the last streaks of sunset. Stars glittered overhead like chips of ice. No sound came from outside the circle, no whickering of ponies, no shuffling of hooves, no call from Niall, checking if he was still here. He wondered, if he walked out again, if he'd be in his own time. But the idea of such a magical switch seemed faintly ridiculous when he thought of Sorcha's eyes peering into his soul.

If you've not changed, there's naught for you at home. He'd changed, he assured himself. But he wasn't sure Sorcha would agree that he'd changed enough.

He made another circuit inside the stones. The pressure on his chest had not stopped since he'd stepped inside, as if the stones themselves pushed him away, warned him to leave. But that was foolish. He laid his hand on one of the monoliths. Its rough surface scraped his palm. A tingle shot up his arm. He yanked his hand back, and moved to the next one, but didn't touch it.

He couldn't walk in circles all night. Moving to the center, he lay down on the hard, cold ground, pillowing his head on clasped palms, and staring up at thousands of stars, dancing in place. They stretched across a night sky bigger than he'd ever known. He became smaller and smaller under them, imagining the whole universe spread out.

And who made that universe?

His father had loved camping for this very reason. Shawn remembered lying side by side in their sleeping bags on cool spring nights, staring up. "Man is so arrogant," his father had said. "We're so small, and we don't even know it."

Shawn's past hummed around him like a beautiful dream—the wealth, his home on twenty acres with a stream and waterfall, floor to ceiling stone fireplace, crowds screaming when he came onstage, girls squealing, shouting his name and flashing his picture. He rubbed his hand through his hair. It wouldn't impress anyone now, dirty, ragged, and tied in a leather thong.

But he felt peace, watching the stars wink. He hadn't thought of those girls in months, hadn't missed them. He missed Amy, his music, his mother. *Let me call my love to* me. The melody sang through his head. He wasn't sure where it had come from. He closed his eyes. Amy was strong behind his lids, Amy at the keyboard in his music room. "This chord," she'd said. "At the bridge. What if you threw in a minor chord instead?" He liked it, he used it, and they kept arranging together, for his combo, his quintet, the orchestra. She had a unique touch with harmony and counter melodies. He felt a little better, knowing she'd be getting royalties from those albums. *Let me shower her with love, and give her cause to sing.* He hummed softly.

Rob thought he had some talent at arranging. He'd be right there, wanting to work with her. Really, Shawn thought, maybe all the genius of the arrangements *had* been hers. Maybe the orchestra would continue to get what he'd thought was his trademark style.

He opened his eyes. Thousands of stars rushed in, pressing close, filling the sky. The seven stones loomed around him. There was no sound in all the earth but his own breathing. He must have disappeared back into his own time. He smiled. He wasn't far from Inverness. He'd find a road, have them call the police, call the States, Amy, his mother. He'd get the first flight home, make it right with her. He'd check in some archives or museum, see how Niall and Allene had fared. He hoped Red would be happy at Glenmirril. He liked the kid. He'd miss him. He'd miss them all! Niall was the brother he'd never had. He felt a friendship with him he'd never felt before, not with Rob, not with anyone.

Because you respect each other. Who did you respect in the orchestra?

Amy? Rob? Jim? He'd seen himself as smarter, funnier, more talented than any of them, rescuing them from their own mediocrity. He'd seen only one person as his equal, sharing his values, views—and desires; equally clever in lies. But he hadn't called it lies. He'd called it discretion; friendship.

Except for one thing. This time, he heard the voice audibly, soft as a snowflake settling to earth.

He sat up, and spoke out loud, angry. "What one thing? How was she not my friend?" She'd been there to talk to, been there when he was lonely.

A friend wouldn't help you hurt someone you love.

He swallowed hard. The stones towered around him. He liked her. She was fun, in every way. She cared about Amy.

More than she cared about her own fun?

He bolted to his feet. His hands clenched in and out of fists, pacing the stone cage. She'd never let it slip, never hurt Amy.

But these things have a way of coming out. How will Amy feel then?

The lump in his throat grew with the sudden certainty that Amy would find out, one way or another. And this time, he cared how she would feel, not how he would cover his tracks. The frozen grass crunched under his feet as he paced the stone circle. He'd buy her that horse when he got back, and a really great violin. That's what she wanted. He'd give it to her!

Anger pounded his head like the witches on *Bald Mountain.* She could have said no. She could have been a better friend to Amy. Everyone knew what *he* was like, after all, but did *she* have to add salt to Amy's wounds? The chattering violins crescendoed in his head, higher and higher, as he stormed back and forth across the circle.

Anger at her?

He sank to his knees. It was anger at himself he felt. The other women were bad enough—anonymous, faceless women Amy would never meet; even Celine—he'd lied to Celine, convinced her she wasn't betraying Amy. Celine, despite her clear infatuation, had been insistent she would have nothing to do with him while he was seeing Amy.

But why her, both of them knowing it would hurt Amy?

He tried one last defense–a good offense. He shouted up at the stars, "It's not as bad as what You did! You let him kill my father who never hurt anyone!" The words hung in the cold air.

The chill came back, but it came from inside. God's silence, breathing down in the pulsing of the stars, reprimanded him. *You owe Celine an apology, too.* He'd lied, used her, broken her heart. He dropped his face into cupped hands. *God, I can't do this. It's too many apologies, too many people, too many ways I've messed up. Maybe I should just stay here.*

Maybe it was too late. He lifted his hands from his face, looking up. The stars had faded, the sky lightened to gray in the east.

Is that what you want?

He didn't know what he wanted. He watched, minutes ticking by, as the gray canopy crept up the heavens, till pink sky etched the mountains black, and the stones around him glowed. Even as the light grew, so grew the understanding that it would take more strength to go back, to face Amy, to apologize, than to stay here. He wanted to make it up to her. But he didn't know if he was that strong.

He didn't know if he *wanted* to be that strong.

He closed his eyes, not wanting to stay, not wanting to go, drained. He tried again with God. "Even if I wanted to talk to You—and I don't—I wouldn't know what to ask for."

Thy will be done.

Shawn heard the words clearly. He didn't know if he spoke them to the invisible god of if they were spoken to him by that invisible god. "Just give me some sort of life back. I'll try to be nicer. I already told You that."

Pink dawn blazed across half the sky, lighting it clear to the top, chasing the dark of night away. Shawn sagged against a stone, spent. He hummed the flute solo from *Bald Mountain*, chasing away the night and the chattering witches, wondering which century he'd walk out into.

And which one he truly wanted.

CHAPTER FIFTEEN

East of Inverness, 1314

Shawn took a deep breath, looking one last time around the towering stones. Pink and orange wisps of cloud blossomed over the eastern mountains. Mist drifted lazily across the frosty grass. He stepped out from the circle of stones, staring at the empty landscape, the rolling hills, trees in the distance. Nobody in sight. His heart kicked up its tempo, in jubilation and fear! He was back! He could apologize to Amy.

Fears crowded in on him as fast as the elation. She had every reason to throw his apology in his face. She might have found someone better. He didn't want to face all the other people he'd hurt.

But he had to get there. He scanned the horizon, thinking which way to walk. North, in the same footsteps he would have walked with Niall, around the tip of Loch Ness, and down into Inverness. There might be a town before then. He'd come to a highway. He'd....

A sound caught his ear.

He turned to the stones at his back, and heard it again. There were footsteps, and a man rounded the stones.

Shawn stared with a faint feeling of unreality at Niall, holding the reins of the two ponies.

Niall came forward, dropped a hand on Shawn's shoulder. "I'm sorry," he said. "And I'm sorry to say, I'm not."

Bannockburn, Present

Beaumont's eyes stayed on Brian, steady as a snake, throughout the interview in the psych ward, sitting in a bright pool of morning sunlight. Brian barely noticed, so eager was he to talk with the owner of the Claverock sword. Between his schedule, talks with hospital personnel regarding the man, and acquiring permissions, it had taken some doing to make the arrangements, but he had good news. "I'll be visiting you twice a week until they feel you're ready to go," Brian explained enthusiastically in Beaumont's archaic language. "You'll have to re-learn modern English. Starting next visit, 'tis all I'll speak. You'll have to keep your appointments. We have to figure out who you are and where you came from. You must be a professor, a historian, maybe an archaeologist." He grinned, slapping his hands together in enthusiasm. "I can't wait to learn all you know. I'm an avid historian myself, by profession and passion. You've a sword with Claverock's rearing lion on it!"

"Why would I not?" The man stared steadily. "I am the Lord of Claverock. I was born and raised there."

Brian smiled. "You must not say such things. They'll not release you."

The man stared at Brian. His stone face betrayed no emotion, though something inscrutable flickered deep in his eyes. "But I do live at Claverock."

"No one lives there." Brian laughed. "'Tis a ruin!"

"A *ruin*?" The word came out like a small explosion. "Are you mad? It is the finest castle in Northumbria!"

Brian smiled at the irony of a man who believed he knew Longshanks questioning anyone else's sanity. But he should have remembered that and broken the news more gently.

The man's thick, black brows creased over his nose. "Do you take me for a fool?"

Danger tingled through Brian. He brushed aside the nerves, saying "Not at all! You were hit hard in the head. There's been some brain injury."

"There's naught amiss with my brain." Beaumont rose, paced to the window, and stared out a long while. Finally, he turned. "What befell Claverock?"

"'Twas destroyed in the Jacobite Rising."

"Destroyed!" He took an agitated step forward, then stopped. "What is Jacobite?"

"The Jacobites were attempting to restore James...."

"I know no James!" Beaumont interrupted. "What happened after Bannockburn?"

"Bannockburn, aye." Brian chuckled. "There seems a lot of interest in that battle lately."

"Explain." Beaumont seated himself.

Fear tremored through Brian once more. He was being ridiculous, he told himself. The man sat on the couch, imperious and arrogant, but completely placid. "A mate of mine came to Creagsmalan not long ago. He had a girl with him; they were quite interested in a man called Niall Campbell who fought at Bannockburn."

"Niall Campbell of Glenmirril?" The arrogance dropped for a moment from Beaumont's voice. "You are acquainted with him?"

Brian laughed, a high-pitched giggle. "Not personally, you know now! He's been dead these seven hundred years."

"Seven hundred years," Beaumont murmured, the words as soft as the hiss of a snake. "'Tis not possible."

"More possible than *not* being dead these seven hundred years!" Brian giggled at his joke.

"What are they called?" Beaumont's voice snapped back to its usual steel.

"What are *who* called?"

"The man and girl who were asking after Campbell."

"Angus. Amy."

"Angus, Amy." Simon repeated. "Very good. And Bannockburn. The English destroyed Bruce's pathetic army, and then...?"

"'Twas not quite how it happened. Edward ran off the field. In fact, he was accompanied by Henry de Beaumont." He chuckled. "An ancestor of yours?"

"My uncle," Simon answered.

Brian frowned. "You must not say such things, if you wish to be let go."

Beaumont smiled, a thin, humorless tightening of the lips. "Of course I jest. Now, tell me every detail of the events following Bannockburn. Leave aside nothing."

Glenmirril, 1314

Shawn stopped his pony, looking down on Inverness. In warmer months, the sea would host a flurry of fishing boats, and the ship-building yard would bustle. Bruce had long since destroyed the stone castle of King David. It looked nothing like the Inverness he had known, the Inverness where he would one day walk through a cobblestone alley to pawn Amy's ring, or stumble drunk past Inverness Castle swinging a bucket of money with Caroline. He might have stumbled right past the ghostly echoes of the Black Friars in their Dominican Friary.

He wanted to be there, in his own time. Yet the understanding that had dawned in the stones clung to him. He wasn't sure he was strong enough to go back, to face all he'd done to Amy and so many other people.

"Very different, aye?" Niall sat astride his pony at Shawn's side.

"The river's the same," Shawn said. It felt good to have one man in this world who understood what he'd come from.

"'Tis hard to believe what it will become."

"Yeah, well." Shawn looked down the bank, guessing where the concert hall would be, where he'd swagger in, demanding they change the poster above the desk. "Guess we better *put the pedal to the metal*." He used English on the last words.

"*Pedal?*"

"*Gas pedal.* Makes the car go faster. They're expecting us."

They guided their mounts to the bridge crossing the Ness. As the sun waned and they came into Glenmirril territory, Shawn pulled his hood over his face, sinking into the persona of Brother Andrew. Joy rose in him at their first sight of Glenmirril's thick stone walls, jutting out into the Loch on a spit of land, as evening fell. A sentry called from the parapets as they approached, and Niall shouted his name.

"Ready to finish your honeymoon?" Shawn grinned, his disappointment briefly forgotten.

"Honeymoon?" Niall asked.

"Enjoying being married."

Niall laughed. "Aye!" He waved to the second sentry who appeared, and waved more enthusiastically as a flash of red hair burst up beside the two guards, waving back wildly. More faces appeared. Shouts rang out. The portcullis creaked as they cantered down the snowy hill toward the drawbridge dropping to greet them. Even as it met the edge of the moat, Allene burst from under the rising portcullis, and hurtled across the bridge. She skidded to a halt, looking from Niall to Shawn.

"You don't recognize your husband?" Niall chided her. He threw his leg over his pony and grabbed her around the waist. "Mind you, he's still got my hair. They must see only my face." He bent to kiss her as more people crowded the gate. He smiled, waved, and crossed the drawbridge, holding her hand and the pony's reins. He touched his hood, keeping it pulled around the tell-tale shorn hair. Shawn followed, leading his own pony, his head down and hood carefully covering his face. He was once again Brother Andrew, under vow of silence. He was relieved to see Christina standing to one side, regal and slender, her head high, her veil hiding all but a touch of glossy black hair.

Red burst through the crowd to take his hobin, reprimanding him. "You should have let me stay with you, Milord!"

"Don't call me that," Shawn hissed. But under his hood, he smiled. He was glad to see the kid again. It touched his heart, to have been missed.

MacDonald appeared, shouting greetings, demanding they be given room to get through, and hastening them to their chambers. "A hot bath," he shouted to the servants. "Send food." The heavy door fell to, sealing the four of them into their secret.

Niall pulled off his coif even as he snaked an arm around Allene's waist, his eyes glowing, pulling her close again.

MacDonald studied his hair. "Can it not grow faster," he demanded. "Now stop kissing her till you've some privacy!"

Niall winked. "You cut my *honeymoon* short, what did you expect?" Allene ducked her head, beaming and blushing all at once.

"What's a *honeymoon*?" MacDonald barked.

"Enjoying being married. Leave us alone for a few weeks and you'll be happier with my hair."

"You're impertinent!" Though he spoke to Niall, MacDonald glared at Shawn.

"He's the one all over her!" Shawn protested. "What are you looking at me for?"

Niall grinned more broadly still. A knock sounded on the door. He looked to Shawn, who had taken off the monk's robe. "You've my hair. Toss the robe over." Shawn tossed the gray robe, and Niall yanked it over his head, pulling up the hood as MacDonald opened the door. Allene stepped to Shawn's side as four burly menservants hauled in bathing tubs.

"One in each room," the Laird ordered. "Brother Andrew will be wanting a hot bath, too."

"Very kind of you," Shawn couldn't resist saying. "Brother Andrew deserves a hot bath after all he's done for you. You should give him a bag of gold, too."

MacDonald threw him a dirty look.

"Milord." The men bobbed their heads at Shawn. Shawn grinned, nodding back. A parade of women bearing buckets of steaming water followed. Niall melted into the wall, head down, hands tucked in his sleeves. The women finished, and Shawn took his prerogative as Allene's supposed husband to shoo the crowd out. "You can come out of your shell now," he said to Niall.

Niall tore the robe off. They shook hands, and Shawn disappeared into his own room, happy for once to be left in peace, to soak in the steaming water before a blazing fire, and look forward to a night indoors, under warm furs. It wasn't the home he'd wanted to reach, but it was better than the open road. And goading MacDonald was getting to be even more fun than goading Conrad.

Inverness, Present

I sink happily into lazy days of naps and board games and walks to a small pub for hot chocolate with Gavin and Hamish. Mairi admonishes them to quiet down, and stop pestering me. But I like their energy. They remind me of my young cousins, playing football with Shawn and jumping for the gifts he brought them. They keep my mind off the professor with my crucifix, our failed searches, and the question of what now?

Mairi is motherly, baking, splotches of flour on cheeks and elbows, hugging her sons, laughing with red cheeks, and forever pushing back a dark curl that insists on falling over one eye. She assures me she is there to listen, but doesn't pry.

Christmas Eve arrives. Angus gives me a keyboard. Tears prickle the corners of my eyes.

He beams. "Will you play?"

I touch the keys. O Holy Night flows from my fingers. I feel Shawn by my side, the day we arranged it; him pushing for thirteen chords, humming the trombone's bass line; setting lit tapers on his mahogany table beside the veal cutlets he'd prepared for us.

"Beautiful!" Mairi carries in cookies, scenting the room.

I smile through guilt. They don't know I inadvertently summoned Shawn. It feels wrong. I switch to I Wonder as I Wander.

Angus and I walk to midnight Mass. Snow floats around us like a snow globe; it crunches under our feet as we turn along the river. Electricity dances in the air between us.

"What?" Angus squeezes my hand, looking down and grinning.

I smile; the feelings stir more deeply. "Nothing."

"It's something," he teases. With a twinkle in his eye, he pulls me around a corner, against a brick wall. The feelings grow. I look over my shoulder, like a teenager afraid of being caught.

He glances around. "I'm sorry," he says, "I didn't realize...."

My confusion shows.

"It's Eden Court," he explains. "The last place Shawn played. I've upset you."

"No." I glance at the theater. "I didn't even notice." I laugh. "That's good, right! It's just...." My cheeks flush in the cold night. "We're headed for Christmas Mass."

"So we are." He laughs, too. "And lucky we've a long, cold walk."

The Gothic stone church, rising on the banks of the River Ness, greets us with winking candles and sweet incense. On the altar, half a dozen Christmas trees soar to the ceiling, twinkling with white lights. Men flock to Angus, pumping his hand, clapping his back. A young couple whispers greetings. People stare at my bulging coat. My face grows hot. I stare at my shoes. He wraps his arm around me, introduces me, beaming, and my cheeks cool.

The choir bursts into song; trumpets and trombones shout joyfully. Angus glances back, squeezes my hand. As priests and acolytes march down the aisle, my mind leaps to Shawn. Is he celebrating a medieval Christmas at Glenmirril? Do they have trees, or exchange presents? Gray guilt crouches on my shoulder, to be thinking of Shawn here, now. I stare at the pew before me.

Mass ends with another blast of triumphal brass. We join the flow of parishioners to the snow globe world outside. A pair of little old ladies pierces me, and my obvious pregnancy, with narrowed eyes. "Mrs. MacGonagal," Angus whispers to me; he waves to her. "She invites me now and again for dinner."

"I don't think she'll be inviting you anymore." My spirits, already burdened by guilt, sink further. "Angus, you shouldn't have brought me. You've cost yourself friends."

He shrugs. "Will I cast stones at you, Amy? I've done exactly what they think I have. Just not with you. I love you and I want you by my side." He kisses my nose, and waves to the other lemon-faced old lady. She tightens wrinkled lips at him, raises her nose, and turns away as snow drifts, sparkling, into her blue-rinsed hair.

CHAPTER SIXTEEN

Bannockburn, Present

Rob arrived first, carrying a vegetable tray, and admiring her black outfit. Sparkles dusted the hem and left sleeve. Her hair hung to her waist in a thick braid. "You look great," he said.

"Doesn't she?" Angus came down the narrow hall from the kitchen. He held out a dark amber bottle, sweating with condensation, to Rob. "Good to see you. Have a Guinness."

Rob shook his head, his jaw clenched. He edged past Angus and the festoons of garlands, taking his vegetables to the kitchen.

Amy looked down the hall after him. The corridors of Glenmirril flashed in her mind; she wondered if they were also festooned with garlands. "I'm sorry," she whispered to Angus.

"'Tis not yours to be sorry." Angus didn't lower his voice. "You did nothing." He wrapped his arms around her.

The doorbell screeched. They broke apart, Amy reaching for the door. Sinead and Siobhan stood side by side on her doorstep, in matching red dresses. Matching black curls bobbed in ponytails; they held out matching gifts in identical red foil paper, grinning mischievously. Amy smiled. They'd had their fun, and now their mother gave their matching ears a yank, saying, "Behave, mind!" She pushed them back toward the kitchen, making way for the sudden flood of students, parents, and neighbors.

Soon, the house rang with laughter, songs, Sinead's brother playing reels on his violin, and phone calls to and from the States, to Rose, her parents, Celine, Aaron, Dana. "Rob's here," she told her. She squeezed through the crowd to find him in the kitchen, and passed the phone over. Pressing a hand to one ear against the noise, he slipped out to the back yard. Amy stood alone in her kitchen; counters and garbage overflowed with cups and boxes and wrappers from vegetables, crackers, and sausages. She felt, abruptly, the loss of the Christmas party she would have attended at Shawn's home. Glenmirril would have minstrels, venison, herb-scented rushes on the floor. Shawn would be in the thick of it all, quaffing ale and enjoying himself to the fullest—every morsel, every dance. She shook herself from her longing, and stretched on tiptoe to take down the crackers sent by the orchestra.

She jumped at the touch of hands on her waist. "They're all in the front room," Angus whispered. He took the crackers from her hands.

Her heart gave a jump. She laughed. "Someone could come in."

"Then we'd best hurry." In the corner behind the table, he kissed her, taking his time. Shawn fled her mind. She wrapped her arms around Angus's neck, returning the kiss. Angus pulled back, grinning, and they returned to the party. It flew into the evening with a dizzying whirl of conversation and laughter. Sinead's brother's fiddle grew more lively, while guests took turns singing. Finally, by twos and threes, people slipped away, glowing with happiness, into the night. When the last guest left, Angus patted the back of the couch. "Rest your feet."

She was halfway to the couch when she suddenly pushed herself back up. "Rob!" she said. "When did he leave?"

Angus looked around, as if Rob might be hiding behind the couch. He stuck his head out the living room door, peering down the hall. "No, he's gone," Amy confirmed. "He left without saying good-bye." She sank to the couch. "What in the world is *he* mad about?"

Angus took her hand. "He thought he'd look for Shawn for a wee bit, and then you'd go home with him, grateful and thoroughly besotted with him in his shining armor."

Amy sighed.

"Never mind him," Angus said. "Sit tight while I get you tea."

He returned almost immediately, laying a large, manila envelope in her lap. "'Twas on the table." She looked from its blank face to his, inquiringly. He shrugged.

She slit it open and tipped it. Her ring and crucifix tumbled out. Relief flooded her. "Thank goodness," she breathed, as she pushed the ring onto the finger that had been so long bare.

"Good to have them back?" Angus dropped the crucifix over her neck, lifting her heavy hair out of the cord.

Amy nodded. "They're my only tangible proof I'm not crazy."

"There's more." He pulled out a sheaf of papers, topped by a hand-scrawled note from Rob, and handed it to her.

Someone saw Shawn in Aberdeen. Thought you'd care, but you were busy in the corner with Angus.

Her mouth tightened. "*That's* why he's mad." She handed it to Angus.

His eyes flickered over it. He crunched it into a ball and tossed it aside.

"Do you think other people see it the same way," she asked. "My boyfriend disappears, the father of my child, and I jump right on to the next man?"

"Well, no, you've not jumped on me." He spoke so dryly, she missed the humor till he said, "More's the pity." He grinned. "But Rob needn't know that."

She laughed.

"Besides, he was *not* your boyfriend." Angus took her hand. "You'd broken up with him. Rob is hurt. Don't let him steal your peace. Let's see what the professor says." He ran his finger under the words on university letterhead. "Style accurate for time claimed," he murmured. "Correct in all details. One of twelve made by the Monks of Monadhliath."

"Niall mentioned them," Amy said in excitement.

"I've heard the name," Angus said. "But I know little about them."

"Do you think the monk he traveled with was from Monadhliath?"

"Seems a good guess." Angus slid the sheet to the back of the pile, revealing a letter from Historical Scotland. They read silently, and Angus turned to her, smiling. "The experts agree they're exactly what you say. And look." He held out the report, stabbing with a thick finger at a line halfway down. "There's a blessing and prophecy associated with each of these crucifixes."

"Does it say what are they?" Amy asked.

"Here." Angus turned to a sheet of stationary with a muted, tie-dye background. Strong strokes of purple ink, said, *I'd like to tell you about the blessing and prophecy in person. I'll be down to Stirling for Hogmanay, if you can meet then. Helen O'Malley*

Glenmirril, 1314

Glenmirril closed in on them for the winter. It wasn't the stark existence Shawn had dreaded. The walls felt safe, tall and imposing, shutting out enemies and the loch's chilling winds. Torches and blazing hearths gave heat and cheerful light to every room. Tapestries appeared on the walls for warmth, filling the castle with vibrant colors. Adam's widow stopped before them with her daughters, pointing up, telling the stories woven into them. Garlands and extra candles decked the great hall for the season of Christ Mass.

The dreaded daily Mass upon which the Laird insisted didn't seem as bad as Shawn remembered from Stirling. He looked forward to Red's presence, kneeling at his side. He even found it relaxing, knowing it would be his only rest for many hours. Latin incantations drifted through his head as soothing as burbling water in a fountain, now and again taking on meaning as Allene resumed tutoring him in Latin and French.

Posing as Niall, he worked with Colin, Lachlan, and Owen, training boys, reviewing the armory, and talking to the smith about repairs to weapons. Red and the Laird were equally happy with Red's new work in Glenmirril's stables, and when Red wasn't with the ponies, he tagged after Shawn, dutifully remembering to call him Sir Niall.

With Niall living out of sight until his hair grew, Shawn sat with Niall's mother and sister at dinner, encouraging their reminiscences, so he could repeat them as his own memories if need be. Musicians played after meals, and Shawn looked forward to his turn with the harp.

"Your music is much changed these days," Lord Morrison commented after dinner one night.

Shawn grinned. "I've been out and about, meeting people, hearing new music." He touched his fingers to the strings and played some Air Supply, weaving a little *Sumer is Icumen* into the verses. But he made a point of having Niall teach him more of the usual repertoire, including the *Falkirk Lament*.

Allene spent her days in the room with Niall, joining Shawn for meals with a smile that confirmed she was happy to have Niall back, and no one objected when they ate and left the hall quickly.

After one meal, Niall's mother cornered him as he hung Niall's harp on its peg. She was a tall, thin woman, beautiful for her years, with smooth skin, a swan-like neck and silky strawberry blonde hair braided and drawn up under a barbet. A blue surcoat fell to her slippered toes. With a recorder piping a lively tune in the gallery, she gripped his shoulders and peered at him. "You're changed, Niall," she said. "Since your injury retrieving our cattle, you often seem...different."

Shawn inclined his head respectfully. "I trust for the better, Milady." He kept his face straight. "Do tell Brother Andrew he's been a good influence."

She cocked her head, trying to decide if this was a jest, of the sort for which he was known. She smiled then, kissed his cheek with dry lips, and said, "I've a concern, Niall. I asked Allene about the crucifix, and she doesn't have it."

"The crucifix?" He vaguely recalled something about Niall giving a crucifix to Amy.

She frowned. "Aye, the crucifix from your father. Surely you're not so changed you've forgotten your promise to wear it always and give it to Allene at your marriage?"

"I've not." Shawn was already thinking up a story to explain its absence.

"Then why did you not give it to Allene?"

"Why?"

"Yes, Niall. Why?" She looked stern. "You were ever one to keep your word. Where's the crucifix?"

"I lost it while I was with Douglas." Years of lying paid off. Words poured out. He met her eyes with sorrow for his loss. He took her hands in his, his body language telling her his grief matched her own. "It was torn off in a fight with a Sassenach. I was lucky to escape with my life."

Allene appeared at his side, her hand fluttering to his arm as light as a butterfly. "Niall." She emphasized his name. "You didn't tell me about that."

"I'd no wish to upset you," he said. And to Niall's mother, "I'll ask the monks to make me another one."

Allene smiled. "Now, you must be sure to tell me the *whole* story. *Upstairs.*" She turned to Niall's mother. The woman had become pale. "My Lady," Allene gasped, taking her elbow. "What is amiss?"

They ushered her to the nearest bench, easing her down. Her hand went to her chest, and she closed her eyes. "Niall, did you not keep it safe under your shirt? The monks cannot replace that crucifix. Had you no idea?"

He dropped to the bench beside her, sobering. "No. Tell me."

Stirling, Present

Amy and Angus ran laughing, hand in hand over a centuries-old stone bridge, crossing what had been a moat, to escape the singing, dancing, and shouting of Stirling's Hogmanay crowd. The lively music of a piper and his band followed them down the hill. At the graveyard, Amy stopped, gasping for breath, a hand to her growing stomach, and looked back. Spotlights swooped over the ancient stone fortress above.

"Rob will be fine." Angus led her to the cemetery. Tombstones shone white in the moonlight.

She shivered, thinking of Rob, left behind in Stirling's courtyard.

"Is that for being in a graveyard or the cold?" he asked.

She nestled into his arm. "Both." A deep-winter weekend with Shawn's mother flickered across her mind. It had been colder, but the wind here cut, with the damp chill of the sea. She pulled her hat tight. The day had passed in a pleasant laze of playing violin, and lounging on the couch while Angus rubbed her feet and told stories of his childhood. Only Rob's daily visit marred the day. "I guess he'll be hurt," she sighed. "But he invited himself."

"He did, at that; he'll be fine. Here's an interesting tombstone." Angus stopped before a large Celtic cross, rising above their heads. An angel knelt in profile on its side, wings arched high, holding a carved marble bouquet. Angus touched gloved fingers to the faded etching, squinting to read. "Alex Campbell." Amy's heart leapt at the name. "1767-1800, beloved husband, father, blacksmith." Angus turned to her. "Ironic. We've searched far and wide for anything on Niall Campbell. D' you think this could be one of his descendants?"

"His brothers died before Bannockburn. He mentioned a nephew." Amy touched the etchings. "But Shawn was living under his name; this could be *his* descendant."

"Makes you question all you know of your own genealogy." Rising, Angus led her deeper among rounded tombstones and towering crosses, stopping occasionally to read names or decipher dates. "It makes me think on how I live my life," he said, "when I think of the people behind the names." He stopped at a bench, dusting off the snow. They sat, looking across the moonlit landscape, under acres of stars tossed across the city-lit sky, toward Ben Lomond and the Trossachs. "Were they kind? Were their children sad or grateful when they died?"

The beat of a rock band thumped down from the castle. Angus wrapped his arm around her.

She laid her head on his shoulder. "Maybe there's really no chance, anyway."

"Of him coming back? I'd never have thought any of it possible." After another minute, he said, "One of my mates found Shawn's marks at Stirling."

Amy sat up straight, staring at him. "I didn't find anything there."

"No, you wouldn't. The current buildings weren't there in 1314. My mate is working on older parts. Once he knew what to look for, he found two."

"*Two*," she breathed. "When did you find out?"

"He called just before I came for you. I doubted Rob wanted to hear it."

"Definitely not," she agreed, and leaned back into his shoulder, contemplating Shawn's presence at Stirling. Singers joined the backbeat at the castle above them, their microphoned voices drifting down unintelligibly. A young couple ran down the path, clutching one another's arms, and laughing. They glanced at Amy and Angus on the bench, and ran faster. "It's strange," Amy said, "to think Shawn or Niall might be right here in this spot, seven hundred years ago. It's like listening for ghosts."

Angus laughed. "We *are* in a graveyard. Let me see that crucifix again." She lifted the leather thong over her head. Angus took it. "Twelve hundreds." He turned it over, and ran a finger down the white line on the back. "Hard to believe."

She cupped her hand around his, and they studied it together. The tiny figure of Christ was carved from the same piece of wood, each feature in exquisite detail. He wore a crown such as the Bruce might, the crown of a warrior king rather than a prince of state. Each minute rib stood out, and the gash in his side gaped. The artist had carved each finger, each fold of the cloth at his waist. His arms stretched out in an almost relaxed fashion, a nail piercing each hand. He gazed upwards. Amy turned it over, seeking any indication of its artist. "Niall said the monks made it for his father."

A sudden chill shook her. She glanced up at the castle shining in the spotlights. The music had grown louder. "We should get back," Angus said. But first, he leaned in to kiss her, a long, slow kiss in the moonlight, the kind that left her wanting more. He grinned. "You won't toss me over for Rob now?"

Amy laughed, her eyes and her insides both warm. "*Definitely* not now."

He took her hand, helping her off the bench. "Watch, now. 'Tis a wee bit icy."

"Look out!" Amy exclaimed. He turned, colliding with a girl running down the path. A wild gypsy skirt swirled around medieval-style leather boots. Dreadlocks sprang from her head. The crucifix flew from his hand, landing in a soundless puff of snow on the path. The girl stooped to grab it, apologizing. She looked at the crucifix. Her eyes went wide. "The Monadhliath Crucifix!" she said. "You can't possibly be Amy and Rob?"

Glenmirril, 1314

Allene all but dragged Shawn to her chambers, slamming the door and yelling for Niall. "Keep your voice down," Niall called, from the wide window sill where he played the recorder.

"Were you playing *A-Train?*" Shawn demanded.

"With some improvements." Framed by the gray stone arch, Niall demonstrated a fingering.

"You can't improve *The A-Train,*" Shawn said indignantly.

"I think we've weightier matters," Allene bit off. To Niall, she said, "Your mother's quite beside herself and rightly so. Did you not know about the crucifix?"

"It goes up higher when you start the bridge." Shawn reached for the recorder.

"Not with my improvements." Niall held the instrument back out of Shawn's grip, nearly out the chilly casement.

"What are you yapping on about?" Allene snapped at Shawn. "Did you not understand the importance of your mother's—his mother's—words?"

Shawn's hand dropped. He turned to Allene. "Actually, no, I don't see the importance at all. And that, by the way, is very different from not *understanding.* It's a silly superstition."

Allene's hand flew to her mouth. "How can you be so ignorant," she gasped. "Have you no respect for the saints!"

Niall swung his feet to the floor and came to her, laying a reassuring hand on her shoulder. "He will when he understands."

"Dream on," Shawn told him. "It's pretty gruesome."

"What does that mean?" Not waiting for an answer, Allene snatched the recorder from Niall, and pushed him into a chair at the table. "That crucifix was not made by the monks of Monadhliath at all. Niall, 'twas not just any crucifix."

"Yeah, you're better off rid of it." Shawn shuddered. "You're not going to believe what's in that thing. Amy is going to *freak* when she finds out!"

Stirling, Present

The girl's long dreadlocks fell around the crucifix like a hemp curtain. "The Monadhliath crucifix!" she exclaimed. Her print skirt swirled around leather boots. "Where did you get it?"

"From a friend. I'm Amy, but this is Angus, not Rob." Amy glanced at Angus. His eyes were on the woman, his hand extended for the crucifix.

With a longing gaze at it, she placed it in the wool palm of his glove. He eased it back over Amy's head and tucked it inside her sweater.

"Sorry." Moonlight flashed off the stud piercing the girl's tongue. "They're just so unusual. Only a dozen were made, representing the twelve apostles."

A shiver racked Amy, as the cold worked its way under her coat. "How do you know about Monadhliath?" she asked.

"I know I *look* like I'm eighteen, but I'm Helen O'Malley, professor of medieval studies." She thrust her hand out to Amy and Angus in turn. "We were going to meet tomorrow, but...do you have time now?" Her eyes shone with excitement.

Amy looked to Angus questioningly.

"I'm dying to hear more," he answered.

"Come down the street. I'll buy you a drink!" Helen beamed. "You look like you're after dying of cold."

Minutes later, crushed in a booth at the back of a crowded pub, the excitement of the chance meeting, the warmth of the packed bodies and a hot coffee, all brought a glow to Amy's cheeks. She wrapped her hands around her mug. The tea's warmth trailed down her throat and curled in her stomach like a cat before the hearth. With the boisterous Hogmanay crowd buzzing around them, Helen launched into the story.

"St. Columba left Ireland in the sixth century. Lots of stories why— plagiarism, wars, promises to save souls, seeking solitude—finding a desert in the sea, they called it, in those times. He went to Iona."

Amy and Angus exchanged glances.

Helen missed it, caught up in detailing the various theories about Columba's journey to Iona. From anyone else, the tangents might have annoyed Amy, eager as she was to hear about Niall's crucifix. But Helen, an earth mother with piercings and a Ph.D. passion for early Christianity, captured her attention. Apart from her looks, she might have been Rabbie, telling his stories as Niall had described.

"Columba went up Loch Ness to the Pictish chief, Brude, where Urquhart now stands. Everyone knows that story," Helen said enthusiastically.

Amy had read of King Brude barring his gates against Columba, the bolts springing back at the saint's prayers, and Brude's subsequent conversion. But she smiled at the woman's assumption that everyone knew the story.

"What's less well known," Helen added, "is that Columba went on to Glenmirril. Are you familiar with it?"

"Very." Amy felt Angus's eyes on her.

"Fascinating place. People see things there. I'd not go in it at night." Helen shuddered. "That American musician who disappeared, now, they said he spent the night there and wasn't the same afterward. Not the first time I've heard that sort of thing."

"Really?" The baby chose that moment to kick hard. Amy gasped, laughed, touched her stomach.

"Due soon?" Helen smiled at Angus.

"Six weeks." He smiled at Amy, his eyes reflecting the tiny candle flame dancing on the table. "Columba, Glenmirril?" He squeezed Amy's hand under the table.

"Yes. He stayed there a few weeks." Helen returned to her narrative.

That lord, too, was converted, and so enthusiastic that he demanded Columba send back monks to nurse his newborn faith to maturity. Through the years, as the wooden stockade gave way to stone walls, and the fortress grew into a motte and bailey castle, as children were born and grew and died, the monks were as much a part of castle life as the hills and loch.

As more revelers sought the warmth of the pub, and the noise grew, Helen leaned forward, recounting miracles and prophecies of Columba and his monks at Glenmirril. "A few centuries later," she finished, "a lord granted them land, across Loch Ness, but they never forgot their roots with Columba."

"I haven't found any of this on the internet," Amy said.

"No, you wouldn't," Helen replied.

Angus raised a hand, summoning a waitress. "Something to eat?" he asked Amy.

Amy blinked at the noisy pub, so engrossed had she become in Columba's miracles, in the loch and hills and life of Glenmirril.

"Anything for you, Helen?" Angus asked.

"Oh, fish pie?" Helen looked around as Angus ordered, seeming as surprised as Amy to find herself in the pub. "They're very ascetic." She jumped back into the topic. "Small and private, even today. They copy manuscripts by hand, pray, and farm everything they need. They're strict vegetarians, probably as a result of the blessed knife."

"Which was what?" Amy asked.

"Columba blessed a knife, somewhat absent-mindedly, while he wrote." Helen's piercing clicked on her teeth as she spoke, drawing Amy's attention with its rhythm. "Only later did he ask if it would harm man or beast. When the monks said it was for slaughtering animals, he put a blessing on it, that it would never harm men or cattle. They found the poor butcher boy outside, struggling with all his might to kill a cow for the monks' dinner. Columba's blessing prevented him doing so.

"So they melted it down and used the metal to coat farm tools, so no one would be harmed by them. And believe it or not, this relates to the crucifix."

The waitress arrived, setting out fish pies and coffees. Amy dug into hers, grateful to fill her stomach, while Helen continued. "Those implements eventually went to Monadhliath, and when they were too old to serve, they were again melted down. Did you notice the bands of metal around the vertical beam of the crucifix?"

Setting down her fork, Amy lifted it from inside her sweater, and pulled it over her head. Helen dug rhinestone-studded glasses from inside layers of clothing. Delicate chains dangled alongside her cheeks when she donned them. "Here!" She pointed triumphantly. "And here." Thin bands circled the beam, top and bottom. "Now, see the back?" She turned the crucifix around, revealing the inlaid white shard. "Apart from yours, I've only ever seen one of these.

Most of the twelve are lost. This is just incredible." Excitement hummed in Helen's voice. "Did you ever wonder what it was?"

"Stone?" Amy guessed. "Wood?" It shone, a soft gleam, in the candle light. Beside them, a large man shouted with laughter, and the whole group slugged down their pints.

Helen leaned across the table. The candle flickered over her features. One of her dreadlocks fell forward. "It's a relic. It's bone from St. Columba himself."

Glenmirril, 1315

It was another week before Christina, gowned in garnet red, her glossy hair swept back in a headdress, approached Shawn after dinner, drifting toward the bench where he sat after playing the harp. It was the first time he'd seen her clearly and close-up. She had a smooth, porcelain complexion. Fine eyebrows arched over eyes even deeper blue than Amy's, framed by thick, black lashes. She was as beautiful as the melodic, husky voice he'd heard in the confessional. He felt the light leap up in his eyes.

Allene glided across the rush-strewn room, skirting a juggler in blue and green, and patting a hunting hound's great head on the way. She leaned close, her small hand on the shoulder of his heavy tunic. He tore his eyes from Christina. "There's a little affection I didn't expect," he teased, as her red curls brushed his cheek.

"Dream for," she said in English.

"That's dream on."

"Regardless, 'tis not affection, but a reminder you must do naught that would put Niall in a bad light."

"She says to the man who earned Niall knighthood."

"Who says? I said it."

"Just an expression. And here I thought you were jealous. Whatever." He winked at her. "You should kiss me so people don't think you're mad at him already."

She kissed his cheek swiftly.

"That won't convince anyone." He grinned, enjoying taunting her.

"Dream for, and keep your hands and eyes to yourself," she murmured. As Christina seated herself, Allene moved away, skirting the juggler once again, to rejoin her father.

Christina offered her hand. Shawn kissed her fingertips. It set his lips tingling. "Milady." His father would have loved this!

Christina smiled, showing deep dimples. "The likeness continues to astound me," she said softly.

Shawn, too, lowered his voice, leaning close, flirtation forgotten. "You understand no one knows there are two of us."

She nodded. "The Laird paid me a visit ere my cloak came off. He was most clear."

Shawn looked around the great hall. With the meal almost over, their table was deserted, though people, dogs, and servants milled and scurried around the hall, some talking, some watching a juggler whirl knives. Allene and the Laird watched him from their place at the head table. Satisfied they had a few minutes, he turned back to her. "How much did he explain?"

"Only that no one knows there are two of you."

"How much has Bessie figured out?"

"Bessie is enamored of her savior, Fionn of Bergen. It has not gone over her head that the man called Niall—you—looks very like him. However, she shaved Fionn, and you've a full head of hair, so she believes Fionn was in the dungeon, MacDougall saw the resemblance but was mistaken, and that MacDonald, for his own reasons, helped me rescue Fionn. I told her Fionn returned to Norway and warned her to speak no more of it."

Shawn shook his head. "Even *I* might have a hard time keeping all these stories straight."

Christina studied him. "You don't speak like a Norseman. Where *do* you come from?"

"Now that's an interesting story," Shawn said, "and one I don't feel like re-telling. For now, we'll just say we're both here, we're both Niall." At the far end of the hall, a pair of men rushed in, escorted by one of MacDonald's men. They rubbed their hands together. Snow fell from their cloaks. Shawn glanced at them as they hastened to the head table, then turned back to Christina. "How did they treat you?"

She lowered her eyes.

"Did he hurt you?" Shawn demanded.

Red crept up her cheeks. "My father-in-law is none too well liked here. But he did stay Duncan's hand."

Shawn studied her flushed cheeks and lowered eyes. "For what price? I haven't forgotten what you hinted to him to get him out to that glen."

"Not so high as that. The chaos in the glen, your quick wits at Niall's wedding, and James Douglas's demand for my speedy return all gave me the miracle I prayed for."

At the head table, Hugh rose and headed toward Shawn. Allene picked up her skirts and hastened to the stairs in the corner.

Shawn snorted. "We cause a little chaos, my quick wits as you say, Douglas's demands…no miracle there."

She smiled. "And was it man's doing that brought together two men who look exactly alike, to cause such confusion? Are you always so quick to take credit from God?" Shawn studied her face, the depth of her eyes.

Hugh clapped a hand on Shawn's shoulder. "You're needed below."

Stirling, Present

"A bone?" Amy's insides went cold. The baby kicked, sending a ripple across her abdomen. "A *human* bone?"

"'Tis very common." Angus slid an arm around her shoulder. "Relics of saints. Bones, bits of clothing, pieces of the true cross." He took a mouthful of fish pie.

"But St. Columba was the sixth century," Amy protested, her food forgotten. "How did they get his bones in the late thirteenth century?"

"Oh, 'twas made much earlier than that." Helen waved a hand. "The history you sent is just wrong."

"But Niall said it was made in 1297," Amy said. "Niall's the friend who gave it to me."

"Maybe Niall himself didn't know its true history," Angus suggested.

Helen returned to her story. "Of the dozen, we can trace only a few. One went back to Iona, one to Beauly. Two to Glenmirril—one to MacDonald in 1296 when Edward came through on his way to Urquhart. It seems to have granted a miracle, so a year later, his steward, James Campbell...."

Amy started, her fork clattering to her plate. Past and present swirled around her for a second.

Helen stopped. "It's ironic you got it from someone named Niall, because that was the name of James's youngest son. James went to Monadhliath specifically because Niall was his only surviving son of seven. James gave them a year's wages, and they gave him the crucifix, with a blessing." She straightened, donned an unsmiling face proper for quoting ancient blessings, and intoned: "'May this crucifix, by God's gracious mercy and St. Columba's intercession, draw together father and son for their mutual protection and benefit.'" In the dim pub, with candlelight casting shadows across her face, she became, for a moment, an ancient prophetess, rather than a dread-locked, tongue-pierced young professor of the twenty-first century.

Amy's mind leapt to the train, to Niall telling her of the men of Glenmirril returning from war, his tall, slender mother keening over his father; bagpipes skirling; heavy wax candles flickering over his father's body in the chapel, while he huddled, a child of eight, beside his mother through the long night. "But James died a year later at Falkirk." The words slipped out, softly.

Helen cocked her head. "Few people know that detail."

"We've been researching," Angus explained quickly.

"Father and son." Amy leaned forward. "It didn't protect James. He died right after." She turned to Angus. "It makes sense, doesn't it?"

"What are you on about?" Helen demanded. Beside her, the Hogmanay crowd shouted with laughter and called for more beer.

"I need to call Shawn's mother." Amy said to Angus. "His father did some genealogy."

"Shawn? Wait, stop!" Helen's hand came down hard on the table. "Shawn

Kleiner, the musician? You knew him?"

"Are you all right, Amy?" Angus squeezed her hand under the table. "We can leave."

"No." Amy spoke as if from a dream. "He was my boyfriend," she told Helen.

"O.M.G!" Helen spit out the letters, a black-nailed hand to her mouth. "I am *so* sorry. I hope I've not said anything stupid."

"No, it's okay." Flustered, Amy gulped her lukewarm coffee. "He *wasn't* the same when he came back. Do you know how I can trace Niall Campbell's descendants? Do you have a card so I can contact you again?"

"We have some genealogy at the university." Helen reached under the table, and came up with a card in tie-dyed swirls. Amy barely noticed the medieval script. Niall's and Shawn's identical faces wavered before her eyes.

"It starts to make sense," she said to Angus. And to Helen, "You said there's a blessing *and* a prophecy. What's the prophecy?"

"Oh, the prophecy, now," Helen leaned forward, her eyes wide. "That's been lost for centuries. If there's any hope of finding *that*, it's with the monks themselves."

CHAPTER SEVENTEEN

Glenmirril, 1315

With an uneasy glance at Shawn, Conal turned to the Laird and bowed. "I'll choose men immediately, My Lord." He and Morrison swished their cloaks behind them and disappeared into the dark tunnels.

Darnley clapped Shawn on the shoulder. "We've need of you here, Niall. The young men need looking to." He followed the others. The dungeon room stank of cold decay; the damp dug into Shawn's bones. But he, Hugh, and MacDonald remained behind.

"What just happened here?" Shawn asked. He'd just taken part in a meeting lit by heavy flickering torches, with the wizened Lord Morrison, Lord Darnley, MacDonald, Hugh, and Conal. Glenmirril, Bruce's messenger had relayed, must send men sooner than expected to fight John of Lorn at the Isle of Man. Morrison and Darnley had argued back and forth about who to send, Darnley insisting Niall knew Bruce's ways best, while Morrison, casting sideways glances at Shawn, pressed for Conal to go. Through it all, rivulets of condensation dripped from heavy, moldering beams above.

"Were you not listening?" MacDonald snapped. "Come along now." He led Shawn, still protesting, into the dark maze of dank tunnels.

"What you're about to see," Hugh rumbled, in his version of a whisper, "is not to be spoken of to anyone."

Hugh's torch crackled near Shawn's ear. "Get that thing any closer," Shawn hissed back, "and I'll burn to death before I get a *chance* to speak to anyone."

"You speak of it," Hugh muttered, "and burn to death is exactly what you'll do. We've done well for ourselves, keeping a few secrets."

"Mind now." Ahead, the Laird lowered his torch. He seemed for a moment to disappear into the dark wall.

Shawn squinted and saw he'd turned down a narrow tunnel. The ceiling pressed close overhead. With his stomach lurching at the thought of rats in the dark, and Hugh nudging him from behind, he followed the hastily moving flame. It veered left, and finally stopped. MacDonald rapped sharply on what Shawn first took to be the wall. But as he approached it, he saw it was a door, smeared over with dirt. It swung open, revealing Niall's face.

"Curiouser and curiouser," Shawn muttered in English.

"Is that proper grammar in your time?" MacDonald asked.

"Not even close. Unless your name is Alice." Shawn followed him through the door. He stared in amazement. "And maybe mine is, because I've just gone down a rabbit hole." The low ceiling that had left him claustrophobic outside in the tunnel exploded to two stories high inside. "Holy subterranean cathedral, Batman," Shawn whispered. The whole place, he guessed, was three times the size of the great room in his own home, back in his own time. A dozen torches flickered from black sconces in the walls, illuminating a worktable laden with hammers, planes, drills and an adze. Pieces of wood lay on the table, or stood on the floor, surrounded by curls of wood shavings. In the far wall was a large recess. Dozens of tiny candles in colorful glass holders lit a life-sized carving of Christ, hanging on the wall in the niche. A kneeler stood at the feet of the figure. "It's the Bat Cave!" he said.

Hugh scratched his head. "There are no bats. Why would ye say such a thing?"

Shawn didn't answer. He was running his hand over a harp frame, six feet tall. Something that must be the base sat on the work bench. He looked to Niall.

Niall shrugged. "I told him about Celine's harp. Perchance you can tell him how the pedals work."

Shawn studied the tools on the table. There had been a man in his father's re-enactment unit who specialized in woodwork. He'd once helped Shawn make a birdhouse, which he'd later painted with his father and mounted in a tree in their back yard. "Who uses these things?" he asked.

Hugh and Niall both looked to MacDonald, who glared at Shawn.

"What?" Shawn protested. "I'm just asking. What's wrong with asking?"

Niall cleared his throat, and Shawn saw he was grinning at the Laird, who still looked surly. "I suspect," Niall told him, "that his time is different and he'll think naught of it."

"Very different," Shawn said. "We don't have amazing underground secret caves in our homes." His words bounced back to him in rich harmonies. He walked the length of the cave, touching the walls, the sconces, the torches.

"In our time," Niall said, following him, "lairds don't do woodwork. 'Tis a menial job."

Stopping at the recess with the crucifix, Shawn turned, studying MacDonald. Understanding grew. "This is your workbench?"

"He's quite the gift." Hugh boomed the words like a challenge, defying Shawn to laugh. They echoed as if Hugh sang a concert.

Shawn smiled—his century's finest engineers would spend millions for these acoustics—as he looked up at the carving hanging in the niche. "Yes, he does." He turned back to them. "Niall's right. In my time, no one would think anything of you doing woodwork. They'd be impressed you're so good at it." He glanced at Hugh. "This place is supposed to be secret. Don't you think someone might hear you?"

MacDonald shook his head. His shoulders relaxed. "'Tis far underground. No one hears anything from here. Now, we've weighty matters to discuss with Niall."

Niall leaned against the work table, his arms across his chest. "Allene said only that a messenger has come from Bruce, before rushing me down."

Hugh and MacDonald exchanged a glance before MacDonald spoke. "Bruce needs our men to sail immediately to the Isle of Man."

Shawn looked from one to the other, perplexed by the sudden tension in the air.

Niall's skin appeared to take on a waxy sheen, and his shoulders to stiffen, but a dozen shadowy torches in a great cavern were hardly the best lighting. "Then I'll take the men to the Isle of Man," he said.

Shawn heard the heightened pitch of his voice. Battles were their normal fare, making Niall's tension inexplicable.

"Lord Morrison is of the mind Conal ought go this time," MacDonald said. "I'm inclined to agree."

Niall's face became as stiff as his shoulders.

"'Tis for the best, Lad." MacDonald spoke sadly, as a father to a son.

Niall glanced at Shawn, and back to a spot on the wall above MacDonald's shoulder. "As you wish, My Lord. Have I your leave to go?"

"You have."

Niall bowed, anger quivering in his body. He took a torch from the wall and stalked out of the cave, disappearing into the dark maw of the tunnels.

Hugh and MacDonald gazed at one another. A silent conversation passed between them.

Shawn cleared his throat. "He's pissed that someone else gets to risk life and limb? Are you people crazy?"

Hugh turned to him. "Peace, Shawn, 'tis none of your affair."

"Holy hidden chambers, Batman, it becomes my affair when I've just been allowed in on your secret Bat Cave."

"There are no bats," MacDonald snapped. "Is there ever a day you are not impertinent and foolish?"

"Third Monday of every month if I try hard," Shawn belted back. "I usually don't. But if I'm in on the secret cave, don't you think that entitles me to be part of the *in-crowd* here and know what's going on?"

"What's an *ink rowd*?" Hugh looked to MacDonald. "Something new that happened while I was hiding in the forest?"

"I should think not," MacDonald answered. "He's just being impertinent."

"I'm just saying, I'm sort of stuck with you people now. So what's up?" When they didn't answer, Shawn plowed through the facts, and all he'd learned since waking up in Stirling, and abruptly his eyes opened wide. "Isle. Water. He's just been demoted because he's scared of water."

MacDonald's demeanor flushed into a dark scowl. "I'll not have you speak so of Niall. 'Twas better for Conal to go for reasons beyond your understanding."

"Oh, no." Shawn shook his head, even as he warned himself he ought to stop while he was ahead—and still had one on his shoulders. "No, I nailed it, didn't I?" His voice bounced off the high ceilings. "Why don't you let me help him?"

Bannockburn, Present

My stomach twists as my phone rings Carol's, thousands of miles away. I hate having to tell her, each time we talk, that Rob has found nothing. This is her son, her only son. She'll be having breakfast, at this hour, in her sunny breakfast nook, maybe scratching her Great Dane's ears while her coffee maker burbles. Shawn and I built the oak bookshelves under the tall windows there, and organized books on cooking, birds, and gardening. He was funny, attentive, loving. We walked through the woods behind her new house that evening, hand in hand, and sat beside a creek, building our future.

The phone clicks, jolting me from memories.

"Carol?" The knot tightens in my stomach. "Happy New Year!"

"Amy! Happy New Year! How are you?" Carol's words have always sounded like a warm hug. But these days there's grief behind the warmth.

"I'm good." I feel Bruce's ring on my finger. I haven't told Carol about Angus.

"You're due soon. Is your mother coming to help?"

"No." I don't spell out my reasons for not asking her, or admit she's too busy with charity work, anyway.

There's a silence. Then Carol says, "I'll come. If you'd like." Hope brightens her voice.

My mind jumps to the office upstairs, covered in maps tracking Niall and Shawn. I can't let Carol see it. But I want Carol here. It's easy enough to lock the door. I smile. "I'd love it." Happy times with Carol rush back—helping her move, talking over coffee, looking through old photos. "I have so much to tell you," I say. But telling her about Angus will be hard.

"Rob calls every week," Carol says.

My grip tightens on the phone. I know she knows. "I didn't want to hurt you," I say. Rob's accusation stings. "I wasn't looking."

"Put on a cup of tea and we'll talk like we always did, okay?"

I head down the hall, my shoulders already relaxing. She always knows how to make things better. I turn on the water. "I'm filling the kettle." I click the knob on the stove. The flame whooshes and licks up around the edges of the kettle.

"I love my son dearly." Her voice catches; she takes a breath and speaks forcefully, as if beating back tears. "I pray every day for a miracle to bring

back the Shawn I knew. But I don't expect you to be alone your whole life. How's your tea?"

"Getting there." I reach, clumsy with my size, into the cupboard, and drop a teabag in my cup.

"He's good to you?" Carol asks. "His name is Angus?"

"He's wonderful." I lower my voice. "I was afraid you'd feel I'd forgotten Shawn."

"There's no forgetting Shawn," Carol says. She hesitates, then asks, "How will Angus feel? About me being there?"

I smile. "He'll like you."

The kettle whistles; damp mist shoots to the ceiling. I make my tea, and settle at my small table. Sunlight streams in the window from the garden. Carol talks about charity work and friends, while I sip tea and imagine Carol doing likewise in her breakfast room with the lace curtains, looking over a garden with bird feeders. "Can I ask a favor," I finally say. "Could you send the genealogy James did?"

"For your child?" Carol asks.

I pause. "Yes." The lie bothers me. "Sort of. Angus and I had an idea...a little different angle...." It's still a lie, and a lousy one. I stop while I'm ahead. "Could you send it soon?"

"The computer is in for repairs," she apologizes.

My heart sinks.

"I'll bring it when I come."

She'll be here soon enough. The tension in my shoulders eases. "It means a lot to me." My hand rests on my stomach. My baby twists under my hand. I can't tell Carol it might mean a lot to Shawn, too.

Glenmirril, 1315

Men and horses and crying women filled Glenmirril's courtyard while the sky was still gray overhead. Conal wheeled his garron, pacing up and down among thirty men, some mounted, some holding children in a last embrace, or kissing their wives. Lachlan stood in the shadow of a wall with Margaret, their noses touching, whispering farewells.

Conal rode up to Shawn and slid from his horse. He clapped Shawn's shoulder. "Niall. You'll lead the next one. All know you are the better fighter and leader." Conal seemed to be apologizing.

Confusion assailed Shawn; he was happy to keep a healthy distance between himself and medieval warfare. Then he remembered: Niall would feel shame at being passed over. Shawn put what he hoped was proper gravity on his face, and tried to think what answer would best serve Niall. "I've got plenty of work here," he said. "Think naught on it." He liked the sound of that phrase. He had to hold back a pleased grin.

Owen glanced up from tightening his pony's saddle strap, and cast his eyes down quickly when he saw Shawn catch his look. Shawn understood. Though no one spoke, they all knew why Niall wasn't going. He felt a rush of relief that he was here in Niall's place, that Niall himself didn't have to face the covert glances.

Shawn stepped to the center of the courtyard. "Mount up!" he bellowed at the top of his lungs. The men would see Niall with his head high. Maybe they would question their assumptions, and think they had it wrong. All around, a shout went up, as the last men hauled themselves onto their horses.

"We'll hold the Isle of Man for the Bruce!" Shawn pumped his fist in the air, and his cry echoed in the voices all around him, and he swore the men's faces lightened, relieved to see Niall in good spirits. He gripped Conal's hand, slapped him on the shoulder, and spoke as Niall would speak. "God go with you!"

Bannockburn, Present

In the days before Carol arrives, I walk through gray streets, bundled against January's chill, and huddled under a big umbrella, to doctor's appointments. I review my trips with Angus and jot notes on the time lines on the office walls. I research the battle of Jura, and, hand angled against the map on the wall, trail vivid yellow highlighter up the blue waterways from Ayr to Jura. Bruce took his men up the eastern passage; Angus Og to the west. I wonder if it was Niall or Shawn in that boat, and which path they took.

I join every genealogy site I can find, too impatient to wait for James's genealogy.

I return to visiting the church, sitting sometimes for hours in the quiet, and once again haunting the field, early in the morning, where I last saw Shawn and Niall. Ethereal mist rises off frosted grass. I wish I could step in among its ghostly shapes, find among its trailing tendrils some soul, lost between times, to tell me what happened to Shawn and Niall. Mist curls around my leather boots. I practice and teach and rub the silky ear of the velveteen rabbit between my fingers, thinking what to name this child, and I wonder how this became my life.

Carol arrives on a cold, windy day—not that there's any other kind in Scotland in January. She hugs me tightly at the airport, and steps back to search my eyes. I shake my head sadly. There was no news when she left the States twenty hours ago, and there's none now. On the train, she gives me the genealogy, packed in a large manila envelope. I take it with hope. Could it really go all the way back to the 1300s? Could it really tell me if Shawn and Niall are father and son?

She gazes out the window at the passing countryside. Just as I stayed, to be near Shawn and Niall, it means everything to her simply to be here, where her son was, where she hopes he still is. I can't tell her he is indeed here. Just not in this century. I hate withholding information. But I can't tell this insane story to a grieving mother.

A ham and noodle casserole waits in the crock pot at home. She smiles. "Did you know this is my favorite?"

"I remember Shawn going out of his way to make it for you once."

I serve up rich creamy noodles while she pours us water. I join her as she prays over her meal. Lifting her head, she says, "You said you and Angus were working on a different angle."

I stare at my hands, not knowing what to say, and revert to the nervous habit of twisting my ring.

"How unusual." Carol's heightened pitch breaks through my quest for a sane answer.

I glance up. She's reaching to touch the red stone. Panic flutters in my heart.

"You always wear such delicate jewelry. Can I see it?"

I can't think of a reason to say no. With shaky hands, I slide it off my finger and push it across the table.

Carol studies the wide gold band. "Where did you get it?"

"Shawn." I clear my throat. "Shawn gave it to me."

Carol squints at the inscription inside. "Robert the Bruce?" She looks up. "Of Bannockburn fame?"

I nod guiltily, furiously wishing I'd learned anything from Shawn about making up stories.

"Is it real? How would Shawn get his hands on such a thing?"

"Um...I don't know." Strictly speaking, it's true. I have no clue how he got it.

"He was obsessed with Bannockburn before he disappeared. Does this have anything to do with what you're following? You said there's a chance I'll get my miracle."

"Yes, something changed in him." I stare at my nails, cut to the quick for violin.

Carol hands the ring back. "I'll see him again." Despite the hopeful words, her eyes brim with unshed tears. Her nails drum a syncopated rhythm on the table, and she says, "I sound crazy, but...." She hesitates, and then throws the words out in a rush. "Does the genealogy you wanted have anything to do with it?"

I think guiltily of the locked office upstairs as I pick among possible answers. Yes, sort of, and no, not really require impossible explanations. No is an outright lie. Fortunately, she sighs, and sinks into memories.

"I read it sometimes, after James died."

I slip the ring back on my finger, grateful for my reprieve, and thinking about the manila envelope stuffed with names, eager to see what they'll add to mine and Angus's paltry pile of clues.

"It's fascinating seeing Shawn's traits in his ancestors." Carol smiles into

a distant world. "*Adam Stewart was a violin maker in the early 1900's. Family lore says his mother, Annabelle, sang beautifully.*"

"*Like Shawn,*" *I say.*

"*Yes.*" *Carol sighs.* "*Shawn has a wonderful voice.*" *She reminisces about her only son, about his love of music from the time he could pull himself up at the piano and, barely reaching the keys, make splatters of sound. Tears glisten in her eyes.*

I hold her hand, listening. I'm safe from questions. She's safe from the frightening truth that that little boy is trapped in a world of maces, lances, and dungeons. She is safe from hearing that perhaps her only son died on the end of a medieval noose, hands bound behind his back, slowly choking to death.

Glenmirril, 1315

"Back to this water thing." In his favorite, if chilly, spot in the arched window of Niall's solar, Shawn plucked chords on Niall's harp, a gentle accompaniment to the slapping of gray waters on the shore below.

"What water thing?" Niall lowered the recorder. Allene looked up from her sewing, a frown creasing her forehead. She gave a small shake of her head.

"This thing about you and water. You think I don't see the way you're sulking since Conal left, leading the men you think you should be leading?"

Niall rose from his seat, dropped the recorder on the chess table, and, with a glower at Shawn, stalked into the bedchamber, slamming the door.

"That's not going to help!" Shawn shouted after him.

"You've as much tact as Edward Bruce with a comely lass!" Allene threw down her sewing on her lap.

"Thank you." Shawn jumped down from the windowsill and swung the harp onto the couch. "But trust me, if that were true, I'd have gotten Niall into the water by now."

Allene half rose, the *leine* sliding down her lap. "You've not a shred of humility."

"Thank you again." Shawn laid his hand on her arm, becoming serious. "I know you both think my time has nothing to offer, but we do know a lot about helping people with their problems."

Her face remained icy with disapproval. "You must not shame him."

"I can *help* him, Allene," he said softly. "What face is there to save? Everyone knows."

She stared at the floor.

"Let me try," he pleaded.

Her shoulders relaxed a little.

He pressed his case. "It would have cost him his life, last June, refusing to take the loch. Is this what you want for him forever?"

She shook her head, and the wilt of her head told him he'd won.

"I want you to start walking on the shore every morning," he said. "When he's in his room and sees. Look happy. Be everything he fell in love with, always by the water."

"How can that help?" Allene asked.

"Do it," he said, and went to the bigger obstacle—Niall.

He found Niall in his room, staring out the arched window at the loch, his back stiff with anger. "Start small," he said.

"What d' you know of anything?" Niall said bitterly.

"I know if I can do it with a horse, you can do it with water. I got thrown and kicked in the head. What happened to you?"

Niall's shoulders tensed under the woolen tunic. He made no answer.

"It doesn't matter." Shawn joined him at the window, leaning on the broad sill. The loch slapped slate-gray waves on the shore below them. "Start by imagining you're sitting by the shore, toes in the water. Think of good things when you look out at that loch. Harps and Allene and, well, I'm told I'm not humble, so let's be blunt, how lucky you are to look like someone as good-looking as me."

He waited for Niall's comeback. When it didn't come, he turned from the water to study him. Niall's face had gone chalk-white.

"Harps," Shawn said. "Allene. Heather on the hill. You have to try. It's going to end badly if you won't."

CHAPTER EIGHTEEN

Glenmirril, 1315

"We'll go through the dungeons two more times," MacDonald said. "Then you'll show me you can do it on your own."

"This is better than a cruise in the Bahamas," Shawn muttered. "Fine. Then, the favor I asked." At the Laird's glowering eyebrows, Shawn launched into campaign mode, using all the techniques that had gotten him, at the tender age of 24, everything he wanted from the orchestra's veterans. "I took good care of your daughter and turned the history of this whole country. I brought you the best stable boy you've ever had. I saved all your skins, not to mention Niall's neck—a couple times now—and earned him knighthood." MacDonald held up a hand, but Shawn was a stone tumbling downhill, gathering momentum. "And I'm going to get him over this water thing. Whether he likes it or not. What I'm asking is next to nothing. I understand your concerns, but the Bat Cave is perfect. And if anyone *does* hear, we explain it with a ghost story."

He would need this, when he got back to his own life—and if the tower wasn't working anymore, he'd find another way.

"If you're done," MacDonald roared, "and if you've remembered you're not in your own time and will respect my authority here!"

"Yes, sir." Shawn lowered his eyes, trying to look contrite. But *contrite* was not in his repertoire. He was already formulating his next attack, and his backup campaign with Niall if that failed. If he couldn't convince Niall, he'd work on Allene. Then there was Hugh....

"It seems you've won my daughter over. And Niall. They sing your praises, though I still find you impertinent and peculiar."

"Yes, Sir." Shawn tried not to smirk, his mind jumping ahead to showing Amy he still had it, when he got home, to winning her back.

"Show me you know the dungeons, and you'll have an hour a day."

Through his surprise at the easy victory—it took half the fun out of it— Shawn remembered this was not the orchestra and he'd be wise to thank the man humbly. "My Lord." He bowed his head. His heart hammered with anticipation. A grin spread across his face. It had been too many months. "Thank you."

"Mind you, it saved your life once, nobody knowing this," the Laird said. "It must be in complete secrecy."

Shawn laughed out loud, his head thrown back. Rarely had he imagined playing trombone something that could be done in secret. But the dungeons had given him that unexpected gift. He would regain anything he'd lost in these months, become even better, and return to win Amy over again.

Bannockburn, Present

Carol leaves the next day for the battlefield and grocery store, telling me to stay home and rest. The door has barely shut before I race with Shawn's family tree, to unlock the office, glancing over my shoulder as if Bluebeard might catch me. Safe inside, I set out names by generation, starting with Shawn's father and immediate ancestors on the table by the door. Niall's name is on a card on the table under the window. The space between them lies empty I begin filling them in, a card for each name in James Kleiner's family tree.

How did they use their time, *Angus asked in the graveyard.* It makes me think on how I live my own life.

My fingers touch ink, all that remains of Anthony MacKinnon, who rescued his prince at Culloden. I wonder who carried Shawn off the field at Bannockburn, and if he in turn pulled men to safety while fighting with Douglas. It's easy to imagine him doing it, remembering the look on his face as he turned back for the child. Carol would be proud. It would mean the world to her.

But I can't tell her.

I lay out a card for Anthony's father, John MacKinnon, 1698. Is he Niall's descendant, or is the connection elsewhere? I touch the crucifix under my sweater. Would it have passed eventually to him, had Niall given it to Allene as he'd intended? I glance at the clock, mindful of the incriminating maps and rubbings on the wall. I have time. But Carol's history ends in the twilight of the seventeenth century.

I pull up my genealogy sites, seeking connections to the names Carol brought. Soon I'm lost in the mid-1600s. Generations explode exponentially. By the tenth generation, 1650, one site tells me, Shawn will have 1,024 ancestors, and a cumulative 2,047 members of the family tree. Any one of those two thousand might be the one descended from Niall. By the early 1300s, he'll have two million ancestors. What am I doing, I ask myself. Doesn't the blessing suggest Shawn and Niall are related? Given the events? What do I gain by proving it? I sigh, admitting I'm pursuing it because it's all I have. It makes me feel like I'm doing something.

But the ever-expanding branches of the family tree loom over my head. Working backwards is impossible. I told Carol that Angus and I were thinking of something else. I gave her hope, and now I have nothing to show her. All I've done is make my office even more incriminating. Maybe I should take it all down. Remove the card with Niall's name. But then, if something occurs to me, I won't have my maps and time lines.

A knock jolts me.

Pain flashes through my distended stomach; my heart trips into a quick staccato. My hand jumps from the pulled stomach muscle to my racing heart. I scan the office for anything too impossible to explain—which is everything—and crack the door, trying to smile nonchalantly as I block Carol's view of maps, time lines, and charts, of the rubbings of Shawn's mark tacked to the wall. "Carol!"

She frowns. "Dinner's on."

"Dinner?" I glance at the clock; its small hand inches toward six. "I didn't mean for you to make dinner," I apologize. "I lost track of time." I'll just squeeze through and pull the door shut behind me.

But Carol peers through the crack. "The genealogy?" she asks. "What are you doing with it?"

I can't think of a reason to keep her out. Not even one. I open the door warily. The maps on the walls—I'll say they're the professor's. Carol's hand falls on the charts near the door. Slender fingertips touch her husband's name and date of death.

I tap the table, farther down, drawing her attention from sorrow. "I tracked down a James Stewart from 1652, who has to be the son of the James Stewart already in the records. I got stuck at his wife, Christina."

"It keeps going over here." Carol turns to the window.

"Oh, no, that's...." I move to block the table.

But she has seen. "Niall Campbell?" Her face puckers. "That's who Shawn called himself at the concert. Why?"

I lick my lips. "I was curious." I twist Bruce's ring, wishing I'd learned from Shawn's skill at lying. "I wondered why, too. If there was some connection."

"I imagine he just made it up." Carol, ever-peaceful Carol, looks agitated. She glances at the ring.

I force my hands off it. She knows it says Robert Bruce inside, knows Shawn threw it to me, knows 'Shawn' had an obsession with Bannockburn. "No." I try to distract her from the ring. "Niall Campbell was real. He lived at Glenmirril in the 1300s."

"Glenmirril, where...." Carol's hand covers her eyes. "I'm sorry. It wasn't your fault."

I stare at the floor. "I left him there."

"And something happened to him."

"Yes. And Niall lived there. And he later said he was Niall. I just thought maybe...if I knew why...." I stop. "The crucifix he gave me came from Glenmirril."

"Shawn gave you a crucifix?"

I curse my runaway tongue. "He just—yeah, he did. It's nothing." My heart is pounding, hoping she doesn't look too hard at the time lines and maps detailing Niall's—Shawn's?—travels with Douglas and Bruce. "We should have dinner before it gets cold."

"It's very unlike Shawn." Lines crease the corners of her mouth. *She closes her eyes, presses her fingertips to her forehead. "This has something to do with where he is now?"*

Sweat prickles my temples. "I don't know."

Carol sways. Her eyes flutter open. "The professor you told me about— Helen O'Malley—would she have more genealogy?"

I stare, surprised Carol would suggest it. But he's her only son. She'll grab any straw. At least I can reassure her. "She might. I've been waiting to hear from her." I slip through the door, pulling it shut behind me, grateful she didn't notice the maps.

But fast on the heels of relief, a new thought hits me, like the rumbling of a tympani, steadily growing. My hand freezes on the door knob. Fear flutters deep in my stomach, like the faint pianissimo tremor of a flute's trill. If the crucifix draws together father and son, it's not only Shawn and Niall who are affected.

Glenmirril, Shore of Loch Ness, January 1315

Shawn led MacDonald through the dungeons, his smoky torch flickering against damp stone walls. Their soft leather boots moved silently over the dirt floor. Shawn paused only briefly when the walls branched, before turning left. The ceiling became so low he had to hold the torch before him, and the tunnel narrowed till their shoulders brushed the walls. It made another, abrupt left. Shawn followed smoothly, knowing what to expect. And there, at the end, was the wooden door smeared with layers of dirt to disguise it in the unlikely event anyone wandered this far.

MacDonald produced a key, a large metal thing that entertained Shawn's modern senses. He juggled the sackbut, wrapped in oilskin, briefly before handing it to Shawn. He twisted the key in the lock, and opened the door.

Shawn stepped in, still amazed at the size of the room. "'Twas a cave," MacDonald explained. "I found it years ago when I was a wee lad. I built the door to keep it my secret." His eyes twinkled, and Shawn saw in a flash why the Laird liked Niall so much. They were kindred spirits, though Niall was not yet weighed down with unending war, the deaths of his children and wife, and the care of his people.

He smiled, his liking for MacDonald leaping like a mountain goat up a hill. And he wondered, what would forty years in this environment do to him? He turned sharply from the thought—he'd be going home—and gazed around the underground chapel. MacDonald set the wall torches ablaze, casting light over his long work tables, bench and stool.

"How did you get all this down here?" Shawn asked.

MacDonald smiled, running his hand over the table with a touch as tender as Shawn reserved for his Jaguar. "What the harp does for Niall, woodwork does for me. I bring things in at night. Sometimes Niall helps. It has served well, having secrets."

"So I've noticed." Shawn crossed the cavern, to where candles flickered under the life-sized crucifix. Skirting the kneeler below, he touched the body, the wood as smooth as pearls, and turned to the Laird. "You made this?"

MacDonald nodded, beaming.

"Your talent is wasted. You may have noticed we have different views about God in my time. At least, I do. But I know a masterpiece when I see it." He gazed up to the ceiling, and the wide space between the walls. "The acoustics are incredible." He returned to the worktable, where the Laird had laid the sackbut, and soon had it in his hands, working the slide in and out. Its brass bell gleamed in the flames of the candles and torches.

"I've kept it in good condition," MacDonald said, "for the day someone would play it."

"Why didn't you let me right away?"

"You must surely understand the need for trust here. You can't play it in the castle where we'd have to explain who is doing so. And I couldn't take you here till I trusted you." The flames from the wall sconces reflected, tiny gleams, in his pupils. "'Tis but five of us, now, who know of this place."

Shawn lowered the instrument. "Thank you." Tightness squeezed his heart. He doubted anyone in the orchestra would trust him with their lives, for this room and its secrets could mean life and death. He pulled back from the thought as from the lip of a great chasm. He lifted the sackbut, closed his eyes, and put himself in the audition room, the day he'd become Conrad's principal trombonist. With ease born of practice, he drew in a slow, relaxed breath and poured it back in a long, shimmering B flat, smiling as golden sound filled the cavern, echoing back with harmonies more glorious than those in the greatest concert halls.

MacDonald frowned as he slid up to the D. "Allene led me to believe 'twas a wee bit more impressive than that."

"Allene was in shock, watching Niall do anything at all with a sackbut," Shawn said. Some months ago, under the scrutiny of an English guard and Iohn, Niall's traitorous friend, he had played sackbut to prove he was not Niall Campbell. He smiled at the Laird's assumption that two notes was all the sackbut could do. But, a true performer, he continued warming up, savoring the moment he would launch into *Flight of the Bumblebee* or *Blue Bells*. He slid through a few more lip slurs, and some slow scales, before drifting into the third movement of the Davison *Sonata*. It seemed appropriate here, the simple, mournful arrangement of *O Come, O Come Emmanuel*.

With his eyes fastened on MacDonald's Christ, he gulped a lungful of air, his chest swelling with a power different from the physical labor of the past months, letting the sackbut sing. *And ransom captive Israel.* The low, sweet sound reverberated through the cavern. Candles and torches cast shadows over Christ's face, bringing the eyes to life in the flickering light.

That mourns in lonely exile here.

The words lilted in his mind as the slide flowed with the music. He was intensely lonely, for his life, for Amy, for the child he might never meet. MacDonald added his voice, singing softly, *Until the Son of Man appear.* Shawn almost stopped, broken by the thought of his own exile. Niall would call it Divine Providence, telling him something. But it had been his choice to play the piece, no guiding invisible god. He kept playing, savoring the sweetness of the high notes filling the chamber, his eyes closed, pouring his loneliness into every phrase.

"Beautiful," MacDonald breathed, when he finished. "Play the piece you played for the Sassenach."

"*Czardas,* by Monti," Shawn said. "He won't be born until the 1800's. He was a one-hit wonder. I'm a little rusty after a few months, but it should still be pretty good." He lifted the sackbut, played the slow, poignant introductory notes, and sailed into the lively gypsy music. Again, he closed his eyes, rejoicing in the feel of the slide in his hand, in the deep breathing that relaxed him and drove away everything else. He saw the gypsy woman dancing before him, that day, her lips smiling, skirts swirling, deep brown eyes inviting, as he'd skipped in circles with her, all the while playing.

He saw Amy, the first night he'd played this piece with the orchestra. She'd usually avoided him, but they'd met in the hall afterward. She'd given grudging admiration. "You're an incredible musician."

"Then you'll go out with me?"

"Dream on." She'd walked away. *Dream for.* He smiled at Allene's attempt to copy his idioms, the sackbut spinning through a multitude of sixteenth notes, dancing and skipping, and sliding, finally, into a slow coda.

He lowered the instrument, pleased he hadn't lost his touch, and grinned at MacDonald. "Is it as good as she said?"

"Unbelievable!" MacDonald gaped. "I'd not have guessed it could do such things."

"Neither did I, the first time I heard it played on trombone. How about this?" He launched into *Flight of the Bumblebee,* throwing in some buzzing noises and clicks and hums just for fun. "Sound like a bumblebee? Try this—Darth Vader." He played the Imperial theme, filling the cavern with the dark animosity of the evil lord.

"I'd have you play that next time MacDougall shows his face."

Shawn laughed in delight. "That's exactly who Darth Vader was...is...will be! The MacDougall of the 51st Century."

"You know what happens that far in the future? You said...?"

Shawn laughed again, filled with the thrill of playing. "No, it was a movie. I told you about movies, like plays—mummeries. Here's another good one."

He spent an hour, the time flying, playing jazz, classical, movie themes, hits from the 80's and 40's and 50's off his albums, thinking about Amy, about his mother putting a crisp bill in his hand each week for his lesson, until his teacher refused to teach him *Blue Bells of Scotland.*

MacDonald listened with rapt attention. "I believe now you were a great bard in your day," he said. "You've a gift I couldn't have imagined."

"Thank you." Shawn lifted his arm out of habit. But he had no watch. "I guess it's time to go." The long lines of admirers and women flitted through his mind, the adulation. He wrapped the sackbut in its oilskin, feeling more pride in MacDonald's approval than he'd taken in the squeals and screams of girls. "They loved me," he said, not knowing why and, embarrassed, changed the subject. "Do you think you could make a wooden case? You don't want the slide getting nicked, or it won't play. Even a little dent."

"I can do that." MacDonald lowered his head. "You believe you can help Niall?" he asked quietly, and Shawn realized it cost him something, to admit a need to a commoner, an outsider. "About the water?"

"Start small," Shawn said. "Have picnics on the shore with Allene. Look happy. We have to make him associate good things with that loch."

"You've no idea what happened there, have you?" MacDonald asked.

"No. What?"

"'Twas an awful day, worse yet for Niall, but a laddie still, seeing such a thing."

"Could you be more specific?"

MacDonald shook his head. "It doesn't matter. We'll try."

Bannockburn, Scotland, Present

"You sure about this?" Alec glanced warily at the stocky man, now dressed in a suit. "He seems kind of dangerous to me."

Brian waved a hand. "Deluded, but harmless." He'd thoroughly enjoyed talking history with the man, though he asked more questions than he answered.

"You're keeping the sword where he can get at it?"

Brian laughed. "If you're afraid he'll kill me, I doubt he needs a sword to do it. Quit worrying."

They opened the door. Simon stood quietly, looking as incongruous in the dark blue suit as a bull in a tuxedo. His hair had grown since Brian had last seen him. The close crop of black curls now covered the edge of the scar, though he was freshly shaved. Orderlies stood on either side of him.

Alec leaned close. "You've a bad habit of seeing the best in people, Brian."

"I see what's there," Brian retorted. He lowered his voice. "I'll be fine, Mate. You notice I've convinced him to speak the language?" He didn't add that he'd also had to convince him he'd be out sooner if he didn't announce, in modern English, that he knew Longshanks personally.

The director of the facility stepped forward, shaking Brian's hand. "'Tis highly unusual. I had some talking to do to convince them."

"I'm grateful," Brian replied. "But you couldn't hold him indefinitely. The only issue here was a language barrier."

"A man who speaks only medieval tongues?" The director shook his head. "I think we've a bigger problem than a language barrier."

Brian tapped his head. "Brain injury. He must be a professor of languages, and the blow to the head took the modern language right away. I'm helping him re-learn, and we'll figure out who he is."

"No one's reported him missing." The director put a sheaf of papers on the table as he spoke. "You'll need to bring him back for his appointments every week."

Brian nodded as he thumbed through the papers, scanning the minutiae of the agreement, and signed. He looked up to Beaumont. "Ready?" He used modern English.

"You have my things?" Beaumont responded as if speaking to a valet.

"In my car," Brian answered.

"Car?"

Brian handed the papers to the director. "I'll keep in touch." He led the way out of the concrete walls that had been Beaumont's home for months.

In the lobby, Brian marched up to the glass doors. They slid open. "We'll go home and get you set up in my spare room," he said, pulling his keys from his pocket. "Then an early dinner, and...." He stopped, aware that Beaumont was no longer by his side. He turned. Beaumont stared quizzically at the wall of glass.

Glenmirril, Shore of Loch Ness, January 1315

MacDonald kept Shawn busy. He started the day with Mass in the chilly kirk, the sounds of Latin flowing over his ears with meaning emerging from the words, rather than the rhythmic burble it had been a few months ago. From there, he took boys to the field beyond Glenmirril's drawbridge—the field that would one day hold a reproduction of a giant trebuchet and a concrete sidewalk —and supervised their attacks on the pell, urging them to greater strength and speed against their mute opponents. He propped little boys, who would be in elementary school in his time, onto wooden 'horses,' armed them with wooden lances, and had older boys pull them at top speed over frosty grass. Niall walked at his side, the silent Brother Andrew, head down, hands in sleeves, murmuring, "Watch them. Heels down," and, "See Taran? He can hit the pell harder. He doesn't yet understand his life depends on it. He's never seen real battle."

At noon, Shawn wolfed down bread as he jogged through the damp tunnels, a smoky torch burning his eyes in the dim maze, to his tryst with the sackbut.

An hour of scales, jazz, classical, or whatever struck his fancy, left him energized. He carried the torch back up into the light of day, where Hugh handed him the reigns of a pony with Lachlan's youngest brother waiting, gripping its pommel. After an hour working with the child, thinking how amused Amy would be at the sight, he led the pony to the stables in the southern bailey, and boosted the boy down. He wondered what Amy's cousins were doing, if they still loved football, if they ganged up on their father, five on one, the way they had on him when he and Amy visited.

The boy gave a grin, showing a crooked tooth, and scampered off, eager for the hot cider Bessie would be bringing from the kitchens. Shawn was hungry, but Red was nowhere to be seen.

He leaned against the stall door. "Old MacDonald wouldn't approve, would he?" he asked the pony. The animal slurped from its water trough, ignoring him. "Come on." He patted its rump. "Give me a neigh-neigh here or a neigh-neigh there, anything to let me know you're not really ignoring me. 'Cause it looks to me like you are." The animal shook its mane. "You know, I'm Shawn Kleiner. Nobody ignored me." Despite the chill in the air, he'd worked hard and was hot. He yanked his vest off, standing in his bell-sleeved shirt. "Or should I say, nobody *will* ignore me in seven hundred years." The animal chomped its hay. "Work those boys hard!" Shawn imitated MacDonald. "If you're soft on them now, 'twill go harder on them in battle."

His stomach rumbled. The smells of venison and pigeon pie and bread warm from the ovens came from the great hall, across the bailey and through the gate. Niall's place would be empty at the head table, waiting for Shawn to fill it. He didn't want to be Niall. He wanted, just for a few minutes, to be himself, even if it was only with a pony who ignored him. At least nobody was calling him Sir Niall.

A rustle at the door drew his attention. In the dim light, a slender woman led in a black mare. It was Christina. Shawn drew back into the shadows. She led the horse to its stall, singing softly to it.

Shawn smiled. Amy would do the same thing. But a twinge of guilt followed quickly on the private pleasure of listening to her sing. She wouldn't like to know she was being watched. He stepped out of the shadows. "Hey."

She spun, and on seeing him, moved quickly to the door. "Red will see to the hay."

Shawn laughed. At her blank look, he realized she had no idea why he was laughing. "Hey." He spelled it. "It's what we say in my—um, country—for hello. Not what horses eat."

She smiled, and he liked her all the more for laughing at herself.

"Are you in a hurry?" he asked. "You don't have to run away because I'm here." He became suddenly aware that he'd been working all day. He lifted his arm and gave an exaggerated sniff. "Yeah, I guess I'd run, too. If you can just wait seven centuries, I'll put on some *deodorant*."

Her mouth quirked up. "What is that?"

"Keeps you from smelling like you've been working hard all day when you've been working hard all day."

She laughed, a quick flash of white teeth in the dim stables, but took another step toward the door.

"Wait." He moved forward. The two of them stood face to face in the doorway, the gloom and rich smell of hay and horses inside, the evening sky spangled with a pale moon and the first stars, and fresh air outside. "Can I take you to a *movie?*"

"A *movie?* What's that? Does it also keep one from smelling?"

Shawn laughed. She wasn't calling him Niall. She knew who he was, and hesitated, not leaving quite yet. It felt good. "A movie is like old Rabbie's stories, but with people acting them all out."

"A mummery?" she asked.

"Yeah, like that." He checked the non-existent watch not on his wrist. "Next showing is in ten minutes, seven hundred years."

"What's this about seven hundred years?"

He shrugged. "Just a jest. We could hang out till it starts. Talk. Or something. What do you do in this time? Could you come to Niall and Allene's chambers, and we could talk?"

She shook her head, but faint color rose in her cheeks, telling him she was feeling the same attraction. She looked down at her hands, clutched together as Amy might have done. "I must go." She seemed, at all other times, calm and in control, not the nervous type.

"We can't talk?" Disappointment grew heavy in his chest, as it hadn't since the days Amy refused to go out with him.

"We're alone," Christina replied. "'Tis not proper."

"Yeah. Okay." He stepped back, confused at the morass of emotions flooding him, at the desire, the disappointment over Christina, when all he wanted was to get back to Amy. He watched Christina's blue cloak swish across the southern bailey. At the gate leading to the northern courtyard, she looked back once, and hurried through. His heart and stomach lurched.

He'd teased Amy for being Victorian; so what in the world was he thinking, wanting to talk to someone centuries away from being even that up to date? It was just that she knew his real name, he decided. She was attractive and had a melodious voice, and he could be himself with her, crack jokes about *movies* and *deodorant*. He grinned. *Deodorant*. Not the smoothest line he'd ever come up with. But her smile made him think it hadn't been a line at all, just a genuine, light moment of humor that had made her smile.

He went to the water bucket in the corner of the stable, splashed water on his face and under his arms, pulled his vest back over the stained shirt, and followed her to dinner in the great hall.

Oban, Scotland, Present

The houses, the city, the speeding metal wagons Brian called *cars,* the steadily burning sconces that lit with the touch of a finger to a wall, Brian's detailed accounts of events after Bannockburn, his casual discussion of events hundreds of years in Simon's own future—it all convinced Simon the roly-poly man spoke the truth, as impossible as it seemed.

Simon looked around Brian's home. It was neither hovel, nor castle, but something impossibly in between, similar to rich merchants' houses in town, but with a patch of smooth gray stone onto which Brian pulled the *car.* Beaumont kept his face passive as the irritating man fluttered around what appeared to be a kitchen, though nothing like the bustling chambers below his castle. It was bereft of servants. It confused Simon. Brian carried authority. He'd secured his release, taken charge, signed documents like a noble. Despite being soft and weak and clearly never having fought in battle, despite flab hanging over his belt and high-pitched laughter, he carried himself with the confidence of one in charge.

Yet he had no servants.

He prepared his own food like a serf.

That alone, the impossibility of such a thing, would have convinced Beaumont he was indeed far beyond the bounds of his own time. He would heed Brian's advice to perfect this mad version of English they used, and stop speaking of his king. He would become whoever it was they thought he was—a *professor?* A *historian?*

Brian turned from a large metal object, a pan in his hand, and slid four round chunks of what appeared to be meat onto a circle of stone sitting on the table. "Eat, eat, eat!" he chirped, as irritating as the birds that insisted on ruining spring mornings with their foolish cheer.

Beaumont seated himself at the table in a rickety wooden contraption that hardly deserved to be called a chair. It was as weak and insubstantial as everything about these people. The men carried no weapons. The towns had no fortifications. The meal in front of him was hardly fit for a villein, let alone a knight in the king's service. There appeared to be no second course, let alone a third or fourth.

"I can make more if you're still hungry," Brian offered. He seated himself in the other chair, at another stone circle filled with food. He jabbed a pronged metal object into the meat.

Beaumont copied him. "Tell me more of the time after Bannockburn."

He listened throughout the meal. He asked questions while Brian cooked more meat over a flameless brazier and took a bowlful of greens from a large white box that glowed inside. He probed for details while he wolfed down carrots. Brian, for all his softness, knew a great deal, and spoke with enthusiasm of the defeat of the English. Beaumont held his anger in check. It was impossible that so small and ill-equipped a nation could defeat the flower of

England, Edward's great knights and mighty chargers! He'd ridden beside his uncle that hot summer day, looking back to see heat rising in shimmering waves off thousands of cavalry marching smartly behind them; sunlight glaring off endless ranks of spears and helmets and shields, till he had to look away from the blinding light. The very earth had shaken with the might of England flooding over Scotland's border; men laughed and boasted of their coming glory on the field of battle. Only days later, on the morning of battle, he'd sat silently astride his horse, watching across the field as the Scots' pathetic priest walked back and forth before their dismal few, as if they actually *expected* God to take the side of a king who defied the Pope. The priest could not even afford shoes and thought God Almighty would favor him! Bah! "What happened to Edward?" he asked.

"Eventually—Isabella and her lover killed him!" Brian spoke as if relaying an great tale of adventure, his eyes shining.

"Murdered?" Beaumont asked.

"Oh, aye, in the most awful way!" Brian rubbed gleeful hands together. "A hot poker up the bum!" He laughed. "Or so they say. There are those who question the story."

"So...Isabella," Simon whispered. His uncle had never trusted her.

"Not the wife any of us would want," Brian laughed, clearly thinking himself a man of wit.

Irritation washed through Simon, along with a strong thirst for ale. He disliked the weak drinks here. He swilled down the water Brian set before him, as there was nothing else. He hoped it wasn't fouled. Brian gulped it with gusto and seemed none the worse for doing so. As Simon sipped his own, his mind spun. He'd jumped forward in time; how it could happen, he couldn't guess, but he was smart. He'd made a knowledgeable, if irritating, acquaintance. Between that and his own intelligence, he'd get back. And then it would pay to know how things had played out. Brian's voice drifted to the background as Simon reviewed all he'd learned of the days and years after Bannockburn, thinking what information would most raise him in Edward's esteem.

He leaned forward, interrupting Brian's story. "Tell me more of the immediate aftermath of Bannockburn. Who helped Edward? Who were his enemies?"

Brian looked startled. "I told you all about Bannockburn."

"I want more," Beaumont replied. "Where did Edward seek refuge when he fled the field? Who sheltered him? When did he return to take his vengeance on the Scottish dogs?"

"Well, I told you everything I know off the top of my head."

"But you have access to more information. Take me to it. I want to know everything."

Brian frowned. Beaumont wondered what was going through the man's mind. As long as he provided the information, however, Simon didn't care. A plan was forming in his own mind. "And Angus and Amy. You'll take me to speak with them."

Brian hedged. "I believe Amy wasn't going to be in Scotland long. She may have left already."

"Find out," Simon instructed. "And make arrangements for my journey to Castle Claverock."

CHAPTER NINETEEN

Bannockburn, Present

"You're quiet." Stooping by the hearth, nursing a newborn fire, Carol looked up to Amy, seated on the couch.

With her teacup warming her hands, Amy smiled weakly. "Lots on my mind."

Carol smiled understandingly. "Both of us."

Angus was due any minute for dinner. But the worry over him and Carol meeting paled beside her realization, several days ago, that her own child might be affected; her worry over whether *father and son* literal or figurative, if the crucifix would affect any child of Shawn's or only a boy? Her thoughts spun around Glenmirril's tower, the night with Shawn, when the fog in the courtyard had been so thick, and later, with Angus, when she'd seen a medieval soldier on the stairs. Had the blessing been pulling the child, and Amy, too, back in time? It scared her, even though she *hadn't* been pulled back.

But she couldn't tell Carol any of it. She would simply stay away from Glenmirril and the battlefield—although apart from the day of the re-enactment, nothing had happened there. She changed the subject. "I haven't heard from Helen."

Lines etched Carol's mouth, the only clue to her stress. "She'll write soon."

The doorbell chimed over her words, a descant to the crackling melody of flames. They glanced at each other. A tide of guilt rolled through Amy's stomach, to be replacing Carol's missing son right before her eyes, even though Carol had suggested it.

The doorbell chimed again.

Carol rose, brushing soot from her hands. "Let's not leave him in the cold." She smiled, but the lines around her mouth deepened.

Moments later, Angus stood in the entry, kneading his dark knit hat in one hand and clenching a plastic-wrapped spray of lilies in the other, while Amy made introductions. He stuck the flowers out to Carol. They bobbed their orange heads. "I'm sorry." He stopped, then tried again. "I'm sorry for your trouble."

"Thank you." Carol accepted the flowers, laying a hand on his arm.

"Thank you for all you're doing to find my son. And being here for Amy." She reached up to embrace Angus. "She said you like chicken."

"My favorite." He broke into a smile. "I smell it now, do I not?"

Carol took his arm. The lines around her mouth softened; the smile reached her eyes.

As they filed down the narrow hall, a knock sounded on the door. Amy glanced from the door, to Angus and Carol. "Rob." For once, she was glad to have him appear. She wasn't sure she could stand the trio of Carol, Angus, and her guilt.

"I didn't set a plate," Carol said. "You didn't tell me you invited him."

"I didn't." Amy opened the door. Cold air billowed in with Rob. He stamped snow from his feet, shutting the door. He gave Angus a hard stare as he edged past Amy's rounded stomach. "Carol!" He held out a dozen pink roses. "It's good to see you!" He hugged her, kissed her cheek, and pressed the roses into her hand alongside Angus's lilies. He noted them with a glare, which he spotlighted on Angus before ushering her into the kitchen and holding her chair. "I see you were about to eat."

Glenmirril, January 1315

At Shawn's request, Christina was brought to his and Niall's chambers. She arrived in clothing befitting her position—an underdress of silk, overlaid by a finely woven cotehardie of dark blue. Her black hair hung in shimmering waves from under a barbet. She offered her fingertips for the customary kiss, lowered her eyes, and joined Allene at the altar cloth she embroidered. Niall was with the Laird in what Shawn now termed the Bat Cave, though they both insisted there were no bats.

"Allene is here, we're chaperoned," Shawn reassured her. "It's perfectly acceptable now, isn't it?" How Amy or Dana or any of them would laugh to hear Shawn Kleiner reassuring a woman they were well chaperoned. And the funny thing was, he had no such intentions toward her. Regal women had never put him off. He'd always felt their equal and then some. They were a game, a challenge. *Had been,* he corrected himself. But it was something else—a bearing that suggested making advances on her would be akin to scribbling a mustache on the Mona Lisa. Even he wouldn't do such a thing.

She threaded a strand of bright blue silk through a needle and raised her eyes to his. "You speak differently in private. Why?"

It gave him pause.

"He's not of these parts." Allene stitched gold onto an angel's wing. "As he must be Niall, he speaks carefully in public, less so among myself, Niall, and my father."

"Maybe I should be more careful in private, too." Shawn boosted himself up into the windowsill, and propped his feet on the opposite wall, watching them stitch. Sunlight poured through the heavy glass. "It would prevent mistakes in public."

"We've become accustomed to it," Allene said, "and might miss your colorful language."

Shawn snorted. "I've been far less colorful, out of respect for the knives and swords you people play with, than I'm used to."

Allene smiled, and bowed her head over the angel, moving to the halo.

"Tell me about yourself," Shawn said to Christina. "How'd you end up married to the Dark Side?"

"Dark side?"

"That would be the charming Duncan MacDougall."

"He's not so charming." Allene pushed her needle in and out in a steady legato flow.

"Yeah, I got that," Shawn cracked. "I was engaging in sarcasm."

"I lived here briefly after my parents died." Christina glanced up. "Before I was betrothed to Duncan and went to Creagsmalan."

She had to have been quite young. Shawn bit back a comment about jail bait. To be fair, he thought, Duncan had only been a few years older. "How did you recognize Niall?"

"I remembered him as a boy, a wee bit older than me. He left for his foster family soon after I arrived."

"It seems a long time to remember a face, especially when he'd grown up in that time." Shawn watched her intently.

Christina took another three stitches before answering, her eyes locked on her needlework. "Niall is memorable. The boy who lost six brothers and his father, running a little wild, getting into mischief, pulling pranks."

Allene smiled. "Despite his mother's best efforts and fervent prayers before the Blessed Sacrament."

"But he was kind." Christina looked to Allene, who nodded. "He'd a knack for getting into mischief that never hurt anyone, that wasn't cruel. He ever stood up for the boys that others picked on, even when it meant getting a black eye himself."

"Colum, the smith's son, was quite the bully," Allene said, "and larger than Niall at the time."

"Has he a family of his own now?" Christina inquired.

Allene shook her head. "He died at Methven, barely a man."

Shawn translated to his own culture. The unlucky Colum had almost certainly been a mere boy. Maybe Red's age. "How did you recognize Niall all those years later?" From his perch in the window sill, he steered the conversation back to his questions.

"By the grace of God, I met the messenger bringing news to Duncan to watch for Niall." She smiled. "So I did. Though 'twas a trick, with his hair so changed and a great Viking mustache."

"Why did you take such a risk for Bessie?" he asked.

"Duncan was harming her."

"What do you do when...." He almost asked sarcastically, *when you're not playing punching bag for Duncan.* It seemed tactless, even cruel, though it wasn't aimed at her. "What did you do with your time?"

"I ran the castle, fed the poor, embroidered, and sketched."

Shawn glanced at the easel near the window. The portrait on it was startlingly lifelike.

"And I prayed."

He liked her smooth, mellow voice, and the way Gaelic's guttural sounds rolled gently from her tongue. He pushed, partly just to hear more of it. "Why did they give you to Duncan?" Her story came out, her voice rolling like a clarinet up and down a melody. Lord Morrison was her kin. They'd hoped to gain peace with MacDougall through marriage. She was well born, but, lacking parents, in need of a good marriage. "Duncan qualified as good?"

Allene raised her head, pausing in her work. "He's a noble name, a good home, position. It was meant to build alliances, to end the feuding."

Shawn stared at her, dumbfounded, thinking of a hot poker on Christina's leg. "It wasn't exactly a good home."

"'Tis a fine castle," Allene objected.

"You're jesting!" He stared at her. "You're jesting, right? See, you regard the stones as the home. We regard the stones as the *house*, and the *situation* as the home. Good house plus bad people equals bad home."

"Did you give Amy a good home?" Allene challenged. Christina's needle paused, for less than a second, in its stitching. She raised her eyes to Shawn, and lowered them immediately back to her work.

"She didn't live with me. She had her own home."

"She had her own castle?" Allene dropped her embroidery to her lap, her eyes wide.

Shawn laughed. The sun poured over his shoulder, striking copper from her hair and flashing off the gold thread. "We don't have castles. We have houses that are nicer than your shacks, but smaller than your castles. She had hers, I had mine."

"Like Christina MacRuari? Head of her own clan?" Allene asked.

Shawn shook his head, holding back more laughter. "No. She's not head of any clan. She just has an apartment. Just her."

"An apartment?" queried Christina.

"Okay, kind of like your houses in town."

"A woman living alone!" Christina's eyes were wide in amazement.

"They go about in their underclothes," Allene added helpfully.

"We do *not* go about in our underclothes!" Shawn argued. "It's just the fashion."

"I'd have Niall show you the pictures he drew," Allene said to Christina, "but they are quite scandalous!"

Shawn rolled his eyes.

"No servants?" Christina pressed.

"Not one."

"Who makes her breakfast or draws her bath?" Christina asked in disbelief.

"She does it herself." Shawn's eyes twinkled, but he dared not explain to Christina the modern technology that allowed Amy to draw her own bath.

"A woman living alone," Allene mused. "'Tis hardly to be believed. Was she not lonely? Would you have given her a good home had you married her?"

"I will when I get back."

Allene stabbed her needle through the altar cloth, and brought it back up, piercing him equally with the force of her gaze. "You didn't answer the question."

"I will when I get back." The cold stones bit into his back.

Christina lowered her work. "Amy is your betrothed?"

The corner of Shawn's mouth quirked up. "You care?" He knew he was flirting, baiting her, and tried to stop himself. It wasn't fair to her or Amy. "Technically, no, she's not my betrothed, but I hope she will be."

"Would you have been regarded as a good marriage prospect in your... place?" Allene asked.

"I'd say he would." Christina's needle flashed again, trailing rich purple silk through a border of grapes. Her eyes stayed on her work.

"You know naught of me," Shawn replied, copying their speech. "Why would you think so? I don't have a castle. Or anything of my own for that matter."

"You are kind and courageous."

"Am I?" Shawn gazed out the window, over the loch's winter waters thrashing as if Nessie's tail churned them, protesting the cold. Pines grazed the sky on the opposite shore, rising in the east. "You're about the first to think so." He turned back to Allene. "Yes, I would have been considered a da..." He stumbled on the precipice of the *M*. "A darn good catch. Right up there with Edward. I was rich, I was in charge. My hair was clean every day. Women threw themselves at me and took my picture."

Christina cocked her head, even as he realized his mistake. "They stole your paintings?"

"They wanted paintings *of* me," Shawn clarified. "When I walked out in public, they uh...had them painted."

"You sat for that?" She looked at him with interest. "How very odd."

"Our painters paint very fast. Then they wanted me to sign my name."

"You're having me on. On someone else's work? Is that not immoral?"

He looked to Allene, begging for some help. She smiled and bent over her work. "Yeah." He skipped explanations in favor of the original question. "I was considered a pretty good catch. I had my choice of beautiful women." Six months ago, it would have been a boast. Now, it was a statement. It seemed like a different life, a different person he described.

"Then Amy must be very special indeed."

"Yes," Shawn said, and fell silent.

Allene and Christina leaned close over the snow-white cloth, comparing work. "See, the grapes must end up under the angel's feet," Allene said.

Christina pointed with her needle. "Mine may be coming in a bit high. I'd best keep them close to the edge." She studied her work with a small frown, and they went back to pushing needles through the material.

After several minutes, Christina looked up, to Shawn lounging in the stone window sill. "Duncan did me one kindness. He allowed me a yearly pilgrimage to Iona." She scrutinized his face as she spoke. "I go every year in June." She paused, as if waiting for a response, and he had the unnerving feeling, as he had the night MacDonald sent him out the window, that she expected her words to mean more to him, to elicit some reaction.

"I'm sure it's very nice." He wasn't sure what she expected.

She cocked her head. "'Tis often cold and windy even in June. I'd have thought you'd know that."

He shrugged, mystified. "How would I know that? Except for what Niall tells me, I don't know a whole lot about med...about your part of the world."

Allene sighed. "And Niall will never go to Iona. Not as long as it means crossing water." She knotted her gold thread securely on the back of the altar cloth before snipping it off with a dainty pair of scissors.

"What a mess," Shawn remarked of the tangle of threads.

"'Twill come out right on the front." Allene threaded sky blue silk through her needle, unconcerned about the mess.

"Why do you go to Iona?" Shawn asked. He wanted, mostly, to hear more of her voice. She was a musician's dream. If he could capture her voice and put it in an instrument, he'd be wealthy. Men would pay fortunes to hear it over and over again.

"To pray." Her raised eyebrows suggested it was obvious.

Shawn glanced from one to the other. Niall's question—why had he carved Iona on Hugh's rock—niggled.

"St. Columba built his monastery on Iona," Allene explained. "'Tis a holy place."

He dismissed Niall's question. He hadn't carved the word, and a random carver, somewhere in seven centuries, had nothing to do with Christina praying at Iona. It was just coincidence. "You really got scre—a bad deal with Duncan. Why do you pray when that's what God gave you?"

"Do you expect only good from Our Lord?" Christina chastised. She spoke lightly, and he felt no criticism. "I've beautiful clothes, a home, good food, a warm bed. Even with Duncan, I had my every need met, which is more than some women with husbands like him can say. And God has answered my prayers and delivered both me and Bessie from him. I'm very blessed. Naturally I'm faithful to God. And if I weren't so blessed, I'd be faithful still, for He'd have His reasons."

Shawn had no answer, at least not one he'd offer these women, who clearly would never see reason. Their needles sparkled in the winter sun, the angel's halo took shape in a shimmer of pale gold, and the trail of grapes crawled further across the hem.

"I often prayed all night at Columba's shrine." Again, Christina looked to him, waiting.

"Don't your knees kind of hurt in the morning?" he asked.

"Shawn, you're impudent and disrespectful!" Allene set her embroidery down hard on her lap.

"Why is that impudent?" he demanded. "My knees hurt when Niall made me pray all night. And it didn't get me anything, either."

Allene rolled her eyes. "You're hopeless, you are. You know naught of God and His ways." She resumed her work. "Did you hear nothing Christina said about thanking God for your blessings?"

Shawn snorted. "Such as they are. I kind of liked my life as it was."

"A life of wealth and power and women admiring you," Christina mused. "Why the secrecy regarding your home?"

"MacDonald thought it could be handy," Shawn said. "And it seems to have been."

"So you'll live as Niall for the rest of your life?" Christina asked. "Or will you go back to your country?"

"I hope to." He sighed, leaning his head back against the gray stones.

Christina smiled, plying her needle. A long trail of grape clusters now stretched across the linen, waiting for the curling green vine that would connect them. "I hear you are an accomplished musician. Will you play?"

He took the harp from the peg on the wall, and returned to the windowsill, tuning it. He touched the strings, played a few arpeggios, and warmed up with a dance piece Niall had taught him, before turning to *Castle of Dromore*. He wondered what Celine would say to see how he could play the harp now. But thoughts of her filled him with shame. He'd lied to her, too, used her shamelessly when he was angry with Amy. His thoughts drifted to Amy, of the hours side by side in his music room, with the sun pouring in the tall windows, glancing off her dark hair, and her flowery scent coming alive in the warm sun.

"You sing sometimes," Christina said.

He switched pieces, running up and down arpeggios, and began, in English, in a soft bass. *"I'm here in my bed with my head on the phone."*

"I speak English quite well," Christina interrupted, "but what is *phone*?"

"Pillow," Shawn said. "I'm here in my bed with my head on the pillow." His fingers trailed up and down another arpeggio, remembering the day he and Amy had arranged the song. They'd gone to the beach afterward, running and splashing in the water under a hot summer sun. He sang again. *"I think of calling you, but it's so late and you're so far away."*

"D' you miss home? D' you miss Amy?" Christina asked softly.

Shawn studied her smooth ivory skin, dark hair setting off blue eyes, fine bones, and regal bearing. A thin scar trailed down her cheek, a match to the one on her ankle. He wondered how many others he didn't know about. Long, thin fingers plied the needle. She asked nothing in return for her troubles, betrayed no concern over it. He saw something in her he'd rarely seen in a woman. He couldn't name it. But he thought he knew what it was. She was what Amy had been, before he'd bullied it out of her. Stealing someone's character and strength—was it any better than burning her with a poker? He lowered his eyes to his hands, moving on the strings.

Christina lifted her eyes, waiting for an answer.

"Yes, I miss home, and I miss Amy."

Bannockburn, Present

It's a nervous dinner, the four of us packed around my tiny table, in my tiny kitchen just right for one. We bump knees seating ourselves, and bump elbows reaching for food.

Carol is nervous about Angus's response to her and her response to him as he takes her son's place in my life. She loves me as a daughter. She wants his goodness for me. But it has to hurt. She glances uneasily between him and Rob.

Angus is nervous about meeting Shawn's mother. He doesn't want this kind, gentle woman to know what he thought of her son. He knows he's stepping into her son's shoes. Yet she asked him to come. How could he have said no? Antagonism bristles between him and Rob.

Rob leans close; touches Carol's arm; speaks as if to the bereaved. "Would you like chicken? Can I pour you tea?" He is auditioning for the role of Beloved Son. I'm embarrassed for him.

"I'm fine, Rob, thank you." She squeezes his arm back and pours her own tea. "Thank you for all you've done." She turns to Angus. "Have you seen his office?"

Angus shakes his head. "I haven't." His lips are tight.

I pray Rob won't mention my office.

Carol dishes boiled potatoes onto Rob's plate. "Angus and Amy had an idea about genealogy."

I close my eyes. No, Carol, don't.

Rob coughs into his napkin. His eyebrows shoot up. "Genealogy?" He glares at Angus, who glares back.

"Shawn's grandmother came from Skye." Carol glances between them. "They thought maybe...."

Angus reaches abruptly for the chicken.

"Did you want more?" I ask loudly. "It's good, isn't it?"

"Aye!" Angus agrees enthusiastically. "You're a grand cook, Mrs. Kleiner!"

"Call me Carol." Her cheeks glow with pleasure. "James loved to cook. It's his recipe."

Rob looks suspiciously from me to Angus.

My nerves jump, praying he won't press the issue, here in front of Carol. "I'll have to get that recipe!" I reach for the carrots. "Something in the spices?"

"Oh, yes," she agrees with more enthusiasm than the question deserves. "He was a master with spices!"

Rob tries to meet my eyes. I avoid his, telling Carol, "I'm arranging Ma Vlast *as a violin solo!" I lean forward, as enthralled as if I've won a new house.*

"Are you?" she asks with the same out of proportion interest.

"Smetana's grand, now, is he not!" Angus declares.

"Do you even know who he is?" Rob glares at him.

Angus tries valiantly for a smile, but only manages a smirk. "The father of Czech music. He composed piano pieces, orchestral works, and operas. I particularly like his Doctor Faust.*"*

I look down at the creamy-white potatoes on my plate, hiding a smile. I told him this when I started working on it. We listened to Doctor Faust *together.*

"And," Angus leans forward, "he shares a birthday with your Dr. Seuss!"

Rob turns to Carol, clearing his throat loudly.

"Rob, I have something for that cough." I stand as abruptly as I can, squeezed in this small kitchen. My stomach bumps the table, jarring plates and silverware and cups crowded shoulder to shoulder on it. I go down the hall, knowing he'll follow.

He's right behind me. I shut the door to the front room. The fire crackles in the hearth, a warm contrast to the gray skies glowering through my lace curtains.

"Genealogy?" he hisses. "You were stressed, Amy! She's afraid! Don't tell her this crazy story!"

"I haven't!" I say irritably. "But you're giving her false hope!"

"I'm supposed to do nothing," he demands, "because you think he's in a time warp?"

I purse my lips, holding tight to angry words that want to fly out and beat like Hitchcock's birds around his head. Because, really, I know how crazy it sounds. How can I be angry at him for thinking it's crazy when it is? I plant my hands on my hips, turning from him. My phone trills. I snatch it up, a blessed distraction from impossible discussion.

I get only the first half of hello out before Helen O'Malley's voice bursts into my ear, a high-speed string of Scottish slang I can't follow. Her excitement is impossible to miss. As are her words, "Genealogy to the 1200s!"

I hear a crack that is without a doubt gum snapping. I fling the words, "Where? How?" into the breach.

"I searched my files," Helen explains, "and found more names. I asked around and what with one thing and another, it was turning into a wild goose chase."

"I didn't mean to put you to any trouble," I apologize, but I'm leaning forward, as excited as Helen. Rob paces the room, throwing me questioning looks.

"No, 'twas great craic, going to this old castle in Clachnaharry."

"Where?"

"Near Inverness. 'Twas brill! An eccentric old woman on a windswept cliff with a dozen cats and two ornery goats in the yard! She has the family history of Clan Stewart, straight back to the Campbells!"

"The Campbells of Glenmirril?" My heart skips. "How...can...." I draw a breath, calming my thoughts. "Can she send it?"

"It's all hand-written," Helen says. "She never leaves her home. But she says bring you 'round. I think this is everything you wanted!"

I press my hand to my stomach. I'm due in just weeks. Sometimes babies come early. It's a long drive. But if Shawn is descended from Niall, so is this baby. I need to know. There are hospitals all over the country. "When can we go?" I ask.

We make arrangements. I hang up, defending myself to Rob before he can draw breath for his assault. "Carol asked if she could find more."

Rob shakes his head. "How have you explained this to her? Amy, go look at this Clan Henny family tree thing, if you must, but at least hold off telling Carol until you find out more."

My lips tighten in annoyance. But this once, I think...maybe he's right.

Glenmirril, January, 1315

Central heat had never been so cozy as the furs, or so comforting as the crackling flames in the hearth casting dancing fire-shadows on the closed bed curtains. But Shawn lay awake, his mind filled with Amy, Rob, his child. It bothered him more each day, not knowing if he had a son or daughter. Wondering—what would he do if he got back and found Amy married to Rob? Rob was no good for her. Really, he wasn't. But what would he do about it?

Christina drifted into his thoughts. She was here. She drew him like no woman ever had. He lay in bed, smelling the burning wood, listening to the crackle, exploring the thought. It wasn't quite true. Amy had drawn him in much the same way. But Christina was stronger. Wisdom and age emanated from her, despite being younger than him. He wouldn't dare pressure her as he had Amy. But then, it was hardly fair to compare the two, he thought. Christina had an entire world backing her. Amy had had an entire world backing her down.

They were sending to a bishop for an annulment, and she would be free to re-marry. It was easy to imagine spending his life with her, if he was caught here. Strange, he thought, because she was different from any woman he'd ever known. She kept her eyes off him. She refused to be alone with him. She spent her time helping Allene manage the castle, walking with Bessie in the gardens, bringing food to the poor. She prayed for hours on end. They had nothing in common.

Nothing.

He tried to imagine kissing her—touching her. But even thinking about it felt like sacrilege. He felt like a peeping Tom. He rolled over angrily, punching his pillow into place, and turned his mind back to Amy. He'd promised himself he would be faithful to her, and he would be.

CHAPTER TWENTY

Clachnaharry, Scotland, Present

"It reminds me of *Annabel Lee*." Amy peered through the rain-streaked windshield of Angus's car, from the ancient castle to the bleak hillside running, like smeared paint in the gray storm, down to a dark shore pounded by crashing waves. *"In a kingdom by the sea...."* Wind rocked Angus's small car as it jerked to a stop.

"Or apart from the water," said Helen from the back, "you could imagine Heathcliff walking out the front door." The three of them squinted through lashing rain at the decaying stone tower and massive curtain walls, all hung with dead, drenched ivy and looking as if it wished to crawl into its own peaceful grave to rest beside centuries of past owners.

The torrent pounded, a drum roll over their heads. "Are we hoping it'll let up long enough to run in?" Helen asked.

"Can't," Angus sighed. "They expect me back at work before June."

Suddenly, the castle door flew open. A tall, lithe figure waved, glowing white between the gloom of the interior and the gloom of the day.

"We'd best hurry before she catches her death." Helen threw her door open and dashed, yanking a wool shawl over her head as she ran. Amy clutched her laptop case close and pulled on her knit hat, useless though it would be against the downpour, and hurried behind, a hand to her swollen belly. Angus sprinted at her side. The woman ushered them into a dim hall with clucks of concern, and slammed the door against the wind.

Amy pulled off her damp hat. A white cat twisted around her ankles. Puddles formed around her boots. The pale glow of a wall sconce shone on wood paneling topped by faded floral wallpaper. The fluttering old woman in white gripped her elbow and led her into a room lined with floor to ceiling bookshelves. A fire roared in a hearth nearly big enough for a man to stand in; it fought futilely against somber skies glaring in through leaded glass. On a tea caddy, a china teapot in whites and pinks puffed billows of steam. A quartet of matching cups and saucers danced a dainty minuet around it. A calico cat curled in sleep on the caddy's lower shelf.

The woman, her white hair piled high with tortoise shell combs, gripped

Amy's hand with soft'fingers and spoke quickly.

Amy cocked her head, and turned to Angus, questioning.

Angus grinned. "She says welcome, she's Honora Stewart, she's a wee bit to show you, and will you take tea."

"In Gaelic?"

His smile broadened. "In English."

Honora spoke again, patting Amy's stomach and grinning at Angus. She threw back her head and laughed—exactly as Shawn always had.

Amy blushed. She turned to the woman, curious if her own English sounded as foreign to her hostess. "I'd love tea, thank you."

Honora pulled her to a couch and pushed her down, fingering her hair, smiling, and chatting in sounds reminiscent of Shawn's Gaelic, though the words *family, Glenmirril, Campbell* and *cuppa* now jumped out. Honora turned to the tea cart, pouring streams of amber into the cups, and passed them around. Amy slid the laptop down beside the couch. She jumped as her fingers brushed the warm fur of another cat.

Accepting his tea, Angus joined Amy on the couch. "She said her family come from the Campbells, generations back, and kept a history." Thanking Honora, he raised the delicate cup, little more than a thimble in his big hands, to his lips.

Honora had no sooner poured her own tea than she set it down, and crossed to a glass-fronted book case. She pulled out a large scroll. Turning to a mahogany table with a lamp hanging over it, she beckoned them.

Angus set his tea down. Helen leapt, her damp skirt swirling in teal waves around her ankles, to help. They battled briefly to get the scroll rolled the vast length of the table, before pinning its corners with books. Honora gestured to Amy, chattering. She grasped her hand, hurrying her along, and pointed to the web of boxes and lines—hundreds of names stretching across the parchment. "See here, noo," she said, with a heavy roll of R's. Amy found herself acclimating to the thick accent. "Christina Stewart."

Amy leaned down, hardly daring to hope. Her finger fell on the name. Disappointment edged out elation. "This Christina Stewart was born in 1742."

"But there was another Christina Stewart," Angus reminded her. "Let's compare it to what you brought." He crossed the room to take the print-outs from her laptop case. They compared names, finding match after match in the 1700's.

"This is it!" Amy exclaimed. "These *are* the same Stewarts!" She raised her eyes to Honora. "You're part of this tree?"

Honora spoke rapidly, turning to Helen at Amy's uncomprehending stare.

"She's the many-times great granddaughter of the man who made this chart," Helen translated.

"I've bickies on the cooker, now am awa tae fix 'em. Ye look a' tha' aw ye want, aye?" Honora patted Amy's belly, and flitted through a dark-trimmed doorway.

Amy's eyes went to the top of the chart, dense with Jameses, Thomases, and Williams, in the late 1200's. She moved to the second tier, skimming the old parchment for Niall's name. Beside her, Angus did the same. "1290," Amy murmured. "That's when he said he was born." A black cat jumped onto the table and stretched languidly along the edge of the family tree, staring, unblinking, at Amy.

"You know who Shawn's ancestors were," Helen said. "Trace them back, instead. You're sure it's Niall Campbell? By the way, I did more digging. Your crucifix was lost on the raids with Douglas."

"Lost in a raid?" Amy frowned.

Angus put a warning hand over her fingers. She bit back her question, *Where would that story come from?* As Helen swished around the table to the other side of the chart, he murmured, "'Twas a treasured possession. Niall would have to explain its disappearance."

"He didn't like lying," Amy whispered back.

Angus grinned. "He could hardly say he left it in the twenty-first century, now, could he?"

"Here!" Triumph rang in Helen's voice. "'Tis the Stewarts you need, aye? You got as far back as, who?"

Amy thumbed through her genealogy. "James Stewart, 1684, Eamonn Docharty, 1639, Mungo MacKinnon, 1575." She offered the papers.

Helen studied them briefly, before announcing, "We'll start from there, will we. Angus, you take the left, Amy, the middle, and I'll follow the right side." She clicked the overhead lamp, casting light and shadow over Shawn's family history.

Almost immediately, Angus straightened.

"What?" Amy asked.

"There are MacLeans in his tree. And they're from my family's part of Scotland."

"There are?" She laughed. "Don't tell me I stumbled from one branch of the family right into another?"

"See here." He pointed. "One of the James Stewarts married Christina MacLean, daughter of James, son of Robert and...."

"What?" She straightened, rubbing her back. Something twisted around her ankle. She glanced down to see a ginger cat purring against her leg.

"Robert and Joan. Joan...." He touched her shoulder, his eyes shining. "Is a Campbell!"

Amy's eyes widened. "You found the connection?"

"There were many Campbells," Helen warned. "What year is she?"

Angus leaned down, squinting at the spidery script. "1618-1640."

"Dead at twenty-two," Amy murmured.

"Childbirth, most likely," Helen replied.

"Who does she lead to?" Angus followed the trail with his large, square finger. "James, 1588, Robert, 1563."

"'Twas a large clan," Helen warned again. "There were many branches."

"Robert, son of James, circa 1539." Angus's voice rose a half step.

"James was Niall's father's name," Amy breathed.

"James was the son of another James, born 1514," Angus continued. "Brian, 1485, Angus, 1442." His voice rose again. "Another James, 1412!"

"We're still a hundred years off," Amy cautioned, but she leaned in, her stomach pressing against the mahogany table.

"Robert," Angus said, "Another James, 1341, son of James Angus, born March 1317."

Amy's hands clenched one another tightly. "1317! That has to be Niall's son! He'd have been twenty-seven." She held herself forcibly from bouncing in excitement, straining to read the tiny script. "Who are James Angus's parents?"

Angus reached to adjust the overhead light.

"Is it Niall and Allene?" Helen asked, as breathless as Amy.

Angus straightened, frowning. "Christina Morrison of Glenmirril?"

Amy shook her head. "No, that's not right. It was Allene. Records can be messed up in 700 years."

"Especially on the maternal side," Helen added. "Who is his father?"

"Duncan MacDougall born in 1290."

Amy shook her head in disbelief. "Not the *thieving* MacDougalls?"

Glenmirril, January, 1315

Shawn woke early the next morning. The winter sun was not yet up, and the heavy bed hangings would have kept it out of his eyes anyway. Iona sprang to mind. He sat up, shivering as the furs fell away, dreading the moment his bare feet hit the chilly stone floor.

But hunger called. He hit the floor running, and all but leapt into his hose and leather boots. He shivered in front of the weak embers of the night's fire as he pulled a heavy woolen vest over his shirt. He stirred up the flames and threw on another log and some kindling. In an hour, he and Niall would practice fighting. But now, Niall was on his way to church. MacDonald would be here any minute, pounding on the door, yelling for Shawn to get up and move.

Shawn paused, in poking the fire. Christina would be at Mass. He grabbed Brother Andrew's robe, threw it on, and flung the door open to see MacDonald's fist raised, ready to thump the door.

"You're up!" he said. "You're even dressed!"

"Ready for Mass!" Shawn grinned. "What took you so long?"

Clachnaharry, Present

"The thieving MacDougalls?" Helen demanded.

At that moment, Honora sailed through the arch from the kitchen, bearing cookies steaming from the oven. "Oh, aye, the MacDougalls, thieves through and through! Always stealing our cattle." She clucked her tongue.

"Now how does anyone know whose cattle they were?" Helen's hands went to her hips.

"They were the MacDonalds' cattle," Angus said. "The question is, *is* Duncan of the same MacDougalls? I've no idea what other he'd be of, but then why is he at Glenmirril? Why would Christina not have gone to Creagsmalan?"

"But this can't be right," Amy objected. "If James Angus is Duncan and Christina's son, then Niall and Allene can't be Shawn's ancestors. And they have to be."

"Why?" Helen asked.

Honora set the cookies on the tea cart, saying over her shoulder, "See here, there's a question mark by Duncan MacDougall's name. There's doubt as to James Angus's paternity."

"Why would they think it was a MacDougall at all?" Amy asked, ignoring Helen's question.

"No one knows. Aye, 'tis Duncan MacDougall of Creagsmalan." Honora handed her a cookie, chirping. "Eat, eat, eat!"

"He can't be the father of a child born at Glenmirril," Angus insisted.

"But the father is in doubt," Honora reminded him. "Which is odd, for there are records of her marrying Duncan MacDougall."

"A second husband?" Helen said. "It would hardly be unusual, with war and disease, for her to be widowed and re-marry."

"Christina," Angus said around a mouthful of cookie. "Think back, Amy, to Brian's stories at Creagsmalan. Wasn't that the name of the wife chasing her husband away from the mistress? Quite the shrew?"

Amy nodded. "Yes. So maybe she married Duncan, and went back to Glenmirril after she was widowed?"

"Come to think of it," said Angus, "Remember the placard at Creagsmalan? I told you it was wrong because Duncan MacDougall was killed at Glenmirril. *Before* 1317."

"But he could still be the father," Helen pointed out. "So why the question about his paternity? Is this about the blessing? You think Shawn is Niall's descendant because of that?"

Amy and Angus's eyes met. They silently questioned one another.

"It seems you do." Helen didn't wait for an answer. "Why? You said a friend named Niall gave it to you. What's that to do with Shawn?"

Amy bit her lip. "It's a long story." She felt the feebleness of her response. Shawn would have changed the subject. She turned to Angus. "We need the prophecy."

"I've no idea how," Angus said.

"The only way," Helen said, "is from the monks. And there's only one way to get any information they have."

"What's that?" Amy asked.

"Hike in," Angus said. "There are no roads."

"What, no highways?" Amy clarified.

"I mean *no roads a' tall.*"

"Everywhere has roads," Amy insisted.

Angus laughed. "Perhaps in America. No, we'd drive to the last town, leave the car, and hike. And you can't go hiking just weeks before giving birth."

Oban, Scotland, Present

Brian pushed another document toward Beaumont.

Simon was wearing on his good humor. For maybe the first time in his life, he wanted to snap at someone. The man had announced at his last appointment that he *remembered!* He was a historian! He'd studied Bannockburn. He dutifully spoke modern English, gaining ground quickly. But he ate huge quantities of food, never offering to help with the cooking or washing up. He refused showers or deodorant, till Brian's head swam with the earthy odors emanating from his bedroom. He refused Brian's offer of a razor, letting his beard grew in black and curly. It gave him a dark, dangerous look. It was disturbingly easy to imagine him wearing the armor found in the locker, wielding the sword now hidden under Brian's bed.

Simon had pestered Brian endlessly for a horse, and, when refused, accompanied Brian to the Creagsmalan archives. He spent hour upon hour there reading old documents, and fuming at Brian that they were useless, as if it were Brian's fault. He hounded Brian imperiously, demanding to be taken to Claverock, until Brian had irritably given in, regretting his decision to get the man out of the psych ward. It was true he didn't seem mad; but Brian wondered what he'd expected to learn from him. He couldn't trust anything he said, anyway. Who knew how affected his brain was by the injury.

"This is all?" Beaumont glared at Brian's latest offering.

Brian swallowed irritation. "'Tis the last, aye. What is it you looking for?"

Beaumont rose from his seat, not answering.

Brian studied him, curious. His behavior was strangely like that of Angus and Amy. They'd all—Angus, Amy, and Simon—been at the re-enactment, where many people had reported strange incidents. But he couldn't think why that left them all digging for scraps of history like nuggets of gold. He rather hoped Simon had forgotten his mention of them.

Hands on hips, jaw tensed, Beaumont scowled at the ancient documents as if they defied him. Abruptly, he swung his bull-shaped head on Brian. He gestured, a barely controlled flinging of the arm, at the papers. "This is not enough! You *must* know more!"

Brian backed up a step; wanting Simon's wrath anywhere but on himself. What would it hurt, he thought, to volunteer Angus's name? In fact, Angus might relish such a meeting. He was sure he would, come to think of it. He craved the details as history as much as Simon. They were kindred spirits. Angus would thank him!

Beaumont regarded Brian with such intensely dark eyes that Brian almost expected to see his tongue flicker out, forked and deadly. He shook himself. His imagination had very much gotten the better of him since this stranger had come into his life.

"Those you called Amy and Angus," Simon said slowly. "Bring them to me."

Uneasiness inched down Brian's spine. Amy was pregnant; vulnerable. He didn't like the thought of Simon near her. He wondered how irrational he was being.

CHAPTER TWENTY-ONE

Bannockburn, Present

Practice, teaching, and growing exhaustion took over Amy's days. Though the blessing and unknown prophecy and all her research tumbled through her mind day and night, there was nothing to be done about it. Her e-mails with Angus, more and more, concerned his work and hers and the coming baby.

A distant relative of Shawn's, at Carol's request, sent more genealogy. "She spent time in Scotland researching," Carol said, as they sat side by side, fitting names in the chart like puzzle pieces.

Amy's finger fell on a lone MacDonald in the group. "They used to be close," she said.

"Who?"

"MacDonalds and Campbells. Hundreds of years before the Glencoe Massacre." She couldn't say *Niall had so much love and respect for the Laird of the MacDonald clan.*

Rob appeared for dinner on a regular basis. "I've got a lead in Aberdeen," he said one week, and the next, over Carol's apple-spiced pork chops, "Someone saw him in Fife. I know this one's going somewhere."

Amy pushed at her mashed potatoes with her fork. She lifted her eyes to Rob's, when Carol rose to remove brownies from the oven. They locked silently, a wordless battle, her plea not to get Carol's hopes up, and his angry rejoinder not to tell her crazy stories.

Carol turned from the sink, lines etched around her mouth. "Rob, tell me about it later. You two go to the front room while I clean up."

"He's in Fife," Amy hissed, in the front room. "He's in Aberdeen. He's supposedly all over Scotland, Rob, always just two feet ahead of you." She yanked back from his reach. "You're not going to find him!"

"And you are, looking at moldy books in musty archives!" He reached for her again; she pulled back again. "You're due any day, Amy. You need rest. Let me stay here till the baby's born. I'll drive you to the hospital."

"Rob, please." She sank to the couch. "Angus is coming."

"He's in *Inverness!*" He turned to the hearth, blinking rapidly, his jaw tight. "How fast does this guy drive anyway?"

"Listen to yourself, Rob. I know you hurt, and I wish I weren't the cause." She watched his tense back. Her own ached terribly. "But I don't feel the way you want me to feel."

"You did the morning we went back to get him from the tower—before he came out all confused and hurt and playing St. Shawn." Bitterness hung on every word.

"I was surprised! I was confused!" She twisted, trying to ease the discomfort in her back. "I was flattered to find out after two years of Shawn acting like no one would want me, that someone did, but I never meant to lead you on. I have apologized for hugging you and holding your hand." She pushed herself up off the couch. *"But I never so much as kissed you!"*

"I bet Angus has done a whole lot more than kiss you." Acid laced his voice. His blue eyes bit into hers.

Heat flared up her face and raced back down, leaving her cold. Her heart pounded. "How dare you assume!"

He jabbed at the fire with the poker. It scraped the brick and sent a spark shooting up the chimney. "I'm sorry," he muttered.

Her heart slowed. "I don't get it." She pressed a hand to her aching back. "You're going to hate Angus forever but you're spending your time and money trying to get Shawn back? You don't get me either way."

"At least Shawn was there before," he snapped. "But it seems like you'd take any guy off the street before me."

He fell silent; so did she. She was seeing Angus, smiling down at her with coffee in his hand, his eyes dark and piercing. The fire crackled, casting shadows on the walls. A warm wave rippled across her abdomen. She put her hand to it, frowning.

"Are you okay?" he asked. "Is it labor?"

"No. I don't think so. It doesn't hurt."

He turned back to the fire, his hand on the wall. She touched his shoulder, noting how his hair had grown to his collar. "Rob," she said. "Angus has done nothing to you." When he didn't answer, she asked, "Is it really about me, or is it about your pride?" She stopped, drawing in breath, as another wave rippled through her.

He turned back, gripping her shoulder. "You sure you're okay?"

"It doesn't hurt," she insisted. But her hand stayed there, on the lower curve of her stomach, feeling it tighten. She looked him in the eye. "Please, Rob, see Angus for the good man he is. Open yourself to someone else."

He edged away from her, looking into the fire. Its warmth touched her toes. Its light glinted off his hair like silver. Another warm ripple tightened her stomach.

"Rob, will you get my suitcase," she whispered. She wanted Angus. She wanted Shawn. She bit her lip, ecstatic and lost all at once. She touched his hand. "Rob, call Angus. Please."

"Carol!" he yelled. "Carol, her suitcase!"

Oban, Present

A phone call couldn't hurt, Brian thought. He picked his phone up off his desk. Angus could make his own decision. He might *want* to meet the man.

He set the phone down. He'd locked his bedroom door last night—as if that would stop Simon he thought ruefully. He had to remove him from the house. Angus was just the man to talk to. He picked the phone up again. He could call the hospital instead, ask them to come and take him. Angus, like Alec, had often warned Brian he saw too much good in people. Brian had laughed it off, saying a cop saw the worst of humanity, and Angus should be less cynical.

Still...he set the phone down. He didn't want to admit to Angus that he'd possibly done something very foolish. He lifted the phone to dial the hospital. A sound in the kitchen caught his attention. He looked up.

Simon stood in the doorway.

"You're sending word to those of whom you spoke?" Simon's voice was as smooth as cured leather.

Brian's eyes skittered away. "Um, yes, I called," he lied.

"Called?" Simon asked. "I didn't hear you. Are they near?"

Brian rose to his feet, wanting nothing more than to be away from the man. "I have an errand. Excuse me."

Simon's muscled body filled the doorway, his black beard making him look dark and dangerous. He didn't move.

Brian imagined Simon as nothing more than an assistant at the archives, one who hadn't a clue how to handle the papers. "You'll have to move."

Simon chuckled. "No. I won't have to."

The smile slipped from Brian's face as he searched for an answer. But there was no answer. The man was threatening him. And, Brian imagined, quite capable of carrying through on whatever, exactly, the threat was.

"I wish to speak to this man," Simon said, as if speaking to a simpleton.

Brian cleared his throat, willing his voice not to squeak. "I've called. He's...out of town. He'll be back...later."

Simon reached out a large hand, planting it like a lead vice on Brian's shoulder. "And Amy. Where is she?"

Glenmirril, February 1315

Shawn scraped his chair back from the table and page after page of Latin phrases. "Don't you think I've learned enough?" he demanded of Brother David. "It's not like Niall ever speaks this stuff in conversation. And it's lousy for flirting." Outside, rain drizzled, as gray as the castle walls, a spattering treble ostinato to their every conversation and every move and every piece played on the harp and recorder. It hadn't stopped for days.

"Come now." Brother David pushed a hand over his tonsured head, his monkly patience stretching thin. "Pick up your quill and try again."

Allene paused in her stitching.

"I know it, you must know it," Niall added from the window seat. "Although we could work with swords if you prefer."

"There's no time for that," Shawn grumbled. "Christina will be here soon." In his own time, he thought, it would be called double dating. The four of them, often with Brother David and Hugh, spent a great deal of time together in Niall and Allene's chambers. They played chess and tric-trac—much like backgammon—or sang while he and Niall played the harp and recorder. Now, they waited for her to return from bringing food to Adam's widow. The weather had warmed in the last two days, and they hoped to go riding and hawking—if the rain would only let up.

"You're irritable of late," Allene remarked. "Is summat amiss?"

"Something's very amiss." He ignored the quill Brother David offered him. "Amy's due soon. My child. And I won't even know if I have a son or a daughter." He rose from the chair, and paced the room. As he passed behind Allene, he leaned close, saying, "I feel disloyal." He felt uneasy enjoying the time with Christina.

"Amy will not be born for seven hundred years." Allene lifted her head to follow his pacing, puzzling over his dilemma. The rain pattered off and sunlight broke suddenly through the window, lighting her hair. "Brother David, can a man be disloyal to one who does not yet exist?"

Brother David stabbed the quill into its holder, giving up on any more instruction. "Oddly enough, such a question never arose in my studies."

Niall tipped his chair back. "Amy will be grateful for your new faith, though she may point out to you that the altar is directly ahead, not off to the right with the women."

"You wanted me to sit still in Mass," Shawn snapped.

Allene's eyes widened. "Is that how it is?"

"He's become very devout." Niall grinned. He finished cleaning his fingernails with his dirk, and pushed it back in his boot. "Have you not noticed he's early to Mass now? Every morning, without your father dragging him from bed." He turned to Shawn. "D' you know which book Father read from this morning?"

"Just trying to do what he asked," Shawn grumbled.

"So no doubt you know if the Gospel was Isaiah or Ruth."

"Niall!" Allene glared at him. "You're cruel."

Brother David covered a cough with his hand.

"Isaiah." Shawn spared a glance at Brother David, his brown-robed back bent and his shoulders shaking. "What's wrong with him? Does he need the *Heimlich* maneuver or something?"

Brother David straightened, his face grave. "I believe the Gospel was from the *New* Testament this morning. Perhaps 'tis different in your time."

"Sit still in mass," Shawn groused. "That's what he wanted." A heat rose in his face that he hadn't felt since his first adolescence crush. "Anyway, Amy may not exist in chronological time, but she exists in my past and hopefully in my future, so to me, she exists."

"But what if we never find a way to get you back?" Allene turned to Niall. "Is he to live as a monk forever?"

Niall shrugged. "We have tried, Allene. And how he lives, as long as he's here, is your father's decision."

"My father listens to you."

"Sometimes," Niall said.

"Niall, we must make him see that Shawn can't be expected to live this way forever."

Niall grinned. "You'd like him to have a wife who can nag him, too?"

A knock on the door stayed Allene's answer.

It would be Christina. Shawn turned his back, hiding the quiver of excitement, deep in his stomach, at the thought of going riding and hawking with her.

"Shawn!" Niall grinned, as Allene crossed to the door. "You look nervous. Surely 'tis not about hawking."

Shawn scoffed. "I'm not scared of a little bird."

Bannockburn, Present

Giving birth for the first time is terrifying—not knowing what's happening, or what to expect.

It's more terrifying in a foreign country, where nothing is what you expect, anyway; where the driver is in a panic, fearing you'll deliver in the back seat if he doesn't blaze through traffic, and you fear that, in his panic, he'll forget to drive on the left.

But it's the most terrifying when you fear for your child's safety, in light of an ancient crucifix and blessing.

I close my eyes, ignoring Rob's muttered exclamations, feeling Carol's reassuring hand on my shoulder. I shut out all but the warmth rippling across my abdomen. It doesn't hurt. It's supposed to hurt. Everyone says so. I'm afraid I've made a mistake; afraid they'll send me home, afraid I'll look foolish; afraid to tell Rob to turn around, in case I haven't made a mistake.

I want Shawn. I'm mad at him for abandoning me to face this alone. Furious! It's irrational. He didn't choose to disappear in time. I don't care.

I want Angus. I'm scared, and he's the only one in the world who can understand my deepest fear: what the crucifix and blessing mean to my child. Now, I can protect this baby. I can stay away from places that might pull us away. If it happens, I'm there, to shield with my life. But years from now, will I lose my child to the same brutal world that took Shawn, that can kill in a heartbeat?

The blessing says father and son. *Maybe a daughter is safe from this blessing that's really a curse.*

Rob screeches up to the hospital entrance, jumping out, shouting, "It's okay, Amy, it's okay, I'll find someone!" A nurse comes running with a wheel chair ; another warm wave ripples into pain; sweat breaks out, cold and prickling, across my forehead. I pray for a daughter.

Near Glenmirril, 1315

With a shriek, the hawk plummeted, a black silhouette against the blue winter sky, its sharp beak diving at Shawn. He yelped, threw his arms over his head, protecting himself from a flurry of wings flapping around his face, and sharp talons grappling for him. Hugh yelled. Wings thrashed. He dropped to the ground, shouting, "Get it off me!"

Hands yanked at him, Niall shouted, and Allene said, "Get up now, Shawn, the bird is on Niall's arm."

He climbed sheepishly to his feet, looking with blazing cheeks from Christina, who stared at him in wide-eyed shock, to Brother David, who stared at the ground, his mouth small and tight against his clear attempt not to laugh. Hugh made no such pretense, but guffawed loudly, slapping his thigh. "I've not seen aught so funny in years!" he declared.

"The thing is too stupid to know the difference between a man and a *rabbit!*" Shawn declared indignantly.

"The way you threw yourself on the ground, nor can I." Niall grinned, as he tugged a hood over the bird's head. He whispered soothing sounds at it.

"You're comforting that murderous thing?" Shawn demanded. "*It* attacked *me!*"

Allene smiled. "It did not attack you, Shawn. It was trying to return to your wrist. You've the leather glove."

"You must trust it," Hugh added. "It is well-trained."

Shawn glanced at Christina. She looked from one to the other, and back to him. "You've never been hawking!" She said it as he might once have said, *You've never watched TV!*

Color blazed up his cheeks.

Niall slapped him on the shoulder. "He'll learn."

"Aye." Hugh wiped tears of mirth from his eyes. "Hopefully before he disturbs the poor bird too much."

"Come now." With a hasty glance at Christina's still questioning face, Allene said, "Let us be on our way."

An hour later, with a brace of winter hare, and Shawn still trying to shrug off the sting of his faux pas before Christina, the party rode down a hill to a loch sheltered in a deep hollow. With the lower elevation and the sun high in the sky, it was almost warm. Shawn glanced from the loch to Niall, and edged the party closer to the rocky shore. "It's like spring in Minnesota!" He stretched his arms, his face lifted to the sun. In college, after a long winter, he'd be crossing the quad in shorts and t-shirts in this weather.

Brother David helped Allene spread tartans over the pebbly shore, as Hugh dug in his pony's saddle packs for bannocks and meat pies. Christina gathered berries in her cloak and re-joined them. "Great place," Shawn commented, avoiding Niall's eyes. "I spent every summer at the loch with my dad. Fishing, swimming." He stopped. He couldn't mention water skiing. "Good times!"

Christina smiled. "Where was that?"

"In my country." He felt the glances exchanged among the others. Niall extended a hand to Allene, and they wandered off along the shore.

Hugh cleared his throat. "Eat, Christina. We've a long ride home. Brother David, will you have ale?"

"I will." The monk drank deeply from the skin.

Christina looked from one to the other, and back to Shawn. "Tell me more of your country. You say you were wealthy, yet you didn't ride or hunt or hawk."

"I had people to do it for me." Shawn hoped his cheerful voice would dissuade her. He could make a joke of it, turn her away from the subject.

"You had men to ride for you?" she asked doubtfully. "That makes little sense."

"I didn't need to hunt," he said, avoiding a direct answer.

"All men of rank hunt," she objected.

"I didn't have time." He made a show of pushing a bannock into his mouth, saying, "Mm, mm, does Bessie know how to make bannocks, or what? Brother David, how about that reading this morning, hey?"

"No time to hunt?" Christina persisted. "What were you doing?"

Brother David busied himself eating. Hugh climbed to his feet and shambled off along the shore.

"Doing?" Shawn stared at the meat pasty in his hand. "Things. Just like I do now." He wanted to tell her. She knew his real name. But he wanted more, wanted honesty between them. "I played *trombone*."

"*Trombone?* Is that a *game*?"

He looked up, into her dark blue eyes, and laughed. "No. It's an instrument, like a sackbut, only bigger."

"So you were a minstrel?"

Shawn stared out over the blue loch glittering under the winter sun. "Yeah. I guess."

"You traveled?"

Shawn nodded.

"But you were as wealthy as a king? I've never heard of a wealthy minstrel. How can this be?"

"Because people all over the world knew me and wanted my music."

"I've never heard of you here in Scotland," Christina objected.

"Okay, everywhere but Scotland."

"Come now!" Her eyebrows dipped with warning. "I'm not so provincial as that, and my husband and father-in-law were well traveled. They'd have heard of you if you were so well known."

She looked to Brother David, who turned away, looking as guilty as ever a man did. "I begin to think," she said slowly, "that everyone but me knows something."

"I'm sorry." Shawn stared at his hands. Brother David rose and wandered back up the hill, still chaperoning, but no longer in danger of being questioned. "Christina, I *want* to tell you the truth. But I can't."

"Are you a spy of some sort?" she asked.

Shawn shook his head, eyes on the tartan.

"Why else would you be unable to tell the truth?"

He cleared his throat. "Because it's too hard to believe. I played sackbut, and I traveled the world and earned lots of money. It's all true, even if you never heard of me."

She bowed her head and spoke softly. "Tell me about your home."

He told her about his house, leaving out details of modern refrigeration, ovens, and flush toilets. He told her about his twenty acres of fields, forest, and streams, and the small waterfall, leaving out how much Amy had liked to walk there, hand in hand, with him.

Her voice became softer still. She studied her hands resting on her jewel-blue skirt. "Tell me about Amy."

"She plays violin," he said. "We played together in an orchestra, a group of a hundred musicians who all play together."

"I've never heard of such a thing. And what is a violin?"

"Like a lute," he replied. "Or a rebec."

"What drew you to her?" Christina held out a bannock to him.

Shawn reached for it. Their fingers grazed. He yanked his hand back, trying to ignore the way his heart pounded out a pair of *allegro* eighths where there should have been only *andante* quarters. He closed his eyes, not wanting to see the delicate pink he knew would be brushing her cheeks at the touch of their fingers; feeling he could hide his own emotions, if their eyes didn't meet. Christina, he was sure, was envisioning something more courtly and noble than anything he'd given Amy.

Behind closed lids, he saw Amy again as if for the first time. It was the day he'd auditioned. He'd pushed past the receptionist's desk into the back halls, and there, coming toward him was a beautiful girl, with porcelain skin, and lively eyes. She walked with a tall, broad-shouldered man, laughing at something he said, the sound as pleasant as bells tinkling in a morning breeze. The man's teeth flashed white. It was clear, in the crinkle around his eyes and the way he leaned close, that he was captivated by her.

Shawn's heart had knocked in his chest, much as it had done just now with

Christina. Amy had worn jeans that day, and a royal blue t-shirt that set off her hair and complexion. It was nothing like the edgy styles and bold attitude he liked. Her demeanor screamed *wholesome*. To him, it was a four letter word. His father had been wholesome, *good*, even, and that hadn't worked out so well for him.

She and the man brushed by, not even noticing him. He turned to look after her, and saw the thick black hair flowing to her waist, and wanted to follow her.

"Her voice," he said, lost in the memory. "The look on her face when she plays her violin. She's beautiful. Was. Will be."

"Will be?"

He opened his eyes, disoriented to find himself not in the cinder block back mazes of the concert hall, but in the Highlands with a medieval woman sitting in her jewel-blue gown beside him. He laughed. "Just jesting." He changed the subject. "There are millions of beautiful women. Why do you think a man is attracted to one and not another?"

"Something in her that he needs," Christina replied.

He frowned at her echo of Dana's words, seven centuries from now. "She trusted me," he said. "She believed in me." The others hadn't, he realized. They'd just wanted his limelight, the notoriety, the moment's thrill. "She saw good in me."

"We all need that," Christina answered.

"I trusted her. I could always count on her." The cruel irony of his words squeezed his heart tight, as he realized how much he valued that, and how little of it he'd given her in return.

They sat in comfortable silence. A winter bird trilled in the distance; a cow lowed back a response, before Christina asked, "What does she look like?"

He hesitated only a moment as the realization struck him. "Like you, in a way. She has long black hair all the way to her waist." He stopped. "I guess that's not remarkable in your time. I mean, here. But for us, it's unusual."

"Black hair?" She frowned.

"Long hair. Most women cut it short."

"Are they ill?" Christina asked. "Or have they taken vows?"

Shawn laughed, delighting in sharing his world with her, even though it was impossible to explain. He shook his head. "It's just the fashion."

"There can be no such place where women live alone and go about in their undergarments and cut their hair short," Christina insisted. "Where minstrels are as wealthy as kings and as widely known as the Pope."

"Yeah, I sure was." Shawn snorted. "One billion Catholics hid their daughters when I came to town."

She leaned forward suddenly. "Why will you not tell the truth?"

Shawn sighed. He picked up a rock and threw it, hard, into the loch. "It *is* the truth. Everything I've said is true. It's just not the whole truth, and you wouldn't believe the rest of it, anyway. Does it matter?"

"It matters a great deal, knowing all of you are keeping secrets." She stared away at the loch, and whispered, "It hurts."

Shawn hung his head, hating the half-truths. This time, they hurt him, too.

Bannockburn, Present

"It's a boy, Amy!" Angus brushes hair off my temple, whispering in awe as if I've single-handedly built mesas and splashed sunrise over the desert.

"A boy?" My heart pounds. I shake my head, denying.

"He's beautiful," Carol gushes.

Angus lays my son, bare and pink, on my chest. Carol gazes down at the tiny face with joy—the first real happiness she's had since Shawn's disappearance. I touch his hair, thick and black like mine. He struggles to gaze up at me. It's Shawn's face, looking up with dark, curious eyes. He blinks sleepily. His eyelids droop shut. He gives a little shuddering sigh and relaxes against my shoulder. Tears sting my eyes. He doesn't even know what trust is, yet he trusts he is safe in my arms, that I will protect him.

I close my eyes in prayer that I can. If this blessing means anything, if Shawn and Niall are related—and they must be, despite the mysterious James Angus who should have been the connection—then he's in danger. I need to go back to the States, to safety. But I can't leave Angus. I can't abandon Shawn in a brutal era. I can't leave myself to explain one day to my son why I abandoned his father. Will leaving the crucifix in a drawer protect him? Or is the blessing itself the real catalyst?

"What is his name?" Carol pulls me from my fears.

"James," I say without hesitation.

She gazes down at me; she blinks suddenly, and presses a hand to her eyes, half-turning from me. She squeezes my hand, a wealth of emotion in the gesture, and whispers, "Thank you."

I run my hand over his skin, as soft as a rose petal, unsullied by life. As my hand slides off his shoulder, I see it: a ginger brown birthmark covers his shoulder blade, blazing out from the middle of his back, like a flame...or an angel wing.

Near Glenmirril, January 1315

They sat in silence for a time, Shawn's thoughts in turmoil. He'd promised himself he'd make it up to Amy. Yet here he sat, and wanted with all his heart to continue sitting, with someone else. At the far end of the loch, Allene and Niall appeared, hand in hand, and shortly afterward, Hugh came from the other direction.

Shawn clapped his hands and jumped to his feet as they neared, hoping to shake Christina's despondency—and his own. "I was just telling Christina more about my, uh, country," he said. "Ever hear of the Polar Bear Plunge?"

"I've never heard of polar bears at all." Allene turned to Brother David, coming down the hill. "Have you, in your travels and studies?"

Brother David shook his head. "What manner of bear is it?"

"Big and white." Shawn raised his hands over his head, demonstrating. "They live in the north and swim in the arctic sea. In my country, we prove our manliness by jumping in lakes in the winter." He threw off his cloak. "Come on, Niall! Let's go, Hugh!" He yanked his vest and shirt over his head, shaking in the chill and laughing at the shock on Allene's face. "Last one in is an out of tune shawm." He stripped his trews, down to the baggy braies, laughed at the disbelief on Hugh's face, and the gasps from the women, and raced at the shore. "You move your arms over your head," he shouted back. "Kick your legs, keep them straight, and next thing you know, you're swimming!" The first of the icy water hit his ankles, sending shocks of cold up his legs. "Come on, Niall!"

"You're mad!" Hugh shouted from the shore.

"You'll catch your death," Allene added. "Come out, Shawn!"

Shawn lunged forward, gasping as cold bit into every part of his body, laughing, pulled him back to the winters he'd done the polar bear plunge with his father, raising money for some charity or other, while his mother protested, laughing, on shore. He threw one arm over his head, then the other, pumping his legs, swimming to the middle of the chilly loch, before diving under and turning back. The water felt almost warm by the time he reached shallow water again and burst into the near-freezing air, racing for his fur-lined cloak. He shook his head, sending a spray of sparkling droplets over the others, as he wrapped it around himself.

"You're mad!" Niall shouted

But Shawn noted he was smiling, not pale, or agitated.

"I'd have to be to hang out with you!" Shawn scooped a handful of water, and flung it at Niall. "Give me a paid day off and I'll teach you how to swim. Best times of my life were out on the water with my dad."

Bannockburn, Present

I wake from restless sleep, from dreams of the crucifix, of maces, swords and nooses; of filthy, sweaty, men in leather jerkins, frantic men pressed together under a mining cat, digging, digging, digging, as arrows hail down. My son is a child, on the field outside Carlisle, lost and scared amidst the battle. Shawn is there, under the mining cat. I'm reaching...reaching...reaching across time, unable to protect him, begging Shawn to save our son, but my voice is silent.

Still, something calls him. He turns. He sees the child. Unhesitating, he leaves the shelter of the cat; runs, hunched over. A bullish English soldier, with a large, black beard, turns toward James. An arrow streaks across the wet sky.

A man bellows.

I jolt upright, breathing hard! The crucifix lies on my chest. The window shows the deep cobalt sky of pre-dawn.

"Sh, now." Angus sits, squeezed on the narrow hospital bed, beside me. He brushes my hair from my sweaty temple. "What is it?"

I see Shawn frozen in motion, reaching for a child he doesn't know is his. "It seems wrong that Shawn doesn't even know he has a son."

He strokes my hand, his face thoughtful. "Aye, it does, at that."

"Where is he?" I hate the tremble in my voice.

"Shawn?" Angus sounds surprised.

"James." I know my fear is irrational. If James had disappeared, Angus wouldn't be sitting here calmly. But I am scared. The dream is strong; the English soldier is menacing. I struggle to sit up. "Where is he?"

"In the nursery, sleeping peacefully. I wish I could give you the same." He looks so sad as he strokes the back of my hand. "What can I do to help?"

I stare out the window. A few lonely stars struggle to glow above the city lights. My hand drifts to the crucifix, my thoughts to the blessing and unknown prophecy. "I need to go to Monadhliath," I say.

He's silent.

I twine my fingers in his, turning to him. "Do you understand," I ask, "that if Niall and Shawn are affected by a genetic connection, it affects James, too?"

It is he, now, who stares out the window. "I saw it immediately."

"Why didn't you say anything?"

"I didn't want to worry you."

"I'm worried," I say. "This isn't just Shawn anymore. It's my son. I need to know what I'm dealing with!"

"Monadhliath is a long hike," he says doubtfully. "You've just given birth."

"Tell me what to do to get ready," I say. "I need that prophecy."

CHAPTER TWENTY-TWO

Glenmirril, 1315

Niall stood on the third floor, looking down through the arched window into Glenmirril's courtyard. The torrential downpour of the morning had given way to a weak stream of winter sunshine. Water dripped from the eaves; puddles dotted the courtyard. The gray hood of Brother Andrew covered his face, but he stayed back from the window, lest anyone look up. He watched men pour over the drawbridge, counting, praying he'd reach thirty, thinking of their wives and children. From his vantage point, he saw a bandage on Owen's head. But he rode upright, and laughed at something Lachlan, riding beside him, said. Taran's one-eyed father followed, sliding off his pony. He embraced his wife and clapped Taran on the arm before yanking him, too, into a rough hug.

Niall watched. He was grateful for the time with Allene. Still, he'd been passed over. Shame burned in his cheeks. Everyone knew why Conal had gone. He tried to imagine letting Shawn teach him to swim—tried to imagine the day he would prove them all wrong. But even the thought of going into the loch made his legs shake; made his stomach turn.

Darnley rode in, his horse splashing sparkling droplets of water from a puddle. He lifted a hand in greeting to MacDonald, and shouted something to the men behind him. They guffawed.

Niall wanted to be there, with his men, where he belonged. Instead, it was Conal who helped the blacksmith's son, with his arm strapped to his body, clamber awkwardly off his garron. And it was Shawn, who still had the longer hair the castle folk expected of Niall, who moved among the men, patting ponies, shouting orders to stable boys, directing the chaos as if born to it. He yelled and pointed, and Taran scrambled up the wooden stairs into the great hall.

A flock of boys erupted from the southern bailey, Red's curls vivid among them, racing to be first to lead the exhausted garrons to well-earned rest. Lachlan gave a sudden whoop and deserted Owen to gather Margaret in an unseemly embrace that would have been sharply reproved by MacDonald in any other circumstance.

A hand fell on Niall's sleeve. He jumped, grabbing quickly for the hood.

"'Tis but me," Allene said softly.

He turned away, wishing she would have stayed in their chambers, rather than catch him watching covertly. There were twenty-five men in the courtyard now. He scanned the crowd below, and found two more.

She took his stiff arm and pulled it around her waist.

He found the last three, and his tension eased. "We mustn't have a maid come along and see Sir Niall's wife with Brother Andrew," Niall whispered into her barbet.

"The maids are far too busy to be up here," she answered.

"Someone may look up."

"My hair is covered. They'll not recognize me."

They watched in silence as Conal spoke with MacDonald and turned to Shawn. "'Tis strange," Niall mused, "to watch him. Is this what it would be, to watch oneself from a distance?"

"Perhaps."

Three stories below, Conal placed a hand on Shawn's shoulder. They spoke, heads bowed close, before Shawn threw his head back with a laugh that carried to the third floor. Shawn shook Conal's hand, slapped him on the back, and said something that made Conal laugh in turn. Shawn beckoned Red, who grabbed the reins of Conal's pony, and the two men turned together for the great hall.

"My father bids me tell you he's meeting Conal, the lords, and Shawn and will be up to speak with you shortly."

"I should have been there." Niall stared at a droplet of water clinging to the eave over the window.

"Your hair hasn't grown in."

"We could have come up with a story. You know that's not the real reason." The droplet swelled, separated itself from the roof, and plunged to the courtyard below.

She looked up at him, surprise on her face. It was as close as anyone in the castle had ever come—apart from Shawn—to speaking the truth. "Shawn says he can help you," she said softly.

Niall scoffed. "I'm to go in the loch in February?"

"Remember all he said," she replied. "Think of good things by the shore. Remember how he moved his arms. You've ever been able to learn from watching. Think on it now."

Footsteps sounded on the stair, hurried and light. Niall and Allene sprang apart as Christina appeared at the top of the stairs, her face white.

"Christina!" Allene spoke in alarm. "What is amiss?"

Christina turned, pointing at the stairs. She moved her mouth, but no words came out. She stumbled, her hand falling on the handle of the door into Niall's chambers, and stood, staring back at the stairs.

Niall grabbed his dirk, throwing himself between Christina and whatever was coming. But the man who appeared at the top of the stairs made him catch his breath. His fingers went weak on the knife.

Scotland, Present

Home from the hospital, life spins into high gear. Monadhliath and the prophecy are my constant companions through laundry and midnight feedings and diaper changes. I've never changed a diaper in my life. I'm bleary-eyed with lack of sleep, though Carol does shopping and dishes. In his few short days with me, Angus takes me car-shopping. As I drive a fire-engine red Renault off the lot, I tremble in elation and fear: elation at my new car, at my ability to care for myself and my child; fear of driving on the left—and fear at this next step in building a life here.

While James stays safe with Carol, Angus has me drive around town, and down the highways in February's drizzle. I graduate from terror to exhilaration. To think how I shook, that night I drove the few miles from Glenmirril to our hotel in Inverness, on an empty highway! Freedom and confidence grow in me. I see, with sorrow, how far my life with Shawn had moved from what love should be—building one another up, helping one another grow. I only grew weak with Shawn. I grow strong with Angus.

As we drive, we discuss how the blessing affects James. Do we take him along to Monadhliath, or leave him with Carol? "It draws father and son together for their protection," *Angus insists. "He'll draw Shawn into our time, not the other way around, because that would be for Shawn's protection. And they need to be together, for anything to happen, aye?"*

"As far as we know," I agree.

"Monadhliath is hard to get to even today," he says. "Niall and Shawn were at Carlisle, Stirling, Cambuskenneth, Creagsmalan, Northumbria. If Shawn was ever at Monadhliath, it was in June, when he and Allene may have stopped on their way to Hugh's camp. When else would they even have time to go to such a remote place?"

We conclude it's safe to take James with us in April.

"So," Angus says. "That's solved. Lunch." He directs me down a highway, around a round-about, through a small town, to a pub. A dozen roses wait on the table. We celebrate my success with lemon shrimp. My heart is in my throat, feeling loved, protected, and cherished. After lunch, in a brief interval of sunshine, Angus leans back against my new car, damp with the recent rain, grinning down at me. I touch his short, dark curls, and want nothing more than to stay in this moment, with him, forever, as he looks down at me with such pleasure.

Glenmirril, February 1315

"Father!" Allene burst into the great hall. She ran through beams of sunlight pouring through high windows, turning the rushes on the floor to gold, and fell to her knees before the table, her eyes averted from the lords, whose faces would be heavy with disapproval at her interruption. Shawn rose from his seat. MacDonald laid a hand on his arm, and he lowered himself.

Allene gripped her father's hands. "Please, Father, please forgive me, but...*Niall*...his people are trying to reach him."

"His people?" demanded Lord Morrison. "What mean you?"

MacDonald and Shawn became still, but for their eyes meeting.

"She means naught," said the Laird. "She has been ill. Niall, escort your wife to your chambers. Immediately."

Only Shawn heard her whisper, "Thank you, Father. *Thank you.*"

Shawn hurried around the table, his cloak stirring the rushes. She gripped his arm, trying to appear ill, even as they wrestled over who would drag whom more quickly from the hall. With the door shut on the lords, she crushed his hand in hers, flying for the stairs, all pretense of illness abandoned, as he scrambled after her. She threw open the door of her chambers, slamming it behind them so quickly Shawn had to open it again and release his cloak.

Turning to the room, he saw none of the pandemonium he had expected. The sun had broken from the clouds, skimming past a half-finished drawing on Christina's easel, and turning the room to a sunny, silver oasis of peace. Niall stood silently by the table, his arm around Christina's shoulder. Shawn stepped forward quickly, laying his hand on her other shoulder. Her face was bone white against her black hair, everything about her utterly still. "What is it?" he asked. "How can they...?"

"The window," Niall whispered.

Shawn raised his eyes to where they both stared. At first, he saw only a shimmer of light dancing through the panes of glass. "It's just...."

"No, look. Listen." Niall breathed out the words.

Shawn stepped forward, squinting, and caught his breath. He saw a man now, his own six feet, with a broad chest, ruddy cheeks and short black curls. He was hazy, ghost-like. "Why do you think he's my people?" he asked. "I've never seen him."

"His clothing." Niall didn't take his eyes from the man.

Then Shawn realized—twenty-first century clothing was still normal enough to him, it hadn't registered, despite months in tunics and cloaks and leather boots laced to his knees. The man wore a heavy blue peacoat.

"He's been calling your name."

"Shawn, are you here?" The man's deep, gruff voice held a heavy Scottish accent. Its modern sound fell strangely on Shawn's ears.

"He speaks English." Christina turned to him. Her fingers squeezed his arm. "Are you from England?"

"No." Shawn's eyes remained locked on the man. He stepped forward, directly before the hazy figure, and said, "I'm here. Can you hear me?"

The man made no response, but peered into the room. A frown flickered across his face, he muttered, and wrung a dark knit cap in his hands. "She had a boy!" The voice echoed as if down a long tunnel, but the words were clear.

Shawn's breath came hard and fast. "Amy," he whispered, and more loudly, "I'm here. Who are you?" *He had a son!*

The man glanced out the window, then studied one of the walls. "That's where the tapestry is, of you being chased by MacDougall," Shawn said to Niall. "Do you think he's looking at it?"

The man turned again. "She named him James, after your father."

Shawn squeezed his eyes shut, fighting the hot tears that pierced them. His heart tripped over a beat and sped up again. She'd remembered him!

She'd honored his father.

"Shawn, she wants you to know," the man called.

"He's been saying it for ten minutes." Allene's fingertips fell on his forearm. Shawn's hand crept over hers, tightening.

The man returned to the window, gave his message again, and wandered across the room, drifting through the settee. Christina gasped. He stopped at the fireplace and spoke again. Shawn called to him several more times, with no response. Christina was still and white as a birch tree. Shawn put his arm around her. "It's okay. He's just giving me a message."

The shimmering shape walked through the door without opening it. They ran, heedless of two Nialls being seen, and threw open the heavy wooden door to stare after him, trailing misty silver through the gray stone hall. He shimmered and faded from sight.

Niall yanked them all back in the room. They stared at one another. Then Niall grinned, clapped him on the shoulder. "You've a son!"

Shawn grinned, frowned, paced the room. "I have a son," he said. "James." He laughed. "I have a son!" He spun to Niall. "Who the hell was that guy? That wasn't Rob." He stared out the window briefly, then turned back to the group. "Does this mean she's still in Scotland?"

He looked at Christina, staring at him with her eyebrows drawn in a delicate crease. Niall and Allene, too, looked at her, and Niall said, "Come, Allene."

"'Tis not proper!" Allene protested.

"Proper can fly to the wind this once." Niall pulled her along to the bedchamber, shutting the door between.

"Christina?" Shawn removed his cloak, and wrapped it around her shoulders. "Are you okay?"

"Tell me who you are." Her tone brooked no evasions, no lies.

He sighed, turned his back to her, staring out the window.

"What kind of man are you?" she demanded. "You receive messages from ghosts in peculiar clothing, and Allene calls him *your people*. You've a child with Amy. You didn't tell me that."

"I didn't...." He stopped, and tried again. "I wasn't...." He faced her. "How can I tell you the truth?"

"You said you weren't married. Yet she has your child."

He laughed, short and harsh. "Uh, you know how that happens, right?" Anger flashed through him at her condemnation. "I think you're jealous."

She flushed.

"It's not like it doesn't happen here," he added, instantly regretting his unkind words. "Didn't Edward Bruce himself get into a little trouble that way? I never claimed to be a plaster saint."

"But I didn't think you were such a man. You seemed kind and good, not like Edward Bruce, not a man who would leave a woman alone with child."

"I really had no say in leaving her." He recognized the lie, even as the words came out. He knew what he would have done, last June, if he'd ever let her say the words *I'm pregnant.* He would have pushed her to end that pregnancy, too. He would have threatened to leave her if she didn't. He bit his lip, the gesture reminding him of Amy, and stared at the floor.

"Were you exiled?" Christina asked.

"No. Well, yes, in a manner of speaking. I don't know."

"You don't *know?*" Her voice rose. "Certainly one *knows* if one has been exiled or not! Where do you come from? I want the truth, and then I'll tell you what I've withheld."

His head shot up. His eyebrows knit together. "You can't possibly have anything to hide."

"I knew you before I saw you in the confessional," she said. "I knew there were two of you. I've hesitated to say it, for fear of being thought mad. Because I didn't understand. But he's not the first ghost I've seen. And 'tis not the first time I've seen him. Now tell me everything if you want my story."

Glenmirril, February 1315

Shawn paced Niall's solar. Christina perched on Allene's settee, giving no quarter. He tried to think how to tell her. He wondered if she had a knife on her and might stab him for lying. He had to laugh at the irony that the craziest story he'd ever told a woman in his life was the one that was actually true.

"I'm waiting," she reminded him tartly.

"Okay, before I start, I want to remind you that Allene, and the Laird will all back me up. Brother David, too. And Niall especially. He's been there."

"Where? Where you come from?"

"Yes, where I come from. You know his reputation for honesty."

She nodded.

"Okay, then. No slapping, no knives." And he told her of the twenty-first century, of Amy leaving him in the tower, of waking in Niall's place.

She listened, her face pale despite his heavy cloak over her dress.

"You're not acting very surprised," he said. "You don't believe a word I'm saying, do you? You saw his coat. It's like nothing that exists today."

"Call Niall in," she said, "and I'll tell you why I'm not surprised."

Soon the four of them resumed their places in the solar.

"I told you I go to Iona each June," she said.

Niall and Shawn exchanged glances. Shawn wondered if he, too, was thinking of the message on Hugh's rock. But there could be no connection.

"I often prayed through the night in Columba's shrine," she continued.

"Yes, Iona. I got the feeling you expected some reaction from me."

She nodded. "But you say you've never been there."

"Not in this time, or my own."

"And yet, I've seen you there. And Niall."

"I've never been there!" Shawn protested.

Niall started off the couch. "The *Isle* of Iona?"

Allene frowned. "'Tis not possible."

Shawn held up a hand, commanding silence. "Let her finish."

"It happened first when I was seventeen. It had been a bad year with Duncan."

"Was there any other kind?" Shawn's own anger surprised him.

Christina ignored him. "One of the nuns suggested I'd not want to pray that night. 'Twas June 8."

"The night we switched the first time," Shawn said.

"But he died just past midnight," Niall said. "'Twas the wee hours of June 9, that we switched."

"As the prophecy says," added Allene. They all looked to Christina to continue her story.

"When I said I would pray as usual, she pulled me aside and told me, 'Iona is a thin place. Strange things are seen in the chapel. I don't wish ye to be frightened, child.' I told her I'd not be frightened, as it is a holy place of God and naught would harm me. She was old. I didn't believe her."

"But you did see something?" Shawn leaned forward.

"I saw a woman with long black hair, braided down her back. Her head was uncovered. She wore a cloak with sleeves—you call it a coat?—much like the man tonight, but long."

"That's Amy." Shawn and Niall looked at one another. Allene's eyes met Christina's, and they looked back to the men. Shawn closed his eyes, squeezing them tight. "Amy's never been to Iona either, as far as I know."

"She's holding a child," Christina said. "An infant."

They stared at each other for a minute, before Niall said, "Go on."

"In the darkest part of the night," Christina said, "'twas quiet in the chapel, just me, the crucifix, candles burning. There were cries outside, a gust of wind, though it had been a still night. At first I ignored it. But the wind became so strong, it sounded like to blow the place down. I rose to see what was happening. But when I opened the door, 'twas still outside."

"You heard no wind?" Allene asked.

Christina shook her head. "I thought perhaps it had died suddenly, and I returned to praying. But soon it started again. I went to the door a second time, and again it was calm. The third time, I heard voices. I saw shadows running in the dark. I shut the door quickly, thinking to hide, thinking of the days Vikings raided and raped and murdered. But as I turned to the altar to ask God where I could hide, I saw men in the chapel. They were like ghosts. They fought one another, their faces in concentration. I backed against the wall, afraid, but they paid me no heed. They were silent, though I heard shouting outside, though I saw their mouths moving as if they themselves shouted.

"When I realized they wouldn't hurt me, I watched more closely and saw two of them were identical. I watched, thinking they looked like someone I knew. Then they were gone."

Shawn rose from the table, pacing.

On the couch, Allene clutched Niall's hand. "But it never happened." She turned to Niall. "Surely you've not fought on Iona and kept it from me?"

"Speaking for myself," Shawn said, "I have never fought with Niall on Iona. I've never been there at all. It was me and Niall?" He turned to Christina for verification.

She nodded. "I stood against the wall for some time after the vision disappeared, trying to calm myself, trying to pray, trying to think who the men looked like, and I finally knew 'twas Niall Campbell I'd known at Glenmirril. When I'd watched him long enough at Creagsmalan, I knew 'twas the same man I'd seen several times, for it happens each year."

"But I've never been there," Niall repeated.

"How old were we?" Shawn asked.

"Much as you are now."

"Then was she seeing something that *will* happen?" Shawn asked.

"It can't happen, for I'll not go to Iona," Niall said. "Even if I so wished, I'll be with Bruce in June."

"And yet, she saw it," Shawn said. "A year ago, I'd laugh. But we're standing here in February, the month Amy was due—will be due—and a man appears saying she had a son. What Christina saw means something."

"Might she have seen things that happen elsewhere?" Niall asked.

"There would be no reason for men to fight in Columba's shrine," Allene added.

"What about this guy?" Shawn asked. "The one we saw here just now?"

"When I turned," Christina said, "he stood at the door, watching. Just watching. Do you know him?"

"No," Shawn said. "No clue."

"Wait!" Niall snapped his fingers. "'Tis the man who came to my room—your room—at the castle, about the counterfeit money."

"He's a *cop?*" Shawn used English where he had no medieval Gaelic.

"What is a *cop?*" asked Allene.

"Police. The law. The constable."

"You were in trouble with the law?" Christina gazed at him sadly. "What kind of man *were* you?"

"Look, it was an accident," Shawn said. "Someone gave me fake money, I didn't have real money to replace it with or I would have. And this guy was going to beat me up, and Amy would have found out...do we have to talk about this now? Was it cops we were fighting? It was only sixty pounds."

Allene gasped.

"That's nothing in my time," Shawn told her. "It's like a couple little coins, that's all. It's not possible they wanted me so badly over sixty pounds that they figured out a way to chase me across time. This makes no sense. Besides, I'd go with them. I *want* to go home. I wouldn't fight them." He turned back to Christina. "Who *were* we fighting?"

Christina frowned. "I've no idea. Each year, I watch the two of you, and I look at the man in the back of the chapel, also watching. I've paid no heed to the men you fought."

CHAPTER TWENTY-THREE

Killin, Scotland, Present

I drive with Carol to Killin. Carrying James in a front pack, we let ourselves into a field behind the schoolhouse. A shaggy Highland cattle snorts indignantly, and bolts away. "He's as scared of us as we are of him," I say in amazement.

Carol laughs nervously. "What if he realizes he's bigger and has horns?"

We climb a stile and ascend S'ron na Claichain's gentle slope toward the summit. But, reaching what we thought was the summit, we discover another, higher peak beyond it. We shrug and continue climbing, determined to reach the real summit—only to discover it, too, is merely a stop along the way. At the third summit, we discover there's a fourth. "Like life, isn't it?" Carol quips.

"Very," I agree, thinking back on all the mountains I have conquered over the years. I have begun to see there will always be another. I'm sore, but elated the next day. I still hurt a week later when we trek to Alloa castle. By the time we make the long climb up Ben Cleuch, I've lost the maternity weight. My legs have become lean and defined. We're walking toward Castle Doune when I get a call from the States that feels like a summit in my new life. Carol hugs me in joy, and we celebrate with a sponge cake when we get home. But I hold the secret close, eager to tell Angus in person.

Glenmirril, February 1315

In the chapel, with Red beside him, Shawn's eyes drifted to Christina's back. The gospel, or psalms, or whatever it was, filtered through his mind, *nolite thesaurizare*, a few words here, a sentence there, as he stared at Christina's hair falling in glossy cascades down her back. *...et ubi fures....*

Rain drizzled down the chapel windows. His mind had always been a leaping brook, never a quiet stream. But today, his thoughts floated on the incense, back to Amy. A Scottish cop had called to him from the empty halls of twenty-first century Glenmirril, telling him he had a son. That same policeman would at some time stand in Columba's shrine, watching him and Niall in a fight in which they'd never engaged, against unknown opponents. It made no sense.

But it must mean Amy was in Scotland. *Ubi enim est thesaurus tuus ibi est et cor tuum. For where your treasure is, there will be your heart,* his mind translated. She wouldn't call the Inverness police from the States and ask them to send a man to Glenmirril calling for him. So who was the guy?

The *Kyrie* drifted to the arched ceiling. Another streak of rain trailed down the window. Father lifted his arms before the crucifix. Christina's face lifted; her waves of black hair shone in the light.

Shawn tried to picture his son. He'd have thick, black hair black like Amy's. Maybe he'd have Amy's nose or her delicate ears that he loved. Maybe he'd have Shawn's temper and scream a lot, keeping her up at night. Maybe he'd have his father's laugh, and make her smile. *There will be your heart....* He hoped Rob would at least love the boy, take good care of him, maybe teach him to play piano, take him fishing and camping. He bowed his head. *God, I know I haven't exactly been on speaking terms with You. I still sort of think You deserve that. But they say You're a forgiving God. Would You find it in Your heart to somehow let me see him? Just once? Even though I'm still mad at You?*

Castle Campbell, Scotland, Present

We trudge, Angus, Carol, and I, through the rich smell of winter decay meeting spring rebirth. A creek gurgles beside us, a pleasant soundtrack. James wakes more often than he did on earlier walks, peering intently over his front pack with big, bright eyes, at brown ferns draping over the path. We cross a wooden bridge and climb a steep flight of stairs, half hidden under last winter's sodden leaves, and suddenly, a lawn opens before us.

"I give you Castle Campbell!" Angus sweeps his arm wide, presenting stone walls and a high tower. Spring has not yet breathed life into the bare limbs, brown shrubbery, and fallow garden that surround them.

James twists in the carrier, letting out a squeak. I draw in deep breaths, after the long climb, as I admire the castle looking out over the Scottish hills. "I need to feed him."

"You two go on," Carol says. "I'm going to look around."

Angus slides his hand into mine. Settling James to nursing on a bench in the sun, I say, "I have a surprise!"

A corner of Angus's mouth lifts in wry humor. "You've had many."

"But this is a good one!" I protest, laughing.

Angus pats James's head. "I'd have to say this turned out to be a grand one."

Warmth bursts around my heart. Our eyes lock, losing track of time.

He strokes my fingers, smiling. "What is it?"

"A friend of a friend heard me play on Shawn's CDs. He wants me to solo

on his next recording."

The smile grows on Angus's face. "Congratulations. And you think you're not good enough!"

I look at Bruce's heavy garnet ring. "Shawn once told me he's a professional, he knows when people are good or not. He would say Adam did some fast talking for me. Or his friend couldn't find anyone else."

"Or maybe he was afraid to let you out of his sight because he knew what he did when he was out of yours." Angus strokes the black down of James's hair. "What would you say to Shawn now?"

I smile, seeing how I've changed. "I'd say Adam's friend knows a good player, too. I'd say if he doesn't like my playing, other people do. Why couldn't I say that to him before?"

"You loved him." Angus twists a long strand of my hair around his finger. "You trusted him."

Silence wraps around us, but for a bird singing in the castle gardens, and James nursing. When his gulping slows. I lift him to my shoulder, thinking of Shawn. He was terrible. He was wonderful. I loved him. I'd started to hate him. He's trapped in a brutal world. My son will grieve his father one day. So many conflicting emotions.

Angus rubs my back. "You've time for one more hike before we head to Monadhliath," he says. "What have you planned?"

"Jedburgh to Selkirk to Melrose."

"That's a full day," he warns.

"I want to be ready." On my shoulder, James sighs. He's falling asleep. I know we've gone over it and over it, but as my son breathes peacefully on my shoulder, I can't help but ask, "You're sure he'll be safe?"

"Positive. Shawn would have to be there, for starters, and odds are a million to one."

Reassured, I ask, "Have you heard from Brian or any of your friends?"

"I haven't." He pulls out his phone. "Let me call him."

Oban, Present

Beaumont threw himself onto the couch in Brian's solar. He needed a pell to swing at, a quintain to charge, a page to berate, a dog to kick. Instead, he had this pathetic hovel, daintily decorated as if for a gaggle of ladies, but totally bereft of such fair company. The man Angus, who promised to hold more information, was still away on his journeys. Brian deflected his questions about the woman, Amy, who appeared to be Angus's wife or betrothed—Brian was quite evasive. And this latest castle to which Brian had taken him had held no useful information—though it had been deeply satisfying to see the home of his long-time rivals in ruins, and read of their demise. It was only a shame it had taken until the 1600s for their well-deserved fate to catch up to them.

He'd wanted to stay the night and visit another castle, but Brian had insisted on returning home.

Home! Simon cast a disdainful glance at the weak chairs that would collapse if a man sat on them in his armor; past the white lace hanging at the windows. It was unsuited to his likes, the meals paltry servings of but one course, no men with whom to talk and boast and laugh, no jugglers or bards, nothing but Brian's fleshy, round face and sometimes a thin piping excuse for music rising from a black box that was more annoying than entertaining or rousing, as music ought to be.

Brian stalked past him, throwing his jangle of keys on a table and tossing an irritable glare at Simon. Simon glared back, making an internal vow the insolent man would pay for his disrespect—as soon as Simon had no more use for him.

The fat man waddled angrily into one of the back chambers. Simon thumped his arms across his chest. He was hungry. But rather than prepare food, the churl threw himself down at the desk in his office, his back to Simon, and began writing. A bullish snort erupted through Simon's nose. His chest heaved. Brian remained engrossed in his work. Simon rose, too irritable to sit, and slipped into the small garden in the back. It was as pitiful as the rest of this hovel, a minuscule courtyard with a few wretched flowers. Simon paced the patch of grass, rubbing his bearded jaw as he considered his next move. He knew where the Scots would strike, and the births of Edward's children. He would appear as a seer to his king. He'd have power. But he had to *get there,* first. And how he was to do that remained unanswered.

From the window came the sound of Brian's *phone* ringing. Simon looked up to the brick wall. In three steps, he crossed the grass, and stood on the flowers under the window, listening.

Glenmirril, 1315

March blew through with no lessening of the fierce winds that kept the castle folk indoors as much as they were able. Shawn helped Red in the stables, after training the boys, enjoying his bright mind and cheerful tales of his days with the farrier. The boy taught him more about horses, and he taught Red to play the recorder.

A messenger arrived, chilled and miserable from his long ride in steady rain, hunched into his shaggy garron. The bishop had annulled Christina's marriage. Duncan MacDougall was in a fury.

Christina received the news with her usual calm, though she laid aside her needlework moments later, and with a graceful incline of her head, departed Niall's solar. With a glance at Allene and Niall, Shawn slipped out after her. He trailed behind, padding silently on leather boots, to the chapel. After waiting in the hall for a time, he let himself in, and knelt in a pew at the back. Rain pounded the windows, dimming the chapel. Candles flickered in shrines on either side of the altar, jewels in their blue and red and green holders. Minutes ticked by. The steady pounding of rain decrescendoed to a miserable drizzle. He missed his chance to play sackbut in the Bat Cave. Incense hung heavy in the air. She knelt, head bowed, without a shadow of motion. The rain stopped. Light filtered through the stained glass window.

At last she stood, and stared at Shawn with unseeing eyes. Wet streaks trailed down her cheeks.

He went to her, touched her cheek. "Why are you crying? You're free."

"I'm crying *because* I'm free," she whispered.

He wrapped his arms around her, letting her cry on his shoulder. "You've no idea what it was like," she said. It was the only reference she'd ever made to his cruelty. "God has seen fit to answer my prayers."

A second messenger arrived, trailing in snow from the mountains he'd crossed. The Bruce would hold parliament at Ayr in April. MacDonald must send a representative. Plans kicked into high gear to send Niall, with his hair finally grown out, and Brother Andrew, to parliament.

Shawn played the sackbut every day—show tunes, solos, jazz, pops from every decade. What he didn't have memorized, he sounded out and added to his repertoire. He made up new pieces.

Niall and MacDonald escorted Allene and Christina down to the Bat Cave one day. "Why d' you insist on calling it that?" MacDonald grumbled. "I've told you and told you, there are no bats!"

Shawn performed a concert. He described for them, with expansive gestures, the magnificent halls he'd played in around the world, the acres of seats, the sea of faces beyond the lights.

"The lights burn steadily, with no flames," Niall explained to Christina. Like Niall, every detail of Shawn's world fascinated her.

Shawn laughed with joy at having an audience once more. He loved sharing the music. He loved their amazement at what a sackbut could do. He played *Czardas, Laughing Brass,* and *Sing, Sing, Sing*, hitting the glisses with vengeance. "Let me get Red down here and teach him drums," Shawn said. "That piece is a thousand times better with Gene Krupa's drum solo."

"What's a Krupa?" Allene's head tilted, her hands paused in the act of clapping.

Shawn laughed again, knowing of all his performances ever, this one would forever hug his heart close. In his last hours on earth, it would be the one he remembered. He didn't want it to end. He didn't want to be at a party afterward. He wanted to be right here, with his friends, doing what he loved.

But he didn't object when the rest of them filed out of the room, leaving him with Christina. Her hands touched his chest, feather light. He kept his hands at his side. "I understand why women wanted paintings of you. There's an energy, a life, to your playing. People want part of that, any way they can."

He wanted to kiss her. He wanted her to stay on her pedestal of purity.

And MacDonald might poke his head back in at any moment.

"Thank you." He slid her hands from his chest, and led her to the door, where Niall and Allene waited with the burning torch to lead them back to the upper world.

Oban, Present

Brian jolted at the sound of his phone. He grabbed it, saw Angus's name, and looked around in haste. He'd managed to put Simon off with stories, excuses, and fake attempts at reaching Angus. He'd called the hospital from work, and Alec was starting the process of re-admitting the man. Simon had been peaceful of late—apart from being in a snit over this latest failure. Still, he didn't need Simon hearing this conversation. But there was no sign of Beaumont. Brian answered the call, his voice coming out in a nervous squeak on hello.

"Brian, mate!" came Angus's gruff voice over the line. "How's things?"

"Grand, just grand!" Brian glanced at the door for any sign of Simon. "And yourself?" He only half listened to Angus's reply, deciding whether to tell Angus about Simon. But Angus might want to meet him, and Brian thought that a very bad idea.

"Did you turn up more on our man Niall Campbell?" Angus asked.

"Well now...." Brian jumped at a creak from his kitchen. But his home creaked aplenty. He checked. His living room was empty. "Something *has* come up. I'd rather not discuss it on the phone. I could meet you somewhere." He glanced at his schedule. "I've Tuesday off."

"I'm in meetings all day," Angus said. "And Amy will be at Melrose."

"Melrose?" Brian glanced back into his living room. Simon was nowhere to be seen. Breathing easier, Brian slipped back into his office, shut the door, and seated himself at the desk by the window. "Amy will be at Melrose Abbey Tuesday?"

"Aye. Will you meet her there?"

"I'll let you know." They said good-bye, and Brian hung up, considering the long drive.

♫

Under the window, Simon smiled. It seemed Amy wasn't quite so far away as Brian had intimated. He looked down at the single bloom he hadn't stood on, and ground his heel into it, crushing it into the dirt. Brian would not be meeting her. He stroked his bearded jaw, laying his plans. His fingers stilled in the thick, black curls.

CHAPTER TWENTY-FOUR

Oban, Scotland, Present

"Selkirk. James Douglas hid there with his men." In Brian's tiny kitchen, with the early morning sun turning the walls a rosy shade of pink, Simon threw the full might of his repertoire of disdainful tones behind the words. "'Tis vital I see it. I remember working there; going back would help me recover." If Brian had feathers, they would be ruffling, nay, bristling, in indignation, Simon thought in amusement.

But the little man, frying sausage and eggs at his *stove,* could only glare and snap back, "I'm well aware of where James Douglas hid. But I've work to do."

"You may do it after you've brought me there. You're free today."

"Take a bus." Brian took a plate from a cupboard and slammed his breakfast onto it.

Simon let out a patient sigh. "You know I'm unable to do so." He had no idea what a bus was. "I believe the doctor instructed you to do all in your power to help me remember." He laid a hand on Brian's shoulder. "I shall really have to insist."

Brian twisted away, studying Simon. Fear lit his eyes. Simon liked that. But his words were, "You shaved. Why now?"

Simon smiled. "I don't wish to scare off the lasses now, do I?" He wondered if this Amy was fair.

Scotland, Present

Dawn climbs out of bed long after Carol and I hit the road. Excitement fills me. I've come to love the long walks through the Scottish hills and countryside, and this will be our longest yet, a full day's walk. But more—it's an emotional milestone. I've reached so many summits already, learning about the crucifix, the blessing, the prophecy, the family connection. It's awful to think of stopping now. Yet from my new vantage point, I also see dangers I didn't see before. My hands are stuck on the wheel, but my heart is reaching, wanting to touch James's soft hand, as he sleeps peacefully in his car seat in the back. I smile, thinking of his bright eyes looking up at me, and his toothless grin, and funny, short yelp when he's happy.

Today's walk is the last summit, the longest walk, the hardest task, before I face Monadhliath, a peak from which, hopefully, knowledge will open like vistas before me, showing me clearly what all of this means to James. I hope my visit to Monadhliath will tell me whether or take him home to the States—leave Angus, abandon Shawn, desert Carol to her grief, to protect my son—or whether it's safe to stay here, continuing the search.

As sunrise bursts gloriously into the car, Carol pulls a book from her tote bag. She flips through, and stopping at a well-worn chapter, says, "There's so much history here." She reads out loud about Jedburgh, our first stop. From there we'll walk to Selkirk, and on to Melrose. "It's too bad we can't spend much time there," she says. "As it is, we'll barely reach Melrose before dusk." She grins at me, then. "And I hear some dark and mysterious things lurk at Melrose at night!"

I laugh. "If there's one thing I don't worry about, it's vampires." My laugh fades. I would have once laughed at the fear of my son disappearing in time, too. Who knows what I should be afraid of.

Oban, Present

With the morning sun piercing his eyes, Brian backed slowly out of his driveway, frantically searching for an answer. Why Selkirk? Why now? Why the decision this morning to shave? It was out of character. Simon had steered him, hand on shoulder, out to the car. Brian braked in the narrow road in front of his home, deciding which way to go. He felt Simon's eyes boring into him. He swallowed, shifted the car into drive and pulled forward, still unsure what he would do. He felt his phone snug in his right hip pocket. He wondered if he could dial by touch, with the phone tucked down against his leg, out of Simon's sight. Or he could drive to the police station. Or the hospital. Yes, he decided. He'd go to the hospital. The decision made, he felt lighter and eased out onto the main road.

He felt Beaumont's eyes on him. He watched the road, fighting the tremble pinching his spine. He felt as he did when he had all but one piece of an ancient document, when that last piece held the key that would tie the rest together. Something was very wrong. His mind spun around Selkirk. Tuesday. And suddenly, he knew. Amy would be in Melrose today, just seven miles away.

He veered onto the highway, glancing at Simon. Simon's eyes flickered to the crossroads and the street sign. "We're going to Selkirk?" he asked. "This is the way to the hospital."

Brian scratched his neck. "Um...yes, I have to...um...stop there and get something. I have to...."

Simon's hand fell, light as a scrap of ancient parchment, deadly as Bruce's battle ax, on Brian's shoulder. "I dislike being lied to, Brian. Go to Selkirk."

Glenmirril, 1315

"We have to find out more about the crucifix." In the Bat Cave, Shawn looked from the Laird, in a heavy leather work apron, to Hugh, bracing a piece of wood on the work bench, to Niall, picking out tunes on his harp.

"I'm not sure how you expect us to do so." At the workbench, the Laird lifted his head from the harp pillar, his hands still on the adze.

Niall's song died away. "What's brought this on?" he asked.

Shawn's hands went to his hips. He turned away from them, staring at the life-sized crucifix, lit by the flickering candles and the wall sconces. Christ stared down at him sadly.

Setting aside the harp, Niall drew near. "Why now, Shawn?"

Shawn stared up at the crucifix for a full minute, trying to formulate words, before he said softly, "Christina. Red. I have to get away."

"While you still can?" Niall asked.

"Before I hurt them more, dammit!" Shawn erupted, spinning. "That boy thinks I'm his big brother! His parents died, the farrier was killed! The longer he hangs around me, the more it's going to hurt him when I disappear, too!"

At the work bench, Hugh and the Laird watched, as still as one of the Laird's own carvings.

Shawn gestured at the parts of the harp. "Look at this! I'm teaching you how to build a harp. Our lives are becoming too entangled."

"Too entangled?" The Laird looked to his brother. They both shrugged.

"Would that we'd kept you in a dungeon?" Hugh asked. "He did offer to lop your head off and you declined."

"Yeah, funny, that," Shawn returned. "And actually, he offered to hang me. And it was more of a threat than an offer. You're not seeing the problem here? You don't get what I'm saying?"

Standing at the foot of the crucifix, hands on his hips, Niall stared at the floor.

"You're coming to care about others," the Laird suggested, "and it discomforts you."

"No!" Shawn exploded. "You're all getting too dependent on me! You know, I'm going home, I'm leaving, and it's better to do it now, before things get messy!"

None of them answered.

"Well?" Shawn demanded. "You can't keep me here!"

The Laird laid down his adze, and wiped his hands on his leather apron. He rounded the workbench and put his hand on Shawn's shoulder. "'Tis not a matter of keeping you here, Lad. I simply don't know how to send you home. I've no idea what you wish to know of the crucifix, or how you plan to learn it."

The Road to Selkirk, Present

Brian scanned the road ahead. It crawled high into isolated hills, devoid of traffic. His mind scrambled, panicked, for a place to stop. He couldn't fight the man. He couldn't outrun him. But he certainly wouldn't drive him to meet Amy!

Simon's fingers dug into his shoulder.

He twisted in the driver's seat, grimacing. There had to be a place he could hide, a cave, a ravine, something! He scanned his memories of the surrounding hills. And suddenly, remembered! There *was* a place! Just ahead. A cave he'd once explored with some archaeologists, finding remnants from the time of Bruce. If he was going to do it, it had to be now.

"Don't think of defying me, Brian." Simon purred like a panther. "No one defies the Lord of Claverock."

Brian's heart fluttered. The man was mad! Did he dare? He thought of Amy, alone at Melrose, with an infant. And Simon approaching her. He slammed the brake and wrenched the wheel, throwing Simon against the windshield. The car skidded on the rough shoulder and ground to a stop. A glimmer of sunlight flashed ahead. It was another car coming! He snapped his seat belt, dislodging Simon's hand, and scrambled out, waving madly. The car flashed by. He spun, seeing Simon's door open, and ran as fast as his short legs could carry him, fumbling in his pocket for his cell phone. It slid between his pudgy fingers as he pushed himself up the hill through springy heather, fighting the trembling of unaccustomed strain in his legs. There was no sound from below. He dared hope it would be this easy to escape this madman! He resisted the urge to look back, warning himself to keep running. He inched the phone from his pocket. It slipped. His other hand scrambled to grab, and caught it. He pushed himself farther up the steep hill. His breath came in short, sharp pants as he tried to run and unlock his phone at the same time.

No sound came from below. Pain lanced his side. He climbed another three feet, heather scraping his jeans. The phone lit up. He punched the screen frantically on *contacts.*

The phone tumbled from his hand, into the brushy arms of the heather.

He stopped, eyes wide, nostrils flaring, and finally looked down the hill. Simon was only fifty meters away, and moving fast. Options flashed through Brian's mind—grab his only connection to help, or run. He couldn't outrun Simon. He dropped heavily to one knee, digging in scratchy, springy brush.

"You can't get away!" Simon bellowed. His face reddened in anger.

Brian searched to the right, praying. Rich loam gouged up under his fingernails. Simon came like a bull. Thirty meters. If he couldn't find his lifeline, he'd have to run, *now!* He fought to remember where the cave was. His heart pounded.

Suddenly, his fingers closed around slick, plastic casing. He shot to his feet and ran, almost to the tree line now. The cave was a tiny abscess wedged in the hillside over the crest, if he could just find it before Simon reached the top. The trees closed around him, dulling the glare of the sun. Rich pine aromas filled his senses. He ran, his legs dragging, protesting, and dropped to the other side of the hill, rolling, praying. He slammed to a bone-thudding stop against the sappy trunk of a pine, looked around, and breathed a sigh of relief, recognizing it. The phone clenched tight in his fingers, he glanced at the hill—no sign of Simon— and darted behind a tree, around a rock, and squirmed into the small, tight opening of the cave that had held a few sparse medieval remnants. There, he tried to slow and quiet his breathing as he punched a frantic text into his phone, begging Angus for help.

The Road to Melrose, Present

We walk for hours, talking and taking pictures of the hills rising around us. We take turns carrying James. I never get tired of the joy of his warm body pressed to mine, my arms wrapped around him, his inquisitive looks over the edge of the front pack, his happy squeals. I barely have words for the emotions I feel at seeing the joy on Carol's face. She has had so much grief, these past years—her husband murdered; her son, in the wake of his father's death, following a path against everything she believes and taught him, her son disappearing. James has given her joy again. She touches his head, as she carries him in the front pack, talks to him. He lifts his face, looks at me, and squeals happily. Gratitude bursts in my heart, explosions like fireworks. I'm blessed. I'm grateful.

We visit abbeys and castles. We stop in a pub for lunch, a relief from the chilly early spring. James sleeps peacefully in my arms. Carol takes out her history book. "The slaughter at Berwick!" she exclaims. "Longshanks only called it off when he found one of his men killing a woman as she gave birth?"

I nod. "Angus told me about it." I touch James's cheek, profoundly grateful he is here, in a time that's safe, where such men don't exist.

She reads, lifts her head, and says, "Legend has it, it was the Lord of Claverock. We should go see Claverock."

A shiver goes through me, despite the warmth in the pub. "I'm not sure I'd want to. When Rose and I went to the Hermitage, it was as if Lord Soulis's evil still hung in the air there."

Carol lays the book down with a sigh, the pages open to the story of Lord Claverock. An image of a medieval knight, helmet in arm, with a thick, curling black beard, adorns the page. He glares up at me from the page, his stance belligerent, angry. "Whatever we put in the world," Carol says, "the repercussions last a long time. It's why James did the things he did. He constantly stopped for stranded drivers. It scared me. But there are two boys alive today because he stopped. A woman with twins—just babies—stranded with a blizzard bearing down. I had to let go of my fears and see that bigger picture."

    Over the open pages of the history book telling of the evil lords of Hermitage and Claverock, I lay my hand on hers. "And his good deeds did end with the worst. How do you make sense of that?"

    "By looking at that bigger picture." She lifts her eyes to somewhere beyond the pub's ceiling, and, amazingly, smiles. "I believe everything happens for a reason. I visit Clarence every month."

    "Clarence...?" I'm afraid to say it. James sighs and curls closer into my body.

    "Clarence who killed James." She sighs. "Speaking of evil, right? But he isn't. Some people do evil because they're evil. Some people do it out of their desperation to escape the evil being done to them. It was a moment of panic and desperation on his part. Not like Lord Claverock." She shakes her head decisively. "No, I've only heard of evil. Clarence saw it face to face."

The Road to Selkirk, Present

    Beaumont crested the hill. It was easy to move silently, without the *chink chink chinking* of chain mail to give him away. He smiled as he scanned the wooded hill below. The man was fat and soft. He couldn't go far. He must be hiding behind a tree; probably pissing himself somewhere, trembling, behind one of the boulders that lay tumbled around the hill, amongst the pine trees, like beads tossed from a giant's sewing basket.

    He could easily walk to Melrose from here. But Brian's defiance could not go unchecked. "Brian," he purred. "I want help. I'm not going to hurt you." He peered under the pine boughs; inched silently down the slope, searching left and right. "Brian," he called, "come out before you die out here. You know you can't fight a wild boar by yourself."

    He waited, listening. If he didn't find Amy at Melrose Abbey, he still needed to know where she dwelt. A bird cawed loudly and took flight, lifting off a branch. It shook dapples of sunlight on the decaying leaves of the forest floor. He hadn't expected the pathetic half-man to be so patient. He gave a grudging nod of approval. It made the hunt more entertaining, at least a bit of a challenge.

    He took another three soft steps, scanning the trees, trying to guess where such a fool could hide—for he certainly couldn't have run far. A chittering erupted. Simon turned, watching a squirrel jump from limb to limb overhead. He shielded his eyes against a spear of sunlight stabbing down between two branches, and turned a complete circuit. The landscape was familiar.

    He'd been here! He knew it!

    He padded softly eastward, edging down the slope, and turned back, studying the shape of the hill, and the hills out beyond it, comparing it to where he knew Brian's house and the hospital to be, to all the places he'd known in his own time. Slowly, the memory came to him. He'd come through with

Longshanks, back when England had a king of whom it could be proud, when they still held the Scottish rebels firmly by the throat. They'd come on their way to talk with MacDougall. They'd camped here, on this very hill.

He took another step to the east. There had been a cave, big enough for himself and several of his knights to shelter in. He wondered if it might still be here; if the weasel of a man could possibly know of it. He studied history. Perhaps he did.

Simon took four more silent steps. The entrance to the cave had been halfway up the hill, between two of the large, lichen-covered boulders, not far from a stream. He stopped, listening for the trickle of water.

There was nothing.

But streams could dry up. He tried to remember anything else that would locate the cave. It had to be where the rat had hidden.

He moved farther, studying the slope, listening. A deer raised its head. Its ears perked. It gazed at Simon and, suddenly, bolted.

Another five steps—and Simon saw a pair of scruffy white boulders patched with moss and lichen, smaller by far than he remembered them. But they were a pair. He inched closer.

The Road to Melrose, Present

I stare at the picture of Lord Claverock. Malice glints from his eyes. Here's a man who enjoys wielding power and inflicting pain—just because he can. I stroke James's downy black hair. Becoming a mother has changed me. I'd rather come face to face with evil a thousand times than let it near my son. My arms tighten around him. But there is no evil like Lord de Soulis and Lord Claverock in this time and place. As long as I can unlock the secrets of the crucifix, he's safe.

Melrose calls me, a place of mystery, with its beautiful ruins reaching for God, century after century. It's my final stop on the way to Monadhliath, which will give me, I hope, the key to protecting him and rescuing Shawn. Angus is sure he'll pull Shawn forward, not the other way around, and Shawn isn't going to be at Monadhliath in April, anyway.

Hills on the Road to Selkirk, Present

Brian lay trembling in the cave, trying to stifle his breathing. From outside came the soft sounds of Simon pushing through the woods.

"Brian." The smooth, evil sound caressed Brian's ear. "You can't fight a wild boar alone."

Brian held back the nervous giggle that welled up in him. The man was an idiot. There hadn't been wild boar roaming this area for centuries. The sides of the small cave closed within inches of his round body. The air came to him in hot, stuffy gasps. It had once been larger, archaeologists believed, but a cave-in many years ago had destroyed much of it. He wished, irrationally, that it was still larger, even as he reprimanded himself that it made no difference.

It did, he thought. If it were bigger, he could hide in a shadow. He could at least move, strike out, in some way. As it was, he was wedged on his stomach, his face inches from the cover of foliage that hid any sign of the entrance, even more defenseless than he would otherwise be. He wondered how crazy the man really was.

He tried to quiet his mind, to push aside his fears, to focus, to listen. Outside, he heard a squirrel chattering, but no more sound from Simon. He tried to think. The man thought he was a medieval knight. That was grand—now how to use that?

A bird cawed outside.

His left leg began to itch. The rich smell of decaying vegetation filled his nose. Still searching for an answer, Brian pulled out his phone, checking for any response from Angus. There was nothing. He looked again and saw why: his phone had no reception here in the cave. He shoved it in his pocket, frantic!

He was alone with a madman, and no thought how to use Simon's insanity to help himself. He squeezed his eyes shut, trying to think of something, to think outside the box, to think what a man who thought he was a medieval knight would do. He saw nothing but black behind his lids. In the dark, the smell of hot, moldering leaves grew stronger. His right leg began to cramp.

A twig cracked outside his hiding place. He held his breath. Simon couldn't possibly know about this place!

The foliage lifted. Simon peered in, black eyes glittering in a snake's version of mirth.

Glenmirril, 1315

"What about this?" Shawn proposed. "The monks of Monadhliath made the crucifix, right?"

"Aye," the Laird agreed, warily.

"They keep records, right? If anyone knows...."

The Laird shook his head decisively, his white-streaked beard and hair shaking like a mane. "No! Niall must be at Parliament. How would we to explain to our men that they're going by way of Monadhliath?"

"They accept your word," Niall reminded him.

"Shawn can certainly think up a story," Hugh added.

"Thank you, I think," Shawn muttered.

"We haven't time," the Laird protested.

"Think now." Niall stepped forward. "To go to Ayr by way of Monadhliath will take little more time than going direct. Two days, maybe?"

"Niall, 'tis not possible!" the Laird insisted. "We've work to do here!"

Shawn started to object, but Hugh turned to his brother. "Think now, Malcolm. Hasn't Shawn saved Niall, earned him knighthood, rescued Christina? Hasn't he brought you Red, who seems to have St. Francis's own touch with our garrons? And Bessie who is a fine help all around the castle? Can we not spare two days in turn?"

"'Twill not be two days," the Laird objected. "You'll need time at Monadhliath itself."

"Four days, at most," Niall amended. "Travel and learning what we can. What if we promise you no more than two days there?"

"A day," the Laird countered.

Shawn started forward, protesting. "A day isn't en...."

Niall held up a hand, even as he bowed to the Laird. "My Lord, a day it will be."

With a sigh hovering between success and defeat, Shawn accepted it. He had no clue what he hoped to find there, himself. But knowing something, anything, was still a step forward. He would have a day in Monadhliath.

Hills on the Road to Selkirk, Present

Simon reached down, grabbing Brian by his shirt, tugging, yanking.

Brian scrambled, fighting the ache in his leg, the stiffness in his neck.

Simon threw him to the ground as easily as a bundle of hay. Brian sprawled, rolling a foot, and coming to rest against a boulder. He squirmed, twisted, and clambered to his feet.

"I want your help," Simon informed him, "and I'll have it. Tell me where to find the man Angus. Tell me where the woman, Amy, dwells."

"No." Amy was vulnerable, alone with an infant. "No!" *Make something up!* he raged at himself. *The man has no way of knowing!*

"Oh, yes." Simon said softly. In a step, he was behind Brian, wrenching his arm up behind his back.

"The States!" The words came out as a shout that disguised the gasp of pain.

"The States," Simon asked. "What is that?"

He thinks he's a medieval knight, Brian reminded himself. *Use that!* "Our planes," he grunted, leaning forward over his big belly, trying to relieve the pressure on his arm. "I'll take you to the airport. I'll get you a ticket. You can fly there."

Simon pressed harder on the arm, till Brian could feel his face going pale and cold with pain. "You've lied to me already," he whispered, and suddenly roared, "I'm supposed to believe I can fly! Bah!" His curling black hair brushed Brian's ear. "Now: where do Amy and Angus dwell?"

Brian said nothing.

Simon increased the pressure on his arm. He stumbled, falling to one knee. A cry escaped his lips.

"Have you ever had your arm broken?" Simon asked casually. "'Tis not pleasant, I'm told. It can be avoided if you simply tell me where they live."

"I don't know...." Brian stalled.

Crack!

Pain blasted through his arm, and exploded in his head. He heard a moan, as if from far away, and the pressure on his arm disappeared, replaced by agony. He sagged; his good arm dropping into the decaying leaves.

"That's your warning." Simon knelt on one knee before him, grasped the hair at the nape of his neck, and yanked his head up, staring down coldly into his eyes. "Where does she live?"

Brian watched, floating in a nightmare of pain, as Simon's hand moved. The hand drifted upward. Sunlight glinted off metal. He would do the same to Amy.

"It needn't end this way, Brian." Simon raised his hand. The knife touched Brian's throat.

Brian closed his eyes, waiting for the cold slice of blade across his skin, ripping into cartilage. He would bleed out quickly. It would hardly hurt. He whimpered, hating his own weakness.

"You're not going to tell me?" Simon asked.

Brian hesitated. He could warn Amy. He could contact her, tell her to get away. He was weak, he decided. He was a coward. But he still wouldn't endanger her. "She went back to the States," he whispered.

"Foolish man!" Simon's hand, with the knife, jerked fast and hard.

CHAPTER TWENTY-FIVE

Melrose Abbey, Present

Beaumont leaned on the stone wall, studying the skeletal remains of the abbey. He'd last seen it in 1307, when he rode past it with the great Hammer of the Scots. He would learn what he could of its demise, he thought. It might help him appear to Edward to prophesy the future. He glanced up at the sky, taking on the deep blue of twilight. The delay it had taken to deal with Brian, and to walk those extra miles, irritated him. Still, smug satisfaction filled his heart, as surely as the wad of cash, retrieved from Brian's car, filled his pockets.

The evening breeze brushed his bare cheek. A younger, cleaner face would be more palatable to the girl, he thought. He watched her from afar—it must be her, walking with an older woman, for the place was otherwise deserted. From this distance, he guessed her to be a bit taller than average, and slender. Desire stirred inside him.

He followed the fence, keeping them in sight as they wandered amid ancient tombstones that milled about the abbey like soldiers unsure who to fight next, leaning, as if exhausted from battle, across the misty field. People whispered of creatures of the night that rose with the gloam in this place. It didn't scare him. He wondered, though, that it didn't scare Amy. He watched her, wondering how to deal with the unexpected presence of the older woman. They turned, and he saw she carried an infant, bundled against the cold, on her shoulder. His eyes narrowed. It made her vulnerable. He pondered the many ways he could use that, even as he searched his mind, for the twentieth time that day, for any knowledge he'd gleaned, that would explain this girl's interest in a long-dead Scottish knight—or a way to get that information from her.

She handed the child to the woman, kissing it as she did, and the woman turned and left. Amy was alone.

♫

My arms feel empty with James gone. So does my heart. But he'll be happier in our warm room in the hostel. I want a few minutes alone. Graveyard grasses squelch under my feet as I explore leaning tombstones, and buttresses.

I'm avoiding the abbey itself.

Finally, alone in the twilight, I approach the ruins. I stop just inside, looking down the long aisle to the altar. It's like the hall of God Himself, dwarfing me as I stand between massive pillars soaring up to the partial roof high above. Mist curls along the floor. Everything reaches for God, the walls stretching to the velvet, cobalt sky.

I stand motionless. I have no right to go up close, not after ignoring God for so long, not after messing up so badly. Evening sun pours down through the massive Gothic window rising high above where the altar once stood, haze all around; it seems to call me, tell me to come forward this time, rather than stay at the back like I do at the church in Bannockburn. I move slowly, past side chapels with tombs, under the stone gaze of saints carved into the ceiling, looking down.

I'm surrounded by the tombs of those who have gone before, by a thousand years of saints and sinners, all of us one before God. It's comforting, thinking of them, thinking of Angus's question—how did they live their lives? As I stand between them, I think some did better than me, and some worse, yet we all ended up in this great ruin of an abbey together, all of us just trying to do our best in this world. I'm a small part of the whole vast experience of mankind, we're all here together, they're by my side, saying it's okay, encouraging me to keep going. I feel God reaching down to me, in the last misty swath of sunlight pouring through the window at the far end.

Everything has pulled me toward this moment: Shawn, Glenmirril, Niall, Angus, finding Shawn's mark at Creagsmalan, following Shawn and Niall's path. "The Author takes great care with our stories," Angus once said to me. "I do believe He makes all things work together, to the smallest detail."

It's true. I'm changed from who I was, or thought I was, last June. I used to think the things Shawn did said something about me. Now I see they tell me only who he is, and when I see myself as good, it's easier to forgive him and let go of the anger. To just see him as another poor human being struggling up the path of life like everyone else, trying to carry life's burdens, and sometimes, not doing so well. Just like sometimes, I haven't done so well.

I think, as I stand in the hazy beam of light pouring down, of Shawn spending this past year with Niall. And I wonder if he's changing as much as I am.

♫

His lips curved up in a tight smile. God smiled on him. He entered the gate, and, eyes on the ground, ignoring her, began to study the tombstones himself. He gave it time—a quarter of an hour, he judged—before he let his footsteps meander toward her, under one of the abbey's soaring arches. She stood as still and silent as the tombs around her, staring up at the hazy light pouring through the great window. Her hair woven into a long, thick braid.

"You're very young to be interested in such old places."

She jumped at the sound of his voice, and spun.

He smiled, a small smile, a shy smile, the one that reassured the laundress and young girls in his own time; the one that told them he was quite different from the bold knight they feared, really very approachable and gentle. She was comely, he noted. Perhaps he had more use for her than merely information.

She didn't smile.

He lifted the corners of his mouth a bit; let the wrinkles deepen around his eyes. "They say dark things wander Melrose by night, but I assure you I'm not one of them."

Her face lightened. A laugh slipped from her mouth. "I hope I wasn't looking at you like you were."

"You'd not be the first," he said, with self-mocking humor. He knew himself to be of fair looks when he chose to be winsome.

"It was your accent," she said.

His smile slipped. He thought he'd done well copying Brian's speech.

"No, I don't mean that badly," she added hastily. "It wasn't a criticism, just...." She laughed, and said, "I don't suppose you speak Middle English?"

"Middle English?" he queried.

"Medieval English," she clarified. "Like the 1300s."

Something lurched in his chest, as it did when an enemy sword struck him a glancing blow in battle, a thrill of danger and wariness. Her precise naming of his time confirmed his instinct. She knew something.

"I'm being ridiculous," she said. "It's just...something about your accent reminds me of a friend."

"I'm a historian," he said carefully. His mind jumped to Niall Campbell, over whom she had so much concern. "I do in fact speak...middle English."

Her shoulders relaxed. But she frowned

He changed the subject. "We're both interested enough in Melrose Abbey to be out on such a cold day when no one else is about. Perhaps I could take you for a wee drop and we could compare notes?"

♪

Warmth settled around her, a relief from the cold wind outside. It had been a long walk. The ache was settling in her thighs, and she missed James. She watched curiously as the man across from her dug in his pocket and set a handful of bills on the table. "Bring her what she wants," he told the waitress, without looking at the woman.

Once again, something in his vowels reminded her of Niall's speech. Niall had been a quick learner and an excellent mimic. But it had taken him time to copy the inflections and tones of the orchestra members' American speech. This man spoke with tones that were neither quite Scottish nor quite English.

"What'll you have, Love?" the waitress's pencil poised over a small pad.

Amy drew her attention from the man. "Coffee," she said. "With cream and sugar." She glanced at the pile of bills on the table. A twenty lay on top. It seemed a curious amount to put out for coffee. "And a cinnamon roll."

The waitress jotted on her pad and looked to the man.

"Coffee. And a cinnamon roll."

He spoke with assurance and Amy thought she'd been hasty in hearing anything of Niall in his voice.

He turned to her. "Simon Beaumont. And you?"

"Amy Nelson." They stared momentarily at one another. She cleared her throat. "So what is your interest in history?"

"I'm a professor." He smiled.

She was about to ask for details when the waitress pushed out from the kitchen, a tray on one hand. Matching ceramic mugs in forest green sent steam curling toward the rafters. The woman placed their coffee and cinnamon rolls before them. Amy reached for a long, slender packet of sugar.

Simon gripped the handle of his mug in one hand. "In my studies, I've encountered an interesting individual named Niall Campbell. You've heard of him?"

Amy lowered her eyes to her cup, busying herself with stirring glistening grains of sugar into the black coffee. "I've *heard* of him." She tried to think, as she poured creamer into the mug and trailed her spoon through, what this second coincidence meant. Niall was hardly a major figure in history. The odds of someone else knowing of him were unlikely at best. She raised her eyes.

Simon frowned, as if in deep thought, one hand clamped on the handle of his mug like a beer stein. "He was at Bannockburn. I believe some unusual events happened there. I hoped you could tell me more."

"About Niall?" It was more a stall than a question, as she pondered the oddity that anyone else in this day should care much about him *and* appear at Melrose the same time she did.

"Niall Campbell, Glenmirril, the strange events at the battle." He smiled disarmingly. "Anything."

Amy considered her answer. She couldn't tell the whole truth. "I don't know much about Niall. The battle, well, I could tell you what led up to it and why the Scots won."

Simon, snorted. "Because the English were led by a fool!" He lifted his mug and gulped. His vehemence surprised her. Something about the way he tossed back the coffee jarred her—a blues chord in a Mozart Sonata. He slammed his mug on the table and swiped the back of his hand across his mouth. "He was a fool from the start." He studied her a moment, his eyes steady and unnerving, before saying. "You don't speak like the rest. Do you live near?"

Amy frowned. "The States."

"The States?" He leaned forward, smiling. "Where is it?"

Doubt flashed across her mind. She tried to enunciate. "The United States. Across the ocean."

"Of course!" He laughed. "I misheard!"

Her shoulders relaxed; she realized tension had crept in. She smiled, herself. It was hard not to in response to his good humor. He was not Niall. He wasn't a time traveler. She was seeing craziness around every corner.

Simon took a big bite of his roll, gulping with a bulge of his Adam's apple. "What roused your interest in the time?"

It was no secret. Yet caution flared in her. "That musician who disappeared at Glenmirril."

"Glenmirril?" His eyebrows rose.

She nodded. "It got me interested. That's all."

The waitress appeared with the coffee pot, filling her cup. She added milk, dragging the spoon through.

Simon stared at her so intently, his black eyes narrowed, that she found her hands sliding under the table, twisting the ring on her finger. She forcibly put her hands back on the table.

Simon glanced at her hand, at the ring.

She slid her left hand over her right, covering it.

Simon bit into his roll, chewing slowly this time, leaving her to wonder what was going through his mind. A thoughtful frown creasing his forehead, before asking, "What do you know of Glenmirril? I believe the Laird's men fought at Bannockburn?"

"Yes." Her doubt grew. Historically speaking, Niall was bit players, a single ping of a triangle never heard by the audience in the screech of trumpets and roar of trombones. "I really don't know more than that."

"I would think you would."

She stared at him. "Why would you think that?"

He answered with a question of his own. "Do you know who *could* tell me more?"

She hesitated a moment, irritated with his failure to answer her question, before deciding it couldn't hurt. She took Helen's card from her purse, offering it over the mugs and rolls. He took it, glanced at it, and up again at her, questioning. "Helen O'Malley. Her phone number is there," she explained. "She's a professor of medieval history."

"Very good," he said. "Have you a phone?"

"Of course."

"May I use it?" He smiled. Once more, his face lightened and lost years.

It reminded her of the times Shawn had twisted her emotions back to his will with a smile of innocence and joy in her presence. She'd found herself smiling in response every time, anger and suspicion melting away. She tried to hang onto the suspicion now. But he wasn't Shawn. She couldn't spend her life being suspicious. What did she think he was going to do? Run away with her phone?

"Please?" His smile grew, like an impish child. "I'll be hasty."

She found herself smiling at the foolishness of her own fears, and reached for her phone.

"Will you call for me?" he asked.

Maybe he was near-sighted, she thought. She squinted at Helen's number on the tie-dyed card, dialed, and offered the phone back to him.

He glanced at it, then pressed it to his ear.

Helen's voice came almost immediately through the instrument. "Amy! I was just thinking about calling you!"

Simon looked confused momentarily before sunshine once again came out in his eyes. "Helen! I'm with Amy. My name is Simon. She said you might be able to help me with my study of Niall Campbell and Glenmirril."

As he arranged to meet Helen the next day, Amy finished her roll, her mind turning to the boots she needed to buy for the hike to Monadhliath. He handed the phone back, giving a slight bow. "We must meet again. Where do you live?"

CHAPTER TWENTY-SIX

Glenmirril, 1315

"You leave on the morrow." Christina stood at the window in Niall and Allene's solar. Gray skies glared through windows streaked with drizzle. "Brother Andrew will not be able to bid me farewell."

Shawn could be himself with her here. In public, he must treat her with nothing more than the kind reserve Niall would show. His initial irritation at such limitations had become sincere wishes on his part, not to harm Niall's reputation or make anyone pity Allene having a philandering husband. He didn't want to break the trust between them or cast doubt in anyone's mind of their love for one another.

Christina had removed her headdress, a move Shawn suspected might be considered daring here and now. But he wasn't sure. He cocked his head, trying to figure her out: a woman who exuded purity, whatever a man thought of that word; a woman who prayed and served the poor, who followed every rule of propriety, refusing to be alone with a man. Even now, Allene worked in her bed chamber, out of sight, but with the door open.

But her eyes held something when she looked at him. He knew the look well from his past. She'd held back, consenting to be alone with him, if only for a moment, in the Bat Cave. She'd touched him there, if only a little.

"I still have feelings." She seemed to read his mind. "I said something once to Niall in a moment of foolishness. I understand you tell one another everything."

"Only what we need to know publicly," he said. "I don't think he told me anything foolish you said."

She glanced toward the bed chamber where Allene worked. Her voice dropped to a whisper. "I told him if I didn't fear for his life, I'd dare find out what it's like to be kissed by a kind man."

He cleared his throat, taken aback at such a bold admission, and asked, equally softly, "You wanted Niall to kiss you?"

"I wanted to know what a kiss might be like from *any* kind man." She stared at the floor, color high in her cheeks.

"Not necessarily Niall?" Blood pounded in his head.

"I didn't know, then, that he was betrothed." She lifted her eyes. "He risked a great deal for me and Bessie."

"You helped an awful lot, and you suffered more than a dungeon for it."

She lowered her eyes. "'Tis over and done. Does Niall dwell on his time in the dungeon?"

"No."

"No more will I dwell on Duncan. But you're leaving. Bruce may summon you to war. Do you have war in your time?"

"Plenty. But it's far away. Nobody has to go unless they sign up for the military. I didn't."

"You may not be back," she said.

"I wish you wouldn't be so blunt about it."

"I'd miss you. What does it mean for a woman not yet born to have just given birth to your son, yet will not do so for centuries? And not know if you'll ever return to her? Is it the same as being betrothed?"

"I ask myself that all the time." He turned from her, staring out the rain-streaked window. "I treated her badly." The far shore had become green in the last week. The snow had melted. "I wasn't much better than Duncan."

"Surely you didn't beat her or burn her. Surely you were kind?"

"I was very kind. I bought her things, I took her places, I left her love letters and flowers all the time. I'd never have hit her, much less burned her. You'd be thrown in jail for doing that in my time." His voice dropped. "There are other ways of being cruel. I cheated on her." It was the first time he'd said it aloud to anyone. He waited for her shock and disapproval.

"Does it not say a great deal about you that you feel badly about it?" Christina asked. "'Tis common enough for men to take a mistress."

Shawn winced. "Niall thinks we have no morals in our time. But we *don't* consider that normal. People expect faithfulness. I lied to her." He stared at the floor. "And it wasn't one mistress. It was lots. And really, I don't think you want to hear more. At least, I don't want to tell you more. I'm not the nice guy you think I am." He lifted his eyes.

They stared at each other.

Christina said, "Perhaps you weren't, then. And perhaps you misjudge yourself now. You asked if I still want the same thing. No, I no longer want just any kind man. You and I are both torn, and I think confused about the contradictions we see in one another."

"Yes." He turned to stare out the window again, his hands gripping the stone sill to keep them off her shoulders, out of her hair. Here, in this time and place, it would be nothing more than a kiss, so much less than anything he'd ever done before. "I promised myself I'd be faithful to her," he said. "Completely faithful. The longer I'm here, I realize I may never get back, and it seems senseless. But if I follow my heart, and I do get back, I leave someone else hurt here, don't I?"

"There are no promises in life," she said. "We live each day knowing it could be our last. Allene is even now carrying a child."

He turned from the window, questioning.

Christina smiled. "Aye. And Niall must go, knowing she may be left alone."

Shawn turned back to the outside scene, the loch's waters more glorious blue in the crisp early spring, than they had been all winter. White crests tipped the choppy waves. Would he never be able to be faithful in his heart, he wondered? "It's different," he said. "Leaving for war, wanting to come back, that's different from *trying* to leave...forever...for another woman."

"Aye, 'tis different," she agreed. "It has meant a great deal to me, knowing you. I want what will bring you happiness."

"Isn't that what you've always wanted?" He tried to hold back his anger, but failed. "Everyone else's happiness? You sacrifice yourself over and over." He faced her, arms across his heavy vest, his hands clenched to himself, with Amy in the front of his mind, almost visible before him.

"As did Christ, whom I follow."

He studied her. Her eyes were the deep, lively blue of the loch, her skin pale and smooth against her jet black hair. He wanted to give her a platitude: *There will be a nice guy for you.* But he didn't want there to be anyone else for her. He wanted to be the one. And he wanted to be faithful to Amy. He wanted to show Amy he was the man she'd believed in. And he wanted to do something right for his son.

"Are you so different?" she asked.

"Very different," he said. "I never claimed to follow Christ. I don't aspire to follow Christ. He and I are not friends, to put it mildly."

"Yet you are sacrificing yourself even now. You are behaving as Christ."

A corner of his mouth quirked up in dry humor. "Believe me, I'm feeling anything but Christ-like right now."

She blushed. "Which is what makes you so. You do what is right, despite what you feel." She bowed her head. "I shouldn't have come."

"Yes, you should have." He pulled her close, wrapped his arms around her, his cheek against her hair. "It means a great deal to me."

♫

Shawn lay in bed that night, trying to wrestle sleep from wakefulness before their pre-dawn departure, contemplating why Christina's affection meant so much to him. Outside, rain rattled the windows. Because she believed in him, he decided. He'd confessed his faults, and still she loved him. He smiled, wrapping her love around him with the rest of his soft, warm furs. Amy had loved him and had faith in him. But she'd never faced his faults head on. And when she saw them clearly, she'd left him.

He rolled over, savoring his last night indoors, hoping spring would bring dry nights for sleeping. That wasn't fair, he chided himself. Amy had known his faults, had lived with them, and loved him and had faith in him through plenty, and he'd squeezed that love around the neck till he choked it off himself. Of course Christina could love a man who *had* done bad things—to someone else—but no longer did. Amy had been trying to love a man who continued to lie and cheat.

She'd been right to leave him. Had she not, he'd still be that man, and he doubted Christina would be so impressed with that. It meant a lot to him, knowing Christina waited and prayed for his safe return. To know that he mattered to someone. He hoped he still mattered to Amy.

Scotland, Present

The woman looked like a demon, Simon thought, with snakes springing half-heartedly from her head—lifeless snakes with neither eyes, nor tongues. Simon wasn't sure if that made it better or worse.

"Helen O'Malley, glad to meet you!" In the doorway, she flung out her hand, bold and brash as any man, though the skirts twisting around her ankles assured him she was, in fact, a woman.

"A pleasure." He shook the proffered hand with the minimum contact necessary.

"Our pride and joy, the best archives in the Highlands!" Her face glowing, she led Simon into a cavernous chamber, detailing its holdings as she led him between ranks of metal cabinets, to a long, gleaming oak table. "I set out some things." She handed him a large pair of white gloves, chatting the whole time, and adding, "We're rather proud of our collection, now."

Edward's blind harper could see that, he thought irritably. He smiled. "Justifiably so."

"We've documents dating back to the late 1200s. We've a few from even before Longshanks stole our state papers. Longshanks!" She made a sound of disdain.

The small hairs rose on the back of Simon's neck. How dare this snake-haired wench speak so of that great man! But he kept his face impassive. He donned the gloves, noting the array of parchments and newer, whiter documents, some clipped with little ornate swirls of metal, some with handwritten script, some with squares of yellow paper stuck to them.

"Funny you and Amy meeting up like that!" Helen plunked herself down opposite him, with no attempt at feminine grace, into a chair as large as Bruce's throne—but not as large as Edward's—and scooted forward, leaning half-way across the big, wooden table. Simon noted the exposed skin. His tongue caressed his lip. Oblivious, Helen opened a large, leather-bound volume as she launched into a story about Amy. Something clicked in her mouth as she spoke, drawing his attention to her lips. They were the shape of a bow, but an unnatural dusky purple, as though she weren't receiving enough air. As she nattered on, he saw the metal ball lodged in her tongue. He wondered if it had been a punishment of some sort. But she didn't seem ashamed of it. Indeed, she made a quip at which she laughed, sticking out her tongue in what he presumed was meant to be playful fashion, very much as if she *wanted* him to see it. Between that and the Medusa hair, he resisted the urge to shudder. The only thing he could say on her behalf was at least she wore a proper skirt, long enough to nearly cover her ankles, which was better than any other woman he'd seen in this bizarre time.

Also, she talked. A lot. Getting information from her would be easy—finding out where Amy lived, among other things. Amy had given an evasive answer, when he asked, and hurried away, looking over her shoulder.

"But then, you've come to read, haven't you, Love?" Helen reached into the folds of her clothing, pulled out a jewel-studded object, with tiny, round bits of glass, like windows, each one just large enough for one eye. She pressed the thing onto her nose, and gave a bright smile.

The room fell silent but for the scratch of Helen's *pen* on a pad of yellow paper, a soft humming in the background, the rustle of paper against wood, and Helen's occasional murmured explanation as she slid something to him. Simon lost himself in the stack of manuscripts—familiar thick vellum and elegant script, so refined compared to the scribbles of these future people. It filled him with pain and pride both, to see how worn some of them looked, and yet how sturdily they had survived the centuries.

He read carefully, repeating the words in his head in his several languages, settling the details firmly in his mind, to carry back in time with him, as soon as he figured out how to get there.

She slid another one over. He read with interest the account of Longshanks' victory over the Scottish dogs at Berwick. He smiled, remembering the day, the women cowering before him, bent over their ugly urchin spawn; the way he'd slashed through the weak, pathetic fools who had tried to block him. The only thing that had marred the day was Edward's touch of weakness, when Simon had been dutifully dispatching a woman before she could birth another traitorous bastard.

But he knew this part! The smile slipped from his face, the memory sliding away. He needed to know more of what happened *after* Bannockburn, or something, anything, about Glenmirril or Niall Campbell. He pushed the paper aside. "What have you from more recent times?"

"Recent?" Helen lifted her head from her reading, setting the snake-like ropes of hair quivering. She seemed dazed, as if he'd just wakened her from a dream. She removed the diamond-studded bits of glass from her eyes. "But you asked about medieval times."

He cleared his throat, irritated with himself for the slip. "More recent than 1296. Say the latter half of 1314, 1315, 1316."

She shot out of her seat, speeding across the room toward a cabinet. "Right here." She opened a drawer, rummaging inside.

"Or anything to do with Glenmirril or Niall Campbell."

"Niall Campbell?" She turned abruptly, blinking at him like a cat. "He does keep popping up!" She laughed, her head thrown back. A pinprick of light bounced off the metal stud in her tongue. "I mean, even *considering* I'm a professor of medieval history." With a folder clutched in one hand, she returned to the table.

"Apart from a passing mention in some ancient manuscript or other," she said, "I'd barely heard of him till that re-enactment, and suddenly, he's everywhere! What brought about *your* interest in him?"

Simon cleared his throat. "I've long had an interest in lesser-known historical figures. I'm a professor."

"Which university?" she asked, her eyes bright with interest.

He realized his mistake. Being a professor herself, she would know the universities in Scotland—he wondered how many there were. "You'd not know of it," he said. "'Tis far away. In the...United States." He hoped this United States, across the ocean, was far enough that she'd not know its universities. He hoped it *had* some universities.

She cocked her head. "Is that how you know Amy? From the States?" Before he could answer, she added, "You've not got an American accent."

"Indeed not," he agreed smoothly. He had no idea where this *American* thing had come from, and spoke before she could question him further. "What have you there?"

"This just came up from Glasgow." Helen laid it before him. "I've not had a chance to read it, but Professor Fraser tells me it's interesting. Though apart from James Douglas, no one important is mentioned." The metal ball in her mouth clacked once and fell silent. "I'm away to get coffee. Do you want anything, Love?"

Simon shook his head. He watched her leave, ruffled layers of skirts swishing, and turned to the document.

The Year of Our Lord 131—. The date was smudged, obscuring the last number.

To My Lord Douglas, Greetings and Good Health, We met Sir Simon Beaumont of Claverock....

Simon stopped, staring at his own name. Pride trilled through his body, as powerful as the rush before battle. His name—his!—stood here in thick, black ink, seven hundred years later! Indignation flared on the heels of pride. No one interesting indeed! The woman was a fool! He was important enough for his name to have stood through time, here for all to read of his mighty deeds!

We met Sir Simon Beaumont of Claverock on the road, coming with his men as you predicted. We engaged him in battle, though he outnumbered us.

If it was James Douglas to whom the author wrote, then it must be a lone surviving Scot, writing to tell of the defeat of his army at Simon's hands! This was exactly the kind of knowledge Simon wanted!

The battle went poorly, My Lord. I fear young Wat will not be coming home. Jamie MacPherson will not be fighting again, such is his injury. We lost several others, too, early on.

Simon smiled, as pleased with himself as if he'd actually fought the battle, although it must be in his own future, since he didn't remember it. He drew a deep breath, at the realization. If this letter spoke of a battle he had not yet fought, that meant he would get back! He pressed his gloved finger to the vellum, reading.

I fear, My Lord, the outcome would have been different, but that a young man suddenly burst over the ridge on a great charger, letting out one short, sharp, piercing scream, and threw himself into battle, hacking and slashing. He rode straight at Beaumont. My men, whose hearts had begun to falter, took courage, and threw themselves back into the fight. Soon our fortune turned.

Simon frowned; the frown that warned his men they had angered him. But they weren't here. There was no one at whom to direct his anger. They should have fought better! They were *Englishmen!* But the battle would turn. The Scots were still outnumbered and his men the most skilled fighters in all the land.

When finally I saw no more of the enemy, I turned and saw this young knight fighting with all his strength against Beaumont. They were afoot now, their helmets off. He had long hair, as black as your own. But for its color, I would have thought 'twas Sir Niall Campbell of Glenmirril, for the face was his.

Simon raised his eyes to the ceiling, his fingers and thumb pressed to either side of his chin. Here was Niall Campbell again. He would find the man, when he got back, and learn more. And he would certainly speak again with Amy. His gut said she knew the man. Did that mean she herself came from Glenmirril of the fourteenth century? Was she caught here? His hand dropped from his chin, falling on the edges of the parchment.

The young knight fell to his knee, but as Beaumont moved in to kill, the man thrust his sword upward, piercing Beaumont's chain, and Beaumont fell dead.

Beaumont's heart slammed against his sternum; his palms became clammy. He shook his head, denying. But as quickly, his lips tightened in a satisfied smile. Forewarned was forearmed. It wouldn't happen.

The young man, despite his victory, fared poorly. We sat him on a rock, noting his injuries. We asked his name, that we might send word to his people. He said he was called James, and would say no more. We removed his mail and saw a distinctive brown mark on his left shoulder blade, flaring out in the shape of flames or a wing.

Simon scanned the rest of the letter, full of inconsequential details of the man's army, weak, womanly concern for their injuries, and not another mention of himself. He stood up in disgust, glaring at the white walls, his hands planted on his hips. It didn't matter. It wouldn't happen. He'd find the man, James, with the flame-shaped mark on his back, and kill him first. Easy.

Glenmirril, 1315

The scene had become all too familiar—the smells of leather, horse and sweat, the jingle of harnesses, soldiers crowding the courtyard spattered with the reminders of last night's rain. As Brother Andrew, Shawn waited quietly under his supposed vow of silence, while Niall, Hugh, and MacDonald strode through the mist with Conal, checking details before their departure. Beside him, Red patted a horse, calming it, and warming its nose. April had not brought Florida weather. But woolen tunics, leather armor, and thick cloaks would keep them warm.

Niall's sister, Finola, hugged her son, Gilbert, trying not to weep. Niall's mother kissed Niall on each cheek and she and Finola held hands, watching their sons prepare to leave. Taran hugged his mother until his father patted his arm, telling him it was time to go. Allene and Christina huddled in fur-lined cloaks against the castle wall, watching while the men formed columns, ready to make the long trek to Ayr for Bruce's parliament. Shawn turned to them. His hood concealed his face, but he could see from under it, see Christina watching, smiling, her eyes warm.

The portcullis screeched. The drawbridge grunted, it's heavy chains groaning as they lowered it inch by inch over the moat's black waters. Father raised his hands over the men. They fell to their knees in the mist, beside their horses, while he blessed them.

Shawn touched Red's shoulder, bidding him silent farewell, and turned to the women. Niall kissed Allene, hugged her tight. Shawn saw his hand drift to her stomach, and the meeting of their eyes, a warm and intimate gesture hidden from all others. His own eyes went to Christina. She blushed, smiled, and lowered her head. She was right. Brother Andrew could not tell her good-bye. But her kerchief, the deep sapphire of so many of her gowns, was tucked in his sleeve. He tugged his hood over his face, bowed his head, and guided his pony into step behind the men, turning his thoughts firmly to Amy.

Scotland, Present

"Something wrong, Love?"

Simon jumped at the bright chirrup of Helen's voice. He spun to face her, wiping the anger off his face as he did. "'Tis naught!" he said as brightly as if he were attending one of Edward's magnificent feasts.

"You looked angry." The pungent aroma of coffee rose from the cup in her hand. The jewel-studded eye piece hung from a thin, gold chain around her neck. She smiled, but her head cocked to one side, a question shouting from her eyes.

"Not at all." He tapped the parchment. "Merely...perplexed."

"'Twas interesting, then?" She sailed, in her layers of skirts, across the

room, lifting the eyepiece, and hooking it over her ears. She set the coffee on
her desk, and leaned over the document. After several minutes, she made a little
noise, and looked up at him. "Interesting indeed, but I've bad news for you. It
seems you're dead!" She threw her head back, laughing in great, gusty
chuckles.

He forced the corners of his mouth into tightly upturned knots, attempting
to look as though he appreciated her pathetic humor. "A sad day," he agreed,
"but that it seems I've not only survived the assault after all, but lived a good
seven hundred years beyond it."

She laughed harder, placing a hand on his arm. "Oh, my, Simon, I did not
think you'd much of a sense of humor." She removed the eyepieces, wiping at
tears of mirth with the back of her hand. "Well, I did go to school with a Robert
Bruce, which hardly surprises anyone. And there are plenty of James Douglases
running about, aye? Still, it gave me a wee start, seeing your name there."

"And with the very Niall Campbell we were discussing," Simon said. "Can
you tell me no more about him?"

Helen shook her head. Her skirts, the vulgar snakes of hair, and the glasses
on the delicate chain all trembled with the vigor of her motion. "Amy's the one
who could tell you. I was quite surprised, now, how well acquainted she is with
yer man."

Simon's eyes narrowed. "Amy?"

"She's a font of knowledge on him, though I never did gather where she
learned so much. She didn't tell you?"

"She did not indeed," Simon confirmed. "She said in fact, that she knew
very little and you know more."

Helen laughed. "Well, now, people underestimate themselves and think that
because I'm a professor of medieval history I know every detail of everyone
who lived in the time. But really, she knows a great deal. Did she show you the
crucifix from Monadhliath?"

"The Monks of Monadhliath?" Simon wrinkled his brow, trying to think
how they might come into the story.

"Aye, you know of them!"

"Indeed," Simon said dryly. He'd never much cared for them. "She
possesses one of their crucifixes?"

"One of the twelve!" Helen's face brightened. "You're familiar them?"

"Each has a blessing and prophecy." He remembered the day Edward
overheard one knight asking another why they'd marched right past Glenmirril.
Edward had stopped, out of sight around a corner, Simon at his side, listening as
another answered, filled with wonder, of the mist rising to hide the castle, and
how the foolish old laird attributed it to his crucifix from the monks. "She has
one?"

"Aye, as did Niall Campbell. And the irony is, she was given it by a friend
also named Niall."

A thrill tremored through Simon's body, as it had in the moment he knew where Brian had hidden himself. He kept his face passive. "Did she, indeed?"

Helen nodded energetically. "I'm surprised she didn't show it to you. She wears it at all times."

"She's aware of its history?"

The woman nodded, setting the springy ropes of hair bobbing, in a strangely syncopated dance. "Aye. I sent her the information and talked to her myself." Just as the snakes settled down, she shook her head, setting them to quivering again. "'Twas the strangest thing, her boyfriend disappearing at the re-enactment, and her with a wee bairn on the way, and all she can think of is Niall Campbell and this crucifix. I've been scratching my head over it for some time, now, I have."

"Her...boyfriend?" He repeated the word carefully.

"Her beau, her young man." Helen's eyes gleamed with excitement. "That American musician who disappeared at the re-enactment—surely you heard of it?"

"He disappeared at the battle?" Simon's mind spun furiously, putting the pieces together. "She said he disappeared at Glenmirril."

"No, no, *no!*" Helen waved her hand. "She *left* him in Glenmirril overnight—not that anyone would blame her! The things I've heard about his catting after women! What he did at that hotel in Edinburgh! People only wonder why she didn't do it sooner. And he came back odd in the morning, a concussion, and...."

She spoke so quickly, that between her accent and the unfamiliar words of her time, he gathered only broad sketches. Shawn Kleiner, a minstrel of some sort, had slept in Niall's castle and woken up, behaving strangely, with an arrow wound. "Are arrow wounds so unusual?" he asked.

Helen stopped mid-sentence, staring at him with wide eyes. The clacking in her mouth ceased. The snakes quivered in surprise and fell still.

He guessed arrow wounds *were* that unusual. He let his mouth splash into the grin that never failed to charm women. "But I jest. Continue, pray."

Her look of surprise crumpled into a smile. "Aren't you funny now? Yes, he had an arrow wound. Or so the telly said. And he was obsessed with the Bannockburn—imagine being obsessed with something that happened so long ago, and him an American, no less, and he was determined to get to the Trossachs to find a man named Hugh, to bring him to the battle. And at his last concert, he played harp instead of trombone and told the audience he was Niall Campbell of Glenmirril."

"Did he now?" Simon asked dryly.

"'Tis mad, sure!"

Simon's mind flew at the puzzle as fast and furious as a shower of arrows. Shawn Kleiner, obsessed with Bannockburn, playing the harp, and calling himself Niall. Amy, calling Niall by his first name as if she knew him personally, being given a crucifix, like the one Niall Campbell had owned, by someone named Niall. Her caginess in not telling him about the crucifix.

"Did she tell you she's going to Monadhliath to talk to the monks?" Helen's words snapped him from his ruminations.

"No," he replied slowly. "She did not." She'd left a great deal unsaid. Had he given her reason to suspect him? He didn't think he had. Clearly, she had her own secrets, and he very much wanted to know what they were.

"Sure an' you should go with her, now," Helen said with enthusiasm. "They can tell you all about the crucifixes, and hers in particular. There was a prophecy and blessing associated with each. I gave her the blessing but she wants the prophecy. Let me call...." She rummaged in her skirts.

Her hand flashed out, holding up a small bit of paper. She squinted at it. "Ah, yes, I'll call now, will I? It's quite a hike now, you know. How are you for some hill walking?"

"I should be able to manage." Simon smiled, an easy, genuine smile this time. He looked forward to doing some isolated walking with her, where he could perhaps persuade her to be more forthcoming.

CHAPTER TWENTY-SEVEN

Inverness, Present

Angus lifted James from his car seat, cooing to him. He wrapped an arm around Amy, and kissed her. "How was the drive?

"Scary! They're all driving on the wrong side of the road!"

He laughed. "But it feels grand to be able to do it, does it not?"

She reached into the car for her backpack, smiling. "Very!"

Angus ushered her into his kitchen, where dinner waited in the crockpot. After dinner, he lit a fire in the hearth, settled James in the crook of his arm, and began reading one of Hamish's books in Gaelic, pointing out pictures. "*Tha e ag iarraidh curran,*" he read, in his gruff voice. "He wants a carrot."

Amy curled next to them.

Angus looked up, smiling. "You catching all this?"

She shook her head. "Shawn loved speaking it, but he never told me what anything meant."

"It's about horses," Angus explained. "See here, *eich.* Maybe a wee bit advanced, but they like listening now, don't they?"

James batted a chubby pink hand at the book.

"So do I." Amy leaned into his arm.

At last, Angus settled James on a blanket with books, and his rabbit. They pored over maps and double checked their hiking gear. "Wool socks. Water bottles." Angus lifted each article out. "Matches." James babbled on the blanket, trying to grab his rabbit, as Angus pushed a roll of socks into a side pocket. "You don't mind this Simon character coming along?"

Amy fit a small metal canister of matches into another pocket. "No."

"After I hung up with Helen," he said, "I thought, sure and we've been looking forward to the time together, and I've ruined it."

She shook her head. "We can go another time by ourselves. But...." She stopped, her hand with a canteen resting on her knee.

"What is it?"

"We need to remember to fill this up in the morning." She clipped the canteen to a loop on the side of the backpack. "He struck me as a little strange."

Angus sat back on his heels. "How so?"

"I don't know. Like he wanted something." She reached for the cooking kit, hesitating again. "I wondered if he could tell us something about what happened." She clipped the cooking kit to another loop, and gave her head a sharp shake, thinking of Shawn and her mother telling her she imagined things. "No, I'm being ridiculous. I had this crazy idea I somehow stumbled on the one other person in the world who actually knows, first-hand, what happened to Niall and Shawn."

James squealed, a short, sharp, staccato sound, slapped a palm against the floor and wrinkled his brow at her.

She rubbed his back, murmuring, "He said he speaks Middle English."

Angus touched her arm. "You're not being ridiculous."

"Yes, I am." Amy pressed her fingers against her forehead. "I didn't meet another time traveler. It was a chance meeting. Even if there *is* another such person in the world, he didn't just *happen* to show up at Melrose at the same time I did."

"Quite likely not," Angus agreed, "but if you think something was odd, it was."

Amy bit her lip, staring at the half-loaded packs. She touched James's hand, and his face relaxed into a toothless grin. He let out one short, piercing squeal, and grabbed for his rabbit's ear.

"Okay, then?" Angus pressed.

She nodded as they replaced flashlights, t-shirts and diapers. He was just a professor. There was no reason to read more into it. It had bothered her, on leaving the pub, to see him staring after her. But maybe he simply had no social skills. Regardless, Angus would be there. They were safe. She wedged three packets of food into the top of her pack. "And the family tree." Their arms touched as they looked over the sheets copied from Honora, scanning the web of Stewarts, MacMillans, and Campbells branching over the paper and all of Scotland.

"And this is part of my family history, too," Angus mused. "'Tis amazing to think I'm descended from the cheating Duncan MacDougall and the screaming shrew Christina chasing him through the dungeons."

"Does this mean I need to call you 'My Lord'," Amy joked.

"'My Dear' would be fine." He touched her hair, paused, and glanced over at James. "He's fallen asleep." He snapped off the lamp, leaving the room bathed in only the firelight's glow.

Amy stroked the top of James's head, his black hair like down under her finger. Angus reached for her hand, lifted it to his mouth, and kissed each finger. Amy closed her eyes, drawing in a deep breath. His hand crept into her hair, and he pulled her close. Papers crackled under her.

"We're ruining the family tree," Amy whispered.

He leaned close to her ear. "I like to think we'd make it better."

Tingles of delight shot through her. But she tugged at the papers under her back. "We'll have to reprint them. You said you're a practical man."

Angus grinned. "What I said was, I'm a practical man *except* when it comes to the Glenmirril Lady." He tossed Shawn's genealogy aside, and kissed her again. She returned the kiss with fervor, her hands in his hair.

"I love you," he whispered.

She became still, the emotion pounding inside her. "I love you, too."

Beside them, James took in a shuddering breath, and settled back to peaceful sleep. Angus lifted his head, supporting himself on one arm, studying her in the flickering shadows. "Where does this end?"

"Are you ready for it to end?" she asked.

"We've searched ley lines and standing stones and followed genealogy and an ancient blessing, with no success." He stroked James's head. "Is it too much Shawn in our lives?"

Angus rolled onto his back, pillowing his head on clasped hands. "I suppose I've begun to wonder how long our lives *can* revolve around him."

"Then why were you willing to do this?"

"For you. For James. For a chance to hear history first hand. I'm still assigned to his case." He studied her face. "But, to be honest, because it just doesn't seem real, anymore."

"It doesn't feel entirely real to me anymore, either," she admitted. But the idea of quitting was as uncomfortable as a cheap violin. The fire crackled softly beside them.

He squeezed her hand. "I'm sorry. This is James's father. Carol's son. I shouldn't have said anything."

Monadhliath Abbey, 1315

As pink-tinged clouds sank in the west, Shawn, Niall and their thirty men arrived at Monadhliath, cold from the steady drizzle. The monks swung open high wooden doors, and the abbot from Shawn's last stay ushered them in. Torches lined the monastery's stone walls, giving light and warmth after their cold ride. "'Tis good it is to see you again." The abbot clasped Niall's hands. "I trust you are feeling better than last I saw you."

Niall smiled, turning to Brother Andrew with arched eyebrows. "I trust anything odd I did at the time was a result of the head wound."

"The singing master made something of the *Kyrie* you sang in the hall."

A snort came from under Brother Andrew's hood, and his head bowed lower still. Niall turned back to the monk. "Did I? I've no memory of singing in the hall. The head wound, you understand. You'll find me much improved, no doubt." Allene would kick him, or yank his ear hard, if she heard him goading Shawn like this when he couldn't defend himself. He smiled all the more broadly. "I've business with the abbot and we'll be on our way."

Monadhliath Mountains, Present

Knowing Angus did mountain rescues was one thing. Seeing his knowledge, strength, and expertise firsthand, was something else altogether, Amy thought, as he reached down, while carrying his own backpack and James in the carrier on his chest, his forearm flexing, to grip her wrist and help her up another steep slope. She was grateful she'd done so much hillwalking, as they climbed boulder-strewn slopes and descended into forest-green glens. Wool socks kept her feet warm inside new boots, but the backpack weighed heavily on her shoulders. They'd been going since morning. Simon charmed them with tales of history, as vivid as if he had lived it, along with asking dozens of questions. A recent head injury, he explained, had caused him to forget a great deal. He stuck close to Amy, quick to offer a hand as she struggled up rough ground. She'd been wrong, she told herself. And yet—his solicitousness left her uneasy.

In the early afternoon, they reached a clearing in a glen.

"There was a village here, hundreds of years ago," Angus said. "See there." He pointed through a sparse stand of birches, to crumbling remains. "And there." To its east lay another ruin, with enough stones left to show where the walls had met at an angle.

"Cogaras," Simon said.

"You know it?" Angus asked.

Simon smiled tightly. "I've been here. There was a lying, sniveling innkeeper—Fergal. A traitor to the throne." He coughed. "So history says."

Amy and Angus glanced at one another, before Amy looked up the slope awaiting them. It was covered with bracken and boulders and trees just beginning to show green leaves. In the carrier on Angus's chest, James squirmed and began to fuss.

"It seems like a good place to stop and feed him." Amy lifted the blanket to give him a kiss.

Simon sighed heavily.

"You're free to go ahead," Angus said. "'Tis not far now."

Simon's eyes lingered on Amy a moment before he said, "I think I shall," and headed down the remains of a road, up the next hill.

"I don't know what to make of him." Amy slung her pack to the ground.

"He certainly knows his history." Angus wiggled out of the baby carrier and passed James over.

Amy found a low, crumbling wall, and settled against it to nurse. She shielded her eyes, squinting up the mountain. Simon had disappeared over the crest. Angus swung his metal-framed pack to the ground and sat down beside her. "If Shawn and Allene crossed the loch as Niall says the Laird would have wanted, they'd likely have come right through here."

"I've been trying to imagine what it would have been like for them," she admitted.

"They were in danger," Angus said. "They'd have traveled by night."

"It would have been when he first arrived." She smiled. It was easy to see him struggling up these hills, wearing leather boots like Niall's. "I bet he was sore, complaining. He raised grousing to a fine art." She didn't add, he'd likely been conjuring up ways to get at Allene. She wondered, here where maybe he'd passed, did he try to kiss her? He's Shawn Kleiner, she chided herself. Of course he tried. The thought soured her stomach. She changed the subject. "It's hard to imagine a village here." She looked around the glen. More remains, no more than earthen mounds, stretched out in rough approximations of foundations.

"We spent the night here once, on a rescue." Angus spoke softly. "I felt ghosts all around, when the mist came up in the evening, but happy, as if the people of years past loved it here and wouldn't leave."

Amy shivered. But the place did have a happy feel. She soaked in the rise of green hills strewn with boulders. It was nothing like the stories she'd read, months earlier on the internet, of Angus's mountain work—stories he still hadn't told her himself. She snuggled closer into his shoulder. "Tell me about your rescues."

"Rescues?" He laughed. "There's not much to tell. He's done, aye? We should get moving."

They gathered James back into traveling mode. He nodded off to sleep against Angus's chest as they climbed the next slope, leaving the glen far below. At a small stream, Angus took her hand, and they hopped over. The cooking supplies in his backpack rattled. James squeaked as Angus landed on the other side.

"After how many years?" she finally prodded. "Of course you have stories."

"Aw' right," he relented. "Once we spent two days on Ben Nevis in winter, searching for a lost hiker. Clive got frostbite, but he pushed on, wouldn't quit."

"You did nothing," she teased. "Just stood around admiring bluebells?"

He grinned back over his shoulder. "We work together. We do our job."

She stopped on the rocky slope. The words slipped out, a quick breath of words. "I found stories on the internet months ago."

He turned, the toe of one boot dug into the earth, one hand gripping a tree limb, ready to hoist himself up. "Why did you not tell me?"

She shrugged. "I hoped you'd tell me yourself." When he only stared, she added, "Shawn caught a boy touching the grill at one of his barbecues, once. All he did was yell, *Hey, look out!* But he told it for weeks, like he'd done something incredible." She tucked her hand inside the stiff crook of his elbow. "You really did, and you say nothing."

Angus continued to stare at her silently.

"Some members of your team were especially courageous," she said softly.

"There was nothing courageous about it." He turned, gazing up the hill. "I didn't save him."

"Save who? You laid on your stomach in the snow for hours, holding on until someone came."

Angus hoisted himself up by the tree branch. He paused, his back to her, and she wondered if he was going to walk away again. James gave a baby chortle. He turned, reaching down for her, still gripping the tree limb tight in his other hand. She pulled herself up, finding herself at the crest. The mountain breeze whistled in her ears.

"Ye must take in the view!" Angus spoke in awe.

They stared down on a garden paradise, nestled in a mountain glen. Orchards and pines surrounded a sprawling complex. "The church steeple, see," Angus said. "There's the graveyard, hundreds of years old, and over there, the new wing."

The abbey far below filled her with exhilaration. She could hardly believe she was seeing the place that had fueled her hopes and imagination for so long. But Angus's evasions didn't go over her head. She laid her hand on his arm. "They got him out," she said. "You *did* save him."

Angus tugged the blanket up around James. After a long silence, he spoke softly, as if whispering from a nightmare: "There was a boy." He wrapped his arms around James, bending close over the baby. "I could see him, down below, the whole time. In pain, calling for his father." A tremble rippled across his back. "He died while I watched. He died while his father begged me to do something. I couldn't."

She hated the pain in his voice. She touched his sleeve. "Aren't you always telling me I take on too much guilt?" she asked. "You didn't take that child into the mountains in winter."

He sank onto a boulder. She dropped down next to him. His head fell on her shoulder. He was still, but she knew it was coming out inside. A gust of wind shot up the mountain slope. Angus tightened his arms protectively around James, bundled under his blankets. "I'm just a musician." Amy bowed her cheek against Angus's coarse, dark hair. "I don't save anyone's life. Ever."

"You've no idea," he said. "When I've watched a child die before my eyes, when I couldn't save him, what music does. You save souls." He lifted his head off her shoulder, studied her face with eyes dry and red. "People like me, Amy, we need people like you, too."

CHAPTER TWENTY-EIGHT

Monadhliath Abbey, 1315

A crucifix like Niall's own dangled from the abbot's slender hand, silhouetted against the fire blazing in the hearth of his office. "'Tis the last of the dozen," he said. "They're relics, each holding a bone of St. Columba."

"Gruesome," Shawn muttered under his cowl.

"He does poorly with his vow of silence, does he not?" the abbot remarked.

"He does," answered Niall. "Precisely why he needed to take it. So one of these was given to the MacDonald, and one to my father?"

"You'd have been too young to remember Longshanks coming through. He left death and destruction in his path, going up Loch Ness. MacDonald himself came here, asking for prayers. We gave him one of the crucifixes. Your guards were on the parapets that day, the men turned out for battle, the women and children in the keep, praying."

From under Shawn's hood came a snort.

"Bless you," Niall said. "We'll have to give you broth of lizard tongue for that cold if it doesn't stop."

"They saw the sun glinting off Longshanks' army as it came," Brother William continued. "They rolled boulders up to the ramparts and heated oil." A log snapped and broke in the hearth. The flames crackled, a pleasant accompaniment to the story.

"I do remember," Niall said. "I was five or six. Alexander and I carried rocks to the parapets."

"Aye, well, a strange thing happened. A mist formed. As Longshanks' army came closer, it rose higher, till it covered Glenmirril top to bottom, even the Laird's banner waving on the parapets."

"Oh, for Pete's sake!" Shawn burst out. "Mist in Scotland is *hardly* a miracle!"

"Your vow of silence, Brother Andrew." Niall said.

"*Cillcurran, Cillcurran, rose by the sea,*" Shawn sang softly.

"What manner of monk is this!" Brother William asked.

"Brother Andrew," Niall snapped, "stop this nonsense!"

"Does he mock God's works?" Brother William demanded.

"The mist rose around beloved Cillcurran," Shawn threw his arms out in lyrical ecstasy.

"Brother Andrew!" Niall warned.

Shawn sank back into his chair, singing softly, *"And took my true love from me."*

"You'll be confined to your cell," Niall warned. Behind him, the fire spit bright sparks onto the hearth.

"Mist in Scotland," Shawn harrumphed. "Some miracle."

"'Twas dry for weeks beforehand," Brother William barked. "D' you know naught of weather? 'Twas so thick and tall it covered the whole castle." His voice rose. "Have you ever seen such a mist, Brother Andrew?"

"I apologize, Brother William," Niall said. "He is not of these parts. He has trouble understanding our ways." He returned to his concern. "There was a blessing with the crucifix. Was it the same for each of the twelve?"

"No. Each was given a different blessing and prophecy, years before they were given to anyone."

"My father knew the blessing and prophecy attached to his?"

"Oh, certainly. The blessing, now let me think where those records are." He turned to the heavy oak desk, rummaging through with irritating deliberation. Shawn and Niall gave each other a hard stare and settled back to waiting, while Brother William moved on to a shelf, and from there back to searching the desk drawers. He pulled up a parchment, unrolled it, and studied it for just a moment. "I have it!" he announced, and in a move designed to push them to the edge, marched out of the room with no further word.

"And took my true love from me." Shawn pushed his hood back, laughing at Niall's irritation.

"Show some respect in a house of God," Niall snapped.

Shawn added an improvised line. *"This mist is hardly a mystery."*

"You'll show respect to Brother William as well." Niall paced the small chamber, scowling. "What is this *Cillcurran*, anyway?"

"A Scottish castle on an island that disappears into mist when danger threatens. It was—will be—a musical, a mummery with singing and dancing."

"Yes, well, interesting, but don't scoff at miracles. Were you there?"

Shawn snorted.

"You're becoming quite adept at that sound," Niall said. "Perhaps you ought to try actual language so you don't forget how to use words."

"It's been misty here almost every bloody, God-forsaken day since I arrived in your miserable time!"

"That's because it's *rained* almost every day since you inflicted yourself and your bloody, God-forsaken ways on my time!" Niall jabbed at the flames, sending up a spray of sparks.

"I don't have to have been there to know that mist in Scotland is as natural as breathing. It would be a miracle if there *wasn't* mist in Scotland," Shawn retorted.

"I *was* there, and I've spent my whole life here, so perhaps I know a wee bit more about it than you. Mist is *not* normal if there's been no rain. As there hadn't been. 'Twas a dry year. I was young, but I remember the concern about the crops. And this mist was *not* normal. It covered everything, like a shroud, the entire castle."

"Cillcurran..."

The door scraped against the stone floor. Shawn yanked his cowl up, shadowing his face. Brother William entered, casting a dirty look at Shawn, hunched in his chair, before joyfully announcing to Niall, "'Tis looking quite worn. It was waiting to be re-copied!"

Niall joined him, helping smooth out the parchment on the desktop. *"May this crucifix by God's gracious mercy and St. Columba's intercession draw together father and son even across oceans and time for their mutual protection and benefit."*

Brother William frowned, then repeated it slowly. "Draw together father and son across time?"

Niall turned to Shawn, raising his eyebrows.

Shawn's pulse raced. Cool sweat slicked his palms.

"It makes little sense," Brother William mused. "It must mean in their time of need...."

"It means exactly what it says." Shawn enunciated each word.

"It can't. I'll have Brother Owen adjust it."

"That's not a good...." Niall started.

Shawn rose from his chair, speaking ominously from the depths of his hood. "Brother William, have you no faith in God and prophecies? Brother Owen must copy it exactly as it is."

"It makes no sense!" Brother William glared, a general in his war room, into Shawn's faceless hood. "As abbot, I will give Brother Owen instructions as I see fit. I'll not have visiting monks of unknown origins telling me what I must do."

Monadhliath Abbey, Present

"Visitors!" The monk, younger than Amy had expected, beamed from one to the other as he threw open the great wooden doors of the monastery. "We get but few!"

Amy and Angus glanced at one another, a secret smile passing between them. They had finished the hike, holding hands, and now they stood, in the same stone foyer where Shawn and Allene had stood seven hundred years before.

"Come along—your friend is waiting! I'm Brother Fergna." The monk ushered them down the hall, Amy looking around in awe as they passed a small chapel opening up on one side. Shawn, Allene, Niall—they'd all been in this very hall! Perhaps Niall had prayed right there in that chapel.

Brother Fergna threw open a heavy door, revealing a dim office. Simon sat in a wing chair beside a huge hearth with a blazing fire, his legs stretched before him, his chin resting on steepled fingers. But he seemed ready to spring. His eyes rested on Amy. "I was just telling your friend," the monk said, "that we've rooms for you as long as you like." He gestured to a couch and another wing chair by the fire.

As Angus eased James from his carrier, Amy glanced around the abbot's study. It looked as it must have for centuries. Dark panels lined the walls. Heavy beams supported the ceiling. She wondered if Allene had sat in this room, warmed her hands by this fire; if Niall or Shawn had sat in this room. The air shimmered with the possibility of their long-ago presence.

"Tell me," the abbot broke into her thoughts, "what brings you this way?"

Amy looked to Angus with raised eyebrows.

"You know the story best," he said.

In his wing chair, Simon watched her steadily. Cold tingles danced in her arms. She turned to the monk, lifting the crucifix from under her sweatshirt.

Brother Fergna leaned forward to see; his eyes widened as she laid it in his palm. "One of the missing crucifixes!" He sank into a swivel chair before a heavy roll top desk and lifted his eyes. "Where did you get this?"

"From a friend." Amy watched him. If she'd doubted Helen's story, his reaction confirmed it.

Angus leaned forward. "We were told you would know more about it."

Simon's eyes moved to the monk's hands, where the crucifix lay.

"Aye." The man turned it over, studying the relic in the back. "Our records go back to the 1100s."

"Amazing!" Amy breathed. "There's so little left from that time."

"'Tis our ministry." Brother Fergna raised his eyes. "We copy by hand. We keep the art alive. Where other records have been lost, information can often be found here. Columba was a scholar and a writer. So are we."

"We're looking for the prophecy associated with this crucifix," Amy said.

"Aye, we'd have that to hand." Returning the crucifix, Brother Fergna rose. "Wait a bit." He disappeared out the door.

"You didn't mention the crucifix when first we met." Simon's voice hummed, smooth as velvet and rich with bass undertones like the throaty purr of a lion. She almost felt she saw a smooth, taupe tail swish behind him.

She shrugged. "I forgot." She was being foolish, she told herself. He had done nothing out of line.

Simon rose from his chair, and stalked to the dark, heavy shelves. He moved restlessly before the leather-bound tomes, his head turned to study the titles. The fire crackled loudly.

A young monk, round and cheerful, bounced into the room, pushing a cart carrying hot tea, honey, and whiskey. "Brother Fergna will return shortly!" He beamed at them, and left again.

Rising, Angus handed James to her, and lifted a bottle. "*Uisge-beatha?* It'll warm you up."

"Tea's fine." She touched James's petal-soft cheek.

Angus poured tea for Amy, and whiskey for Simon, who downed it in one gulp, held out his glass for a second, and returned to his perusal of the ancient volumes on the shelf.

James gurgled, his face lighting with a toothless smile, and reached a clumsy hand for her face. She smiled back. She looked up fleetingly. Angus gazed at James as if at his own son. Her heart warmed, loving him. He raised his eyes to hers, and smiled.

James squirmed suddenly, letting out one of his short, sharp screeches that stopped as abruptly as it started.

Simon turned slowly, staring at the baby.

"He's very red," Amy said. "Can you get something lighter out for him?"

Angus dug in his backpack for another outfit, while Amy pulled the pint-sized turtleneck over James's head. "There you go," she cooed. "Better?" He leaned into her neck, cooing happily. She patted his bare back, and glanced up.

Simon stared at her son, his eyes narrowed.

Discomfort tremored in her stomach.

Simon took a step away from the bookshelf. "What's that?"

"What's *what*?" Defensiveness sprang into Amy's tone.

"On his shoulder?"

Amy slid her hand over the birthmark. Her eyes cut to Angus. The fire flickered shadows across the plane of his jaw.

"It's in the shape of flames." Simon took another step forward. "How very unusual."

Amy's arms tightened around James. He let out another short, piercing screech.

Simon's eyes narrowed.

Angus cleared his throat. "Is there a problem?"

"Not at all." Simon smiled, and sipped his whiskey. The fire snapped its teeth against the dim room. "It seems, in fact, that God smiles upon me. I believe he's called...*James?*"

Monadhliath, 1315

Niall all but pushed Shawn through the rain-darkened halls of the monastery and onto the narrow cot in his cell. "You will in future do as you're told!"

Shawn bolted straight back off the bed. *"He cannot change that prophecy!"*

"He is the *abbot*. You have voiced your opinion. I will speak to him again. But you are not to make trouble."

Shawn stabbed a finger at Niall. "Tell him to get his head out of his...."

Niall swatted Shawn's finger away and pushed him back onto the cot. "You'll not speak like that in a house of God."

Shawn shoved himself back off the cot. "If he changes that...."

"What does it matter? We know what it says."

"But *Amy* needs to know!"

"Who's to say she'll ever find it, up here in a remote monastery. This place may not even exist in seven hundred years! At the moment, you've embarrassed me with your disrespectful attitude. You'll stay here while I speak with Brother William." He slammed out of the room.

Shawn whirled, ready to punch the nearest wall. He stopped, glaring at the stones that were eminently un-punchable. He planted his hands in anger on the narrow window sill, and stared out at the rain trickling down from gray skies.

Monadhliath, Present

The door scraped open, breaking the tension in the room. All eyes cut to the doorway. A draft fanned the fire. Brother Fergna bounded in, in his brown robe, waving a sheet of paper. "The prophecy, as given to James Campbell in 1297. Or at least, as it has, hopefully accurately, been copied."

Amy's arms, around James, loosened. He sighed and snuggled into the warm crook of her neck.

"Funny thing about copies and translations," the abbot said, "one wrong word changes everything. You really must use common sense." He chuckled. "This one was a doozy, had you taken it literally."

At the shelves, glass tumbler in hand, Simon watched the monk.

Her eyes alight, Amy reached for the sheet—an oxymoron of crisp white ten pound printer paper in the ancient monastery. They'd come a long way for these precious few words.

"Go on, read it." Angus leaned forward.

Simon became still.

She lowered her eyes to the words. "May this crucifix, by God's gracious mercy and St. Columba's intercession...." Her voice trailed off.

Angus finished. "Draw together father and son for their mutual protection." He looked to Brother Fergna. "This is the blessing. We already had that."

Brother Fergna frowned, reaching for the sheet. "You're right. 'Tis not what I was thinking at all. I clearly remember summat about salvation through the Son."

"It sounds more a platitude than a prophecy," Angus said.

"'Twas redundant," Fergna mused. "It didn't seem much of a prophecy to me either." He studied the paper, a deep crease between his eyebrows, and when it yielded no answers, said, "We'll look again in the morning."

"Do you have other records associated with the crucifix?" Amy asked. "Or the Campbells? James or Niall?"

"Aye." Fergna nodded. "We've plenty."

"Is there some connection between Iona and Glenmirril? Or Iona and Niall Campbell?"

"Apart from Columba's crucifixes, none of which I'm aware. But we'll look after dinner. If there's naught else you're wanting, we've a hot meal and warm beds for you. You're welcome to join us for prayers."

Monadhliath, 1315

"Aye, the prophecy, then." Brother William glided to his desk, muttering about monks of unknown origin. With irritating deliberation, he thumbed through scrolls and parchments.

Niall waited, tamping down growing impatience, while Brother William moved from desk to bookshelves, searching. *Google,* Niall thought. *Search.* He forced himself to pray silent *Paters* while waiting in the chair by the fire.

"Here we have it!" Brother William lifted a document victoriously to the firelight. "'Tis looking poorly. I'll have the monks copy this one as well."

"What does it say?" His heart quickening, Niall jumped from his chair to take the edge of the parchment.

He'd barely caught the words before Brother William harrumphed and snatched it away. "Quite repetitive," he said. "All these *boys*, all this *saving*. 'Tis senseless. It must mean a man who was lost *for* a time."

"Have faith." Niall's voice came out with a frantic edge. He was already repeating the precious words over and over in his mind, memorizing. "Columba knew more than we." His mind raced. Amy had Columba's crucifix. And Shawn now had a son who must certainly be near that crucifix at all times.

"Lost in time, 'tis mad! Clearly a monk was overtired when he copied this. I'll have Brother Owen adjust...."

"I don't..." Niall started. Shawn was right. Amy would need the prophecy.

Brother William fixed Niall with a stern gaze, a general astride his horse staring down at a foot soldier. "Sir Niall, knighted by Bruce you may be, but *I* remain in charge at my abbey. God's grace will guide me aright. I will have the prophecy copied into language that makes sense. We are saved by the Cross. Clearly that is what it means."

Niall swallowed. "Aye, sir." Amy might never find the monks of Monadhliath in her own time, anyway, even if they survived that long. He would simply have to think of another way to leave her a message.

Brother William stalked from the office, charging on to his next conquest with a stiff back, taking the parchment with him.

"Amy," Niall said aloud. "I promised. I'll do what I can."

CHAPTER TWENTY-NINE

Monadhliath, Present

"Brother Eamonn wrote most of the originals. He'll help you." In the archives, Brother Fergna smiled fondly, patting the arm of a tall, gaunt, and very elderly monk. His cheeks were sunken, his hair reduced to a few silky, white strands combed over his pate. His eyes twinkled with cheer as he regarded the newcomers.

"Brother Eamonn." Fergna raised his voice to be heard by the old friar. "This is Simon Beaumont."

Eamonn's hand lingered in Simon's. Watery blue eyes assessed. "Simon Beaumont." His voice rustled like autumn leaves. He smiled. "A pleasure to meet you finally."

Simon raised his eyebrows. "I believe you have me confused with another."

Still smiling, Eamonn turned to Amy, shaking her hand, and touching James's downy hair.

When he moved on to Angus, Fergna leaned close. "Brother Eamonn is fond of Brother Jimmy's brew. He knows these archives better than any man, but his sense of reality wavers at times."

He left, and Eamonn led them in a slow shuffle into the archives, through rows of cabinets and drawers, amidst ancient stone walls. Amy followed Simon, rubbing James's back as he snuggled close on her shoulder. "How much of this monastery was here in the late 1200s?" she asked.

"The archives is new," Brother Eamonn gazed around the stone interior. High Gothic windows let evening sun in at the far end. "'Twas built in 1567, the cloisters in 1793. The church is the original from 1235. We're so remote, we were spared during the Reformation."

"The...Reformation?" Simon asked.

Angus turned in surprise. "Martin Luther's ninety-five theses?"

"Of course." Simon nodded. "I misheard."

"Terrible time," Eamonn rustled in his creaky voice. "We like to think 'twas another of Columba's miracles, though none so dramatic as the fog at Glenmirril." He shuffled past a cabinet, patting it like an old friend. "Malcolm

MacDonald himself came on that occasion, seeking God's protection. Fine, Godly man. A mighty warrior in his day, too."

James squealed his eighth notes of glee on Amy's shoulder. Simon turned, regarding him. Amy's lips tightened, staring back. "Babies make noise," she said.

Simon smiled, a smooth upturning of his lips. "My apologies. I'm unaccustomed to weans."

Eamonn touched a cabinet. "The writings of Owen MacLeod. He took refuge here during the Jacobite risings in 1703. Fine young man, tall and strong, though he talked a blue streak; had difficulty with silence at meals."

"In 1703?" Amy asked.

"Aye, early spring he arrived." His fingertips grazed another cabinet. "Brother Wilfred. A small man with the stamina of a bull. He stopped only to eat, pray and sleep an hour or two. He copied four Bibles that year." He stopped at several more cabinets, telling of the men whose writings they held. "Our William was one for the brandy," and, "Poor Brother John, from the age of twenty thought he was dying of one illness or another. He outlived them all, strong as a horse at ninety-six. Worked the field all day, and knelt before the altar afterward. Slipped away as he prayed."

"Niall Campbell came here," Amy said. "He was...."

"Aye, Niall," the old monk wheezed. "Quite a character. A sense of humor you must hear to appreciate. He visits now and again."

"Visits?" Simon's voice spiked with interest.

"Visits?" Brother Eamonn stopped, turning and blinking uncomprehendingly at Simon. "Who?" Reaching the far end of the archives, he stopped before a cabinet, and gently lifted some papers from a drawer.

Simon's eyes narrowed.

"'Twas on the way to Parliament they came." Eamonn laid the papers on a table, and pulled on a pair of gloves.

"They?" Amy exchanged a look with Angus, wondering why Niall would detour to Monadhliath on his way to parliament.

"Who came with him?" Simon asked, his voice as smooth as cured deerskin.

Eamonn lowered his gaze to the parchments. "Niall often traveled with a monk called Brother Andrew." His gloved fingers trailed the ancient ink.

"His confessor?" Amy patted James's back.

"Ah." Brother Eamonn winked one blue eye. "Brother Andrew was not his confessor. He was a monk of *indeterminate origins*. An *unusual* monk, and most irreverent."

"How so?" Angus asked.

Simon watched the old monk steadily.

Eamonn scanned its spidery script, before announcing, "Here! He sang of carrots and churches."

"Carrots and churches?" Angus echoed.

"Aye." Eamonn squinted at the parchment. "So it says. 'Twas when Brother William told them of the Glenmirril Miracle. The abbot was quite perturbed." The old monk tapped the paper. "He suggests Niall not bring Brother Andrew back, if he see God's grace as cause for jest. There was further upset when Niall asked that Brother Andrew stay a wee bit, promising he would prove useful. There's a note here." Eamonn leaned close, squinting. "'So long as he does not sing irreverent songs at improper moments,' writes the abbot." Eamonn sat back, chuckling.

"It seems unlike...." Amy glanced at Simon. He turned his unblinking eyes on her. She changed her words. "From all I've *read*, Niall doesn't seem the type to press a disrespectful monk on a monastery.

"What other records have you on Niall and Glenmirril?" Angus asked.

"A fair bit." Eamonn opened the nearest cabinet. "Mind the hands now. Put on the gloves."

Simon turned to Amy. He inclined his head in a small bow. "Will I take the child so you can read?"

She shook her head. "He's fine, thanks." She hoped she'd kept her voice even, and not let slip her revulsion at the thought of him touching her baby.

She settled James on his thick blanket, batting at his toys, and seated herself beside Angus at a table against the wall. Simon took a table in the middle of the room. Brother Eamonn distributed ancient documents and new copies—Latin to himself, Gaelic to Angus, and English to Amy. "Though 'tis middle English." He cocked an eyebrow at Simon, as he laid a file before him. "You can read it?"

"I'm quite literate," Simon said curtly.

"Certainly you are." Eamonn shuffled to a chair across the table from Simon.

Amy's hours in archives paid off. With the heavy smell of old parchment surrounding her, she worked through an account of Brother William's arrival as abbot in 1313.

Eamonn lifted his withered head. "Niall was fluent in Latin, Gaelic, French, and English."

Amy hid a smile, wanting to add, "Medieval *and* modern."

"Here it is, Amy." Angus drew her attention, pointing with a white-fingered glove. "Niall Campbell, born 1290, married Allene, nee MacDonald, October 29, 1314."

"They say Allene was quite beautiful." Brother Eamonn lifted his head again. "Curly red hair. She stayed here several times. Had a wee temper."

"That's in the records?" Amy asked.

Eamonn touched the parchment tenderly. "They're like family." He returned to his work.

"Sons." Angus said. "James, born August 1315."

"Not James Angus, though?"

"No." He paused a moment before continuing. "William, November, 1316. A daughter, Amy."

Her insides jumped. She leaned over to see.

Light fell through the stone windows, onto spidery script. His hand covered the edge of the parchment. "You made an impression on him. Though it appears she was stillborn. Died...." Angus stopped, looking at her questioningly.

"No." Amy glanced at Brother Eamonn. His spindly, brown-robed shoulders hunched over his work. Simon, too, was engrossed in reading. "I want him alive in my mind," she whispered.. "I left him less than a year ago, a young, single man, proposing to me." She didn't add, *strong, attractive*. But his presence came back to her in a way it hadn't for months. She saw him on the catwalk behind the theater, knife in hand, every muscle taut; onstage in his own clothing, telling the audience exactly who he was, turning to meet her eye, saying, *This is who I am*. She smiled, admiring the chutzpah. "Now, in thirty seconds, he's become a father, he's lost a child." She glanced back at James, babbling on his blanket. It hurt beyond reason to think of him being born dead. "Can you imagine waking up tomorrow, I'm gone, and someone is telling you how my whole life played out? When I died?"

"I understand." Angus's hand edged farther over the parchment.

They sat in silence. It was too easy to picture Niall, bearded maybe, bowed in grief over a waxen-faced child. She wondered if Shawn had held their children. Maybe if—when—he came back, he'd tell her stories about them, as he'd amused the orchestra with stories of her cousins.

Angus turned to Eamonn, bent over his papers. "Tell us about the crucifix," he said.

Eamonn shook himself, seemingly emerging from a dream, blinked, and lifted his eyes to the ceiling. "'Tis the story of James Campbell, Niall's father." His creaking voice carried them to a faraway time. James Campbell had been an outgoing man, good-looking and smart, with an enviable position as Malcolm MacDonald's steward. He had a bonny daughter and seven fair lads, the youngest called Niall.

Amy felt Simon's eyes on her. She kept her own firmly on Eamonn.

James was a man who could support his large family—if any of them survived long enough to need support. But one by one, they died of illness or injury. Two were executed by the murderous English.

Amy glanced at Simon. His lips tightened.

Each death took more of the humor from James's eyes and added to the stoop of his lanky shoulders. "In 1296, word came that Longshanks was on his way, burning and destroying. Malcolm MacDonald saddled his horse, summoned his men, and rode hard to Monadhliath, asking for protection for his people. He was given one of Columba's crucifixes, with a blessing and prophecy, and a command to lead his people in prayer. This he did, and on the day Longshanks passed, a heavy fog rose, hiding the castle from view." Eamonn stared up into the shaft of sunlight slanting through the far window, once again lost beyond the archives.

"How does James Campbell come into it?" Angus prodded.

Eamonn turned from his study of the sunbeam, blinking at Angus as if he didn't recognize him. Suddenly, he smiled. "Ah, James. Well, 'twas shortly after the miracle that Alexander, his sixth son, drowned. James thought sure if the monks could give MacDonald a miracle, he'd get one for himself, and beg that his daughter and wee son, Niall, be spared. He threw in a prayer for his country, the threat having come so close. The real miracle, perhaps, is why the monks parted with one of the few remaining crucifixes for such a request."

"Six sons dying?" Amy said. "That seems dramatic enough to warrant helping him."

"Children often die."

Amy jumped at the sound of Simon's deep bark. On his blanket, James startled, and settled back to sleep with a whimper.

Eamonn shrugged his bony shoulders. "'Twas indeed common in those days."

"But *six* of them!" Amy protested.

Simon snorted.

"Perhaps it moved them." Eamonn grinned, adding wrinkles to his withered face. "Or perhaps James gave them a large sum of money. The abbot spoke with him about buying miracles, Jesus's sacrifice, and what would he himself sacrifice for his son and country, and sent him home with the crucifix."

"What was the prophecy associated with this one?" Simon demanded.

Amy glanced at him, surprised at his urgency.

"Ah, now, that's here somewhere." Eamonn scanned the archives with watery eyes. He shuffled a few parchments, muttering, "'Father and son...mutual protection.' Tragically ironic, when you consider James died shortly after at Falkirk. There is no miracle recorded with this particular crucifix."

Amy and Angus glanced at one another. Disappearing in time, she thought, might certainly count as miraculous.

"Niall came here asking about it," Eamonn continued. "He'd greatly upset his mother by misplacing it."

Amy touched the small ripple of the cross under her clothing. She hadn't thought how anyone else—Niall's mother, or Allene—might feel about him giving it away. Simon watched her. She dropped her hand. "His brother drowning," she said. "Is that why Niall's afraid of water?"

Simon's head swung to her, his eyebrows dipping.

"Was." Angus murmured. "*Was* afraid."

On his blanket, James whimpered. Amy tore her eyes from Simon's dark gaze, and crossed the room to scoop him up onto her shoulder.

"Aye." Eamonn nodded arthritically, making no note of the wrong tense. "Niall did not much care for water. He was on the shore that day. Though he did well at sea against Lame John."

"Iain Bacach?" Simon rumbled. "They fought? When?"

"Not until June," Eamonn wheezed. "Still time for you to get there." He cackled, and it was easy to believe he'd had too much of Brother Jimmy's special brew. "Time. Sage and thyme. Time makes sage."

Simon leaned forward irritably. "Certainly My Lord of Lorn triumphed."

"Now perhaps he will or perhaps he won't." Eamonn winked, and lowered his head to his documents.

"An event seven centuries past is surely a matter of did or didn't," Simon said, "not will or won't."

Eamonn raised his gaze to the far end of the chamber, where evening sun turned the stone walls silver.

"My good Friar," Simon said sharply, "I have spoken."

Amy stared at him in surprise.

"Mr. Beaumont," Angus began.

Drifting from his reverie, Eamonn stilled Angus's words with a raised hand. He turned pale eyes on Simon. "What if," he said slowly, his voice creaking like dry leaves in autumn, "what if it's taken many men who will never be seen, never known, never recorded, to keep history *as it should be*?"

Amy's arms tightened around James. "What do you mean?"

At the table, Simon Beaumont watched the old man steadily.

Brother Eamonn's pale lips curved into a smile. His eyes flashed, a brief flare in which Amy saw a man younger and stronger; a man in battle. His eyes cut back to her, settling back into filmy age. "I mean," he whispered, "if one could see all the possibilities in any moment of time—how a battle might turn on the smallest detail—what if a man stood at that intersection of history, a man out of time, to make that detail happen? What if a man tried to use his knowledge of the future to change the future? What if someone else prevented that change? Because he only *stopped* a change in history, because he himself caused naught, would history even record his existence?"

Angus's brow furrowed. "Why would history not record that as it happened? And if such a thing wasn't recorded, how would we know?"

"'Twould be known to those with second sight," Eamonn replied, "in thin places where more is seen than history knows."

Simon's head turned slowly, staring at James. Amy's hand tightened on his head. He whimpered and squirmed.

"*Are* there such places?" Simon turned back, leaning across the table. "Where one could know what might have been? Where one could see the possibilities?"

Eamonn studied the man. His back straightened. "If there were? What would one do with such knowledge?"

A slow smile touched Simon's lips. "That would depend on the man, wouldn't it?"

The room darkened abruptly as a cloud slid across the far window.

"It would," Eamonn replied. "Which is why if I knew such a thing, I'd hesitate to tell." His faded eyes wrinkled suddenly into a smile and he melted back into his arthritic stoop. "But then, 'tis a fool's game we play. No such place exists." He quirked one eyebrow at Simon. The gesture reminded Amy of Shawn and Niall. "However...."he turned his gaze on Amy. "If there were such a place, there might be those who *must* know. The sacrifice is not only the men who die in battle, but the mothers and wives who let them go...indeed, insist they go...to their death knowing there is no other way to save thousands, even millions."

Amy's lips tightened. James squirmed in her arms. He let out a short, sharp, screech.

Simon startled, and cast one lingering look on James, irritation crossing his face.

Amy rubbed James's back, shushing him. A shiver trembled in her heart.

"Where would such a place be," asked Simon, turning back to Eamonn, "if such a place existed."

"*If* such existed," rustled Eamonn, "'twould be here or Glenmirril. Our friend Niall seems to have a great interest in telling us what may or may not have been." He leveled his gaze on Amy.

Fear shot down her spine.

Eamonn's eyes drifted slowly back to Simon. "One would be advised to be very, very cautious what one does with that information—if it were true—and never overestimate oneself."

Simon chuckled. "I've not done so yet."

♪

"I'm sorry." Angus looked around the small cell, bare but for a cheerful fire in the hearth, a small wardrobe, a crucifix on the wall—an almost-double bed. "I didn't realize they assumed." They returned to the hall. It was empty—a furlong of stone walls with an arched window at one end, spilling down moonlight. Angus headed to the nearest corner and peered around. He came back, shaking his head. "I've no idea where to find him." He heaved his backpack into the wardrobe. "I'll take the floor."

"No, I dragged you into this," Amy protested.

"You've James to think about." He pulled back the heavy duvet for her, before easing James from her arms.

She sat on the edge of the hard mattress to remove her hiking boots. The crackling flames fought against the chill to warm her toes. She glanced around for somewhere to change.

"I can step out," Angus said. "But you'll be warmer in your clothes."

"Yes, it's chilly in here." Taking James, she settled him to nursing while Angus removed his own boots. Soon, James's eyelids fluttered closed. Amy lifted him to her shoulder, rubbing his back. Angus joined her, and they sat silently, pressed close on the bed while the fire cast flickering shadows around the dark room, and over Angus's dark hair and the stubble on his jaw, with James's even breathing as a soft drone to its crackling melody. Amy relaxed into

Angus's arm, smiling. "Can you imagine, if Shawn stopped here on his way to Hugh, what his dinner was like?"

"A hundred monks," Angus said.

They fell silent. Amy watched the flames dance in the hearth, seeing beyond them to the night she and Shawn had spent, less than a year ago, in the time-ravaged courtyard of Castle Tioram. Over a picnic dinner there, he'd sung about carrots. *Baked potatoes, peas and carrots, eat them with your ham!* He'd circled around her and the picnic basket, crooning into an imaginary microphone, flinging his hair back, parodying himself onstage, till she'd laughed, forgetting her apprehension about sneaking into forbidden castles. *Eat your onions, eat your mushrooms, you should try some yams!*

They laughed at age-old joke as they ate, and planned his next album, a collection of Broadway musicals, as they climbed Tioram's ramparts, through cool air fragrant with the green vegetation clinging to the gray stone walls. With the sea splashing up around its rocky base, shutting them off from the world, he whispered, "The album starts with *Wait for Me* from *Cillcurran.* For you." He sang the opening song from the musical about the mysterious Scottish island; sang softly, his rich bass caressing, asking would there be an empty place in her heart when they were far apart. His words, his arms around her waist, warred with the call from a woman, just hours earlier. A producer, he said. His producer was a man.

But she wanted to believe in him that night.

The bed squeaked. Angus ran a finger down her jaw, jolting her back to the present. She gave a small gasp as his face and shorn curls in the flickering shadows replaced Shawn's flowing chestnut hair glinting in moonglow. "You're beautiful," he said. James peered up at him, and he touched the back of the baby's hand. James clutched his finger. Angus smiled.

Warmth crept up Amy's cheeks. She couldn't hold back a self-conscious grin. Her stomach fluttered, torn between pleasure in Angus beside her, and guilt that she'd been thinking of Shawn. "Let's get some sleep," he said.

CHAPTER THIRTY

Monadhliath

Amy lay sleepless, thinking of Angus on the hard floor. A moonbeam floated through the narrow window. The ghosts of Niall, Allene and Shawn hovered around her. But the cloister, where she and Angus slept, had not been here in their time. "There *was* a cloister," Brother Fergna had explained. "Just not this one. But the courtyard hasn't changed. Nor the church, but that a few statues have been lost, and we added stained glass in 1532."

She had barely drifted off, sliding into dreams of faceless robed monks gliding the halls, when James stirred, wanting to nurse. She stroked his cheek, thinking of Shawn. If Niall's guess was right, he'd been here with Allene in June of 1314. Maybe he'd slept in the room that had been on this spot. Maybe Niall had. Her senses sharpened, as if she might hear them. But that had been June, not April.

James finished nursing, and with a soft sigh, drifted back to sleep. Her thoughts returned to Angus on the floor, Angus in the glen confessing his grief, Angus holding her hand proudly in church despite the disapproving, puckered mouth of Mrs. MacGonagal. She touched the crucifix under her shirt, thankful for him.

Footsteps shuffled outside, faint and faraway, a *swoosh* that blossomed like the finest crescendo and diminished again, the monks going to prayers. Vigils, matins? She couldn't stand her own wakefulness. She rose, pulling on her boots and lacing them. On the bed, James smiled in his sleep. She donned her coat, and gathered him up.

"Angus," she whispered. He didn't move. She hesitated, wanting him to have the comfort of the bed, but not wanting to disturb his sleep. "Angus?" When he didn't respond, she stooped, clutching James, to pull the blanket over his shoulder. She touched his cheek, rough with stubble, then slipped into the hall.

Her boots brushed the flagstones silently. Moonlight shone through the window. Distant chanting echoed down the hall. A dozen monks appeared from the right. They turned the corner and filed through a wooden door. She stopped, feeling like an intruder on something private. But Brother Fergna had invited them.

The night snaked icy fingers around her arms, drawing her out into a cold, silver patch of moonlight in a cloistered walkway, empty and silent. James sighed. She patted his back. Mist curled across the grass and twisted like vines up the columns supporting the covered walkway. The chanting grew, dozens of basses and clear, floating tenors. The hair rose on her arms.

She continued down the cobbled walk, past a black iron rail. Beyond it, tombstones and Celtic crosses pierced white mist. A body floated above the gloam. Cold shot down her arms. With her breath coming in cold gasps, she realized it was just an effigy.

Just!

It was eerily lifelike. She hurried to the church.

The chanting reached out, wrapping her in the warmth of men's voices. Shawn had sung bass. She pushed through the towering doors, studded with brass and leather. Moonlight poured through dark stained glass high in the stone walls. The monks knelt, row upon row of homespun hoods, backs bent in homage.

Their chant—*Deus magnus Dominus*—enveloped her with the champagne-golden glow of Heaven's rays. Their voices lifted a step—*de—e—os*. James twisted. A prickle inched up her spine, squeezing her neck between cold fingers. She moved along the wall, with huge marble columns opening to the pews on her left. A shrine opened on her right. A face stared from beyond the shimmering candles. She jumped, her heart pounding. The chanting fell a step. *Quoniam ipsius est mare.* It was another effigy, one of a dozen life-sized figures, staring down sternly. Candles flickered under them, throwing shadows up on their faces.

Et siccam manus ejus formaverunt.

She touched the crucifix through her sweatshirt. James cooed. His eyes gleamed in the candlelight. She passed the shrine. The moon glistened, a sharp-edged, silver-white crescent, through the open window, gilding the edge of each monk's robe. Their voices rose. *Venite, adoremus, et procidamus.* Her eyes played tricks in the moonlight, in her exhaustion after the day's long hike and sleeplessness. The monks shimmered, misty and ethereal in the candlelight. She backed into a niche where a statue had once stood, transported to another world, another time, by the chanting and incense and candles flickering on stone walls.

In the last pew, a monk turned, faceless beneath his hood. He pushed the cowl back, and rose from his knees, his hand reaching for hers. She gasped. Her stomach lurched.

Shawn stared back. A heavy beard obscured his jaw. His eyes, that had once sparkled with gold and confident humor, gazed with longing, all laughter gone. Shawn had been a bully no one wanted to cross. The man watching her had the bearing of a lord, carrying the weight of his medieval world; a man used to fighting a life no longer in his control. His eyes and jaw softened as he looked at her. She lifted the baby off her chest, holding him out. James stretched his hand from the folds of blankets, and laughed. Shawn stared at him. His face lengthened, saddened. His fingers touched James's. He shimmered. "It's your son, James," she said. The stained glass dropped a ruby gleam of moonlight over his hand. "Come home, Shawn." She looked back up to his face.

"He's a beautiful child." Brother Eamonn's voice scratched like dry leaves over a crypt. "You're welcome to join us. Or I'll walk you back to your room."

Monadhliath, 1315

Shawn sank bank into his pew. Nerves hummed up and down his arms. Around him, the chanting continued. *Quia ipse est Dominus Deus noster.* Two pews ahead, Niall turned, raising his eyebrows. Shawn yanked his hood up, covering his tell-tale features. He turned again to the wall where she'd stood, a hazy figure.

He'd thought at first it was one of the life-sized statues that stood in niches along the walls, a Madonna holding a child, hair flowing down her back. Then his tired mind had registered the twenty-first century jacket, and her face. Amy. A trick of his eye, he warned himself, of exhaustion from the hard day's ride from Glenmirril, followed by a sparse meal and being woken in the night for nocturnes. But she held the child out to him. The boy stretched out a hand. Shawn touched it, feeling petal-soft skin under his war-roughened fingertips. He knew, even before she spoke, her words floating in misty tendrils through the chanting. *It's your son, James.*

The softness faded and his hand lay on a stone carving of a child, held by the Madonna in the niche.

He'd retreated to the pew.

Niall continued to watch him. He swallowed, the loss welling up. Every moment of that first rehearsal, of seeing Amy in her chair behind Peter, rushed back to him. He'd turned himself upside down, walking in on his hands, staring upside down to see if she was looking. Every moment of the first evening, when he'd slid the plane ticket under her door, came to him in Technicolor, the soft peach hues of her robe, the old lace adorning her couch, the antique tea kettle covered in hand-painted flowers, and the reward of her smile, finally bestowed on him.

He wanted her back with everything in him. He wanted his son. *James.* He wanted them to be a family. He crossed his arms on the back of the pew before him, and dropped his head on his arms. More even than waking last June to find himself stitched together with medieval thread, everything in him hurt.

Quadraginta annis offensus fui generationi illi. The chanting wrapped around him, a soft healing bandage.

Monadhliath, Present

Numbness slicked her insides. She heard herself talking, words floating in the air overhead, saying *Shawn* over and over, as Angus rushed into the office. Brother Eamonn, fragile as old parchment over bones, took James as she collapsed in a chair, eyes unblinking; Angus on one knee, pushing a tumbler of whiskey at her. She shook her head. "I'm nursing."

Angus touched her cheek. *We've formula for him. You're in shock.*

I'm not over stressed! Her arms trembled. *He's here.* The words echoed over her head.

Drink, he said. *You're in shock.*

She gulped. It burned. *Shawn's here!* It hit her stomach hard, words tumbled out again, between tears, *I saw Shawn.*

Niall Campbell, Angus told Brother Fergna, and to Amy, *Why did you go alone? Why didn't you wake me?*

His voice echoed through a tunnel.

She thinks she saw him. Amy. His voice came more loudly through the haze. *Remember it was Niall.*

She watched him gulp a tumbler of whiskey himself. *Are you okay?*

Warmth spread through her stomach. *I saw him, Angus.*

I'm not saying you didn't. His voice was a tough rope, pulling her up to reality. *How many monks were there?*

Dozens. A hundred.

We're only twelve. Eamonn's rustle of a voice floated as if in a dream. He leaned his head over James, crooning.

Angus rose abruptly. *I could have lost you and James!* He paced an agitated lap of the room, saying, *He's not supposed to be here!* Turned, eyes blazing, on Brother Eamonn. "How could this *happen*?"

The monk stopped his rusty lullaby. "'Tis a thin place, Monadhliath. Many of us see things that cannot be explained by modern wisdom." He chuckled softly. "Or lack thereof."

"But Shawn...Niall...*Niall* was supposed to be in *June*, not April! Why is he here?"

The old man swayed by the fire, a wisp carved from a willow tree, holding her son as if they might blow over any minute. "'Tis not only possible to see those who walked here," he whispered, "but if the Lord wills it, especially probable, here at Monadhliath. Niall is quite taken with us. He's here often, as if searching." James let out a squeal. Brother Eamonn bent his head, offering a bony finger for James's plump hand to grip, and resumed his rustling song.

Angus's mouth tightened. He refilled Amy's glass. Past and present swirled around her; she felt herself and Angus and Shawn and abbots and monks all crowding the room. She felt irritation. She felt lips pursed in disapproval. She tipped her glass, the whiskey warming her. Pleasant calm floated over her.

Angus rose to his feet, poured himself another glass, belted it down. *Has anyone ever disappeared here?* His words floated pleasantly over her head.

The old monk chuckled. *Not yet.*

Angus poured himself a third drink.

♫

"The whiskey hit her hard," Brother Fergna mused. "'Twas one of Jimmy's more potent batches, sure. "You can manage, now?"

"Aye," Outside their cell, Angus clutched James in one arm, his other around Amy.

She sagged against him, murmuring, "I saw him. Why didn't he come back?"

Angus reeled with the past half hour. He'd been jarred from sleep by Brother Fergna pounding on his door, to find Amy and James missing, and raced through dark, ancient halls, fearing the worst, to see Amy pale, dazed, saying, *Shawn, Shawn,* over and over. Fear for James jostled with shock at seeing Amy's feelings for Shawn blaze as hot as the fire roaring just inches from Eamonn's robe.

"I've got them," he assured Fergna now. He ushered her into the moonlit cell, wondering if he'd done more harm than good, insisting on that whiskey, and kicked the door shut behind them.

Her head dropped to his chest, James cradled between them. "I saw him," she whispered.

"Amy." He tried to right her, tried to reach through the haze of whiskey, tried to keep his mind on what mattered: James's. Not Shawn. "You said there were dozens of monks."

"He looked so sad," she said.

Irritation trembled like ripples in water. A lifetime of bad behavior, and the git had but to *look sad,* and her heart was right back in his selfish hand! *There were bigger problems*, he reprimanded himself. James whimpered in his arm. He walked her toward the bed. "Amy, there are only a dozen monks here."

Her head lolled onto his shoulder. "Mm, dozens, a hundred." Her hand crept up his arm, feather light.

He jumped at the electric zing her touch shot through him, fighting back the smile. They had a problem.

"I'm hot." She slithered abruptly from his grip, onto the bed, and tugged her sweatshirt up over her head, revealing a silky red tank top kilted up at the waist.

He looked around in frustration, wrestled a drawer from the dresser, and, one-handed, pulled a sweatshirt from his backpack to fold into it. He settled James under his blanket in the makeshift crib and joined Amy on the bed. Before he could speak, she slid her leg up over his thigh. Sensations shot through his body. But he pushed her away. "Amy, stop now! Do you understand you were being pulled into Niall's time? You and James?"

She laughed, and raked her hand through her hair. "I'm not in Niall's time, am I?"

"We need to go. James was being pulled back!"

The smile slipped. She frowned, focused her eyes on the ceiling. "Everything's spinning," she said weakly.

"Do you understand?" he pressed.

She rose unsteadily to her feet, and crossed the narrow space between the foot of the bed and the hearth, to the window. A wafer-white moon shone through leaded glass. "It's dark," she said. "We can't go."

Angus came behind her, his arms encircling her. He gazed out into the night, to stars flung by the thousands across black, velvet night. She was right. It would be foolish to take her and an infant into inky wilderness even if she were sober. People got lost, and died, in such circumstances. He glanced over his shoulder, at James in the drawer. People got lost, and died in medieval Scotland, too. Especially babies.

She pressed a hand to her forehead. "This wing is new. Shawn can't be here."

Angus didn't remind her there had been other cloisters, that perhaps Shawn and Niall's rooms *had* been right here. He looked out into the moonlight. There was no way to get her and James safely away. "We'll leave at dawn," he decided. "Let's get some rest until then." He guided her to the bed.

"We're going to sleep together?" She twisted into him, nuzzling his neck.

He grinned, even as he emphasized, "We're going to *sleep.*" He added, more softly, as he sat her on the bed, "Together. With James. Where I can hold onto you both if Shawn comes back." He removed his boots, and knelt to remove hers. She sat, in the red camisole, with her hair falling in long, dark tangles to her waist, watching. He eased the second boot off her foot, and joined her on the bed. She collapsed like a rag doll onto the pillow, looking up through eyes bleary with whiskey, and smiled. He stroked her hair.

"The room's spinning." Amy squeezed her eyes shut. A moment later, she spoke softly. "He's changed."

Angus swallowed irritation. "'Tis not *real,*" he said. "You're making him what you wished him to be."

"It *was* real." She touched his bare arm, warming him as much as the whiskey did.

He brushed her cheek. "What's real is I've loved you and James selflessly every step of the way." She was drunk, he reprimanded himself. But his thoughts demanded to be spoken. "What you had with him was a fantasy world, where he gave you a cheap bauble and called it love."

Amy shook her head, her hair fanned across the pillow. "He'd *love* James."

"Would he?" *Stop,* he told himself, but anger boiled out. "James mightn't *be* here *to* love! What's real with him was other women, lies, self-centered ego!"

"I know. I know that." She closed her eyes, and murmured, "The room is spinning."

Angus let out a breath. "You're guttered."

"I'm not guttered." She pulled him down to nibble his ear. "What's guttered?"

"Out of your pickle. Jaked up. Hammered. And you are." He smiled at her breath tickling his cheek. "Though it has its benefits."

You were right about the...whis...whisk...whiskey." She laughed softly into his neck. "I don't feel shocked."

"I suspect you're not feeling much of anything."

"Mm-hm." She grinned. "Yes, I am." She ran her hand across the black t-shirt stretched over his chest.

Sensations shot through him, bringing a grin to his face. "Mm, aye, whiskey can do that." His breath came more quickly than he liked. But he pushed her hand away. "Now stop that."

"Why?" She inched her hand under his t-shirt, giggling.

"Because I need to get James!"

She grabbed him on either side of his face and pulled his head down. Cool night air and the spicy scent of whiskey clung to her. He gave in, breathing deeply as she ran her hands up and down his back. She pulled his hand under her camisole, onto soft, warm skin. Excitement shot through him. But he yanked back, slowing his breath forcibly, and pushed himself up on one arm. "Have you ever had whiskey at *all*?" he asked.

She threw her arm over her eyes, giggling. "No. But you had three. You're a triplet drunker." She laughed, wiping tears from the corner of her eyes. "A triplet drunker!"

"That's grand," he muttered. "Drunken musician humor. Have you ever been drunk at all?"

She ran her hands through her hair, arching her back. "Uh-uh. I think I like it. It feels good."

"Not in the morning, it won't." Angus shook his head. "I shouldn't have given you the second."

"I'm fine." She laughed, rolling her head. "I know what I'm doing."

"Aye, you're just sober enough to know, but you *are* drunk enough to do it."

Her voice dropped. "Don't you want me?" She slid his hand back onto bare skin.

His eyes fell on the thin, low-cut silk. Her hair spread like black velvet beneath her and tousled around her pale face. Her eyes shone in the firelight. His insides raged with wanting. "Very much," he whispered. The feel of her skin burned his hand; the taste of whiskey on her lips called him back for more. He held himself back. "But I want more than this. I want all of you." He spoke in a rush, wrapping her in his arms, burying his face in her hair. "I want your heart for all time. I want to be a husband to you and a father to James. I know I came into your life too soon, but I'm offering you something real, Amy, real love that *gives*."

"I love you," she whispered. She touched his cheek. "Make love to me."

He drew in breath. She'd asked.

But he shook his head, forcibly against his own desire. "When you weren't staggering under Brother Jimmy's special brew, you said you wanted to wait. Are you going to marry me?" His breath hovered, waiting; waiting for her to choose him over Shawn reaching for her in the chapel.

"Yesssss," she slurred. "Are you going to make love to me?"

She'd said yes. Temptation coursed through him. Her skin was soft. She was only half drunk. She knew what she was saying. He pushed himself off her abruptly. "Tell me again in the morning when the whiskey's worn off."

She ran her finger across his lips, setting his senses tingling. "Promise."

He opened his mouth to answer, but her hand dropped to her chest and a shuddering snore rippled the air.

Angus sighed. He smoothed the hair off her temple, alabaster in the moonlight. She'd agreed to marry him—even if she had followed it up with a drunken snore. Not quite how he'd planned to propose. Not as reassuring as a sober promise. He slipped out of bed to lift James from his drawer. Back in bed, he slid his arm under her, cradling her head on his shoulder, as he cocooned James, safe between them. His thoughts settled, with James's peaceful breath against his neck. Her agitation—it was only the shock of seeing a ghost, not any real feelings for Shawn. She'd broken up with him, before he disappeared. It had been Niall she kissed backstage, not Shawn. She'd seen Shawn for what he was—hadn't she? Angus had never doubted her feelings for himself.

He pushed the worries aside, declaring them irrational, and turned his thoughts to the future. He'd done nothing with his money but save, these years since Julia. That house in the country was still for sale. He'd get her a horse. He'd teach James to swim. They'd have more children. He could see them, playing on moors, climbing hills vivid with heather; he sank into the dream, hearing them laughing and calling.

"Mum!" one of the boys shouted. "There's a man coming!" He pointed.

Shawn strode over the hill, his leine fluttering out beneath a leather jerkin, leather boots laced to his knees, a claymore strapped to his back. He strode down among the girls with their long black hair and boys racing from the nearby loch. Amy came from the house, smiling, calling for them. Her eyes fell on Shawn.

He stopped.

The children froze, looking from Shawn to their mother.

Her smile slipped. Her hand flew to her mouth. She burst into tears, and ran; ran across the moor, ran to him, into his arms, clinging to him, sobbing, kissing him, her hands pressed to either side of his face.

Angus jerked into wakefulness. The sunny hill and children melted into the moonlit cell, the soft crackle of embers, and Amy, tossing restlessly at his side. His heart pounded as the scene replayed itself, as she left him over and over, flew into Shawn's arms, crying, crying for a man who had cheated on her. He lay awake the rest of the night, thinking of James and Shawn, and the life he wanted with Amy.

CHAPTER THIRTY-ONE

Monadhliath, 1315

Niall and Shawn faced one another over a flickering candle in Niall's dark cell, identical in their auburn beards and hooded robes. Outside the window, stars glowed in the night sky. In the halls, doors opened as Niall's men headed to the dining hall to break their fast before their ore-dawn departure.

"She's here," Shawn insisted.

"You were touching a *statue!*" Niall's voice rippled with irritation.

"I was touching *my son*. He was born in February. This baby was about two months old."

"'Twas a long ride. We're tired and hungry."

"You of all people shouldn't doubt what I saw. Find a reason for me to stay. Music. I can do music for them. I can sing it, play it, copy it, whatever they need. But I'm not leaving till I've left a message for her. Something more solid than scratches on stone this time."

A bell tolled outside, calling the monks to prayer.

Niall's eyes blazed. "You will do well to remember that I am in charge."

Shawn's anger grew. "*You* will do well to remember that I belong to the twenty-first century and a woman I left alone and pregnant, *not* to Glenmirril. I don't fall under your authority."

"Everyone at Glenmirril falls under MacDonald's authority, regardless of how they came to be there. And by proxy, when he is not here, mine." The bell tolled a second time, reverberating through the small cell.

Shawn closed his eyes, seeing Amy's face, feeling the petal-soft skin of his son. "You knew her. You cared for her. You did what you could for her yourself. Let me do what I can. She deserves that." His voice dropped. "After all I put her through."

Outside the cell came the soft clicking of dozens of doors opening and closing, dozens of shuffling feet.

Niall's jaw tightened.

Shawn planted his hands on his hips. He closed his eyes, seeing Amy strong behind his lids, and spoke softly. "You will have to physically drag me out of here, which is going to result in every monk in this place and all your men seeing my face and yours together. Do you have an explanation ready?"

Shawn opened his eyes, piercing Niall with his gaze, and lowered his voice still more. "I don't care if you do it because I threatened you or because you care for her," he breathed, "but let me stay and leave a message for Amy."

Silence stretched between them. Niall squeezed his eyes shut, hands on hips. He nodded. "You can stay. For *Amy's* sake."

Monadhliath, Present

I move through haze, clutching James to my chest; my arms ache with holding on...air shimmers with the burnished amber of Brother Jimmy's whiskey and the soft glow of a thousand medieval candles lighting the chapel. The chant of a thousand monks calls like Sirens...my head spins...drunken delight. At the back of the chapel, Angus reaches for me.

The Gloria echoes through the lofty sanctuary. James fades in my arms with each rising note, and re-appears as the melody falls. Shawn and Niall turn, two identical faces among a thousand monks, staring, staring, staring at me. Shawn reaches, pulling James through shimmering champagne streams of chant, clutching him to his own chest, kissing him; my mouth opens in protest, and Angus, behind me, falls to the floor, reaching down, down, down, to Shawn, to James, trying to pull him back, hanging on to me, wrist to wrist, I'm dangling over an abyss, my legs swinging in air, reaching for James, shouting, no sound comes out. James floats away with Shawn on a river, around a bend out of sight, and back in sight around the next bend.

I leap, landing with a jarring thud! *flailing, scrambling upright, the sheet twisting around my legs. "Where's James?" Quick, short staccato accented words of panic. "Where's he?"*

Cold sweat slicks my palms. Gray-pink sunlight filters through the casement. Angus, by the wardrobe, spins when I cry out, sees James in the drawer, and drops to the bed beside me, taking my hand. "He's fine," he says. "I changed his nappy and fed him. I've checked on him every minute while I've been packing our things."

My heart slows. I smile at the image of his tender care. I feel for the crucifix; my fingers touch smooth silk. I glance at Angus as I tug the skimpy camisole down at my waist.

His mouth quirks up. "What are you laughing at?" I demand.

Angus hands me my turtleneck. His smile disappears. He's become the rescuer. "We need to get him out of here."

I yank my shirt over my head, and push my feet into my boots, glancing at James. He didn't *disappear last night. But that means the time switches are erratic, unpredictable. I lace the boots, swish, cross, swish, cross, watching James, as if he might fade before my eyes. But something else happened last night. I glance up at Angus, tall and broad in the doorway, his jaw swarthy. A lifetime of walks by the River Ness, my hand warm in his. Warmth rushes up inside me.*

"He's ready to go." He yanks the drawstring tight on his backpack.

He proposed to me. Tell me again in the morning he said. I want to fly into his arms, saying Yes, and yes again! Yes, I still mean it this morning! But it will have to wait till James is safely away. I gather him up gently, smiling at the sleepy way he twists his mouth into a yawn, stretches his arms, and blinks up at me. He smiles.

Angus touches my back. "Let's go."

Monadhliath, Present

In the pearl-pink dawn, with chilly mist curling around his ankles, Simon ran his hand over one large tomb. He stooped to study the inscription, tracing the worn engraving with his finger to be sure, and was relieved to see it was in the 1400s.

"'Twould surely be distressing to find a friend among the dead."

He jumped at the sound of his own thoughts, spoken aloud. The elderly monk stood, as tall and as thin as his dry, reedy voice, his hands inside the voluminous wool sleeves, flanked by two chipped angels. Simon rose. "Surely I'm unlikely to do so. Are they not all from centuries past?"

"Indeed. The abbey is alive with the ghosts of centuries past. 'Tis a strange place we live, with untold secrets."

A motion at at the end of the cloister caught Simon's eye. The man, Angus, strode from the sleeping cells, his hiking gear on his back. Amy came after him, the child on her shoulder. Simon started forward.

"They'd like a new room," Eamonn said placidly. "Our ghosts disturbed them in the night."

Simon relaxed. He lifted his lips into a thin smile. "Perhaps your ghosts would sleep if their secrets were told."

"Perhaps I *will* tell," Eamonn replied. "Monadhliath's secrets may be what you seek."

Simon glanced after the couple, disappearing into the front wing. But the old man dangled a precious jewel. He turned back. "What knowledge have you of what I seek?" He didn't hide the sneer in his voice.

The old man meandered, his shoulders stooping, among the leaning tombstones. The towering angels swallowed his words. Simon moved closer, straining to hear. He wished he could hit him over the head, see him sprawl in the tall grasses, blood trickling from his temple, and be done with his riddles. He *would* do so, once he had the man's information.

"She doesn't know, herself." Eamonn touched a lichen-covered knight, stretched atop a tomb, staring endlessly at the dawn, oblivious to the birds that sang.

Simon followed him around the sepulcher. "Doesn't know what?"

"Neither do you, I believe. But you very much need to, now, do you not?" The monk wandered deeper into the graveyard, till the cloister disappeared behind towering Celtic crosses.

"I know a great deal," Simon replied. "But I'm ever amenable to learning more. What is it you think I need?"

"A way home." The man turned, facing Simon. A breeze lifted five filmy strands of white hair off his scalp. He touched the beads hanging at his belt. A crucifix swung at the end of them. "A prophecy, a blessing." The monk turned, shuffling around a tall Celtic cross.

Simon followed, barely catching his next words.

"And what was the last thing? A crucifix, perhaps?" Eamonn glanced down at his beads, and back to Simon, and laughed. "But not this one. Perhaps I can give you the one you need. She's unaware 'tis missing. Tonight, after the monks have left evening prayers, aye?"

♫

In the front office, the round young monk looks up from stoking the fire, and cheerfully hurries off to find Brother Fergna. Shawn, whiskey, nightmares, waking to packed bags! As Angus shrugs his pack to the floor, I sink into the wing chair. My mouth tastes of old whiskey. My stomach is queasy. I was sliding into Niall's time. My arms tighten around James. We're in the oldest part of the monastery. Shawn might have sat here, in this very office, before this very hearth. Would he be here first thing in the morning, after our midnight encounter, in his own time? Why was he here in April, anyway? It was June he came through on his way to Hugh. Did Brother Eamonn know? Why didn't he say so? I remind myself he can't know every detail of the past seven hundred years. And that's not the problem, anyway. The problem is: Was James in danger? He didn't disappear. But we don't know he won't, next time.

Angus wanders the book shelves, touching old volumes.

My mind turns to Shawn, caught in a world of death and dismemberment. I see his eyes on me last night, begging. After all we've put into it, to abandon him, leave Carol to her grief, leave James never understanding what happened to his father—it hurts.

Angus paces.

"We're leaving," I say.

He nods, absently.

I rise, James sighing on my shoulder. I touch Angus's back. "He's in my arms, Angus, he's safe."

Angus stops before the blazing fire.

"Is it something else?" My mind flits to his promise last night. He had a lot of whiskey. Is he re-thinking it?

"I'm assigned to his case." He speaks tersely. "It's my job to find him."

He doesn't have to spell it out. My heart hurts. He's the most honest man I know. What can he tell his superiors, or Clive, when he's supposed to be working on the case?

"It's everything!" He turns, suddenly. "I put him in danger." He touches James's head.

Anything he might have said is stopped by the office door flying open. Brother Fergna enters, smiling. "'Tis a pleasure, it's been!" *he says.* "I do hope you found answers"

"The prophecy hasn't turned up?" *I ask.*

Angus looks at me in surprise. "Forget the prophecy," *he says.* "We need to walk away from this. For James."

I close my eyes, the weight of it all as heavy as the ancient timbers. The fire crackles in the hearth, as it has for hundreds of years, over paneled walls that have been here since Niall's day. A cool draft touches my cheek. I jolt, opening my eyes. Angus's hand is warm on mine, his eyes begging.

Eamonn shuffles in. If a shuffle can be frantic, his is. He sounds out of breath. But then, he's always wheezing. "I've not found the prophecy," *he sighs. His pale blue eyes gaze somewhere beyond my sight. I glance behind, half expecting to see monks from Monadhliath's past. There's no one there, of course. A cold finger trails down my arm as a draft sloughs through the chinks in the door.* "Though," *he adds,* "I found something in the archives you'd surely like to see. 'Twill take but a moment."

I glance at Angus, torn between curiosity and the desire to get James out of here.

"James is quite safe," *Eamonn says in his rusty half-whisper.*

His words startle me. What does he know?

"He'll be with you for many years," *he adds.*

Angus glances to Fergna, who says, "A thin place it is, but your son is quite safe."

"I'll wait here with him," *Angus says.* "But hurry. Please."

James whimpers. His fingers dig into my hair.

Amy....

I whirl, searching, but the fire crackles, undisturbed. Angus doesn't react. Eamonn's eyes return from wherever he wandered. I wonder if he'll remember to look for the prophecy. James's whimper turns to a cry. "Sh," *I whisper.* "What's wrong?"

"Sign the guest book." *Brother Fergna offers a pen.* "We'll send you the prophecy when we find it."

I'm soothing James. Angus signs. When he finishes, I pass James over. James sticks his fist in his mouth, and buries his face in Angus' neck, as I follow Eamonn's slow shuffle down the stone halls.

Monadhliath, 1315

Niall rode from the monastery, at peace with allowing Shawn to remain. It had taken some talking. Brother William did not much care for 'monks of unknown origin,' as he repeatedly called Brother Andrew.

"Trust me," Niall had insisted. "Glenmirril and Monadhliath have ever been on the best of terms, aye? I know he's peculiar. He's not of our parts and doesn't know our ways, but he's no threat. I've my reasons for asking."

After a great deal of hemming and hawing, and a list of terms, Brother William gave in.

With much grousing, Shawn agreed to Brother William's terms, which Niall relayed to him in his cell. "No disrespect. No questioning his authority," Niall reported. "No singing unintelligible songs."

Still, it was not with complete peace that Niall rode away, followed by his thirty men through the rain-soaked valleys and mountain passes to Ayr. His conscience nagged. He had not told Shawn the prophecy.

Monadhliath, Present

Eamonn gestured proudly at three thick piles of parchment on the table. "The music Niall copied!"

"Niall copied music?" Amy reached for white gloves. "Why would he do that? When?"

"He stayed that April," Eamonn said.

She glanced up at his wrinkled face, shining with joy at his news. "Which April?"

"The April after Brother Wolfred died, naturally. Why would he stay before? Now, I've work to do." He tottered from the room.

Amy lifted the first parchment, covered in four-line staves, awed at its age. Mythical creatures, in vibrant reds and blues and golds, crawled up the side of the page. Twisting vines, still jade green after so many centuries, curled like a tall, thin S, around the front leg of the large illuminated A at the beginning of the song. It seemed to shift momentarily, into a trombone, and twist back into a vine. She scanned the Latin text. *Deo*—God. Another word or two jumped out, but mostly, it was meaningless.

As she scanned the notes above the words, the diamond-headed neumes Niall's quill had brought to life so long ago, the song came alive in her head. She hummed slowly, as monks would have chanted it. Something was wrong. She hummed again, wondering if she'd missed an interval, gotten the wrong key signature, or gone off key. But it was major. She frowned. She couldn't go wrong with a minor inversion. In the silence, she tried again, eyes closed, concentrating.

The melody hit her!

Her eyes flew open. An invisible fist punched the wind from her chest. She shoved herself off the stool. It clattered to the floor behind her. She turned abruptly, pressing her fingers to her forehead, trying to slow her breathing. Niall had not copied these!

CHAPTER THIRTY-TWO

Monadhliath, 1315

Shawn immediately saw the impossibility of living under a hood for a month. "You were right, Brother William," he announced when he joined the abbot in his office. "Brother Andrew is nothing but trouble. I've decided to stay and help you, myself."

"I can't say I'm displeased," Brother William huffed. "We need help. Brother Wolfred dead these two months, and no one to replace him. We need music for services and music copied. Now as to your duties...."

If Shawn had expected a quiet month, the schedule Brother William rattled off, as he led him through dawn-washed halls, quickly disabused him of the notion. He would play harp for chants, masses, matins, lauds—Shawn lost track of the names. "You'll practice daily, in addition to copying." Brother William led him to a cavernous stone chamber, filled with rows of tall, spindly stools before desks on tall, spindly legs. Tall windows let in rosy dawn. He stopped before a particularly battered desk piled high with old, worn music. "You may start." With a curt bow, Brother William turned on his stern heel and departed.

With a sigh, Shawn took up his quill, grateful for Allene's insistence on learning to use one. A template to lay out staves would have been nice, but he managed to create a passing resemblance, on fresh, new parchment, to what was on the old.

Cool drafts blew around the monks' ankles as they hunched, copying Bibles and psalters, hymnals, and local records. Shawn leaned over and whispered to the short, fat monk at the next desk, "Why do you do this?"

"We are historians and scholars," the monk whispered back. He was little more than a boy, but already tonsured. "We keep records of marriages, births, and deaths, at the castles with whom we are associated, and all events at the abbey. We've records back to the days of Columba himself."

"And you just keep copying and re-copying the same things forever?" Shawn arched one eyebrow. It seemed an insane waste of so many lives.

"Aye, Sir Niall. 'Tis our ministry, keeping the people's history."

An older monk shot them a stern look, and the boy bent to his work. Shawn rose to sip his dipper of water from the communal bucket, long past worrying about germs, and trailed back to his desk. The early morning sun shone gloriously through the stone casement. He stared at the psalm before him. Diamond-headed neumes slid up and down four staves over Latin text.

"Sir Niall, you are lost in thought," Brother William's sharp voice crackled like gunshot behind him.

Shawn jumped. The man was young to be an abbot, hardly older than Shawn himself. Every inch of his bearing spoke of control. Shawn wondered what had drawn such a man to a monastery.

"I know 'tis a favor you do us," Brother William added, "but there is much to be done. Brother Wolfred was ailing and had fallen far behind."

"Aye." Shawn sighed, and dipped his quill in the ink, carefully laying four staves for a psalm, leaving room for a large, illuminated letter. He couldn't just scribble *Amy, help! I'm caught in 1314,* and expect generations of Brother Williams to let it reach her. It was a useless message, anyway; there was nothing she could do. He tried to think, while he copied Latin text beneath the notes, what he really needed to tell her.

Amy, I'm sorry, I was stupid, please forgive me.

But the vigilant Brother William would see such words and dispense with them. Or change them to what he deemed they must really mean.

Shawn dipped his quill in red ink, and placed the first neume, eyeing the original for shape and size. He switched to black ink and continued the long row of notes, as identical as he could make them. He hummed while he copied, working through Glenn Miller's greatest hits, while the sun rose higher, all the while pondering how to leave a message for Amy, one that might slip by Brother William and seven centuries of his successors. He sanded the parchment and shook it dry, leaving it on the worktable for the monks to once again store away wherever they put these things.

A bell tolled. Without a word, the monks shuffled, straightening quills and inks, and setting things in order for the afternoon's work. It was lunch time. Shawn fell into line beside the short, fat boy. It felt like being in school again. "Nobody but Brother Wolfred did music?" he asked.

"We've no musicians. Only Brother Wolfred could read music."

"Whisht, quiet now," admonished the older monk.

Yes, it felt just like being in school. But Shawn smiled. The boy had just handed him gold.

Monadhliath, Present

I don't know much Latin. But I know the text below the diamond-headed neumes doesn't say what the melody does. I made so many mistakes, I'm so sorry, can you believe me?

I draw slow breath, fighting the punch to the solar plexus. Give me one last chance; please don't leave me.

I arranged it with Shawn for his brass quintet. I know every word. He knows I know every word. I see his eyes, the sad desire in the chapel, as his message whispers against my heart. I'm so sorry, can you believe me?

Tears sting my eyes. Give me one last chance; please don't leave me.

I slap it away, as if it burns. A Gregorian chant follows. But the next manuscript sings out. Don't forget me when I'm gone.

I went to hear him play at the jazz club. I suggested a better chord progression afterward. I couldn't resist. He was so arrogant, so unaware he could miss a chance for perfection. He challenged me. "You think you can write?"

I know, staring at the ancient manuscript, that he remembers every detail of that day, as I do. I went to his half-timbered mansion. He wanted trombones on every line. "Don't be stupid!" I said. "You have to move the melody around."

"This is a powerful piece," he insisted. "It's begging for trombones."

We argued. He wrote it his way. I wrote it mine. We glared at each other and stamped out into an early spring, unspeaking, down a dirt road muddy with melting snow, past a field guarded by a wilting snowman, under clouds as angry as our faces. The rain started as we reached town, large drops, quarter notes on beat one; beats one and three, and suddenly a spray of triplets spattering short and sharp and light and fast, in a burst of sun shower. He laughed, grabbed my hand, and ran, pulling me under an overhang, spun me into his arms, and kissed me. Everything in me stood on end, electricity zinging through every nerve. No force on earth could have torn me from him, least of all my lingering fear he was a player.

Half a world away, in an ancient monastery, I press my hand to my mouth, still feeling that kiss, feeling the rain pour down. I turn, almost fearfully, to the next manuscript. You take my breath away.

We arranged this one together. We played it at our first sell-out concert. You're beautiful tonight.

He gave me flowers. I have so much to say. My love for you grows day by day.

He left a note in my case: You're beautiful. Can I see you after the concert? *Signed with the S.*

If you'd seen the things I've seen, if you knew where I have been.

Celebration backstage. I wake up and you're not here.

Champagne flowing. Who left who, was it me or was it you?

We'd never had a sellout concert. Don't forget me through the years.

He had to leave to record an album. I drove him to the airport. Don't forget me when I'm gone.

He kissed me in the car. Don't forget me in the time between.

"You'll never leave me?" he asked, a strange desperation in his voice. The chorus sings over and over, Don't forget me through the years....

*I wipe at tears with shaking fingers, wipe harder. Wipe my nose with my sleeve...*in the time between.

I hear sounds of gulping. Don't forget me….
Of sobbing. When I'm gone.
I see him, trapped in a bubble in time, pounding, calling, pleading. Don't forget me….

Monadhliath, 1315

Copying took longer when Shawn transcribed from memories of music that wouldn't exist for centuries, rather than from the parchments before him. He placed each neume carefully, to the steady rhythm of the rain spattering the windows high above, a note over each Latin syllable. Future monks and abbots would read the words. Amy would read the melodies. They'd worked together on the albums. She knew every word. He copied a chant from Brother William's pile, and another for Amy. Another plainchant, three more messages for Amy.

Brother William leaned over his shoulder, nodding approvingly at the neat copies, the accurate Latin text, and notes that looked to him like any other music notation: a meaningless jumble.

Monadhliath, Present

She heard her name. And Angus had his arms around her, pulling her from the parchments, from the memories; pulled her close. "Amy? What happened?"

Tears flowed down her cheeks. James, in Angus's arm, kicked and let out a screech. "What's wrong?" Angus tried to comfort her while holding James. He glanced at the music scattered across the long work table. Colorful letters illuminated the first word of each piece. Black staves, stretched across creamy vellum, with diamonds leaping across them, like gymnasts on bars. He turned her from them, as if those strange animals might slither off the paper like medieval scarabs and crawl under her skin.

They already had. Shawn's plea was under her skin, a splinter in her heart. He pulled her from the room. Shawn followed, reaching for her arms, her hair, gripping her fingers, reaching for James in Angus's arms. Angus bustled her to the front room, seating her before the crackling fire, and turning for the tea cart. Wind gusted down the chimney and roared back up, sending the flames higher. She stared into them, feeling every memory of Shawn, each sensation his songs stirred up.

Cradling James in one arm, Angus deftly set out a china teacup. "What is it?" he asked over his shoulder. "You were looking at chants." The silver coffee pot poised in his hand. James mewled in his arm.

"No," she said. "I read music like you read Gaelic. The Latin said *Agnus Dei*. The melody said, *Please Forgive Me.*"

Angus set down the tea pot. He shook his head, as if trying to dislodge something.

"*Tell Me What Love Is,*" Amy's voice came out choked. They'd worked on it in Hawaii. "*Don't Forget Me.* Do you know the lyrics?" Shawn had sung it in Tioram. She swallowed, remembering the way he'd held her that night. "*I Will Remember.* It's all music we arranged together." She didn't tell him that each one left her with powerful memories, of Shawn's touch, Shawn's laughter, Shawn's kiss.

James fussed. Amy crossed the small office, taking him onto her shoulder.

Angus dropped into the chair by the fire, his hands clenched together till the knuckles turned white. "He's seven hundred years gone, and he's sent you love letters."

He'd seen her reaction. She couldn't deny the power of Shawn's message. Shawn had never shown any weakness. The thought of him afraid, begging her across centuries not to forget him, had torn open the floodgates. On her shoulder, James whimpered again.

Angus raised his head, staring at James. "Let's go. Now." He rose, taking her hand. "Think of James."

Amy closed her eyes, the weight of it all as heavy as the ancient timbers around her. The fire crackled in the hearth, as it had for hundreds of years. A cool draft touched her cheek. She jolted, opening her eyes. Angus's hand was warm in hers, his eyes begging.

The door flew open. "The prophecy!" Brother Fergna burst in, waving a sheet of paper as if rallying an army. "We found the prophecy!"

Angus watched her. She felt Shawn's presence, saw his brown eyes with the gold flecks as surely as if he stood before her, waiting, begging. Maybe the prophecy held the key. She met Angus's eyes.

"What about James?" he said softly.

"It doesn't hurt to read it," she objected. She felt Shawn's hand stretch out to her. *Don't forget me.* Her heart pounded more swiftly. "James might want it someday."

"Is it just about James?" he asked.

"Is it?" she returned.

He said nothing.

"Angus, it's what we *came* for," she protested.

His lips tightened. Brother Fergna glanced between them. Angus heaved his backpack up onto his shoulders and strapped the baby carrier to his front, waiting for her decision.

CHAPTER THIRTY-THREE

Monadhliath Mountains, Present

"Are you going to walk away again?" I fling angry words at Angus's back as he strides over the rough moor. He's been marching, unflaggingly, for an hour. "You'll have to stop eventually," I call.

He turns, his hand protectively on James's head. I sling my backpack to the ground, and drop to a large boulder, challenging him to leave me. I unscrew my canteen and take a long draft. "I don't get it." I wipe my mouth. "What does it hurt to just have *it?" I hear the defensiveness in my own voice, and I know I'm right—it* doesn't *hurt just to have it, but I'm fighting guilt. I know my reaction to Shawn's music hurt Angus badly.*

Angus heaves a sigh. He eases James out of the baby carrier. I spread a blanket on the ground, where James lies on his stomach, bundled in his little sweatshirt, batting at spring grass. My stomach rumbles. He opens his backpack, pulling out homemade bread and goat cheese. Brother Eamonn pressed them into our hands as we passed through the gatehouse, back into the world.

I want to touch his dark, short curls. But everything in him shouts Keep Away. *His hands, holding bread, cheese, and a knife, sink to his knees. He stares up at great white clouds scooting across blue sky. He seems to pick among thoughts, discarding, searching again. He produces four short words. "You're going to continue."*

I shake my head, denying. "I haven't...." But it hurt, horribly, walking through those gates, leaving Shawn behind. I know how I am with a hard piece of music. One more measure, I tell myself; one more phrase. Will I remember only that Shawn faded away, leaving James safe? Will I remember only his eyes full of longing? Will I open the prophecy, telling myself just one measure? Ponder what I read—one more phrase. Put a foot back on the trail?

I leave my boulder to sit beside him, my legs curled under me. I take the knife from his hand, spread thick cheese, and hand him the bread. He eats silently, and drinks from his canteen, while we sit together, separated by our thoughts.

"I have to quit." He wipes his mouth, and brushes the crumbs from his

hands. *"It means abandoning you and lying to my superiors, pretending I'm on the case when I'm not."*

"Angus...." Everything in me hurts for him. I doubt he's ever lied in his life.

"But I won't do anything that might harm James." He turns to me, angry and pleading for understanding all at once. *"I rescue, Amy, it's what I do! Yet I took a foolish risk."*

"You didn't! We thought...."

"He's in danger," he snaps.

Is it my guilt or seeing the truth? My words slip out in a faint pianissimo. *"You're afraid you are, too."*

Angus turns away. *"Should I not be?"*

The sun inches to its zenith.

"I'm sorry, Angus. It wasn't deliberate."

"No, but it was real."

His pain tears into me like Shawn's lies never did.. *"So is everything I feel for you,"* I protest. *"So was my promise."* I slip my hand into his. *"The whiskey has worn off."*

He turns to me, wary.

"You said...." Bashfulness creeps over me. *"...tell you again...in the morning...when the whiskey has worn off."*

His jaw tenses. *"You can't marry me when he has such power over you."*

"It was shock," I say. *"It was unexpected. He's James's father. Carol's son."* I'm speaking frantically. The truth is, my reaction to Shawn's music stunned me, too, left me reeling with the depth of my emotions. But I feel the same for Angus!

He watches a hawk circling above. *"Aye, but what happens when he comes back? To us?"*

"Angus, it doesn't matter," I protest. *"I want to be with* you.*"*

He rises. *"It matters to* me.*"* He pushes the bread into his rucksack.

"Angus?" I whisper it, not wanting to believe this. *"You can't take back a proposal."*

"We both have things to think about." He gathers up his backpack and James.

"I haven't even opened the prophecy," I object.

"But you will." He marches away over rough ground.

My anger rises at his stiff back. *"You can't take back a proposal!"* I shout.

Monadhliath Abbey, Present

The couple was gone!

Simon watched their places as the handful of monks filed in for supper. They bowed tonsured heads over steepled fingers for prayer, clearly not expecting the seats to be filled. The blood began a low simmer in his veins as the soup that passed for a meal was placed before him, as his mind traveled back to the incident in the cemetery. The old man had lied to him. He'd deliberately led him deeper amongst the ruined stones, tempting him with gems of knowledge. The simmer rose to a slow boil as he realized they had many hours head start, and would have many more; for he couldn't set out into the hills with night falling.

He watched Eamonn, who never looked up from his soup. When the meal ended, the monks filed out on cat's feet, silent leather shoes brushing age-worn stone floors.

Simon paused in the hallway, watching as they turned the corner, heading for the church. He could do nothing with all of them together at prayer. Besides, he must let his anger cool. He must do nothing foolish, and he certainly wanted to kill the man. The archives, he decided. Sooner or later, that's where Eamonn would go.

Simon went first. He let himself in as the sun dipped below the sill of the Gothic window, casting a golden sheen on the walls and cabinets around him. He waited, silently, as the archives grew dark, between rows of cabinets where he would not be seen, pondering, as he waited. The crucifix was important. Else why would a monk would steal it?

The great wooden door creaked. Eamonn shuffled in. He touched the wall, raising pale, yellow light to life, and turned his head on his wizened neck. He lifted watery blue eyes, staring directly at Simon.

Simon's gaze shot to the rosary beads hanging from his belt. The crucifix was not there.

The monk's eyes lingered on Simon, betraying no fear.

"'Tis odd, a monk stealing a crucifix," Simon moved close, leaving less than a thumb's breadth between himself and the monk's rough woolen robe. "Pray tell, good brother, why you would do such a thing."

"Thou shalt not steal," Eamonn intoned, not drawing back. He was taller than Simon, but slight—a twig to Simon's trunk—and frail. He should tremble in fear. He didn't. "I'd not do so but for great need."

"You've no need of another crucifix, here in this holiest of places," Simon replied.

"This thinnest of places," Eamonn corrected.

"Thinnest." Simon paused on that. "Where worlds come together."

"Here of all places, they do."

"It seems you know things." Beaumont's voice slid out smooth as a mountain cat purring.

"One learns a wee bit in eighty years." Brother Eamonn's hand drifted over the smooth surface of a cabinet holding dozens of lives. "One learns even more, perhaps, in seven hundred years."

Beaumont's eyes narrowed. "What exactly do you know?"

Eamonn chuckled, a wheeze deep in his chest. "Now we've hardly time to tell *all* I know. Shall we speak only of your own history?"

Simon glanced at the cabinets, and back to the monk who had not the sense to cower. "It seems," he said, "that the history written here may change. And it seems there are those who live in the places between time, seeing all possible outcomes."

Eamonn shook his head. His robe scraped his wrinkled neck. "There are many possible outcomes, but only that which actually happens will, in the end, be recorded here."

"Will be?" Beaumont's breath alighted on the old man's cheek. "Or already is?" He circled the monk, glaring at his silky, white strands of hair. "There's a letter to James Douglas, written in the 1300s. Might it cease to exist?"

Eamonn chuckled. "'Tis useless, trying to escape one's fate. 'Tis rare that it works."

"But then, there are rare men. Could not fate be escaped if one knew the players, if one of those players was but an urchin? How could such a one stand against a great knight?"

"Behind every urchin is a mother bear."

Simon laughed, his head thrown back. "A woman cannot stand against a great knight."

"Your arrogance will be your undoing." Eamonn sighed, as if speaking to a child.

Simon ignored the monk's words. "I gather that until recently, your records told of a bitter loss for Scotland, a complete slaughter of her finest lord." He snorted. "Such as they were. Yet today, your records tell of great victory."

"Do they?" Eamonn turned his back, wandering down between the rows of cabinets.

"The other monks think you mad," Simon mused, following him. "But I begin to think you the sanest one here. Tell me—what if a man could read here, what transpired in centuries past, and then go tell those kings their future?"

"That man would be thought a seer and acquire great power."

"Even so," agreed Simon. "Was there ever such a man?"

"There is such a man."

Simon licked dry lips. "Is his story in these drawers? Is it different from that which I've read?"

"His story is not yet complete." Eamonn stopped his shuffle, turning to Simon.

"If his story played out seven hundred years ago, it is complete," Simon returned forcefully. "Show me the drawer!" He gestured angrily at the cabinets. "I'll read it myself."

Though Simon's breath stirred the hair above his ear, the old monk stood immobile. He spoke softly. "'Tis often wiser not to know one's own future."

Beaumont's lip lifted in a sneer. "I've no fear. You, however, ought to." He circled Eamonn once more. His shadow swayed like a snake, in the yellow light, over the cabinets and floors. His finger inched under the old man's collar, probing about his neck. His sneer slipped into a snarl. "Where is it?"

"Where is what, My Lord?" Eamonn stared straight ahead.

Beaumont started. Then he laughed. "Ah, you *do* know."

"Know what, My Lord?"

"How did you know?" Simon asked.

"Prior to your arrival with the young couple," Eamonn said slowly, "I saw you wearing chain mail, with a black beard, full-grown."

Simon stroked his jaw. Two days' stubble rasped against his thumb. "I've never been here before."

"You will be. I believe 'twas...will be...1316, 1318."

A sound like a growl rose from Simon's throat.

"Forgive an old man. 1319?" Eamonn smiled. "Or 1315."

"Why did I come?" Simon demanded, holding tight to his anger.

"You sought Niall Campbell." Eamonn sighed, a sound as thin and fragile as the fluttering strands on his bald pate, and turned his back to Simon, moving further down the rows of cabinets. "Your men storm through, shouting, yelling."

"You've seen this?" Simon stepped stealthily closer, eyeing the back of the man's neck, where his thumbs would press as his fingers squeezed the withered neck, pressing the life from him as peasants pressed wine from grapes, leaving only shriveled skins behind. But first...he would get information.

"I've seen a great many things." Eamonn chuckled suddenly. "Of course,'tis only the wine. Brother Jimmy, Brother Jimmy! Perhaps a wee bit strong for me."

Beaumont made a harsh sound in his throat. "Enough games, old man. Where's the crucifix?"

Eamonn's pale lips narrowed in a tight smile. "Where it will keep many safe. Really, what good has come of the death and killing?"

Beaumont laughed. "For me, a great deal. Were you hoping for a miracle conversion here in the archives?"

Eamonn smiled, lifting his eyes to the sliver of moon shining in the window. "Stranger things have happened."

Beaumont snorted. "Let us have done with pointless conversation. Take me to the crucifix."

Eamonn didn't move.

Beaumont grasped his elbow, jerking it behind his back.

Eamonn let out a sharp gasp. His face went pale. He whispered, "I'm no good to you dead, now, am I?"

"None whatsoever," Beaumont purred. "However, if I don't get what I want, I'm none the worse for your broken carcass at my feet."

"And once you get what you want, there's naught to stop you doing so anyway," Eamonn responded.

"Well, now," Beaumont suggested, "I propose a deal. You give me the crucifix and I'll leave."

"I'm to trust the word of a man who would harm an old man and a child?" Beaumont gave a sharp jerk on his arm.

Eamonn gasped more deeply this time. He drew a second, slower breath, then laughed his dry laugh. "I've very little time left, anyway. 'Tis possible I'm not so concerned with death as you think."

"Nobody likes pain." Beaumont pressed on the arm. "The crucifix."

"You're sure you're wanting this?" Eamonn asked. "You're playing with forces stronger than your own."

"Take me there, Monk," Beaumont snarled.

"Very well." Eamonn nodded. "Come along." He touched the wall, plunging the chamber into darkness.

Inverness, Present

"You're back!" Clive looked up in surprise as Angus entered the small office.

Angus tried for his usual good-natured grin. Despite the long hike and drive, he was restless. He'd walked to the station through the cool night, thinking to comb Kleiner's files for a reason to close the case. But he couldn't tell Clive that. "The monks are vegetarians," he said, instead. He snapped a dead leaf off the wilting plant on the filing cabinet, and tossed it in the trash. "Had to come home before I starved." He sat down to his computer, and typed in his password.

"Mm." Clive threw a wealth of skepticism into the single syllable. "Good hike?" He kept his eyes on his own computer.

"Not bad." Angus opened the Kleiner file. A page sprang up documenting Shawn's antics at an Edinburgh hotel last June. How could Amy be anything but grateful he'd disappeared, along with his lying, cheating, trouble-making ways? But she had been distraught. Over him.

Clive snorted. "Yep, sounds like a guid time."

Angus tapped fiercely at his keys. Coming here was no better than pacing his living room, rehashing things. Maybe worse. His fingers became still on the keys. He *should* talk to Clive. It was his case, too, after all. But it was difficult to explain the situation without mentioning not-quite-ghostly visions and time travel. And he certainly couldn't explain his fear for James, which was the only thing that could possibly justify his decision to lie to his superiors.

"It must be bad. You're not even taking the piss out of me." Clive pushed back from his desk. "I'm knocking off. Give me a ring if you want to come 'round for a Guinness."

Angus sighed. "I might do. Thanks, Mate."

Monadhliath, Present

Simon followed the shuffling old monk down stone halls that looked exactly as they would in Simon's own time. The man stopped repeatedly, one gnarled hand resting on the wall, his head lowered, drawing deep breaths. Simon tamped down growing impatience. It mattered little how much the old man stalled, he had no choice but to hand over the crucifix and tell all he knew of its powers. And if Simon was in a good mood when he finished, the old man might remain alive another year or two to guard his musty documents.

The monk stopped at a heavy door, half-turning his skull-like head. "'Tis not too late to walk away."

Simon grunted. The man shrugged weak shoulders under the coarse, brown robe. He pushed at the door. A small sigh of effort escaped his lips. Simon waited, offering no help. The door creaked, letting in cold tendrils of mountain air. They crossed the cobbled courtyard path, past the graveyard, and the chipped angels rising above the mist. He wondered, as they passed a marble sepulcher glowing in the night, if the switch would happen on touching the crucifix. It couldn't, he decided. Otherwise the chit, Amy, would have disappeared. He planned his moves. He'd kill the monk just for fun, take the crucifix, find the girl, kill her spawn, and then figure out how to use the crucifix.

The monk pushed at the kirk door, a towering wood affair. Darkness swallowed them, but for moonlight casting a silver tinge on the walls and bouncing a gleam off the back of each pew hulking in the dark. Incense hung in the air. The monk shuffled, stopping now and again to rub the arm Simon had twisted.

"Hurry up, old man," Simon growled. The holiness in the air restrained his roar of impatience snarling to be loosed.

"'Tis not yet time." Eamonn stopped before an empty alcove that must once have held a statue.

"It's here?" Simon grabbed the back of Eamonn's wrinkled neck.

A harsh pant came from the monk's throat. But he wheezed placidly, as if they strolled through a field of bluebells. "I'm thinking, I'm thinking. Forgive an old man's forgetfulness. 'Twas at night I came."

Outside, a bell tolled, low and mournful, as if summoning forth the very ages.

Simon knew the sound. His rage slammed like a wild animal against its chain. He grabbed the monk's shoulder, spinning him, slamming him against the wall. Eamonn's pale eyes watered. He sagged. Simon pinned him to the centuries-old stones. "They're coming for prayers, you scoundrel! Get the crucifix now or 'twill go poorly for you before they arrive."

Eamonn smiled, despite the blood running down his temple. "Aye, My Lord. 'Twas in the pew."

"It had best be." Simon jammed the monk's arm up behind his back, till he heard the snap of a bone.

Eamonn's face went pale, glowing in the dim church. "Bide a moment." His voice crept over his vocal chords. Pain hung like gossamer on each syllable. He eased himself between two pews, his arm limp at his side.

Simon watched. He could hardly run. If he didn't hold the crucifix, dangling from his hand, in the next moment, Simon would kill him and flee before the monks filed in.

Suddenly, the old man lifted his head, shouting in the voice of a warrior, "Niall!" Then he sagged to his knees.

Life erupted in the vast cavernous church. Simon spun. A man with golden-brown hair stared at him, his head cocked to one side, watching Simon curiously. His mouth moved silently. Simon wondered if it was like the *telly* in Brian's house, when the sound was off. But this man appeared real, and close, and his hand moved to his hip. Simon backed up, tensing to spring, and glanced back. A hundred monks filled the pews, a hundred brown backs, a hundred tonsured heads.

Simon spun back to the man reaching for his weapon. He shimmered, as if pierced by moonlight. The doors at the far end of the church creaked. A dozen chanting monks filed down the center aisle.

Simon ran.

Inverness, Present

The door clicked. Angus's shoulders sagged, released from the tension of pretending. He took Amy's picture from his bulletin board. Her dark eyes smiled at him. The planes of her high cheekbones echoed those of the Glenmirril Lady, as did her thick, black hair falling to her waist. Guilt washed over him. He was abandoning her to deal with this on her own. She would quit, he assured himself. She wouldn't risk James.

But alongside his worry about James, marched the image of her repeating Shawn's name, and crying over his music. In nine months of talking, e-mailing, driving through England and Scotland, visiting ruins, laughing, sharing deep feelings and ideas, Angus had never doubted her feelings for him.

But it all centered on Shawn, a voice whispered insidiously in his ear.

No, he decided. It hadn't. He refused to believe she was capable of using him or pretending like that. She'd broken up with Shawn. She'd been in shock. That was all. She'd agreed to marry him.

She was drunk, the voice hissed maliciously.

No, he argued. She'd meant it. He believed that.

He stabbed at his keyboard, closing the reports. He was sick of the eejit grinning at him from the monitor, and he still had no idea what to tell the chief. He'd have that Guinness with Clive and come at it fresh in the morning. He took out his phone. He'd go get piss drunk with Clive. He hadn't done it in years. Why not? There was no one to care. No wife, no girlfriend. No child.

He yanked his office door closed and stopped, hand on the knob. *He* cared. Mairi cared, his brother-in-law, his brother, his parents cared. Hamish and Gavin looked up to him, and would copy him one day. He shoved the phone in his pocket and headed down the hall with a sigh. Right. Laundry, then.

"You're up late, Inspector."

The bright voice jolted him. He stopped, staring at the girl at the front desk. She had jet black hair bobbing in a ponytail, cornflower blue eyes, and freckles sprinkled across her nose.

"Claire." She held out her hand. "I've just started."

"Angus." He shook her hand. "Pleasure to meet you." He forced a smile. Her phone rang. Grateful for the diversion, he escaped out the front door. Who was he kidding? Laundry sounded miserable. He'd had a hell of a weekend. A few drinks never hurt anyone. He pulled out his phone. The door flew open behind him.

"Inspector!" Claire called, breathless. "They're asking after you!"

Bannockburn, Present

Sleep eludes me. Hiking and driving since early morning should have left me too exhausted for anything but settling James and collapsing. Instead, the events of the last 48 hours gnaw on my mind, a restless tiger batting its prey. In an act of love for Angus, I haven't opened the prophecy. Like a flute solo after the last of the audience has left, it's a beautiful gesture—but meaningless.

I roll onto my left and stare past the crib, out the window, to the white moon snared in black branches. Shadow buds, the hope of spring, are a sad contrast to my dying hope. We found Shawn. Angus asked me to marry him. This is where the soundtrack should have burst forth with triumphal brass and violins rising in a sea of emotions, marking the happy ending.

Instead, it's merely the end. Of everything. Shawn touched his son, and faded away. And if James is the key to rescuing Shawn, but doing so endangers him, then Angus is right, and I have to abandon someone I loved to a brutal world on that maybe.

Is there a way to find out just how much danger James is in? I roll to my right, searching for sleep away from the moon's glow. My worries follow me. Angus is upset. I plump the pillow. I don't blame him. He loves James. But Shawn and the prophecy—my act of taking it—have laid diminished harmonies under what should have been my joyful song. He asked me to marry him. I said yes. Yet we parted badly. And now I'm alone with this problem.

I roll onto my back. James sighs, blissfully unaware of danger. I shoulder fear while he sleeps. I think of my mother, far away in her bed, sleeping peacefully after a charity event, oblivious to my worries. Carol sleeps in her room; I shoulder the burden for her, too. But she's here, which helps me do this for her. But what am I doing for her? Her son is trapped in a killing world, and

I lie here, not even reading the prophecy that might save him.

I sit up, swinging my legs over the bed. Moonlight stamps a white square on the wall over the dresser. I wonder how Shawn is sleeping, up at Monadhliath, in his own April. Is he exhausted from his hike? Is he lying awake staring at this same moon, reliving our meeting? Does he feel despair at his failure to cross back, or hope at how close he came? Does he worry about pulling James in?

I wonder how Angus is sleeping. I have no doubt he's as restless as I am. I consider sending him a text, a soft whisper in the night, loud enough to let him know, if he's awake, that I miss him and love him, soft enough to let him sleep if he actually is.

But he doesn't want to hear from me.

I take the crisply folded sheet of ten pound paper from the dresser. It glows in the dark room. I tap the sharp edge against my knee, as I stare at the trio of framed pictures on my dresser: me and Angus by Mairi's Christmas tree; me and James—the same photograph hangs over Angus's desk; me and Shawn at Tioram. It's a twisted minuet of rights and responsibilities, duties and obligations, love and risk, who deserves what. Angus has loved me purely and selflessly. He deserved better than seeing me cry over someone like Shawn. But Shawn is in danger; Angus isn't. Shawn acted out of brokenness; it doesn't make it right, but neither does he deserve to die on the end of a rope or by any of a thousand other horrible, medieval fates. James deserves his father; yet, I may endanger him by trying.

I press a hand to my throbbing temple. I consider calling Rose. But I know what she'll say. Just reading it doesn't endanger James. *The throbbing slows and fades. I unfold the paper, lifting it close. My eyebrows furrow. I go to the window, standing over the crib where James sleeps, verifying in the moonlight that I read right. I close my eyes in frustration. There's only one person who can help me.*

As I ponder the problem, my phone rings. My heart thuds twice, seeing Angus's name.

"Amy," he says when I answer. "I'm on my way back to Monadhliath." His voice cracks. "It's Brother Eamonn."

Monadhliath, Present

Simon watched from the shadows of a pillar as the monks clustered around the prone body of the fool. He considered storming into their midst, strong-arming them, demanding answers. He could overpower all of them, most of them advanced in years, none of them warriors. But he held still, watching. They might be of use, yet. They hadn't seen him. They'd been too busy whispering, and shouting about the old man's heart, rushing to and fro, and the arrogant Fergna punching a *phone.*

As Simon watched, there came a pulsing beat from the sky. Eleven monks looked up to the ceiling, as did Simon. There was naught to be seen. Fergna lifted his skirts and marched for the huge wooden doors. Men burst in, Angus among them. Simon's brow wrinkled, wondering how he'd gotten back so swiftly. Perhaps he and the girl had returned? The men behind Angus pushed in a litter on wheels, and slowly, with commands among themselves, lifted the body, as carefully as one would tend a prized warhorse, onto the cot.

Cautiously, with speed, they raced away with the withered carcass. Let them rush. The sooner they left, the sooner he could search for the crucifix, and its prophecy.

♫

When the monks returned to their cells, Simon began searching the church, the vestry, the nave, around the remaining statues, in and around and under each pew, in the sacristy. His anger grew with each failure. The child had slipped from his hands! The crucifix was not to be found! At least the old man was dead!

When the monks returned for prayers, he searched Eamonn's beloved archives, cabinet after cabinet. Anger burned, a hot, slow simmer, in his chest. He had a mind to tear the place apart, destroy Eamonn's precious records, rip them, shred them, burn them!

But he stood motionless, a wildcat contemplating its prey. The records might contain useful information. The crucifix might be hidden amongst them. It would not do to burn the very treasure he sought. No, he would leave the place intact. He set back to work, searching each drawer methodically, perusing documents from his own immediate future, learning bits and pieces about Edward that might prove useful, but not finding the crucifix.

He searched Brother Eamonn's cell, turning up scanty white bits of clothing. He held them up, examining them, and tossed them aside. A shelf held dozens of books, filled with Eamonn's spidery, thin scrawl. The dates stretched back sixty years, into firmer, stronger script. The bedside table held a rosary and prayer book. Seething, he felt under the thin mattress, and beneath the bed. Nothing.

A bell tolled. Doors opened and closed; a soft swish and rustle told him the monks were going to morning prayers. He slipped into Fergna's office, searching in the flickering light of the fire, through drawers of unidentifiable bits of metal and stretchy bands and the tawdry *pens* with which these people wrote, and through shelves of scrolls and parchments and books. There was no crucifix, and no prophecy. He closed his eyes, his jaw tight. Where would the old man have put it?

He stood before the fireplace, sending up its warm wood scent, thinking. The bell tolled again, calling the monks to break their fast. He slipped out and joined them.

"Where is the good Brother Eamonn?" Simon asked Fergna as they entered the dining hall. He kept both glee and fury from his voice, sounding humble and merely curious. The old man had paid—that was good.

"He's taken ill." The abbot barely glanced at him, speaking brusquely as his ten remaining monks gathered around the long, wooden table. "He's at hospital in Inverness."

Simon's heart pounded at this news. "He's alive?"

"Barely," Fergna clipped.

"How very good," Simon lied. He bowed his head over his gruel, hiding his anger. Couldn't the old fool even die properly! But then, he still had information. Simon swallowed the watery mess, sitting amongst a group even more silent than usual, with one of their own missing. When the bell tolled, summoning them to chores, he said. "I'll be in Inverness. I'd feign give my regards to Brother Eamonn."

"How kind," replied the monk dryly. But he named the hospital, and Simon began the long trek down the mountains. He puzzled, as he went, how Angus had returned so quickly. There were no roads for their *cars*. But it didn't matter. He laid his plans as he moved steadily over paths worn among the heather, and down slopes scattered with boulders. He'd find Eamonn, learn where the crucifix was hidden, and get the prophecy. He'd kill the monk, then find and kill the child. It shouldn't be difficult. He'd return to his own time, regale Edward with his prophecies, and soon have king and kingdom, both, in his palm. He was doing the poor sod a favor. Without his ineptness on full display, perhaps Isabelle and Mortimer wouldn't be driven to murder him after all.

As he edged down a steep slope of greens and browns and purples, Simon chuckled. There *might* be worse ways to die than what dear Isabelle had in mind, but Simon was fairly sure *he* couldn't think them up. Yes, he was doing Edward a favor, taking his kingdom.

CHAPTER THIRTY-FOUR

Ayr, Scotland, 1315

Niall, Hugh and their thirty men flowed, with ever-growing numbers of others, over hillocks into the town of Ayr. They arrived barely on time, hampered by steady rain and hills treacherous with thick mud. Douglas arrived from his nearby lands. Great lords filed in from north, east, and south, giving Ayr the feel of a fair day, with peddlers selling food and ale to the gathering army, children darting and shouting among the newcomers, horses snorting and nickering, and the smells of sweat and damp wool and horseflesh filling every street.

Niall felt, still, the sting of being passed over for the Isle of Man. Here, in Ayr, war plans would be laid. As much as he wanted to be back with Allene, he needed to be here, ready to fight for his king—to redeem his failure.

The sun blossomed from behind clouds as earls and lords crowded St. John's, important in their fine tunics, heavy cloaks, and gold chains. As Niall took his seat beside James Douglas, he searched the faces in the hall. Down the table, Edward Bruce boasted to a bearded companion of his latest female conquest. Walter Stewart, no older than Niall himself, leaned close in discussion with Bruce's aging friend, Neil Campbell, the lord of Loch Awe.

"He must be forty if he's a day," said Hugh at Niall's side.

"Aye, and suffering from a life hard-lived." Niall felt for him. With Bruce, Douglas, and others, he'd spent years in the wilderness and war camps while Niall had been growing to manhood safe behind Glenmirril's walls and with his foster family. "D' you see MacDougall?" He scanned the great hall.

"He'll not be here," Hugh murmured.

James Douglas leaned over. "Christina was returned safely?"

"Aye." Niall pulled his attention from the gathering lords.

"She is under our protection," rumbled Hugh.

While Hugh and Douglas spoke, the young Earl of Menteith clapped Niall's shoulder. "Campbell, I missed you at Man."

A band tightened around Niall's chest. He thought of Shawn in the courtyard, and put on a smile. "Conal's turn for fun. I had things to take care of at home."

"Being newly married and all." The Earl grinned knowingly.

Niall gave a hearty laugh, such as Shawn might give. But shame churned in his gut. He was grateful Hugh was talking and hadn't heard. Thankfully, a staff rapped on the stone floor, ending the conversation. The Constable's voice rang out. "His Grace, King of Scots, Robert the Bruce!"

The lords rose. Bruce entered, back erect, his auburn hair circled by a thin ring of gold. His scarlet and gold tabard shone even among the fine garments of Scotland's nobility. He seated himself on the dais.

"The Honorable Patrick Cospatrick, Earl of Dunbar," the Constable announced.

The door opened, admitting a tall and striking young man. He strode to the dais, and knelt before Bruce.

"As powerful a sign as can be that Bruce is strong," Douglas whispered.

Niall's eyes flickered over Dunbar, barely thirty. His royal lineage showed in his straight back. He had long sided with Edward Carnarvon, believing the English king the safer bet in protecting his lands. Only ten months ago, he had sheltered Edward after Bannockburn, helping him escape in a fishing boat. The shame that had risen with Menteith's words grew. Niall hated to think if he was ever called upon to rescue anyone by boat.

Bruce and Dunbar both rose. "Welcome back to my peace, Cousin," Bruce declared. "Your lands are returned." The scribe's quill flashed over parchment, recording the moment. There were those who questioned Bruce's wisdom in accepting Dunbar back into his peace, cousins though they were. Niall breathed a silent *Ave* that Bruce might have the right of it.

As the Earl took his seat, Bruce nodded to Abbot Bernard, who stepped forward as chancellor. "The matter of negotiations at York. My Lord William, Bishop of St. Andrews, rise."

Niall became still. This was the real crux of parliament. He would go home to Allene or redeem himself in battle.

An elderly bishop, tall, gaunt, and stooped, rose laboriously from the Bishops' bench, bowing stiffly. "Your Grace, they refuse our terms. Edward maintains he is Lord Paramount of Scotland."

Edward Bruce erupted from his seat. "Did I not say we must pursue them and fight!"

Robert shot him a stern glare. "Sit, Edward. My Lord Bishop is speaking."

Edward thumped back into his seat, glowering.

From the lords' tables, the newly-forgiven Dunbar rose. "My Lord Bishop, what were our terms?"

Bishop Lamberton bowed to the Earl. "Recognition of our realm as an independent kingdom. Robert the Bruce as lawful king. English troops withdrawn from Berwick-on-Tweed. Assurance that England will interfere no more in the affairs of Scotland. They could hardly be easier, My Lord."

"We must fight," spoke Sir Niel gravely. "They understand no argument but steel." He exchanged glances with Edward Bruce. It was, perhaps, the first time the two had agreed on anything.

The Earl of Lennox shook his head, his bushy white beard brushing his chest. "Patience, Your Grace. Edward Carnarvon is besieged. His lords of the north murmur against him. They've no desire to fight us, so busy are they fighting amongst themselves."

Edward Bruce chuckled. "As they've oft ridiculed us for doing."

"Let us pray," Douglas murmured to Niall. "that Bruce's mercy has ended *that.*"

"Please God," Niall returned.

"They say," boasted Edward, "that many an English knight harries Northumberland in our names. We appear to be everywhere and a greater threat than we actually are."

Lennox, glaring at Edward's interruption, turned again to the king, who leaned back in his throne, his chin on one hand. "Your Grace, King Edward is under pressure. He is near breaking. Continue our present tactic of raids, and treating for peace, and we shall soon have it." He lowered his bulk into his seat.

Edward erupted, docile as a charging bull. "My Lord King! Regarding those tactics, I've good news."

Niall's eyes flickered from Edward to the king, who lowered his eyebrows, but said nothing. Edward gave a caricature of the expected bow of respect. "Your Grace, the Irish hate the English as much as we do. Perhaps more. They are ready to rise, and need only leadership. Give me two thousand men and with Ireland, we will press England till they accept our terms."

Niall's stomach lurched. Of the places he did not want to fight, Ireland— anywhere across water—headed the list. He blinked away the image of Alexander's white face.

Bruce's gaze rested briefly on Niall, and returned to his brother. "How do we know the Irish kings will follow?"

Niall found his own gaze intent on Edward, whose face betrayed a flicker of uncertainty. Then he grinned. "Certainly they will. They hate the English."

Niall's mind leapt ahead, reaching Bruce's own conclusion, even as Bruce spoke. "You have spoken with them." It was not a question. "Without consulting me."

Niall dared hope. Bruce would not agree to a venture worked out in secret behind his back.

"Only sounded them out," Edward hedged. "We've spoken here of the possibility. *Someone* needed to know where they stood."

"That somebody, by rights, would be the King of Scots," Bruce suggested sharply. "Furthermore, the kings of Ireland would not commit to us unless we've committed something in return. As *I've* made no commitment, who has?" His hand tightened on the arm of his throne.

Hugh leaned close, murmuring, "Edward has forced his hand, for he'll not make a public break with his brother."

"Cleverly done," Niall returned. He meant no admiration.

Edward looked at the floor, abashed, but only for a heartbeat. Then he raised his eyes and threw his shoulders back, swishing his cloak against the stone floor. "*I* have."

Bruce raised his eyebrows. "You have committed my armies without consulting me?"

Around the table, men exchanged looks.

"Mine," Edward corrected. "As Earl of Carrick, I command my own men."

Bruce stared down the brash Earl of Carrick till he blinked and dropped his gaze to his leather boots. Bruce turned his steel gaze, then, around the assembly. Men studied their jeweled hands on the table, or branches fluttering new green leaves outside the arched windows. The Lord of Loch Awe coughed.

"My Lord Campbell," summoned Abbot Bernard.

Campbell rose, looking his forty years and more. He was thin to the point of gaunt, his hair lank and gray. But he spoke with strength, sparing a sharp glance of disapproval for Edward Bruce. "Your Grace, though I protest the manner in which it was done, I believe leading the Irish against England is the answer."

"We need peace," protested Lennox.

"Needing it will not make it so!" Edward Bruce shot to his feet, pounding the table, eyes blazing.

"There are procedures!" Bruce roared at his brother. "Sit down!"

Beside Niall, Douglas heaved a sigh. "He was ever a hot-headed fool."

Bruce turned to Douglas. "What say you, My Lord? We are assembled not to soothe my ego, but to choose wisely for Scotland."

Douglas stood. Color rose in his cheeks. He did not look at Bruce. "Your Grace, lead the Irish. Pressure England on all sides: I in the north, Angus Og on their coasts, My Lord Earl of Carrick in Ireland. They will have to yield."

"Angus Og has no love for Edward Bruce," Hugh whispered. "He'll not care to ferry Edward to Ireland."

It gave Niall no comfort. His stomach turned. Bruce's gaze swung around the assembly, over fur-lined cloaks, gold chains and heavy beards. Niall wanted to shrink into his seat. He had no wish to be asked his opinion. He feared learning whether he would advise for the good of Scotland, or for his own comfort.

"They are close to yielding, Your Grace," Lennox insisted.

Bruce's attention moved across the room. "My Lord Hays."

Gilbert Hays rose, avoiding Bruce's gaze. "Fight, Your Grace."

Niall watched Bruce. Though his face betrayed no emotion, Niall imagined what it must cost him to have his closest friends advise him to follow his reckless brother's path, deceptively taken. Bruce nodded heavily, and Niall, reluctantly, agreed. Lennox was far too optimistic. Bruce bowed his head momentarily. Then he lifted his eyes. "The Earl of Carrick will go to Ireland."

The tension in Niall's chest eased. He had not been asked his opinion.

"I'll send some of my own men." Bruce searched the room.

The vice clamped once more around Niall's lungs. He wanted to melt away, to avoid being chosen to cross that sea. Sweat prickled his forehead.

But Bruce turned to his nephew. "Thomas, you'll lead my troops in Ireland. But first, we've another problem. John of Lorn is gathering his fleet in the Sound of Jura. We cannot we allow this."

Edward Bruce rose to his feet. "We *cannot* go to Jura first! I must be in Ireland before the end of May."

"You'll sail to Ireland in May," Bruce said smoothly. "Ross, you and Angus Og will transport him, and return immediately. My Lords of Dunbar, Ross, and Glenmirril, bring your men back by early June, ready to sail for Jura."

The room wavered before Niall. Blood roared in his ears as Alexander's bloated face rose before him, white as the soft underbelly of a fish.

Hugh leaned close, his voice softer than it had ever been in his life. "Niall, ask Shawn for help. You must."

Inverness, Present

"Thank you for calling." In Eamonn's room, Amy set down the car seat, in which James slept. She hesitated a moment before touching Angus's arm.

He slid his hand over hers. "Of course I'd call."

The tension in her chest eased. She laid her head on his shoulder. They fell silent, watching Brother Eamonn's withered form under crisp, white sheets. A bandage covered his left temple. Tubes snaked into his right arm. A cast covered his left arm, shoulder to fingertips. "Do they know what happened?" she asked.

"I suppose he got dizzy, lost his balance, and tried to break his fall. Hit his head on the pew."

She slipped her hand from under Angus's to touch Eamonn's sunken cheek, praying for him. She'd barely met him, but he'd worked his way into her heart with his slow smile, dry humor, and easy acquaintance with those who had walked Monadhliath's halls. If he slipped away, his knowledge went with him— including knowledge of her son.

Angus cleared his throat. "'Twas a long night. I'm away for coffee. Would you like some?"

Amy looked up. "Yes. Thank you."

He'd barely left before a dry whisper rasped the air. "I thought he'd never leave."

Amy jumped. "Brother Eamonn!"

He chuckled. His laughter slipped into a short, dry cough, but his faded blue eyes twinkled.

"You've been awake?"

"Do we know," he whispered, "if we are sleeping and all our thoughts a dream?"

"Or talking to one another in a waking state?" Amy finished.

Eamonn smiled. "If only Plato had passed through Monadhliath. How I should have liked to talk with him. Though most feel a doctor is who I ought speak with." He chuckled.

"They're wrong." Amy tugged a chair close to his side. "Brother Eamonn, I need to ask you something."

"I must *tell* you something," he whispered. "Guard the crucifix."

She touched it, through her shirt, with her free hand. "I do. But James...."

He gripped her hand with surprising strength. "Protect it!" Trembling, he lifted his head, piercing her with pale eyes. "It has great power; power which is dangerous in the wrong hands."

She leaned forward. "Will it get Shawn back?" She remembered he didn't know who Shawn was.

But he nodded, settling back on his pillow.

"You knew?" she asked in surprise.

"Aye. Niall was at Parliament that April." The machines at his side beeped softly. "There's some row between you and the Inspector."

"Over James," she said, not entirely liking herself for pressing a sick old man. "We're worried about his safety." In the carseat, James whimpered, squeezed his eyes as if preparing to cry, and settled back into sleep.

"No man is ever safe," Eamonn mused. His eyes clouded over, drifting to a world Amy couldn't see.

"*Can* the crucifix pull him into Niall's time?" Her heart pounded, desperate for assurance. "The prophecy...."

Eamonn's gaze returned from wherever he'd been. He frowned up at her, as if unsure who she was, before declaring suddenly, firmly, "James is safe."

She wondered if he knew which James he was talking about, or to whom he spoke. "How can you be sure?" She found herself squeezing his hand. "History seems to change."

"Only for some." He regarded her. "Sixty years of reading records; some stories never change. Take James where you will. He'll remain with you for many years."

"You're sure?" she pressed.

But he closed his eyes, a silent coda.

The smell of mocha hazelnut floated to her. She turned. With a small, sad smile, Angus offered a Styrofoam cup. "Coffee?" Their fingers brushed, recalling the first day behind the Heritage Centre; she felt sick to think it was all over, so quickly. Angus gazed down at Brother Eamonn. "Still asleep." In the car seat, James stirred. Angus stooped to lift him out, onto his shoulder. "You've had a long night, too. I've chicken in the crockpot at home."

Monadhliath, 1315

Shawn Kleiner locked in a monastery for a month: he expected it to be his own personal hell. At least in the castle there'd been beautiful women to look at. Caroline would be horrified at the waste of his talents. Amy would be surprised and pleased. But busy days passed quickly. He enjoyed playing for the monks. "Show time," he laughed to himself as he took his place near the altar, his fingers lilting out soft melodies as rain pattered against stone casements high above. And though they were hardly the screaming girls of last year, their quiet appreciation, a hand on his arm, thanking him with, "It's been years since I've heard anything so beautiful," and "Bless you," meant just as much. Someone loved what he gave. Nothing else mattered. Between parchments, practicing, praying, and performing, his hands and mind stayed busy.

He pushed himself not only to attend every service—matins, lauds, all of them—but to spend extra hours in the chapel, hoping to see Amy again. More Latin sank into his ears, but no sight of Amy.

"Ye've returned to your normal reverence in chapel," the fat, young Brother Phillip said, as they processed into the chapel one night. The moon, for once, shone clearly in the windows, freed of its cloudy prison. The pews stretched out on either side, and thick granite pillars soared upward, supporting a massive vaulted ceiling. Torches and candles flickered everywhere, casting dancing shadows over red stone walls.

Shawn laughed inwardly at Brother Philip's belief in his reverence. Even now, he was envisioning the line of monks banging themselves on the foreheads. "You're too young to have known me," he said.

"They spoke of ye."

Shawn filed into place beside the boy and knelt. Incense wafted from the altar. He bowed his head, joining his voice to the plainchant. Philip would be disappointed to know he was not rapt in holy awe, at least not of Christ. He spent services contemplating Amy, Christina and the men around him. They had become individuals, no longer tonsured clones in matching robes. They were short, fat, tall, thin; some were naturally bald, while others shaved their heads frequently. Brother Philip struggled with silence, preferring enthusiastic chatter. Brother William stalked the abbey like a medieval MacArthur, using words with swift efficiency. Brother Ambrose tottered with blue-veined hands on a sturdy oak staff; his words curled softly around his listener like mystical vines. Brother Fillan, strong as a grizzly, would have done well as a lumberjack in nineteenth-century Oregon. A few were slow, placed in the abbey by caring relatives, but most were bright, with skills and talents that would have served well in the world outside.

Shawn spent services, between asking God for another glimpse of Amy and his son, perplexed why these men and Christina, who could have anyone and do anything, spent their time with a silent, invisible God, chanting, praying, sending up incense to Someone who never paid them any heed.

That same someone also paid no heed to Shawn that he could tell. But an urge took hold during vespers, one he couldn't shake, and he sought out Brother William the next morning.

"Your family history?" Brother William seemed only mildly mystified that 'Niall' would want to look at such a thing. Shawn thought he himself was much more mystified than Brother William.

"Brother Fillan," Brother William summoned the burly monk. "Show Sir Niall his family history."

The towering Fillan led Shawn through the halls, beneath arches pouring in cold April sunshine, to the records chamber. He looked better suited to chopping timber, but he honed in on a shelf, and soon had a stack of Campbell and Glenmirril parchments laid out.

Shawn knew the names. Now he paged through verbal portraits of Niall's family. James and Thomas—drawn and quartered by the English. His stomach turned. Their visit here, a year before their deaths, was recorded, with requests for prayer. Much good it did them, Shawn thought dryly. Robert died in infancy. A summer illness swept through Glenmirril, taking Adam and William. Finally, Alexander waded into the loch when the girl watching them turned her back. A separate hand had scrawled at the bottom of the parchment. *Young Niall watched as they pulled Alexander out. He didn't speak for a month. Pray for him.*

Inverness, Present

The sun slid down its western slope before Simon stared up at the massive infirmary. There were no guards. Still, finding one man in such a fortress would be a task. Entering the place, he decided, would be a good start. A foyer opened up, as impressive as Edward's great hall, showing a myriad of passages and doors and stairs—any of which might lead to his prey.

"Can I help you, Love?" a bright voice chirped.

His eyes traveled to the source of the sound, and lit on a perky young girl. He let his features soften, and moved toward her, leaning in, as if she were the only girl in Scotland. Her eyes didn't light up. She looked him up and down, and he remembered he'd spent the day traveling. His unshaven jaw must be quite scruffy. These people valued bathing above gold. He let his smile deepen. "My apologies, My Lady. It's been a long journey to see my friend."

Her wariness thawed. She tilted her head with a sympathetic smile. "Has it, now?"

"It has," he replied. "A dear friend. I hope you can tell me where he is. I've come such a long way to see him. Brother Eamonn."

"His surname?"

"Surname?" He gave an internal curse. If monks had surnames, he certainly didn't know Eamonn's. He gave a chuckle. "Is that not funny? I've known him since I was a child, when he taught me the catechism. I've no notion of his surname, now I think of it. But surely you haven't many frail, old monks here?"

"Most likely not, Sir." She blinked owl-like eyes at him. "But he'd not be in the computer under *frail, old,* or *monk.*"

Simon held back his irritation. It was not useful. "He arrived late last night."

"Hm." She pursed her lips, tapping a pen against the edge of the desk till he wanted to snatch the thing and break it in two. "Last night, you say."

I most certainly did and you heard me, you foolish wench. He smiled. "Last night, yes, from Monadhliath."

"Oh, *him!*" She sat up straight, the pen slapped one last time on the desk, and her face lit as her fingers flew to the dozens of tiny, clicking letters on the board before her computer. "He was airlifted in. Hold on now, and I'll have that!" Abruptly she turned, staring at the clock on the wall behind her. "Oh, I'm so sorry! Visiting hours have just ended!"

"Visiting hours?" Anger swelled Simon's voice. He cleared his throat, trying to sound more pleasant. "What are *visiting hours?*"

"You can't see him until evening."

"Where is he?" Simon demanded. He would go, regardless.

She tilted her head, her eyes narrowing. "Come *back* at *seven.* Your name?"

His lips tightened, deciding how he would get the information, with or without her cooperation.

"Your name, Sir?" She spoke crisply.

At that moment, a short, sharp squeal pierced the air.

Simon turned. Walking out the front door were Amy, and Angus, carrying the child. He smiled. God did, indeed, look upon him with favor!

♫

Simon followed. He couldn't simply walk up and throttle her nasty spawn. But what was the best approach? The child gazed over Angus's shoulder, blinking at Simon with large, dark eyes. Simon scowled at him. He let out a short squeal. His mouth split into a toothless grin. Angus patted his back, shushing him.

He would follow them and find their dwelling, Simon decided. But they walked to a car. He changed his plan as swiftly as tactics on a field of battle. "Angus!" he shouted as the man reached for the car.

The couple paused, then turned.

"Simon!" Angus sounded surprised. "You didn't stay on at Monadhliath?"

"Only overnight." Simon's eyes traveled to James, contemplating how he could get at the child.

The girl, glancing at him, took the infant. She opened the car, and slid him inside.

Simon's lips tightened. The car would speed away; he'd have no way of finding them again.

"What are you doing here?" Angus asked.

Simon assessed him. A man so weak as to carry infants could hardly be much of an obstacle. He would rush him, break his neck, and kill the child. He smiled, taking a step back for momentum. "Hoping to see the good Brother Eamonn, as perhaps you were yourself? His heart, was it?"

Angus frowned. Amy watched him, saying nothing. Simon felt a tremor in his heart, wondering what she knew or suspected. It surprised him that the stare of a mere girl should unnerve him.

In that moment of hesitation, she spoke. "Angus, we have to go."

The man gave a tight nod, and rounded the car.

"You'll return to see Brother Eamonn?" Simon called.

"Maybe." Amy slid into the car and slammed the door.

Simon watched through the window as she gestured with apparent agitation. Angus pulled out his phone, and spoke. They drove away. Anger simmered, white-hot, as Simon planned his next move. The child had slipped his grasp for the moment, but the monk remained in the hospital, and 'visiting hours' began again soon.

CHAPTER THIRTY-FIVE

Monadhliath, 1315

Anticipating Niall's return, Shawn found excuses to scan the southern glen, thinking how to warn Niall he couldn't be seen. As the sun climbed toward noon early in May, its rays finally glinted off helmets. As they drew nearer, Shawn saw Glenmirril's blue and white banner flapping above them. He strode to the abbey's great front door, reminding himself he was, to the abbot and monks, Sir Niall of Glenmirril.

"My men are coming," he informed the porter. "I'm going to meet them." He didn't ask. He could only hope it was a normal thing for a future laird to do. With Brother Andrew's robe secreted under his shirt, he hurried through the gatehouse, fearful of being stopped. In a copse, he yanked the gray robe on, shadowed his face with the hood, and hastened to meet Glenmirril's party.

Niall held up a hand, halting his men, and spurred his garron ahead. He slid off, a hand connecting solidly with Shawn's shoulder in greeting. "Did you see her again?" They strode over spring grass, under the monks' apple trees.

Shawn ignored the question. "You realize it was impossible to live under a hood for a month."

Niall stopped. His face darkened. "So I've supposedly been here this whole time. Doing what?"

"You're dressed all wrong, for starters," Shawn said. "The monks expect you to be dressed like me."

"And my men expect me to be dressed like me."

"Okay, we'll send them ahead and figure something out."

"What if the monks and my men compare notes?" Niall demanded. "You've made a bollox of this!"

"You try living under a hood for a month!" Shawn shot back.

Niall shook his head, seeing Shawn's original problem and the new one he'd created. "My men can't stay here tonight. They can't hear from the monks that I've been here all along. We'll move on apace up the road. Tell Brother William that Hugh has returned and you'll leave immediately to join him. As soon as you're out of sight of the abbey, put the robe back on. Though I'm disappointed not to see him again."

Shawn snorted. "Yeah, Brother William's so warm and cuddly. I'll miss him like an iceberg in my bed."

Niall grinned. "He's a good heart. He keeps the abbey in order. I'll take the men to the wood. Tell Brother William we must reach home."

The thing was not so easily done as said. Brother William objected strenuously to driving the men on without rest. Shawn thought the men themselves might not care for it, either, though they wouldn't argue with their de facto laird. Brother William insisted Shawn wait long enough for him to pack a hefty sack of turnips and bannocks for the men's dinner.

It gave Shawn time to go to the copy room and say good-bye. "Brother Philip." He gripped the boy's hand. He'd miss his enthusiasm. "Brother Fillan." He slapped the lumberjack's back. "If you get tired of the monastery, we've got room for a man like you at Glenmirril." He stopped at his copy desk, touching the towering stack of music, dozens of messages to Amy. *God, please, I did my best for them. Could You watch over these for seven hundred years? That's nothing to you, right? Make sure she sees them? Please?*

Inverness, Present

Angus's kitchen feels like warmth and home. Chicken bubbles in the crockpot, reminding me of happy times with him. I wonder, did he plan on us living here? Or buying a house together? I'd have been happy with either. I wanted only to be with him. His steadfastness. His humor. His quick smile. The dark shadow on his jaw in the evening. But time traveling ghosts and my traitorous emotions have slammed a minor chord to the end of our short symphony.

Angus swings the crockpot to the table, and slides a ladle in it. In his car seat, James lets out a short squeal. Angus's face softens. He stoops, and lifts him, crooning. James's face lights up. He gives a great belly laugh.

I spoon chicken, in creamy white sauce, onto my plate. "Am I being paranoid? About Simon?"

"Better paranoid than sorry."

"You're sure they'll take care of it?"

Angus smiles. "They trust my instincts."

I poke my fork at my chicken.

He reaches across the small table for my hand. "I'm sorry." *His words are husky.*

"I'm sorry, too. I didn't...." *I stop. I can't pretend Shawn didn't affect me. No words are adequate. I know in my heart I want to be with Angus, but I also know how I'd feel if I saw him so emotional over Julia. I clear my throat.* "Brother Eamonn promised me James is safe."

"We don't know how lucid he is," *Angus reminds me.*

I have no answer. I push at the chicken.

"You read the prophecy?"

"I wrestled with it." I force down a bite of chicken, untasted.

"But you did."

I raise my eyes. "Just reading it doesn't hurt him."

He strokes James's cheek. "I can't endanger him."

I stare at chives floating in Alfredo sauce. "He seemed lucid. How do I balance all these competing needs? James, you, Shawn, Carol?"

Angus lifts his eyes. "If you quit for me, you'd hold it against me in some corner of your heart." He looks down at James in his arms. "So might he, one day."

"But I hurt you by continuing. I might *endanger James. I don't even know if it's possible to bring him back. If I called it off...?"*

"I want what we had." He touches my hand. "But right now, we don't."

"Choosing you, for the rest of my life means nothing?" Anger flashes through me. But at least we're acknowledging it now. "If you *disappeared, I'd be just as upset."*

He stares at his untouched food. "You must do what gives you peace of mind."

I glare at my chicken, angry with myself, angry with him, angry with this weight on my shoulders. I'm a musician. I play my part. Suddenly, I'm forced to write the parts, to choose who solos, and who gets written out.

He touches my hand, speaking softly. "I protect, Amy. It's what I do. But I can't protect you from this. Find a place of peace, and think carefully."

Highlands, 1315

Shawn and Niall rode side by side toward the northern tip of Loch Ness, along the same route they'd taken last December. "Lot nicer this time of year," Shawn said. Birdsong replaced the cold slough of last November's wind.

"And a break from the rain, hopefully," Niall added.

"It's sure made the forest green," Shawn commented. "I thought Scotland was known for its rain."

"Aye, perhaps, but we've had a good bit more than normal, and if it doesn't stop, 'twill ruin the crops." When Shawn didn't respond, Niall asked curiously, "Your crops never fail?"

Shawn shrugged. "There's always food at the store."

"Here," Niall said, "If crops fail, people die. I suspect you've never seen starvation."

"No," Shawn admitted. The breeze shuffled green leaves more gently than last winter's rattling of skeletal branches. It was hard to believe, in the day's warmth, that anything as evil as starvation could ever touch them.

"Did you see her again?" Niall asked. There was comfort in Hugh's presence, the hum of the men's conversation behind them, the creak and chink of their small army.

"No. But I left dozens of manuscripts, telling her what I need to." The horses loped along, flexing muscle beneath them.

"Won't Brother William dispose of them?"

Shawn smiled. "Brother William reads Latin. Amy reads music." He laughed. "In the meantime, you're going to have monks chanting Toto." He sang a bit of *Africa*, slowing it to a plainchant.

Niall smiled. A red fox darted from the undergrowth.

"You?" Shawn asked. "What happened at parliament?"

Niall's smile faded. "I am to take Glenmirril's men to the sea battle against John of Lorn."

"A sea battle, like, what, on water?"

"Sea battles often are." Niall's voice reflected no humor. He looked pale in the summer sun.

Words chanted through Shawn's mind: *Niall watched as Alexander was pulled out. He didn't speak for a month.*

Inverness, Present

The girl at the desk looked up when Simon returned at seven.

"Brother Eamonn," he reminded her. "What did you say his surname is?" He might need it on another occasion.

"I didn't," she returned. "His visitors are restricted. Your name, Sir?"

He understood in a flash. There was a list. He could be quite sure his name wasn't on it.

"Your name?"

"Simon Beaumont." If he wasn't on the list, he had a plan.

"Not here." She blinked up at him like an owl.

"Certainly they forgot me," Simon purred. "I was with him just prior to his accident."

The girl stared up at him blandly. "You're not on the list, Sir."

He leaned over the desk, charming her as he would a laundry wench. "It would please me so if you were to add me. Surely you can!"

She didn't blink. She didn't smile. Her cheeks did not turn rosy at the attention of a knight in the king's service. "No, Sir, I can't."

Anger stirred in his gut, the same anger he'd felt at the boy in the streets of Berwick, so many years ago, who defied him; or the girl in the orchard who'd spurned his attentions. His hand drifted to his waist, but the knife wasn't there. He strained to keep the smile in place. "Surely 'tis not difficult. I'm quite concerned for him and would fane give him my regards."

"You'll have to talk to his doctors."

"Where might I find them?"

"They'll be in tomorrow." She spoke crisply, dismissing him, stabbed at a button on the desk, and bent over her work.

"I was not through speaking to you," he purred.

She rose from her seat. Fear flickered in her eyes. He liked that.

"Sir," a deep voice said behind him. "The doctors will be in *tomorrow.*"

Simon turned to stare up at a giant of a man, as tall as Longshanks, and built like a warhorse. His hand rested on his hip. Though Simon didn't recognize the short, black object there, he knew the posture of a man about to unleash a weapon.

"You'll have to leave." The man's voice rumbled like war drums across a battlefield.

Simon gave a slight bow, and strode out the door, conscious of eyes on his back. Amy's agitation, Angus's phone...he knew how this had happened. Angus was a sheriff of some sort. He should be easy to find. Angus would add him to the list in order to protect the child. Then he'd kill all three of them, and visit Eamonn for the crucifix.

Highlands, 1315

"You've had a poor excuse for a honeymoon," Shawn said. The horses jolted beneath them, their feet clopping on stony passes in the rising hills. "You have a child on the way. You should be with Allene."

"Is that how war works in your time?" Niall asked. "Here and now, my king commands me, Shawn. England will not relent her assault on Scotland because I've a child on the way."

"The Laird doesn't lead his men anymore?" Shawn guided his horse around a boulder, and back into a shady copse of trees climbing up the mountainside.

"He's aging. He's needed at Glenmirril, now that I'm available."

"When do you leave?"

"Early June."

"Here's the deal." Under guise of ducking a low-hanging limb, Shawn organized his words. "I've got nothing to do. How about I go in your place?"

Niall stared. His mouth moved once and stopped. Their ponies crested a hill and began their descent. He tried again. "This is war."

"Yeah, I managed to get through one war with just a little scratch, and all those raids with even less. This time I know what I'm doing, thanks to you and Hugh bullying me with your silly toy swords. So I'm good, right?" In the narrow glen at the bottom of the hill, they stopped at a stream. The horses lowered their heads, drinking with slapping sounds of their velvety lips. Birdsong trilled overhead, a pleasant duet to the ripple of the stream.

Niall stared up the hillside, swallowing. Never had a man offered to risk death in his place. *No greater love than this has man.* He swallowed again. Shawn made no pretense of following God.

He could accept, with an off-hand comment, perhaps, as if it were not an earth-shaking gift. He could stay with Allene. Alexander's bloated face swam before his eyes. He gripped the reins, white-knuckled on the pommel, his jaw hard. He could avoid water once more.

But there was no flippant way to accept.

And he had not told Shawn about the prophecy. *In St. Columba's chamber.* Heat warmed his face. He needed to tell Shawn, send him home. He needed to overcome his pride and ask Shawn for help.

"Come on, where's your smart-ass comeback," Shawn said. "You know I'm right. You go home. I'll kill time, no pun intended, since I'm stuck here anyway. No one's the wiser. Where's the downside?"

From the hill above came the voices of Niall's men. Shawn glanced back and flipped the hood of Brother Andrew over his face.

My integrity. My honor. Niall didn't say it. Shawn, with morals little above the Sassenach king, had just offered to risk his life while Niall shamefully withheld information that could give him his life back. Niall snapped the reins, and guided his horse up the path, not looking back.

The Trossachs, Present

The hiker is nervous, climbing the hills in his ponytail and Birkenstocks. He steals glances at me from behind little round glasses. We make uncomfortable small talk. He tells me how Shawn was chasing phantoms, last June. He's perplexed I don't share his concern. I don't have energy to pretend, as I follow him up steep paths under tall, cool pines, contemplating the decision before me. This is the place of peace I have chosen, to weigh competing needs, to seek wisdom in deciding the fate of all of us, of James and Carol, myself, Shawn, and Angus..

We're both relieved when we reach the clearing. The hiker clears his throat. "I'll...be back...?"

I nod absently, murmuring thanks. The firestorm of the last ten months rushes over me. Shawn was dead. Then he was alive, but beyond my reach. Now, his fingers are touching mine across time, begging me, and I'm here, standing before his message on Hugh's great stone wall, The Heart.

I gaze, awestruck, at the ring of supple birches reaching for blue sky high above. It's a cathedral carved from trees and sky and water. Shawn lived here! I touch a gnarled tree, thick and knotty as an old man's fingers. I imagine Shawn and Allene coming into camp after their long hike. The soft melody of a creek comes to me, and the rhythm, like brushes on a snare, of a loch, lapping at a rocky shore. I search beyond the trees, and there it is, wide and blue. Maybe Niall and Allene held hands here. I drop to the rocky shore, my arms wrapped around my knees.

I'm alone, while they're together, there, then. But I feel them here, amidst the swaying birches and firs. Agitation slips away with each deep breath of fragrant pine. I feel their strength. I think of Shawn's father's murder, and here where Shawn walked, I understand how deeply troubled he was. He tried. But he was so broken. I can't take it personally. The pain of the last years drains away.

I see how guilt has driven me: I left him. I put him in that brutal world. I have climbed mountains and sought ancient monasteries and hiked to this long-lost camp in search of my own redemption. And I find it, for here by the loch, Peace lays a tentative hand on my arm. I left him, yes. But I didn't put him in that world.

I had to walk away. Nothing would have changed if I'd stayed that night, but now, something has healed him. As I sit by the loch, listening to the water ripple as it has rippled for hundreds of years, as it rippled when Shawn and Niall and Allen sat here, Healing gently eases Guilt off my back.

I toss a rock into the water. Water laps in widening circles, till the outermost ring sloshes at my feet. Peace steals over me about Angus, too. I hurt for him. I hurt for myself. I hurt for the future we promised each other in a monastic cell. But it's not just about me, or him, or us. It's about Carol and James and Shawn. It's about whether it's right to abandon someone to their fate.

The peace that touched me tentatively now sits down on this rocky shore, and throws an arm around my shoulder. I'm ready. Strengthened by the presence of those who lived here, I return to the clearing. I stop at the stream, looking across to Hugh's beloved Heart. It's whiter, where Niall scrubbed it, last summer. From this distance, I see Shawn's words. Closing my eyes, lost in pine and birdsong, I see him carving in the night, while rough, wild men sleep around the fire's embers. Did he look over his shoulder, wary of Hugh rustling in his sleep? Did a guard come? Did Shawn hide his knife, make small talk? Did his heart beat faster, was he scared, was he cold? I wonder if he considered the billion to one odds anyone would ever see his words?

And yet—miraculously—Niall did. And now, I do; I stare at them, scratched into Hugh's beautiful white rock.

A. So Sorry.

I see the sorrow in his eyes at Monadhliath, the carefully inked manuscripts begging for forgiveness, and know he has changed beyond all recognition. I see, too, that I'm fooling myself if I say this is about Carol and James. I want him back. In my heart of hearts, I desperately miss his humor, his generosity, his vitality. At the same time, I miss Angus. Part of me wishes he'd never walked into my life. But if he hadn't, I wouldn't be here. He's made most of this happen, in a sad cycle of cause and effect where his very presence brought about the things that hurt him.

I touch my phone, in my pocket. I want to call Rose, run to her, ask her what to do. All those years, she was there, protecting me in ways I couldn't comprehend, from things I couldn't see. I think about protection. I protect James and Carol. All these years, Rob and Conrad and everyone in the orchestra protected me. They were wrong, but it came from love. And Angus. He's protected me from the start, standing between me and Clive's question, between me and Mrs. MacGonagal's condemnation. He's given me absolution and healing from things I barely knew I needed healing from. But here in this clearing, where changes came over Shawn, where the proof of that change is carved deep in the Heart, I ponder Angus's words: I can't protect you from this decision.

The phone is heavy in my pocket. I can throw away the prophecy and call Angus, right now.

I cross the stream. Up close, the words are indecipherable scratches. It comforts me to touch them, to know Shawn's hand was here, to stand where he stood. I drop my head against the rock, against the letters A—So Sorry, *and* Iona J.

I'm exhausted from months of searching, months of failure. I want to give up and go back to Angus.

I hear Shawn calling, begging; I think of James who might never know his father; of Eamonn assuring me he's safe; of all the good and bad, the pain I've caused Angus and the pain of missing him, and I stand here, my head against the rock, tears running down my face, till I realize the hiker is in the clearing. I try to wipe my face, try to pretend it isn't what it looks like.

He inches closer in his Birkenstocks and Bermudas, wary of my tears. He glances sideways at me. "1314?" *He touches the letters.*

I nod. Questions burn in his eyes. He's seen the news, he can guess who Shawn K is; he knows my name.

"What...what does Iona J mean?" *he asks.*

"I don't know." *I wipe at tears. And here in Hugh's camp, where Shawn called men to fight for Scotland, I know what I must do.* "That's what I'm going to find out."

CHAPTER THIRTY-SIX

Glenmirril, 1315

Allene's eyes flickered from Niall on one horse to Brother Andrew on another. Rain drizzled down. The castle folk cheered for the returning men, heedless of the damp day. Niall threw himself to the ground, grinning as he pulled her into his arms. "You still don't know your own husband?" he whispered. "Are you well? And the bairn?"

He pulled her through the tanners and bakers and wives and children who filled the courtyard to greet the returning men, to the great hall where her father and Glenmirril's lords waited. He threw off his wet cloak, and shook his head, flinging droplets that hit the fire in the hearth with a sizzle. Shawn trailed them, silent and faceless as Brother Andrew, and faded against the wall in his wet robe. Niall knelt before MacDonald. MacDonald's eyes went from Niall to Shawn.

"'Tis me, My Lord," Niall murmured, rising.

"Allene." MacDonald's eyes flickered to her. "Send for food. Niall, sit." He acknowledged Shawn, who melted back, gray robes against gray stone.

"My Lord." Darnley looked hard at Shawn.

"He'll stay." MacDonald brooked no argument. "Niall, tell us of Parliament."

Niall summarized the succession agreement, while women piled the table with food.

"Stewart is a fine man," said Morrison. "Bruce chose well. Now if she but bears a son quickly."

Nods went around the table. Scotland needed an heir stronger than Marjory, but not so rash as Edward. The men dug into trenchers while Niall told of Edward's sly tactic to push Robert into leading an Irish rising. "He says he can do it with two thousand men, and the Irish will do the rest."

"Bruce ought to cool him off in a dungeon," muttered Morrison.

"He cannot afford a public break with his brother, and no other heir," argued Darnley.

Niall stood, commanding silence. "Angus Og and My Lord of Ross will move Edward's army to Ireland. He's placed his own men, however, under Randolph. They leave anon, and the galleys return to take men against John of

Lorn. I have but days to choose men and return."

Silence fell around the table.

Darnley and Morrison looked at him gravely, and turned away.

Niall smiled, a tight, grim smile. He knew what they were thinking. They all remembered the day on the shore. He could let Shawn do it, showing them all they had no cause for censure; capturing their amazement once again. He lifted his head, lifted his head as Shawn had in the courtyard at Conal's departure last January, and spoke with confidence, "We begin preparations immediately."

♫

Bed curtains closed Niall in a warm, dark cocoon with Allene, muting the steady thrum of rain against the castle walls. His hand rested on her rounded stomach. Men died in battle. He wanted to know, and raise his child.

"Something's upsetting you." Allene's laid her hand on his. "Is it going on the galleys?"

"'Tis naught," Niall said.

Thunder rumbled outside. When it passed, she said, "Clearly summat is amiss." He remained silent. She pushed again. "What did you learn of the crucifix?" When he didn't answer, her hand tightened over his. "'Tis the crucifix, is it not?"

Niall sighed, the air rushing from his body.

She lifted her head from his chest. "You found something?" At his continued silence, she sat up. "Niall, it worries me that you'll not say."

He sat up, turning away from her. "The thing is, we don't know what it means."

"We? You and Shawn?" Thunder clapped. She jumped, and drew herself up in the bed.

"Me. I don't know what it means."

"You didn't tell him? Why not?"

"I wanted to be sure, I wanted...."

"What did you learn?" she demanded.

"There was a prophecy and a blessing linked to each of the twelve crucifixes." He rubbed his forehead, frowning. "'Tis unfair to tell him, maybe get him chasing after yet another fairy hill, if it means naught."

She grew still. He tightened his jaw, resenting her quick mind.

"You've a guess how to get him back and you've not told him."

"'Tis a great difficulty, getting there."

"Where?"

He grimaced, not wanting to say it. "Iona."

"Iona!" Allene drew in a sharp breath. "As Christina said."

"It seems so," Niall agreed. "But I must be with Bruce at the time."

"What time?"

"The Feast of St. Columba. Early June? I don't know the day."

"You had but to ask!" She threw herself from the bed, grabbing her wrap, and yanking a torch from its sconce, stormed through the dark solar to Shawn's room. Rain pelted the windows. Thunder rolled, a long, low growl.

"Stop, Allene, what are you doing?" Niall followed her.

She pounded on Shawn's door. "Open up!"

"Stop it, Allene," he hissed. "You've not even heard the prophecy."

She pounded again. "Open the door, Brother Andrew."

"We don't know what it means," Niall said more loudly.

She whirled, her hair flying, the torch high. "Well, it's his life, he's a right to not know right along with you!"

She raised her fist to pound again. Shawn caught her wrist. He squinted bleary eyes. "Are you sleeping, are you sleeping?" he sang. "Yes, I was, yes I was." He rubbed his eyes, looking from one to the other. A bright flash from outside lit the room like the noon sun. "One," Shawn said, "Tw...." Thunder erupted with a crack so loud Allene jumped and squeaked.

Niall reached to steady the torch wavering in her hand. "How can you sleep through this?" he demanded of Shawn.

"We have them all summer in Minnesota." Shawn leaned into the windowsill, peering into silvery sheets of rain lashing the window. "Aren't they great!" He turned back to Niall and Allene. The torch threw sharp shadows across their faces. "But if you've finally come to your senses and decided to ditch him for the better looking identical twin, I'm happy to be woken up."

Allene rolled her eyes and snorted. She stuck the torch in a bracket.

"You're picking up bad habits from him!" Niall leaned against the wall with a thump, glaring.

"Yeah, well a pleasant good evening to you, too." Shawn boosted himself onto the windowsill. "Have you at least got something to eat or drink in exchange for waking me up?" Lightning flashed, illuminating the bare table. "Not a Dagwood sandwich in sight," he muttered. "And six hundred years until refrigeration." A peal of thunder shook the castle. "What do you want?"

"Tell him, Niall." Allene turned to Shawn.

Niall threw himself into a chair at the table, casting a look of irritation at Allene. "It could have waited till morning."

"You'll be busy in the morning."

"I was busy *now*, sleeping!" Niall bit out.

"We were *not* sleeping," she snapped, and suddenly blushed, looking to Shawn. "I didn't mean...."

He cleared his throat. "You were presumably talking about things I need to know right now."

"Aye," Allene said, with a little less force. "He says you heard the blessing but not the prophecy."

Niall closed his eyes, pressed his palms into them, and recited: "*'A boy will be his redemption. And on the feast of St. Columba in St. Columba's chamber, the door of time will open and the man who was lost in time shall be rescued by his son with my crucifix.'"*

Nobody spoke.

Niall opened his eyes. Shawn stared at him. "*When* were you *going* to *tell* me?" he asked softly, an accent on each angry word.

"I was trying to sort it out," Niall mumbled.

"What's to sort out? When's the feast of St. Columba?"

"I don't know!" Niall shot from his chair, and set to pacing.

"Early June," Allene volunteered. "My father will know the exact date."

"And where is St. Columba's chamber?"

Thunder rolled outside, weaker than it had been. Allene glanced out the window and clutched her arms more tightly about herself.

"As it happened the first time in the tower, I recall he had a room here centuries ago." From the window arch, outlined by moonlight, Niall tossed the words over his shoulder.

"But given Christina's vision, it surely means his chamber on Iona." Glancing at Shawn, Allene tugged the shift more tightly about her rounded stomach.

Niall stopped his pacing, jabbing his hands onto his hips. "This is the problem, Allene! The man stayed many places. It happened in our tower, it happened at Bannockburn, near his relics. How would we know 'tis Iona?"

"But Christina *saw* both of you in the chapel—his chamber—on Iona."

"Meaning what?" Niall countered. "Even if Iona is the place, we need the crucifix *and his son.* How are we to get Amy there? Scrawl on the wall, *Amy, bring the bairn to Iona,* and perhaps a note to the maidservants, *Do not scrub clean for seven hundred years?*"

"Your sarcasm is not appreciated." Allene turned her nose up.

"Whatever it means," added Shawn, "I had a right to be in on the guessing game. It is my life, after all."

"So I told him," said Allene.

"Allene, I'm sorry." Niall put his hands on her shoulders. She shrugged them off.

"How about an apology to me?" Shawn snapped. "It's *my* life you withheld information about."

"I didn't withhold it. I was trying to figure out what *to* tell you."

Shawn snorted.

"Oh, stop that," Niall barked. "I'm sorry. Are you happy?"

"Almost."

"I can do no more. Columba had chambers all over Scotland."

"Then maybe it doesn't matter," Shawn said. "Maybe any of them will do, as long as Amy is there with James and the crucifix."

"Father and son!" Allene looked from Niall to Shawn. "Niall, what was the blessing?"

"*'May this crucifix, by God's gracious mercy and St. Columba's intercession, draw together father and son for their mutual protection and benefit.'"*

"Fat lot of good it did," said Shawn. "How long after your father got this crucifix did he go to Falkirk?"

"You've the tact of a Jedburgh axe," Allene snapped. Almost as an afterthought, she added, "They say he's the image of his father." She stopped, looking from one to the other, from their identical chestnut hair to their matching eyes, noses, mouths, in the torchlight.

"The genes run strong in our family," Shawn murmured. He'd said it to Caroline, after the poker game in which he'd gambled away his trombone. He and Niall studied each other.

"This means you're my great-great grandson!" Niall arched an eyebrow. "You'd best mind your manners, as that makes me not only your future laird, but your elder and your grandsire."

"Better be nice to me," Shawn retorted. "I'll choose your nursing home."

Niall laughed. "What is this *nursing home?*"

"Where they stash old folks."

Allene studied Shawn, frowning.

Shawn slapped a hand on his forehead. "I kissed my own grandmother!"

Allene blushed a deep maroon and spun quickly, staring out the window. Niall tried to look stern. "Don't worry." Shawn added. "I will definitely never look at her again as anything else." He shuddered. "No offense, Allene. You're beautiful and all—Scottish bikini team, you know—but you're still my great-great grandmother. Or so it would appear."

"So now we know why the first two switches happened." At the window, trickling with rain, Niall shifted the conversation back to safer ground. "And it seems we've a good guess how to try for a third."

"But if this is a miracle associated with Columba's relics," Allene asked, the red in her face receding, "d' you really think we can control it? Miracles are not under man's control."

Shawn snorted, looked at Niall's glowering eyebrows, and said, "Sorry, Gramps."

"You'll not call me gramps," Niall stated. "'Tis improper to address your elders so."

"You're the same age!" Allene said in exasperation. "Stop this nonsense."

Niall and Shawn smiled at each other.

"All the same," said Shawn, "there's no such thing as miracles. They're just unexplained occurrences. I told you that."

"St. Columba was known for his miracles," Allene returned. "And this unexplained occurrence as you name it, happened with his relics on hand, in accordance with a prophecy and blessing. I say that's God's hand."

"No." Shawn shook his head. "There must be another explanation."

"In the meantime," Niall said, "what do we do with the information. Come the feast of St. Columba, I'll be on my way to Jura."

"I said I'd go for...." Shawn stopped. "I can't go to Iona or even the tower here, if I'm heading off to fight Johnny Reb."

"John *of Lorn*." Allene corrected. "You said you'd go in Niall's place?" Her eyes lit up. "He could stay here? He'd not have to go on the galleys?"

Niall turned stiffly, staring out the window. Alexander's face floated behind his eyelids. He felt as sick and decayed as the seaweed that had clung in his brother's hair. He could almost feel the lurching of the ships and the waters swallowing him, filled with whitened corpses tangled in rotting sea vines. But if Shawn could volunteer a huge risk for his sake, he could do no less. Behind him, the moon slid, a silver ship, from behind clouds. His voice came out taut as a Welsh archer's bowstring. "I go with the Bruce. He goes to Iona on the Feast of St. Columba."

Iona, Present

Back from Hugh's camp, my decision firm, I shift into high gear. I hunt the internet for Columba's prophecies, collecting them like rare gems, one by one from far-flung sources. Angus? I'm afraid to call. I text. He sends jokes as he once did, historian jokes, archaeologist jokes. But they're cold and clipped, wedged into the spaces of the new wariness between us. I don't speak of Shawn. He doesn't ask.

But Shawn is on my mind as I practice for the upcoming album, play on the floor with James, try to read Hamish's Gaelic books to him, teach lessons, do laundry, and buy groceries. I receive an invitation to sub with the Scottish orchestra. Damnation of Faust. I add it to my practice, and head to the library seeking more of Columba's prophecies.

"You need to get away," Carol says. "You're strained."

We sail to Iona, where we push through the salty breeze, down Iona's main street, to the wild hills beyond the abbey. I hold James to my chest in his carrier. Rocks jut from scrappy grass that ripples in the wind. "It's like Shawn," Carol says. "Rough, wild, unruly, but there's something deeper here."

"There certainly is," I agree. I'm seeing him at Monadhliath. James squirms, lets out his distinctive staccato cry, and by unspoken consent, we find a boulder to sit against. As James nurses, I look down over a silver, sandy beach. Seagulls screech overhead.

"They call it a 'thin place,'" Carol says. "I understand why Columba chose it." She watches the rolling surf. Sorrow settles on her face like a veil. "You said I may have gotten the miracle I prayed for with Shawn. Why?"

I choose words carefully. "He left me a message."

"A message? When?"

"It sounds crazy." I hesitate on the brink of telling Carol the impossible. There's still time to appear sane. But Carol leans forward, waiting. I rush in. "Look at these." I pull Columba's prophecies from my purse.

Carol scans them. Doubt shows on her face. "We're not really an age that believes in prophecies, are we?"

"What about miracles? You prayed for one."

"That was just a person changing sort of miracle, not a...." She lifts the paper in frustration. "A Red Sea parting sort of miracle. What are these?" Her red-rimmed eyes, plead for a sensible answer.

I inch another step toward the truth. "They're St. Columba's prophecies. Please—just tell me what you think."

Carol clasped her hands against her lips, staring out at the gray waves crashing on the shore.

"Please, Carol."

She blinks twice, wipes her eye, and reads them more carefully. "The last one," she says.

My heart picks up a beat. That's the prophecy concerning the crucifix. "It jumps out?"

"The rest are specific predictions, specific people. The last one is a general statement."

"That's it," I whisper. "How did you pinpoint it so fast?"

Carol shrugs. "You read them off this list?"

"No. The last one is from Monadhliath. I found the rest on the internet."

"When you see them all at once, the contrast is obvious. What is this about?"

I tug inside layers of clothing, hampered by nursing James, but I pull out the crucifix. Carol lifts the weight of my hair to slide the crucifix off. She studies it, turning it over, while I explain its background. My excitement grows. Maybe I can start telling the truth to Carol, too.

"So Niall—whoever he was—and that's what Shawn called himself at the last concert—gave this to you?" She presses fingertips to her forehead.

I nod. "That's a relic of St. Columba on the back, and that last prophecy is associated with this crucifix."

"But that prophecy can't be genuine, because it's not like his others."

"Then where did it come from?" I ask. "Is it a fake? Did someone make it up and attribute it to Columba?"

Carol frowns. "I don't know. I don't understand everything you're telling me. I don't understand anything you're telling me. Did you write it down wrong when you got it from the monks? Did they copy it wrong?"

I dig for my phone, clinging to James, then stop. "I can't."

Carol touches my arm. "Angus?"

I nod. It's become so natural to turn to him.

"Amy, what happened?"

James twists, batting the blankets away. I pull them back, protecting him from wind and sand. "I found out something about Shawn at Monadhliath. I reacted."

She's stares out to the waves a moment before asking, "He's afraid he'll lose you if Shawn comes back, isn't he?"

I nod unhappily.

"Shawn is like Ride of the Valkyries," Carol says. "Wild, exciting. Angus is Pachelbel's Canon, steady, enduring." She squeezes my hand.

"He's sure I prefer Valkyries." I watch a couple pass, hand in hand, kicking bare feet in chilly waves.

"Call him," Carol said.

"About the prophecy?" I shake my head. "I can't."

"Angus has devoted plenty of energy to my son. We'll figure out the prophecy on our own."

My cheeks turn red from more than wind. "I've e-mailed and texted. He gives me short answers."

"Sometimes," Carol says, "people need to know just how much they matter. I'll take James for a walk."

James finishes nursing. Bundling him tight, I hand him over. "Thanks." I trust Carol knows I mean for more than taking James.

Carol smiles as she accepts the bundle of blankets, cooing at the pink face showing through.

Alone on the beach, I stare at my phone a moment before dialing. I clutch it to my ear, breathing silent prayers as the sound echoes down the line.

"Inverness police department," comes a girl's voice.

"Hi." My voice comes out as a squeak. I clear my throat. "Can I speak to Inspector MacLean?"

"Aye, he's just arrived."

In the brief silence, I fight the urge to hang up. He doesn't want to talk to me. With good reason. I watch slate-gray waves, hoping this is the place of miracles it's reputed to be.

"Inspector MacLean." The rough voice I love comes over the line.

"It's me." I smile.

His silence unnerves me. Finally, he asks, "Is everything aw'right?"

I rub my thumb on Bruce's ring. "Apart from missing you." He doesn't answer. I swallow over a hot lump in my throat. "Are you busy?"

"I'm due for lunch. If it's to do with Shawn, I'm done."

A sifting of silver sand rises in the breeze, dances across the shore and settles again. "It's a Shawn-free conversation, Inspector MacLean." I strive for lightness. "If you can't abide by that, I'll have to hang up."

There's a quick intake of breath. "What do you want, then?"

"How's your day been?"

"Busy." The word comes out as cool as the wind tugging at my hair.

He's silent long enough I think he's hung up. "Angus?"

"We'd a cat up a tree." A little of the frost thaws from his voice.

"You're joking." I rise from the boulder, missing James, but feeling free, and cross a stretch of scrubby grass sloping to the shore. I kick off my shoes, despite the cold, and walk, feeling sand like silk between my toes.

"'Twas the sergeant's neighbor. His son fears police, so he sent me."

"He knows you're good with kids." Wind sends a veil of sand dancing around my legs. His voice washes over me, telling about the department slagging him over his hazardous duty. I like his gentle, self-mocking humor. This is what it would be like for us, without Shawn.

"And you?" His tone degenerates back to one such as he might use with a disagreeable aunt, to whom he is merely being polite.

I swallow the ache. "We took a ferry ride."

"How was it?" He doesn't ask to where.

"Rough. The waves are something else."

"Aye, they'd be that, in April." He clears his throat; his next words fill with emotion. "You and James are well?"

I sink into his familiar warmth, telling him about the ferry, the captain admiring James. Niall's aversion to water fades to a long ago world. Only James and Angus matter. "I'm playing Damnation of Faust with the RSNO," I tell him. I hope he'll come.

"It'll be grand," he says, not offering to. It's only that it's a long drive, I tell myself, as we talk about Gavin and Hamish. But by the time I hang up, I'm smiling, feeling warm inside. I'll give him a little more space, and invite him to the concert.

Pachelbel's Canon. I know this, as Iona's sea chills my feet. Even if Shawn returns. The real question is, can Angus believe it?

Inverness, Present

As Angus hung up, he glanced at the wilted fern on top of his cabinet—he really needed to take care of the poor thing.

Clive entered, tossing a note on his desk. "From Claire." *A Simon Beaumont was asking after you. Said he'll come back.* "He's intent on seeing you. This is the second time he's been by."

Angus glanced at the note before scrunching it and tossing it into the small metal trashcan. "Nothing I can do if he doesn't leave a number." The man didn't sit well with him. He turned his computer on. Down the hall, an officer shouted, dragging in a perp, who protested his innocence in colorful Glaswegian. Footsteps raced down the hall amid clanging and yelling. As his computer booted, Angus stared at the picture of Amy and James over his desk. Their conversation drifted through his mind. He found himself smiling, even as he warned himself it didn't change anything.

"Things better with Amy then?" Clive picked up a small rugby ball off his desk and tossed it.

Angus caught it one-handed, not looking up, and slammed it down on a pile of paperwork. "She's playing with the RSNO next week." He wasn't sure if it was better, or worse. He'd let his barriers down. But it didn't change anything about her feelings for that eejit, or the danger to James. If she'd quit the search, she would have said so. He sighed, thinking he'd have done better to keep his distance, but he'd missed hearing her voice.

The secretary came through, her ponytail bouncing, and dropped a pile of mail on his desk with a cheery, "Morning, then, Inspector! How's things? Morning, Lieutenant!" and passed on.

"I think she fancies you," Clive said. "Will I tell her you're still seeing Amy or that you're free?"

Angus rifled through the envelopes. "You're irritating, Chisolm. It's a wonder your mother didn't drown you with the kittens the day you were born."

Clive laughed. "I couldn't talk yet. The poor woman didn't know. Listen, mate, she's had a bad year." Clive wheeled his chair over, plunking his elbows on Angus's desk. Angus edged a pen out from under his arm. "You wrote the reports yourself, when her boyfriend disappeared."

"*Ex*-boyfriend. She broke up with him."

"Only just."

Angus stared straight ahead.

"Whatever happened between you," said Clive, "cut her some slack. Why not surprise her at that concert?"

Angus tapped his own pen, considering. "Maybe I will," he said.

CHAPTER THIRTY-SEVEN

Glenmirril, 1315

"Allene, I need to talk to you."

Allene glanced around the empty solar, looking slightly panicked.

"Oh, come *on*," Shawn protested. "This is stupid! Have I ever touched you?" At her pointed look, he added, "Apart from that! I've kept my hands to myself for a year. You really think I'm going to try to seduce my great grandmother?"

"'Tis scandalous," she replied primly. "Others don't *know* naught is happening behind closed doors."

Shawn shook his head in irritation. "Where's Christina?"

"Taking food to the poor. I'll call Bessie."

He shook his head more vehemently. "I need to talk about Niall. Bessie is going to find it a little odd for Niall to be talking about Niall. Come on, this is ridiculous. I just need to talk to you."

She settled back on the divan. The sun had emerged, after heavy morning rain, and splashed through the window, flashing off her gold thread. She eyed him warily. "Speak quickly before Hugh or my father comes."

"This is ridiculous," he muttered again.

"You haven't time to complain," Allene sniffed. "What is it you wish to say?"

"This water thing." He hoisted himself into the window seat. "I'm leaving. You have to keep helping him."

"What more am I to do?" Allene laid the embroidery on her lap, her eyebrows furrowing. "I've been going down as you told me."

Before he could answer, the door flew open. Shawn leapt to his feet, turning his back to hide his face.

"Shawn wanted to speak with me about Niall, Father," came Allene's voice quickly.

Shawn spun. Hugh and MacDonald stood in the doorway, their faces dark. "Ah, for cripe's sake," Shawn snapped. "Quit looking at me like that! I'm fully clothed and so is she. The door was unlocked. You really think...?"

"'Tis improper!" MacDonald slammed the door.

"'Tis *ridiculous!*" Shawn shot back. "I'm trying to help Niall. I'll be gone in a few days, anyway."

"You'll follow our ways until then," barked MacDonald. "I'll not have questions raised about my daughter." MacDonald glowered at Shawn before rounding on Allene. "Why did you not call Christina?"

"She's feeding our widows, Father."

"Bessie, then," said Hugh.

"If Bessie heard me talking about myself...." Shawn started.

The Laird lowered his eyebrows.

Shawn stopped talking.

"What is important enough to risk my daughter's reputation?" MacDonald demanded.

"Niall and water."

"He'll get over it," MacDonald said.

By the door, Hugh folded his arms across his chest. He stared at the floor.

"He's got a *phobia*," Shawn argued, using modern English where medieval Gaelic failed. "You have to...."

"*Phobia?*" MacDonald repeated the foreign word.

"Irrational fears. They don't just go away. He lives by water. If I were staying—but I'm not. I'm telling Allene what to do."

MacDonald and Hugh glanced at one another.

"He's often been right," Allene reminded her father. "'Tis no harm in listening."

"She's a point," Hugh said.

"He shouldn't have been alone with her!"

"Father, what harm can there be to my reputation? Anyone would think I'm with my own husband."

"But you *aren't* with your own husband!" MacDonald roared.

Allene heaved a breath. "Father, I promise I will never again be alone in a room with him. As it concerned Niall's welfare, I told him to speak quickly, and he'd but started when you burst in. Will you listen?"

"It's not to happen again," MacDonald emphasized, before turning to Shawn. "Speak."

"Get him to come down with you. Keep edging closer to the water. Convince him to put a foot in. Just a toe to start."

Hugh and MacDonald exchanged glances. "We can do that," Hugh said.

"Do any of you know how to swim?" Shawn asked.

Hugh and MacDonald exchanged raised eyebrows. "Swim?" MacDonald nearly shouted. "In the *water?*"

"I've tried it on dry land in my more drunken moments," Shawn deadpanned. "It's easier in water."

Hugh spoke as if to one soft in the head. "D' you not know there's a creature in there? 'Tis not healthy to be in the loch when you don't know what swims with you."

"I find it healthier to *swim* with unknown companions," Shawn said, "than to sink with them. Besides, apart from on dark nights, who really believes in the Loch Ness monster?"

From the looks exchanged by the other three, it was clear they did.

"St. Columba himself saw it," MacDonald said.

Hugh shook his head, unconvinced. "Very few swim at all. Do you?"

"Like a fish," Shawn said. "Let me teach you. I'll have you swimming in no time. Then you can teach Niall."

"Certainly neither of you is afraid to go in the loch," Allene said, "not after you made Niall—Shawn—cross it on a stormy night in a little currach!"

"'Twas a year ago, Allene!" MacDonald snapped. "I'd no other way to send him, and you know yourself, he'd have been dead had he gone his own way, as we both know he'd have done."

"How will we explain Niall out in the water teaching one of us to swim?" Hugh asked.

"We'll go at night," Shawn said.

"The guards walk the parapets. They'll see us."

"You're adept at thinking up stories, are you not?" Allene asked Shawn. "Make one up for the guards. They'll not see your faces clearly."

"Okay, then!" Shawn clapped his hands, grinning. He'd won, without any of them admitting they'd given in. "Who will it be?"

A gruff snort erupted from MacDonald, making it clear he would not compromise his lairdly dignity.

"I will," Hugh said.

"Okay, then, you got a swimming suit? I'm guessing not. We'll go in these funny little drawstring pants that pass for underwear around here."

"What's wrong with our underclothes?" Allene said indignantly. "What d' you wear in your time?"

"Allene!" Shock rang in MacDonald's voice. "Ye'll not discuss undergarments with a man!"

She tossed her head, and jabbed her needle through the altar linen, muttering, "There's naught amiss with our undergarments!"

"Tonight, then," Shawn confirmed. "We'll go out the tunnel by the Bat Cave. Can we get Niall to watch from the shore at least?"

"We'll try." Hugh didn't sound optimistic.

"Try hard," Shawn ordered Hugh, and turned to MacDonald. "Tell your guards we're checking fortifications, in case MacDougall sends men across the loch to mine in."

MacDonald glared. Hugh lifted a hand to his mouth and turned his back, busying himself with staring out the window.

"Please?" Shawn said. "I mean, it's just a suggestion. Will it do?"

"'Twill do nicely," MacDonald said.

Glasgow, Present

The heavy Scots and Glaswegian accents around her only heightened the familiar excitement of concert night, of concert black, and flowing onstage with a hundred virtuosos.

"Is your boyfriend coming?" Sarah, her stand partner for the evening, fell into step beside her. They'd enjoyed a coffee together after the last rehearsal. In showing pictures of James on her phone, Angus's picture had appeared.

"It's a long drive from Inverness." Amy skirted the issue of whether he was her boyfriend. She wasn't sure herself. She changed the subject. "I love hearing *Damnation of Faust* sung by a native speaker."

"You'd never guess English isn't her native language," Sarah said admiringly, as they filed between chairs rapidly filling with musicians. "I took French all through university, and I still muck up the grammar."

Amy smiled as she squeezed between two violinists warming up. "I just got a bench for my keyboard. Made in China. It's warning label says, 'Do not stand in stool.'" She set their music on the stand.

Sarah laughed. "Aye, the wrong preposition changes everything."

Amy settled her long skirt, and tucked her violin under her chin, joining her A to the swell of instruments tuning. Excitement rose. It was just her and her violin, one small piece of the incredible precision instrument of a symphony orchestra.

The conductor strode onstage with bows, applause, greetings, and a swish of his baton. Her last thought was her wish that Angus would have come, before she slipped into the drama of Faust. Her bow flashed up and down. The music grew, thundering and crashing, as Faust, eager to save Marguerite, signed his soul to the Devil, represented by a trombone. Shawn had loved that part. "Fits me, doesn't it?" He'd winked and laughed.

Her mind wandered the dimming halls of her life with Shawn. The crucifix *must* be connected to him. He had certainly gone astray for a time. *Do not stand in stool.* The man who sang Faust drew breath, filling a huge barrel chest with air. Sarah flipped the page swiftly and bent back to bowing. *Prepositions change everything.* Amy leaned into a flurry of staccato notes, sparkling beneath the tenor. *At time, by time, in time.* She glanced at blinding footlights that turned the audience into a dark mass, wishing Angus had come.

Marguerite joined her mezzo-soprano to Faust, singing in French. Shawn had loved trans-lingual word plays. *Cean—love, fault, crime.* "Ironic, isn't it?" he'd asked.

"Why can't a word mean what it means?" she'd complained.

"Words never mean just one thing," he'd said.

Marguerite's voice rose; bows streaked, oboes wailed. The orchestra began its descent into hell. Amy, in the sea of violins, fought a quickening fray over her strings. Her thoughts spun from the music to Angus. She missed hearing him read Gaelic to James. Mephistopheles and Faust battled with rising arias.

The brass groaned and rumbled. Amy's eyebrows furrowed; her bow flashed through sixteenth notes. How would she translate Faust from French, knowing nothing of its background? She wouldn't think it meant a literal descent into hell. She would translate according to her own paradigms. She would translate it....

She sucked in air, a cold wash of realization. Her thoughts bounced from Shawn, to Angus, wishing he had come; to the prophecy, to James at home with neither Shawn nor Angus in his life, before she got her mind firmly back to the black flurry of notes. She couldn't afford distraction.

The piece finished with a heavenly chorus, rows of angels in white singing, and the audience burst into applause. The conductor bowed, swept his arm over the orchestra, while Amy itched to reach her phone. The applause stretched out endlessly, with multiple curtain calls summoning Marguerite, Faust, and Mephistopheles back for bow after bow.

One of the angels pressed a gargantuan bouquet of roses into Marguerite's arms, while Amy tried to control her eagerness to reach her phone, to call Celine, to tell her!

Finally, the applause died from a roar to a swell, to a smattering, and the musicians began to gather their music and rise. She had to tamp her impatience as violinists milled and blocked her way, chatting as they loosened their bows. Backstage, musicians and well-wishers swarmed around her. She clutched her violin close, protecting it from the press of the crowd. Finally, she reached the sanctuary of the green room, and in moments had her phone out. Still holding the violin, she stabbed at Celine's number.

"Amy!"

She only registered Sarah calling her name.

"Amy?" Celine's voice came over the phone, groggy with sleep.

"The prophecy, Celine!" Amy said frantically.

A hand touched her arm. "Amy, look who's here!"

She felt Sarah turning her, even as she rushed the words out. "Celine, I need that prophecy in the original Gaelic!" She lifted her eyes and sucked in her breath. Angus stood in a suit, clutching a bouquet of mixed flowers.

Glenmirril, 1315

On the moonlit scrap of rocky shore behind Glenmirril, Shawn shook fresh spring leaves and twigs from his hair as he pushed through the brush-covered mouth of the tunnel. Hugh was already on shore stripping off his vest and shirt. Bare-chested and looking more than ever like a grizzly on its hind legs, he looked to the parapets.

"They'll accept the Laird's word." Behind Shawn, Niall emerged from the tunnel.

Shawn looked up. Four stone stories above, a man patrolled the walls.

Moonlight glinted off his helmet. He raised a hand in greeting, and kept going.

"See." Niall rose, brushing the filth of the tunnel off his vest, and tugging twigs from his hair. "Searching for underwater boats! Where d' you think up such things?"

"Jules Verne thought them up," Shawn said. "Or maybe it was H.G. Wells. The United States Navy made it happen during the Revolutionary War. Or maybe it was the Civil War."

"The MacDougalls could hardly think up such a thing," Niall snorted.

"Doesn't matter if they could or not. All that matters is your guards up there believe it. You coming in?"

Niall laughed easily. "You got me this far. Don't push your fortune."

"You don't know what you're missing," Shawn said. "And it's 'don't push your *luck*'."

"Luck is fortune, is it not?"

Shawn rolled his eyes, his own shirt skimming over his head. "Whatever."

"Whatever," Niall mimicked. "Does this word actually mean anything in modern English?"

"It speaks volumes." Shawn yanked at his trews, till he stood at Hugh's side, both of them in baggy drawstring underwear hanging to their knees, that not even Marky Mark could make look good. "Do you think you could get all those women who sew all day to embroider some palm trees on these?"

"Palm trees? What are they?" Hugh waded into the water.

"Tall skinny trees with huge leaves at the top."

"You stitch them on your *braies?*" Hugh shook his head, giving the impression of a lion waking.

"They're symbolic of sun and sea. Good times, easy living."

"No wonder you're all so immoral in your century if you've time to embroider trees on your *braies*. The devil makes use of idle hands."

"We are *not* all immoral," Shawn snapped. "Who said we're all immoral?"

Hugh jerked his head at Niall, seated on the boulder, watching.

"I am *not* immoral," Shawn told him. "A little amoral at times, but that's completely different, don't you think?"

"No," said Niall.

"Well, I do. Amoral. Adjective. Knows how to have fun. We know how to swim, too, which is more than I can say for you two lunkheads."

"Lunkhead," Niall mused. "Lunkhead. I must use that on Lachlan."

"I already have." Shawn followed Hugh into the water. "Therefore, you already have." He cupped his palm and flung a small tidal wave at Niall.

Niall laughed as a few drops reached him. "Better fortune next time."

"We haven't all night," Hugh complained. He'd gone in past his waist. "I hope the guards aren't watching you two. They'll not believe we've any concern about MacDougall."

"Okay, then," Shawn said. "First step. Are you listening, Niall? Face in water." He stuck his in deep, and came up, laughing and shaking his head, flinging moon-speckled droplets across the silver-glinted surface of the dark loch. "See? Easy." It felt good to be in water again. He threw himself in, laughing at the chilly shock, and swam what he guessed was a pool's length out, and back to Hugh. "Come on," he said. "Put your face in."

Hugh did so.

"That was only the tip of your nose," Shawn reprimanded.

"I can't breathe underwater!" Hugh objected.

"You don't breathe. You hold your breath."

After a few failed attempts, Shawn tried another tack. "Sing as you put your head in."

"Sing what?"

Shawn heaved a sigh. "Anything. Niall, what should he sing?"

"*Sheik of Araby.* Everyone should sing *Sheik of Araby.*"

"Thank goodness I got *some* twenty-first century sense into your medieval head." Shawn sang the first line. "Now watch. When I stick my head in, you'll see bubbles come up. Air can't go *in* my mouth when it's coming out."

Singing the not-yet-composed jazz standard, in an unwieldy and off-key bass that made Niall laugh, Hugh stuck his head under water. He came up with a wide grin. "It works!"

"Of course it does!" Shawn grinned, resisting the urge to look to shore for Niall's reaction. "Now try this."

The lesson progressed with setbacks and accomplishments, till, an hour later, Hugh could dog paddle twenty feet out and back. He emerged, shaking like MacDonald's wolfhounds, onto shore, beaming, bellowing, "Niall, 'tis easy! 'Tis fun! Come and try!"

Niall shook his head. "Our ideas of fun differ greatly, Hugh." He headed for the entrance to the tunnel.

Shawn sighed. He was leaving in days. He hoped what he'd taught Hugh was enough.

CHAPTER THIRTY-EIGHT

Bannockburn, Present

Amy woke early the next morning, lacking the usual afterglow of a performance. She stared up at the white ceiling. Angus had made a great effort, and that's what he heard from her. Not *You came!* or *I love you*, but...*I'm thinking about Shawn.*

His face had fallen; he'd wheeled through the crowd backstage. She'd rushed after him, trying to protect the bouquet and violin against her body, calling, "Angus, I'm sorry." He was halfway down Buchanan's cobbled street when she reached the cool Glasgow evening, her bell sleeves billowing, skirt swirling around her ankles.

"Angus!" She stopped halfway down the stairs. She couldn't chase him with a violin. She returned to the green room, depleted and angry, put her instrument away, hurried through polite greetings, and made the long drive home. It was bad luck, bad timing. But there was no taking the words back. She still needed the prophecy in Gaelic. Something beyond her had made the decision. She'd known, in Hugh's camp, there would be no turning back.

Swinging her legs from the bed, she tucked her robe tight, checked James in his crib, and went to her office. Soon she had the request sealed in an envelope. Thirty minutes later, wearing a long forest green sweater against May's chill, and her leather boots, with James in the carrier on her chest, and her hair braided the length of her back, she scooped yesterday's mail into her purse, and set out through Bannockburn's twisting streets to drop her letter in the post box.

With James snug in his wrappings, peering up with bright eyes and grins that reminded her of Shawn, she turned for the battlefield, that held so many memories—of Shawn, of Niall; of Angus standing over her, offering a mocha hazelnut. She spread James's blanket, took her familiar seat on the tree stump, and pulled the mail from her purse, while James babbled and reached for green grass. Power bill, a note from the professor reminding her of his return in July, and—she smiled—a letter from Conrad. She slit the envelope and pulled out a card in the shape of a grand piano.

My Dear Amy. Conrad's writing flowed, a work of art typical of his age, across the card. *I miss you, and worry about you, but Rob and Celine assure me you are well and your son is beautiful. I forbade them to tell you, on pain of an entire season of twelve-tone music, because I wanted to surprise you. We're coming for another tour in June! I want you to solo. Choose a piece, arrange it with Rob. We can't wait to see you. Love, Conrad.*

Glenmirril, 1315

"I feel bad. It feels wrong to just walk away." Shawn's voice echoed in the Bat Cave. He winced as Christina applied a poultice to his shoulder. He'd lost concentration while drilling one last time with Niall. They had practiced daily in the cave. It afforded space, and allowed Niall and Shawn both to fight free of the confining robes of Brother Andrew.

"Though the monks fight well enough in their robes," Hugh had said.

"Monks fight?" Shawn had asked in astonishment.

"If they must to protect their flock, why would they not?"

Shawn's opinion of them shifted again, though he couldn't say how. He jerked at the touch on his arm.

"Hold still now." Christina's throaty voice called him back to the present. Her words bounced off the high walls.

"You must ever watch that feint." Allene's hands rested on her rounded stomach. "You must be quick."

"Yeah, I figured that out," Shawn grumbled. "What do you know about sword fighting anyway?"

"My father taught me well," Allene said. "He didn't wish me to be defenseless, should the English ever breach Glenmirril."

"Really? You can fight with a sword? Show me what you got."

"You're injured."

"Niall will be back soon," Christina murmured. "He'll be most displeased to find you fighting in your condition."

"Excuses," Shawn said. "You both know she can't deliver on her big talk." He grinned. "Don't worry, I'll go easy, you being pregnant and an old granny and all."

In a flash, she had Niall's wooden practice sword, raining blows on him.

"Stop that, now," Christina said mildly, still trying to daub his arm as he laughed and threw up his hands to ward off her blows.

"All right, let's go!" He jumped to his feet, snatching up his sword. "I promise I won't hurt you."

"I make no such promise in return." Allene smiled. "Best not be over confident. I've seen you fight. You've not seen me."

"I know women weren't taught to fight in medieval times."

She smiled. "Are you ready?"

"Bring it." He stepped into his stance. She whacked him on the arm before he finished. "Hey, I wasn't ready," he snapped.

"Think you Lame John will wait till you strike a pretty pose?" She whacked him on the other arm.

"Hey, you're not...."

"Defend yourself!" She gripped the wooden sword with both hands, her face becoming a mask of concentration, swinging and wheeling the weapon over her head. Two blows struck him forcefully, before he managed to fight back. She blocked and parried almost as well as Niall, all the while backing him into her father's work bench. The sword blurred over her head and struck his shoulder, sending his weapon skittering to the floor.

As he reached for it, she bought her sword down on his neck.

"Ow!" He yanked back, barely getting his weapon, and flew at her. Her sword whirled again. He blocked it, and drove her back, swinging. She parried, swung, blocked, pushed at him, and swiped at his legs, catching him hard in the shin. He swore, dove at her, grabbing the wooden sword by the blade to pull her in, and spun her around till he gripped her around neck and rounded stomach, restraining the flailing weapon. "Okay, who's so smart now? You're stuck, aren't you?"

"Aye," she said. "You'll be a great danger to the Sassenach, if you can grab real blades in your bare hand after having your leg and head lopped off."

"My...what?"

Christina laughed. "Had she been wielding a real sword, you'd have lost your head some time ago."

The door burst in.

"What are you about!" Niall demanded, seeing Shawn's arms around Allene's neck and pregnant stomach.

"Careful now." Allene squirmed against Shawn's grip. "You'll kick his head. I lopped it off near the workbench."

Shawn released Allene. "I was teaching her a little about self-defense."

Christina smiled. "Come now, Shawn. A man of honor is truthful. She also cut off your leg. Come back and let me see if there's aught more to be done for that arm."

"Shawn, has a lady bested you at fighting?" Niall couldn't resist a grin. "And she with child, no less!"

"Exactly why it wasn't a fair fight! Look at this bruise you left on my arm." He yanked up his sleeve, showing the purple blotch. "You and MacDonald would take turns removing my limbs one by one if I did that to her."

Christina pushed him back onto the worktable, tugging his sleeve up, and returning to her ministrations. "Now, you were saying, before Allene lopped off your head, that you feel bad about walking away. You meant going to Iona while Niall goes to fight Lame John?"

Shawn nodded.

Niall grunted. "'Tis decided. MacDonald agrees. This is our war, not yours, and you've a chance to try to for home."

"How are you going to get on those galleys?" Shawn asked.

"I believe I'll walk on." Niall picked up the fallen sword, examining it for nicks and splinters. "Your only concern is that we leave tomorrow to get you to Iona." He nodded at the sackbut, in its case on the Laird's worktable. "Will you play for us one last time?"

Shawn regarded him. But Niall's stance and expression firmly closed the subject of water. Shawn turned to the workbench, and opened the wooden case the Laird had built. The golden instrument nestled on a velvet lining Christina had sewn for it. Emotions swirled in him. He wanted his life back—the crowds, tuxedos, lights. But he'd miss his life here. He wanted to show Amy he'd changed, to see her and touch her again. He wanted his son. And he'd miss Christina. He wanted his place in the spotlights on the world's great stages, with the world's greatest musicians backing him up—and he'd miss the glorious, unearthly echo of the sackbut throughout the bat cave.

He tried to smile, but it didn't reach his eyes. He lifted the sackbut, fit in the mouthpiece, and with a deep breath, he blew a slow and mournful *Don't Cry for Me Argentina;* a haunting *Music of the Night.* He filled his lungs, pouring his pain into crashing crescendos.

"Your music is filled with grief." Christina spoke softly, when he stopped. "Are you not happy to be going home?"

He nodded, staring at the floor with unseeing eyes. "Yeah. I'm happy." He settled the sackbut back into the wooden case, trailing his fingers over the satin sheen of the bell. Christina and Allene stood together, watching. Niall turned his back, his head bowed. Shawn surveyed the room where he'd spent so much time. In the recess at the far side, the life-sized Christ hung on His cross. Candles flickered below it, glittering gems of blue, red, and green. He yanked his gaze away and patted the case. "I'll buy a sackbut when I get back," he said. "It's been fun. Trombones are bigger. You'd love the sound."

There were several minutes of silence, before Allene said, "It's getting late. Dinner will be served."

"I'm not having dinner all cloaked and hooded my last night here." Shawn ran his hand along the Laird's workbench, touched his tools, and the half-finished harp.

"Go as you are," Niall said. "I'll stay here."

"You must say good-bye," Allene added. "Owen, Lachlan, Gilbert—they're your friends, too, even if they don't know. You must certainly say good-bye to Red."

Shawn smiled. He thought about being back in his own time, maybe finding Owen's and Lachlan's graves, knowing their life's stories in the blink of an eye, when tonight they were young men with everything ahead of them. The smile flitted off his face.

"Shawn?" Christina took a step toward him. "You're going back to all you love."

The thought of seeing Amy and James erupted in his heart. He glanced at Christina with an equally strong twinge of guilt. "Yeah. I am. I'm going to get my job back and play on all the great stages of the world. I'm going to tell Amy I'm sorry. I'm going to show her. I'm going to raise my son and be a good father."

Her eyes met his and skittered away. Then she met his gaze firmly. "You must go home to her, Shawn, if you can."

He lowered his eyes, staring unseeing. "There are two problems," he said.

"Which are?" She drew another two steps closer. Allene and Niall drifted away to the crucifix, leaving them alone.

"In your vision, you saw both of us. But only I'm going."

She shrugged. "Who can know what I saw? Maybe 'twas not to be taken literally. The other problem?"

He gazed mutely at her.

Christina took another step. He turned his back. "Don't," he whispered.

But she touched his shoulder. "You'll be a good father. You'll be a good husband to Amy."

He spun, gripping her, pulling her tight against his chest. "I told you not to touch me," he whispered gruffly in her hair. "I'm going to love her right this time." He held her, his heart pounding. Her arms wrapped around him.

From across the cave came the sound of a throat clearing.

Shawn pulled back, looking into Christina's damp eyes.

She laid her hand on his chest. "You've prior obligations and promises. There's naught more to be said."

"'Tis time to go, Shawn," Allene said softly.

Shawn nodded, stepping back from Christina. But his eyes didn't leave her.

Bannockburn, Present

"Why not *Loch Lomond?*" Rob asked. Sunlight poured into his front room, over a drafting table and stools.

Amy resisted the urge to slap her pencil onto the orchestral score paper, covered in a thick spray of notes. "Conrad told me to choose. I did." She studied the score, tried a few chords on her keyboard, and jotted them into the flutes. "We've scored the solo and half the accompaniment. I'm not changing my mind."

"Yeah, okay. How 'bout filling out this chord in the brass?" His pencil poised over the first trumpet staff.

"I like it open there. It suits the music."

He jotted in rests, and laid his pencil down. "I just don't get why you're so stuck on this piece."

"I like it." Amy didn't look up as she penciled in a rhythm for the snare. She wasn't about to tell him it made her glow, remembering Angus singing in the misty solstice dawn, the melody rising hauntingly over the standing stones. Neither would she admit she'd been foolish to choose a song that made her miss him even more than she already had.

"Just saying," Rob said.

Over and over, she wanted to say. But she held her tongue, leaning over the score. Her hair fell like a curtain between them. They worked in silence, Rob occasionally sipping coffee. Their arms brushed one another. Rob's pencil paused. Amy felt his eyes on her. She turned away, trying a different inversion on the keyboard.

"Amy?" His voice dropped a minor third.

She closed her eyes, wary. "What?"

"I'm sorry...about Angus."

She waited for his offer to fill that empty spot in her life.

"We'll have bagpipes in the balconies." He marked a note. "They'll harmonize the end of your solo."

"Yes." She studied his profile as he jotted in notes. "I'm impressed."

Leaving Glenmirril, 1315

Shawn's pony jingled through the forest, a blur of greens and browns from under Brother Andrew's hood. Raindrops from the morning shower clung to every leaf, and the sweet smells of a freshly washed world filled the air. Niall had covered the plan carefully. Shawn would travel with his company, who were well accustomed to the silent Brother Andrew. When they passed Loch Linnhe, Shawn would slip away and travel to Iona alone. MacDonald had gone over the geography repeatedly with a map and a dozen lectures.

"'Tis a long way," Niall warned. "Keep going southwest. Stay clear of castles or towns. 'Tis all MacDougall's land."

"Just what I need. Crossing MacDougall's land is the only way home."

They said their good-byes the evening they reached Loch Linnhe, with dozens of campfires blazing in the glen. Niall gripped his hand.

"It's becoming familiar," Shawn said. "Uh, I can't entirely say I've been thrilled with all of this, but, well, you know, it could've been worse."

Niall mirrored Shawn's rueful grin. "Give my blessings to Amy and the child."

"Yeah. And...thanks. For everything. Leave me a historical trail or something, okay? I'll look you up in the history books. Have a good life."

The sun dipped in the west. In late May, there weren't many hours of darkness. With shadows reaching for him, he had to hurry. Campfires crackled. Ponies snuffled. Laughter and talk floated on the air.

"Watch for the guards," Niall said. "They do their job well. God go with you."

Shawn hesitated. The words meant something to Niall. "You, too." He clapped Niall on the back and melted into the trees, leaving it all behind.

Monadhliath, Present

"Brother Lewis." Brother Fergna addressed the elderly monk who had taken over the archives. "The couple who visited—the wife would like the prophecy linked to her crucifix in its original Gaelic. Copy it and send it to her, please."

"Aye." Lewis tottered to the archives, and found the prophecy. He studied it, a frown creasing his brow. It made no sense. It was redundant. He set pen to paper, copying in the neat script he'd learned years ago, giving great care to the aesthetic flow of ink.

When he finished, he ambled along the stone hallways, through the cloisters with fresh spring grass, and Brother Colum bent over his flowers. In the abbey office, he found the guest book. Brother Lewis copied the address carefully onto an envelope, and inserted the prophecy. "God go with ye," he said, and left the envelope with the bundle awaiting the youngest brother's hike down to the outside world next week.

Scotland, 1315

A hand fell on Shawn's shoulder. He heard the whisper of steel on leather and Lachlan's voice. "Name yerself."

Shawn squeezed his eyes tight. Iona, home, Amy, James—they all slipped from his grasp. "It's me, Niall."

"I thought ye were back at camp."

Shawn smiled ruefully. "I guess I got turned around in the dark."

"Good thing I found ye. Ye were heading into MacDougall territory."

"Good thing," Shawn agreed. "Look, how about you finish your patrol? Now that I know I was going the wrong way, I'll be fine."

"My Lord, 'tis dark. Your mother expressly asked me to watch you, as you've been so different since your head injury."

"My *mother?*" Shawn threw his head back and laughed. "I'm a warrior and a lord. Surely I don't need my mother posting a nursemaid by my side. Go on, Lachlan. I'll be along."

"My Lord Niall, your men love you. Since the head injury, and your sometimes erratic behavior, we all watch you more closely."

Shawn sighed. "I'm fine, Lachlan. Go back to camp." He shut his eyes for a second, and opened them again, staring at Lachlan. The man had been a friend to him; a real friend, not like Rob. He didn't want to send him away. But he spoke sternly. "That's an order, Lachlan." Pain stabbed his heart.

Lachlan turned. Shawn listened to the rustle of the trees. The sound stopped almost instantly. He knew, as if he could see in the dark, that Lachlan waited and watched. He cared for Niall. Shawn stood another five minutes, listening for the sound of Lachlan leaving, and trying to think who, in the orchestra, would care and wait that way.

The silence stretched. Insects hummed. He heard the man breathing. He sighed, and pushed his way through the firs, back to camp. Lachlan's soft footfalls paralleled his own, guarding his beloved Lord and unwittingly destroying his chance to reach his own loved ones. Shawn followed the path slowly, hoping for a chance to escape.

Inverness, Present

"Morning, Inspector."

Angus, his feet propped on the table, pulled his eyes from the television in the corner of the break room, to glance at Claire in her tomato red cardigan and black hair tied up in a short, bouncy ponytail. She looked too young to be out in the adult world. But then, he reflected, he was feeling that way more and more lately, especially since Monadhliath.

"I left some mail on your desk. And one of those donuts with the sprinkles you love. And your coffee. Mocha with hazelnut."

He smiled, nodded absently, and turned back to the television. "It's nearly a year since the renowned musician Shawn Kleiner disappeared," a woman announced in crisp accents. In a clip from last year, the camera closed in on a crowd of Americans surging through Edinburgh airport, smiling, excited, laughing. Last year, the unit had watched it live. Angus closed his eyes, not needing a replay to remember Shawn bursting from the hall, smiling, waving, dragging the girl with the long black hair behind him, stopping when he saw the cameras, and putting on a show of kissing her.

"Can he not see he's making her uncomfortable," one of the women officers had demanded.

Angus's eyes had lingered on the girl, as she pushed him away, flushed with embarrassment. He'd never seen anyone so pretty. And—he sat forward, recognizing her—it was the Glenmirril Lady. The violinist Charlie had called about in such a fluster was the notorious Shawn Kleiner's *girlfriend*? His heart sank even as he sternly reminded himself it was nothing but coincidence, anyway. Then Kleiner's cocky mug had filled the screen, answering reporters' questions until the weather came on. Angus had turned his attention to the meeting regarding Shawn Kleiner's arrival, and put the girl out of his mind.

"I hope you don't mind," the young secretary said, "but I thought you'd want this right away."

Angus's eyes snapped open, yanking him back into the present. He kicked his feet to the floor. Claire held out a creamy envelope. "Thanks." He took it, without interest, letting it fall in his lap. He should have seen it, he thought. Although never given to fantasies, he'd seen her on television, and been jolted at her resemblance to the Glenmirril Lady. He'd seen her distressed at the hospital, and his knight in shining armor syndrome had grabbed him around the neck and throttled his usual common sense out of him. It had gotten worse when Mike described her sitting alone at the battlefield every morning. He'd taken a foolish detour from his usual firm-footed contact with terra firma, and reached for a dream.

He glanced at the envelope: the Monks of Monadhliath. He rolled his eyes and dropped it back in his lap. He'd had enough of Shawn, and Niall, too, and had no intention of letting them out of that envelope and back into his life. He glanced at the telly, still playing last year's video. The camera settled on Shawn, and Amy beside him. Her hair hung in thick waves down her back. Angus fought the ache. He'd been a fool, thinking he could ever replace a big name like Shawn Kleiner in any woman's affections.

Chisholm burst through the door, talking about a rugby match in Glasgow. His eyes fell on the television. He snapped it off, dropped into a vinyl chair beside Angus, and grabbed a donut from the box.

Angus turned on him, all his self-deprecating thoughts spearheading on Clive. "What are you telling me? Quit moping because I should have seen she's out of my league?"

Clive shrugged. "It's not like you know an opera from an aria."

Angus couldn't resist a brief glimmer of his usual good humor. "It would appear you know it even less."

"What's that mean?" Clive bit off half the donut. His cheeks bulged.

"An aria is *part* of an opera, ye eejit."

"Oh. Well, no, I wasn't going to say she's out of your league. She isn't."

"Look at her." Angus gestured at the blackened screen from which she'd disappeared. "She's talented and beautiful, she's used to a big star, and I thought I had something to offer. A little house in the country and a horse!" He snorted. "Why I thought she needed *me* for that, I don't know."

"You're being too hard on her," Clive said around the donut. He gulped, and spoke more clearly. "How long was she with him?"

"Two years and more."

"Pretty intense years, aye? Worked with him, did all those albums together, had his child. He's gone less than a year, traumatic circumstances, and it seems something happened up at Monadhliath." He bit off half the remaining donut and brushed a flurry of crumbs from his uniform, smearing in chocolate. When Angus neither confirmed nor denied, he added, "Strange things do happen in these old places."

"What happened," Angus said tersely, "is that I saw she'll always be in love with him."

Clive coughed into his hand, not quite smothering the word, "Julia."

Angus tapped the envelope on his knee. "I'm not crying over Julia."

"At ten months, you were moping something fierce."

"When did you become the love doctor?" Angus demanded.

Clive ignored the jibe. "Does she love you?"

"Aye." Angus leaned back, remembering her eyes on him, the first night he'd kissed her.

"There it is then." Clive stood, and walked to the door.

"As much as she's able."

Clive stopped, his hand on the door knob. "They'll be in Inverness in June. I'll be buying you a ticket."

"Last concert didn't go so well," Angus murmured. But Clive had disappeared. Angus followed, dropping the envelope in the pile on his desk.

Scotland, 1315

"Home again, home again, jiggity jog." Shawn cocked a grin at Niall.

As he and Lachlan had neared camp, he'd given up, crashed into the wood, pretending surprise at seeing his friend again, and slipped away from Lachlan on pretext of nature calling, long enough to sneak around the clearing, calling for Niall in a harsh whisper, before the two of them might be seen together.

"'Tis not God's will," Niall sighed, as Shawn wiggled back into Brother Andrew's robes. "Yet. 'Tis sorry I am." Clouds slid across the face of the moon, and the first raindrops began to fall.

CHAPTER THIRTY-NINE

Bannockburn, Present

Questioning the villeins clogging Inverness's streets yielded results: the girl, Amy, lived in Bannockburn. She'd been *on the telly,* hadn't she now, and sure she wasn't married to any copper in Inverness. *That musician* had been her boyfriend. Brian's cash had long since disappeared, but it was easy enough to take money from others in lonely alleys. Simon used a handful of bills to buy passage to Stirling on a snaking, metal wagon called a train. The walk to Bannockburn gave him time to ponder. Bannockburn had been a small place. It may have grown, as had Stirling, but certainly it was small enough still that people would know Amy. An unwed woman with a baby? Scandalous!

An hour later, he hadn't escaped the houses and roads of Stirling, yet signs said he was in Bannockburn. He stared doubtfully at the endless spread of houses. It had grown more than he'd anticipated.

Still, the child had to go. Long hair wasn't so common in this time, he'd noticed, and she was still a trollop with a child. People would be eager to gossip and point her out. He approached a woman pushing a cot on wheels, containing a screaming child. "Excuse me." He used his most genteel manner. "I seek Amy."

The woman stopped the cot inches past him and turned back. "Amy? I dinna ken any Amy." The child screeched, and she moved on.

"Amy," he expanded to a short, round woman. Gray frizzles jumped from her head like an old crone who had hacked off her long strands. "She's so tall," he held up his hand, "long, black hair, and a child." The woman gave him a look that, in his own time, would have gotten her head lobbed off, and moved on without answering.

"She's unwed and has a child," he told the wench he saw next—a girl with raven hair, a scandalously short skirt of leather, and black boots to her knees.

"Oh, gawd!" The girl rolled her eyes. "Unwed and has a kid! How *awwwful!*" Something bulbous and pink erupted from her mouth in a large, opaque bubble. He stared in horror as it grew. The protrusion burst with a snap. She sucked it back into her mouth and laughed. "Gawd, not like ye'd catch *me* bein' unwed and havin' a kid, now!"

"How impertinent!" he snapped.

She guffawed, as coarse as a peasant woman, and strode away, calling over her shoulder, "Yeah, I been called worse. Good luck with your Amy, Love!"

His hand snapped to his side, seeking his sword. There was nothing there.

A young man bumped into him and strode by, not asking pardon or even noticing he'd bumped into a knight, a lord! Simon's anger bubbled. But killing them in the light of day would not help his mission.

He found a market. Two loud urchins, with bobbing black curls and matching red coats skipped in front of the place. One of them arched her hands over her head and did a jig of some sort, something rustic and uncouth. He scowled at them. They giggled and danced to the side, barely jumping out of his path. *Vile Scots!* Maybe he could get back *before* the battle and make that fool Edward *listen,* and wipe out this accursed race! Certainly, when he held the throne, he would see it done right. Destroy them before they produced such ill-gotten likes as those on the street!

Inside the store, equally rustic, uncouth women picked food off shelves, loading small metal carts with boxes, bottles, and vegetables. They chatted and called to one another and laughed. "Who's in command here?" he demanded of one red-cheeked woman.

"In command?" She seemed dumbfounded by his question.

"To *whom* might I *speak*?" His irritation grew.

She gave a *harrumph!* and strode from the store without answering, calling, "Girls, come along now!"

"Sir, might I help you?" A lass leaned over a counter.

She didn't look in charge of her own petticoats, much less this market. But there was no one else. "Amy," he barked. "She lives here. Where would I find her?"

"Ex*cuse* me, Sir? Amy? Could you be more specific? She lives *where*? Nobody *lives* at the market."

"Bannockburn." He let his displeasure show. It was usually enough to put fear into fools.

She only looked blank. "There are many Amys in Bannockburn, Sir. Do you not have a surname?"

"Long black hair, a child. She plays violin. Why would she have a surname?" She was a menial sort.

A discordant pair of giggles erupted at the doorway. He spun, glaring at the street vermin with black curls. They covered their mouths with their hands in identical motions, and dashed away.

"I'm sorry, sir," the girl replied. "I don't know any Amy." She glanced at a woman waiting with one of the metal carts, and tapped the side of her head.

Simon's anger boiled. Though he'd never seen the gesture, the look on her face spoke clearly. She would pay.

Ayr, 1315

The streets of Ayr rang with the whine of the whetstone sharpening blades and the shout of the butcher to his boys. Bruce's soldiers pushed through servants racing to bring flour from the mill. The hammering of metal rang out as the smith repaired weapons and shields.

Niall pushed through the crowd, hefting a keg on his shoulder, and leading four of his men, bearing similar loads, to the docks. Dozens of ships waited there, sleek and low in the harbor, to carry Bruce's men to battle against Lame John. They bobbed on the water, Angus Og's pennants flapping at prow and stern. They sailed in three days. Niall sped his steps, racing against the image of Alexander's face, and determined to carry the cask onboard this time. It was only a ship, after all, wooden planks beneath his feet. He wouldn't even be touching water. As the dock raced up on him, his heart sped. His palms became cold.

"You!" His fingers closed on a lad's collar. "Take this, while I talk to your father about the bannocks." He shifted the barrel to the boy's shoulder, and turned, chiding himself. Next time, he assured himself. He *would* carry the next barrel onto the ship. He had three days. He had time.

He stalked back into town, retrieved another keg, and carried it to the ship. Shawn appeared at his side, Brother Andrew's gray hood shielding his face. He leaned close, in the way they'd developed, and murmured, "How are you going to get on that ship when it sails, if you can't even get on when it's beached?"

"I'll walk on," Niall snapped.

"Uh-huh. You're whiter than the sail even now." Shawn let his disbelief cudgel the air. "Try thinking about Scotland instead of your damned pride, and either let me help you, or let me go in your place."

Niall stared grimly at the bustle aboard the bobbing ship, men in tunics and leggings running, the ship master shouting, sailors swinging from masts high above the deck.

"Lots of people have phobias," Shawn said softly, to his stiff shoulder. "No big deal."

Niall's hand tightened on the keg on his shoulder. "I've no problem."

"Show me," Shawn said. "Get on."

Niall turned, staring into the depths of the gray hood. Their eyes locked with a clash of wills. And Niall turned back to the low-slung galley, bobbing in the water. Its sail rippled in the coastal breeze. He snapped at Lachlan, just coming off the ship, "Get this one, too, Lachlan! Brother Andrew, we've work to do." He stalked off the dock.

Bannockburn, Present

After the elderly Mr. MacPherson tottered out the door with his purchase,

Colleen counted the money in the cash drawer, and locked it away for the night. She made a quick call to a friend down in Glasgow before heading out into the narrow lane behind the store. It had gotten late enough that even in this northerly latitude, the first stars shone against dimming sky in the narrow band above the store and its neighboring house.

"Would you like to tell me now where Amy is?"

She jumped, her heart thumping, at the low voice, and spun.

The man from earlier stood so near her, she could feel his breath on her cheek, his eyes burning in the dark.

The man was mad! "Go on wi' you! I don't know any Amy." She tried to squeeze past him, but he moved, blocking her. Her breath became still. Her fear grew. She pushed suddenly, harder, and in an instant, her arm was wrenched behind her back, a hand clapped over her mouth. "Nobody defies the Lord of Claverock," he hissed in her ear.

Ayr, 1315

Waking from his rest, Shawn glanced out the window. But nearing Midsummer day, sunlight brightened the sky almost around the clock. It might be morning or evening. Regardless, it was time to become Niall. Rising, he helped himself to ale, bread, and cheese from the table, and donned Brother Andrew's robes. Amy drifted through his mind. He should have crossed back. He should even now be holding his son. And he should be thinking of some way to get Niall on those boats. But Niall continued to refuse all help, insisting he would simply walk on when the time came.

There was little time for worry. Brother Andrew had acquired the task of bringing meals to Bruce and his commanders. Shawn collected a basket of food and a jug of wine from the kitchen of his lodging, and hurried out, down a narrow lane running behind the town's shoulder-to-shoulder half-timbered houses. A clothesline flapping with linen shifts, and a chicken yard later, Bruce's voice floated from the back window of his lodgings in a tavern. "Douglas must know," he rumbled. Irritation spiked his voice. Shawn stopped, listening. "Who can we spare?"

Angus Og spoke, energy exploding through the open window, unconcerned for who might hear. "We've few enough men as it is, your Grace! There's no one!"

"Douglas must know, ere he finds himself surrounded," Bruce insisted. "A younger man, a boy? Someone from the town?"

"We need someone we can trust," Angus Og replied. "It must be one of our own."

"Exactly who we cannot spare with this latest word of Lame John's army. And, they're gathering fast. We must leave sooner than planned."

Shawn slipped between two houses, to the front of the tavern, breathing thanks. Fate had handed him the opportunity. Inside, luck was once again on his side. The tavern was empty. He ducked behind the counter, hid the food, and tore Brother Andrew's robes over his head. A moment later, he entered Bruce's war room.

"The Bard of Bannockburn!" Bruce hailed him. "I was expecting your monk. Join us."

"Your Grace, I've no time," Shawn returned. "There's a great deal to be done." Worse yet, he expected Niall himself any minute.

Angus Og chuckled. "Rumor said you'd no sea legs, Campbell. Yet I've seen you on and off my ships as if born to them."

Shawn cocked a smile. He'd spent his childhood on Minnesota's lakes. A galley at dock hardly tested his abilities. "Rumors are funny things, My Lord," he said. "You see the truth before you, no?"

Angus Og chuckled again. "You do seem comfortable on them, not the green-gilled fish I'd heard of."

"I was on my way to find Brother Andrew, seeing as he's late with your meal," Shawn said, and with a quick breath, jumped into more dangerous territory. "I couldn't help but hear you through the window. If you've need of a messenger, Brother Andrew is your man. We can spare a monk from battle, can we not? He's to be trusted as well as I." He resisted the urge from elementary days to cross his fingers behind his back, desperately hoping Niall himself did not show up, or overhear voices through windows as fortuitously as he himself had.

Bruce and Angus looked at each other, considering.

Shawn held still, wishing they'd get on with it before Niall turned up. The sun had crept lower, casting grayer shadows outside than it had on his way in.

Bruce stroked his beard. "Not a bad idea," he mused. "What say you, Angus?"

Shawn's toe itched to tap out a staccato demand for speed. Footsteps fell outside the window, and only the need to verify it wasn't Niall kept his eyes open, rather than staring at the heavens behind closed lids. The baker passed by the window in the lane outside. Shawn let out a slow breath.

"He's an odd one, Brother Andrew," Angus replied.

"But very trustworthy," Shawn said. "And fast. He'll deliver the message quicker than...quick. He's your man."

"He's under a vow of silence, is he not?" asked Bruce.

"He's never been good at that," Shawn said.

"So I've heard," Angus said. "The man is forever leaning in, whispering to you, when he should be silent."

"It's why we had to extend the vow to two years," Shawn said. "However, it means he'll not hesitate to give Douglas the message, even if he must speak."

They chuckled and nodded. More footsteps sounded in the narrow alley behind the window.

Shawn's palms erupted in sweat. Niall would kill him if he found out. "My

Lords." He spoke softly, in a rush, desperate not to be overheard. "Truly he is perfect for the job."

"I believe you are right," Bruce said. "Inform him."

Shawn's brain shimmied up a wall, searching for an excuse not to do the telling. "My Lord, I am due at the docks. As you know the mission yourself, you can explain it better than I, and send him on his way 'ere the sun sinks lower. Douglas must get this message!"

Bruce considered, leaving Shawn to fret another few eternal seconds, before nodding. "Aye, he'll be along anon. I'll tell him."

Another quick tread of footsteps sounded outside the window. Shawn gave the quickest respectful bow he could manage, and tried not to look as if he were running from a king's presence. He snatched the robe from behind the counter, thankful the innkeeper was still away, and raced for the alley, tugging the robe over his head as he ran. Still blinded, his arms flailing in the sleeves, he slammed into someone and stumbled back against the stone wall.

He yanked the robe down, struggling to keep his face hidden. It would be impossible to explain Niall Campbell trying to pull on a monk's robe while running down an alley.

"I did hear your luck is legendary," growled an angry voice.

Shawn dropped a heavy breath of relief, and edged back the hood. "Niall," he hissed. "Thank God it's you. This damn alley is Grand Central! Change, fast!"

"What is Grand...?"

"Sh! They can hear through the window." As quickly as he'd pulled the robes on, Shawn tugged them off again, shoving them at Niall. "There was a problem." Talk fast, give them no time to think. Lies were his forte. "Almost caught." By the time Niall had a chance to think it through, he'd be on the road to Douglas. Even now, the monk's robe was sliding over his head. "Bruce's food is behind the counter in the tavern. Brother Andrew is late. Hurry and they might only chop off half your head. They're pissed. What is Niall doing?" He put his hand on Niall's shoulder, turning him, keep him moving, keep talking, give him no time to think!

"Bringing ale on board."

"I'm off. Get the food to Bruce and get a good night's sleep." He strode down the alley, trying to mind the dignity of the name Sir Niall Campbell, while escaping any chance of Niall asking questions, or the wrong Brother Andrew being sent to Douglas. All was silent behind him. As the alley opened to the harbor, he dared look back. Niall had rounded his own corner, gone to meet an unexpected twist in his life.

Bannockburn, Present

"You're sure nothing else came?" Amy rifled through the mail a second time. In the front room, James slept peacefully on his blanket. She stooped to kiss him, and headed to the kitchen.

"That's all there was." Carol turned from the sink, up to her elbows in hot soapy water. "What are you waiting for?"

"The prophecy. I asked the monks for the original Gaelic. It's been two weeks." Amy picked up a drying cloth. She circled it around and around the bottom of a plate.

"They had the right address?"

"I think so." Amy slid the plate into the cupboard. The memory hit her. Angus had signed the guest book.

"Shawn's been gone nearly a year." Carol stared into the deep suds. "A seven hundred year old prophecy isn't going to change that. Angus is here and now. Have you heard from him?"

"No." Amy dried the next plate more roughly than necessary, slid it into the cupboard, and gathered carrots, knife, and cutting board, her back to Carol to hide her tightening lips.

"Call him," Carol advised. "What can it hurt?"

"It can hurt *him*." Amy slashed the knife up and down, slicing the carrots into a cascading row of coins so uniform even Shawn would have approved. She wondered if he missed cooking. He'd loved his kitchen.

"It's not the carrot's fault," Carol said with humor as soft as the April mist outside the window.

Amy paused, the knife resting on the cutting board. In the front room, James chuckled. Amy glanced up, imagining him gripping his rabbit's ear or reaching for one of Hamish's books. Shawn was missing it all. And the only chance she knew of getting him lay with the translation, which, if it was anywhere outside of the monastery, must be with Angus.

"I can't...." She stopped. She couldn't tell Shawn's mother she couldn't do that. She wasn't even sure what Carol knew or thought of the prophecy, regarding Shawn. Her jaw tightened, hating the secrets and evasions; hating the headache that grew with trying to keep track of who knew or believed what. She wondered again how Shawn had lived that way. But he was as type A as they came. She suspected he'd thrived on the challenge and viewed it as a thrilling game, trusting his famed luck never to get caught.

Carol touched her hand.

She let out her breath.

"Just ask him," Carol advised. "Then ask him how he is. Invite him down."

"Okay." Amy laid the knife down, and wiped her hands on the kitchen towel. She headed down the narrow hall to the front room. James looked up as she entered, and squealed happily. She sank to the floor, rubbing his back. He laid his head on his blanket. Her stomach knotted itself, torn between finding Shawn—James's father, Carol's son, someone she had loved—and hurting Angus.

She took out her phone, considering possible words. Maybe she'd get his voicemail; but then she'd have to call again. That would be even worse. With a sigh, she hit *Call*. Her stomach curled into a tight coil as it rang. It was wrong to drag him back into this. It was wrong to abandon Shawn. It was wrong to leave James fatherless if she had any choice. She stroked his downy hair. He turned his head, looking up to her with a sleepy smile. He let out a soft sigh as his eyelids fluttered into sleep.

"Hello."

She jumped at the sound of Angus's voice on the phone. Under her hand, James, too, startled. "Angus...." Her words came out on a quick breath. The memory of him rubbing her hands in St. Oran's chapel came back to her, like a cat rubbing against her leg. She smiled. "How are you?"

"Grand. What did you want?"

Her smile slipped. She wanted more than the prophecy. She wanted to fix all that was broken. His abruptness told her he wanted none of it. She cleared her throat. "I sent to the Monks of Monadhliath for the original Gaelic prophecy."

He didn't answer.

"I just need to know if they sent it to you by accident," she said hastily. "I'm sorry, Angus. I wouldn't have bothered you. I mean, I wanted to, but I didn't know what to say. I hoped, at least having a reason to call, it didn't have to be just about...."

"Something was put on my desk," he interrupted. "I'll forward it."

"Thank you. But I hoped...."

"I'll put it in the post," he said. His voice softened. "I'm sorry, Amy. I wish I were a better man." The phone clicked in her ear.

She dropped the phone to her lap, hating herself for hurting Angus again, and relieved the prophecy would be on its way. She lifted the phone, and typed a text.

Ayr, 1315

Niall entered the tavern, head bowed, and found the basket and jug stashed behind the counter. "That yours?" the innkeeper asked.

Niall gave a silent nod, collecting it, and carried it, monk-like, to the Bruce's room.

"The not-so-silent Brother Andrew!" Angus Og's voice burst through the doorway. "We'd thought to go looking for our dinner."

Niall bowed silently, and set the food on the table, his head low.

"We've a mission for you, Brother Andrew." Bruce reached for a hunk of cheese. "You know where to find Jamie Douglas?"

Niall nodded. His heart picked up a quick beat. James Douglas was speeding through Jedburgh forest on his way to another series of lightning strikes against the English. With a fast horse, he could find him and be back on time to sail.

Bruce sliced off a piece of cheese with his dirk. "I'm given to understand you're more than willing to break your vow of silence when necessary."

Niall kept quiet, though he fumed at Shawn's callous disregard for the gravity of a monkish vow. He gave a nod—a silent nod.

In the narrow field of vision left by the hood, Bruce's hand tapped a scroll on the desk, then pushed it toward him. "Deliver this to Sir James. The English are heading north to meet him. He must be warned. Understand?"

Niall nodded, accepting the scroll.

"Make haste, good brother. God go with you." Angus Og slapped Niall on the back, and Niall faded away, out the door, for his own garron in the stables. There would be no rest for him tonight.

In the stables, with a blanket tucked under the saddle and food stowed in his sporran, Niall thought of Shawn. There was no way to get word to him of this development. It occurred to Niall, slipping the bridle over the pony's head, that a leisurely return to Ayr would spare him boarding those ships. He beat away the thought, ashamed. It crept back, whispering in sultry tones. *You could say there was trouble; bandits.* It would be easy. He scratched the pony behind the ears. It nuzzled him, hoping for an apple. "I'd not do that to Shawn," he murmured. "'Twould be wrong."

Of course, he thought, there was the problem of Shawn keeping his face hidden the whole time, trying to row and fight without the hood slipping. So maybe 'Brother Andrew' *would* have trouble on the way. He'd get back, switch places with Shawn unseen, and order Shawn into hiding till the men returned, because this wasn't Shawn's fight. Hiking his robes, Niall mounted the animal, and gave it a smart kick, driving it hard for the eastern hills. The sun streaked the western clouds pink and orange, and turned the western isles to small black humps in the sunset-painted sea behind him. He'd ride hard and be back on time to switch places with Shawn and sail for Jura.

Inverness, Present

Angus reached for the envelope, with the curling letters reminiscent of a long-ago time.

"Don't be a fool." From his desk, Clive regarded him. "Tell her you're sorry."

"I haven't done anything," Angus objected.

Clive snorted. "Except walk away when she needs you."

"She only called for her post."

"If you'd sent it immediately, she'd not have had to call."

Angus's phone beeped. He glanced at the flashing text icon.

"Bet that's her." Clive jotted a note on his report. "Think she gave you a piece of her mind for cutting her off?"

Angus's mouth tightened. Worse, he thought, she might be sending her pain. He didn't want to hurt her, but he wasn't satisfied with being second, and second, no less, to a selfish, self-centered, irresponsible git. He stared at the envelope from Monadhliath. Shawn didn't deserve it. And he feared for James's safety.

"Would you ever look at the damn text," Clive demanded. "If you don't, I will, and I'll use more appropriate language than she has to tell you what she thinks!" He reached across the gap between their desks.

Angus snatched the phone away. "Why didn't your mother leave you off at an orphanage," he snapped.

"Somewhere in China so I wouldn't have to put up with you?" He opened her text. *You're a better man than you think you are. I miss hearing about your day.* His stomach knotted. He missed hearing about her day, too. *I'm sorry. Love, Amy.*

He bowed his head, a hand over his eyes.

"She chew you out?" Clive asked.

"No." He lowered his hand, wrote *forward* and her address on the creamy envelope.

"She should have."

Angus handed the envelope to Clive. "Put that in the post before I change my mind."

CHAPTER FORTY

Ayr, 1315

"All aboard!" Shawn shouted. The din around him rivaled a packed stadium shouting for a winning team. The sound of swords clanging, shaking in the air, and men bellowing for Lame John's head threatened to lift Shawn off his feet, to float him over the cool mist writhing on the surface of the sea. He glanced uneasily to the eastern hills, stained with sunrise. But Niall would be long gone, much too far away to hear the clamoring.

Men filed past him in the narrow longship, stowing gear under their seats, like medieval crowds thronging onto an airplane. Angus Og's black device snapped from the highest mast. Shawn took his oar. Twenty men shoved around him, grabbing oars. "Let's get this show on the road!" he shouted.

Lachlan looked at him with furrowed eyebrows. Shawn laughed, thrilled to be in a boat again—a longship, no less, hardly his father's canoe—ready to sail for open water, and a stiff salty wind blowing his hair.

"It's an expression," he told Lachlan. "It means let's move." He laughed with joy. He should be furious with Lachlan for thwarting his return home. But Lachlan's concern for Niall touched the heart he would once have proudly sworn he didn't possess.

"Aye!" Lachlan grinned, taking the seat beside Shawn, and gripping the thick handle of the oar.

Ronan, with his stringy, red beard, sat on the bench in front of them with Taran's father.

"Owen," Shawn bellowed. "Take the drum. Give us a beat."

Owen picked up a massive cudgel, while the ship master jumped aboard, hollering for order. Mist drifted across the water, sparkling pink and orange with the rising sun. Shawn hoped Niall was loving his pony ride half as much as he was loving being on water. He hoped Niall wouldn't be too angry. He hoped he'd survive Jura in few enough pieces to still care.

"At your oars," the ship master bellowed. The tide pulled the galley from the dock. Its prow swung, and soon it was gliding to sea. The ship master called out again. "We follow Angus Og to open waters, but then we sail north." He paused, looking from one man to the next, before shouting, "Between West and

East Loch Tarbert, we drag the galleys overland!"

A hush fell over the boat; then a commotion exploded. Men laughed, *hoo-ahing*, waving fists in the air, and chanting, "Bruce, Bruce, Bruce!"

Shawn turned to Lachlan as they tugged their oar. "It's different, dragging a boat overland, but they seem a little overawed."

At the front of the galley, Owen pounded the drum. The heavy thud reverberated in Shawn's chest. Lachlan's eyes widened; his arms flexed, dragging the oar.

Ronan turned on his seat. "You don't mind Magnus Barefoot?"

"Uh, no." Shawn touched his head, the constant excuse he and Niall used for anything they should know but didn't. "That old cow raid injury, you know. I know men from seven hundred years in my own past better than I know Magnus Barefoot."

"Magnus was king." Lachlan spoke in staccato bursts, to the crisp beat of Owen's drum. Salt wind rushed past Shawn's face, cooling the sweat on his arms. "Of Norway." Owen's cudgel pulsed. "Two hundred years ago." Thirty men heaved oars in time.

"Magnus Barefoot sounds older...." Shawn stopped, remembering two hundred years ago was the 1100's, not the 1800's. Men sang to the beat of the drum.

"He invaded Scotland." Lachlan grunted as they yanked their oar.

"Par for the course around here." The wind rose, whipping Shawn's hair in his face. Owen picked up the beat.

"King Malcolm offered him," Lachlan continued. "All the islands. Off the west coast. Navigable by ship."

The singing quickened. Sweat dripped down Owen's face, as he pounded and sang with the men.

"Mind, now," Lachlan continued. "Kintyre is part. Of the mainland. Magnus sailed. Up the east coast. As we're doing. Into East Tarbert. Then sat at its helm. While his men. And the wind. Sailed it over land. To West Tarbert."

"Great story." Shawn heaved on the oar. Spray kicked into his face, hot in the rising sun. The galley skimmed the water, as a burst of wind billowed the sails overhead. "But why do they care?"

"You're forgotten much," Taran's father said sadly.

Sweat beaded Lachlan's jaw. "Islemen believe. When their invader does the same. They've no chance. When they hear the Bruce. Has come overland. They'll not even fight."

Shawn smiled, both at the superstition and at his significantly increased chances of survival against men who didn't fight. But he couldn't resist asking, "They really believe that?"

"Aye."

They fell silent, their energy consumed by rowing. A new thought occurred to Shawn. If he was killed in battle, if men saw Niall Campbell die, what would become of Niall, who would then have a hard time explaining his own existence? He sighed, and pushed the thought from his mind—it was too much —in favor of memories of Amy, standing in the monastery, holding their son. A flash of blue caught his eye. Christina's kerchief had slipped from his sleeve.

Lachlan glanced down and grinned. "Sure an I'm smiling, too, thinking of my own bonny wife waiting at home for me!"

Bannockburn, Present

"Did ye hear, did ye hear, Miss Amy!" Sinead bounced into Amy's front room, her hair a mass of black curls. Her fingers flew to the latches of her violin case. "Colleen at the market, she's disappeared! She's not been to work or come home for two days! Her mum's desperate!"

"Colleen?" Amy tightened the screw on her bow. The creamy envelope, with *The Monks of Monadhliath* in the upper corner and Angus's scrawl across the right half, had arrived as Colin walked up the path two hours ago. Amy had itched, through his lesson, and through Ella's chatter about her new puppy, and Ben's worry about his audition for university, to rip it open. She set her mind firmly on Sinead's concern. "Did she go visit a friend maybe, and forget to tell anyone?"

"Maybe." Sinead's bow flashed up and down. The d minor melodic scale flew out, the notes skipping in the air around them. Sinead grinned at Amy and, without stopping, danced into the accompanying thirds exercise. She finished with a flourish of a blues riff, and dropped the violin to her side. "I took that off Shawn's album. Do ye like it, Miss Amy?"

Pain shot through Amy's heart as Shawn's mischief and joy both shone through Sinead's eyes. She was his kindred spirit, though cloaked in innocence. Amy wondered what Shawn would come back as—if he got back. The pain flitted away, replaced by peace in feeling his joy for a moment. She smiled. "I like it very much, and he would, too. He had a lot of fun playing music."

"Do ye think he's dead?"

Amy's smile disappeared. "No." But there were many ways to die in medieval Scotland. He may have fought at Jura or in Ireland. He may have died either place. She chose her belief and spoke resolutely. "No, I don't think so."

"So where is he?"

"Sorting things out." He was with Niall. He was okay. She glanced at the envelope, shining in the sunlight slanting through the lace curtains.

"Do ye think Colleen is dead?" The light left Sinead's eyes.

Amy touched her shoulder. "Two days is too soon to worry."

"There was a man talking to her." Sinead's violin dropped to her side. "He was mad she didn't know who you were."

"What?" Amy tilted her head.

"He was at the market askin' after you. He had black hair."

"Simon?" Amy asked, more of herself than Sinead.

"I don't know, Miss," Sinead said. "He wanted to know where to find ye."

"Well, why didn't you tell him?"

"Because he was rude. Who is he, Miss?"

"He went to Monadhliath with me and Angus." Amy frowned. "He's a historian."

"He looks like a fighter. I can see him easy, carrying all that heavy medieval armor and weapons. Did you see how thick his arms are?"

"No." Amy shook her head abruptly. "We should get to your lesson."

Sinead's smile flashed out. "I should play slower and listen to the tone."

Amy returned her smile. "Now why didn't I think of that?"

Sinead grinned, lifting her violin. A long, slow note, warm with vibrato, filled the room.

An hour later, bundled in her Aran sweater against the evening breeze, Sinead headed down Amy's walk, swinging her black case. Amy raced back to the front room, and tore into the envelope. Minutes later, half a dozen Gaelic language sites revealed her new problem. "Of course," she muttered. "I should have known."

Ayr, 1315

Niall guided his pony over the last ridge and looked down, over a vast orchard bursting with fresh June leaves, onto Ayr. Mist hung in its streets and hovered around its stone walls. He pushed the cowl back, studying the scene. Something was wrong. It was too still—no bustle of men, only a lone boy running between the bakery and tavern, the lowing of a cow and the lusty call of a rooster.

He'd ridden hard. But the journey to find Douglas, deep in Ettrick Forest, and back, had left him time to think. Something about Shawn running breathlessly down the lane, fumbling into the robe, hadn't sat right. It had been on the way home with the message safely delivered, that he'd put the pieces together. Shawn had been out of the robe. Shawn had been in the tavern with Bruce's food. And Shawn had been in an awful hurry. He had become more sure, as his pony climbed yet another hill, that Shawn had known Bruce's intention. But it would serve no purpose, as *Brother Andrew* would return on time to sail.

He lifted his eyes to the harbor beyond the town. Waves swept up onto the shore, unhindered by Angus Og's fleet. Niall's fingers tightened on the reins. Remembering the frantic look on Shawn's face, he understood. Shawn had known they were leaving early. The pony skittered under him, irritated by his tension. Niall's jaw tightened, his eyes narrowed.

Bannockburn, Present

"Helen, it's me, Amy."

"'Tis grand to hear from you!" Helen exclaimed. "How was Monadhliath? That Simon, now, he's a character, is he not!"

"Definitely." In the evening sun slanting through her office window, Amy smiled, grateful to have reached Helen this late. "I got the prophecy in the original Gaelic."

"Did you now! That's grand! Did you need help translating it? I can find you Gaelic speakers."

Amy could imagine Helen clapping her hands in glee. She smiled, even as she stressed, "It's the *original* Gaelic."

"The original?" There was a half measure of silence, before Helen said, "Oh! Medieval. Or...earlier?"

"Exactly," Amy said. "Do you know anyone who could help me?"

"Well, now," Helen replied, "there are only so many who read medieval Gaelic fluently."

Amy held her breath, waiting.

"Ian MacNutty, he's away on sabbatical," Helen mused. "And Charles Fraser is in hospital. A stroke, I believe. He's lost some memory. But Mark Sutherland, yes—I'll try him and have him ring you, all right, Love?"

"Yes, that's great," Amy said. They said their good-byes. She closed the lid on her lap top and rose, touching the maps and time lines on the walls. Maybe Mark Sutherland would bring the happy ending to all of this. She thought ahead to the coming days. She had to finish the arrangement with Rob, send it to Conrad, and practice for the upcoming album.

She wanted to scour the internet, in an attempt to translate it herself. But the monks didn't even know when the crucifix had been made—*sometime after Columbkille's death, I would say*, Brother Eamonn had remarked mildly, betraying no clue as to whether he intended the comment as a joke. They knew even less when the prophecies and blessings had been written. The language could be as old as the sixth century, or as new as the thirteenth. She had no idea if a man fluent in medieval Gaelic would be able to read the Gaelic of seven centuries earlier. But she was certain she couldn't. She turned off the light and headed for bed.

Jura, 1315

The ring of axes on trees echoed through the pre-dawn forest. Bruce stormed through mist shouting instructions. Shawn worked at the far end of the glen, swinging an ax while the night, which had never turned black, lightened to gray. The smell of sweat and pine filled the air. Blisters rose on his palms. They had rowed through the night, up Kilbrannan Sound between Arran and

Kintyre. Sweat trickled down his back under leather armor. He suffered in silence as they felled trees throughout the morning, bringing down tall, straight pines and skimming off their limbs, till they had a ship's length of rollers lined up on the shore.

"Haul it up!" Bruce shouted. A cheer rose, despite a day and night's hard work. Men flung ropes down from the first galley, snaking out and down into eager hands. Dozens of men grabbed them. Their bodies shone with sweat, their muscles strained against the ship's weight. Shawn stomped with twenty others, knee-deep in cold waters swirling through his breeks, pushing the ship. It jarred onto the first log, ground onto the second, scraped land, and lifted onto the rollers. Men cheered, hauled, pushed, pulled, shouted encouragement in a battle against fatigue. They all knew the belief of the Islemen.

A stiff breeze ripped across the narrow isthmus. "Now we sail!" cried Bruce. Lachlan scrambled up a rope ladder, up the sides of the galley streaming with sea water, onto the deck, and unfurled the sail. The wind caught it. Once again, men cheered, as the wind lightened their load, pulling the galley for them. With a dozen tonsured monks, Shawn grabbed one end of a great felled pine, as the stern of the ship rolled off. They hoisted it, and raced ahead, sliding it back under the prow. Over and over, with muscles screaming for rest, they stumbled and ran with massive trunks, while the men before them hauled their ropes like beasts of burden, grunting and shouting in the pine forest. Shawn longed to tear off his leather, let some air at his sweating body. But nobody could see his back, bare of the scars they knew Niall to have. The monks remained robed. If they could do it, so could he.

Finally, the first men hit the icy water of West Loch Tarbert. More piled in, heaving at the ropes, till the boat slid off its rollers, skimming into glassy dawn waters. Pink mist curled up around the ship's sides. A ragged cry of victory rose.

With a tight time limit to meet Angus Og, sailing northward into the Sound of Jura, they jogged, twenty men carrying each roller, a mile back across the narrow stretch of land, for the next ship.

By evening, Bruce's fleet floated proudly in West Loch Tarbert. Bruce pushed on. "The Lord of the Isles is waiting on the other side. We've no time." They stumbled in exhaustion back into the galleys, plucked up their oars, and rowed to Owen's drumbeat, to meet the Islemen and John of Lorn.

Aberdeen, Present

Amy found herself barely breathing as Professor Sutherland scanned the prophecy. It had taken a week of phone tag, and another week of schedules that didn't mesh, before he could meet. She'd tried to be content with the routine of lessons, and time with James and Carol, but she couldn't resist several fruitless forays onto the internet, and into a book store, searching for anything that might help her read ancient Gaelic. Her attempts only left her more frustrated. She found no evidence that it said anything other than what the monks had told her it said.

She sent a text every third or fourth day to Angus, telling him she was thinking of him, and hoped he was well. He didn't answer. She supposed it was her penance, making a fool of herself, but she hoped it mattered to him, knowing she thought of him.

Professor Sutherland looked up. His face was young and smooth, with a touch of five-o-clock shadow on his jaw. "It's quite old." He frowned. "I don't wish to lead you wrong, as 'tis clearly quite important to you. There are words and constructions with which I'm not familiar. No, I'd prefer you take this to a specialist in ancient languages."

"What do you *think* it says?" Amy asked.

He gave his head a sharp shake. "I've no wish to give you bad information." He reached for his phone, punched a few buttons, and scratched at a note card, glancing from his phone to the paper. He pushed it over. "Professor Jamieson is our top expert in medieval Gaelic."

The Sound of Jura, 1315

John Lorn and his men gave battle, even if the Islemen didn't. It should have been a swashbuckling tale Shawn would tell his grandchildren—whatever century they happened to be born in—of Angus Og's and Bruce's fleets closing like jaws on either side of Lame John's; ships crashing together and rocking apart, leaving gaps to open sea, through which several men plunged; of salt water spraying high, men shouting, swarming onto enemy ships, of seagulls screeching and wheeling, of heat and weapons clanging, arrows flying, maces whirling over heads, crossbows, a trumpet calling orders over the fray, the screams of the injured, the smell of blood, and the sad cry of the gods as the skies drizzled over it all.

It wasn't swashbuckling adventure.

It was pain and death. It was madness.

It was necessary.

As dusk fell, as the sounds of battle faded, as John of Lorn was disarmed and clapped in irons at the prow of Angus Og's ship, as the cry of victory spread among Bruce's men, from ship to ship, across the sound, Shawn slammed his sword into its sheath and turned, accounting for his—Niall's—men in the gathering gloom. One, two, ten, fifteen. He found Ronan, and some of his fear fell away. He found Owen. He counted twenty-six.

But Lachlan—he searched, his fear leaping back, growing, as he ran across the rain- and blood-slicked deck, rocking on the sea, from stern to prow, shouting, "Lachlan," calling to his men, "Where's Lachlan?" until he heard the cry from Owen, and slipped and slid to where the man knelt in rain and blood, cradling his friend's head in his lap. Owen looked up to his chief; tears streamed down his dirty, bloodied face.

"No!" Shawn dropped to his knees in a pool of blood. He shook his head, denying. "No." Despite drizzle crying from the sky, sweat trickled down Lachlan's pale face.

Shawn raised his head, bellowing at the god he didn't believe in, somewhere high in those dark clouds that blotted out the stars. *"No!"* He swore. *"Give him back!"* A hand, clammy with sweat and blood, slipped into his. He lowered his gaze to Lachlan, grasping his hand.

Lachlan clutched his stomach, panting in short gasps, as he clung to Shawn. "Niall, Margaret is with child. See my bairn is cared for."

Ronan slid to his knees on the wet deck, with a water skin. Owen stroked his friend's forehead. "Ye'll be home to care for them yerself." He took the skin and lifted Lachlan's head, easing water into his mouth. Then he lifted his own head, shouting, "The relics!"

Shawn tried to keep his eyes off the jagged gash, oozing with ruby blood, showing pink flashes of organs. When Lachlan closed his eyes, Shawn hissed at Owen, "Don't give him false hope. Nobody could survive this!"

"Whisht," snapped Owen. "Ye survived worse. D' ye think miracles are only for ye?"

"There was no miracle," Shawn argued. "They sewed me up. I told them to wash first."

Owen soothed a damp edge of his shirt over Lachlan's glistening forehead. A boy ran with a gold box. A monk hustled behind, dropped to his knees and gripped the crucifix on his neck. His eyes closed; his lips moved in silent prayer.

"Yer injury was far worse than this," Owen said.

"That can't be," Shawn protested.

"Have ye not seen yer own scar, man?" Owen demanded. "From side to side? They say half your insides were spilling out."

"Impossible." Shawn stared, mesmerized despite the bile in his throat, at Lachlan's intestines, at blood welling inside. Even modern medicine couldn't save him.

The monk murmured; his hand sketched a sign of the cross over Lachlan.

"Pray for another miracle, Niall," Owen whispered.

Shawn swallowed. He didn't believe in miracles. And without one, this man would die.

Rain drizzled in sympathy.

Edinburgh, Present

With Professor Jamieson's busy schedule of classes, research, and speaking engagements, it had once again taken time to get a meeting. Now he sat like a great, grizzled bear behind an incongruously small desk, clear but for a brass pen holder and green ink blotter with a single yellow sticky note tucked under one triangular corner. Framed sheepskins adorned the walls. There were no family pictures. Nothing that might make a man smile. And he didn't. He glared at the prophecy, while Amy waited in a hard, straight-backed chair.

"Is this a joke?" Professor Jamieson's voice boomed in the small room, jolting Amy from her thoughts. His white eyebrows, like foaming white crests on a stormy ocean, crashed dangerously close to the bridge of his nose.

Amy drew back. "Of course not! What does it say?"

He scoffed, pushing it across the desk toward her. "'Tis nonsense. Either you're having me on, or someone's messing with you."

"I've read the English translation...." Amy tried.

Professor Jamieson waved one meaty hand in dismissal. "Whatever you read, I can assure you 'twas wrong."

"You can't just tell me what you see there, however ridiculous?" Amy asked.

"I'm a busy man." He rose to his full height, rounded the desk, and gestured toward the door. "I've no time for games."

CHAPTER FORTY-ONE

Ayr, 1315

"Brother Andrew returned but hours after ye left," the daughter of the house informed Shawn, when he arrived back in Ayr. "He's been quiet this past week, Milord."

"About time." Shawn swung his cloak off, shaking rainwater from it. The thought of a warm, dry bed was heaven. "He's had a wee problem with his vow of silence." He grinned. "Got something to break our fast?" His father would have had fun talking like that. The girl dimpled and blushed. All sorts of good feelings rushed Shawn's head.

But as he headed down the narrow hall to the back room, clutching a basket of bread and cheese in one arm, he twisted Christina's kerchief into a tight cord between nervous fingers. He forced himself to unwrap it and tuck it back in his sleeve, staring at the scarred wooden door. Niall would be mad. In fact, mad wouldn't begin to describe what Niall would be. Well, too bad. The stubborn fool couldn't see beyond his own nose. He'd have been worse than no use on a sea voyage, certainly no good to the cause of Scotland he claimed to champion. And there was nothing he could do about it now. Shawn straightened his spine, put on the smile that always got him off the hook with Conrad, and threw open the door.

Bannockburn, Present

"Why, is it not Amy?"

Leaving the market, Amy spun at the deep voice, the impossible-to-name accent. "Simon!" She gripped her groceries tighter. *He was rude,* Sinead had said. The man before her smiled as warmly as the May breeze brushing her shoulder. *Did ye see how thick his arms are?* She glanced at his arms, revealed by a blue t-shirt. They were taut with muscle—like Niall's.

"I hoped to meet you." He pulled his hand from his pocket.

Amy stepped back, her heart hammering.

But he held out his hand, smiling. "I got this for your lovely son." A small white rabbit sat in his palm.

Amy shifted a bag of apples to her left hand to accept it.

But Simon drew his hand back. "What am I thinking? Your hands are full. Let me help you carry those home."

Colleen had not yet returned to the shop. "I'm not going home," she said. "They're...for a friend."

"I'll help you, and then we could have tea at your home and talk about Niall Campbell."

"I'm sorry," she said. "I have...errands...after that." Sinead's words flickered across her mind. *I can see him easy, Miss, carrying all that heavy medieval armor and weapons.* He'd been at ease with the ancient documents at Monadhliath. She *did* want to talk to him. "We could meet tomorrow," she said hastily. "There's a coffee shop." She pointed down the street. "I have something to show you. Eleven?" She backed up a step, fearful he would follow her home.

He nodded. "Eleven. Can I not help?"

She shook her head, and turned, hurrying down the street, past rows of attached houses, in gray, brown, and sandstone stucco, each with a little garden and wrought iron fence. She looked back. He stood outside the store, watching. Abruptly, he began walking after her. She veered into the roundabout, and turned onto Whins Road. Ina had a friend here. But she couldn't remember which house. Her mind wrapped around James as tightly as her arms wrapped around the groceries, as if the force of her thoughts could protect him from all she imagined Simon to be. His offering was ridiculously inappropriate for a baby—something a medieval knight might choose after seeing James with his rabbit.

Amy's heart pounded. Her arms ached with the weight of the groceries. She glanced over her shoulder. Simon was nowhere to be seen. She ducked into the only yard that had a shed, and edged behind it. Her thoughts swung the other direction. Picking poorly for a child was hardly proof he'd shot through a time portal. Probably most historians had no idea what to give a child.

You imagine things, her mother had always said, with a cheerful, dismissive laugh. *Why would you think such a thing?* Shawn had asked, pain in his eyes that she could doubt him. She leaned her head against the shed, waiting, trying to silence her breathing, and praying.

Ayr, 1315

Niall was not Conrad. He bolted off the bed, and seeing who it was, threw the hood back, revealing a face as dark as Jura's blood-washed seas.

"Hey, you missed the boat." Shawn laughed, dropping the basket on the table. He flung his cloak onto a hook. "Get it, missed the boat? That was some trip. Sorry you...."

Niall's fist rammed into his jaw with a thud that sent him stumbling against the wall. Shawn gripped his jaw, pushing himself to his feet, and swung his fists up.

"Don't ever try that again," Niall roared.

"Thank you would have been more appropriate," Shawn roared back. "What the hell did you think you were going to do? Have a sudden miracle cure?"

Niall swung again. Shawn blocked, and aimed for Niall's stomach.

Niall grabbed his arm, wrenching it behind his back. "'Twas not your decision to make."

"I did not make that decision." Shawn grunted, doubling over under the pressure on his arm. "Bruce did."

Niall shoved him, releasing his arm. Shawn stumbled, caught himself on the table, and whirled, fists up.

But Niall seemed satisfied. "At your suggestion," he said. "And you made sure I'd be the Brother Andrew who turned up."

"It was time to switch." Shawn glared at Niall, massaging his aching arm. "Luck of the draw. You got the message to Douglas, and everyone now thinks you're a master on water to boot. What harm is done?"

Niall's eyes narrowed.

"What?" Shawn demanded. "All for Scotland, right? I served Scotland, you served Scotland, all's well. Why are you glaring like that?"

"How did you know I was sent to Douglas?"

"Well, I—where else would Bruce send someone?"

"You warned me of the window. I've been wondering why you'd go into the tavern as Niall when you were supposed to be Brother Andrew. You heard them and offered Brother Andrew's services, did you not?"

"Dumb luck," Shawn insisted.

"Why did you hide the food behind the bar?"

"I told you, an emergency, someone nearly caught me. I had to get out."

"I'm not Amy. Save your lies." The storm clouds on Niall's face did not relent. But his fists fell.

"What else could I have done?" Shawn demanded. "You clearly weren't going on those ships." But he lowered his voice. "They're going to wonder why Niall and Brother Andrew are shouting at each other." He rubbed his jaw. "And now we'll have to explain how Niall has a bruise appearing and disappearing every few hours."

Niall glowered. "No. You'll be Brother Andrew till it goes away."

Shawn shrugged. "Less work for me. How are you going to explain that you can't do twenty-hour days anymore?"

Niall shook his head in irritation. "I'll work like an ordinary man for a few days. 'Twas a long journey and a hard battle."

"Not really," Shawn said. "All our men saw I was energetic and in good spirits leaving the galleys just now. Despite the infernal rain."

"You're impertinent and rude," Niall snapped.

"And I earned you knighthood and made you look like Superman and Paul Bunyan rolled into one. Have it your way. Means I get some vacay." He rubbed his jaw again, giving his own dirty look. "I hope you haven't upset any of the Laird's plans by bruising up one of his Nialls."

Niall grunted, thumping himself into a chair at the table with the bread and cheese. He didn't offer any to Shawn. "It'll be gone before we get back. Tell me what happened."

Shawn helped himself to cheese. "Let's start with Lachlan."

Bannockburn, Present

"James is okay?" Amy tried to speak lightly, as she burst through the front door, juggling groceries. But panic heightened her voice.

"He's fine." Turning from the stove, Carol's eyebrows furrowed in concern as Amy brought in milk, apples and bread. "What's wrong?"

"Nothing." Amy set the canvas bags on the table. "Just checking."

"You were gone a long time. I was getting worried."

"I ran into Simon." Amy put away the milk. "He hasn't, um, been here, has he?"

"The man who went to Monadhliath with you?" The crease in Carol's forehead deepened. "No. Why?"

Amy shrugged. She'd waited for forty minutes behind the shed, fearful of Simon lurking around the corner, waiting her out. She'd considered calling someone. But Angus was two hours away and didn't want to talk to her. Carol had James and would lead Simon directly to their door. Rob would wrinkle his forehead and worry about her mental health. And what would she tell any of them? *He offered to carry my groceries?* Besides, if Simon were indeed lying in wait, speaking into the phone would bring him to her hiding place. Finally, admonishing herself she couldn't hide behind a shed for the rest of her life, she'd crept out cautiously, to an empty street, and feelings of utter foolishness.

Upstairs, James squealed.

Amy rushed up the stairs. In his crib, James lifted his head, pushing his chest up on sturdy arms. He blinked large, liquid eyes, and gave a toothless grin. Eamonn, she reminded herself, had promised he would be with her for many years to come. She picked him up, pressing her cheek to his soft, black hair. It didn't matter if she was wrong about Simon. He had no reason to be near her son or know where she lived, even if his intentions were as pure as an angel's thoughts. She would drive to their meeting tomorrow, and see if he could help with the translation. But he would stay away from James, no matter who he was.

Tioram, 1315

Niall's company rested at Castle Tioram with Christina MacRuari. Pleasant as Shawn found it, playing Niall that evening, listening to stories in the great hall, watching jugglers and acrobats, playing harp—pleasant as it was wandering the gardens that night—it was still life on the road, with no one, not Amy, not Christina, to make it home.

He longed for his bed at Glenmirril, as he roamed Tioram's rain-dampened courtyard, robed as Brother Andrew. He remembered clearly what it would look like in seven hundred years, broken down and lonely on its wind-swept coast. He remembered every detail of the night he would spend here with Amy, exactly where he would sing to her by the picnic basket. The stars would dance overhead on a clear night just as they did tonight. He remembered painfully, the text message to the writer in New York. Debra? Jo? It soured his heart, knowing he'd hurt Amy, broken her trust and love, for a woman whose name he couldn't even remember.

He touched the gray stones of the courtyard wall. Fresh ivy clung to it, drops of rain shining like diamonds on each leaf, not the dead vines that would shroud dry crumbled walls centuries from now. Laughter drifted from the sparkling new great hall, ladies and knights laughing at the jester's antics. The smell of roasting venison drifted out.

Amy felt like a dream slipping from his grasp. His son, James, felt like a whisper on the wind, a rumor he could only hope was true. He climbed to the ramparts, following the same path over newly cut stairs with sharp edges, that he and Amy would clamber up, one day, over broken chunks of stone and sprouts of trees pushing through the dirt in between. He stared out at the starlit sky, contemplating miracles—who got them, who didn't, his own aversion to believing in them.

"Your songs have become sad of late." Niall appeared beside him, leaning his arms on the wall. They gazed over the dark spill of water, pushing in and out, fjord-like, along Scotland's rocky coast, trailing past Tioram's island and wandering further inland.

"My life has become sad of late." Shawn didn't turn.

"As will everyone's, for a season."

"Spare me the lecture. At least you're heading home to Allene."

"Only long enough to deliver Lachlan." He, too, stared across the inlet. "At least you're alive."

Shawn snorted.

Bannockburn, Present

Amy parked two blocks beyond the coffee shop. It would be obvious, if he followed her for that far. Simon waited in the shop. Two coffees sat on the table

—the same table where she'd sat last summer with Angus. He seemed innocent; an injured man with a memory problem, just as he claimed; benevolent, even, with his boyish cheeks.

"You didn't bring your son." He smiled. "How disappointing."

Amy's nerves danced. She took her seat, searching his eyes. They were pleasant, bereft of any guile. "His grandmother took him to England," she said.

"A shame." He didn't seem overly concerned. "They'll be back soon?"

She shook her head. "Next month."

"I bought you one." He gestured at the coffee. "What was it you wished to show me?"

Her nerves settled somewhat at his lack of concern over James's supposed absence. She reached into her purse for the sheet she'd copied that morning. She was paranoid, she admitted, but she didn't want him to snatch her only copy and leave her with nothing. "The prophecy in its original Gaelic."

"Which would be from the 1300s or earlier," Simon said.

Amy nodded. "You seem well-acquainted with medieval languages. I hoped you could read it."

Simon took it brusquely. His smile disappeared. Amy watched him. Many people became serious when their work absorbed them. The same change always came over Shawn when he put pencil to score paper. Her mind flickered to Colleen, still missing. It didn't mean she was dead, and even less that Simon had anything to do with it.

Simon raised his eyes. The hard jaw softened into a smile. The clear blue eyes lightened and soft wrinkles appeared at the corners. "I'm afraid either our dear Monks have pulled a cruel jest on a fair lady, or they've been played for fools themselves."

Amy leaned forward. "What does it say?"

Simon took a long, slow sip of his coffee. He wiped his lips with the back of his hand. "It's naught to do with the crucifix." He leaned back, quoting, "In days of yore comes a great king who leads his people on a white horse." He smiled, lifting a hand in apology. "It seems you made the trip for nothing."

Amy pulled the sheet over, scanning it. Angus had taught her the words *eich* and its medieval ancestor, *ech.* Neither was there. She raised her eyes, keeping her face blank. "Which word means horse?"

He pointed. His finger landed on *mac.*

Amy stared at the word—*son.* She cleared her throat, pulled the paper from under his finger, and folded it. "How disappointing." She was a lousy actress, she thought irritably. She slid the prophecy into her purse, wondering why he'd lie. But if he was going to, she judged it best to let him think he'd fooled her. "I've wasted your time." She tried to look disappointed.

"I'm sorry I couldn't help." He smiled blandly, and she suspected he, too, was a poor actor.

"Thanks, anyway." She swung her purse over her shoulder, and reached to shake hands.

He clasped her hand with both of his. "Surely you're not going so quickly?"

"I have things to do." She pulled her hand free.

"Let me walk you. A lady surely should not walk alone?"

"Nowadays we do. Very different from 1314." She swore he started.

Then he smiled. "Certainly. Still, such fair company. May I bide with you a ways?"

Her heart fluttered. He'd done as she'd predicted. And who used the word bide? She swallowed. "I'd love that, but I drove. My house is ten miles away."

"I thought you lived in Bannockburn."

She laughed as she took her keys from her purse. "Who told you that?"

He followed her down the street, chatting amiably in the late May sunshine. At her car, he suddenly snapped his fingers. "Perhaps you could give me a ride! I'm going that way!"

"To Glasgow?" Amy named a town at random.

"Yes."

Her fingers trembled on her keys, threatening to drop them. She clicked the fob. "I'm sorry, I'm going to Edinburgh." She opened the door hastily, slipped in, and clicked the lock.

He knocked on the window. He was no longer smiling.

With shaking fingers, she pushed the key in the ignition, and turned it. *Drive on the left, stay on the left,* she reminded herself frantically, desperately afraid of making a mistake in her agitation, and pulled away with Simon calling out in the road behind her.

CHAPTER FORTY-TWO

Glenmirril, 1315

Astride his pony, staring down at Glenmirril, joy returned to Shawn, a slowly-blooming summer dawn, a warm glow at odds with the gray clouds overhead. Christina waited. He felt her kerchief snug inside his sleeve. He sighed, hating his divided heart. But he was lonely. And the memory of her warm smile reached over the stern parapets, drawing him.

Niall clapped his robed shoulder. They snapped their reins, a sharp crack, and followed the men down the wooded slope. Banners snapped on the walls. Trumpets sounded. With groaning chains, the drawbridge inched away from the gate house walls. Shawn dreaded the next hour, when three women would learn they were widows, and the rest learned their men were leaving again almost immediately for Bruce's siege at Carlisle.

The clouds slid apart, curtains opening on blue sky. The drawbridge inched away from the gatehouse arch, showing a crescent of light. He anticipated Christina's smile, her arms, his hands in her thick black hair as he held her close, the pleasure on her face at seeing him back. She *would* be pleased, wouldn't she? They'd been gone more than two months. The countryside burst with life, crops reaching for the sky, lambs and calves, bluebells carpeting the hills, squirrels and fox peering from foliage and darting away.

What if Christina had been married off again?

He chided himself. Iona wasn't going anywhere. They would plan ahead, and next June, he'd go. He had no business hurting Christina, no business holding up her life. And he'd vowed to be faithful to Amy.

The drawbridge thumped to the lip of the moat. Trumpets blared. Men clattered across the bridge, hooves clopping, harnesses creaking. Women shouted in the bailey. MacDonald appeared, raised a hand, parting the crowd and sending them back against the walls as men flowed in, splashing through puddles in the courtyard. Women and children strained on tiptoe, searching faces. Allene waited beside her father, pale, serene, her hands on her very-pregnant belly.

Shawn watched, feeling her fear, wanting to reassure her, but Niall sent his men ahead to their families. "Do you always think of the people first?" Shawn murmured. The men must not hear Brother Andrew break his vow of silence.

"Always." Niall's eyes rested on Allene. "She understands our place is to serve."

Shawn stared straight ahead. Allene and Niall wore the finest clothes, slept in the finest beds, ate at the head table. He had never considered what they gave in return. Niall went first into battle while the smith stayed home safe. Niall traveled to Stirling in all weather, invaded Creagsmalan, and risked his enemy's anger, and Allene waited in fear, with a smile on her face as she carried food to the poor, returning to a lonely bed while the steward and his wife slept together each night.

The first keening of a lone woman skirled up from the courtyard, thin and cold in July's heat. Shawn closed his eyes. His heart pounded in rhythm with her pain. A second voice rose, wailing with the first. Then there came a cry of joy as a woman found her husband, alive and strong. Shawn swallowed, thinking of Lachlan. It couldn't have happened.

More horses clattered across the bridge, two of them dragging a man's pallet. Shawn scanned the courtyard, seeking Christina. He found her, comforting one of the keening woman, while Allene, heavy with pregnancy, lowered herself awkwardly beside the injured man, wiping his face. She glanced up the hill, and returned to her work, as the man's wife fell on her knees beside him. Niall watched Allene's every move.

Ronan hugged the widow Muirne, her children clamoring around, hugging his scrawny waist.

A third wailing voice rose in the summer heat, clashing in a distinct tri-tone with the others. The hair rose on Shawn's arms. Everywhere, women flew to their returning husbands; children danced around their father's knees, clinging to their hands, or were scooped up to be hugged tight against leather armor muddy from the road.

The horses immediately before Shawn and Niall now whickered, and moved forward.

"Margaret is waiting, Lachlan." Niall grinned at the man at his side. "She'll not be too hard on St. Columba for sending you back, aye?"

Lachlan laughed, though the action made him grimace in pain. "Perhaps she'll accept her fate and not bribe another saint to do the job right this time." His face was pale. He sat his pony poorly. But he rode into Glenmirril on his own.

"There goes the miracle you don't believe in, Brother Andrew," Niall said softly. A smile played around the edges of his voice. Not waiting for an answer, he clucked to his mount, and headed down the hill.

Shawn followed, dismounting in the courtyard on time to help Lachlan down from his garron, into Margaret's arms. He turned, tugging his hood tight as the crowd pushed on every side. The shrieks of the newly widowed pierced his ears. Pipes wailed, drums beat. His eyes fell on Christina, scooping up a crying child, pressing the girl's head against her shoulder, swaying to and fro, her own face in anguish as the child cried. She lifted her eyes, staring into the depths of his hood. He inclined his head slightly, acknowledging her, and, dropped to his knees in the damp earth beside one of the injured men. Many people needed care.

Edinburgh, Present

Amy and Rob waited at the Edinburgh airport. "It feels like yesterday we were getting off this same plane," she said. The day stood out in her memory. Shawn had burst into the airport with loud cracks, throwing his arm around her, shouting witticisms to fans gathered at the gate, kissing her till she pushed him away, cheeks flaming. She wondered what he was doing now, if he was at Glenmirril, maybe dining in the great hall with Allene. And she wished Angus would acknowledge any of her texts, the last one telling him she was meeting the orchestra.

"Did you ever imagine, that day, that life would change so much," Rob asked. "I feel like a different person." He looped his arm around her shoulder.

She looked up to his pink-tinged cheeks, and white-blonde hair. He'd made no critical comments about Angus, asked no questions. He hadn't been to her house in a week. "You are," she said. "Me, too."

A commotion erupted at the end of a hall. People stirred. "He's coming," a woman whispered. A gaggle of girls jumped up, peering past security. "Zach Taylor! Zach!"

Rob and Amy looked at each other, restraining laughter. "He's actually a very down to earth guy," Rob said. "He's got a wife and two kids. A quiet house in the suburbs."

The orchestra appeared, a mass of jeans and sweatshirts. Dana strained on tiptoes, her auburn curls framing her face. She waved frantically, yelling, "Amy! Amy!" and pushing through the crowd. They hugged tightly. She turned to Rob, grasping his hand. "Any word about Shawn?"

A group of brass players appeared, greeting Amy enthusiastically. "I've missed you!" Jim enveloped her in a bear hug. His white mustache tickled her cheek, making her laugh. Celine with her blond hair shimmering down her back, Aaron, Peter, all the people she'd been close to for three years, pressed in, asking questions, demanding pictures of James, hugging her, till tears poured down her cheeks.

An ear-splitting squeal erupted from the group of girls.

"Zach!" Rob lifted his hand high. His face lit up. A tall man with clean-cut dark blond hair, strode down the hall looking like a boy out of school. He held a young woman's hand; each of them carried a tow-headed girl on one hip, smiling good-naturedly at the screaming girls.

"Rob, how are you?" Zach asked.

Rob pulled Amy forward, introducing her. Zach shook her hand, introducing his wife. "Kristin, and my daughters, Emma and Sophie. I'm so sorry about what happened."

Kristin clutched her hand. "I've looked forward to meeting you."

Amy smiled, feeling the warmth, and thinking how different it could have been with Shawn.

Glenmirril, 1315

"The Feast of St. Columba comes every June, no?" Hugh's voice bounced off the walls of the Bat Cave.

Shawn, Niall, and Hugh turned as one to MacDonald. He knelt under the crucifix, staring into dozens of dancing flames below it for a time, before saying, "Why one Feast of St. Columba is better than another, I'd not know. You'll try again next June."

Relief leapt in Shawn's heart. But Niall spoke cautiously. "But why would Amy take the child to Iona on Columba's feast? What is obvious now was not when I read it. We must return and leave a clearer message."

"Whatever you saw there in my time is what's there," Shawn said. "But I didn't carve anything about Iona at all."

"So did someone after you carve it?" asked Niall. "Is it an uncanny coincidence, or must we go do it? But if we did—do—we'd certainly do it right, aye? Why would we leave a message so hard to decipher?"

"Why not go back to the abbey and leave it where we know Amy will be?"

"But we also know I'll go to Hugh's camp and give her the message," Niall said.

"And though we know she'll go to the abbey," Hugh pointed out, "it doesn't mean she'll find what you left."

Shawn fingered the long polished frame of the harp. "So we do both."

MacDonald sighed. "I don't know your world, but here, we've much to do. D' you not understand what I'm sacrificing already, giving Niall time to go with you?"

"I'll go by myself," Shawn said.

"You don't know the way. The rock or the abbey. You may stop at one or the other on your way home from Carlisle. Choose." He pushed himself up from the kneeler with a grunt, and headed for the door. When he opened it, Christina stood with a torch in one hand, the other raised to knock. He and Hugh left, while Christina, her eyes lowered, entered. The sweet scents of heather and fresh rain floated in with her, and Shawn suspected she'd been making rounds to the poor again. Niall drifted to MacDonald's workbench, picking out tunes on the harp.

Given the closest thing to privacy they'd get in 1315, Christina sat beside Shawn on a bench under the shadow of the crucifix. For a time, they said nothing. Her hands lay in her lap. His stayed clenched between his knees, his head bowed. "I'm sorry," she finally said.

"Really?" He quirked a corner of his mouth. "You seemed sorry to see me leave. Aren't you glad I'm back?"

"I'm sorry you're disappointed. I'm sorry you're hurting. Know you so little of love?"

He lifted his eyes to the crucifix. It really belonged in a church, he thought. Such a masterpiece should not be hidden away in a cave. Strains of an air from *Sir Tristrem* floated from Niall's harp. "You tried to convince me there are miracles," Shawn said. "I saw one."

"Did you?"

"You saw Lachlan ride in. He should have been dead." He described for her the battle, the injury.

"Do you believe now?"

He shrugged. "No." It had eaten him from the moment he'd watched the mortal wound heal before his eyes, from the moment he saw Lachlan regain color and struggle to his feet. It had eaten him as Lachlan rode beside him—grimacing and pale, yes, but a man who should have been dead, left behind and buried with his fallen comrades. "I saw it. I know what it means. But I can't believe in my heart."

"Why not?" she asked.

He frowned, trying to answer the question for himself if not for her. The sound of the harp drifted over them. "If I believe in miracles," he finally said, "if I believe what I saw, then I have to face that God didn't see fit to give a miracle to my father, who was good. If anyone deserved one, ever, it was him."

"Miracles aren't about who deserves one, but who needs one."

"He needed one to save his life."

"'Tis not merely our lives God wishes to save."

Shawn turned to her, puzzling. "What else is there besides our lives?"

"He wishes to save *our souls* that we might spend eternity with Him."

Shawn's forehead puckered. He stared at his hands clenched between his knees. "I just can't understand." He stared at Christ on the cross. For the first time since his father's murder, he *wanted* to understand.

Inverness, Present

Simon hadn't found where Amy lived. People were talking about the missing wench. Only yesterday, he'd heard two women, gossiping like fishwives on a street corner, describing the stranger—him—who had been at the market the day she disappeared.

His anger mounted with each failure. He couldn't stay in Bannockburn. But, he reminded himself, he'd gotten the important information. He knew when and where the switch would happen. *St. Columba's Chamber.* The old Laird had been ridiculously proud of the saint having, centuries past, spent a night in his castle.

He had only to get the crucifix. If he had to break down walls to reach the old monk, he would. He once again boarded the snake-like wagon. He stretched his legs as it slithered north to Inverness, his eyes closed, plotting a way to reach the monk, should he still be guarded by The List.

"He's been discharged," the girl at the desk told him.

"Where might I find him?" Simon leaned close, giving his most winning smile. She was young and fair, not the shrew from the last time, and her blouse hung low enough to make his smile quite genuine. He might come back for her.

She smiled back, showing deep dimples. "That's confidential, sir."

"I'd so like to bring him a gift." Simon let his eyes meet hers with longing.

She glanced down. A small giggle came from her lips. "I'm not supposed to."

"He used to visit me when I was a child and bring me such lovely prayer books," Simon sighed. "I hate to think he's alone, wondering why I don't come now, in his time of trouble."

"You're so kind," she said in a breathless rush. Her fingers flew over the keyboard. She stretched toward him, her breath tickling his ear, and whispered the name of the place.

He smiled, let his fingers graze the back of her hand, and thanked her. "It means the world to me, and to him." He turned to go. The lass from last time, the shrew with the prim little eyepieces, rounded a corner. She stopped, staring hard at him, her mouth in a firm line of disapproval. He smiled, and headed out the door to kill Eamonn.

Carlisle, England, 1315

July passed with downpours, thunderstorms, drizzles, mist, sprinkles, sun showers, and every other sort of rain the weather gods could think up. It passed with brutal medieval weapons, the boredom of a siege against Carlisle, and the less boring, far less pleasant, screams of men pierced by arrows from Carlisle's archers. But at least, thought Shawn, this time Niall was at his side, someone who now and again called him by his real name.

Fast on the heels of a hard ride to join Bruce, Shawn, dressed as Niall and leading Ronan, Owen, Conal, and Hugh, raided the Bishop of Durham's manor at Bearpark with James Douglas. His father's ghost, though not yet conceived, grappled with his conscience. Raiding bishops wasn't done in polite society, not even by such as Shawn Kleiner. When he saw the bishop's gold rings and chains and heavy gold plate and tapestries and expensive rugs spill into the bags of James Douglas's men, his guilt eased. The bishop had not convinced Edward of the immorality of attacking Scotland, of slaughtering women and children at Berwick. Perhaps his gold, funneled into Bruce's war machine, would.

Other days, Shawn covered his hair with a coif, shielded his face in Brother

Andrew's hood, and spent hours felling trees in the drizzle, and crafting them into the belfries and sows with which Bruce would assault Carlisle. On those days, Niall sacked Hartlepool with Douglas.

By night, one or the other of them played harp by the campfire, while men thrust chunks of English beef, sizzling, and dripping juices, over the flames. Rain dripped off the trees above as they sang of ancient victories and heroes. The harmonies of the harp reverberated in Shawn's fingers and through his body, healing him from the exertions and bloodshed and screams of the wounded that each day brought.

By the light of the fire, after the rest had fallen asleep, Hugh, Niall, and Shawn remained. Through the chirrup and hum and symphony of the night insects, came a messenger from Glenmirril, touching Niall on the shoulder. He turned, laying down his harp, and accepted the missive wrapped in oilcloth. His eyes turned to Shawn's, deep in the monk's hood, and to Hugh's. Niall hesitated, his fingers touching the seal.

"You'll change naught by not looking," Hugh said.

Shawn looked at him blankly, not understanding.

"In your time," Hugh explained, "you await good news of a new bairn. We await news." He cleared his throat and started into the fire. "We'd not expected it so soon."

"Oh." Shawn's heart felt, for a moment, trapped in a fist, unable to beat. Allene, with her vivid red hair, her quick words, and happy laugh, Allene who had stabbed him, and curled into the safety of his arms while soldiers stomped overhead looking for them, who had danced with him at their wedding, flown to Niall in joy, knelt with difficulty at the side of injured men—he'd never even stopped to consider that she might not survive childbirth. *Everybody* survived childbirth.

He raised a hand, heavy as his heart, to Niall's shoulder. He wanted to say, *She's fine!* But he knew Hugh was right. Niall ripped at the seal abruptly, and held the parchment near the fire's weak light. The moments dragged on, before his shoulders suddenly slumped, his head bowed.

"No...." Shawn whispered.

Hugh touched his shoulder. "Niall? Not Allene?"

A shudder racked Niall's shoulders. He drew a huge breath, and whispered, "I have a son. She's alive." He lifted his face. In the firelight, tears of gratitude streaked down his face. "I couldn't have borne to lose her. Thank God."

CHAPTER FORTY-THREE

Carlisle, 1315

In the moonlight, after everyone drifted to sleep, Niall lay awake thinking of Allene and his new son, smiling up into the stars. He was blessed. As the fire died to embers, he heard a rustle among the men. Turning, he saw Shawn creep away. He rose silently, following. He wasn't surprised to find himself in a tangle of trees edging the River Caldew. On the shore, Shawn stripped off his shirt and breeks, and in his baggy braies, waded into the water.

The trees rustled. Hugh lowered himself to the ground beside Niall. "Will we watch that no English snipers get him?" he whispered.

Niall laughed. "He still doesn't understand our time, does he?"

Hugh chuckled. "'Tis one reason I believe your story, lad. No one born to our life would be so careless."

They watched Shawn scrub himself before diving in, and slicing through the water to the center of the river. Niall watched his arms stroke, memorized the curve of the elbow, the angle of the wrist, felt the rhythm of the arms swinging one over the other in his own muscles, though he didn't move.

"Go on," Hugh said. "Ask him to teach you."

Niall gave a short laugh. "I will." He rose, went to the shore and, pulling off his boots, put his feet in. Alexander's face reared up, the hair streaming as his head hung back in death over his father's arm. Sickness rose in Niall's throat. The shaking started in his legs. He closed his eyes. *Harps. Allene on the shore.* Alexander's face pushed through. The water curled around his ankles like moldering burial shrouds. He fought the desire to snatch his feet away. *Harps, Allene.* His fingers curled as if about harp strings, picking out *Blue Bells* as he'd played it that night in Inverness with an orchestra at his back. His breathing slowed. He let his mind drift to the motion of Shawn's arms, up and over his head. *Knees straight, point your toes.* He felt it in his own muscles.

"It's not so bad, is it?"

Shawn's voice jolted him. The water was warm for just a heartbeat, before it twined like entangling seaweed again. He jerked his foot out, backed up to the shore, and made himself laugh. "Very pleasant till an English archer shoots you. You'd best come out now."

"Yeah, I'd best." Shawn shook his head, flinging water. "Nothing feels better than a midnight swim. Come in and I'll teach you. Sing in the water, remember?"

"Another time." With a guilty glance at Hugh, Niall slipped away through the woodland.

♫

Through the rest of the siege, Niall ignored Shawn's nightly swims, and Shawn said no more to him. For ten days at the end of July, Shawn and Niall took turns assaulting Carlisle's gates with Bruce and Douglas. Rain hammered down as steady as the stones and arrows hurling over the city walls. On dry nights, they tried to mine under, but rain filled every tunnel. Shawn emerged from his efforts beside Taran's father smeared in thick mud, shivering in his soaking tunic and trews.

They dragged the new belfry, towering higher than the city walls, dozens of men hauling thick ropes that slipped through their hands in the drizzle. Other men protected them with shields raised against the arrows, darts, spears, and rocks flying in a steady barrage over the wall. But the wheels stuck in mire; the tower refused to budge. Conal, straining on the rope just ahead of Shawn, dropped suddenly to his knees in the mud, with a piercing scream. Shawn shouted, grabbed him by the shoulders, and stumbled under his weight, hauling him beyond range of arrows, dreading the feel of one lodging in his own back at any moment.

Niall, in Brother Andrew's robe, darted forward, shouting, "Conal!" Shawn hissed a warning at him, and he fell silent as they carried the groaning man, gripping the arrow in his side. Rain slicked their faces and plastered Conal's hair to his forehead. Hugh shoved through the soldiers, taking up his share of the burden. Mud streaked his face and leather armor and caked his beard. "He'll be aw' right," he told Shawn.

"All right, are you mad?" Shawn looked at him in horror. "He's got an arrow sticking out of his side."

"Nothing vital," Hugh said. "He'll live."

"Don't forget to wash it!" Shawn's voice came out sharply, driven by rising fear, for himself, for the men, for the women waiting at home, for Amy maybe, by some miracle, waiting for him in the twenty-first century.

They spent the next day filling the moat—with hay and corn that had rotted in the wet weather, with any debris they could find. Everything sank into the swirling dark waters. They floated a bridge of logs over the moat. It sank, while Harclay's men lobbed stones and arrows from above. One grazed Taran's father's leg, tearing open a bloody gash. He gritted his teeth, squeezed his one eye shut in pain, and made no sound.

They attacked one gate with vigor while Douglas led a surprise group to another, throwing up ladders. More Scots died. Some were captured.

After ten days, with many dead and wounded, Bruce called off the siege. They retreated, leaving their war engines, leaving captured Scottish knights in the hands of Carlisle's governor, Andrew de Harclay.

"So much for leave no man behind," Shawn hissed, as he and Niall pounded north with their men. Another downpour, rolling steadily on the green and gold leaves overhead, guaranteed the men would not hear him. "In my time, the Marines leave no man behind! We *left* them!" The depth of his anger surprised him.

"What would you have us do?" Niall demanded. Men turned in shock, to see him snapping at a monk. He looked up with irritation at the gray skies drenching him, shook water off his overhanging hood, and lowered his voice. "How many good men did we lose already, and never got close to getting in? Would you have us lose another hundred or thousand, for naught?"

"They'll kill them!" Shawn said.

"They're knights," Niall replied. "They'll be ransomed."

"We hope." Shawn shivered in his robes, wet, miserable, and angry.

"I thank God there are no new widows at Glenmirril," Niall murmured.

"Plenty of them elsewhere in Scotland after the last ten days." Shawn's mind drifted to Amy, left alone.

Hugh reigned up beside them. "We're near the camp. Go now, do the job and catch up."

Inverness, Present

She had just enough time before the concert to stop at the station. The girl at the desk looked up. "Oh!" she said, with a small intake of breath. "You're wanting Angus?"

Amy nodded, wondering how the girl knew, and why she looked so upset.

She lifted her phone. "Inspector, your Amy's here to see you." She nodded, said, "Yes," and hung up. "He says go on back."

Amy trailed slowly down the hall, feeling the secretary's eyes on her back. She had a thing for Angus, Amy was sure of it. She wondered if he returned those feelings. Had he really moved on that quickly? Despondency settled on her shoulders. She knocked tentatively at the door at the end of the hall.

It swung open. "Grand to see you, Amy!" Clive said. "Angus, it seems I've a coffee run to make."

"Aye, just what you were thinking when you pulled up your reports just now." Angus didn't look up from the papers scattered across his desk. One big hand clamped down on a sheet while he pressed a pen to it, so hard Amy thought he'd break the tip.

"'Tis indeed!" Clive agreed heartily. He pulled the door behind himself, shutting her in the small office with Angus. It wasn't big enough for the nerves shooting between them. His pen dropped to the desk. He stared at the papers.

She reached a hand toward his shoulder; pulled it back.

Silence prickled the air.

"What do you want?" He stared forcefully at his papers.

"I think I upset....what's her name...at the desk."

The tendons in his neck stretched taut. "Claire." The word was as terse as an A string strained to a D.

"So...um...." She shifted the envelope from one hand to the other. She had no business saying the cutting things she wanted to say. *I see I'm easily replaced.* He'd seen she still had feelings for Shawn. *Even James meant so little to you?* "I...um...yeah. I guess it's a good thing we didn't get married, if she gets upset about me just being here."

His head snapped up.

Amy's head dropped. She stared at the envelope, crisp and white against her black skirt. "I'm sorry." The words came out low and husky. "I had no business saying that."

He said nothing.

She cleared her throat. "Is she your girlfriend or something?"

"No."

When he didn't elaborate, she said, hopefully, "I have a solo tonight."

He stared at his bulletin board.

"I chose it and arranged it," she tried. "You might like it. I could get you tickets. For you and Clive, Mairi, Hamish...."

"Why did you come?" he interrupted.

"Because I miss you!" she erupted. "All those texts meant nothing?"

He looked pointedly to the envelope in her hand.

She sighed, holding it out. "I need your help."

He glanced at it, and back at her.

"I know it's wrong to ask you," she said. "And I *do* miss you."

He said nothing.

"A professor of medieval languages said it's a joke and wouldn't help me. Simon read it and lied to me."

"Lied?" Angus cocked his head.

"He said it was about a king on a horse. There's no *eich* or *ech* there. When I asked him to show me the word *horse,* he pointed to *mac.*"

"What makes you think I can do anything with it?" Angus asked.

Amy shrugged. "You know people. You know the language. I haven't said a word about this to you in two months. But I have no one else."

He straightened the papers on his desk.

"He's still James's father," Amy whispered. "And Carol's son." When Angus didn't answer, she laid the envelope on the desk. "I'm sorry for bothering you. I *did* want to see you, too. For yourself. Good luck...with Claire."

She reached for the door.

His voice stopped her. "Who was the professor?"

She turned, studying his face. It was blank. "Professor Jamieson. He looks like a bear who just packed on the weight and crawled into his cave for winter hibernation."

His lips tightened. She wasn't sure if he was annoyed, or trying not to smile.

"Uh...he's not your best friend from school or something, is he?"

Angus smiled. "No."

"Okay." She hesitated, but he said nothing more. "I'm sorry for bothering you. I'm sorry for...everything." When he still didn't answer, she left, back down the long narrow hall, with Claire at the desk trying to look as if she wasn't watching, though she glanced up, and ducked her head again repeatedly, steady as a metronome.

Amy walked to the theater, deciding what to do next—or if there was anything she *could* do. Shawn might not even be alive. He might find his own way back, as Niall had. But if she couldn't translate the thing, she was stuck.

Highlands, 1315

With Hugh leading the men north, Shawn and Niall veered east. "It makes no sense we'd leave half a message," Shawn insisted.

"So does someone else carve it later?"

"That can't be," Shawn argued, "because we're on our way to do it now." The horses' harnesses creaked and jingled under the late summer forests, through foliage lush with the recent rainfall. "For that matter," Shawn said, "I didn't have much time to carve at all. What I did wouldn't have lasted so long. So we'll carve that deeper and leave a detailed message telling her to go to Iona on June 8."

He glanced at the green leaves overhead. He'd last traveled this route pursued by English soldiers, and nursing a wound from Allene's knife. His face grew warm. He barely recognized the man who had kissed her, and pushed for a great deal more, by the stream.

After a brief sleep, Shawn and Niall reached Hugh's camp at dawn. Shawn studied the clearing where he'd lived with Hugh, Will, Adam. Mist crawled along the ground, over a hollow that showed where their campfire had burned. It was here Shawn had lived out the changes that had come over him in Fergal's hidden cellar; here he'd made the decision to fight to protect Allene. He smiled, remembering Hugh heaving a sword at him, expecting him to catch it in midair as Niall would have.

Further on was the stretch of meadow where he had learned to swing a sword. He grieved Adam, wishing he could have lived in a world where he never had to fight, where he never would have died pierced by a Welsh arrow, a world where he would have met his son. He was glad they were even now on their way back to Glenmirril, where Niall, at least, would see his new son.

A glimpse of loch peered through the forest. He'd gritted his teeth there on the shore, biting leather while Allene stitched his leg together from the wolf's long claws, and sat with her in the long evenings.

Niall cleared his throat, and Shawn had the disturbing sensation that he followed his thoughts. "I didn't really have much choice but to pretend to be you." He answered unspoken words. "I could hardly tell her where you'd gone or if you'd be back." He shivered in the early morning chill.

"Did you kiss her?" Niall asked.

Shawn shook his head. He couldn't elaborate on why not.

The camp felt empty, desolate. Silence hummed around them, dancing down on the sunbeam cutting through the leafy branches above. "Makes me think of Sherwood Forest."

"What's that?" Niall asked.

"Where Robin Hood lived." Shawn was relieved Niall was willing to leave the subject of Allene. He couldn't explain to himself his change of heart, much less convince Niall. He quoted, instead, all he remembered of a poem of Robin Hood.

"But who *is* he?"

"No one knows. If he existed, it was around this time. Give or take a century. Or two." Shawn dropped the pony's reins and moved to Hugh's rock.

Niall snorted.

Shawn cocked a grin over his shoulder. "Losing your vocabulary?"

"A century or two makes a wee difference."

"Whatever. He was medieval. The Earl of Huntington, some people say. This clearing, all empty of everything I knew, reminds me of the poem." He studied what he'd left, seeing just how pathetic his scratches were.

"Imagine how I felt, finding it in your time. He was English?"

"Yeah." Pulling out his knife, Shawn began etching the letters deeply. "He stole from the rich and gave to the poor."

"The Sassenach always were thieves." Niall dug his own knife into the letters on the right.

Shawn shook his head. "You're missing the point. He was a good guy."

"He was a *Sassenach*."

"Fine. We'll call him Angus of Ettrick, and I'll tell you the stories." As they worked, the sun climbed higher, burning off the mist and warming them till they tore off their vests, working in their linen shirts. "*Stout-hearted England.*" Shawn recited, as the poem drifted back to him from many years ago.

"*Cold*-hearted England," Niall scoffed. He touched letters now gouged an inch deep. "Brutal, vicious England." Behind them, the ponies shuffled, and nibbled at vegetation.

"Hey, I didn't write it."

"I'll find a fish or squirrel," Niall said. "We'd best start the part about Iona." He wiped a hand across his brow and headed to the stream for a drink, before setting out into the woods.

Shawn carved another ten minutes before taking a break to sip from the creek. A rustle sounded in the forest. He squinted into the trees. A fern rustled. Shawn's hand tightened on his knife. Niall was out there. There'd been no outcry. They were alone in a great wilderness. Only wild animals could threaten them, and if he'd fought off a wolf eighteen months ago, he could do it now with one hand behind his back. He crossed the clearing, reassured, and began carving the *A* of *Iona*.

CHAPTER FORTY-FOUR

Inverness, Present

"I could easily kill you." Simon sat at a small, wrought iron table, in a garden, with the old monk, his legs stretched before him.

"Ah, but then you'd have trouble getting home." With a withered, shaking arm, Eamonn poured coffee from a silver urn into a tiny, china cup. "Sugar?"

"No, thank you. You understand if you don't give me the crucifix, I'm no worse off for killing you."

"True. But sadly, I'm not so holy a monk. I've been known to lie—at least by omission."

Simon sighed. He lifted the ridiculous tiny cup to his lips. At least the coffee in this time was good. "On what matter have you misled me?"

"I haven't the crucifix." Eamonn lifted a medallion hanging about his neck, fiddling with a button on it. "'Tis at Glenmirril."

"And how would it have gotten there?"

"You see...." Eamonn paused for breath, then gave a small chuckle. "Pardon an old man. I do have difficulty talking some days. Where was I?"

Anger darkened the edges of Simon's vision. "The crucifix...."

"*Aye!*" Eamonn pounced as if he'd found a great treasure. He clutched the white medallion. "Amy...the crucifix. I do apologize, I *believed* I had the real one, back at Monadhliath. You do remember our talk there? Such a mix-up! Amy had it after all." He burst into a dry cough.

"Amy had it?" Simon demanded. The old man was faking it, putting off the moment of his own death. Not that an extra few minutes mattered one way or another.

"Amy?" Eamonn asked.

"Amy," Simon growled. "The crucifix. The real one, the one associated with the prophecy that promises a door of time shall open on the feast of St. Columba."

"Is *that* what it says?" Eamonn blinked like a child offered candy. "Why that's tonight, is it not?"

"It's at Glenmirril?" Simon pressed, the anger building.

"Oh, the *real* crucifix." Eamonn tapped at the white medallion again. "The real one?"

"Yes, the real one!" Simon snapped. "Quit playing the fool!"

Eamonn twisted a finger in his ear. "Gruel?"

"Where at Glenmirril?"

"The food here is quite good, not gruel a'tall."

"*Where is it?*" Simon ground out.

"Well, now, there's a story there." Eamonn pressed a hand to his mouth, and entered a prolonged bout of coughing.

Simon regarded his doubled over body coldly.

"Forgive me. I'm so sorry." The old man righted himself, wiping at his eye. "You see what happened was this." He pressed bony, shaking fingers to his forehead, as if struggling to remember. "Amy discovered she had it."

"So you said. How does she know she has the real one?"

"The bone in the back," Eamonn answered. "She looked and after all this to-do...." He laughed. "Silly, isn't it, My Lord, how these things happen. But aye, she had the real one, and so she went to Glenmirril last Tuesday, or perhaps the day before? It may even have been...."

"It doesn't *matter* when it *was*," Simon roared. "Is that where the crucifix is now?"

"Well, yes, you are so very right, My Lord. It matters not a'tall when it happened." He squeezed the white medallion around his neck. "You see, she went there, seeking Niall."

"With the crucifix?" Red hot anger began to rise in his vision, fueled by his many failures these past weeks. It should have been a simple matter, killing a child and an old man!

"Certainly! How else would the times cross?" He leaned forward abruptly, his eyes alight. "Though if you believe in miracles, they can't be controlled, can they?"

"I've no interest in your theological musings."

Eamonn's eyes sharpened. "You ought, for 'tis miracles of which we speak, and miracles with which you wish to meddle." He gave a sudden, inane cackle. "With. Which. Wish. Which...."

Simon leaned across the delicate wrought iron table, to grasp the monk's robe. A tea cup skittered to the edge of the table, teetered, and fell to the cobblestones with a crash and splash of coffee over the bricks. "Is the crucifix there?"

"Glenmirril's a large place." Eamonn yanked back with surprising strength. "One must know where to look."

"Tell me." Simon spoke patiently, almost kindly, as if to a foolish child. "Death can be quick and painless, or slow and unpleasant."

"So it can," Eamonn agreed. "And I should hate...."

"*Where?*"

"'Tis in the chapel."

Simon pondered the information. "How would you know?"

"She told me."

"So I can kill you now and go retrieve it."

"Oh, you could, you could!" Eamonn agreed cheerfully. "But then you'd not know the rest."

"You're almost entertaining enough to keep alive for another few minutes," Simon said.

A creak at the far end of the garden caused them both to look up.

An orderly stood in the gateway.

"Send him away," Simon murmured. His fury grew with the effort to hold it in.

Eamonn pushed himself up from his chair, his hands trembling against the small table. "I will do that, My Lord. But you don't actually need the crucifix."

"You said Amy took it to bring the times together."

Eamonn waved a hand. "She was mistaken. You need only be at Glenmirril at midnight tonight. Now, I'll send him away."

"Tell him from here," Simon warned, rising. But he saw it was too late. He could do nothing in front of the guard. He watched in fury as the old man tottered across the short stretch of lawn, two steps, three. The man in white, a huge hulk of a man with great muscles bulging under the short sleeves of his white shirt, closed the gap. He took the monk by the elbow, giving Simon a hard stare. He lifted something from his belt and spoke into it.

Moments later, two more large men appeared. "Sir, you'll have to leave now."

Simon's anger erupted in a stream of foul, medieval insults.

Trossachs, 1315

In the forest, Niall closed his eyes, listening. The cry of an osprey sounded overhead. The brook chattered over rocks along the edge of the clearing. He stepped carefully over branches and leaves, a stone and his slingshot at the ready, and waited.

A deer appeared silently, from the forest. He thought of the great stag that had stood in the clearing almost a year and a half ago—many centuries from now—while he scrubbed Hugh's rock, uncovering Shawn's message to Amy. This deer was nothing like that stag. But it was too large to bring down with a slingshot. A squirrel darted up a tree. He readied his stone. It shot from its sling, knocking the animal from its perch. He smiled, thinking of Shawn's futile attempts to copy him. "Yeah, well, you couldn't get around an international airport," Shawn had retorted.

Niall scooped up the dead animal, and headed back to the clearing. Halfway there, he heard the ponies whickering and stamping. He stopped. He knew that sound. Something had made them nervous. He took his next steps carefully, keeping his leather boots off twigs that might crack. Allene and his newborn son filled his mind.

Inverness, Present

The green room filled with the orchestra, arriving by twos and threes in jeans and t-shirts. Singly or in small groups, they approached Amy, patting her arm—*good to see you again*—or hugging her—*it's great to be back.*

"It's like a wake," Amy whispered to Celine. They stood near the counter, where pastries, tea, and coffee languished, ignored.

"Well, it really is." Celine replied. She took James, cooing back at his toothless grin. "How are you, James?" She looked up at Amy. "It's been a year."

"To the day," said Aaron.

Amy took her son back, kissing his forehead and bundling him on her shoulder.

"It's starting!" Peter called. They joined the rustle of bodies toward the television. Amid shushes, quiet fell. Peter adjusted the volume and joined Amy, Celine, and Aaron.

A bright-eyed reporter squinted in the sun; delicate blue blossoms rustled in the fields. The great statue of Robert the Bruce stood guard behind her, gazing out protectively over the country he'd saved. "It's almost a year since the renowned musician, Shawn Kleiner, disappeared during the re-enactment of the Battle of Bannockburn," she told her audience. The orchestra members nodded silently. A picture of Shawn filled the screen, his official orchestral photo, holding his trombone, in full tuxedo, and looking serious. But even in this photograph, his eye held a look of mischief waiting to burst out. Someone patted Amy's back. She bit her lip and closed her eyes. It hurt to look, and even now, a year later, it was a double pain, missing both Niall and Shawn, and the pain compounded by guilt for feeling faithless, fickle, and confused. The situation with Angus didn't help.

"We have with us today his friend and former colleague, Rob Carlson, who is leading the effort to find him." The reporter turned to him. Sunlight danced in his blond hair. He swallowed, and looked from right to left. Amy lowered her eyes to her son.

"Mr. Carlson," the reporter asked, "What is the status of the investigation?"

He looked into the camera. "We're, um, following leads right now that he's been spotted in Aberdeen, but so far, Julie, there's been no trace. We have a toll, uh, toll free number where we can be contacted if you have, uh, information." He swallowed hard.

"I've told him and told him," Amy whispered to Aaron.

Celine patted her arm. "Can you blame him for not believing it?"

Another picture of Shawn flashed on the screen, a photograph taken shortly before the orchestra had left for Scotland the previous year. His long hair blew in the wind, and he squinted, laughing, into the sun.

"Can you tell us about the events of last Midsummer's day?" the reporter asked Rob.

"He, um, spent the night in a castle ruin," Rob said. His eyes darted from side to side as he recapped the events of the previous summer leading to Shawn's disappearance.

"The police have speculated that he deliberately walked away from his life," the reporter suggested. "Thousands of people do it every year. They do not want to be found. Is that a possibility?"

"No," Rob spoke with certainty. "Shawn had everything. Talent, money, fame." He stared directly into the camera. "He had a beautiful woman who loved him. He'd be insane to walk away from that."

Trossachs, 1315

The sound jerked Shawn's head from his work. He'd just finished the *J* for *June*. His pony skittered, a quick troika on nervous hooves, and yanked its head back.

Shawn raised his knife, scanning the woods. A man appeared across the stream; then a second, and a third. Rough beards covered their jaws. He recognized the clasps on their cloaks: MacNaughtens. Allies of the Comyns and MacDougalls.

"What've we here?" The largest of the three crossed the stream. A knife dangled in his hand. The other two slid dirks from their belts. "Is it *Sir* Niall of Glenmirril?" A fir tree behind them rustled. A fourth man stepped out.

"Got any more friends hiding in the woods?" Shawn kept the icy fear in his stomach, not letting it show in his voice. He thought of Allene, waiting at Glenmirril with her new son, for Niall to come home.

The first man crossed the clearing. Shawn eyed the knife. "Wouldn't MacDougall like to catch up with ye?" the man asked.

Shawn scrolled through his options. Surprise was always handy. He decided against shouting for Niall. He would be back soon enough. He hoped.

Inverness, Present

Like hundreds of times before, Amy joined the flow of tuxedos and long black dresses onstage. It was comforting to take her old place behind Peter's empty chair, to hear chords shimmer off the harp like a Thomas Kinkade waterfall, and know it was Celine. She smiled at Dana, running up and down arpeggios on her French horn. The rumble of the timpani was Aaron, his black lock of hair falling perpetually over his forehead.

Peter stepped onstage to applause, and gave the tuning pitch, his head bowed. The strings picked it up, moving from high to low. Woodwinds followed, and finally the brass. It was hard to believe Shawn wasn't among them. Peter seated himself and turned, smiling. "It's good to hear you behind me again."

She reached to clasp his hand. "I was just thinking the same thing."

A burst of applause cut their conversation short as Conrad came onstage, beaming.

A concert like Shawn's, yet different, followed. Zach had all Shawn's talent, energy and wit; none of his edginess. Amy smiled as she played, catching glimpses of Kristen backstage, on one knee between her daughters, pointing out their father to them.

She plucked out the staccato reports of *Go Home with Bonnie Jean* and sailed into the lyric melody of *Brigadoon*. At intermission, she changed into a royal blue evening gown, with sprays of silver twisting, vine-like, across the bodice, to play her solo, the song that would forevermore call to mind a glorious winter morning with Angus. She wished he were here to hear it. But he'd made it clear it was over.

Trossachs, 1315

From the hill beyond the stream, Niall watched. Two men stood belly to belly with Shawn. A third and fourth waited across the stream. From his vantage point, Niall could see two more hiding in the forest. His eyes locked on them, while he prayed. *My Lord God, I want to see Allene again. I've not even seen my son. If you can let Shawn see his, across seven centuries, surely You can get us out of this and home to see mine.*

Shawn's voice carried over the stream, and up the hill, though Niall couldn't make out words. His attackers did not appear amused. Niall analyzed his options. Brute force did not seem a good one, not at three to one. No way of using their likeness jumped to mind.

He fingered the leather sling dangling from his hand. The men hiding in the woods waited some distance from one another. He fit a rock to his sling. A moment later, the first man crumpled to the ground, closely followed by his companion. Now it was four against two. If he hurried.

Inverness, Present

Alone in his office, Angus propped his stocking feet on his desk. A small television on Clive's desk broadcast Amy's concert. The new star, Zach, danced through a lively version of *Jock O'Hazeldean*. The camera closed in on Amy, leaning into her music. Her hair hung loose, the way he liked it best. He watched, entranced by the concentration on her face.

He swung his feet abruptly to the floor. Papers cascaded off the desk. He leaned to pick them up, frowning at the envelope from Monadhliath. The orchestra finished its piece. People applauded, someone spoke, but his mind was on the monks, on Shawn, Niall, and Amy. Clive was right. He was expecting too much of her in less than a year. His gaze traveled to the picture of her and James pinned to his board. Papers had inched over the photograph. He moved them aside, so he could see Amy again. Clive's most recent lecture came back to him. *You take a chance every time you're called to a rescue. Isn't Amy worth as much?*

"*Do you understand Kleiner might be back?*"

"*He may be back, he mayn't. You take a chance either way. Is she worth it?*"

The orchestra burst into song again, a piece from an old musical about Scotland. Angus picked up the envelope, tapping it on his knee in time to the bouncing notes. He squinted at the television, seeking a glimpse of her. The camera focused on Zach, leaning back as he played his trumpet; it panned across the trombones, doing some sort of drunken gliss, and skimmed over the violins.

He found her, small amid the sea of instruments, and thought, what could it hurt? If it could help her? *Love is giving,* he'd once told her. *Love is kind.* Hadn't she sent him repeated texts while he snubbed her? The camera focused on the older man sitting in front of Amy, giving him glimpses of her, rapt in concentration, behind him.

The song ended to applause. The television cut to an ad.

Have you ever regretted doing the right thing? Clive had chided him. The words looped through his mind while advertisements played.

Trossachs, 1315

Shawn tried to ignore the sweat gathering under his arms. At the very least, maybe they'd take him away, and Niall would return to Allene and his son—if he didn't stumble on the scene and get himself killed, too.

McNaughton's dirk wove a pattern before Shawn's throat. "I hear ye've a gift for survival. I'll make sure I push the knife deep and twist hard."

"There are no walls to walk through here, aye," said the other man.

Shawn eyed them, the two before him and the two at the stream. He couldn't fight four. He strained his ears for any hint of Niall's return. But he'd been handed his answer. "If anything happens to me, MacDougall's secrets will fall into the wrong hands."

"He was willing enough to hang ye."

"He was willing enough to hang a man he thought was me. He's a fool who quickly forgets. But I don't. Would you see MacDougall brought down? I suspect you share a few of his secrets."

The two men glanced at each other.

Shawn's eyes flickered to the men by the stream. He wondered if they would notice two ponies, or two vests on the ground. He caught a flash of white behind them—Niall's shirt—and breathed more easily. Best to divert their attention and separate them for Niall. "There was a wild boar out there just before you showed up. You might want to see if it's still around."

The two before him looked at each other, questioning.

"You don't want them sneaking up on you. They're vicious."

MacNaughten turned to the men by the stream, nodding at the forest.

Shawn's shoulders relaxed as they separated, edging into deep brush. He pulled his eyes back to MacNaughten, trusting Niall to use the situation.

"I don't believe ye know any secrets," MacNaughten said. "Tell me what ye know and who else knows, or I cut yer guts out."

"Now that hardly seems like a fair deal." Shawn's hand tightened on his knife, praying Niall would act fast.

Inverness, Present

When the ads ended, Amy, an inch tall, stepped onstage in a form-fitting gown as gloriously blue as the waters of the Ness in summer, shimmering in the lights, like the loch itself. Her hair shone. Angus leaned forward. The camera zoomed in on Conrad's back. His arms swooped down, and the orchestra burst into a deep chord, while the trombones, rich as velvet, poured out the poignant melody of *Ride with Me.* His heart jumped to his throat, remembering the day at the cairns, the way she'd smiled when he sang.

She filled the screen, her head down, moving gently to the music. She lifted her violin; the bow poised, her head bobbed four beats, and the bow flashed, her fingers dancing, her eyes closed. He watched, entranced, feeling again everything he'd felt that morning at the cairns with her.

His hands moved, as if on their own, to the envelope. When the camera cut to the blond harpist, he lowered his eyes to the spray of Gaelic twisting across the pages, while the trumpets sang, *If you go to another.*

The camera returned to Amy, her bow bringing the poignant melody to life. She smiled, joy shining on her face, as the harp shimmered behind her. He watched, entranced, until the song drew to an end. She smiled ear to ear to thunderous applause, bowed, shook Conrad's hand, and left the stage. Angus scanned the prophecy. A modern dictionary was useless. Amy returned to stage to shake the concert master's hand. Angus sat back, watching momentarily, before selecting a name off his phone and hitting dial. He got voicemail.

Trossachs, 1315

Niall pressed himself against rough bark, breathing deeply and praying.

When the man passed the tree, searching the thick vegetation for signs of a boar, Niall stepped in behind him, slid his knife across his throat, and eased him silently to the earthen floor. He squeezed his eyes shut, and made the sign of the cross over the dying man. Minutes later, the second man was dispatched the same way. He wiped their blood off on his trews, and crossed himself. It was no different than war. Kill or be killed. He prayed for their souls as he slipped back through the forest toward the clearing. Behind him, a twig creaked. At least one of the men hit by a rock must be up again.

He heard scuffling and shouting, and broke into a run, foregoing secrecy. With his back against the rock, Shawn lashed out, one against two. Niall leaped across the clearing with a shout. The smaller man spun, his mouth gaping only a second before Niall landed on him, stabbing. MacNaughten whirled. In the moment's distraction, Shawn's knife flashed, catching him in the side. He grunted, doubling over.

"Get out!" Niall shouted. "More in the woods!" He grabbed his vest and Shawn's, and sprinted for the ponies, Shawn on his heels. They leapt on the animals and bolted.

Inverness, Present

"Hey, Cuz, I hear you're packing on weight." Angus couldn't help smiling into the phone, though his frustration had mounted each time he'd gotten voice mail, and grown steadily as he'd waited for a return call.

"What are you on about?" came his cousin's gruff voice over the line.

"A bear who just packed on the weight and crawled into his cave for winter hibernation, were the exact words."

A snort that sounded very like a bear erupted into Angus's ear. "Who do we both know who has such a way with words? Not that I'm denying it."

"I'm surprised," said Angus, "that you didn't call straight away and tell me she'd been to see you."

"Who?" The one word sounded like a bull preparing to charge.

"Think back to the day you took me to the Glenmirril archives," Angus said.

"That was years ago. All I remember is, the Rangers won."

Angus tapped his pen. "Ah, 'twas your mate who spent more time with the Glenmirril Lady, was it not?"

"The Glenmirril...." Jamieson's voice trailed off. Two beats of silence grew to four before he spoke again, softly. "She *was* very like the drawing! But how do *you* know she came to see me?" His voice took on a peal of indignation. "Do you *know* what she was asking!"

"Aye." Angus laughed. "I'm holding a copy of it right now, and I'm afraid my medieval Gaelic is poor."

"'Tis a joke of some sort," Jamieson retorted.

"All the same," Angus replied, "I'd very much appreciate if you could fill in the blanks for me."

Jamieson snorted. "She's playing some kind of a game, or someone's playing with her. But if you must...." He rattled off the prophecy.

Angus jotted it down. The implication hit him immediately. He glanced at the clock, his thoughts churning. "Thanks," he said. "I owe you one."

"As long as it doesn't involve me packing on more weight." His cousin rumbled, with what Angus recognized as his version of a laugh.

"We'll go swimming," Angus promised. He ended the call, and stared at the prophecy. It was exactly what Amy needed to know. The question was what to do with it. He wanted to throw it in the trash and never look back. She was better off without that eejit. He glanced at the clock again. He had to decide immediately.

Highlands, 1315

"We have to go back and finish!"

"'Twould be suicide!" Niall trotted ahead, his jaw set. A branch snapped across his face. He swatted irritably at it, too late. "They know exactly where we're going. As it is, we're not safe."

"As it is, I only got *Iona, J.* How's that supposed to tell Amy anything?"

They emerged from the cover of trees at the base of a hill. Niall kicked his pony, sending it loping upward. "Try praying," he snapped. "I've a wife and child waiting for me."

"So do I!" Shawn nudged his pony. It picked its way up through scrub grass, brown heather, and jutting rocks.

"She's not your wife."

"Rub it in. Must be nice to be so perfect. She will be. I'm trying to get back so I can do the right thing. And half a message doesn't help."

Niall pushed his hair back from his forehead. "We've done what we can. 'Tis in God's hands now."

Shawn glowered at Niall's back. He shouldn't, he thought. He'd seen a miracle, a man walking who should be dead. He already knew Amy had stayed in Scotland and by some miracle, would one day go to the same abbey, deep in the wilderness, to which he and Niall had gone.

Niall urged his pony faster toward the pass. Another ten feet, and they dismounted, climbing steep hills, among boulders, tugging the horses behind them. At the pass, they stared down the other side. Hills rolled, a billowing sea of green, purple, and brown to be crossed. Shawn had become used to such distances. By night—if MacNaughten's arrows didn't pierce their backs first—they'd meet the men of Glenmirril, and round the top of Loch Ness. Home was around the corner. Niall vaulted back on his mount, and they edged down the rocky slope, their spirits lifting at putting another mountain between themselves and their enemies.

"How do you think she ended up at Monadhliath?" Shawn asked.

Niall guided his pony carefully over the rough ground. "The only thing that would lead her to Monadhliath is the crucifix."

"So she goes there. How did she even find the way?"

Niall shrugged. "Does it matter?"

Shawn shook his head. "I guess not. Let's say she finds the music I left. She'd understand it in a heartbeat—if she even thinks to look at music. But why would she?"

"Why did I scrub the rock?" Niall asked. "God guides us to do what seems natural at the time, and we find we've stumbled across another little miracle. I did as Hugh would want, and I found your message. What were the odds?"

"I'm thinking there's no reason she'd find any of the marks I've left all over."

"You must trust God, aye? What prompted you to leave them?"

Shawn shrugged. "Desperation." His pony side-stepped a loose stone, made a tripping step downward, and regained its footing. He glanced back up the hill, wary of pursuit. But it wasn't safe to go faster. "I just did. I didn't think about it."

"Sometimes that's God's way of working. We act without thinking. We know Amy will get the message at the rock, but you didn't know that when you left it." They reached the bottom of the slope, and, with a last glance behind, broke into a gallop north up the glen.

Inverness, Present

"Just tell me to do the right thing," Angus said into the phone. He hoped Clive would give him a reason not to.

"What are we talking about?" Clive asked.

"Kleiner." Angus pulled up youtube as he spoke. There was already a clip of Amy's solo. "I can get him back."

"Why would you not, then?" Clive asked. There was a silence, and he said, "Oh." Almost immediately, he added, "It's our *case*. You couldn't live with yourself."

"I couldn't." Angus studied the translation. He could get Shawn back. Or he could prevent it ever happening. Amy would come to accept, some day, that he was never coming back, and he would have the future with her they had dreamed of. *Come Ride with Me* played on youtube, Amy in her sparkling dress, her hair flowing down her back, swaying to the music.

"You've ever done the right thing," Clive said.

"So why is it this eejit who never did the right thing in his life has her heart? And now I'm supposed to help him?" The camera settled on the concert master. Peter Abbot. Angus's eyes fell on the picture of James pinned to his corkboard. *That's Abbot, not Rabbit.* He smiled, thinking of James chewing his rabbit's ear. James would grow up and struggle with his father's disappearance. Angus dropped his eyes back to Jamieson's translation. Carol grieved her son. Shawn himself was caught in a world where disemboweling and dying impaled on a sword were real possibilities. Angus closed his eyes. He would lose Amy and James if Shawn returned. He knew he would.

"Don't change who you are over this eejit," Clive said softly. "You've ever done the right thing,"

"I've ever found it easy to do the right thing," Angus said. "Tonight, I don't."

CHAPER FORTY-FOUR

Glenmirril, Present

They arrived home to the familiar scene of women and children racing to find their returning men. Red flew from the stables with wild abandon, his vibrant mop of hair sticking out in every direction, to hug Shawn and Niall, and care for Shawn's pony.

Exhausted and hungry as they were, Shawn, Niall and Hugh went first to Niall's rooms, to find Allene there, holding the swaddled child.

Shawn was appalled. "Let the kid *breathe!* Let him move his arms and legs!"

"'Tis not how it's done!" Christina said in horror. But her face glowed to see him, and she stood close.

Ignoring him, Niall fell to the divan beside Allene, holding her close, taking the child into his arms.

"His name is James, after your father," she said.

Niall carried him to the chapel to thank God.

Autumn passed with slaughtering cattle and sheep, meetings, sending messengers to Douglas and Bruce, and preserving and storing what little grain had been salvaged from the rain-soaked fields. MacDonald and Hugh paced the storerooms worrying how they would feed their people through the winter, but all their pacing did not increase the stores, and Shawn's own fear mounted as he began to understand there was no Costco.

He played harp and sackbut, and he spent time in the stables, learning from Red how to listen to the garrons. Red came to Niall's rooms and learned to play tric-trac and pluck melodies on the harp. His joy lit the room and brought smiles to the women's faces, despite the war preparations and looming hunger.

The blacksmith's hammer rang from dawn until far into the night, as he and his boys worked by the light of their great fires, with rain drumming down endlessly outside their smithy. Women gathered in Allene's room, spinning, embroidering and sewing—clothes, priestly garbs, shrouds for men who would die in battle. Shawn noted them uneasily as he made his way through Allene's solar, on his way to rouse Niall and trade places. The melody of rain on the window followed him. People talked of Niall Campbell's unflagging energy, as he and Shawn traded off rest, performing the work of two men through drizzly days and torrential nights.

Messengers came through rain and snow with news of Edward Bruce leading the Irish princes against England, burning and slashing through Dundalk and Ardee the previous summer, and fighting in Kells in early November. More messengers came with news of famine, and disease breaking out among cattle and sheep. Food prices were rising, they said. Adam Banaster had revolted on Lancaster's estates.

In the evenings, Shawn played harp in the great hall. Sometimes, he and Niall played harp and recorder in Niall's rooms, while Allene sewed, Christina sketched at her easel, and MacDonald and Hugh played chess. Some nights, Shawn and Brother David bellowed theological arguments at one another, while rain lashed the windows and wind raged across the loch. On the evenings Niall went to dinner, Shawn worked as Brother Andrew, checking stores in the grain houses, buttery, and armory, marking progress on the continuing preparations for war.

Niall slipped away to confer in secrecy with Douglas, during which time Shawn made a point of being seen in the great hall, in the armory, in the courtyard, at Allene's side. He carried Niall's son, wrapped in warm blankets, along the cold, drizzly shore and to the stables to look at the horses. His own son would be bigger by six months. Pain stabbed his heart, as he rocked the five month old James in his arms, stretching out his tiny hand to feel a horse's velvety nose. Amy would take their son to see horses, stretch out his plump hand to touch their noses. He rocked James in his arms, giving him the kiss he couldn't give his own son.

Often, he slipped into the candle-lit chapel to kneel several pews behind Christina, contemplating what drew such a woman to a place dominated by a beaten and bloody man nailed to a cross. Sometimes, he went even when he knew she wasn't there. The silence, and the smells of candle wax and incense wrapped him in peace, even as he stared at the Crucifix with one question burning in his mind: *Why?*

Why did You allow my father to die? Why a miracle for Lachlan and not me? That he healed from something worse than Lachlan didn't feel like a miracle. He hadn't seen the injury; had only woken from it in intense pain. Pain and miracles didn't mix, in his mind. The miracle he wanted, sliding back across time to Amy, wouldn't materialize. *Why did You allow such an insane thing to happen at all? Why are You keeping me here?*

Candles flickered; incense hovered in thin, silent clouds. And no answer came. He dropped his forehead on clenched fists, the word *Why* burning his mind. A feather light hand grazed his shoulder. He raised dry, red eyes to Christina, radiant in royal blue. Her hair glistened from the edges of her veil, jet black against pale skin. "'My God, why have You abandoned me?'" she quoted. "The waiting is hard."

He covered her hand with his. "We're all waiting, aren't we?" She was a woman of rank; it would be to MacDonald's advantage to marry her again. As a woman, she must desire it. But they all waited.

"Maybe I should accept it," he said. "He's almost a year old. I haven't seen her in 18 months. She's probably back in the States, married to Rob or someone else by now. I have a life here." He squeezed her fingertips. She tightened her grip on his shoulder.

"You've a life there. James, Amy. Your heart is there. You must try again next June."

Bannockburn, Present

Rob came that night, letting himself into her kitchen. He kissed James's dark hair, lying sleepily on Amy's shoulder. "How did I do?" His eyes held hope. She hated herself for deflating it again.

"I'm not marrying you."

His face flushed. "I didn't ask."

"You made your feelings clear again on television in front of everyone. You're not going to find him, Rob."

"And you are?" He snapped off the whining kettle. "Looking in museums and at reproductions of books that fell apart hundreds of years ago?" He slapped two mugs on the counter and filled each. Twin tendrils of steam twisted toward the ceiling.

"I know what I saw that day, Rob. Why do you listen to a thousand strangers calling a toll free number and not to me?"

"Because what you're saying is insane."

"Am I the only one who remembers Niall reading page after page saying the Scots lost? We went that day to a re-enactment of the Battle of the Pools, won by the English, and we left a re-enactment of Bannockburn, the Scots' greatest victory."

"That's impossible, Amy. You know it is."

James fussed. She pulled a blanket over her shoulder, settled him to nursing, and managed to sip her tea, calming herself. "I showed you the crucifix and ring," she finally said. "I showed you what he wrote about the crucifix. You verified it for yourself."

"It's a huge leap from *Shawn researched a crucifix* to *Shawn and his medieval twin made a daring leap across time.*"

Amy sighed. "We've been over this. You're not going to find him. I saw Shawn throw himself between a charging warhorse and a child. I *saw* it, Rob!"

Rob circled behind her, rubbing her shoulders, and laying his cheek on her head. She knew him well enough to know the look of grief that would be on his face. "It wasn't a real battle. And even if it was, you and I both know Shawn would never do a thing like that."

Glenmirril, 1315

Shawn almost dropped his chess piece when the door to Niall's solar flew open. Hugh bolted to his feet, jarring the chess table, to shield Shawn's face; then relaxed equally abruptly. "Niall!" he boomed. Allene erupted from her seat, dropping the altar cloth in Christina's lap, and flew across the room, hugging him.

MacDonald and Brother David rose from the table in the center of the room, leaving their maps. MacDonald strode forward, beaming. "You're home! How was the ride?"

"Cold!" Niall pulled back from Allene, grinning. He proffered greetings, bowed over Christina's fingertips, and swung his snow-sprinkled cloak onto a hook, before warming his hands at the fire.

"Shall I call for a bath?" Allene asked.

At the same time, her father asked, "What news of Stirling?"

"We heard Edward Bruce pushed into Dundalk in Ireland."

"Give the man wine before you badger him!" Hugh filled a goblet and handed it to Niall.

He drained it and his face became grim. "My Lord, His Grace requires forty men from Glenmirril to serve Douglas in Northern England."

Silence hung over the group, all waiting for MacDonald to speak. He betrayed no emotion, though the scar across his cheek turned white. He paced to the window, staring out at gray skies, and back, and finally spoke. "England shows no sign of relenting?"

"A year and a half," Hugh muttered. And louder, "Has Edward not enough headaches?"

"We've decimated the north of his country," Shawn said. "His people are starving—they're eating dogs and horses and even each other. He's under attack in Ireland."

Niall glanced at him, a furrow creasing his forehead.

From Niall's bedchamber came the sudden screech of James. All heads turned, watching as Allene hurried away.

"Is it true he has a new favorite?" MacDonald asked.

Niall nodded. "'Tis now Roger Damory to whom Edward gives gifts."

Hugh snorted. "You'd think he'd remember what trouble that caused with his nobles. Now of all times, he needs their support."

"And yet," Niall turned from the hearth, his frown deepening, "this incompetent fool holds us hostage."

"He can't hold out forever," Brother David said. "Turville has caused great resentment in Wales. Edward will soon have rebellion from Llewellyn."

Niall paced the chamber, his agitation increasing. "Yet he'll not let go of this determination to be overlord of a country that never was England's."

"Another winter of raids," MacDonald said, "and 'twill be the end of it, Niall. Edward has angered his barons, his people, even his queen. We control the north of his country. 'Tis but a wasteland."

"And still these stubborn English never learn!" Niall cried. "How many lives has one man's pride cost both countries!"

"Peace, Niall." Allene emerged from their room with James on her shoulder. "'Tis a matter of time."

"How many widows in that time?" Niall demanded. "How many orphans, how many towns burned and destroyed!" He paced the room. Allene rubbed James's back. Snow swirled and stuck to the window behind her. Her eyes closed; eyelashes fluttered against her cheeks, her lips moved. The temperamental Allene was praying, Shawn realized.

"Niall, Lad, we'll change naught by raging," Hugh said. "Bruce and Douglas have the right of it. We must force them to treat for peace, and we'll do our part."

Niall stopped in the center of the room. His eyes fell on Allene. She opened hers. Words flowed through the look they exchanged. As if they had spoken aloud, Shawn heard Niall: *I don't want you to be the next widow. I don't want James to be the next orphan.*

"We'll do what we must for our country, our clan and our bairns," Allene answered his unspoken words. "We grew up under England's oppression. We lost our brothers. We'll give James summat better, aye?"

Shawn swallowed. Her words invoked the ghosts of her brother and Niall's, dying brutally at Longshanks' command. He felt them, though he'd never met them, standing shoulder to shoulder with the living in the stone chamber. He cleared his throat. "Do we both go? Or I can go this time."

Niall and MacDonald glanced at one another. Hugh spoke. "I worried, the whole time at Carlisle, that your hood would slip and someone might see two of Niall. Battle is a poor time to hide a face."

"Fine. I'll go. I know Douglas, I know his men, I know his ways."

"We're trying to get you *home*," MacDonald objected. "'Tis best to send Niall, as he's the one who will remain here. We don't know past June for you."

"I'll go," Shawn said more firmly. He looked at Allene by the window with James. She met his eyes. Eighteen months ago, she would have bristled at Niall being sent away. Now, she met life's hardships more peacefully. Christina, Shawn suspected, had had her effect on all of them.

"Shawn," Allene said, "you mustn't if…."

"You've been married more than a year." Irritation laced Shawn's words. He didn't want another suicide mission. "And he's barely had time to hold his own child. Consider it a wedding gift, some time together."

"If My Lord has decided…" Niall began.

Shawn snorted. "No offense, but it's a crappy decision."

MacDonald's face turned red. Hugh swallowed a grin, and turned quickly to study a tapestry.

"Does it matter who goes?" Shawn pressed, facing MacDonald. "I'm here, right? If he goes, I have to hide out under Brother Andrew's hood and not be seen the whole time. I've never been one to sit around. If I go, he'll be happy to stay in his room all day."

Allene's face flamed cherry red. MacDonald rose, glowering.

Shawn looked from one to the other, the meaning they'd taken from his words dawning on him. He held up a hand. "Look, I didn't mean anything, only that he has something to do…" He stopped. "I'm really sticking my foot in my mouth. You know, in my time…."

"You're not in your time, Laddie." Thunder clouds rolled across MacDonald's face.

"I'm just saying, he'd enjoy…." He groaned. "I didn't mean…."

MacDonald's eyebrows bristled.

"Damn it," Shawn erupted, "quit taking everything I say wrong! He'd *enjoy* staying here."

Hugh turned from his examination of the tapestry. "I dare say."

Shawn glared. "Well, don't. I fight as well as he does, now. I'll go."

MacDonald lowered himself stiffly back into his chair, still glowering.

Hugh no longer bothered hiding his grin. "Any more reasons for Niall to stay, Laddie?" he asked Shawn. "You're an eloquent man. I quite enjoy listening to you."

Shawn threw him a murderous look and thumped himself into a chair.

Bannockburn, Present

Amy's front burst open, jarring Rob's cheek off her head. "Amy!" Angus charged down the hall. He saw Rob's hands on her shoulders, still draped in concert black. "Didn't take you long, did it?" he said.

She jumped up, clutching James. He blinked and let out a wail.

"What's going on!" Rob yelled. "What do you think you're doing?"

"Get milk, blankets, whatever James needs for the night," Angus barked. "Hurry, I know where he'll be."

"You know—what? Milk? Who?" She looked from Angus to the howling James, patting his back.

"Shawn. We've not a second to lose."

Rob jumped into action first, shouting, "Carol, we need help! Amy, bottles!" He swung to Angus. "Can't James stay with Carol?"

"No. We need him. Get diapers."

Carol appeared at the end of the hall, blinking. "Shawn? You know where he is?"

"Blankets," he barked. "Go! The crucifix, Amy, your jacket, trainers." He rummaged in the cupboard, grabbing bottles, turning the faucet on till water billowed out hot.

"You can't give a baby tap water," Amy protested.

"D' you want to see Shawn again?" Angus had the first bottle under the faucet. "It'll not kill him." He pushed the second one under. "Get his bag." Holding the third bottle under the faucet, he yanked formula from the cupboard. "Food," he hollered, capping the bottles and grabbing off the counter. He dug in the refrigerator for sliced meat. "Go, go, go," he yelled as Carol and Rob jostled in the hall. Lifting her black skirt, James on her shoulder, Amy hurried after them, grabbing her tennis shoes as she ran. Angus scooped up bottles, formula, and food. "We'll sort it in the car."

The force of his commands shoved them out the door. "You've the crucifix, Amy?" he demanded. Rob flung James's car seat into the mini, and strapped in a howling James. Carol shoved the diaper bag in the other door. Angus threw the car into gear as Amy strapped her seatbelt, and backed out with a squeal of tires.

CHAPTER FORTY-FIVE

Glenmirril, 1315

"We've something for you before you go to Douglas."

It had taken more talking, but MacDonald had agreed to let Shawn go in Niall's place. He and Hugh would leave at dawn the following day. But now, Allene's voices sparkled with excitement, though he could barely make out her face in the dim underground tunnels. Niall, Hugh, Brother David, and Christina, too, seemed to be suppressing eagerness. MacDonald, leading the group with his torch aloft, looked back, grinning.

"A ticket home?" Shawn asked. "Or a bag of *coal*?"

Niall and Allene glanced at one another. "*Coal*?" Allene asked. Her father veered left and lowered the torch as the walls and ceiling closed in.

"Coal, you know, to keep a fire going? What the bad kids get for Christmas?" In the dank chill of the underground caves in late December, Shawn shivered, despite his fur-lined cloak.

"'Tis a fine gift," MacDonald grumbled. "Would your people not give a warm fire to the *good* bairns?"

"What a peculiar time," Hugh said. "I'd give the wicked children a good thrashing, not a warm fire." He tugged his own heavy cloak close.

Shawn shook his head. "We have central heat. Coal is useless to kids in my time. Not to mention dirty. Forget coal. What do you have?"

At the door of the Bat Cave, MacDonald handed the torch to Hugh before fumbling with the ring of keys. They clanked as he peered in the flickering light, sorting through them, and finally inserted one into the lock. Hugh entered, sharing the precious flame with the torches ensconced on the walls. One by one, they sprang to life, throwing dancing shadows around the cave. Beneath the crucifix, most of the candles had burned out. MacDonald lit one from a torch, and set out new candles he'd brought. Soon, dozens of tiny flames lit the great cross, setting light playing over the honey-colored wood of the man hanging on it.

MacDonald stood by the kneeler, beaming.

Allene and Christina, huddled in vivid blue cloaks, Hugh, Brother David, and Niall all smiled ear to ear, their enthusiasm barely contained.

Shawn looked around the cave, not seeing anything different, and back to them, all still grinning under the cross like fools. "What?" he asked. "You're all obviously expecting me to see this wonderful gift."

"Go on, Shawn." Christina beamed with the rest. "Do you see nothing different?"

It dawned on him they stood on either side of the kneeler, framing it. He cocked his head, and saw it was new.

"A kneeler?" His eyebrows shot up. "I'm wrong, right? I have to be wrong. Why would you give *me* a kneeler?" He studied it. Like the crucifix, it was a work of art, with intricate Celtic knots and crosses carved up the side. Purple velvet covered the knee pad, thick with filling. He touched the high sheen of the arm rest, as smooth and beautiful as anything the Laird had ever created. It must have taken days for the sanding and polishing alone. He looked at them, baffled. "I mean, I know why any of *you* would find this a good gift, but you know me. Despite your best efforts, I'm just not that into God."

Christina laughed, her white teeth flashing in the fire light, and laid her hand on his arm. In another day and age, it would have been a warm hug. "Our Laird is not only artistic, he's clever." She touched the kneeler, near the arm rest. A panel dropped into her hand, revealing a compartment. "We expect you'll leave someday."

"You're confusing me even more." Shawn knelt, examining the latch, cleverly worked in under the arm rest, and the deep recess it revealed. "How does my leaving relate to a kneeler, with or without secret chambers?"

Niall spoke. "You said you'd look us up in the history books, see how we fared. We've already ruled out messages on the castle walls with a request to the servants not to clean them for seven hundred years."

Shawn laughed. "If they're better than you at doing what they're told, that would work."

Allene smiled. "Niall's set a poor example. No doubt the servants will disobey and clean the walls."

"But see," Brother David said, "we can leave parchments here. The cave is well hidden. They've a good chance of surviving till your time. If you get home, you know where to look."

The amusement left Shawn. His heart felt heavy, with something he couldn't name.

"What my clever brother must think next," Hugh thundered, "is how you may leave messages for us in return."

"You want me to?" Shawn asked.

Christina squeezed his arm. "Why would we not, Shawn? D' you really think we've no concern what becomes of you?"

The thing that squeezed Shawn's heart tightened. He blinked rapidly, feeling, for the first time in years, as if tears prickled his eyes. They cared about him. That's what the feeling in his heart was. They loved him. He swallowed, afraid his bass would slip up a tri-tone and betray him. He cleared his throat, thinking down an octave just to be safe, and said, "Thank you. It's the best gift I've ever gotten."

Scotland, Present

"Before you say anything," Amy snapped, in less than the loving reunion tones Angus had hoped for, "don't ever again say a thing to me like 'didn't take you long.' There's *nothing* going on between us, and if there was, it's hardly your business, the way you've snubbed me."

He tore from her neighborhood as quickly as he dared, scanning for darting children. He hit a switch, setting the siren wailing, and eased into the M8's evening traffic. "Aye, well, I'm sorry," he said.

"I *loved* you!" Her voice came out ragged. "I know my feelings are torn, but they're torn between Shawn and *you*." Her heart lurched as Angus flashed into traffic, on what still felt like the wrong side of the road. Fear fueled her anger. In the back, James screamed, his voice blending with the siren. "*I'm sorry*," she muttered. "Weeks of ignoring me, and I get *I'm sorry*." She twisted in her seat, straining to reach a bottle and formula. The car lurched as Angus swerved around two slower cars.

"I thought you might be interested in what I found."

She juggled the formula and bottle, the black skirt billowing around them, while James drew breath, preparing another vocal assault. "I'm sorry," she muttered. "It all happened so fast. You came in ordering and accusing...." She capped the bottle, shook it, and twisted again to hold it in James's mouth. The screaming stopped abruptly.

"I'm sorry," he said, sheepishly. "I was wrong."

She closed her eyes against cars flashing away behind them. The screeching siren pierced her ears. "You said..." She looked at him. "You really think you can get Shawn back?"

He nodded, his jaw tight, skimming around a slow-moving KA.

In her half-twisted position, Amy held the bottle for James. He gripped it between his hands, gulping as if he hadn't been fed since birth. A smile crossed her lips, watching. Shawn filled her mind: lies, love letters; endearments, other women. Traffic thinned. The car passed into a sea of green, fields stretching away on either side. Angus pushed his foot down on the gas. "He doesn't deserve it, especially from you," she said.

Angus glanced in the rear view mirror, eased into a free spot, and shot onto a bridge. Water sparkled below, cobalt shimmering in the blazing evening sun. He stared straight ahead, his knuckles white on the wheel. "I've spent my life rescuing, and never yet stopped to ask if they deserve it."

They rode in silence, but for the shriek of the siren. James settled to calmer drinking, and drifted to sleep. Amy eased the bottle from his mouth, wiped the trickle of milk from his chin, and settled against her seat. "What did you find?"

"Jamieson's my cousin. He translated the prophecy for me. I wish I'd opened it right away." His next words made her wish he'd take her hand, but he didn't. "I hope you can understand this is difficult."

"I'm sorry." She kneaded her skirt between two fingers. "I wish I could control what I feel. I've missed you."

"Him, too."

The siren split like a metal shard through her head. She pressed a hand to her temple. "There's no more traffic. Could we turn that thing off?"

He flipped a switch. The siren sliced off mid-screech.

"Thank you," Amy murmured. "Yes, I miss him. He was my life for almost three years. And it wasn't that long ago."

His hand left the steering wheel, coming to rest on hers. "I should have given you more time."

"Neither of us is to blame for the timing." Pastures flashed by, a dizzying whir of greens. "What does it say?"

"It's in the glove compartment." As she took it out, he said, "Didn't Brother Fergna say it was redundant?"

"Yes. Is it?"

Angus pointed to the page. "It says *boy* at the top, and here at the end, *son*. It would appear redundant, unless he'd known about Shawn, unless he'd seen what you saw at the battle."

"What do you mean?" She studied the jumble of words. "Does it say something about a battle or rescuing a child?"

"I think so!" He turned to her, his eyes gleaming. "Was it a boy he rescued?"

She frowned. "I don't know."

"Close your eyes. Try to remember."

She leaned back, closing her eyes. The horse reared over Shawn, pawing the air. The sword rose high. She bolted upright, jerking against the seatbelt, stunned at how powerful and disturbing the scene still was.

"What did you see?" Angus touched her hand.

Her heart slowed under his touch, but her voice shook. "The same thing I always see. Hooves in the air, right over his head, the sword. He's arching back, trying to get away, and you know what's going to happen, and there's no stopping it."

He squeezed her hand. "Try again. Back the film up to the child."

She tried. It had taken months to rid her dreams of the horse rearing over Shawn. But she tried, and was amazed. "A blanket!" she exclaimed. "It's gray-white. I remember now, the face! It was dirty, tears streaking down."

"How old?"

She squeezed her eyes tight, trying to see. "Five, six."

"How long is the hair?"

"Just touching the shoulders. It's curly, and red."

"The clothing?"

"Leggings. A tunic." Her eyes flew open. "I can't believe this can work! Leather boots. It was a boy! But what difference does it make?"

"The word at the top." Angus pointed, his eyes on the road. He looked smug. She smiled, not blaming him. He knew something. "Like our word save, it has multiple meanings."

"Redeem," she said. "Rob was just saying it—the old Shawn would never have stopped for a child. Does it say something like that?"

"'A boy will be his redemption,'" Angus quoted. "That's what he left off, because what comes at the end is a son—not *boy* this time, but *son*—shall rescue or save. There's that word save again, but saved by a son, or his son, with my crucifix. Do you see how Fergna found it redundant? A boy saves at the beginning of the prophecy and at the end, but if this is Shawn, it's two different boys, two different kinds of saving. One is his redemption, the other physically rescues him."

Amy stared at the words, her eyebrows carving a deep line over her nose. "You're sure? You're not just reading into it like Fergna did?"

He smiled. "It's Jamieson's translation, not mine. We know this prophecy is linked to Niall's crucifix, which connects to Shawn. And now it's specific, like Columba's other prophecies. Why are you not excited?"

"I don't know." She felt a strange let down. "Maybe I was expecting something more direct? More easily understandable? And if it's his son, how could whoever wrote that know Shawn would...."

Angus laughed. "That defines a prophecy, does it not? Knowing things you couldn't. And it *is* more direct. Look at the middle. 'A boy will be his redemption. On the feast of St. Columba in St. Columba's chamber, the door of time will open and the man who was lost in time shall be rescued by his son with my crucifix.'"

A chill shot up Amy's back. "But we could still be reading into it. It was written hundreds of years ago."

"A boy *was* his redemption," Angus emphasized. "The old Shawn never would have done it. He's lost in time, is he not? He has a son, you have the crucifix."

"The first time," Amy said, "the crucifix was there, and Shawn and Niall were together."

"And we think Shawn is Niall's descendant." Taking his eyes briefly off the road, Angus pointed again. "This word can mean descendant. And the crucifix *did* draw them together for their protection. What would have happened to Niall and Scotland, had the switch not happened?"

Amy squeezed her palm around Bruce's ring. "*Niall* would have gone through the Great Glen."

"And his friend would have found him there. And if he'd escaped the traitor, he'd have died of the infection. The switch saved his life."

"But the second time, at the battle—the crucifix wasn't there."

"But it was!" Angus's eyes lit up. "*You* were there, wearing it. And you know what else was there?" She shook her head. He pressed his foot harder on the gas pedal; the car shot forward. "Bruce brought St. Columba's relics to battle. Father, son, crucifix, St. Columba, all the elements together."

"St. Columba's chamber," Amy asked. "Where he built his monastery on Iona?"

Angus nodded. "St. Columba spent time at Glenmirril. Maybe that's why it happened there the first time. But the message on the rock said Iona. They say Columba's buried in the shrine on the side of the current abbey. I'm betting everything that's where the door opens this time. And somehow, Shawn knew."

"But when is the Feast of St. Columba?" Amy gripped her door handle, her heart pounding at the narrowing road and hills racing by.

"A saint's feast is when he died," Angus said. "Columba died at midnight between June 8 and June 9."

A car shot toward them. Angus's wheels squealed as he swerved into the pull-over to let the car pass. Undisturbed, he shot back onto the road.

"That's in a few hours," Amy breathed. "How far is Iona?"

"A few hours. Are you understanding now?"

CHAPTER FORTY-SIX

Northumbria, 1316

The cold woke Shawn long before his shift on guard duty. He sat up inside the pitch black he shared with Hugh. He tugged his tartan close, gathered his bag of oats, and crawled out into the starry night. Embers glowed in the fire pit. He stirred it up, adding kindling. An occasional flake of snow drifted down and sizzled in the heat while he fixed bannocks over the small flames. It was at least warmer than fording mountain passes had been, heading to Jedburgh with Hugh, Brother David, and three dozen of Niall's men.

January had blown in with cold winds and flurries in Douglas's wooded glens and rugged hills. On the fourteenth, they attacked Berwick by land and sea, zeroing in on an unfinished section of the town wall. But moon glow, as bright as a helicopter spotlight, slapped an abrupt coda on the attempt, like a pair of cymbals crashing to the floor. Berwick's garrison poured into the gap in the wall.

After his showing on sea at Jura, Shawn had been assigned to the skiffs in the river running alongside the town. In a move worthy of James Bond, he maneuvered one of the small boats through a hail of arrows and stones, his men raising shields over him as he steered and shouted to Hugh at the oars. He bellowed for Douglas, who turned, and splashed into the river. Sir de Landels followed, protecting Douglas with his own shield. An arrow pierced his back as he pushed James into the skiff. Shawn hauled the fallen knight in, shaking as he shouted orders to Hugh while the man died in his arms.

Douglas blockaded Berwick's harbor with a fleet of galleys and set up camp, hundreds of tents under the snowy trees of Ettrick Forest. His men harassed the English every time they ventured out, till, by mid-February, they'd largely stopped trying.

Now, a stirring came from Shawn's tent. Hugh emerged like a shaggy bear from its lair. "Time for guard duty," he rumbled, in his attempt at a whisper.

Shawn handed him a bannock, checked his sword and knives, and the two set off into the white-washed forest. With a low whistle, they found the night guard and relieved him.

"Tell me more of your time," Hugh said, as they settled on a dark ridge overlooking the camp's eastern flank.

"For starters," Shawn said, "if I were there now, I'd be planning a big surprise for Amy for Valentine's Day."

"What's that?" Hugh chewed the hard bannock.

"A day for love. You never heard of St. Valentine? I'd think in this holy time, you'd know your saints."

Hugh chuckled. "It might be Malcolm knows of him."

"Aw, hell," Shawn said, "maybe he hasn't even been born, yet. Or maybe when Niall and I changed history, it killed off his ancestors and he never will be. I don't even know where he was from."

"What kind of surprises?" Hugh asked.

"Our first year, it was roses, dinner by candlelight, the Merlot she likes. The next year, it was a trip to Hawaii."

"What's that?"

"This incredible tropical island." Shawn heard the smile in his own voice, as he slipped into memories of hot sand and bright sun and lazy days with Amy, much nicer than the frosty ground groping with cold fingers through his breeks. "Like paradise. I took her to this incredible hotel with a *Jacuzzi* in our room."

"What's that?" Hugh scratched his head.

Shawn laughed, finding joy in the memories. "Like those tubs they haul up to our rooms for baths, except hotter, and the water bubbles, and man it would feel good on sore muscles after a day of fighting. But in my time, no one fights."

"No one?"

"They do," Shawn said. "But not in my country. It was just me and Amy, drinking champagne in a *jacuzzi*, looking over the ocean at sunset, and I surprised her with her first *royalty check* from our *CD*."

Hugh shook his head. "What language are you speaking?"

"Twenty-first century English where I need it." He sighed, gazing at the snowy forest, and the eastern sky turning gray. "Guess we should do our thing." They rose and began their patrol of the perimeter, swords and shields at the ready, as he explained checks and royalties and CDs. Walking warded off some of the chill. "Shawn Kleiner," Shawn mused, "spending Valentine's Day with a bunch of medieval warriors." He snorted. "It just isn't right."

A rustle brushed Shawn's ears. He put a hand on Hugh's arm, and they both froze. Footsteps fell again, and they heard a distinct crack of ice and splash from a stream. There came a short whistle, and Shawn's muscles relaxed as surely as if he'd just slipped into that hot tub.

"Come out," Hugh whispered. "'Tis Douglas's guard."

A man stumbled, in russets and browns, from the trees. "De Cailhau and his Gascons!" he gasped. "They've left Berwick!"

Mull, Present

They caught the last ferry to Mull with a flailing of arms, and shouting from the ticket booth to the boat. Angus shot on with a squeal of tires, shouting thanks to the crew's reprimands to watch the time more carefully.

Amy pulled a hooded sweatshirt over her black blouse, switched her heels for tennis shoes, and followed Angus up to the deck. She huddled into the wind, clutching blankets around James. "What do you think it would do to someone?" The wind whipped her words out across choppy waves. Angus leaned close to catch them. She wanted to take his hand, but it didn't seem fair. "Being in a time like that, the things he's been through?"

"Everyone reacts to trauma differently." He pulled her hood up, her hands being full. "I've seen strong men break, and timid women turn to steel. You knew him best."

"The man I saw in the monastery was strong," she said. "Something in the eyes."

"No chance it was Niall?"

She shrugged. "Niall wouldn't have looked at me like that." She thought of him in the alley, and backstage, kissing her. He had been lost and alone, probably as scared of being stuck in her world as she would have been, caught in his. But he was with Allene now. Waves slapped against the ferry. Niall would hate this ride. The sun blazed across the sea. Its brightness gave little clue to the hour, or the time when the door would open. "What happens if we miss it?" she asked.

"We try again next year."

The evening breeze tore at James's blankets. Angus kept his arm around her, shielding them, till they descended to the car. "I hate to think of him caught there a second year," she said, as she strapped James in, preparing for the drive across Mull. "I mean, you could get killed in a place like that."

Coldstream, 1316

They mounted, three dozen men wiping sleep from their eyes, gnawing last night's meat—the only breakfast they would get—and jamming helmets on their heads. Their garrons snorted, and kicked through early morning gloam twisting among their fetlocks as they darted among the trees, picking up speed from a trot to a canter to a gallop. Shawn leaned over his pony's neck, protecting his face from tree branches swooping down low. His sword felt solid on his back, and his knives at home in his belt and boots. A few raiders was nothing. Maybe he'd even pluck a daisy on the way home and stick it in his pony's forelock, since he couldn't give Amy a rose. He could pretend the tough, boiled English beef was a juicy filet mignon from the Strip House. He'd convince himself the ale was sweet Merlot, and kiss his pony on the nose. His animal veered around a birch, ghostly silver in the morning mist. Sometimes you just had to look life in the face, he told himself, and say, *Nice try, I'm going to have a good day anyway.* He patted the pony's neck. "At least I'll kiss someone on Valentine's Day. Better you than the rest of these lunkheads, aye?"

Hugh looked back, peering through the narrow slits running vertically down his helmet. "A quick day's work." His grin showed beneath the nose piece.

"We'll be home for lunch," Shawn agreed. The mist cleared quickly as the day lightened, and they burst from the forest, forty strong. An orb of flaming orange crested the hills, glaring in his eyes as they raced across open farmland, the River Teviot flowing on their left. He lifted his head, free of the swiping limbs, and squinted northeast. What he wouldn't give for a pair of Ray-Bans!

"Stop!" Douglas raised a hand gloved in thick leather. Thirty-nine riders skidded to at a copse, with a stream running a hundred feet ahead. Their mounts blew frosty breath into the February air, and stamped in excitement. Douglas pointed to a ridge.

Shawn's heart dropped.

"That's no handful of raiders," Hugh breathed at his side.

Shawn shook his head, dazed. "It's a whole army." Armor flashed in the rising sun; spears swayed like a living forest.

"They are at least twice as many as us," said Brother David, sitting astride his horse beside Shawn.

The Gascons had seen them. Shawn's heart pounded; the familiar tremble of adrenaline began in his arms. His pony moved restlessly beneath him, feeling the energy of a coming battle.

Across the field, English horses tossed their heads. All the men looked to Douglas. "Do we fight?" Hugh asked.

"Aye." Douglas drew the sword from his back.

"There are twice as many of them," Shawn hissed.

"We do not run from the enemy on our own soil." Douglas stared straight ahead at the army where they'd expected only foragers. He nodded to the man at his side, who unfurled his white banner with the band of blue and three white stars. Across the field, motion rippled through the ranks of knights. Visors lowered. Lances shifted.

Shawn thought of Amy. His certainty, all these months, that he would see her again, suddenly seemed foolish. He thought of stories he'd read where people died in one dimension, but survived in another. He knew if he died on this field, he'd be dead everywhere, every time. He thought of his mother, and hoped Amy would be there for her.

"Put your helmet on," Hugh muttered.

Shawn nodded numbly. This was no different than any battle, he told himself. A trumpet blared across the field. He lifted the helmet, and pushed its heavy weight down tight. Just like the raids, he told himself. But there hadn't been knights charging him then. Just like Jura, he told himself. They'd fought back, there. But there hadn't been knights charging him on those ships. He swallowed. The last time he'd been thrown in among mounted cavalry, it hadn't gone so well.

The charge began. The English rolled like a silver wave across the silver, frosty field.

"The ford will slow them," Hugh said. "Steady, Shawn. We each kill two and we're good, aye?"

Shawn nodded, grateful that at the end, at least he'd been called by his own name. He secured his shield on his arm. Cold breath puffed from his pony's nose. It tossed its head. Shawn hefted his sword.

"Owen," Hugh said, "Watch Niall's back." He stared straight ahead, watching the horsemen charge, their lances pointed. The ground shook. Around him, Shawn heard visors click into place. Horses shuffled, snorted, and shook their manes. Lances and swords emerged, and he felt some safety in the men surrounding him.

Douglas swung his sword lazily at his side, the way Shawn had once swung his trombone, grinning, before a concert. Indeed, Douglas smiled in anticipation, much as Shawn himself did before the hardest pieces. "Take their leaders first," Douglas said. His message rippled down the ranks.

Sunlight flashed off the four score Gascons thundering toward them. Douglas backed up twenty paces from the stream, up the small hill; the motion reflected down the line, thirty-nine horses backing up, snorting, pawing.

"What are we doing?" Shawn asked Hugh

"The stream will slow them," Hugh said. "We'll charge as they cross and the momentum will be with us."

Shawn nodded, seeing only the knight from Bannockburn rising over him, sword flashing down.

"Look to Douglas," Hugh murmured. "Take courage, Shawn. Fight your hardest. He'll bring us through."

Shawn nodded dumbly again, but he watched Douglas leaning forward, eyes blazing, eager to do battle, to take back his country, and he felt something grow hot and strong inside himself; felt strength emanate from Douglas, into his sword arm. His back stiffened.

The first Gascon warhorse stamped through thin ice at the edge of the creek. It crackled and snapped, and a dozen more splashed in, slowing as Hugh had promised, kicking up sprays of water sparkling in the sunlight, hanging in the air as far away as the back of the concert hall from the stage, and Douglas let out a guttural roar, "*A Douglas!*" It echoed among his men, and ripped itself from Shawn's own throat, as he pounded his heels into his pony, hardly needing to, for it was off, speeding toward what it lived for, and the short descent gave momentum to their charge.

Niall's training took over, Shawn's sword rose, he met the eyes of the enemy, peering through helmet slits, as he'd once met the eyes of girls in the audience. The pony pulsed under him, muscle to muscle, part of him, and he met the Gascon with a crash of horse and man and muscle and weapons, and slashed his sword down with all his power, snarling, screaming *A Douglas!* and spun and whirled his sword into the next, rammed his shield into one coming at him from the other side, gripping the horse with his knees as Niall had taught him, driving the sword into an abdomen, steel ringing on armor, driving again; knocking the man to the ground, where ponies trampled him in his armor.

There were two on him. A blood-curdling scream ripped through the air. Shawn spun in panic, saw three on Douglas, and Douglas's weapons whirling in frenzy, his mouth beneath the helmet taut in determination, eyes blazing. "Scotland!" he roared. He shoved through the three, sword whirring, sunlight glancing off it, and drove for de Cailhau. His courage spun like a pinwheel of fire across the field, electrocuting Shawn; he doubled his efforts, striking with sword and shield, spinning, whirling.

Sweat ran cold inside his gambeson. Beside him, Owen fell. Unburdened by the heavy armor of the Gascons, he scrambled to his feet, fighting in the chaos. Shawn jerked his reins, twisted his body, and rammed his shield on the neck of Owen's attacker. The man crumpled, sagged, and his horse bolted as he toppled to the ground, one foot caught in a stirrup. Owen scooped up his sword and scrambled for a riderless beast, heaving himself up.

"Behind you!" Hugh's voice boomed over the roar of battle. Shawn twisted, flinging up his shield. Something heavy crashed on it, jarring his arm clear to the shoulder.

"A Douglas! Scotland!" rang over and over across the battlefield. He gathered his wits, gave his head a sharp shake and thought of Allene and Christina. Anger grew in him, a beast powering his sword, smashing it on his attacker's head, smashing again, and again, till there was nothing but a bloody mess before him, and somewhere, he heard a shout. *"De Cailhau's dead! Take them!"*

The battle changed in an instant. Panic shot through the air like sheet lightning. The man before Shawn paused in the act of raising his sword. Terror flashed in his eyes.

"Your leader's dead," Douglas roared, and Hugh echoed his words, *De Cailhau's dead!* like a microphone. "De Cailhau's dead," shouted the man before Shawn, and jerked his reins, wheeling. The Gascons turned, leaning low, dropping lances, kicking battle-weary mounts. Douglas's men fell on them, shouting, chasing, killing. Two splashed across the small stream and bolted up the hill. Shawn searched the field, energy pulsing his sword arm, hunting the enemy.

He saw only friends. And dead bodies. His horse, beneath him, quivered with excitement, dancing impatiently. And slowly, as he realized the danger was over, so slowly, the energy drained, and he was left gripping a sword that sagged to the ground. Every muscle trembled.

A Gascon stared up at him with unseeing eyes, his helmet knocked off, his head half-severed at the neck. Shawn yanked on the reins. The smell of blood permeated everything. The pony backed up, stumbled on a body, regained its footing, and backed up another step. It splashed one hind leg into the stream, running red with blood. Shawn yanked its head around, till the setting sun blinded him and he shook his head, lowered his eyes against the orange glare, and found himself staring down into another pair of lifeless eyes, electric blue, the upper quarter of the head cleaved away. Gray matter oozed onto blood-stained snow.

"Niall."

The voice came to him, faint and far away. He yanked his reins, and the animal spun, bringing him around to two men piled atop another, limbs sprawled at impossible angles.

"Niall." Owen cantered up beside him, and he heard *Niall!* roared behind him.

Hugh thundered up, grabbed his reins, and their horses raced side by side, deep into the woods. The sunlight faded quickly. Shawn felt the sword slip from his hand, heard the soft thump as it slid into the rising mist and hit the winter-damp forest floor. Trees flashed by, Hugh large at his side, and then he was sliding off the animal, falling to his knees, Hugh pushing his neck down. "Get it out, Lad," he said. "But don't let the men see Niall do this."

The trembling grew in Shawn's arms and moved into his back. He saw the shattered head behind his eyelids, no matter how tightly he squeezed his eyes. "I'm going to be sick," he whispered.

"We all are," Hugh said. "I pissed my pants the first time."

"You were probably sixteen."

"Fourteen."

"I'm twenty-five," Shawn rasped over bile, "and it's not my first battle."

"Lad, you barely lasted ten minutes at Bannockburn."

Shawn's arms shook. He leaned over the frosty grass. He'd been unconscious for days while the Scots picked over dead, mutilated, and rotting bodies for armor, spurs, wealth, and weapons. The reality of what Niall had had to do struck him full force. Nausea reared in his stomach.

"Douglas's raids are not battles," Hugh said. "You were helping Lachlan after Jura. This is the first time you've seen the carnage."

Shawn vomited. Over and over and over.

Mull, Present

"We've an hour's drive," Angus said, as they rolled off the ferry into Mull's rugged hills. "Forty minutes at my speed." The mini shot forward as he pressed his foot to the gas. "Let's review and recap."

"Raids with Douglas," Amy said, "the siege at Carlisle, Monadhliath."

"Niall goes to Ayr," Angus added. "Shawn, as Niall, goes to Monadhliath with an irreverent monk."

"Why is *Shawn* traveling with a monk at *all?*" Amy asked.

"We don't know," Angus said. "We only know he *does* show up with the crooning confessor...."

"Shawn finds he can't replace the crucifix," Amy continued, "then tells the monks he wants the melodious monk to stay with them. Why?"

"Tired of the caroling cleric's canticles about carrots?"

Amy laughed. "Carrots and churches," she mused. "But Shawn stays long enough to copy an awful lot of music. What happens to the bellowing brother?"

Angus shrugged. "Maybe they both stayed?" They fell into silence, contemplating the question. After a bit, Angus pointed south. "Castle Moy is just down there." He grinned. "My family home."

Amy smiled. Her thoughts drifted to Castle Tioram, and Shawn singing over a picnic dinner. *Baked potatoes, peas and carrots, eat them with your ham!* On Tioram's ramparts, he'd sung the beautiful ballad from *Cillcurran.* She smiled, thinking of the beautiful story of the castle protected by mist, and the song so different from carrots....

She straightened. "Carrots!" It had been in Hamish's book. "What is it in Gaelic?"

"Carrot, *curran.*" Angus followed her thoughts. "But there was no carrot church. 'Tis ridiculous. Something was copied wrong."

"No!" She shook her head. "The *church* of St. Oran! *Cill* Oran!*" When his face remained blank, she laughed. "A fog rising on a Scottish castle. *Cillcurran!*"

A corner of his mouth quirked up, but he looked blank. "What's that?"

"A castle...." In that moment, Amy realized the musical had blinked out of existence, into the mists of time, just like its fictional castle—because the Jedburgh Rising against English rule wouldn't have happened. Because Shawn and Niall had changed history and thrown off English rule a hundred years before the Rising would have occurred. She bit her lip. "It was a castle that disappeared in mist when danger threatened." All the beautiful pieces from the musical were gone forever. But the significance of the song left behind overshadowed everything. "They heard about fog rolling in." She felt Shawn's humor across the years. It was easy to imagine the faceless medieval abbot outraged at his irreverence. Laughter welled up in her chest. Even across seven centuries, he could make her laugh. "And he started singing *Cillcurran.*"

"Brother Andrew *was* Shawn." Angus's brows furrowed in thought. After another moment, he said, "By the way, there's one thing I didn't tell you."

Scotland, 1316

May burst with life—lambs, calves, budding leaves—through the long trek home. Shawn led his men down the forest slope, alive with a hundred shades of green and brown, to Glenmirril, eager for the trip to Iona. They passed peasants, weakened with hunger, trying to force hoes through water-logged fields.

After de Cailhau, Shawn had led the men who lit fires, dancing high in the dark night, to alert Sir Robert Neville, the Peacock of the North, that Douglas had heard his boast, and dared indeed to raise his banner outside Neville's home. By morning, Robert Neville had lain dead, and Shawn had escorted Ralph Neville to Scotland for ransom, through rain drumming their muddy path, and rolling like a snare on the leaves overhead.

His thoughts, surprisingly, had not dwelt on blood and massacre, but danced between Christina, Amy, Niall, and Allene. In the evenings, he played for the men, songs of home, valor, love. Rain drizzled on his harp. He did his best to wipe it dry, but the men needed hope and peace. He'd lost all fear of dying. He believed with his whole heart he'd reach Amy. And he'd rather while away the days until next June in action than idle waiting.

Christina played constantly on the edges of his mind, her black hair and jewel-colored gowns, the crisp white linen of her wimple wrapped under her chin. She was what Amy might have been in another time, in a world where he and Dana had never pushed her to be someone else.

He imagined, as his fingers caressed chords from the harp, what their son might look like. At over a year, he'd be walking. Shawn pictured him, with Amy's black hair, reaching a chubby fist for Rob's hand. He glared into the fire. But it was his own fault. And, he consoled himself, he was making it up, about Rob. Amy had never had any interest in him.

"Keep playing, Niall," Hugh said, and Shawn realized he'd drifted into thought. He smiled, grateful for the loss of so few men under Douglas's leadership, and plucked a lively tune.

Now, home at last, he paraded into the courtyard to cheers from the castle folk, dancing in joy at a rare, brief glimpse of sun and the return of their men. Red flew from the stables, hugging him with abandon, as if Shawn were his returning father. Allene played her part, greeting the returning 'Niall,' to the keening of a new widow and skirling of bagpipes. Dinner waited in the great hall. They called on him to play the harp, and Owen told of Coldwater, Cailhau, and Robert Neville. With the skies once again darkening with rain, and fires blazing in the hearths, they told of Edward Bruce being crowned high king of Ireland.

As soon as possible, Shawn left the table with Allene. "Room service!" He stuck his head in her chambers. Niall sat in the windowsill, rain spattering off the window behind him as he picked out *Sound of Silence* on the harp. He set it aside, striding across the room to clasp Shawn's hand. "Enjoy hiding out in your room?" Shawn leered.

Niall bit back a smile, noting Allene entering the room on his heels. "Very much," he whispered. "Though we'll have to say the bairn's early, when her time comes, as I've supposedly been gone these past months."

Shawn turned to Allene, grinning. "Congratulations are in order?"

She blushed, slipping her arm through Niall's. "I don't believe I'll ever become accustomed to your bluntness."

"I don't think I'll get used to your delicacy," he replied. "Babies happen. Why pretend we don't know how?" He laughed at her fiery cheeks. He resisted only seconds before asking, "Where's Christina?"

"In the chapel. Bide a moment." Niall laid his hand on Shawn's arm. "You'll be bidding her farewell. We must leave to make the crossing."

"We?"

"Have you not yet figured out 'tis not safe to travel alone?" Behind Niall, the rain pounded harder against the window. Thunder growled.

"I was going to last time."

"We'd no choice last time."

"Who's going?"

"MacDonald, myself, Hugh, Brother David, two-score of our men."

"Won't it be easier to cross MacDougall's land unnoticed by myself?"

"The decision has been made," Niall said. "We leave before dawn, the day after tomorrow. Get some rest."

Mull, Present

Angus clung to the steering wheel with deliberate calm, swerving around curves and pushing the mini hard over rough roads. More than once, Amy bounced near the ceiling.

"You didn't tell me...?" Amy broke off with a gasp as a car burst around a bend in front of them. It slammed on its brakes, shooting up a spiral of dust, and backed into a pull-over. Angus zoomed past, waving thanks. His jaw tightened in concentration. He pushed the gas pedal down.

Amy checked on James, sleeping in the back.

"'Tis my job," Angus said. "I'm trained to drive quite safely like a madman."

She smiled weakly, her knuckles white on the door handle. "And I'm worried about Shawn getting killed."

Angus grinned.

"What is it you didn't tell me?" she asked, curiously.

"There's no ferry to Iona at this time of night."

CHAPTER FORTY-SEVEN

Glenmirril, 1316

"This saying good-bye is getting old." In the Bat Cave, Shawn smiled ruefully at Christina. "Third time lucky, right?"

"I've a feeling this time," she said. "May God go with you."

"Yeah, may He. I guess."

She touched his cheek and pulled her hand back quickly, dropping her gaze. "Things come aright. They always do."

Shawn thought of Allene's and Niall's brothers, of having been away from Amy for two years. For Christina's sake, he held back his sarcastic comment, asking instead, "What if she's found someone else?"

"I don't understand your time," she said. "You'll do what you think best for her and your son."

"You have faith in me. Like she did."

"And it seems she was right."

Mull, 1316

A dozen reactions raced through Amy's mind. Screaming. Throwing the car door open and announcing she wouldn't go another mile till he explained himself. Demanding to know what he'd been thinking.

"'Tis this or leave him another year," Angus reasoned. "Of course, we can do that anyway."

She burst from her paralysis. "What are you planning to do? Swim? Are you insane? I mean, I appreciate it and all."

He smiled. "I believe this is our chance, tonight, on Iona. He needs the crucifix and his son to go through that door. I borrowed something from the force. It's in the trunk."

There was only one thing he could have borrowed. The blood drained from her face, thinking of the choppy waters. In a flash, she felt everything Niall felt. If the boat capsized, she'd be pulled under, the long skirt tangling around her legs. Nausea twisted in her gut. But her greatest fear wasn't for herself. "I can't take a baby out in that," she whispered. "What if the wind picks up? Just how big is this thing you borrowed?"

"Big enough," Angus said. "It's used for rescues." He touched her hand. "We needn't do it."

"What kind of a person would...?"

"The kind who chooses a baby over a grown man," he said firmly. "None would fault you. I do this, Amy, I'm trained for this. I've life vests for us all. The other choice is wait until next year. No one would blame you for thinking of James." He touched her cheek, drawing her eyes to his. "Least of all me."

Highlands, 1316

"Remember everything I tried to get through your thick skull," Shawn said. "Sing into the water. Fingers together. Legs straight." They rode alone, with MacDonald, Hugh, Brother David, and the men of Glenmirril before and behind. "I want a report in that kneeler that you're swimming across the loch and back each morning."

Niall laughed. "I'll leave such a report if it makes you happy."

"Seriously, you'll leave me letters, right?"

"We will," Niall confirmed.

Shawn looked back for a last glance at Glenmirril. The crest of the wooded hill behind them slowly swallowed it, as their horses jingled under them. His mind drifted back to Red, waving from the stable door, and Christina standing silently in the courtyard, unable to touch him, to hug him good-bye.

"Come now, Brother Andrew," Niall murmured. Shawn lifted his eyes, disoriented at the greenwood all around. "You're going home, aye?"

"What will happen to her?" Shawn asked.

Niall shrugged. "She'll pray, she'll feed the poor. Mayhap one day she'll marry again. Or go to a convent."

"She doesn't belong in a convent," Shawn said. She'd kissed him. On the cheek. He'd kissed her fingertips, slowly, lingering over each one. She'd drawn in a ragged, husky breath and looked at him with eyes that spoke passions the year 1316 would not allow.

"I'm going to a time when she's dead," Shawn said, softly. The reality hit him, as white flowers drifted down, a warm snow shower, on his pony's neck. "I'm going to a time when you're all dead."

Niall laughed, a hearty, happy sound. Hugh and his men looked back, grinning, to see what the joke was. "He says I'll be dead in seven hundred years!" Niall called to them.

"Aye," Hugh said. "In seven hundred years, you'll be antagonizing the poor saints in Heaven, as the divil hasn't the patience to deal with you."

The men laughed, even Brother David, and fell to discussing the pranks Niall might play on the devil and his hapless demons, should he earn his way to their fiery lake.

"I can't believe you're laughing about death," Shawn muttered.

"In two years, has nothing sunk in?" Niall asked. "I'll not be dead, I'll be elsewhere. What you really ought worry over is whether I'll be looking down, seeing what *you're* up to!" He laughed again, his head thrown back. White petals drifted down, landing on his shoulders.

From under the gray hood, Shawn studied Niall, with his garnish of white petals, one caught in his hair. "You could die any day in this world," he said. "Why are you so happy?"

"Because I mayn't have time to be miserable, as you do in your time." Niall clapped him on the shoulder. "I wish you could stay."

Mull, Present

Amy hesitated on Mull's rocky shore. The breeze tugged her hair and swirled her skirt around her tennis shoes. The sun had sunk lower, leaving streaks of pink dancing on the water. The rescue boat bobbed in a rocky outcropping, half on shore. Angus held three life vests.

"Amy," he said softly. "We've not a moment to lose. Either I try myself, with the crucifix, and take the chance he's trapped another year. Or we all go. I'm trained for this. He's safe."

She stared, biting her lip, at the gray waves slashing the shore.

Angus put a hand on her shoulder. "I love him like my own son. I'd not do it if I thought there was any danger. Wait in the car. But I must go now. We've no idea how long this door is open."

She dug inside her sweatshirt for the crucifix, wrestling it over her hair whipping in the wind, and handed it to him. He kissed her, kissed James, and handed her two life jackets. He strapped his own on and pushed the boat into the water. She watched him, torn between dooming Shawn and endangering her son.

Glenmirril, 1316

Christina's fingers lingered on the cool curve of the sackbut. She sat on Shawn's bed, the instrument in its wooden case beside her, angry with her weakness. She should accept the inevitable with the steely grace with which she'd always accepted life; go to the chapel to pray, surrounded by incense and candles sending up faint smoke trails, and the stained glass window throwing down colored bits of light. But she'd become accustomed to Shawn's silent presence behind her, knowing without turning, when he came in. Her place of solace had become a reminder of his absence.

If not the chapel, then she should feed the poor, she chided herself. She could be of service to them and God, rather than sitting idly, mooning over a man who wanted to be with another, a man who had never belonged in her time, anyway.

She pulled out the mouthpiece, turned it over in her hands, and pressed it to her lips, the one thing that had so recently touched his. She closed her eyes, seeing him in the Bat Cave, his eyes close to hers, Christ looming large behind him, and his hand on her cheek. He loved her. But he'd chosen to go back, to care for his son, and a woman he also loved—a woman who should be his wife —to make amends. She loved him the more for it. And it made his leaving hurt the more.

She laid the mouthpiece back in the case and lowered the lid, trailing her hand over the leather covering. She tried to picture Amy. Long black hair. Dark, blue eyes. Fine, white skin. Tall and thin, playing something like a lute with a flattened back, tucked under her chin. Christina drifted from her place on Shawn's bed to the press. She touched the shirts he'd left behind. "They're a little out of fashion in the twenty-first century," he'd laughed. She touched the trews, her fingers lingering on a pair she'd stitched herself. "Trews are especially out of fashion," he'd added. She could almost feel his fingers on hers, as they stood side by side just the night before, deciding what he'd take on the dawn parting. He'd ridden out wearing breeks and a shirt she'd made.

She shut the press with a firm click. She had no right to feel this way about a man who was as good as married to another. "Bessie!" She raised her voice, calling even as she left Shawn's room for the ante chamber where she'd sat sewing or sketching so many times while Shawn played the harp or sang, or argued with Brother David or played chess with Hugh, looking up now and again with a secret smile for her.

Bessie appeared from Allene's chamber. "Milady?"

"Find Elspet to watch the child, please. Adam's widow—her son has taken ill. We must see what we can bring her. And food for the families over the hill. Their crops were hit especially hard by the rain. Come now, we've no time to waste."

Mull, Present

"Wait!" Fighting every instinct to stay safe in the car with James, Amy splashed into the water, soaking her skirt, and climbed over the edge, juggling James and the life vests.

"Your jacket first," Angus said. "Hand me James. Quick!" While she donned the life vest, he took James, now wide awake and peering with furrowed brows at the water. Every gust of wind made him draw a shuddering breath. Angus secured the infant vest around him, and handed him back. Amy huddled with him in the rescue boat's prow. The wet skirt chilled her legs. Angus started the motor, sending the boat bouncing over the water. A wave washed over the side. James started to cry. Amy rocked him, humming as much to comfort herself as him.

Glenmirril, 1316

"I shouldn't," Christina murmured. At her easel, she lowered her charcoal to her lap. Thoughts of Shawn had continued to plague her. His kisses on each of her fingers lingered in her memory, rousing feelings that made her hesitant to go to the chapel. His absence left a hollow in her stomach. She'd fought unsuccessfully, since returning from her rounds to the poor, against re-visiting each place he'd been—the candle-lit Bat Cave, Niall's chair in the great hall where Shawn sat several times a week. She'd touched everything he'd touched, gone everywhere he'd been.

Allene rose from her place by James's cradle, and picked up her sewing. "Shouldn't what?"

"Perhaps I am contrary, but ever since Niall forbade me, I've had a burning desire to go to the tower."

"You can surely understand why that tower makes him nervous." Allene studied the garment on her lap, before choosing thread and poking it through her needle. "I believe Shawn also told you to stay away. He fears we'll be pulled into his world. The things I've heard of it, we'd not like it."

Christina lowered her charcoal. "But if the prophecy applies to those of Niall's lineage, if the switch happens on Iona, and if it requires the crucifix and kin of Shawn's, then no such thing can happen to me."

Allene's mouth turned down. "And surely there's time to finish the sewing ere Niall returns."

"And the men have left. Who is to object if I look?" Christina mused. "Who will even know?"

They stared at each other another moment before Allene set down her sewing. "I'll call Bessie to watch James."

Ten minutes later, they stood at the foot of the tower. Christina's insides trembled as they had the first time she'd ridden a full-size mare. She should obey her Laird. She should obey Niall. She should respect Shawn's wishes.

The keys jangled in Allene's hand. They glanced around, but the few men left in the castle had too much work to notice two women, and no way of knowing, regardless, the Laird's orders concerning the tower. Allene fit the big black key in the metal lock. Inside the mechanism, the bolt scraped. As the door opened, cool air reached out. A foreboding chill shot down Christina's arms.

They clutched hands and squeezed together side by side on the narrow stairway. It was chilly, with the sun shut out and the loch breeze blowing down from above. Gray stones pressed close on either side. Allene's hands, warm on hers, gave her courage. They took the first twisting steps, and stopped, by unspoken consent. "What if it should happen?" she whispered. "What if we should find ourselves in Shawn's world, with *cars* and *planes* and women in knickers? It seems a noisy and immoral place."

"He says 'tis safe and clean," said Allene. "He says there's no war in his country, and children rarely die. Still, I've no wish to find out. But the switch happens on Iona."

"We're no relation to them. It can't happen to us." Christina tried to speak boldly. They climbed four more steps. Christina stopped, staring at the archer's slot. Her stomach dropped. Her hand tightened on Allene's. "No," she whispered. "We must get them back. We must get out of this tower."

Between Mull and Iona, Present

Amy hunkered low in the craft, only somewhat reassured by skies still blue over the streaks of pink in the west, and Angus's insistence that it was perfect boating conditions. She gripped James against her life vest. Niall would appeal to God. She felt with her free hand, searching for the crucifix in the silky folds of her concert blouse, and found nothing there. She closed her eyes, feeling the wind on her cheek. *Our Father, protect us.* The crucifix loomed large in her mind. "Angus," she said, "can I have it?"

One hand on the rudder, he reached inside his vest, and handed her the crucifix. Her fingers played over its surface, the tiny carved Christ. But she was seeing the stone cross in the window of Glenmirril's tower, where Rob had hugged her.

"Are you aw' right?" Angus asked.

Her jaw ached with tension. "It's Rob." She struggled, one-handed, to get the leather thong of the crucifix over her head. "I can't get him out of my mind."

"Of all the men I've never worried of you thinking about," Angus said, "Rob headed the list."

"That's not the feeling I got in my kitchen."

Angus huffed. "I said I'm sorry. Why him, why now?" He studied the approaching shore.

"I don't know." She slipped her hand from the crucifix to grip James more tightly as another wave batted the boat. "I just keep seeing us under the cross window in Glenmirril's tower."

"Go with it," Angus said. "Remember how things came to you about Shawn and the boy? What else happened there?"

"I was upset about Shawn hitting his head."

"What else?" The boat lurched over a swell. Water washed over Amy's feet, soaking her shoes.

"It was a year ago." She pressed her fingers against her forehead, trying to remember. "He said he wasn't sure if he'd rather face Shawn up there, hung-over and mad, or down in the courtyard crazy and carrying a knife."

The boat lurched again. James wiggled against her chest. "Then you went up?" Angus pressed.

"Yes. I was shocked that it was empty." She turned, squinting into the falling sun, a ball of blazing orange silhouetting Iona's hills. "Why am I remembering it now?"

Glenmirril, 1316

Christina and Allene tumbled down the stairs in a flurry of skirts and cloaks. "Lock it!" Christina gasped. "Ink and parchment! We must send a message!"

"Christina, what *is* it?" Allene twisted the key in the lock. "I've been in that tower a thousand times. There's naught amiss."

"Come." Christina pulled her through the stone halls, to her chambers, speaking as Allene pulled out quill, ink and parchment. "In my vision...." She seated herself at the desk, jabbing the quill into ink. "They were fighting before the archer's slot. It happened here. *Happens* here. Who can we send after them?" The quill flashed. *Niall, I was wrong. I went to the tower. There, I saw the stone cross in the archers slot. It is what was in the vision. You and S were on either side of the cross window in your tower at Glenmirril, where Columba had a chamber.* She lifted her head, listening to a sound from outside. "What was that?"

"Children playing," Allene said. "The blacksmith in a temper?" She leaned over Christina's shoulder, reading.

Christina dipped her quill and added, *I leave it to your judgment, but I believe the crossing will be here.*

A jolt on the door jarred them both. Christina's hand flew to her chest, trying to slow the pounding.

"Who is it?" called Allene.

A tenor voice shouted, "A man from MacDougall, Milady!"

Nerves shot through Christina's body. She and Allene stared at one another. "MacDougalls?" Allene ran to the door and threw it open.

In the doorway, the miller's sons wrestled with MacDougall's jailer. At sight of Christina, the man dropped to his knee, speaking in a flurry. "Tell them you know me, Milady! MacDougall is coming!"

"What?" Christina's mind spun, disoriented at the sight of MacDougall's jailer in Glenmirril's hallway.

"He's coming, Milady!" He clung to Christina's hands.

Allene spun to the miller's boy. "Send word to the gatehouse. Raise the drawbridge." The older boy ran. Allene addressed the younger. "Summon Conal and Lord Morrison." The boy bolted. Allene spun to the man on his knees. "Why?" she demanded. "How many?"

"Two hundred." The man turned to Christina. "I escaped as soon as I could to warn you, Milady."

"How far?" Allene demanded.

"His army is a day's march behind us! MacDougall and Duncan will be here first, cause confusion, open the gate."

"Who can we send after the men?" Christina's heart pounded.

"Conal," Allene answered. "Get water and linens, get the women and children to the Bat Cave."

"Where are you going?"

"To take my father's place."

"You can't...." Christina started.

"Take James and Bessie and protect them with your life!" Allene's eyes blazed. "When Conal arrives, send him after the men." She addressed the jailer, scrambling up from his knees. "Come with me."

"Milady?" Lord Morrison arrived breathless at the door.

Taking his elbow, Allene led him and the jailer toward the courtyard, conferring.

In the next room, James whimpered. Bessie appeared in the doorway, cradling him on her shoulder, her face as white as flour. Christina folded the letter she'd written and tucked it in her pocket. She'd been strong under Duncan's cruel thumb. She would be strong now. She stiffened her spine, and spoke calmly, even as she lifted the pitcher from the washstand and scooped linens from the sewing pile. "Take the furs from the bed. We must get the women and children to safety."

"Yes, mum." Bessie's voice trembled like the wing of a butterfly in a storm. She laid James in the middle of the bed, gathered the furs under him, and scooped it all into her arms. He twisted his head and cried. Bessie's trembling lip suggested she was close to doing the same.

"You let Ni—Fionn, the minstrel, out of the dungeon, did you not?" Christina spoke briskly. "We'll do this, too. Come along." She led the way from the room, shouting for the women.

At the end of the hall, Conal appeared, outlined in the sunlight pouring through the window. "Milady?" He hastened to her, glancing at Bessie carrying James and the linens. "The MacDougalls are coming," Christina said crisply. "The men are heading to Iona. You must find them and tell them. Take Red in case either of you is held up." She didn't voice what might hold them up. "The fastest garrons, whatever you need from the kitchens. They must return immediately. We shall be safe in the dungeons. God go with you, Conal."

"And with you." He turned and ran, shouting for Red.

On the second floor, Christina found Niall's mother. "Blankets, linens, water," Christina ordered. "We're under attack. Gather the women and children."

Niall's mother crossed herself, whispering, "Mary, Joseph, and Jesus." She disappeared into her room and reappeared almost immediately, with a water bucket and linens.   One of her women ran after her bearing a pitcher and blankets.

In ten minutes, Christina led a frightened group down to the dungeons, bearing a torch aloft. Musty odor filled her nostrils. In the dank tunnel, some women whimpered; others hushed their children. She turned to them. "Keep your bairns close." Her insides turned watery. She'd never navigated the maze by herself. She hoped she remembered the way. The torch flickered off stone walls. Behind the Bat Cave's doors, they would be safe, but lost in the endless labyrinth, the children's echoing cries would draw MacDougall's men straight to them.

Straightening her back, she glided forward.   With enemy soldiers approaching, these women needed whatever confidence she could muster, for they had none of their own. She stopped at a fork in the paths, unsure. She closed her eyes for a minute, seeing Shawn beside her.

Left.

He'd teased her that it was on that hand people wore wedding rings in his time. He'd taken her left hand, his eyes shining in the torchlight, before they'd both looked away and he'd dropped her hand quickly. She turned left. The walls narrowed. She moved forward, calmly reassuring the frightened women, lifting her fine cotehardie from the damp dirt. In another five minutes, they crowded into the Bat Cave. She found the wet nurse for James, and with a kiss on Bessie's cheek and a hasty sign of the cross under MacDonald's crucifix, turned for the door. Niall's mother caught her sleeve. "Where's Allene? Where are you going?"

"Allene is with the men. She knows her father's will. I'm going to help."

"You mustn't."

"Take care of them," Christina replied. She kissed the woman on each cheek and headed back into the maze beneath the castle. Her hand slipped into her pocket, touching the note. She had forgotten to give Conal the letter. Her heart sank. She had taken Shawn's greatest hope from him. But he, at least, would be safe on his way home.

CHAPTER FORTY-EIGHT

Iona, Present

The rescue craft's rubber bottom scraped Iona's shore. Amy closed her eyes, giving silent thanks.

"You doubted me?" Humor lilted in Angus's voice.

She opened her eyes, grateful for the hills rising behind him, and the white sandy beach. "I didn't doubt *you*. I doubted the waves." He smiled, offering his hand. Clutching James, she hauled herself up. "I understand Niall's feelings, if he saw his brother drown in that." She stopped, one foot in the boat, one on shore, her black skirt dragging in the sand. "Angus, why can't I get the tower out of my head? The cross window? Where did I read those words?"

"What words?" Angus yanked the boat up the shore, out of reach of the grasping waves.

"*On either side of the cross window in the tower.*" She could see the words in her mind's eye.

"'Twas at Glenmirril," Angus said. "I remember, because English was unusual there." He reached for James, taking the weight off her back, as they crossed the small stretch of sand. "The rest was, *I believe the cross will be here.*"

"What did it mean? *The cross will be here?*" Clinging to his hand, she pulled herself up the bank to the road. "The letter had just said it *was* there."

"It doesn't matter now," Angus said. "Here's the Street of the Dead."

They started down the path of flat stones embedded in a grassy avenue. The abbey rose at the far end. Evening sun turned the stones rosy. "It seems it should feel more...mysterious."

He studied her face. "What did it feel like, that night in the tower?"

"Tension," she said. "I told Shawn so in the tower. The hair was prickling on my arms and neck."

"Did you see anything in the tower?"

Wind gusted off the sea. She pulled her hood up. "No I was mad, and scared about being pregnant. Shawn was up in the tower. We were shouting back and forth. But I remember feeling like I was pushing through a crowd, down in the courtyard, the mist was that thick, that high."

Angus looked around at evening light flooding the island, and grass leaning before the breeze, like dancers in green bending and swaying. "It's too peaceful?" he clarified.

Amy nodded. "Nothing like when Niall and Shawn switched." The abbey grew larger as they approached, a sprawling structure reborn from ruins in successive waves of restoration. A Celtic cross towered before a small arched doorway on the side.

"They believe this was St. Columba's chamber." Angus opened the wooden door, flooding the dim chapel with a wide bar of light. Amy eased through an opening no taller than herself. Angus stooped, squeezing through behind her. Amy looked around at the Persian-style rug and green curtains framing a modern wooden cross. A cowbell stood on a table below the cross. She looked quizzically at Angus. "Not quite what I expected. It just doesn't seem possible anything mysterious could happen here." She sat down on one of the few chairs.

Angus handed James to her. "He carved it on the stone. He *has* to be here."

Amy bundled James onto her shoulder, kissing his forehead. He opened tired eyes, squinted at her, and dropped his head against her neck, sighing. Angus paced the chamber, examining a candle holder. Feeling James's breath on her neck, feeling the stillness of the room, Amy's mind drifted over the hundreds of parchments she'd read in the past year. "How would he get here? Would Niall bring him?"

"Traveling alone wasn't safe." Angus wandered to a lectern holding an open Bible. "They'd send a group."

"I guess it would be easy to explain to the group why they're taking a monk to Iona. Assuming Shawn would travel as Brother Andrew." Amy rose, restless. Sand squished in her damp shoes. On the right, a small window let in dying sunlight. She touched the icon in the niche, the wise, sad face of the Virgin Mary on a gold background. "I *know* I've heard of him, somewhere, sometime, before Monadhliath."

"Glenmirril?" Angus suggested.

Suddenly, Amy snapped her fingers. "The professor's books!" She frowned. "But I can't remember the details." She patted James's back as she paced before the cross. Five wooden circles formed the beams, each with a religious symbol carved on it. The word *cross* played through her mind. James squirmed, and squealed.

"Something's wrong," Amy said. "We made the crossing because...." She stopped.

"Amy." Angus's eyebrows furrowed with sorrow. "I don't know what else to do."

"Crossing," she repeated. "Do you remember how that phrase looked on the parchment? Remember it seemed to be saying the writer saw two people on either side of the cross window?" She turned to him, and laying a hand on his chest. "And shortly after, *I believe the cross will be here*. It seemed repetitive, like the prophecy." Her words flew now. "Of *course* the cross was there. The writer had just seen them on either side of it. It's a stone window. It's not like it could walk away."

"But what do you want to *do* about it?" Angus asked in frustration. "It *has* to be here."

"I don't know," Amy replied. "It just won't leave me alone. There was a gap after the second 'cross.' What if it said 'I believe the cross-*ing* will be here?' Can you see it? That space was just big enough for three letters."

"But this is a big jump." He covered her hand with his. James squirmed between them; he arched his back, sucked in breath, and let out a howl.

Resuming her seat in the hard chair, Amy settled him to nursing. "I wish I had my notes." Frustration edged her voice. "It's too much to remember, and it all happened so fast today. What if we're in the wrong place?"

"The prophecy *said* St. Columba's chamber." Angus squatted on the floor beside her, peering into her eyes. "That's here."

"But it's also there."

"He said Iona on the rock."

Amy shook her head sharply. "What if he thinks it's Iona for some reason, maybe based on the prophecy, just like us. Then someone finds out it's not."

"You making a big leap on the *guess* that the letters *ing* were in that space."

"But they *fit!* And with those letters, it makes sense."

Angus rose, stretching his legs. "But *the crossing will happen here* could mean anything," he argued. "It's on a loch."

"Okay, so who crosses the loch?" Amy challenged.

"No." Angus shook his head. "You're starting from a premise and twisting the facts to fit. You can't do that."

"But who would cross the loch?" Amy pressed. "And why *I leave it to your judgment, but I believe the crossing will be here.* Why the doubt? A water crossing, for trade or military, would be planned, right?"

"Maybe it was a surprise attack and they believed the crossing would be there."

"Angus, we're talking the Highlands, 1315. Bannockburn is over. The English have been kicked back across the border. Who crossed Loch Ness to attack Glenmirril?"

"I don't know," he snapped. "But 'tis still a leap."

"But I don't *feel* anything here," she insisted. "The MacDougalls were their only enemies in 1316, and they were southwest of Glenmirril, not across the loch. I know it's a leap, but it *fits.*"

Angus looked at his watch. "'Twill be dark in half an hour. Even if we knew for sure, we're running it close, making this crossing...," He paused at his use of the word, then continued. "...with dark coming on."

"But you're trained for that." Excitement squeezed her heart.

"We may be walking away from the right place," he warned. "You can't assume the one piece we happened to find...."

"No, we found hundreds, among all the archives." James squirmed. She slid him from under the blanket, and lifted him to her shoulder, rubbing his back. Her mind returned to Brother Andrew, and the professor's books. Angus's method had worked with the child on the battlefield. She closed her eyes, trying to see the words on the page, trying to put herself back in that moment of reading it. She'd been sitting in the chair, in front of the bookshelves...she read it later in her notes.... The date had jumped out at her because....

"Angus." Her eyes opened wide. "I was so busy thinking about the word *crossing*, I missed the obvious. The disturbance at Glenmirril—with Brother Andrew—was on June 9th. We *know* Brother Andrew was Shawn. There's no way he's *here* tonight!"

Angus drew in a quick breath. "Let's go!" He threw open the door, casting an eye at the fiery orange sun sinking below Iona's hills. He grabbed James, and they sprinted back down the Street of the Dead.

Highlands, 1316

Sleep evaded Shawn. Amy and Christina hovered at either hand. He rolled over, crushing pine needles beneath his tartan. Amy who had loved him; Amy, whom he had loved as much as he'd been able to; his son, redemption from his mistakes, a new life. Peace. They called him. He opened his eyes to the still night, too dark to see more than black etchings of trees swaying overhead, brushing the twinkling stars, to Gil's ragged snores, erratic in rhythm, pitch, and dynamics, and Niall's deep, even breaths, and Hugh's rumbling ones that seemed, even in his sleep, to burst with life and energy, to want to leap up and fight or throw back an ale, or tell a good joke.

A noise at the edge of the clearing snapped him to attention, every nerve taut. He rose silently, crouching. Hugh's dark hulk, too, rose, tense with listening.

"'Tis me, Owen," came a whisper.

Shawn's nerves remained alert. MacDonald's voice sounded softly in the dark. "What news, Owen?"

"Conal, My Lord!"

A dark shape scrambled down the hillside and dropped to his knee in a patch of moonlight before MacDonald. A boy scrambled behind him, skidding to his own knees.

"Conal?" Shawn stared in disbelief. "Red!"

"Conal?" MacDonald repeated.

"My Lords!" Conal gasped, looking from Shawn to MacDonald. "My Lady Christina bids you return immediately."

"Hush, man!" MacDonald returned. "Have you no sense? You'll bring the MacDougall's down on us!"

"Nay, My Lord. The MacDougalls are on their way to Glenmirril!"

Iona, Present

Dusky blue painted the eastern sky as Amy hurtled into the rescue craft. Sand billowed across the beach in the breeze. Orange blazed like Beltane fires across the western hills. As Amy secured James in his vest, Angus waded into the cold water, pushing off from the shore. The breeze grew. Angus heaved himself into the craft and yanked the engine's pull cord. They were halfway across when the engine sputtered and died. He yanked the cord, and yanked again, his eyes hardening.

"Angus...?"

He ripped the cord a third time. The engine coughed and died.

"This can't happen," Amy said.

Angus cast an eye to the sky, his eyebrows dipping. "Help if you can." He nodded at the oars in the bottom of the boat. He grabbed his own and leaned in, drawing them in powerful strokes. A wave slammed into the boat, shoving it toward Mull. Amy struggled to unzip her life vest, one-handed, in the rocking craft. James squirmed and squealed. She secured him inside her own jacket, and leaned awkwardly for the oars. She shoved them into the locks, dipped them awkwardly into the water, and pulled. "Other way," Angus shouted over the wind. She flailed briefly before matching his motions. The boat bounced hard on thrashing water. Behind her, the first stars dotted the horizon, a handful of glitter flung on blue velvet.

She dipped the oars again, pulling with all her strength. James arched his back. "Hold on," she pleaded.

The wind threw another wave at the boat. Angus took the brunt of it. He shook his head in irritation, sending water flying, speckling her face. "Are we safe?" she asked. "Maybe we should go back?"

"We're past halfway." Angus flung his arms forward, his knuckles white on the handles, and pulled back. The wind pushed them the wrong way. James screamed, twisting inside Amy's life jacket. "Keep rowing," Angus yelled.

His glance at the darkening sky sent chills down her spine. She leaned into her oars, awkward around James's body. The wind shifted at the same moment Angus pulled, and the dinghy shot for Mull, leaping over waves. Amy gasped, as it slammed down again. Her head jolted. Her hand flew to James's back. He shrieked.

"The oar!" Angus shouted.

It wobbled in its lock. She grabbed it, fighting for control. The current yanked at it. A wave crashed over the side, soaking her skirt and chilling her hands. James screamed and flailed his fists against her chest. "I can't do this!" she shouted.

"You have to!" Angus hollered over the wind.

She bit her lip and tugged. Her back hurt. The star-littered velvet reached the top of the sky. The fire of orange sunset died to a small streak behind Iona's hills. Sea water chilled her legs.

"We're almost there," Angus called. With a grunt, he leaned back, and flung himself forward again. The boat shot ahead. A wave doused him. He shook his head, and pulled, not breaking his pace.

James thrashed and screamed. She tried to hum, tried to keep Angus's pace, as rough waters slapped the boat side to side. Wind shoved at her shoulders, bowing her sideways. Something scraped the bottom of the craft. She gave a shout of fear. Angus dropped his oars, leaping forward. "Let's go!" He grabbed her hand, splashed in sea water, heaving her, stumbling, up Mull's rocky shore. "Take care of James."

With water and sand squelching in her shoes, her toes numb with cold, she scrambled to the car, a dark beast crouching on the shore, fumbling with icy fingers to get James out of her life jacket.

Highlands, 1316

MacDonald's army rustled in the deep gray before dawn. They lit their fires out of sight on the far side of the ridge, and cooked their bannocks quickly. "Two hundred," MacDonald mused for the third time, and to Conal, "You're certain?"

"'Tis what the jailer told us," Conal said.

"They're still south of us?"

"We didn't see or hear them on the way," Conal said. Red nodded in agreement.

At that moment, a whistle sounded from the dark wood. The Laird's head shot up. "Lachlan?" he hissed into the night.

Shawn yanked his hood over his face as the man appeared in a beam of moonlight on the edge of the clearing. "An army two miles south, Milord," he reported softly. "Ten score, and not overly cautious."

MacDonald nodded. "Conal's come from Glenmirril. 'Tis the MacDougalls. Tell the men to mount up."

"We've only thirty," Hugh said, as Lachlan faded away into the dark. "How are we to stop them?"

"Douglas would station archers in the woods on either side and ambush them," Shawn said. Men moved around him, dark shapes twisting through gray-white mist.

Hugh glanced around, making sure none of the men were within earshot. "Keep your voice down," he said, gruffly. "Keep that hood over your face."

"'Tis none of your affair." Niall spoke with distraction. "You must go on to Iona, Shawn."

"What about you?" Shawn asked. "His army has to eat, right? Their horses need water. That glen by the loch—they'll have had a long march, they'll stop awhile, lay down their shields, start cooking. We roll boulders down on them like Bruce did at Glen Trool. Follow it with a firestorm of arrows. Bam!"

He slapped his hands together. "By the time they know what's happening, half of them are down."

"Two hundred." MacDonald's voice was as heavy and gray as Scottish rain.

"We re-load and fire, right," Shawn said, "while they're still trying to figure out what just happened. They're out in the open, we're protected by trees. Douglas does this stuff all the time."

"He's right." Niall rubbed his chin. "We can't just run ahead of them all the way to Glenmirril. They're but two miles behind us. We can't meet them head on." He turned to Shawn. "You must go over this hill, far out and around and make for Iona. Take your pony and go."

From under the hood, Shawn stared at him. He closed his eyes, seeing Amy in the chapel, holding their son out to him; seeing Christina back at Glenmirril, with MacDougall coming at her.

"'Tis not your fight." Niall gripped his shoulder. "You must go. We've done aught we can to help you. I'm sorry we could do no more."

Shawn looked south, down the road to Iona and Amy, and north where Red waited to mount his pony and fight with the men, where Christina and Allene and Niall's son would soon be under attack.

Mull, Present

Angus tore open the back door. James jolted and squealed. "It's okay," Amy soothed, and he quieted.

Angus shoved the half-deflated mass of yellow into the back, over James's car seat. "You'll have to hold him."

"That's not safe!"

"'Tis safer than medieval Scotland." He speared the oars in atop the boat.

Amy bit her lip as he threw himself into the front seat. The car lurched backward, rumbled up the small slope, and shot onto the road.

"Turn on the heat," Angus said softly. "You're shivering."

Amy obeyed; she closed her eyes, breathing deeply and trying not think about the dark, twisting roads. Her fingers and toes ached with cold. "Is there a ferry this late?" She wasn't sure she wanted to know. She wanted him to say, *we've gone crazy, let's find somewhere warm and dry, and try next year.* She wanted hot coffee. She wanted James safe in his car seat. But his words, *safer than medieval Scotland* were more chilling than the Scottish sea.

"Aye, there's a ferry," he said. "If the schedule hasn't changed, we might make it."

"Might?" She turned to him. The dashboard lights cast a green glow along his jaw. The heater blew warm air over her sodden shoes.

Angus shrugged. "Columba's feast is June 9." He scanned the road before them, and gunned the motor. "Maybe the prophecy's good for the whole day.

Maybe we try again next year. The records say Brother Andrew was there in 1316, two years after Shawn appeared there."

"I know. I keep wondering if that means we failed this year. Will fail." Amy relaxed against the head rest. She wanted a dry bed and hot coffee. James sighed, and drifted to sleep in her arms. "But then, it's time travel."

"We'll do our best." Angus's voice smoothed her worry as surely as a gentle hand across the forehead. "Get some rest. I think you'll not like to watch this drive." At that moment, headlights flashed around a curve ahead. A car horn blared. Amy flinched, hunching tight over James. Angus swerved into a pull out, muttering, "What are they doing out at this time?"

"I don't think I'll like hearing the drive, either," Amy gasped. But she relaxed her grip on James, zipped her sweatshirt up around him, and tried to relax. The numbers glowed on the clock. "How long until the last ferry?"

"Twenty-five minutes."

"How far are we from the terminal?"

"Twenty-five minutes."

CHAPTER FORTY-NINE

Highlands, 1316

Shawn leaned against a tree, breathing deeply to steady his nerves against the rumble of two hundred horsemen filing into the narrow glen below. Two hundred against thirty. He'd believe it was suicide, but that he'd seen Douglas fight such odds. He had faith in the men around him—the Laird with his red and white-streaked beard, Hugh, Brother David in his robes, Conal, Lachlan, Owen, Red, and the rest.

"The Laird told you to go," Niall muttered.

"I follow your example," Shawn hissed back. "I'll go as soon as we ambush them. Now shut up before they hear us."

To Douglas's methods, he'd added camouflage, convincing the men to smear their faces with mud. Boulders and a host of smaller stones, hastily gathered in the previous hours, lined a wooded ledge high above a spot where the narrow glen opened to a patch of meadow with a clear running stream and small loch.

The sun burned high in the sky. More MacDougalls flowed into the glen. Their captain raised his hand. He scrutinized the loch glittering on his right, and the small rocky shore perfect for fires—exactly as they'd hoped!

Shawn held his breath, feeling the sweat of nerves and the hot day trickle down inside his leather vest and chain mail, and monk's robe. He hoped, prayed, the MacDougalls would be equally uncomfortable in their equipment and shed it. They had no cause for fear in such a peaceful place.

The captain's voice carried up, though not his words. He called out, and the men dismounted, with cheerful shouts from one to another. "How can you be so happy on your way to kill innocent people?" Shawn murmured to Niall. As he said it, his conscience niggled. But that had been war, trying to stop England's aggression. And they had spared any who did not oppose them, unlike the English who slaughtered indiscriminately.

Below, a man stripped off his gambeson, the tunic underneath, and his trews, and waded, laughing, into the loch, splashing water up under his arms. He shouted something and others followed him. The captain yelled. The men in the loch laughed again, and waded out, going for the griddles and oats strapped on their ponies. Others gathered firewood. A dozen removed their chain mail.

Shawn stooped quietly, leaning to his assigned boulder and watching MacDonald. The Laird scanned the army below, watching while another dozen removed their chain, and three more shed gambesons. He glanced at Hugh. They gave one another a nod, and MacDonald lifted his arm.

Shawn shoved his boulder, with a grunt. Down the long line of the ledge, other men grunted and shoved, and thirty boulders rumbled, rolled, and showered onto MacDougalls army. Shawn saw two men crumple under the avalanche before he heaved another rock, twice the size of his fist, and fired it down, and another, and another. The bare-chested man, ankle deep in the loch, threw up his hands. Rocks pelted his bare body. Down the line, Hugh, Brother David, Niall, Red, and MacDonald heaved rocks. In the peaceful glen, horses screamed, men shouted.

MacDonald gave a short, sharp whistle. The barrage of rocks ceased, the hail of arrows began. Shawn yanked one from his quiver, shot, yanked another. The man in the loch fell, pierced. A horse went down, buckling to its knees with bared teeth and a screech of pain. Shawn blocked the carnage from his mind and kept shooting, reminding himself what would happen to Christina if he took pity on these men. They'd have no pity on her.

A horse skittered to the side, rearing, as an arrow pierced its side. A man streaked for his horse, clambering half on, shouting to those behind him, before an arrow struck his neck. Shawn shot until his arm ached, until the last MacDougall fled the glen, leaving their dead behind.

Niall stayed his hand as he reached for another arrow. "They've gone," he said quietly.

"Now what?" Shawn's breath came hard.

"We circle behind the hills," MacDonald answered, "and meet them again. Niall, take ten men to gather weapons from the dead. Shawn, go to Iona. 'Tis an order."

Mull, Present

Despite Angus's urging to rest, and the heater gradually thawing her toes, Amy spent the ride in tense silence, trying to hide sidelong glances at the clock. Loch Linnhe opened up, a dark stretch of inky waters, on their right.

"There's Torsay Castle," Angus murmured. "We're almost there."

"The clock," she said. Twenty-four minutes had passed.

"The terminal's only a mile away." He pressed the gas pedal harder.

"Is your clock right?" Amy asked.

"Why?" He glanced at her.

She pointed. A string of lights, high up off the water, drifted around the headland south of Craignure, moving toward Loch Linnhe.

Glenmirril, 1316

"Fourteen hours, two battles, and I can't wait for round three. It could only be adrenaline." Shawn breathed deeply to relax taut muscles, as he watched the castle below.

"My Lord," Red whispered, "the men are gathering."

Looking down over its high walls, he could see Glenmirril's men gathering in the courtyard. Watching them gather, his heart swelled with pride, hope—and fear. But he smiled at Red. "The MacDougalls don't stand a chance, kid." MacDougall's men milled at a safe distance from the moat.

Beside Shawn, Niall peered out from behind the tree. "You should have gone to Iona. We've tried so hard to get you home."

"Yeah. Well." Shawn looked down onto the walled roof of the gatehouse. A fire burned there, under a large pot. The smell of burning oil came to him on the breeze blowing off the loch. In another life, he thought, he would have cringed at the brutality. Now, he thought only of how many invaders the oil would keep away from Allene, James, and Christina. It didn't ease the ache in his heart that Amy and his own James had once again slipped from his grasp.

Niall grinned. "You've missed your chance to return to a time where such words pass for intelligent discussion." His smile slipped. He stared straight ahead. "Why didn't you?"

Shawn shrugged. He glanced at Red, waiting patiently with his bow. "My legs just wouldn't go." He jerked his head at the men below. The sinking sun cast the shadows of Glenmirril's walls, long and dark, over them. "What are they're doing? They're not making any attempt to cross the moat."

"Aye." Niall beckoned MacDonald, and repeated the question.

"They'd be fools to stand there and get shot when our archers arrive," the Laird said. "That means they've every intention of crossing." His lips pursed grimly. "And that means they know summat we don't."

Mull, Present

Angus pushed his phone at her. "Call the station." She fumbled through his contacts, trying to hold James. "What are you doing?" she asked as she punched *Dial.*

Angus reached for the phone, his eyes locked on the curving road. "Chisolm," he snapped. "I've missed the ferry at Craignure. Call it back. Police business."

Amy clung to James. Angus flung the car around a dark curve. She closed her eyes, fighting panic.

"I *know* I'm not on duty. Can you do it without an explanation?" Angus demanded. Amy opened her eyes, watching his face in the glow of the dashboard lights. He glanced at the clock. "Chisolm, *make something up!*"

He swore, and glanced at Amy. "He's getting the chief. I wish he hadn't."

She bit her lip, watching the road, and wishing Angus would, too. The half-deflated lifeboat wobbled at her shoulder. A pair of headlights appeared. Angus leaned on his horn. The car swerved into a pullout, and Angus flew past.

"What's going on!" The chief's voice burst from the phone. "You're not on duty. What are you commandeering ferries for!"

"Chief!" Angus boomed back. "You've known me for fifteen years. Any chance of trusting me?"

"None. My head will be on the block with yours. What's up, MacLean?"

"You're neck deep in it now," Amy murmured.

He mouthed something at her, a question in his eyes.

"You have no choice," she answered.

Angus swerved around a curve. A dark rise of stony hills jutted out at them. He swung the wheel again. She closed her eyes, happier not to see, and prayed for James's safety. "Kleiner," he snapped. "I know where he'll be. But I have to be on this ferry."

The chief spewed an unintelligible string of agitation.

"Chief," Angus snapped, "I'm driving too fast, one handed, on dark, twisting roads. His son needs to be there. I *can't* explain."

The chief squawked angrily.

"Glenmirril," Angus sighed. "It'll do no good. The child needs to be there. Will you call the ferry back?"

Glenmirril, 1316

In the day's last light, Christina rummaged in the cabinet in Niall and Allene's solar, searching for weapons they'd left behind. The door flew open, slamming hard into the wall. Christina locked her fingers around a knife, spinning to face the intruder. An armed soldier glowered in the doorway, MacDougall's blue and gold blazing dangerously on his tabard.

Christina stepped back, hiding the knife behind her body.

The man in the doorway bellowed down the hall. "I found her!"

Christina knew him. She'd cared for his wife after childbirth. Her fingers convulsed on the knife. Her breath turned shallow and quick. She'd imagined fighting nameless, faceless men. She wasn't sure she could stab a man she knew. MacDougall burst into the room, feet sliding on the flagstones in the hall, his face dark with anger.

"Alexander...." The word barely escaped Christina's mouth over her pounding heart. She hoped he still cherished feelings for her. She hoped, with her heart pounding halfway through her chest, that she could do whatever it took to defend herself.

"If it's a knife behind your back," MacDougall barked, "drop it."

It fell from her trembling fingers, clattering to the floor. He grabbed her arm, thrusting her through the adjoining door, into Shawn's room, and threw her to the floor. He kicked the door behind him and dropped the bolt.

Inverness, Present

Simon paced the cell like a lion trapped in a castle courtyard, alternately shouting down the hall what he thought of the guard's mothers and sisters and ancestors—in English, Gaelic, and French—and shaking the bars in fury.

"You been at it for hours, ye eejit," said the buffoon in the adjoining cell. "Are ye still thinkin' they'll let you out fer callin' their mums names?"

Simon slammed his full weight against the bars, gripping them with hands that had once swung a sword hard enough to slice a head from a body. "Shut your mouth, you villein!"

The man, though safe behind his own bars, backed away. "Villain? All I did was get piss drunk."

"Come here," Simon reached through the bars.

The man took another step back. "You tell me from there what you want."

"How do I get out?" Simon pointed to the cell window, where the light was fading. "I have to be out in the next hour. I'll see you're rewarded well."

"Well, you sit down and shut your friggin' mouth."

"You fool," Simon snapped. "I mean, how do I *get out?*"

"Do like I said, and you'll be out tomorrow. All you're in for is breach of peace, so stop actin' like a madman and quit callin' their sisters—whatever it is you're callin' 'em."

"There must be a way to dig out, break the bars, bribe the guards."

The man shook his head, still backed against his far wall. "Sit down and co-operate. 'Tis only a few hours."

"I've not *got* a few hours," Simon hissed.

The man shrugged. He scooted along his wall, as if Simon could reach him, and laid down on his cot, pulling a pillow over his head.

Simon paced back to the front of his cell, considering the man's words. It was true. He'd been a fool, letting his anger take control. More guards had come; they'd overpowered him, though it had taken six of them, and thrown him in this cell. He watched the man at the desk down the hall. He carried extra weight, and pushed some round cake-like thing into his mouth with one hand while scratching a pen over paper.

"You!" Simon called.

The man glanced up, pushed the last of the cake into his mouth, and brushed his hands. He gulped, and said, "Sit down now and quit your shouting. That's enough of you." He returned to his writing.

Simon returned to his cot, and dropped onto it, hands behind his head. Outside, the sun sank lower. A few hours, the man had said. He would wait. If he couldn't get to Glenmirril tonight, he would kill the child, find the crucifix, and figure out another way back. First, though, he'd kill the fool in the other cell, and the man at the desk. And definitely the monk. He chewed his lip, considering how he could most quickly find Edward, once he returned. He'd have to get through Scotland, now in enemy hands. That shouldn't prove too difficult. The forests were wide and easy to hide in. No one would be looking for him. He'd slip through the forest, a ghost among the Scottish mist, to Edward's castle....

A buzz jarred him. He bolted upright, realizing he'd drifted off. "Not a chance," barked the man at the desk. He lifted his head, and shouted, "Chief! Angus is on the horn. He wants us to send the ferry back to Mull."

Simon sat up slowly, listening.

A burly man strode into the office, snatching up a phone. He held an incoherent conversation, before erupting. "Glenmirril! Are you mad, MacLean? Why would Kleiner go to Glenmirril?"

Simon's fury railed to be loosed. *Glenmirril! It was happening.* He had to fight himself not to storm the bars again. If he stayed quiet, maybe they'd let him out and he could still get there. He pressed himself close, listening.

"Shall I call the ferry back?" the man at the desk asked.

More muffled speech, shouts, and another man burst in. "Go, Clive. They want you at Glenmirril when MacLean gets there." The cake-eating man rose in a fluid motion, and raced for the door. The new man looked at Simon. "'Tis none of your affair," he snapped. "Go back to your cot."

Simon's eyes narrowed. *Cursed Scots!* This man would die with the rest who had thwarted him. Flinging a contemptuous glare, he returned to his cot, planning the death of Amy's child while he waited.

Glenmirril, 1316

"Mind the oil!" Allene snapped at the men on the gatehouse roof. The flames glowed bright in the dusk. Taran threw more wood on the fire while his one-eyed father stirred the oil. The smell nearly choked her. It flashed across her mind that this was Niall's life, smelling boiling oil, and staring down from parapets into the far-away faces of the men for whom it was intended; the faces of men who would kill her, too, if they could. She spared a glance for those men, gathering in the field beyond Glenmirril. "The moat will keep them away, surely?" she asked Ronan.

"'Tis odd, Milady." Ronan scratched his graying red beard. "I'd expect to see them building bridges or hauling dirt to fill it in. They're doing naught. Summat's amiss here. I wonder...?"

He broke off at a sound behind them, and almost immediately threw himself at the man bursting up the stairs, even as he shouted, "Taran, get Milady out of here!"

Allene spun, catching a glimpse of Duncan MacDougall and three of

MacDougall's men behind him. Duncan's teeth bared, his eyes shot fire, his sword flashed. The shock of their presence barely registered before Taran tackled her, dragging her out the far door, while his father and Ronan threw themselves into the fight.

"Let go!" she shouted, yanking backward. For one so thin and young, he had great strength.

"Sir Niall will never forgive me if I let aught happen to ye, Milady. And with child, too!" He dragged her into the shadows of the ramparts.

She heard shouts from the men over the gatehouse. "I can help," she screamed, wrenching against his hand. He pulled mercilessly, forcing her to stumble after him in a half-run despite her best resistance. "Help them," she shouted. "We can't let the drawbridge go down! Stop them!"

Taran pushed her into the dark guard house at the corner of the ramparts. "Take it as the order of your lord himself," he yelled, belying his youth. "Stay there! Think of your child if not yourself!" He slammed the door, and ran back down the parapets.

She shook the grate in the window. He'd locked her in. She watched him run, sword in one hand, knife in the other.

She gave the bars another shake, kicked the door, and threw herself against it, jarring her shoulder. "Kill them, Taran!" she shouted after his fleeing form. She marched once around her small cell, and stopped at the window again, listening. Her stomach sank hard as she recognized the sound of the drawbridge creaking. She spun for the window, to see it lowering inch by inch to admit the enemy. She spun again, wrenching her knife from her belt and started digging at the wood around the lock. From the gatehouse came the sounds of fighting, swords clanging, shouts, a cry of agony. She squeezed her eyes tight, fearing for the boy, begging God, *Not Taran. He's too young!* There came a sound of running feet, and three men in MacDougall's colors fled past her prison.

CHAPTER FIFTY

Glenmirril, 1316

Shadows covered Glenmirril, but it was easy to see and hear the drawbridge inching down steadily, incessantly. Illness welled in Niall's stomach. "Someone was inside." His hand convulsed on his sword.

Shawn touched his arm. "Wait." Under cover of the pines on the ridge, they looked to MacDonald. His face was pale under his heavy beard, the scar white across his cheek bone. "Morrison, Darnley, and Allene are inside. They have lots of common sense." He watched a line of archers file onto the ramparts, dim figures, against the clouds gathering over Glenmirril.

"Please God," Niall murmured. He studied Shawn's face: the stranger who had remained true where his childhood friend had betrayed him. "Thank you," he whispered, and felt Iohn's ghost fade completely at last. There was no way to put the rest into words. He cleared his throat and turned to MacDonald. "Do we charge, My Lord?"

MacDonald shook his head, indicating the action below. The drawbridge thumped to the lip of the moat. On the parapets, a call sounded, and a rank of bows rose in a beautiful line. "We'll run into our own arrows." He motioned, and his thirty men inched down the forested slope, bows drawn, through twists of evening gloam.

MacDougall's men charged the drawbridge. A flurry of arrows showered from the ramparts on either side of the gatehouse. Screams erupted from men and horses. A horse bucked, reared, and tumbled off the bridge, plunging into mist curling up from the moat like a cauldron. Even at their height, the splash of the man reached Niall. He nodded in grim satisfaction. One less threat to Allene and James. Every nerve screamed to chase them down.

Below, the MacDougalls threw their shields over their heads. Mist twined around their legs. A horse went down, blocking the drawbridge. Men shouted, fighting to get the horse up and moving, even as they fended off arrows from above. Flames from the fire over the gatehouse flickered, dancing shades of red and orange against the gathering dusk.

MacDonald edged farther down the hill, silently drawing his bow. Thirty men moved through darkening trees. "But a furlong," Hugh said.

The locust-crowd of MacDougall's army covered the drawbridge, swarming into the gatehouse. *The oil,* Niall thought. Taran and his father would be over the gatehouse at the murder holes, pouring it down. It was impossible to tell the screams of arrow wounds from the screams of men searing in their own armor. He prayed for Allene, even as he inched down the hill between MacDonald and Shawn.

Down the line came the rustle of thirty bows lifting, the whisper of thirty arrows sliding from quivers, and the soft pad of sixty feet. Niall nocked his arrow; the feather grazed his ear. His arm tightened against the pull of the string, straining to be loosed. He eyed his target, waiting.

"Now," MacDonald whispered.

Thirty arrows shot into MacDougall's army from behind, as two score rained down from the castle walls. Horses jumped, men screamed. Niall whipped out a second arrow, loosing it into the dark mass below. Seconds later, it pierced the blue and gold tabard he'd chosen; the man arched, screaming, and fell from his horse. Animals stamped and turned; men twisted in their saddles, deciding which side to cover with their shields. Niall loosed his third arrow, still moving forward. He held the image of Allene and James steady before his eyes. Despite the rain of arrows, MacDougall's army flowed steadily across the drawbridge, hooves drumming like the timpani in Shawn's orchestra. Niall let fly a fourth arrow, a fifth. Beside him, Shawn's gray-robed arm flashed steadily, quiver to bow, quiver to bow, arrows flying almost as quickly as Niall's own.

The last horses charged across the drawbridge, leaving half their number behind, pierced with arrows.

"After them!" MacDonald roared. He slid his bow over his body, grabbing his sword as he ran, unfurling the MacDonald banner and bellowing, "MacDonald! MacDonald!" to warn his archers.

Niall pelted after him, over murky ground, his rage burning deep. At his side, Shawn kept pace, his hood fallen back. "They'll be okay," he said.

Niall tugged his sword and knife as he ran, Shawn, MacDonald, Hugh, and Red all around him, weapons ready to kill.

Road to Glenmirril, Present

"How much trouble are you in?" Amy asked, as Angus guided his mini off the ferry into the inky night.

"Significantly more if Shawn doesn't turn up," he said tightly. "If he does, I'll be okay. Where my career is concerned."

Guilt chewed at Amy's heart. "You must regret the day you saw me."

"Not exactly." His eyes flickered over her and returned to the road. "Get some rest. We've a long drive."

She dropped her head against the headrest, disheartened by his answer, and closed her eyes.

Sleep wouldn't come. She opened them again.

"If he doesn't show up—your job...?"

Angus shrugged. "Too late now."

They fell silent, cutting through fog. Reaching the highway, Angus sped north with abandon. Back in his car seat, James stirred, and settled again. After a time, Loch Ness's dark waters opened up, shining through the mists on their right. Amy fluctuated between relief in knowing they were close, and tensing for action.

"If he comes back," Angus said, "you'll find a changed man. For better or worse, we can't say."

Hills appeared on their left before she spoke. "You think I'll regret it?"

"Will you ever regret doing the right thing?"

She reached over the back seat to touch James's soft hair, and whispered, "No."

"Nor will I. Though I had to call Clive and have him tell me to do it."

She bit her lip, hating all she'd put him through.

The mountains rose on their left, the long, narrow ribbon of Loch Ness stretched like a pool of ink on their right. James sighed in his sleep. He deserved to have his father. She watched Angus. In the glow of the dashboard lights, bags showed under his eyes. "What about us?" she asked. "If he turns up, are you going to walk away again?"

"I don't know." Angus stared straight ahead, his knuckles white on the wheel. "If he turns up, what will you do?"

Glenmirril, 1316

Allene gouged the door with her knife till it became too dark to see, till she realized it was hopeless. She rammed the door a few more times, but only bruised her shoulder. She climbed onto the stone bench against the back wall, and, clutching the bars, looked out to the forested hills across the moat. The sun had faded behind the hill, leaving MacDougall's army a dark mass covering the drawbridge while her father's archers fired into their ranks. The noise split her ears, of men and horses screaming. Then there was a new noise: someone running on the walkway outside. She shouted, jumped from the bench, pounded at the door.

An archer skidded to a halt just past the guard house, backed up, squinted in the dying light, and gasped, "Milady!"

"MacDougall locked me in," she shouted. "Haste!"

He slipped the latch, and she burst out, almost knocking him off his feet. Grabbing her skirts, she raced along the parapets, past the backs of the archers shooting. She reached the gatehouse to find Ronan propped in a shadowed corner, eyes closed, blood running down from his temple over half his face. Taran's father's one eye gazed at the night sky. Taran himself, gasping back tears, shouted, "Milady, help!" He struggled with the huge pot. Embers glowed under it, fiery red against the night. "They've jammed the cogs. I can't get the drawbridge up again!"

"Your father...." she said.

"There's no time. They're in!" He tossed her a rag. "Help!"

Protecting her hands with the rag and her skirt, she grasped the cauldron They tipped it. Bubbling, black liquid cascaded through the hole. Screams erupted below, of man and beast. She squeezed her eyes tight, fighting back tears at the ungodly sound. Hooves pounded, chain mail rang against stone walls. She peered down, seeing the dark macabre shape of a man clawing at himself. Vomit rose in her throat.

"Don't look, Milady," Taran said softly. "Ye *know* what they'll do an we don't stop them here."

She swallowed hard. Her breath came in short, sharp jerks. She pulled her eyes away. Her arms trembled under the weight of the pot.

"Steady, or we'll spill on our own toes." Taran turned, shouting over his shoulder for help.

She heard horses clattering out the other side of the gatehouse, into the courtyard. She wished, suddenly, that she'd stayed hidden in the guardhouse. But there were men dying, and women waiting in fear, protecting her own son. Tears pierced her eyes for Taran's father behind her, staring eternally at the stars; for Taran, doing his duty and comforting her. She couldn't let them down. Oil flowed over the cauldron's lip. She braced her feet against the weight, against the new round of screams from below, as more men rode under the scalding waterfall.

"To the courtyard!" rang out a voice behind her, and suddenly the gatehouse was full of archers, switching bows for swords, pushing through the tight space, one after another, in their white tabards with her father's arms embroidered on the front.

The weight of the pot eased as the last of the oil trickled down. "Go somewhere safe, Milady," Taran reprimanded, but gently, even as he heaved the pot back to its place. "Hide in the guardhouse." He patted his sword, checking it was in place, before stooping at his father's side, kissing his dead fingers, and rising swiftly to run after the archers.

Allene swallowed hard, closing her eyes to the shouts and clash of metal from the courtyard below. This was Niall's life. She had never equated her father's instruction, and wooden swords, to such noise, carnage, smells, injury, and suffering.

"Milady?"

At the croak, she opened her eyes. Ronan reached for her. She squatted beside him, wiping her skirt across his wound.

"Duncan...got away. 'Tis sorry I am."

"You've naught to be sorry for, Ronan. Can you stand?"

With a grunt, she helped him to his feet. He leaned heavily on her, as step by painful step, she led him to the dark guardhouse. "Stay there, out of sight," she said. "Pray for us, d' you hear, Ronan? I'll be back for you." She paused, looking over the cool stones of the tower. Outside in the night, dark shapes fought in the mist. Her heart beat more swiftly. Niall was out there. It gave her courage. She lifted her skirts and ran. Taran's father no longer needed his sword. She pried his stiff fingers from its hilt, and darted for the stairs.

Glenmirril, 1316

Shawn burst through the gatehouse into the sea of men and horses writhing in the courtyard. Brother David charged through the mist behind him, hacking. Red fought at his side, his face a grim mask under his wild hair. The Laird and Hugh leaped ahead, bellowing their war cry. Shawn swung at anything blue and gold. His hood fell back, and Niall appeared, fighting beside him. A flash of red hair appeared through the dark and mist, raising a sword in two hands. "Shawn!" she shouted above the fray.

"Allene, get out!" Niall bellowed. But his jaw was tight, his eyes locked on the man before him.

An ear-piercing shriek split the night. Shawn glanced up at the black sky. A flash of light streaked across it. "Come on, Allene," he yelled. "I'll get you out."

"You get out," she shouted back.

He spun, suddenly, feeling something at his back, and drove his shield, with the blade jutting from it, deep into the belly of a helmeted, faceless attacker. "I'm not leaving," he yelled at Allene. "Are you insane?" He shoved the man off his blade, spinning back to her. Niall was glancing from her to a man on horseback.

Red, despite his youth, battled ferociously with the enemy.

"The tower." She panted, raised her sword against a man coming at her in MacDougall's blue and gold.

The man stopped, cocked his head. "You're a woman!"

Shawn swung his sword like a bat striking a home run, severing his head cleanly.

Her hand flew to her mouth, staring at the head rolling away; she tore her eyes away, and gasped, "The switch happens in the tower."

"What do you mean?" Niall backed up from a mace swinging over a horseman's head.

Shawn whirled his sword overhead and into the man's midsection. A clash of metal on metal rang out. It threw the man off balance. Allene slashed at the horse's legs; the animal buckled to its knees, and MacDougall's man tumbled. Niall dove in, stabbing mercilessly.

Allene yanked him and Shawn into the empty gatehouse. "'Twas the cross window in the tower Christina saw. Go!"

Shawn and Niall glanced at each other, breathing hard, and at the tower. The battle blocked Shawn's path. The moon climbed toward its crest in the sky. "I can't walk out," he said.

"You *must*." Niall gripped his arm. "Amy needs you. 'Tis where your fate lies."

Overhead, something thumped and pounded with a steady beat in the sky. Lights flashed like sheet lightning.

Shawn looked past Niall to the tower, and saw instead, a man charging. Niall spun. Steel clashed. Shawn launched himself forward, felt his knife dig deep in the man's gut. He shook him off and went after another, back into the fray of battle. Across the courtyard, horses whinnied. A child cried; a woman darted from a doorway.

"Go!" Niall shouted, and to the men around them, to MacDonald, Hugh, and Brother David, "Get him to the tower."

"'Tis blocked," Hugh shouted back. "Are you mad!" His sword never stopped swinging, catching a horse in the chest and bringing it down. Sweat streaked his face.

"We knew we might fight to get him to Iona!" Niall shouted back. "Get him through!"

Glenmirril, Present

Angus ripped through strands of mist, skidding into Glenmirril's parking lot. The thrum of helicopter rotors broke the night overhead. Floodlights flashed across the castle grounds. Angus glanced at them and swore. He reached for his seatbelt even as he jammed the gearstick into park. Amy threw open her door. Mist shrouded the parking lot, covering the visitors' center completely, and rose high on the castle walls, leaving the ramparts floating above the white brew. She reached for James, conscious of the passing minutes. Her fingers fumbled on the car seat straps. James twisted, mewling in his sleep. The catch slipped in her hands. She squeezed again, springing the latches free. She scooped him up, torn between gentleness for the child and fear for the father. "Run!" Angus barked, reaching for James.

"He needs to be there," Amy protested.

"Go!" Angus yelled. He took James from her and sprinted. She hiked up her skirt, racing beside him.

"MacLean, what the hell are you doing!" a voice shouted. Clive and the chief emerged from the fog.

"Stay back!" Angus yelled, still running. Gloam swallowed them.

Mist swirled everywhere. A horse reared beside Amy; she jerked back, brought up short. But it was mist, just mist. Her heart slammed against her sternum. Angus grabbed her hand. She fumbled with the latch on the first gate, and shoved. They were through, running down the incline, heedless of the slippery surface. The tower floated ahead. The mist thickened; men appeared in the bubbling cauldron. Fear screamed at her to run the other way. But Shawn was there, he had to be.

"Come on!" Angus barked. The second gate loomed. She yanked the entangling skirt high and clambered over, reaching, even as she landed, for James. Angus passed him over, vaulted himself, took him back and shouted, "Run!"

Rotors pounded overhead, pulsing through her body. Lights flashed down, reflecting off mist, white and more white everywhere. She tripped, caught herself. Something large bumped her and skittered away as she pounded across the drawbridge, into the short, dark tunnel of the gatehouse. She lost sight of Angus, fought panic, kept running. The tower loomed. Something slammed into her, in the empty castle grounds swirling with gloam. She pushed back, panic rising, palms slick with cold sweat.

"'Tis me, Amy," came Angus's voice. "Hurry!"

The path had disappeared. They raced for the tower. A shriek split the air. A shout. Her lungs burned. She ran, fearful of slipping on the wet surface, conscious of time slipping away.

CODA

"I can't watch you die!" Shawn screamed, and spun, coming face to face with MacDougall. His black hair glistened in the moonlit mist. The yellow teeth smelled foul. Shawn's mouth turned down savagely. He threw himself at the man. MacDougall grabbed his arms, lowering his head, pushing back. Shawn looked frantically to the moon, climbing steadily higher. Damp fog twisted around his legs; the shouts of men and clanging of blades skirled in his ears. From somewhere, a steady beat pulsed through his body. He tried to yank MacDougall toward the tower, tried to free his knife hand to stab. But they were locked together. At least it was one less man on Niall. Shawn threw himself one way and another, trying to break the man's grip. He butted with his head, and brought his knee up, catching MacDougall unawares. The grip broken, he slashed with his knife. MacDougall leapt backwards, Shawn followed, three steps closer to the tower. He slashed again.

An arm caught him around the throat, spun him, kicking, to see ten men on four. One lay dead. Brother David tripped over him, landing on his back. His combatant leapt on him, arm raised. Brother David rolled, fluid in his robes, wrenched the man's arm, yanked his knife away, and stabbed him in the back, turning even before the body fell to attack a man fighting the Laird. Shawn's opponent squeezed, lifting Shawn off his feet. Shawn clawed at the arm around his neck. He thrust an elbow back, managing to surprise the man enough to free himself, spun, and drove his knife into the man's gut.

"Go, Shawn, get out!" Niall shouted.

A wisp of green flashed, a wisp of red through the mist, and Allene was dragging him, protesting, pulling him to the tower. Another man leapt on her father. She screamed. Shawn wrenched free of her grip, bellowing, flinging himself on the man. He heard the crunch of bone, and flung the body aside.

Red darted through the mist, pursuing a man.

"Go!"

A child cried, the weak thin cry of an infant. A woman screamed. Allene's jaw locked tight. Moonlight flashed off her knife, flashed again. She had a knife in each hand, pummeling, slicing. The man screamed. A woman darted among the melee, a wraith fleeing the fight, and disappeared into the tower. A bulky man shouted after her.

"Go, you fool!" Niall shouted. "'Tis what we've tried two years for!"

Shawn bolted, knowing Niall was right, but hating himself. He fumbled at the tower door.

Amy reached the tower. The door was shut. Without a word, Angus handed James to her, backed up into mist, and charged. The door splintered.

Shawn scrambled through. Duncan charged after him, snarling, circling, backing him away from the stairs with a sword. MacDougall and two of his men burst in, blocking the stairs. Shawn bellowed, roared, furious. Something shoved him aside. It was the Laird, wielding his sword like an ancient god of war, his mouth grim, swinging like a man half his age, backing the men up the stairs.

Angus shoved James into her arms. "Go, go!" Clutching James, she pushed through misty swirls of bodies in the lower room, ghostly shapes of men shouting, and clashing, clanging, steel on steel, as she climbed the stairs.

Duncan lunged after them. Shawn chased Duncan, swearing, slashing. Brother David burst into the tower. One of the men on the stairs above skidded under the impact of MacDonald's fist, bumping, grabbing for support. Duncan clambered up the stairs, climbing over him, chasing MacDonald. They fought, the Laird and Duncan, in the cramped space, while Shawn tried vainly to help. Duncan shoved, sending MacDonald sprawling down the stairs.

A face reared before her, black-bearded and ugly, yellow teeth. "Angus!" She screamed, a long drawn-out wail.

"Go!" Angus's voice echoed from the bottom of the stairs.

She pushed the man. He grabbed her arm. She gripped James, yanking back, kicking. The man grunted, fell, went rolling down the stairs.

Shawn leapt over Duncan as he tumbled down. MacDonald scrambled up off the floor, and spun. Niall stood in the doorway, panting.

She scrambled upward, stumbling into the open tower. Night air whipped across her face.

"Go!"

Amy heard the shout from below. "I'm here, I made it!" she yelled. The whop-whop-whop of rotors drowned her voice. Thick mist swirled in the tower.

"Go!" the voice shouted again. "Hurry!"

"I said I'm...." She stopped, gulped. It was Niall. Her heart pounded so swiftly she could hardly breathe. Her legs trembled. "Shawn! Shawn, I'm here!" She screamed it, clutching James, tears streaming down her face.

Duncan rolled to his feet and stormed back up the stairs. Shawn broke from the fight, giving chase, bursting into the open night of the tower. His chest heaved from exertion.

Amy jumped back as a man backed in, his black hair swept high on his forehead, his eyes wide, panting. A shoulder bumped her, a flash of black hair, and disappeared into nothingness.

Shawn burst into the tower. Duncan panted against the far wall, his face white, his sword trembling. "What happened to the Lord of Creagsmalan who's so courageous against women and kitchen maids?" Shawn shouted. "Come on, you bastard! Hit me the way you hit Christina."

Duncan snarled, lunged and with two hands swung his great sword at Shawn's head, spinning in a great arc. Shawn dodged.

A swirl of mist flew at Amy. She ducked, cringing, against the stones, shielding James. A sword slammed into the wall above her back. The clang of steel on stone echoed in her ears.

The wail of an infant cut the air. A woman huddled under Duncan's sword striking the wall where her head had been. She rose, gray and shrouded, a ghost, reaching for him. Her misty hand passed through him, her hollow eyes stared, grew darker. He arched backward, out of reach of Duncan's knife, and looked again. It was Amy!

It was Amy!

Thank God, it was Amy in the midst of battle, her face fully formed now, eyes shining with hope, love, and forgiveness. Duncan lunged.

"Shawn!" She screamed. He hacked and stabbed. She grabbed for his arm, his hair, his clothing. Her hand went through his solid form. She screamed again.

He slashed. A man burst in, throwing her against the wall, swinging. Niall crashed in behind them. His eyes caught hers, and she read relief there, as his arm snaked around the man's throat.

She pushed herself off the wall, gripping James so tightly he squirmed and screamed. Shawn turned, his eyes wild. Niall wrenched with an ugly grunt, and threw the body down the stairs. Amy reached across the tower, past the man with yellow teeth. He hacked at her, his lip bared. Niall swung at him. Shawn grabbed her hand. His eyes met hers. His dirk jabbed out, slicing at Niall's enemy. The man wrenched, turned on Niall.

"Leave!" Niall shouted. The man twisted, knocking Niall's dirk from his hand, and driving in for the kill. Amy grabbed the man's hair. It slipped, greasy and long, through her fingers for a moment before catching him up short.

Shawn drove his sword into the man's gut with a loud grunt as Niall sagged to his knees.

"Niall!" Amy screamed.

"Niall!" Shawn shouted, reaching for him, yanking his sword from the man with black hair.

"I'm aw'right." Niall climbed to his feet in sudden silence, but for the beat of the rotors overhead, smiling, showing her. "I'm *okay*. Go now, kiss your son for me. Pray for us."

Shawn's hand gripped Niall's, wrist to wrist. "My friend," he whispered. "Leave me a message. Let me know you're okay."

Niall smiled. "I'll write it on the wall. With a message to the scullery maid. *Do not scrub clean for seven hundred years.* God go with ye."

Shawn dropped his hand, wrapped both arms around Amy and James, and they waited, while tears stung his eyes. He swallowed hard, breathed heavily, and buried his face in Amy's hair. The mist swirled, Niall faded, his hand raised in farewell, and they were alone in the tower, the two of them wrapped around James.

The End

(until Book 4)

Coming Next:

Westering Home

The Battle's Over

To learn more about the world of the Blue Bells Chronicles, about Niall's times—the times of Scotland's Wars of Independence—and about Shawn and Amy's world of music, please visit the author's website and blog,:

www.bluebellstrilogy.com
http://bluebellstrilogy.blogspot.com

For daily doses of medieval history, time travel, Gaelic Word a Day, music, a bit of humor, and updates on the rest of the Blue Bells Chronicles and other books, be sure to LIKE the author's facebook page:

www.facebook.com/laura.vosika.author

For other books by Gabriel's Horn authors, please visit:

www.gabrielshornpress.com

31802707R00258

Made in the USA
Lexington, KY
25 April 2014